EUROPEAN TRAVEL FOR THE
MONSTROUS GENTLEWOMAN

ALSO BY THEODORA GOSS

The Strange Case of the Alchemist's Daughter

The Extraordinary Adventures
of the Athena Club
BOOK II

EUROPEAN TRAVEL

——— *for the* ———

MONSTROUS

GENTLEWOMAN

Theodora Goss

SAGA PRESS

LONDON SYDNEY **NEW YORK** TORONTO NEW DELHI

SAGA PRESS
AN IMPRINT OF SIMON & SCHUSTER, INC.

1230 AVENUE OF THE AMERICAS, NEW YORK, NEW YORK 10020

For information about special discounts for bulk purchases, please contact Simon & Schuster Special Sales at 1-866-506-1949 or business@simonandschuster.com.
The Simon & Schuster Speakers Bureau can bring authors to your live event. For more information or to book an event, contact the Simon & Schuster Speakers Bureau at 1-866-248-3049 or visit our website at www.simonspeakers.com.
Jacket design by Krista Vossen
Interior design by Brad Mead
The text for this book was set in Perpetua.
Manufactured in the United States of America
First Edition
2 4 6 8 10 9 7 5 3 1
CIP data for this book is available from the Library of Congress.
ISBN 978-1-4814-6653-0 (hardcover)
ISBN 978-1-4814-6655-4 (eBook)

For all the girl monsters.
May they conquer the world.

At the end of the world,
they encountered monsters. . . .

CATHERINE: Mary, you're not even going to protest?

MARY: When has my protesting done any good?
When it comes to a book, you usually do as you
please.

CATHERINE: That's not necessarily true!

MARY: Anyway, Budapest is not the end of the world.

CONTENTS

VOLUME I

FROM LONDON TO VIENNA

VOLUME II

FROM VIENNA TO BUDAPEST

VOLUME I

From London

to Vienna

CHAPTER I

The Telegram from Budapest

Lucinda Van Helsing looked out the window. They were coming for her, she knew they were coming for her. She walked back and forth over the carpet, rubbing her hands together, occasionally putting one to her lips. She could feel the sharpness of her teeth, which no longer felt like hers. Yesterday, she had inadvertently bitten her own mouth.

The clock on the mantle chimed. It was almost time for her afternoon coffee. Helga would bring it as usual, and she would stare at the coffeepot, the selection of little cakes. She could no longer eat. She had not eaten for three days.

There . . . what was that, out beyond the linden tree, against the line of privets? A flicker of something black. For the last few days she had seen them, lurking. Frau Müller, the housekeeper, had said there was no one there, but she knew—she could sense them. Yes, they were coming for her, and soon she would be in that place, where no one could find her or know what had become of her ever again.

When Helga, the parlormaid, entered five minutes later, the parlor was empty. A chair had fallen over, but otherwise the parlor looked as it always did. Lucinda was gone.

DIANA: I don't think you should start with Lucinda. You should start with us.

CATHERINE: Why are you telling me how to write
this book?

JUSTINE: I think she's right, Catherine. Forgive me, I
know you're the author, but I think Diana is right.
You should start with us.

CATHERINE: Fine. Whatever.

The Athena Club was meeting, with all members present.

The parlor windows were open to let in the morning air.
It was late summer, and for once, miraculously, London was
warm. Beatrice sat on one of the window seats, reveling in the
sunlight like a happy poisonous plant. "This weather reminds
me of Italy!" she said. How London can remind anyone of Italy,
I don't know.

Mary and Diana were sitting together on the sofa, although
officially they were quarreling. Yesterday, Diana had cut the feathers off Mary's favorite hat with the sewing scissors.

"Why can't I go?" she asked, petulant as a child.

"First, because I can't trust you," said Mary, imperturbable.
Our Mary is always imperturbable. She had already retrimmed
the hat. "And second, because you're my sister, and I want you
safe, here. I'm going, because I'm the only one who knows Miss
Murray. Justine is going, because she speaks French and German."

"But only a little German," said Justine.

"And Catherine is going because it will be useful to have someone along who can bite people."

"I can bite people!" Diana showed her teeth, as though prepared to demonstrate.

"And third, because you need to focus on your studies. You
don't even know where Vienna is, so how can you go there?"

DIANA: I wasn't petulant! I'm never petulant. What does that mean, anyway? I think you made that word up. Are writers are allowed to do that?

MARY: I am certainly perturbable! Catherine, you're describing me as though I were some sort of female Sherlock Holmes, which I am not, thank you very much.

DIANA: That's not such a bad comparison, actually. You're as annoying as he is.

Justine was sitting on the carpet. All our chairs, she said, made her feel as though she were folding up like an accordion. And Catherine, your author, was standing next to the fireplace, leaning on the mantle, looking particularly jaunty in a man's suit.

MARY: If she does say so herself.

That day, Catherine was going to Purfleet to meet with Joe Abernathy. She went once a fortnight, to see if he had any information on the doings of the Alchemical Society or the movements of the sinister Dr. Seward, director of the Purfleet Asylum. After our previous adventures, Joe had agreed to spy for our heroines. And if those heroines keep interrupting me, this story will never get started.

My readers may remember that in the previous adventures of the Athena Club, Mary Jekyll learned about the existence of her sister, Diana Hyde, and the secret society to which their father belonged: the Société des Alchimistes. Certain members of the society had been conducting experiments in transmutation, as they called it: experiments that involved transforming girl subjects in various ways, for their brains were the most malleable, as Dr. Moreau insisted. Female flesh was the easiest to transform. If you looked around the parlor that day, you would see the results.

Beatrice Rappaccini, wearing one of those shapeless liberty dresses she insists are more healthful for the female figure, sat leaning forward, with a ceramic mug in her hand. The window was open not only to let in air, but also to let out the poisonous fumes she could not help emitting. As a girl, she had tended the garden of poisonous plants created by her father, Dr. Rappaccini, until their toxic essences became a part of her. If you stood too close to Beatrice, you would begin to feel faint, and her touch burned.

> BEATRICE: You make me sound so dramatic,
>   Catherine!

> CATHERINE: Well, you are dramatic, with your long
>   black hair and the clear olive complexion that
>   marks you a daughter of the sunny south, of Italy,
>   land of poetry and brigands. You would be the
>   perfect romantic heroine, if only you weren't so
>   contrary about it.

> BEATRICE: But I have no desire to be a romantic
>   heroine.

> MARY: Brigands? Seriously, Cat, this isn't the
>   eighteenth century. Nowadays Italy is perfectly
>   civilized.

Beatrice took a sip of the noxious green sludge she called breakfast, which smelled like Thames water. Because of her unique constitution, she had no need of food. She lived off sunlight and water in which organic matter had been steeped. In other words, weed soup.

Mary Jekyll had finished her breakfast some time ago. She was already dressed in her walking suit; after our meeting, she would walk across Regent's Park to 221B Baker Street, where she was employed by the famous and insufferable Sherlock Holmes as a sort of assistant-secretary-Girl Friday, for which she did not receive enough credit, although she insisted that she was quite well compensated at two pounds a week.

Diana, who had not yet had her breakfast, lounged beside her in disarray—as usual. She had been pulled out of bed just before our meeting, and was still in her nightgown, with an Indian shawl thrown over it. She was whispering to Alpha, one of the two kittens, who was *not* supposed to be up on the parlor sofa, according to Mrs. Poole. But there she was, snuggled into a corner of Diana's shawl. You would not have thought they were sisters, Mary with her hair neatly pinned at the back of her neck, Diana with her freckled face and the mass of red curls she had inherited from her Irish mother. And yet sisters they were, born of the same father in different phases of his being—Mary of the respectable chemist Dr. Jekyll, and Diana of the despicable Mr. Hyde, murderer and fugitive.

DIANA: Oy! That's my dad you're taking about.

By the fireplace, as I have mentioned, stood Catherine Moreau, created by Dr. Moreau out of a puma on his island in the South Seas, where through a long, cruel process of vivisection, he turned beasts into men. There was something foreign about her, with her yellow eyes, the faint tracery of scars on her brown skin. In her respectable suit, she appears to be a civilized Englishman, but at any moment she might be at your throat, white fangs bared.

MARY: Oh, for goodness' sake. Do all writers
    romanticize themselves?

And finally, on the carpet at her feet sat Justine Frankenstein, already in her painting smock. Taller than most men, pale and fair like the Swiss maiden from which she had been created by Victor Frankenstein after being hanged for a murder she did not commit, she was the quietest of us, the gentlest and most delicate, although she could lift a costermonger's cart without assistance. She had a spot of paint on the side of her nose.

JUSTINE: Did I really?

CATHERINE: I don't remember, but it makes for a
    better description. Anyway, you probably did. You
    usually do.

"I do too know where Vienna is," said Diana in response to Mary's question.

Just then, Alice poked her head through the doorway. "Is it all right if I clear away the breakfast dishes, miss?" The question was directed toward Mary. Although we all lived together at 11 Park Terrace, she was still indisputably the mistress of the house.

"Of course it is," said Mary. "You know if you want to, you can always chase us out of the breakfast room—or join us for breakfast." As though Alice would have! *I'm just a kitchen maid,* she kept insisting, despite her role in our previous adventures. *I don't want to be involved in your investigation of this Alchemical Society or whatever it may be, not after almost getting killed last time, thank you very much.* Now she disappeared behind the door, like a mouse.

"Is it all right that I'm staying in London rather than going to Vienna?" asked Beatrice. "I know I could be useful to you."

"Of course you could." Mary stood and smoothed the wrinkles out of her skirt. "But we need you here, to protect Alice and Mrs. Poole, and make sure Diana doesn't do anything stupid. If you do," she looked at her sister, "Beatrice will poison you. So don't!"

"I haven't even had breakfast yet, and you told Alice she could clear away," said Diana.

"It's your own fault for lazing in bed until all hours. Ask Mrs. Poole for something, but don't let her see that you sneaked Alpha up here. And for goodness' sake get dressed!"

Diana kicked Mary on the shin, but not hard—almost affectionately. If Diana had meant to kick hard, it would have hurt.

DIANA: You bet it would!

"Well, I think it's time you told Mr. Holmes," said Catherine. "We've calculated how much the trip will cost, we've decided who's going, we know the train routes. We should leave as soon as possible."

"I know," said Mary. "I'm planning on telling him today. He may be able to give us some advice on how to rescue Lucinda Van Helsing. Anyway, I need to ask for a holiday. We don't even know how long we'll be gone."

And now I think it's time I returned to telling the story in a more traditional way, focusing on one character at a time. However, a story about monsters can never be entirely traditional. And anyway, the nineteenth century is drawing to a close. I believe the new century will bring new ways of writing, new ways of perceiving the world. . . .

MARY: I doubt our readers want a lecture on modernity!

CATHERINE: You're probably right.

Mary smoothed her skirt again, although Diana's foot had scarcely disarranged it, then leaned over to kiss her sister on the head, quickly to avoid being hit.

"All right, I'm off," she said. "Be careful in Purfleet, Cat."

"I'm taking Charlie with me," said Catherine. "I want him to look around the asylum, to see if there's anything going on. We've heard almost nothing for three months—why has the society been so quiet? What can Dr. Seward and Professor Van Helsing be doing?"

Mary shook her head. She did not understand it either.

In the front hall, Mrs. Poole was waiting for her, holding a hat and gloves, with Mary's purse hanging on her arm. Mary wondered again what in the world she would do without Mrs. Poole. The housekeeper had been there all her life. When Mary was a child, Mrs. Poole had been her nursemaid, and as she grew older the housekeeper had taught her how to manage the servants, keep the household accounts, care for her mother as Mrs. Jekyll had slowly descended into madness. Mrs. Poole had been the solid rock upon which Mary could lean in times of trouble.

MRS. POOLE: Oh, please. Miss Mary can certainly take care of herself.

MARY: Catherine may have a habit of exaggerating—or, you know, lying for effect— but that at least is completely and entirely true. I really don't know what I would do without you, Mrs. Poole.

"You did a wonderful job on this, miss," said the housekeeper, looking at the hat. "I can scarcely tell that devilish child snipped all the feathers off."

"Well, to be honest, I think it looks better without them, and I like this black ribbon," said Mary. "It contrasts with the gray felt. Maybe now Beatrice will stop going on and on about the decimation of bird populations for women's vanity." She looked at the hat with satisfaction—she really had done a good job, and saved a few shillings into the bargain. Then, she frowned, worried. "Will you be all right here with Diana, while I'm abroad? You can always threaten her with Beatrice, you know."

"Oh, I can handle Diana, don't you worry," said Mrs. Poole, handing Mary the retrimmed hat.

Yes, she liked it better this way: simple and modern in style. She regarded herself in the hall mirror: pale face, middling brown hair pulled neatly back, middling gray eyes looking solemn, as they almost always did—not an unattractive face, but not a noticeable one either. Gray walking suit, showing the white collar of her shirtwaist. She put on her hat, then pulled on the black gloves Mrs. Poole handed her. "I look like a governess," she said, almost to herself.

"You look like a lady," said Mrs. Poole approvingly. She handed Mary the purse. "If you don't mind, miss, I've put in a recipe for Mrs. Hudson, behind that envelope. She asked about my quince jam, and I promised to give her my recipe, what came with my mother from Yorkshire when Mrs. Jekyll was a bride. I've written it down for her."

"Of course, Mrs. Poole," said Mary. "I'll be back for tea, and I expect Cat will be as well." She checked her purse: yes, the letter from Lucinda Van Helsing was there, beside Mrs. Poole's recipe.

"Bread and butter and cold meats it will be today, miss, on account of it being laundry day," said Mrs. Poole. "I hope that's all right."

"That will do quite nicely, thank you." Mary made sure she had her latchkey—a custom she had introduced that scandalized Mrs. Poole, but how much easier when they each had their own keys to the house! Then she hung the purse over her arm and walked out into the sunshine of Park Terrace.

On the doorframe, above the doorbell, was a small brass plaque: THE ATHENA CLUB. For a moment, she stopped to wipe a smudge off the brass with her gloved finger. Was it really only three months ago that her mother had died, and she had found Diana, Beatrice, Catherine, and Justine?

She turned left down Park Terrace. How peaceful and quiet the old brick houses looked! Until three months ago, this was the only part of London she had truly known. Since then, she had been to Whitechapel, and Battersea Park, and the London docks. She had seen sights that would shock the respectable Mrs. Poole.

Should she go around by Marylebone Road? But her feet were already taking her the accustomed way: through Regent's Park, where Mrs. Poole had taken her to play as a child, and later she had walked with her governess, Miss Murray, reciting the dates of the English kings. The park had been a constant part of her life. Even on days when her mother had been particularly ill, when Nurse Adams had grumbled and Enid the parlormaid had sniffled, and she had not dared leave the house in case her mother had one of her fits, she had been able to see the green tops of its trees over the houses across Park Terrace, waving in the wind. Now she walked along the paths beneath those trees, remembering the day, three months ago, when she had walked from 11 Park Terrace to 221B Baker Street for the first time.

Then, as now, she had been carrying important documents. Three months ago, they had been the documents she had received after her mother's death—her father's laboratory notebook, his letters and receipts, and an account book detailing payments for "the care and keeping of Hyde." She had been convinced those payments would lead her to the notorious Mr. Hyde, her father's former laboratory assistant, who was wanted for the murder of Sir Danvers Carew, a member of Parliament and prominent supporter of Irish Home Rule. But no, they had led her to Diana, Hyde's child, who had been raised in the Society of St. Mary Magdalen, a home for magdalenes—fallen women who were trying to reform amid the corruption and vice of London. Such women deserve much better than the opprobrium they are met with in society, and in the halls of power! No, Mary, I'm not turning this into a political tract. But you know perfectly well how women like Diana's mother are treated. And remember those poor dead women whose murders we solved, but whose lives we could not save. Remember Molly Keane, lying on the pavement with blood pooling around her head . . . The image still haunted Mary at night.

BEATRICE: Did it really?

MARY: Yes. Even now, it still gives me nightmares.

Her father's papers had revealed that the respectable Dr. Jekyll was Hyde, and that his chemical experiments had a deeper, darker purpose. He had been a member of the Société des Alchimistes, a secret society whose adherents continued the research of the medieval alchemists into the transmutation of matter. However, in the nineteenth century they were attempting to transmute, not base metal into gold, but living flesh into— what? Her inquiries had led her to Beatrice, exhibited at the Royal College of Surgeons as a scientific marvel, the Poisonous Girl. Beatrice had told her and Diana about the Alchemical Society and the experiments on young women conducted by certain of its members—Dr. Rappaccini and

Dr. Moreau. Then she had led them to Catherine and Justine, who had been working in the sideshow of Lorenzo's Circus of Marvels and Delights in Battersea Park.

Here Mary stopped to touch a rose, still blooming although it was late August. She bent down to smell it—but it was one of the new hybrids, lacking the old rose scent. No wonder it was blooming out of season. She drew her head back quickly—at its center was a black beetle that had already eaten through some of the petals, leaving the heart of the flower ragged. How could life be so beautiful and yet contain such evil in it? She did not know. Regent's Park basked peacefully under the sun, yet out there, in London itself, were horrors enough for any number of penny dreadfuls.

She was grateful that Mr. Holmes and Dr. Watson had helped them, as the members of the Athena Club had helped the famous detective solve the Whitechapel Murders. A series of fallen women had been murdered in the vicinity of Whitechapel, each missing a part of her body: legs, arms, head. Following the clues to their logical conclusion, they had learned that Hyde was still alive and involved in the murders, acting at the behest of that monster—Adam. Mary shuddered to think of Victor Frankenstein's original creation, who had loved Justine with such a cruel, sick love that he had attempted to recreate her with parts of other women—and then attempted to replace her brain with one that might love him in return. How thankful she was that he had met a fiery death!

But Hyde—she could not acknowledge him as her father—had escaped from Newgate Prison itself, and Mrs. Raymond, the corrupt director of the Magdalen Society, remained beyond the reach of the law. These adventures, and more, are detailed in *The Strange Case of the Alchemist's Daughter*, the first of these adventures of the Athena Club, only two shillings at all the best booksellers.

MARY: That's rather clever of you, inserting an advertiscment. But you haven't mentioned Mr. Prendick, who was also working for Adam, creating Beast Men.

CATHERINE: I don't want to think about him.

And now she had arrived once again at Baker Street, with the cries of the costermongers in her ears—*Onions! Lovely onions!*— *Apples! Ha'penny a lot, apples!*—*Old shoes, patched as good as new!*—Once again, she wanted Mr. Holmes's advice.

She crossed Baker Strcet and rang the bell at 221B. The door was opened almost immediately by Mrs. Hudson.

"Oh, Miss Jekyll, good morning! Do come in. They've been uncommon quiet up there, which means they're working on something, although goodness knows what."

"Thank you, Mrs. Hudson," said Mary. "Mrs. Poole sends her best regards and a recipe for quince jam that I'm told is a sort of state secret." She pulled it out of her purse—no, that was the letter. Behind the letter . . . there it was, a folded slip of paper with Mrs. Poole's handwriting on it. She handed the recipe to Mrs. Hudson. "Now, if you'll excuse me . . ." She rather liked exchanging pleasantries with Mrs. Hudson, but this morning she was in a hurry.

"And how is Alice? I knitted a pair of stockings for her, if you wouldn't mind taking them over, miss—"

"Not at all, Mrs. Hudson. I'll get them from you later!" Mary hurried up the stairs to the sccond floor.

She knocked on the door of the flat, then entered. It was always left unlocked for her on weekday mornings, whether Holmes and Watson were there or not. Usually they were, just finishing their breakfast, but occasionally they would be away on one of Mr. Holmes's cases. She had participated in a few of them herself—not as many as she would have liked, and Watson had not mentioned her in any of his accounts except occasionally as "a lady" who had done one thing or another. A lady whose chance remark had reminded Holmes of a clue (no mention that at the time, she had been pointing a revolver at the baronet who committed the murder), or who had collided with the absconding clerk at an opportune moment (although the collision was of course deliberate). She did not mind . . . much. What would Mrs. Poole think if she were featured in a Sherlock Holmes case in *The Strand*?

> MRS. POOLE: What indeed! Your poor mother would be spinning in her grave. Not that Miss Moreau writing these books is any better. Gallivanting around Europe is one thing, but writing about it . . . It's not ladylike, is all I say.

> BEATRICE: Neither is agitating for the vote, Mrs. Poole, yet you accompanied me to that suffrage rally and almost got yourself arrested!

> MRS. POOLE: Well, men have been running this country for the last thousand years, and where has it gotten us? It's time women had a say in what goes on.

The parlor looked as it always did —an organized shambles, more organized since she had taken over keeping the records of Mr. Holmes's cases, the notes for his monographs, his files on famous crimes . . . The shelves were filled with books that overflowed onto the floor. On one side of the room was a long table covered with the scientific instruments necessary for Holmes's investigations, including a Bunsen burner and microscope. On the shelves behind it were specimen jars with parts of bodies swimming in them—mostly ears. By the window stood a camera on a tripod. On the other side of the room, on the mantelpiece, were skulls of various physiognomic types, all human except the last, which was that of an ape. This morning it sported Holmes's deerstalker cap.

Lying on the sofa was the man himself, Sherlock Holmes, smoking a pipe. Dr. Watson sat in one of the armchairs, reading *The Times*.

"Ah, good morning, Miss Jekyll," said Holmes. "We had some excitement over the weekend and missed your assistance. It was the case of Mr. Lydgate, the Hounslow butcher accused of murdering his daughter and cutting her up like one of his carcasses. Watson did his best, but I could have used a lady's hand to retrieve the murder weapon from a drainpipe into which the murderer had jammed it. Instead, we had to use a pair of fireplace tongs, and even then we almost lost it down the drain."

"And of course your insights, Miss Jekyll," said Watson. "I assure you, we do not value you solely for the smallness of your hand. You cannot be replaced with fireplace tongs."

"You are both in very good humor this morning," said Mary. "I deduce, following the precepts of Mr. Holmes himself, that you solved the case of poor Mr. Lydgate and delivered your murderer to Inspector Lestrade. Probably with a ribbon tied around him, like a Christmas present."

"Ha! She's got us," said Holmes, sitting up and giving one of his rare smiles. Mary had long ago told them not to stand when she entered the room, any more than they would have stood for Charlie or another one of the Baker Street boys. She could not work with them if they were continually bobbing up and down like apples in a bucket. "We wrapped him up in red ribbon and drove him to Scotland Yard ourselves. And it was not Lydgate, as you have no doubt guessed, but the local Reverend, who had gone completely mad by the time we got to him, insisting that he had been sent to divide the sheep from the goats, and poor Amelia Lydgate was a goat, ready for slaughter. Evidently he had seen her with one of his curates in a compromising position, and decided he had been divinely appointed as an instrument of the Almighty. I have no doubt that he would have gone on to commit another murder—the mania had taken hold."

"The man will be sent to Broadmoor, no doubt," said Watson.

"But for the present, we have no pressing cases on hand. There is something—but no, it's not worth discussing yet. So today we might work on that disquisition on ears I hope to present at the meeting of the Anthropological Institute. Ears, as you know, are my fascination."

"Indeed, how can one not be fascinated by ears?" said Mary, trying not to smile. She could not quite tell whether he was joking—he did it so rarely. Now was the time to show him the letter and ask for his advice . . . as well as time off. After all, she would be leaving for Vienna in little more than a week.

"What is it, Miss Jekyll? Out with it. There's something you mean to say." Holmes looked at her expectantly. It always bothered her, just a little, that he seemed able to tell when something was on her mind. Was it her expression?

"And do sit," said Watson. "Wait, let me move that pile of books. You haven't even taken off your hat, and already Holmes has started on one of his hobbyhorses."

Mary took off her hat and placed it atop one of the skulls on the mantelpiece—the one representing the highest intellectual type. She put her gloves on the mantle, with her purse beside them, taking out the envelope with Lucinda Van Helsing's letter.

Then, she sat in the armchair Watson had cleared for her, uncertain how to start. Ah, of course Mr. Holmes could tell something was different today—usually she took off her jacket and got right to work. Even Dr. Watson had noticed. How to begin? At the beginning, as the King of Hearts said in *Alice in Wonderland*.

Holmes looked at her keenly, like a hawk sighting its prey.

DIANA: Oh please!

BEATRICE: He does look like that, actually. It's rather frightening, until you realize what a gentle man he is.

DIANA: When he's not shooting someone.

"When I was a child," she began, "I had a governess named Miss Wilhelmina Murray. She came shortly after my father's death and left just before my fourteenth birthday. As my mother's illness progressed and she required the constant presence of a nurse, I could no longer afford a governess, and anyway Miss Murray had been offered a position at a prestigious girls' school up north, which I encouraged her to take. After she left, we kept in touch by letter, and I always thought of her as a friend." Miss Murray had been her one intellectual companion, the only person who had ever truly encouraged Mary to develop her mental capacities, suggesting books to read, telling her about the world beyond her doorstep. If not for Miss Murray, who would she be now? Certainly not the Mary Jekyll she had become.

"After the events of this past summer, when we solved the Whitechapel Murders and the other girls moved in—after we formed the Athena Club—I wrote to her. I told her everything. And she wrote back. My letter had taken a while to reach her—she was no longer at that school, or even in England. The letter found her in Vienna, for reasons she did not have time to explain. But enclosed with her letter was this." She held up the sheet of paper, with its elegant, foreign handwriting, and read:

> Dear Miss Jekyll,
>   Our mutual friend Miss Murray has told me who you are, and of the Athena Club. You do not know me, but I take the great, the very great, liberty of asking you to help me in my dire need. I am the daughter of Professor Abraham Van Helsing, a doctor and researcher associated with several important universities, in England and on the continent. My father is also a prominent member of a certain Société des Alchimistes. Miss Murray has assured me that you know of this society, and that you and your fellow club members are aware of its activities. I am, against my will and sometimes without my knowledge, the subject of certain experiments carried out by my father. As I result, I am . . . changing. And I am afraid. The one person who could protect me, my mother, is locked away in an asylum for the insane. I am not yet of age, and have no resources of my own or friends to whom I could turn. I do not know what to do. Please, if you can, help me, I beg of you.
>
> Lucinda Van Helsing
Vienna, Austria

When Mary finished reading, she looked up at Holmes, then at Watson. Holmes's eyes were narrowed, his chin on his hands, pipe on the table beside the bedroom slipper that served as an ashtray. It was still burning—well, that would be another mark

Mrs. Hudson would shake her head over. Watson was regarding her with astonishment and dismay.

"My God, Miss Jekyll! They're at it again, aren't they? This is another of their abominable experiments. But the last we heard, Van Helsing was in Amsterdam, where he is a professor at the university, holding appointments in both law and medicine. That, at least, we have been able to discover. Why would his daughter be in Vienna?"

"When did you receive this letter?" asked Holmes.

"A little more than a week ago. I did not bring it over directly because we had to discuss it first—the Athena Club, you know. I'm sure you understand, Mr. Holmes." Actually, she was not at all sure he would. She had been bracing herself for his displeasure.

He frowned. "I am as interested in the doings of the Société des Alchimistes as you are, Miss Jekyll. I wish you had brought me this letter immediately, rather than waiting more than a week, particularly as it concerns Van Helsing, whom we know is a prominent member of the society. You should have brought it at once."

"No, Mr. Holmes." She sat up straighter, if that was possible (our Mary always sits up straight). There was the response she had expected, but he needed to understand and respect that she made her own decisions. "Your interest is as a detective—you wish to prevent the society from committing further crimes. Our interest—that is, the interest of the Athena Club—is personal. Lucinda Van Helsing is one of us, and we mean to rescue her. We're preparing to leave for Vienna—I plan to go, and Justine and Catherine will accompany me."

Out of the corner of her eye, Mary saw Watson raise a hand and open his mouth—he was going to protest, wasn't he?

"Dr. Watson, if you are about to lecture me on how a group of young ladies can't possibly go off to Vienna to rescue one of their own who is in trouble, I shall remind you of the night we stood outside a warehouse at the London docks, preparing to rescue Justine from Adam Frankenstein. We acquitted ourselves quite admirably, I think. So please don't bother."

Watson slouched back into his chair, looking nonplussed. Had she been too hard on him?

"I have no intention of lecturing you, Miss Jekyll," said Holmes. "So may I be permitted to continue?" He looked . . . well, more amused than anything else.

"Certainly," said Mary. At least he did not seem angry. But there was nothing amusing about this situation.

"If I were free, I would offer to accompany you, Miss Moreau, and Miss Frankenstein. That is, if you would allow it." Here he bowed, but Mary did not believe in this display of humility. When had he ever been humble? "However, I am needed here. There is a matter—not this matter of the Société des Alchimistes, but the one I alluded to earlier. It is something my brother Mycroft has brought to my attention."

His brother? Holmes had a brother? It suddenly occurred to Mary that he must have had a mother and father—like ordinary human beings. Of course he must have—he couldn't, after all, have hatched out of an egg!

> DIANA: Although if he had, I wouldn't be at all surprised.

Sometimes it was so easy to see him as some sort of walking, talking automaton. A processor of information, rather than a man. ". . . not certain what it is yet," he continued, and she realized that for a moment, her attention had slipped. How unlike her! "Mycroft does not resemble me, either physically or in inclination. He does not go to and fro upon the earth, making mischief, as Inspector Lestrade calls it, searching for information among the criminal elements. No, he is like a spider in its web. Information comes to him, and when he finds it, he keeps it, often until the right time to act. And he never acts himself, only through others—several times, he has acted through me. A spider, to continue the metaphor, can feel when there is some other insect on its web. That is what Mycroft has described to me—nothing more than faint vibrations on a string. But when my brother asks me to stay in London, I know there is something important afoot. And I need Watson here with me, particularly since I am about to lose you . . . I cannot do without one or the other of you. So no, Watson, you may not indulge your chivalrous desire to accompany Miss Jekyll and her fellow Athenians to Mitteleuropa, although I see it written on your face. It may console you a bit that evidently Miss Rappaccini is staying here."

Once again Watson looked as though about to protest, but Holmes continued. "However, Miss Jekyll, I can nevertheless help you. I am not without resources, even in Vienna."

"Indeed?" What sorts of resources could he have there? Surely the Baker Street Irregulars did not venture so far as the Austro-Hungarian Empire.

Holmes rose and went to the rolltop desk next to the fireplace, where Mary usually worked. It was kept open, although she often had to clear stacks of books and papers off it before it was usable. He pushed on a decorative scroll between two drawers, and it slid open—Mary had suspected it was a hidden drawer, but had never tried to open it herself. She was not the sort to go prying into other people's secret drawers, unlike some—Diana! Don't kick me. I'm trying to write a novel and you're interrupting my train of thought. Holmes withdrew some sort of document. What was it?

He stood looking at it for a moment, then brought it to her. Ah, a photograph. Mary took it from him, holding it by the edges. It was the sort of image used to advertise theatrical performances. An actress in costume, dressed as—a character from Shakespeare, perhaps? A queen, judging by her medieval dress and crown. Cordelia? Lady Macbeth? She was very beautiful.

"Who is this, Mr. Holmes?" The last thing Mary had expected him to keep in a secret drawer was the photograph of a woman. Unless she was a murderess . . .

"Her name, when I met her, was Irene Adler. She is now Mrs. Norton. I knew her only briefly in London, but years later she wrote to me. Her husband had been attached to our embassy in Vienna, and after he died she decided to remain there rather than returning to England. She told me that England had too many painful memories for her. We established a correspondence, which we have since maintained, although we do not write often. But if I write to her and explain your situation, I know she will help you. A letter should reach her by the time you arrive. She has contacts in the artistic and intellectual communities there."

He took the photograph back from Mary, examining it again, his face inscrutable. Then with a brief shake of his head, surely the result of unconscious cerebration, he returned it to the secret drawer.

What mystery was this? Whatever his association with this woman, it was no ordinary matter of business. Mary had never seen him look so pensive, almost hesitant. He had been unlike himself. Even Watson was looking at him strangely.

"Thank you, Mr. Holmes." She did not quite know what to think. "We propose to leave early next week—we are trying to get our affairs in order as quickly as possible—and the journey itself will take another two weeks. If you would also give me her address and a letter of introduction, I can find her in case the letter does not arrive in time or goes astray. I would of course be grateful for her assistance." How could an actress help them? Although she was probably not an actress any longer. Perhaps, if her husband had been attached to the embassy, she might have some contacts in government or at the university who could help them locate Lucinda Van Helsing. At any rate, it would be useful to know another Englishwoman in Vienna. Justine's German was better than she gave herself credit for, but it was certainly not fluent.

"Am I correct in thinking Miss Moreau is currently in Purfleet?" Now he seemed himself again—all business.

Mary merely nodded. He knew perfectly well she was. It was he who had suggested that Catherine should pay Joe Abernathy regular visits, since Holmes, Watson, and Mary were known in Purfleet, particularly at the asylum. And didn't he keep watch over the Athena Club? One or another of the Baker Street boys was always hanging around 11 Park Terrace. Mary could not always see them, but Catherine could always smell them out. That morning, she had mentioned that she was taking Charlie with her. He would no doubt have sent Holmes word of where he was going.

"Then perhaps when she returns you can call a meeting, if you would be so kind as to include Watson and myself. I'm very interested to hear what Dr. Seward is up to—particularly whether he intends to travel to the continent in the near future. If Van Helsing is experimenting on his daughter, I suspect Seward is involved in some fashion. You may remember that Van Helsing was writing to Seward about the progress of his experiments— perhaps this is what he meant? And we can discuss the details of your journey."

She had known this would happen—as soon as she told him about Lucinda Van Helsing, he would take command. If she were honest with herself, and she generally tried to be, she would have to admit that it was one reason she had put off sharing the letter with him for more than a week. Perhaps the primary reason. After all, this was her mystery—the Athena Club's mystery—as much as it was his. Still, how could she protest? He meant well, and after all, he had offered his assistance, which they would certainly need.

"She won't be back before teatime," said Mary. "Until then, since Mr. Lydgate no longer requires our attention, shall we work on ears? I can at least type up the manuscript of your talk." She was getting to be quite a good typist. She had even bought herself a book on shorthand. "And I'd like to make sure his case is properly filed, so all the records are in order before I leave."

"I don't know what we will do without you, Miss Jekyll," said Watson. "We'll be back to the state we were in before you came."

Mary smiled. They would make an infernal—yes, that's right, an infernal—mess. Well, she would clean up when she returned from Vienna. Whenever that might be. . . .

CATHERINE: Our Mary swearing. I'm shocked.

MARY: No, you're not.

She returned the letter neatly to her purse, then finally took off her jacket and sat down at the rolltop desk, glancing just for a moment at the secret drawer. Whatever curiosity she felt could not be satisfied at present. Anyway, she was Mr. Holmes's assistant, and it was time for her to get to work.

"All right, Miss Jekyll," he said. "If you will transcribe these notes I made on Sunday evening. I'm afraid they're all out of order. . . ."

For a long time, there was no sound in the parlor at 221B Baker Street but the scratching of Mary's pen, the rustle of Watson's newspaper, and Holmes's occasional murmurs to himself, all on the subject of ears: "Three inches from top to bottom of the lobe . . . fleshy auricular tubercle . . . particularly prominent lobule, pierced twice . . ."

He had just turned to her, with a specimen jar in one hand, saying in a particularly satisfied voice, "This, Miss Jekyll, is the ear of John Seton, a famous highwayman in the time of the Georges, who was known as Black Jack Seton. He and his men terrorized Shropshire until he was hanged—even now his ghost is said to ride the country roads. You see how it disproves Lombroso's theory that a criminal is immediately identifiable by his ears. Seton's ear is neither large nor prominent, yet he was a thief and murderer. . . ." when Mrs. Hudson opened the door without knocking and Alice stumbled in. Her sleeves were still rolled up, as though she had come directly from doing the laundry.

"Miss, telegram!" she managed, then put one hand to her side, breathing heavily. Had she run all the way across the park?

"Sit down, Alice, or you'll fall," said Watson. "Come, there's space on the sofa." He brushed away flecks of ash.

Mary made her way across the room, dodging Holmes and his precious jar. "Mrs. Hudson, could Alice have some water? And do sit down, as Dr. Watson said. What could possibly be so urgent?" She took the telegram from Alice. She stared at it for a moment, then showed it to Holmes. On the thin, cream-colored paper was written:

LUCINDA MISSING CAN YOU FIND AND BRING HER TO BUDAPEST S.A. ANNUAL MEETING SEPTEMBER 20-24 MUST CONVINCE THEM TO STOP EXPERIMENTS LOVE MINA

CHAPTER II

An Appointment in Purfleet

This time, Mary did not notice the roses. She hurried back through the park with Sherlock Holmes at her side. And to think that she had spent the entire morning on *ears*. She should have found a way to leave as soon as she had received Miss Murray's letter, but there had been so much to arrange: train schedules to consult, accommodations to find, and of course the question of how they were going to pay for it all. They were still not ready; they could not possibly be ready for another week. And now Lucinda Van Helsing was missing.

How in the world were they going to find a girl they had never seen, in a city they did not know, whose inhabitants didn't even speak English? And bring her to Budapest? They certainly had not budgeted for that. September twentieth was only three weeks away. It was all quite impossible.

"Just a moment, Miss Jekyll." Holmes took her arm and pulled her to a standstill. "However quickly you cross Regent's Park, it will not get you to Vienna any sooner. We have left Watson and your maid behind."

Mary looked back. Yes, they had fallen behind. Watson was supporting Alice, who was hanging on to his arm and limping.

"I'm so sorry. And really I don't know how rushing will help. We've lost the person we were meant to rescue. Does it even matter how quickly we get to Vienna? I fear we've already failed."

"You have certainly not yet failed. I recognize this place, Miss Jekyll. It is where, on a May evening, we left the body of the Beast Man that had assaulted Miss Frankenstein. Right under that tree. You, Miss Rappaccini, Miss Moreau, and Miss Frankenstein—and yes, even Miss Hyde, as troublesome as she is—have resources denied to ordinary women, or men either. Do not discount yourselves before you have begun."

Mary looked at him curiously. It was not like him to give encouraging talks. And now he was looking back down the path, waiting for Watson and Alice. She liked his profile. It was lean, aquiline—a determined profile, nothing halfhearted about it. With Mr. Holmes one knew where one was . . . most of the time.

"Forgive us," said Watson as he approached. "Alice's ankle is hurting rather badly, although she keeps telling me it's nothing. I believe she may have twisted it running over."

"I'm all right, Dr. Watson," said Alice, but her face was pale and damp.

"Come on, then," said Holmes. To Mary's surprise, he picked Alice up in his arms—the kitchen maid let out a short but piercing shriek of surprise, like a teakettle coming to a boil—and started carrying her up the path. Mary stared at his back.

"He seems like a machine sometimes," said Watson, "but he has great depth of feeling in him. You saw him with that photograph, Miss Jekyll?"

"Yes, what was Mrs. Norton to him?" It was scarcely polite to ask . . . but she wanted to know.

"Ah, who knows the depths of Holmes's heart? But I believe she was the love of his life."

Mary walked beside Dr. Watson in silence. Somehow she had never imagined . . . But of course even Mr. Holmes must have fallen in love at some point. After all, he was quite a bit older than she was, and he had not lived the sort of restricted life to which she had been confined. She mentally scolded herself for being surprised.

"It was a curious case," he said after a few moments. "At first we thought she was a common adventuress. The King of Bohemia asked us to find her—she had been his mistress, and retained a compromising photograph of them together in her possession. He was about to be married to a woman of his own class and the strictest moral standards. He feared Miss Adler, as she was then, might make their association public, and he asked us to retrieve the photograph. A simple matter, or so we thought. But she turned out to be a woman of uncommon cleverness and integrity. She is the only adversary I know of who bested Holmes."

And there they were at Park Terrace, with Holmes waiting on the front steps, Alice still in his arms. Mary stepped around him and unlocked the door. What sort of woman was this Mrs. Norton? The former mistress of the King of Bohemia! A potential blackmailer! She sounded like a character out of a book. Why would Mr. Holmes be attracted to such a woman? But then men, as Mrs. Poole often said, were incalculable. Mary prepared to dislike Irene Norton intensely.

> MARY: Do you have to put that in? Irene is going to read this.

> CATHERINE: I think Irene will understand.

> MARY: Of course she will. But it's embarrassing.

> CATHERINE: Because it's true. That is, in fact, how you felt at the time.

> MARY: That doesn't mean we have to mention it.

"Mr. Holmes, could you put Alice on the sofa?"

"I'm all right, miss," said Alice, her voice muffled by Holmes's shoulder. "Really, I can walk down to the kitchen."

"Not just yet," said Watson. "I want to inspect that ankle. Miss Jekyll, this room looks quite different than the last time we were here. Surely it was darker?"

When was the last time Mr. Holmes and Dr. Watson had been in the parlor of 11 Park Terrace? Mary was startled to realize that it was almost three months ago, shortly after they had solved the Whitechapel Murders. Yes, the room had changed. "That's Beatrice's doing," she said. Although it was Justine who had painted it blue, with a border of red and yellow flowers just below the ceiling, and several of her paintings hung on the walls. But Beatrice had bought additional furniture, as well as the fabric in a Morris & Co. pattern they had used to recover the sofa and armchairs. She had also bought the blue Chinese jars. She was decorating in an Aesthetic style on a budget, she told them—whatever that meant. At least the parlor wasn't as dismal as it had been after Mrs. Jekyll's death!

Holmes put Alice down on the sofa, with her head on one of the embroidered Turkish pillows—in Beatrice's Aesthetic style. "Doctor's orders," he said, then stood up again and put his hands in his pockets, nonchalantly as though he had not just carried an injured girl halfway across the park.

"Miss Mary! I heard your voice." Mrs. Poole was still wearing an apron, with her shirtsleeves rolled up above her elbows. Her hair was, uncharacteristically, coming down in tendrils around her face. She even had soapsuds on one arm. It was evident that she had come from the laundry tub.

"Alice seems to have sprained her ankle." Mary took off her hat and gloves, then put them on the mantel. "Is Beatrice around?"

"I'll get her," said Mrs. Poole, and disappeared down the

hall—but not before picking up the gloves and hat, no doubt to return them to their proper place. Mary felt a pang of guilt—this was not Holmes's flat, in which hats and gloves and human skulls could be left anywhere. She had not meant to make extra work for Mrs. Poole.

"I believe it's just sprained," said Watson, feeling the ankle in question. "Nevertheless, it will hurt for a while, and you will have to stay off it for a few days, Alice. Can you do that?"

Alice nodded unconvincingly.

"Mary! Have you seen the telegram?" Justine stood in the doorway, her dress protected by a painting smock, which was covered with streaks and splotches of oil paint. She had a scarf tied around her head and was still holding a paintbrush in one hand, its bristles the blue of a Swiss sky—which was in fact what she had been painting. "Oh, Mr. Holmes, Dr. Watson! What a surprise to see you today."

"Yes, I saw it, and I have no idea what to do," said Mary. "Is there any way we can leave in less than a week?"

"The passports arrived today, but we have not yet started packing. And I believe you were going to make arrangements with the bank?" Suddenly, Justine stared at the paintbrush in consternation. "*Mon Dieu*, did I really bring this down? Forgive me, I'll return in a moment."

"Alice, *cosa ti è successo*? What happened? Mrs. Poole told me you were injured." As Justine hurried up the stairs, Beatrice came into the parlor, holding a basket in her gloved hands. As she approached the sofa, they all automatically drew back. Even Watson took a step backward, although he almost immediately stepped forward again, as though to show that he, at least, was not afraid of her. She knelt by the sofa and took a white roll of linen out of the basket, then a bottle of green liquid.

"I believe it's merely twisted, Miss Rappaccini," said Watson. "May I ask what that is, in the bottle?"

"An anti-inflammatory of my own concoction. Yes, I can feel the swelling." Beatrice ran her gloved hands up and down Alice's ankle. The gloves were made of the thinnest, finest kidskin, to her specifications so they would impede her as little as possible. Of course, it was not like making actual contact—but with them on, she could touch without causing injury. "If the gentlemen could give us a moment?" she asked, looking pointedly at Holmes. With a smile, he turned and examined the portrait of Mary's mother over the fireplace. Watson also turned away. Once their gazes were properly averted, Beatrice stripped off Alice's stocking. She doused the linen with the green liquid, then wrapped it around and around her ankle, covering it with another strip so the bandage was both tight and dry. "There, that should make the swelling less."

"Please, can I just go to my room?" asked Alice. She looked pale, ill, and mortified.

"Of course," said Beatrice. "Now you need to rest. No more adventures for you, for a while I think!"

"Shall I carry her down?" asked Holmes, turning back from his minute examination of the portrait.

"No!" said Alice at the same time that Justine, standing in the doorway, now without her paintbrush and smock, said "I can do it."

"Yes, please, Justine," said Alice, with evident relief.

> Alice: I would have died. Mr. Holmes in my room by the kitchen? Indeed, I would rather have crawled down the stairs on my hands and knees!

"Come then, *ma petite*. Put your arms around my neck." Justine lifted Alice even more easily than Holmes had.

"I'll open the doors for you," said Beatrice. Putting the basket once again over her arm, she followed Justine out of the room.

"Miss Rappaccini would make a wonderful doctor, if she were not a woman," said Watson.

"Or poisonous." Diana was standing in the doorway, her arms crossed. "As usual, no one tells me anything."

At least she had gotten dressed! Although Mary noticed that her shirtwaist was untucked in the back and her tie was askew. And had she forgotten to brush her hair? With Diana, one could never tell.

"All right, come in, we need to meet anyway," said Mary. She took the telegram out of her purse. "We need to figure out what to do about this." She put the purse on the mantle, then realized what she was doing—once again making more work for Mrs. Poole. Instead, she sat down in one of the armchairs and placed the purse on her lap. Suddenly, she felt very tired. Really, she had no idea what to do.

Holmes sat down on the sofa across from her, where Alice had been lying. Watson was about to sit next to him when Diana insinuated her way around him and onto the sofa, rather like a cat. Before he could sit, she was already curled into the corner. With a look half of amusement and half of exasperation, he took the other armchair. While his back was turned, she stuck her tongue out at him. Mary shook her head vigorously as though to say *Stop that, you brat!*

DIANA: You can't say "brat" by shaking your head!

MARY: Oh, can't I?

"Why don't you tell me your original plan," said Holmes. "How were you planning to rescue Lucinda Van Helsing?"

"I'll need my file," said Mary. "Everything is in there. It's on the table in the library."

"Here it is." Justine came into the parlor, carrying a portfolio and a small red book. "Beatrice is making up some sort of medicine for the pain, and to help Alice sleep. I put our passports in here just before the telegram arrived. You will see, Mr. Holmes, how organized we have been! I also have the Baedeker."

She handed the portfolio to Mary, who gestured for her to draw the tea table in front of the sofa. When it was in place, Mary put the portfolio on it and pulled out the documents they had spent the past week assembling. Justine added the red book, which had *Baedeker's Austria* written on the cover.

Mary picked up the passports, which were on top of the pile, and handed them to the detective. "According to Baedeker, the passports aren't strictly necessary for European travel, but we need them to establish identity. You see, we don't intend to travel as ourselves." Each passport was a single sheet of thick official-looking paper on which a clerk at the Passport Office had written, in clerical script, that the holder of the passport was a British citizen and should be allowed all the rights and privileges of free passage within the country where it was presented.

"Justin, Mary, and Catherine Frank," said Holmes, reading the passports. "And you, Miss Frankenstein, are to be Justin, I take it?"

"Yes, Mr. Holmes. I would be immediately conspicuous as a woman, simply because of my height. I am less conspicuous—not much more than you would be—as a man. Oh!" As though suddenly remembering, she pulled the scarf off her head. "You see?"

"Miss Frankenstein!" said Watson. Justine's hair, which a week ago had fallen down her back in blonde ripples, the color of a wheat field with wind blowing across it, was as neatly cropped as any London clerk's. As Justine Moritz, the Frankensteins' maid, she had been a pretty, laughing, rather thoughtless girl with eyes as blue as the bellflowers growing on the slopes of the Swiss Alps. As Justine Frankenstein, brought back to life by her father and creator, Victor Frankenstein, she was tall and pale, with a habit of stooping in an effort to conceal her height. She was thoughtful, quiet—it would no longer have been quite right to call her pretty. But as a man, she had a sensitive handsomeness that would be attractive to intellectual women, such as writers for *The Yellow Book*, suffragettes, and dress reformers.

> BEATRICE: I suppose I would qualify as one of those intellectual women for whom you have such obvious scorn! Although I have not written for *The Yellow Book*—I leave that to you, Cat. And I thought Justine was quite handsome as a man.

> CATHERINE: I doubt *The Yellow Book* would be interested in the sort of thing I write!

> BEATRICE: Well, I won't argue with you about politics or literature.

> CATHERINE: That would be a first.

"We intend to go as a family group, a brother and two sisters," said Mary. "It seemed best to choose a name that was fairly common. We thought any of ours—Jekyll, Moreau, Frankenstein—might attract attention. You see, we shall have to buy train tickets, pay for lodgings . . ."

"And how are you proposing to get to Vienna?" asked Holmes, putting his elbows on his knees and tenting his fingers. It was his *I am about to suggest something* pose. *This*, thought Mary with trepidation, *is where he disrupts all our plans.*

"London to Dover, then the ferry over the channel of course, then Dover to Ostend, and from there by a series of trains—"

"Not an express?"

"Mr. Holmes, we can't possibly afford an express. From Ostend we shall take the train to Brussels, then to Frankfurt, then to Nuremberg, and finally to Vienna, traveling second-class when possible, staying at lodging houses along the way. Our route has been carefully planned."

"No doubt, Miss Jekyll. Any planning you do would be careful. But how long will it take you to reach Vienna, traveling in such a fashion?"

"Two weeks," said Justine. "Truly, Mr. Holmes, it is the most rapid means of transportation we can afford. I sold a painting to the Grosvenor. Catherine received an advance for *The Mysteries of Astarte*. Beatrice worked day and night to fulfill a large order from the Royal College of Surgeons. We have all contributed what we can, and Mary has worked out the cost very carefully." Mary looked at Justine, impressed. It was not like her to challenge anyone, yet here she was, standing up to Mr. Holmes! Good for her. She had changed in the three months since they had formed the Athena Club. They all had.

"Two weeks is too long," said Holmes. "Remember that you are due in Budapest by September twentieth if possible for that meeting of the Société des Alchimistes. I do not understand what Miss Murray, your former governess, is planning—or why she wants you there with Lucinda Van Helsing. But you know and respect her, Miss Jekyll, so I assume she is a woman of sense, and there is a reason she has asked you to do the almost impossible. I have an interest in this case: I too am trying to unravel the mystery of the Alchemical Society. I too want to find out what Van Helsing and Seward are up to. If I could go myself, I would. Despite the danger, I am glad you are going, and I hope you will report to me as circumstances permit. But if you wish to be in Vienna as soon as possible, it must be by express. I shall wire for three tickets on the Orient Express to Vienna. As it is a sleeper, you will not need to pay for lodgings. And I shall telegraph Irene Norton your date and time of arrival."

There was silence. "You are all glaring at me," he said. "Even Miss Frankenstein, who never glares. Pray tell me what I have done wrong."

"Ladies, you must forgive Mr. Holmes," said Watson. "He is so often in command that he sometimes forgets it may be disagreeable to others, to have their affairs arranged according to his ideas."

"In other words, you're the great Sherlock Holmes, so no one tells you when you're being a pain in the arse," said Diana. Mary looked down at her clasped hands and smiled to herself, both because it was true, and because Diana had managed to stay quiet for five whole minutes at a time. That was progress.

"You're right, Mr. Holmes," said Mary. She tried to stop smiling—he was not used to being found amusing, much less being called a pain in the arse. "An express would no doubt get us there more quickly. As to whether we can accept your offer, I shall have to consult my fellow members of the Athena Club. We have no president here—decisions are made by agreement of the members."

He looked at her for a moment—he was about to say something. Yes, what was it? She prepared for an argument. But he visibly restrained himself. It would be cruel to laugh at him—he really was trying his best, and the offer he had made was most generous. Granted, its very generosity had felt like an insult. Nevertheless, on the Orient Express, she calculated—if they could finish their preparations quickly and leave within the next few days—they could be in Vienna in less than a week. That would give them two more weeks to find Lucinda Van Helsing and get her to Budapest. It was still hopeless—but it was a week less hopeless.

"Will you be wanting tea, Miss?" While Mary was making her mental calculations, Mrs. Poole had come in, her usual respectable self in a black dress and apron, no longer dressed for laundering. Once they could have afforded a proper laundress, and a parlormaid to help Mrs. Poole carry the tea things, and a footman to move the tea table. . . . Well, that was the past, and there was no sense wishing for it. Anyway, her former parlormaid and footman, Enid and Joseph, were happily married and living in Basingstoke.

"Yes, thank you, Mrs. Poole. Come to think of it, I don't remember ever having lunch. We got the telegram, and then Alice was injured, and we've been sorting through the travel documents. . . ."

"I wish you girls would think more of your stomachs and less of mysteries and adventures," said Mrs. Poole. "If it weren't for me, I don't think anyone would get a decent meal around here."

"That is entirely true," said Mary. "Would you bring it in here, please? We can clear the table."

"And can we have jam tarts?" asked Diana. "I know there are jam tarts." But Mrs. Poole was already out the door and heading toward the kitchen. "I'll help. What's the point of my being here anyway, since I'm not allowed to go, though I'm the smartest and most useful of all of you?" She followed Mrs. Poole out the door, as disdainfully as possible.

Justine looked at Mary with astonishment. "Diana is volunteering to *help*?"

"That I very much doubt," said Mary. "Diana always has a motive of her own for doing anything."

> DIANA: I wanted to make sure she brought the jam
> tarts. She keeps them in a cabinet in the kitchen,
> and when I go down there, she gives me one. I *told*
> you Mrs. Poole likes me best.

MRS. POOLE: The tarts are to keep you quiet, you
devilish child. And I give them to Alice, too, if she
asks.

DIANA: Alice is *insipid*. That's one of my vocabulary
words for the day. Quite a good one, isn't it? I even
know it in Latin: *insulsus*. That means unsalted.
Alice is unsalted.

BEATRICE: Did you ask me to teach you Latin just so
you could insult people?

"You're all here!" At the sound of Catherine's voice, Mary
looked up, startled. Catherine was standing in the parlor doorway. She must have let herself in as well, just missing Mrs. Poole's
pointed disapproval. Although Mrs. Poole might have been more
shocked by how Catherine was dressed than by the fact that she
had let herself in!

"What in the world happened to you?" asked Mary. "You
look . . ." But Catherine's outfit was indescribable. "It's certainly
not what you were wearing this morning. Where is your suit?"

"I can't go to Vienna. Prendick is still in London, and he's been
meeting with Dr. Seward. . . . What, you mean this?" Catherine
looked down at herself. When she had left that morning, she had
been wearing a gentleman's suit, worn but respectable. Now she
was wearing a woman's dress, much too large for her. It was a
faded lavender, and had evidently seen better days. On her head
was a straw hat that looked as though it had come from a scarecrow (it had). Tendrils of hair were coming down around her face.
She rolled back one sleeve to examine a long scratch. "I fell into
some sort of bush and had to steal a dress from a clothesline. The
important thing is that something is finally happening! Seward is

meeting Prendick again next week, at an address in Soho. I have to find out what's going on. Hello, Mr. Holmes, Dr. Watson. If you're sitting here, something must be up. Have you discovered the same thing I have?"

"So Prendick did survive the fire!" said Watson. "We suspected he might have escaped from that warehouse."

"We're talking about Vienna and Lucinda Van Helsing," said Mary. "She's missing, according to Miss Murray, and we need to go find her—why, what have you discovered? You'd better sit down and tell us what happened in Purfleet. Mrs. Poole is bringing tea."

"The God I don't believe in bless Mrs. Poole!" said Catherine, vehemently. "Charlie, you'll stay for tea, won't you?"

Charlie stuck his head around the doorway, then stepped in tentatively, as though venturing into a pit of snakes. "Hullo, Mr. Holmes. I dunno, is Diana here?"

"She's down in the kitchen," said Mary. "Would you rather take your tea down there?"

"Yes, miss," said Charlie gratefully, and disappeared as suddenly as he had appeared, his boots echoing along the hallway.

Mary glanced at Holmes. He had not said anything, but there was that look on his face again, as though he were amused and simply waiting for an explanation. She sometimes found his patience disconcerting.

Catherine took off the straw hat and put it on the mantel— Mary reminded herself to put it away later, before Mrs. Poole found it there. Then she sat down next to Mr. Holmes on the sofa and started to uncoil her hair from the bun that had hidden it under the man's hat she had been wearing that morning, which she had lost—where? And what in the world had happened to the suit? Mary thought about the money wasted. But perhaps it couldn't be helped.

"So what happened? We have plenty to tell you, but perhaps

you should go first. It sounds as though you've had an eventful day." Mary leaned forward, eager to hear what had happened in Purfleet. Justine sat on the carpet and leaned back against one arm of her chair. Holmes and Watson also looked at Catherine expectantly, waiting for her story.

"Goodness, now you're all staring at me. I know I must look a fright. It started well enough," Catherine began.

> MRS. POOLE: Adventures is one thing, but I don't hold
> with stealing. The trouble I had returning that
> dress to poor old Mrs. Potts of Purfleet!

> CATHERINE: Well, I'm sorry, but I had to change into
> something! They were coming after me. Would
> you rather I had been caught by the Purfleet
> constabulary, such as it was?

And now we need to go back to that morning, just after Mary left for 221B Baker Street.

On Marylebone Road, Catherine had flagged down a cab headed in the direction of Fenchurch Street.

"Asking me to transport a ragamuffin like him!" said the cabbie, once they had climbed in. "One of them street Arabs he is, and a pickpocket like as not. I don't know what a gentleman like you is doing with the likes of that one." The cabbie glared at her.

Catherine growled, deep in her throat. But that wasn't going to get her anywhere. "As long as I pay you, my good man, you shall take me where I please and with whom I please. I am taking this poor runaway back to his mother, so he can live a respectable life. Now, Fenchurch Street Station!" She had learned that respectable clothes and a high-handed manner usually get you want you want—in London, anyway.

With an oath, the cabbie turned and shouted "Gee-up." The horse gee'd, and they were off, down the crowded streets of London. The windows were open and it was too loud to talk in the cab, although Catherine distinctly heard Charlie saying, "Poor runaway, my arse."

> BEATRICE: I do not understand why the term "Arab" is an insult. After the fall of Rome, the scientific texts of the ancient world were preserved in Arabic, by adherents of Islam. They added greatly to our knowledge of astronomy, physiology, the art of surgery. Without them, medicine as we know it would not exist!

> CATHERINE: Well, I wasn't about to argue that with a London cabbie, was I?

At Fenchurch Street Station, they boarded the train to Purfleet, taking a second-class carriage. It was empty, so finally they could make plans.

"When we get to Purfleet, I want you to talk to the boys," said Catherine. "Boys always know things. There's the boot boy at the Royal Hotel, to start with. I'll talk to Joe. Three months, and nothing—Dr. Seward hasn't gone anywhere; no one has visited him. We know he's been getting letters with the red seal of the society, but we don't know what's in those envelopes."

"Why don't we just nick them?" asked Charlie. Boys like Charlie are always direct. Their lives on the streets of London require a strict practicality. Any sentiment they may have been born with is quickly lost: to hunger and cold and the danger of the streets. Yet there is nothing like the loyalty, the quick-wittedness, of the typical London boy. The next time you hear the expression "ragamuffin," remember boys like Charlie, who live by their wits because they must, on the scraps society leaves them. They may not be strictly honest, but who is to blame—one poor boy, or the social conditions under which he lives as best he can?

> MARY: I'm not sure Charlie would like being a poster boy for the street urchins of London. He thinks himself a cut above them, you know. The Baker Street boys are very particular as to what company they keep.

> BEATRICE: And yet Catherine is right—these boys are treated shamefully, as pickpockets or worse. Our system of justice is deeply, fundamentally prejudiced against them. Our society casts them out with opprobrium. . . .

> MARY: See, now you've got Beatrice started again!

Catherine shook her head. "Joe is already under suspicion. Dr. Seward sacked him once—when the madman Renfield escaped. We don't want him to get sacked again. He's too useful to us where he is. But the situation feels too quiet—like water when a fish is moving under the surface but you don't see it yet, just a line of bubbles. Those letters are the bubbles. . . ."

She turned and stared out the window. The shops and businesses of London gave way to houses, then to countryside.

"I've never been in the country before," said Charlie at last. "Green, ain't it?"

She nodded. For a moment they sat silent in the *clickety-clack* of the train. Then, "Are you really a puma?" he asked. "If you don't mind me inquiring. Because Diana told me you were, and she can lie something beautiful."

Catherine nodded solemnly. "Want to feel?" She drew up one corner of her upper lip to reveal the canine.

Charlie reached over and felt it with the ball of his thumb. "Blimey! I bet you could do some damage with that." He looked at her in alarm. "You're not going to bite me, are you? Sometimes Diana does, but she can't do much damage."

DIANA: Oh, can't I? Just you wait, Charlie Sutton . . .

"I only bite in self-defense, or when I'm hungry," said Catherine. "Luckily for you, I've had an excellent breakfast." She was amused to note that Charlie still eyed her warily. Well, that was all right. What was the use of being a Puma Woman if you couldn't frighten people once in a while? "Do you want to know what it was like on the island of Dr. Moreau, with the Beast Men? And being left alone on a deserted island? And then rescued and taken to Peru?"

Charlie nodded eagerly.

"Well then, I'll tell you." And for the rest of the trip, she regaled him with stories of her time on the island and what had happened after. If you want to read Catherine's story, you have only to purchase *The Strange Case of the Alchemist's Daughter*, the first in these adventures of the Athena Club, two shillings as I have mentioned.

MARY: I wouldn't advertise too often in this book. Our readers want to hear a story, not advertisements! We're not *Lippincott's Monthly Magazine*, after all.

By the time the train drew into Purfleet, Catherine was only slightly lower than Diana in Charlie's private pantheon—in which the inimitable Miss Hyde reigned supreme as his goddess of thievery and mischief.

> DIANA: Inimitable! I like that. It's going to be another one of my words.

At Purfleet, Charlie left the carriage first and walked along the High Street toward the Royal Hotel, hands in his pockets, whistling as though he were simply strolling through the streets on a fine summer day, with no ulterior motive whatsoever.

Catherine waited a few minutes on the train platform so they would not be seen together in town. Then she followed Charlie up the High Street. She could not see him—he must have gone into the hotel, which was next to a pub called The Black Dog, in the town center. As she passed the pub, she shook her head disapprovingly, already in character. Just beyond the town proper, she turned onto the North Road, passing the gates of the asylum as though they had nothing to do with her. Beyond the asylum was a development of workingmen's cottages. Out of her leather satchel she drew a stack of leaflets. At each house, Reverend Josiah Crashaw, or so she introduced herself, left a leaflet in the hands of the bemused housewife or random small child who might answer the door. The leaflet was titled *Temperance Tract*. Below the title, in large, ornate letters, was written *Drinking Leads to Neglect of Duty, Moral Degradation, and Crime*, and below that was an etching of a man about to strike his fearful, long-suffering wife while his bedraggled children clutched at the hem of his jacket. Anyone who stopped Reverend Crashaw would have gotten a lecture on the Demon Drink and how it had ruined the lives of honest men, and aye, women too! But no one did stop him. At the end of Peaceful Row, the last street in the development, he came to the cottage of Joe Abernathy, where Joe's mother told Reverend Crashaw that she was quite of his mind, and drink was ruining the young men of England, although she didn't think beer was the same as strong liquor and even her Joe, the best of sons, had his pint at the end of each day. Until Joe came out and said, "Ma, can't you see it's Miss Moreau? Come in, quickly. I've been expecting you, miss."

"Well for goodness' sake," said Mrs. Abernathy. "How can I recognize her when she has a different disguise every time? You can sit here, miss, and have yourself a bite of something—it's almost elevenses. And tell us how Mrs. Poole is doing, and Miss Jekyll, and that nice Mr. Holmes."

The Abernathys' kitchen looked just the same as the last time Catherine had visited, with its neat shelves of crockery and Nottingham lace curtains. It had a large table with four mismatched chairs where Joe and his mother took their meals, a sink with a pump handle, and a large black stove that squatted at the end of room like a useful ogre. Its spotlessness was a testament to Mrs. Abernathy's housekeeping skills.

"Miss Moreau doesn't want to gossip, Ma," said Joe while he set out plates with the cathedrals of Great Britain transfer-printed on them. "She's here for information. And I've got something for you, miss. Something has happened at last."

"Tell me," said Catherine, sitting at the kitchen table. The Abernathys' cottage had no dining room, and the parlor was reserved for only the most formal occasions. Everything important happened in the kitchen.

"Well," said Joe, "you know there's been nothing for a long time, not to report anyway. Just letters coming in with those red seals marked S.A. Dr. Seward has been his usual self, and poor Renfield too—eating his flies as nice as you please, and as kindly as ever.

"But on Friday Dr. Seward had a visitor. It was a gentleman from London. I know because I was the one as let him in, and while we were crossing the courtyard I remarked that it was a nice day, and he remarked back that it was cooler here than in London, with all that pavement. He was a gentleman by his voice and manner, although his collar wasn't as white as it oughter be if it was laundered regular, and his suit jacket was fraying at the cuffs. He had a queer, frightened air about him. At first I thought he might be coming for a consultation himself—he didn't seem quite right, if you know what I mean. He had that look the patients get, sometimes. But when I asked who I should say was calling, he said his name was Edward Prendick and he had an appointment with Dr. Seward. I remembered that was one of the names Miss Jekyll told me to watch out for. I would have sent you a letter, miss, but I knew you were coming today."

Catherine sat in stunned silence. So Prendick—Edward Prendick, the man who had watched her being transformed from a puma into a woman, who had taught her to speak and read, who had told her that he loved her and finally deserted her on Moreau's island—was still alive. He had not died in the fire with Adam Frankenstein, nor escaped to the continent as they thought he might have. He was still in London. Catherine did not know what to say.

Mrs. Abernathy brought a plate of brown bread with butter and slices of cold ham, as well as a dish of mixed pickles. "I'll have the tea ready in a minute," she said.

"That's important, right, miss?" asked Joe, looking at her anxiously.

"Yes. Yes, it is." Absentmindedly, Catherine buttered a slice of bread and put it on her plate. She took a slice of ham, then started tearing it with her teeth. "Do you have any idea what the meeting was about?" *Knife,* she reminded herself. *Cut the meat with a knife, eat it with a fork.* An incredibly inefficient way to nourish oneself. How did human beings survive?

"It went on for about an hour," said Joe, making a bread, butter, and ham sandwich for himself. He piled pickled onions and gherkins on his plate. "I tried to listen at the door, but I had my duties and anyway there were other attendants passing. So I heard only the beginning of their conversation. Dr. Seward said something about a meeting in London, and Prendick was against it, which made Seward angry. He was talking loudly, which is why I heard as much as I did. He said something about questioning Prendick's loyalties, and that was when I had to go. So I don't know much more than that."

Across the kitchen, the teakettle started to whistle. Mrs. Abernathy took it off the stove.

"Joe, you forgot teacups!" Mrs. Abernathy set two teacups on the table, then brought the matching teapot, steaming out of its spout. "Do you take milk, Miss Moreau? Joe never does, so sometimes I forget to put it out."

"Yes," said Catherine. She ate the rest of her ham properly, with fork and knife. She did not want to shock Mrs. Abernathy.

"I'm sorry, miss. I wish I could tell you more. But it sounds as though something is afoot, as Mr. Holmes always says. We buy *The Strand* just for Dr. Watson's stories." Joe poured his tea and added a great deal of sugar. It looked dark and strong—much stronger than Mrs. Poole's.

"It's all right. What you've found out is certainly important. If only I knew when and where they were planning to meet!"

"That I can't help you with. But I'll keep a lookout—maybe Mr. Prendick will visit again and I'll be able to learn more?"

Catherine poured her tea, only filling her cup halfway, and added a great deal of milk from the jug Mrs. Abernathy had brought.

"Thank you, Joe. We're all grateful for your help." But the meeting had to be soon, or Seward would have written rather than summoned Prendick. How could she find out when and where it was going to take place? Where would that information be kept? Surely a man as important as the director of Purfleet Asylum had an appointment calendar. Would he write down a meeting with another member of the Société des Alchimistes? Or would that be too secret to record?

"Oh, it's nothing really," he said, his neck and face flushing red. "Anything to help Miss Jekyll—and Mr. Holmes of course."

His embarrassment was almost comical. But Joe had the dignity of large, quiet men, which a red face could not affect. Catherine wondered why he kept working at the asylum, when he could have earned more in one of the trades. Perhaps it was this desire to be of use, to help those who needed his services.

Suddenly, there was a knock on the kitchen door. Joe was so startled that he almost knocked over his chair. "Were you expecting anyone?" asked Mrs. Abernathy. Reverend Josiah Crashaw prepared to lecture the Abernathys, in a loud and obnoxious voice, on the necessity for abstention from all alcoholic stimulants.

But when Mrs. Abernathy opened the door, there was Charlie, glancing furtively behind him at the street, then dodging around her and darting into the kitchen—to her intense surprise. "I weren't followed, I promise you, miss," he said to Reverend Crashaw.

"It's Charlie, one of Mr. Holmes's boys," Catherine explained. Mrs. Abernathy was looking with alarm at Charlie's London finery, a ragged approximation of what a gentleman would wear, too large for him and tacked up so the trouser legs would not drag on the ground. "I brought him with me from London, so he could talk to some of the local boys in case they had noticed anything Joe might have missed. Mr. Holmes employs a small army of such boys, as his eyes and ears about London."

"Oh, well, if he knows Mr. Holmes," said Joe, although he looked at Charlie dubiously.

"Mrs. Abernathy, could Charlie have a cup of tea as well? He was never supposed to come here——we were supposed to meet again at the train station. But if he is here, it's because he has news for me. So." Catherine turned to Charlie. "What is it?"

"There's been developments," said Charlie. "Look what I brought you. Is that bread and butter?" He pulled a bundle of blue cloth out from under his shirt and held it out to Catherine.

She shook it out. It was . . . a dress.

"That's from the asylum," said Joe. "The female patients wear that. Where did you get it?"

Charlie sat down at the table and took a slice of bread, just as Mrs. Abernathy slid a plate in front of him. As he spoke, he spread a great deal of butter on it with the butter knife, without waiting for cutlery of his own. "I went to the Royal Hotel, as you told me, miss, and got friendly with the boots there. Soon we were drinking beer and I was telling him that I wanted to find a job in the country, because a man was after me in London, on account of I refused to turn pickpocket for him. I told him about life in London, making out that it was just like a novel by Mr. Dickens, though it ain't anymore, but country boys are credulous, you know. I could of told him I was Oliver Twist and he would have believed me." Mrs. Abernathy put a knife and fork by his plate, which he proceeded to ignore, and a teacup that he filled almost to overflowing. "Thanks kindly, ma'am." He flashed her a smile, the crooked smile of the London boy, made up of equal parts innocence and impish charm.

"Well!" she said, trying not to smile back, and took a jar down from a shelf. In a moment, Charlie had a pot of plum jam by his elbow, which he spread liberally on another slice of bread and butter. He added a great deal of sugar to his tea and as much milk as the cup would allow, then took a loud slurp.

"So he says the only jobs around are at the asylum, on account of the economic depression. His sister works there as a maid and might know of something. Could I talk to her, I ask him. Surely, he says, and asks the head clerk if he can take an hour, and the head clerk says all right if he stays late to sweep, so we go up to the asylum together and he takes me in the back door and introduces me to his sister, who's doing the laundry." By this time, Charlie was on his third slice of bread and had poured his second cup of tea. "Well, she says they're looking for a boy, and the pay's good on account of having to be around mad people. I tell her I wouldn't mind, mad people don't scare me, so she shows me around and takes me to the housekeeper. I convince the housekeeper that I'm an honest boy, despite my appearance, doing my Mr. Dickens bit, and she says I'll do. But she can't hire me until the director gets back, because himself has to approve everyone, down to the scullery maid. So I ask her where he is and when he'll get back, since I'm eager to start. And she says he's been called to meet with one of the trustees, so he won't be back until teatime!" By now, the bread was gone. Charlie looked forlornly at the serving plate, and then at the final slice of buttered bread in front of Catherine. "Are you going to eat that?"

"So Seward has gone out for several hours! His office will be empty. . . ."

"I wonder which trustee, and what he wanted," said Joe. "There's Dr. Raymond, Lord Godalming, and—no, I've forgotten the name of the other. That's the first time Dr. Seward's been away from the asylum for weeks. If we can get into his office without being noticed, we can see if there are important papers—"

"Not you, Joe." Catherine put the slice of bread on Charlie's plate. "For one thing, it's your day off, so anyone who sees you will wonder why you're there, and remark on it. For another, you're not exactly inconspicuous. No, it's got to be me, which is why you brought this, isn't it, Charlie?" She held up the blue dress, made of a practical cotton poplin that would wash and wear well.

"That's right. You can't get in through the back entrance. There are too many servants about, and they would notice you're not one of them. But maybe you can get in the front way." Charlie finished his third cup of tea and checked to see if there was any more, but the teapot was empty.

Joe had a look on his face—it was the same look Watson had so often. He was about to say, *But it's too dangerous for a lady like you.* . . . That's how the objections always started.

"Joe, I do need your help," she said before he could speak. "I need you to tell me how to get to Seward's office."

He sighed and shook his head. "All right. You'll have to get into the grounds first, but the wall's tumbled down in back, which is how Renfield escaped. It still hasn't been repaired, on account of it belongs to Carfax House, behind the asylum, and the owner of the house is abroad. Most of the women patients are harmless, there for hysteria or harming themselves, so they're allowed to walk on the lawn after lunch. The attendants don't keep careful watch over them, not like with the men patients. So you might be able to sneak in the front door of the asylum. From there it's up the stairs, second door to your left. Dr. Seward's name is written on the door. But miss, once you're inside, one of the attendants might realize you're not a patient. And then what? Anyway, the office door will be locked."

"I don't know," said Catherine. "I'll have to figure it out as I go along, including the lock. Will you show me where the wall has fallen down?"

"All right, if you're determined. But I worry that it's too dangerous for a lady like you—"

"I'm a puma, remember? Are you ready, Charlie?" She stood up, the dress bundled in her arms. She was certainly not going to argue the point with Joe.

"Ready," he said. Where in the world had all that food gone?

How could a boy made mostly of skin, bones, and cunning eat so much?

Catherine looked around for Mrs. Abernathy, to thank her, but Joe's mother had gone into another room, probably to give them some privacy while they discussed what they were going to do. She stuffed the blue dress into her satchel, leaving the temperance leaflets on the table to make room. Perhaps Mrs. Abernathy could make spills out of them, to start the stove. She had no idea what she would find at the asylum, what information might be in Seward's office. Mary would scold her for this adventure, for going into a dangerous situation alone. But if Prendick was up to something, she had to find out what. Why was he meeting Seward in London? Were they going to perform more experiments? Was Hyde still in London as well? If so, she might be able to deliver him to Holmes and Scotland Yard. She could already imagine them all congratulating her on her cleverness and courage. . . .

She slung the satchel over her shoulder, put on Reverend Crashaw's hat, and prepared to follow Joe to the tumbled-down place in the wall of Carfax House. It was certainly going to be an interesting day.

CHAPTER III

Dr. Seward's Diary

Joe checked to make sure there was no one passing in the street. Then they all left by the kitchen door and headed through the back garden, where vegetables marrows and melons were hanging ripe, ready for picking. Joe led them through a gate in the white picket fence that protected the garden from rabbits and deer. Behind the house was a path, with back garden fences on one side and a forest of tall trees, oaks and ashes, on the other. Catherine and Charlie followed Joe down the path, behind the workmen's cottages.

The afternoon sun shone hot upon them. For once, incredibly, England was warm enough for Catherine.

"What do you think of the country, Charlie?" she asked, swatting at a cloud of midges that had risen from the tangle of yarrow and wild carrot at the edge of the forest.

"It's as noisy as London, in its own way," he said, dispassionately. "I couldn't sleep in this racket."

"That's birds and crickets," she said, smiling.

"Yeah, well, give me pigeons and cabs rattling across the cobblestones. And cabbies swearing! This green stuff's all right in its place, and that place is a park. Bloody blooming hell! Something just stung me."

In front of them, Joe snorted.

"What does he know? He wouldn't last half a day in London,"

said Charlie, but in a low voice. He knew better than to anger a man with arms the size of tree trunks.

They had passed the development now: trees grew on both sides of the path. They walked in the shadows of leafy branches. "Carfax House is up ahead," said Joe. "All this used to belong to the Carfax family—Carfax Woods, it's called. But it was sold off for logging, and then the logging company went bankrupt. Don't know who owns it now."

In a few minutes they had reached a high wall of gray stone covered with ivy and lichen. "The gate's a little farther, I think. I ain't been here for a while." Walking along the wall, they soon reached it: an iron gate, rusted and with a lock that had been broken at some point. It made a grating sound when Joe pulled it open and led them through. The other side of the gate did not look much different: it was still wooded, although as they walked along the path, the undergrowth began to disappear. There were the remains of formal plantings, and here and there a moss-covered statue. Catherine realized this had once been a gentleman's park. "There's the house," said Joe. Through the trees she could see a building of the same gray stone as the wall, looming and crumbling at the same time. One wing looked as though it dated back to the middle ages. The other was in the fanciful gothic of the seventeenth century, as though designed by Horace Walpole himself. They were connected by a section in a considerably more modern style. The house looked entirely deserted—its windows, whether medieval, pseudo-medieval, or modern, were dark and empty. Beside it stood a chapel, probably older than the house itself, with a stone cross on its roof.

"After the last of the Carfaxes died out, it was sold to a foreign nobleman. He took possession, and we all hoped he would fix it up and provide jobs for the townsfolk. But after appearing in town several times, he disappeared suddenly, back to his own land they

say, where he had a grand castle. I guess an English manor wasn't
fine enough for him!"

Now they had passed the house and the forest was darker,
the trees closer together, the undergrowth more dense. Light
filtered through the branches, and it was cool under the shade
of the trees.

"There," said Joe. "That's the back wall to the asylum, and you
can see the place where stones have fallen. The stone part of the
wall belongs to Carfax, the brick part to the asylum. I don't know
why Dr. Seward doesn't just get it fixed. It's not as though the
foreign nobleman is going to object!"

The place where the stones had fallen was low enough to climb
over—no wonder it had been so easy for Renfield to escape.

"Why don't they all escape this way?" asked Charlie, looking at
the wall appraisingly.

"Most of them don't know about it. And if they did, most of
them would stay in the asylum anyhow. This world's no place for
a madman. The wall is to keep them safe, not just keep them in,"
said Joe.

"All right, turn around." Catherine drew the blue dress out
of her satchel. Joe and Charlie both looked puzzled. "I need to
change? Out of my clothes."

"Oh!" said Joe, growing red about the ears. Charlie just
grinned. They both turned their backs to her. She wouldn't have
cared if they had seen her in her underclothes, but it would have
embarrassed Joe, at least. Quickly, she slipped off her masculine
attire and pulled the blue dress over her head. It would conceal the
fact that she was wearing men's, not women's, undergarments. It
was certainly not the sort of dress for which one needed a corset!
She suspected that she looked rather like a blue sack of potatoes.
But Beatrice would no doubt have appreciated it as an instance of
rational dress.

BEATRICE: That's not fair, Catherine! One does
    not have to dress in a way that is unflattering,
    or even unfashionable, to be rational—and
    comfortable. How can you expect women to
    exercise their faculties, nay, their rights, in
    clothes that confine them? We shall never be
    men's equals while we lace ourselves into ill
    health and drape ourselves in fabric until we
    can scarcely move. Dress reform is almost as
    important to our cause as the vote.

Catherine took the pins out of her hair and untwisted the tight
bun she had been hiding under Reverend Crashaw's hat. She shook
her hair over her eyes, rather like an unkempt dog, then said, "All
right, how do I look?"

Joe and Charlie both turned back to look at her. "Well done,
miss," said Joe. "I might have mistaken you for a patient myself."

"I'll wait here for you," said Charlie. Catherine stuffed
Reverend Crashaw's clothes inside her satchel and handed it to
him, along with the hat she had been wearing. The men's shoes
would be hidden by the hem of her dress, which dragged on the
ground a little. Did it . . . yes! It had pockets, into which she put
three of the hairpins. They would come in handy later. The rest
she would leave with Charlie.

"And so will I," said Joe, crossing his arms and frowning at
Charlie, as though the London boy had taken his place. Which,
in a way, he had—it was good of Joe to keep watch for them and
send them updates, but when it came to scheming, Charlie was in
a different class.

"No, you won't," said Catherine, looking through the gap in
the wall. On the asylum side, close to the stone wall, ornamental
trees and shrubs had been planted, probably to conceal the wall

itself. Beyond that small patch of wilderness, visible through the rhododendrons, viburnum, and Rose of Sharon, was a broad swath of lawn. She would follow the wall, staying among the shrubbery as far as she could. But eventually she would reach the brick portion of the wall that belonged to the asylum, where there was no cover. Then she would have to cross the manicured expanse of lawn to join the other inmates.

"If anything goes wrong, if anyone notices that Seward's office has been broken into, I want you to have a solid alibi. So what I want you to do, Joe, is go to The Black Dog and make sure everyone there notices you. And I want you to stay there at least until teatime. Can you do that?"

"But what if you need help?"

Men! Why did they always assume their presence would, in some intangible way, be helpful? "Right now, that's the best help you can give me. We need to make sure you stay as far away from this affair as possible. That's what Mary would want."

Aha! That had done the trick—she could tell by the expression on his face. "Well, if that's what Miss Jekyll would have wanted. Just be careful, miss. When you get back, if you follow the path through the woods, opposite to the way we came, you'll reach the front gate of Carfax. From there you turn left onto a road with no name, far as I know. We just call it the road to Carfax. You'll know it's the right way if you see a gravel pit—it was a cut to the gravel pit, originally. And that will take you back to the North Road."

"Thank you, Joe," said Catherine. "I won't get lost, I promise." As though she could! Pumas had an excellent sense of direction.

Reluctantly, Joe turned and walked back through the forest in the direction he had described, presumably toward the front gate of Carfax and the road with the gravel pit, which would take him to the North Road and into town.

MRS. POOLE: You're absolutely right about men, miss. They're all very well in their place, but if I were in a tight spot, I would rather have women with me. They're so much less sentimental.

MARY: What about Mr. Holmes?

MRS. POOLE: Ah well, I'm sure Mr. Holmes would come in handy. But look at how you girls work together, despite your bickering. Someday, I'm sure you'll be as famous as Mr. Holmes.

CATHERINE: If anyone buys our books . . .

Catherine stepped through a gap in the wall where the stones stood no higher than her knees, holding her dress up as daintily as a lady of quality. With a brief wave to Charlie, she turned and crept close to the wall, hiding as much as she could behind the rhododendrons, which gave her good cover with their broad green leaves. There, across the lawn, was the Purfleet Asylum, a brick building, modern and undistinguished in style. She could see a back entrance and lines of laundry drying in the sun, but no one on this side of the building. All the servants must be inside. Hopefully no one would be looking out the windows—at least, no one that anyone would listen to. On the third story, the windows were barred. Behind one of those barred windows was Renfield, the madman, who had been suspected of the Whitechapel Murders. Seward's office was on the second floor, on the right side of the building—it would be the left once she was inside. It would have been easier if she could have climbed up to it without entering the asylum, but there was nothing on the building to climb—no pipes, no ivy. Presumably all the plumbing had been built in, as it often was in modern construction. The ornamental shrubbery that hid the foundations did not extend even to the height of the first-floor windows. No, she would have to go in the front entrance and climb up the stairs, like an ordinary human being. In that office was a clue to what Prendick had been planning with Seward—at least, she hoped there was.

Now she had reached the end of the stone wall, where the band of trees and shrubs also ended. Here the wall turned a right angle, into the brick wall of the asylum proper. And there, across the lawn, were the female patients, just as Joe had described. Some of them were walking, alone or arm in arm. Some were sitting in lawn chairs in the shade of the building. They were dressed as she was, all alike. Where were the attendants? She strolled across the green lawn, trying to look as though she belonged and knew where she was going. Now she could see the front of the asylum. Yes, there were two men in white coats standing close to the front entrance, one of them smoking a cigarette. Even as far away as she was, she could smell the smoke. No one, as far as she could tell, was looking in her direction.

The two women closest to her were standing together, one of them nodding and gesturing to the other in an exaggerated manner. As she approached, the one who had been gesturing turned to her and said, "Oh, hello, my dear, did you get lost?" Her voice was cultivated, and she looked rather like the grandmother in a fairy tale, with white hair in an untidy pile on top of her head. She was as small as Diana, with bony wrists and elegant hands. Her eyes matched the blue of the asylum dress. She might have been the only person on whom that dress was not entirely unflattering.

"Yes, a little. I've only just come here," said Catherine.

"Oh, you'll get used to the routine soon enough. You may call me Lavinia, although I make the attendants call me Lady Hollingston. An impudent lot! I'll have no disrespect from them.

And this is Florence. I don't know her last name because she hasn't said a word since I came here. It's not physical, is it, Florence? Dr. Seward says it's hysterical mutism, most common in young women of marriageable age. She suddenly stopped talking at the age of sixteen, although she writes a lovely Spencerian hand. And she's been here ever since."

Florence nodded. She was a plump young woman with a round face, shy smile, and sad eyes.

"I'm very pleased to make your acquaintance, Your Ladyship, Miss Florence," said Catherine, with a slight curtsey.

"Oh really, Lavinia, please. We have very few formalities here," said Lady Hollingston. "May I ask why you were admitted?"

"Well, you see, I can't stop cutting myself," said Catherine, pulling up her sleeve. On her brown skin shone the faint tracery of scars from Moreau's surgery. "And if I may ask such a delicate question . . ."

"Oh, I don't mind." Lady Hollingston smiled a kindly, gentle smile. Her blue eyes crinkled at the corners. "I murdered my husband, you see. But because of my age and station I was not committed to Broadmoor. Dr. Seward does not consider me dangerous, so he doesn't keep me confined, as I might be elsewhere. He runs such a progressive establishment here, so forward-thinking. I feel quite fortunate to be here, although the fees are expensive. But my son does not object."

"Do the families of the patients pay for them?" asked Catherine, surprised.

"Oh yes, this is a very exclusive madhouse, you see. . . . I don't believe you told me your name? Otherwise they might be in charitable institutions. Most families of means would not want that for their relatives, however mad they might be."

"Yes, I see. My name is Catherine Crashaw, Your Lady—Lavinia."

Florence put her hand to her throat and mimed what was

obviously an apology for not taking part in the conversation. She seemed a sweet girl, although Catherine wondered if she had murdered someone as well.

> MARY: Hysterical mutism is most often associated with trauma, such as an assault of some sort. I learned that in Vienna, when we were discussing symptoms of madness before Diana was—

> CATHERINE: Could you please not spoil the plot for our readers? You can talk about researching symptoms of madness all you want when I get to Vienna. I mean when you get to Vienna, later in the narrative.

> MARY: Well, at any rate, I doubt Florence murdered anyone. It's much more likely that someone did— well, something not very nice—to her.

"Are you by any chance related to the Devonshire Crashaws?" asked Lady Hollingston.

Catherine wondered how Lady Hollingston had murdered her husband. She looked as fragile as a porcelain doll. "Yes, I believe so—distantly. You know, I think I'm beginning to feel faint."

"It's this heat. You should go in and ask for a glass of water with a slice of lemon in it. They really are very accommodating, as long as we obey the rules of the institution. But make sure they put in a slice of lemon—the lemon is very important." Lady Hollingston patted her on the arm.

Florence nodded. How nice they were to be so concerned! And this was of course the excuse Catherine needed. She curtseyed again, then turned and made her way through the patients strolling about or sitting in lawn chairs, wondering what was so important about the lemon. Most of the patients nodded to her, except one young woman who was twisting her hair and muttering to herself.

When she reached the steps to the front entrance, whose doors had been left open, probably to combat the unaccustomed heat, one of the attendants, the one who had not been smoking, said, "And where might you be going?"

Catherine pulled at her hair, twisting it over her face like the madwoman she had just passed, hiding herself as much as she could. "I'm not feeling well, so Lady Hollingston told me to go in and ask for some water. With a slice of lemon, she said." She made her voice as vague and plaintive as she could.

"Oh, well!" He winked at her, while his companion chuckled and then coughed. "If Her Ladyship told you, then of course you must. Lord Holliston pays through the nose for having her whims indulged! I can't think why, since she murdered his pa. But be quick about it."

She nodded, then walked quickly up the steps and into the asylum.

It was just as Mary had described: a large vestibule, with benches along the walls and chairs scattered about, all made of hard wood. The walls were whitewashed, as in a hospital. A corridor ran back into the recesses of the building: from Joe's descriptions, she knew it led to a communal dining room, the kitchens, and servants' quarters. Somewhere in the distance she could smell cooking—mutton and dumplings, she thought, although over it all lingered what was probably a permanent smell of cabbages. On one side of the corridor was a set of stairs leading upward. On the second floor were offices and rooms for patients who were not considered dangerous. On the third floor were rooms for the patients considered dangerous to others or themselves.

Luckily, the vestibule was empty, although she could hear what an ordinary person would not have: the *click-click* of heels coming down the corridor toward her. A faint medicinal smell identified the person with the clicking heels as a nurse. Medicine and cabbages—that's what the asylum smelled like. Up on the third floor, a patient was groaning and crying. But otherwise, the building was silent.

As lightly as she could, Catherine ran up the stairs. Perhaps she should take off her boots? But no, there was nowhere to hide them. She would simply have to be light on her feet.

The second door on her left was conveniently labeled:

JOHN SEWARD, M.D.

DIRECTOR

Now came the part she had been worried about. She pulled one of the hairpins out of her pocket. Would it be strong enough? She hoped so. She pulled apart the two legs of the long *U* until they were almost straight, then bent one into an angular *S*, as Diana had shown her. One bend of the *S* raised the lever, the other would retract the bolt. She put the hairpin into the keyhole. There—she could feel the lever lifting. She turned the hairpin firmly but carefully. And then, with a click, she heard the bolt draw back. She turned the knob, and then . . . she was in. Quietly, with a sigh of relief, she closed the office door behind her and locked it again with the hairpin.

Seward's office was neatly organized: books arranged on the shelves, file cabinet in the corner, a large desk with a blotter and inkstand. On the desk, beside the blotter, lay a single leather-bound book. On one corner of the desk was a phonograph, set to record on a wax cylinder. Good: that meant anything to be found would be appropriately filed. And bad: Catherine did not know where.

The bookshelves would tell her nothing. All the books were thick, bound in leather, with gilding on their spines—medical books, no doubt. There were shelves of paperbound journals, but after one look at them, Catherine knew they would not be helpful either. They had titles like *Journal of the Anthropological Institute of Great Britain and Ireland*. No, the shelves told her nothing except that Seward was an important man, the director of a medical establishment, who tried to keep himself informed on the latest research in his field. She was glad the windows were open, or the afternoon sun would have made the room uncomfortably hot, even for her. She had no idea England could get this warm.

What about the desk? Yes! The leather-bound book was stamped WEEKLY DIARY. She opened it to where the ribbon had been placed. This week, Sunday to Saturday, with this afternoon's appointments crossed out—hastily, by the look of it. And written in the margin, also in haste because the ink had blotted, was written: *Summoned—Dr. R*. Seward did not seem like the sort of man who would have blotted his ink, except in a moment of distraction or distress. She flipped back to the previous week. And there it was, on Friday afternoon, in a neat hand this time, from 1:00 p.m. to 2:00 p.m.: *Meeting with E.P.* So he did keep personal information in this diary—it was not simply business. Now to flip forward. It was all asylum business as far as she could see, including an appointment with Lord Hollingston. Wait—there, a week from today, at 5:00 p.m. *Meet E.P. Soho 7 Potter's Lane*. That must be it, the meeting he and Edward Prendick had been arguing about. She had nowhere to write down the address—she did not want to take anything from the office—so she would simply have to remember it. She flipped forward again . . . more asylum business. Until the last full week of September, which was left blank. On that week was written simply: *S.A. Budapest*. After that, the journal was empty—the rest of September, October, November, and December were not yet filled in.

S.A. *Budapest* had to be a meeting of the Société des Alchimistes in Budapest. But for what purpose? A scientific conference to present data? That's what scientists did, right? Van Helsing had mentioned presenting papers at a conference, and that might take about a week. Although really she was just guessing, and it could be something else altogether. . . . Perhaps she would find more information, or better yet, correspondence with Van Helsing, inside the desk. It had a central drawer and three drawers on each side. The central drawer was locked. She tried the right side: paper for correspondence, with and without the name of the asylum on top; another pen and two bottles of ink; folders of what looked like notes for individual patients that had not yet been filed. The left side contained a bottle of bourbon with two glasses, three starched collars, and a pair of rubber shoe covers, presumably in case of rain.

What about the file cabinet? Catherine went over and pulled open the drawers. They contained only patient files. She searched through several to make sure they were indeed what they appeared to be, but none of them revealed any secrets. Wait, she had almost forgotten . . . surely one of them must contain more than clinical notes. Quickly, she looked under R. There was the folder, marked RENFIELD, RICHARD MATTHEW. It was completely empty. Someone, presumably Seward himself, had removed the contents. Where could they be? Catherine returned to the desk and flipped quickly through the folders of patient notes—none of them pertained to Renfield. There was nowhere left but the locked drawer—any secrets would be in there. She sat down in Seward's chair, which was the sort that rolled on four casters, and stared at the lock. For the first time, she wished that she had brought Diana.

> DIANA: See? You never want to take me, and then you
> wish I were there. I could have picked that lock in
> a minute. Less than a minute.

It resembled the lock on the door, except for being smaller, but . . . it bolted upward, into the desktop. So it wouldn't be a matter of lifting the lever, but of what? Shifting it in one direction or the other? If it was a lever . . .

She simply did not know. But Seward's diary indicated that he would be gone all afternoon, and no one had discovered her so far, so she might as well try.

She took the bent hairpin out of her pocket and inserted it into the lock, trying to feel the moving parts. Yes, there was a lever in there. If she could just . . .

She heard a lock click open. It was not the lock on the desk drawer.

"What the devil are you doing in my office?" There, at the office door, was a man in a gray sack suit, with a bowler hat in his hand and an expression of fury on his face.

With what she prefers to think of as catlike grace but was probably pure panic, Catherine rose and pushed the chair back so that it rolled and struck the bookshelf behind her, then turned and leaped out the window.

> CATHERINE: It was really pure panic, and I would
> have been more graceful if I hadn't been wearing
> that stupid dress. I almost tripped over the hem.
>
> MARY: You're interrupting your own narrative?
>
> CATHERINE: I want to be honest. It wasn't exactly my
> proudest moment. I didn't even hear him coming,

a great clomping man like that. I'm supposed to be
a cat, remember?

Cats are supposed to land on their feet. Unfortunately,
Catherine landed on her back in a clump of azaleas growing by
the asylum wall. It took her only a moment to recover. As quickly
as she could, she pulled the dress over her head and discarded it
under the bushes. They would be looking for blue. Her drawers
and undershirt would not be inconspicuous against the grass, but
at least they were not blue.

She could hear Seward shouting above, and then more
shouting in the corridors of the asylum. But there was no
one on this side of the building to see her, at least not yet.
As quickly as she could, she sprinted across the grass toward
the back of the building, which was also deserted, the laundry
still flapping on its lines. Any moment now they would realize where she had gone. There, finally—she was back among
the shrubbery by the stone wall. She crouched in the bushes,
panting, and then looked back. The two attendants she had
spoken to earlier had just rounded the corner of the building,
and another man, in shirtsleeves rather than a white coat and
incongruously holding a broom, was running out the back door.
He must be a servant of some sort? That meant the asylum had
been alerted.

As quietly as she could, Catherine made her way through the
bushes to the place where the wall had tumbled down.

Just before stepping over the fallen stones, she looked back
one more time. It was difficult to see because a large rhododen-
dron was in her way, so she could not tell what was happening on
the asylum lawn. But so far none of the shouting was headed in her
direction—it was a back-and-forth confusion of voices.

"You seem to have lost something, miss," said Charlie. He

grinned as though he could not help it and handed her the satchel with Reverend Crashaw's clothes.

"Yes, well. I was an idiot, Charlie." Quickly, she once again dressed herself as the advocate of teetotalism. "Dr. Seward came back early and saw me. I should have heard him walking down the hall. I should have smelled him outside the door. What's the point of having superhuman senses if you don't pay attention to them? Instead, I trusted to his schedule, and he caught me unawares. Never trust a man to do what he says he's going to."

"I never do, miss."

There, she was once again outfitted as Reverend Crashaw. She pinned her hair back up with the remaining hairpins and put his hat on over the resulting bun. It was not as tight as it had been, but it would have to do.

"There's nothing more we can do in Purfleet. I think we should catch the next train back to London. What a mess this has been—although I did learn something valuable."

"And what is that?"

"I'll tell you on the train. Come on, if we go the way Joe told us, we'll find the front gate of Carfax. Then we can get back to the North Road and head into town. They'll be on the lookout, but for a woman alone, not two men together." Once they were back in London, she would tell Mary and the others— about the meeting in Soho and the mysterious S.A. at the end of September. What could it mean? What was going to happen in Budapest?

Once again they walked through the woods, Charlie first, brushing branches out of the way. Every once in a while, Catherine heard calls and cries from the direction of the asylum, but she could not make out what was being said. She was tired and hungry and ashamed of herself. Anyone, even Diana, would have done better than she had!

DIANA: What do you mean "even Diana"? You made a
    bloody mess of the whole thing. Of course I would
    have done better.

CATHERINE: I only meant that you're impulsive and
    easily distracted. And yes, I made a blooming,
    bloody mess of it, as Charlie might say. Thank you
    very much for reminding me.

Seward might not have seen her clearly enough to identify
her, but surely the two attendants had, as had Lady Hollingston.
Florence didn't count, since she wouldn't be able to provide
a description—unless they asked her to write one? Hopefully
as Reverend Crashaw she would be able to walk back along the
High Road to the town center and train station without attracting
attention.

There were the front gates of Carfax, taller and more imposing than the rusted, broken ones at the back of the estate. And
they were standing open. Just as she and Charlie were about to
pass through the gates, he stopped so abruptly that Catherine
nearly fell over him.

"Copper," he whispered.

Where? Cautiously, she stepped forward and looked where he
was pointing. Yes, to their left, by the gravel pit, she could see the
lean blue form of a village constable. He was turned away from
them, looking in the direction of the asylum. Could they somehow get around him while he wasn't looking?

"Harry, it's not a woman!" Who had said that? It had been
shouted down the road, from the direction of the asylum.

"What's that you say?" the constable, still turned away from
them, shouted back.

"What are they saying?" whispered Charlie. He could hear

their voices, but not their conversation—it took her puma ears to do that.

> DIANA: Oh, please. What are you going to call this book? *Adventures of the Puma Woman*, by Catherine Moreau?

> JUSTINE: I would read that. I think it would make a wonderful book.

Although they were some distance down the unnamed road, Catherine could hear them clearly, then the sound of running footsteps. She saw the white coat join the blue uniform. It was one of the asylum attendants, the one who had spoken to her when she was disguised as a madwoman. He leaned over, hands on his knees, panting. Evidently, he was not used to such exertions. "It's not a woman, I tell you. Albert found the dress he'd been wearing hidden in the bushes, and the prints in the dirt are of a man's square-toed boots. Lady Hollingston says she spoke to him. Of course she thought he was a woman at the time, but an uncommon masculine one, with a slight mustache. He should be easy to identify—Her Ladyship says his eyes are different colors, one blue, one green."

One blue, one green? Catherine's eyes were neither of those colors—nor did she have a mustache, not even a slight one, thank you very much. It sounded as though Lady Hollingston had deliberately lied—but why? Or was she simply mad and rambling when they questioned her? At the moment, Catherine did not care. Bless Lady Hollingston.

> MRS. POOLE: I made some inquiries afterward, about the Hollingston murder case. Turns out that

      one morning, after not speaking to his wife at
      breakfast for twenty years because he claimed it
      distracted him from the *Financial Times*, the late
      Lord Hollingston looked up from his paper and
      told her that his soft-boiled egg had been left
      in the water a minute too long, and she really
      ought to do a better job of managing the staff.
      She killed him with the carving knife—drove it
      right through his throat. Imagine that! Of course
      murder is wrong, but I can't say as I blame her.
      The first thing he said to her at breakfast, after
      twenty years of silence . . .

"There was a Reverend going up and down the lanes of the development earlier," said the constable. "Some of the womenfolk have been complaining that he scared the children with his descriptions of hellfire. You think that might have been him?"

"I doubt it. A thief isn't likely to go preaching up and down before breaking in, is he? But if you see this preacher fellow, I would keep him for questioning. Who knows, he might have seen something. Check to see if he has one blue eye, and one green!"

"All right. I'll tell Sam to check in the development first—the thief's more likely to have gone that way than into town. And let me know if you hear anything else. Just my luck this happened when I was about to go home for dinner. The missus is going to be upset. . . ."

Catherine pulled Charlie back into the shadow of the trees. It was evident that the North Road was being watched. If the constable saw her, or rather Reverend Crashaw, she would be stopped and questioned.

"Now what, miss?" he asked, looking her up and down. If the constable examined Catherine at all closely, he would know she wasn't a man. He wasn't a distracted housewife, to be fooled by a suit and pinned-up hair. And while he might not think she was the thief who had broken into Seward's office, he would certainly suspect her of something underhanded, disguised as she was. He would probably lock her up until her identity could be established. She would have to explain what she was doing pretending to be a minister. . . .

Catherine leaned back against the stone wall and slid down until she was sitting among the bracken. What now, indeed? She and Charlie were safe here for a while, but to return home they needed to get to the train station, and the only way was through town—or over the marshes that lay between the train station and the development. She immediately dismissed the marshes as worse than the police. Marshes meant water. She hated water, even if it was shallow—and what if they became stuck in the mud? Calling for help would alert the police to their presence. Should she and Charlie go back to Joe Abernathy's house? But if they were seen around that neighborhood, they might cast suspicion on Joe and his mother. They needed a way to quickly, quietly, invisibly, walk down the High Road. . . .

"It's Monday," she said suddenly, tugging at the hem of Charlie's jacket.

"What?" Charlie looked down at her upturned face as though she had gone mad.

"It's a Monday afternoon, and this is England, and the sun is shining."

He still looked at her uncomprehendingly.

"Don't you see, all over this isle of Albion, as Milton or some other poet called it, Monday is laundry day. What do all the good women of Purfleet have hanging in their back gardens, today of all days? Clothes! Clothes on the lines! Let's just hope some of them are dry. Come on, Charlie! We're going to murder Reverend Crashaw."

She stood up, stretching her arms, which still ached from the fall out of Seward's window, and started back through the trees the way they had come. They needed to get back to the path through Carfax Woods, and then to the workmen's cottages Reverend Crashaw had leafleted that morning. All the cottages were in the same style as Joe Abernathy's, built by the same builder: compact, designed to be modern and hygienic, with front and back gardens. And in those back gardens she would find what she was looking for.

As they once again trudged through the undergrowth, back along the way they had come earlier, she agreed with Charlie's conclusion about the English countryside—it was very pretty in its way, but best observed at a distance. If she could not have the slopes of the Andes, then give her a London street with an omnibus! She thought again about what she had seen in Seward's diary. That week marked *S.A. Budapest*—was he planning on going with Van Helsing? She was supposed to leave for Vienna with Mary and Justine—but then who would stay and find out what was going on here? Who would follow Seward and Prendick to Potter's Lane in Soho? Not that she wanted to see Prendick again—far from it. But someone would have to figure out what he was up to. And Seward as well, of course.

Once again they passed Carfax House—this time she thought it looked less ominous, almost comical in its juxtaposition of genuine and imitation gothic. And there beyond it was the back gate with its broken lock. Then the path through the trees, and then, yes, the back gardens of the workingmen's cottages. By this time she was hot and tired, no longer speaking to Charlie, simply pointing the way they should go.

The first of the laundry lines contained only linens. What time was it? She was not wearing a wristwatch, but the position of the sun indicated midafternoon. She was so thirsty. Charlie must be too—his face was pale and damp with sweat. But he followed closely behind without complaining. They crept along the back gardens, between Carfax Woods and whitewashed fences, still among the trees but close enough to see vegetables growing, chickens scratching in the dirt, sometimes children chasing one another and laughing, or playing quietly by themselves. There, in the back garden of a cottage that was a more dilapidated than its neighbors, was hanging exactly what she wanted—a faded lilac dress, several years out of fashion. It was probably worn as a housedress or on cleaning days, but it was perfect for getting past constables. There was no one about here, no children or housewives checking on the clothes, and thank goodness no dogs, so in a moment the dress was hers.

It took only three more houses to find everything she needed: in addition to the dress, a corset, corset cover, and petticoat. Underneath she would still be wearing a man's drawers and undershirt, but on the surface she would look indisputably female. After the disaster of the asylum, it felt good to lead three successful raids, even if they were only on clotheslines.

As soon as she had what she needed, she crept back among the trees, slipped out of Reverend Crashaw's suit, and put on female attire. Although Charlie tightened the corset laces as much as he could, it was still too large for her—its previous owner had been considerably more buxom. The corset cover, which had come from a different line, was a little tight, and the dress was too loose over it all, but that could not be helped. A young woman of Miss Catherine Montgomery's social station was unlikely to have a new dress of her own anyway. Catherine Montgomery—she had used that name before, and it would come in handy again. This was scarcely an ideal place to make one's toilette—there was no mirror, and branches kept catching on her clothes. Once she was dressed, she had to pick burdock off the hem, which dragged a little on the ground, with Charlie getting any burrs she had missed. But the forest, with its dappled light, was as elegant as any lady's boudoir.

She redid her hair in a loose chignon so it would fall in tendrils around her face, emphasizing the fact that she was female, totally unambiguously female, and had not been walking around in a man's suit an hour before, then looked down at herself. "I feel like a giant crocus."

Charlie grinned. "You'll do. There's one thing you're missing. Hang on a minute. . . ."

Five minutes later, just as Catherine was starting to get impatient, he was back. In one hand he clutched a straw hat, a little bent and battered, decorated with silk flowers. In the other he carried a ripe melon.

"Oh, you brilliant boy," said Catherine. "Have you got a knife?"

"Have I got a knife?" he said, incredulous that she had asked such a question. When was he, Charlie Sutton, ever without a knife? In a moment, he had flipped open his pocket knife and carved the melon into slices. "And if you could tell Diana that, about me being brilliant I mean, I would be much obliged. She doesn't think I'm good for much."

"Having a crush on Diana is a really stupid idea, you know," said Catherine. She took the slice of melon he handed her, sucked the liquid until it ran down her chin, then wiped it away with her hand and licked her fingers clean. She should have stolen a pocket handkerchief. "Where did this come from?" She looked dubiously at the hat, then put it on her head, careful not to disturb the coiffure secured with an inadequate number of hairpins. She tied the ribbons under her chin. They were a little frayed at the ends.

"Scarecrow. You look like a maid-of-all-work on her day out."

"That's supposed to be the general impression. And you're my brother, who's reluctantly accompanied me to visit . . . our aged mother?"

"Better make it an aunt. A local copper will know we're not from around these parts."

True. And Charlie, at least, had London written all over him. A boy like Charlie, with his hair slicked back under a hat that had in the distant past belonged to a gentleman, and his general air of self-possession, could have come from nowhere else.

One more slice of melon for each of them, since it wouldn't do to go thirsty. Several minutes later, Miss Catherine Montgomery and her brother, Master Charlie Montgomery, were walking down the North Road. Reverend Crashaw's satchel, stuffed with his clothes, had been buried under an oak tree and covered with last year's leaves. The return tickets and all of Reverend Crashaw's money had been transferred to Charlie's pockets.

As they walked by the asylum gates at a leisurely pace, an attendant leaning up against the wall called out, "Have you passed a man anywhere up the road?" This time it was the one who had been smoking. Presumably, the other was conducting a more active search. This one seemed to be keeping an ineffective lookout.

"No, sir, we saw no one," Catherine called back, in what she thought of as her most dulcet tones. "Would this be the way to the train station?"

> MARY: I don't think you have dulcet tones. Dulcet means sweet. When are you ever sweet?

> CATHERINE: My *most* dulcet tones. I was using the superlative. Everyone has a *most* something, even if it's not very much.

> BEATRICE: I think Catherine can be quite sweet when she wants to.

CATHERINE: I just don't want to very often.

"Aye, turn left onto the High Road and then keep going through town," said the attendant. "It's after the Royal Hotel. If you see a man—a peculiar gent, one eye blue, t'other green—you let a constable know. He's wanted for breaking and entering."

"I will. Thankee, sir!"

They walked to the center of town without seeing any more constables—where had they gone? Presumably they were still searching the development. Here they could blend in with the ordinary traffic of Purfleet. Men rolled carts filled with fruit and vegetables, old clothes, or furniture. Women with marketing baskets looked into shop windows, exclaiming over the prices. A group of school-aged children, just let out of school, ran down the street, laughing and shrieking. As they passed The Black Dog, Catherine noticed a group of men lounging about the door. And there was Joe, leaning against the wall, arms crossed. Even through the noise of the street, she could hear fragments of their conversation. "Stole some important papers, they say—dressed hisself as a woman—eyes of two different colors." So the news had circulated quickly. Joe, who did not join in the conversation, looked anxious.

As they passed, he glanced at her, noticed Charlie, and then examined her again more closely. He almost jumped when he realized who she was. No, Joe was not good at subterfuge. She looked directly at him, as though to say *Yes, I see you've recognized me*, then looked away, pulling Charlie by the sleeve like an impatient older sister. She had a character to maintain, and a train to catch.

As they approached the train station, Catherine saw Harry-the-Constable standing by the ticket office, looking official in his blue uniform and helmet with a silver star. The constable barely glanced at them as they passed, and Catherine breathed a silent sigh of relief. But before they had taken many steps, he said, "Hey there, miss, are you headed to London?"

"Aye, sir. My brother and I are in service there."

"Well, you just watch out," he said, leaning back against the wall of the station. "There's a thief on the loose. We have reason to believe he came from London this morning, and will try to get back there. Stands to reason—in a small place like Purfleet he'd stick out like a sore thumb, while in that den of iniquity, as they calls it, he'd be right at home!"

"Oh, that's terrible!" said Catherine Montgomery. "I wouldn't want anything of mine stolen. Mum always tells me to keep my money wrapped in a pocket handkerchief, in case my pocketbook is took."

"Smart woman, your mum. Well, if you see him on the train, you just tell the stationmaster or a policeman. You can't miss him: He's got one eye green and one blue! You'd think someone so easy to identify would know better than to turn thief. Though I don't think he'll escape us. We're watching the train station and all the roads out of town. If he wants to spend the night in Carfax Woods, I don't mind—let the ghouls suck the blood out of him! But we'll get him in the end."

"Oh, this is going to give me nightmares, sure!" She did her best to look frightened.

"Don't worry, I'll keep you safe, sis," said Charlie, with a reassuring squeeze of her arm. She tried to look grateful. Had he forgotten that she had hurt that arm falling out of Seward's window? Even a light squeeze hurt.

But Harry-the-Constable nodded his approval.

They walked to the bench on the platform, then sat under the watchful eye of the constable, not talking except for desultory complaints about the heat. Catherine was too tired to talk. What a day it had been!

Twenty minutes later, the train to London arrived.

"So the thief with mismatched eyes slipped through Harry's fingers after all," said Catherine, sitting on the sofa in the parlor of the Athena Club, next to Sherlock Holmes. "And then we had to take an omnibus, because no cabbie would stop for me wearing this lavender horror. No, it's cabs for gentlemen like Mr. 'olmes here, and omnibuses for maids-of-all-work in patched dresses! Honestly, I was this close to turning Anarchist . . ."

"For goodness' sake, don't let Mrs. Poole hear you," said Mary. "You know how she feels about loyalty to the Queen."

> MRS. POOLE: You're right about that, miss. God save the Queen! Not that I take Miss Moreau's statement at all seriously. She's got a streak of Diana in her, sometimes.

> CATHERINE: There's no need to insult me, Mrs. Poole. And I have no intention of blowing up Houses of Parliament. At least, not at the moment.

"Clearly, I messed up," she continued. "Seward saw me, although I don't know if he could identify me again. I've lost a man's suit costing at least two guineas, second hand. And for what? I know Seward is meeting Prendick in Soho next Monday, but I don't know what about. What is the Alchemical Society up to now? That's why I need to stay here—I'm the only one who can find out. I think we all agree that Beatrice can't go spying on people—she might poison them accidentally. And Diana—well, just no. And there's something important happening in Budapest toward the end of September, something connected with the society. There was a week marked off on Seward's calendar, the twentieth to the twenty-fourth, with just 'S.A. Budapest' written on it. But again I don't know what. Also, I'm starving. Have you all had tea yet?"

Mary, who had been listening intently, jumped a little. "Mrs. Poole was bringing it. I'll ring for her."

While she rang the bell, which chimed distantly in the kitchen, Dr. Watson looked at the scratches on Catherine's arm. "These just need washing and a bit of alcohol," he said. "You'll be as right as rain in no time, Miss Moreau. And here's hoping we get some rain, soon."

"Catherine, I think we know what will be happening during that week," said Justine. "Mary received a telegram."

"Yes," said Mary, returning to her armchair. "Look, here it is——" She handed the telegram to Catherine and started explaining the events of that morning. Just as she had gotten to the part where Alice had burst into Mr. Holmes's parlor, Mrs. Poole came in with tea, followed by Beatrice, who sat on her customary window seat. Then there was tea for them all, with potted meat sandwiches and Victoria sponge and jam tarts, and green sludge for Beatrice. Only Diana and Charlie were absent. Mary was glad her sister had not joined them—Diana would have complained incessantly about being left out.

"So Mary and Justine will go to Vienna," said Beatrice. She took a sip of her noxious liquid.

> BEATRICE: You don't need to describe it like that. If
> you don't like it, don't drink it——I believe that is
> the English expression? But there is no need to
> criticize my dietary requirements. At least I'm not
> a carnivore.

Catherine scraped the meat in her sandwiches off the bread and ate it with her fingers. She preferred Mrs. Abernathy's way of serving to this fussy procedure.

MRS. POOLE: Well! If you don't like the service, you
       have only to say, I'm sure. You're welcome to eat
       in the kitchen from a bowl on the floor, like Alpha
       and Omega! Or catch mice in the coal cellar . . .
       Mrs. Abernathy is a good woman, but this is a
       lady's residence. In this house, the food is served
       proper.

"I think we can agree that Dr. Seward is planning to attend
the meeting Miss Murray described—the meeting of the Société
des Alchimistes in Budapest. That is his week marked 'S.A.'"
Beatrice leaned forward, elbows on knees, forehead wrinkled.
"The threads of this mystery are beginning to weave together—is
that correct in English? Meanwhile Catherine will investigate Dr.
Seward's activities in Soho. And I—will I simply hold down the
house?"

"Fort. Hold down the fort." Mary took another slice of the
sponge cake. She was hungrier than she had realized.

"It feels as though I am the only one not contributing." Beatrice
looked down disconsolately into her cup.

"But you are," said Justine. "Someone has to look after Mrs.
Poole and Alice, and Diana of course."

"And get telegrams," said Mary. "And make sure we're all com-
municating with one another. We really do need you here, Bea."

Beatrice nodded, looking unconvinced.

"And I think we'll accept your offer to pay for train tickets, Mr.
Holmes," said Mary. "That is, unless anyone has objections?" She
did not like the idea herself, but the situation had changed and all
their carefully made plans must be set aside.

None of the members present objected, although Catherine
raised her eyebrows and then wrinkled her nose, which was her
way of looking displeased.

"Then we'll prepare to leave as quickly as possible. In two days' time, or three at most, Justine and I will leave for Charing Cross Station. And then it's Dover to Calais, to Paris, to Vienna on the Orient Express."

"And you'll be keeping me apprised along the way?" said Holmes. It was not quite a request.

"Of course," Mary replied, more acerbically than she had meant to. He might be paying for this trip, but she wasn't one of his Baker Street Irregulars, to *check in regular with Mister 'olmes.* Then she reminded herself that he was footing the bill and they would owe him—gratitude, if nothing else. So she might as well practice being grateful.

He merely nodded. Once again, he was his usual distant self. Would she ever find out more about the mysterious Irene Norton? Well, she would meet the woman herself in Vienna. She was not particularly looking forward to it.

In a few days, she would be traveling farther than she had ever traveled before. The thought filled her with equal parts apprehension and elation. But rescuing Lucinda Van Helsing—that was the purpose of this journey. It would be no pleasure trip. Rescuing Miss Van Helsing, and then stopping the Société des Alchimistes from experimenting on any more girls. Tomorrow she would go to the bank and withdraw twenty pounds for travel expenses, then purchase a pair of washable gloves and rubber-soled shoes. Justine would need a man's mackintosh. What else? Tomorrow morning she would make a list—there was no reason to worry, as long as she stayed organized.

She did not know, she could not know, that halfway across Europe, Lucinda Van Helsing was locked in a padded cell. And she was screaming.

CHAPTER IV

Crossing the British Channel

Mary stared down at the blue-gray water of the channel, which appeared to be rushing past the ferry although of course it was the ferry that was moving over the water, farther and farther away from England. There were small whitecaps on the waves left in the ferry's wake. Finally, she felt as though she had time to breathe. The last few days had been a mad rush of preparation. She had gone to the bank so they would have money in Vienna and Budapest. She had studied currency conversion tables to make sure they would not be cheated. Francs and centimes for France, the new krone and hellers for Austria and Hungary although evidently the old florins and kreuzers were still in circulation. It all seemed unnecessarily complicated to her, but then so much about traveling seemed unnecessarily complicated.

She had met again with Mr. Holmes, who had made the same journey as far as Vienna and could tell her what to expect, at least that far— "Although Hungary is its own entity, Miss Jekyll," he said. "A strange little country, very proud, with a language that is almost impossible to learn. There, some would tell you, is the edge of civilized Europe! At least you will have one contact in addition to Miss Murray—Irene Norton has responded that she will do her best to help you. When you arrive in Vienna, proceed directly to her apartment." Mary had mumbled her thanks, not quite knowing what to think or feel about Mrs. Norton's offer of assistance.

Finally, she had gone shopping, trying to make sure Mr. Justin Frank and his sister Mary would have whatever they needed on their trip—at a reasonable cost. At the moment, she was wearing a waist bag, and very convenient it was indeed—so much better than carrying a purse. Justine had a carrier bag, which she could sling across her body. They also had a trunk—covered with leather, as suggested in *The Complete Lady Traveler* by Mrs. Miles-Mowbray, who, according to the advertisement, had traveled to every country in Europe and even crossed the Sahara by camel-caravan. At least there were no camel-caravans on this trip!

She should check on Justine, who was below being seasick. How large the channel was! They were completely out of sight of land. She had never seen a body of water larger than the Thames, and leaving England like this made Mary feel both excited and melancholy. Just now the melancholy was uppermost, probably because she had not slept well the night before, and so far the day had been a continual whirl of activities. First there had been saying goodbye to Mrs. Poole, Beatrice, Catherine, and Alice, with their baggage around them in the parlor of 11 Park Terrace. Diana had refused to see them off—she had stayed in her room, saying that as no one cared about her or took her anywhere, she did not want to see any of them ever again.

Mary did not care—well, she cared a little. She had been hurt that her sister had not said goodbye to her, when she would be gone for more than a month. And what would happen in that month? None of them knew. She and Justine were going to the edge of civilized Europe, according to Mr. Holmes. What would they find there? She had no idea.

Beatrice had held their hands in her gloved ones, and Catherine had surprised Mary by embracing both her and Justine briefly. Usually, Catherine was not one to show affection. Mrs. Poole had cried a little, and Alice had sniffled and then hidden her face in her apron. "Dust in my eyes," she said in a muffled voice. Mary had taken one last look around the parlor, pausing especially on the portrait of her mother over the fireplace. This would be her last glimpse of what had been her home all her life, until—when? She did not know when, exactly, she would be returning. Mentally she bade the portrait goodbye and promised it that she would come back . . . once their adventures were over.

> MRS. POOLE: I would have done just the same as Alice, if I hadn't remembered my training. A good servant never gives way to emotion, my father used to tell me when he was alive, bless his soul. You girls going so far away, and not knowing when you'd be back!

> MARY: But we did get back safely in the end, Mrs. Poole.

> MRS. POOLE: Eventually! But the worry I had along the way . . .

> CATHERINE: Can you please do your best to not give away the plot? Like the fact that Mary eventually made it safely home . . . I won't say whether or not the others did!

> MARY: Oh please. If we hadn't made it back, we wouldn't be writing this book. The important thing is, what happened to us on the way?

CATHERINE: It's unbelievable, what authors have to put up with from their own characters. Remind me why I agreed to do this?

MARY: Excuse me. We are not your characters, but fellow members of the Athena Club. And as to why you agreed . . . we need money, remember?

CATHERINE: Oh, right.

Watson and Holmes had been waiting outside with a hackney carriage. Watson had shaken their hands heartily, and Holmes had driven with them to Charing Cross Station. He would have helped with the trunk, but Mr. Justin Frank was able to do all the lifting and carrying necessary.

At Charing Cross, as they were about to board the train to Dover, Mr. Holmes had shaken their hands and held Mary's, she thought, a little longer than necessary.

"I would worry about you, Miss Jekyll," he said, "but I know an Englishwoman with your good sense and observant eyes will always make her way in the world. I look forward to your return, and to hearing about your adventures. Remember that you promised to send regular telegrams!"

"Of course, Mr. Holmes," she said, pleased at the unaccustomed praise, although she bridled a bit at the reminder. Yes, of course she would send telegrams. She had said so, hadn't she?

And then they had taken the train to Dover, where they had boarded this ferry. She checked her wristwatch. In about twenty minutes, they would arrive in Calais. Then they would have to catch the train to Paris, which should get them there in plenty of time to board the Orient Express. Should she check the schedule she had written out for herself? It was tucked into her waist bag. But really she could recite it all from memory: train to Dover departing 9:00 a.m., ferry to Calais departing 11:50 a.m., train to Paris departing 1:15 p.m. from Gare Maritime, through Boulogne and Amiens, arriving 4:45 p.m. at Gare du Nord. Then they would need to get to Gare de l'Est to catch the Orient Express, departing 7:30 p.m., arriving 11:15 p.m. two days later at a train station called Westbahnhof, whatever that meant. Below was written Irene Norton's address, which Mr. Holmes had given her, as well as Miss Murray's address in Budapest, which had been on the telegram. In her waist bag she also had the twenty pounds she had withdrawn from the bank, which left Mrs. Poole with only two pounds in the bank account Mary had set up three months ago for the Athena Club. All of them except Diana could access it—she did not trust Diana with their money. Had she taken too much? But Catherine had said Mary should take as much as she could, that she and Beatrice would manage. Mary double checked everything, then felt silly. The schedule had not changed, the money had not changed—she was just being nervous.

What she should be doing instead was checking on Justine—or her brother Justin, as she must now call him. Justine . . . or rather, Justin had said he just wanted to be left alone in his misery, but it would be a good sisterly thing to make sure he was all right. The last time she had seen him, his face had been positively green. She must make a mental note, so she did not forget in public—he was her brother Justin now.

She turned and started across the deck, toward the stairs that would take her below. The deck was almost empty—the sky was gray with clouds that send down intermittent gusts of rain, and most of the passengers had chosen to sit indoors. But there across the deck . . . surely she recognized that boy, turned away from her and looking over the railing? No, it was impossible. But she knew that back, remembered that posture, hands in pockets.

She recognized the curling red hair under the newsboy's cap, and surely she had seen that cap recently on Charlie? The boy swayed easily with the deck, as though born for sea voyages. He had no need to hold on to the railing.

She walked over to the other side of the deck, although her balance was not as good as his, and stood at the railing beside him.

"I can *not* believe you would do this," she said.

"Why?" said Diana. Now that she was standing next to him . . . her, Mary could see Diana's freckled face under the cap.

She was so angry—so very angry, as angry as Mary ever gets—that she did not know what to say.

"Seriously, why?" asked Diana. "I mean, this is exactly the sort of thing I would do. You should know that."

Which was, Mary had to admit despite her anger, entirely true.

DIANA: That was prime! Mary looked like a goldfish with its mouth open in a great big O.

MARY: Someone should have drowned you at birth.

"How?" was all Mary said.

"Wouldn't you like to know!" said Diana, looking particularly smug. Mary would have liked to slap that expression off her face. "Let's just say you should always check to see if anyone is hanging on to the back of your carriage! The Baker Street boys do it all the time when they're tailing someone. I bet old Holmes would just kick himself if he knew. Outwitted by a girl! I don't think much of Mr. Famous Detective!"

"Well, you'll have to go back," said Mary. "We're not taking you with us. As soon as we get to Calais, you're taking the ferry right back home again."

"Shan't," said Diana. "And you can't make me. If you try, I'll go . . . well, I don't know where. Maybe I'll keep following you. Or maybe I'll stow away on a boat to America! I can go anywhere I want to."

Mary sighed. No, she could not in fact make Diana go back to London by herself. Justine would have to go with her, but without Justine's help, what chance did she have of finding and helping Lucinda Van Helsing? And if she went back with Diana, Justine would have the same problem, in addition to which she would have to make contact with Miss Murray, whom she had never met, in Budapest, a city she had never visited. What in the world was Mary to do?

"Anyway," said Diana, "you know how useful I can be. I wouldn't have made a mess of Purfleet, like Catherine."

DIANA: Seriously. I would have opened that desk drawer, quick as winking. I bet Seward kept all his S.A. letters in there. They would have told us about Lucinda, right enough!

CATHERINE: Can we drop the Purfleet incident already?

DIANA: What? You mentioned it first. You're the one writing the book, remember?

"If they've got that Lucinda girl locked up somewhere," Diana continued, "I can get her out. I can pick any lock that's ever been made."

Which was, Mary had to admit, probably true. "I don't know," she said, although she already knew that, for good or ill, Diana would be accompanying them to Vienna, at least. They were stuck with her. What in the world were they going to do with her on the

Orient Express? Mr. Holmes had only purchased two tickets. . . . "I need to consult with Justine. Come on, she's below."

Justine looked better, or as much better as Justine ever looked. She was always unnaturally pale, as one tends to be when one is a reanimated corpse.

> JUSTINE: Is it absolutely necessary to mention that, Catherine?

"Look what I found," said Mary, holding Diana by the arm. "Evidently, she was hanging on to the back of the carriage the whole way! And then she must have snuck onto the train somehow. And then the ferry. That's a lot of sneaking." She frowned at Diana.

"Hey, let go of me!" said Diana, pulling away. "I came down here willingly, didn't I? I want to help."

"So you propose coming to Vienna with us?" said Justine. She answered in the slightly deeper voice of Justin Frank, who looked both tired and skeptical.

"That's the idea." Diana glared back, defiant.

This was no place to argue, Mary realized, looking around the large passenger cabin. It was, of course, full of passengers: families with children, the fathers reading newspapers, mothers distributing sandwiches, brothers and sisters playing cards or cat's cradle until it was time to eat. Salesmen carrying display cases. Lady travelers in groups of two or three, consulting their Baedekers. Students returning to continental universities after the holidays. It was crowded and noisy, and no one was paying attention to them. Nevertheless, this was neither the time nor place for a serious discussion.

"You can come with us as far as Calais, and then we'll see," said Mary.

"It's not like you have a choice," said Diana. "You can't exactly make me get off the boat in the middle of the channel, can you?"

"Don't tempt me!" was Mary's response.

Diana did not answer. Instead, she sat next to Justine, looking as cross as possible. But for the rest of the voyage, she was quiet and obedient, which worried Mary more than if she had been up to her usual mischief. What in the world was going on in that head of hers?

> DIANA: I'd gotten my way, hadn't I? If I got my way
> all the time, I'd never have to be bad. I would be
> just like Mary.

> MRS. POOLE: I don't believe that for a minute!

When they disembarked at Calais, the first order of business was finding a telegraph office so Mary could let Mrs. Poole know Diana was with them. Here Justine proved invaluable. She arranged for their trunk to be taken to the Gare Maritime and loaded onto the Paris train—luckily they had registered it in Dover, so it would not need to be inspected again by customs. Then she helped Mary exchange one pound for twenty-five francs, which made Mary feel quite rich, at least in French money. Then, although telegraphy had not yet been invented when she had last spoken French as Justine Moritz, she found the way to the telegraph office. Evidently, telegraph in French was *télégraphe.*

When Mr. Justin Frank and Miss Mary Frank went up to the telegraph window and told the clerk what they wanted, they were surprised to learn that there was a telegraph waiting for Mademoiselle Frank. *"Mais oui,"* said the clerk, who resembled a turtle. *"Vous pouvez le voir ici—votre nom est en haut.* Mademoiselle Mary Frank."

Mademoiselle Frank was no less astonished when she read the telegram.

HELLO TO DIANA WILL INFORM MRS POOLE SHE
IS WITH YOU GOOD LUCK GODSPEED HOLMES

She sent a telegram to Mrs. Poole anyway. She had intended to, and she would, no matter what Mr. Holmes chose to do. For goodness' sake, would he continue popping up, like some sort of marionette, at every stage of their journey?

"So he knew," she said to Justine as they walked out of the telegraph office, to where Diana was lounging about and waiting on the street corner. They seemed to have left the gloom and fog behind them—now the sun blazed overhead and on the small shops and hotels of the French town. "He knew Diana had followed us and didn't say anything. Of all the . . ." She was going to say "cheek," but it sounded so rude and ungrateful. Well, she was not feeling very grateful at the moment.

"I'm sure Mr. Holmes had his reasons," said Justin Frank, replacing his hat, which he had taken off indoors. "He usually does, as you know. But we must get to the *gare*, or we will miss our train."

Justine was right, of course. Anyway, Mary was supposed to be the practical one, the one who remembered timetables and how much money they had, so she would be practical, no matter how she felt. What can't be altered must be endured, as Cook used to say, when Mary could still afford a cook. She hoped that Cook was doing well at her sister's in Yorkshire. The change in Mary's fortunes had brought Diana into her life, and Diana was one of the things that couldn't be altered. She was a fact of nature, like thunderstorms.

DIANA: Exactly!

CATHERINE: Or slugs. They're forces of nature too.

DIANA: Slugs don't do anything. They just sit there.

BEATRICE: They will destroy a garden, eventually.
Slowly, slowly, they eat the leaves of the plants,
and then the plants cannot drink in sunlight.
They are as destructive, in their own way, as
thunderstorms.

CATHERINE: Right. Like Diana, who destroys pretty
much everything, eventually.

MARY: How in the world did we get onto the topic of
slugs?

Mary wished she had more time to spend in Calais. It was a
charming seaside town, still quaint and old fashioned despite the
influx of visitors that had turned it into one of the most important ports in France. She could see pastry shops and cafés, some old
churches, and what looked like a bustling market. Farmers drove
their wagons over the cobbled streets. There were fishing boats tied
up at the piers, and in the distance she could see sandy beaches covered with bathing huts. But there was no time, not now.

At the ticket office, Mary bought a ticket for Diana, despite her
protestations that if she could sneak onto the train from London
to Dover, and the ferry to Calais, she could sneak onto the train
to Paris. They'd had enough sneaking for one day, thank you. Her
ticket, and Justine's, had been bought as part of the London to
Paris express package. Luckily one extra ticket from Calais to
Paris was not very expensive, but the Orient Express would be
another matter. Holmes had arranged for those tickets, which

would be waiting for them at the Gare de l'Est in Paris. But what was she going to do about Diana?

Soon they were on yet another train, chugging out of the Gare Maritime toward Boulogne, on route to Amiens and Paris. All the way to Amiens, she, Justine, and Diana were the only occupants of the carriage, so she could lower the window and smell the sea. The day was sunny, the countryside fresh and green—someday, Mary thought, she would come back here on holiday and visit properly. When she didn't have anyone to rescue!

Diana continued on her best behavior, a feat made easier by the fact that soon after they pulled out of Calais, she fell asleep. Mary had brought sandwiches for her and Justine to eat before they reached Paris—two cheese and chutney for Justine, two ham mayonnaise for her. Diana had announced that she was ravenous and eaten one of each before yawning without covering her mouth, lying down full-length on the seat across from theirs, and falling into a deep slumber. Without a word, Mary handed the remaining cheese and chutney sandwich to Justine and started on the ham mayonnaise herself. At least Diana had left them the two apples! With that, they would have to be satisfied until Paris. Mary watched the countryside roll by and Justine studied her German phrasebook. Diana snored.

"How's that going?" Mary asked at one point.

"Alas that my German is so inadequate!" said Justine.

Of course, she would say the same if she were fluent in the language, thought Mary. Justine was constitutionally incapable of self-confidence. Well, whatever German she spoke by the time they got to Vienna would have to do!

JUSTINE: That is not quite fair, you know. I do have
confidence in myself as a painter, although I am

not perhaps in the first rank. And I speak rather
good French. But my Latin is not as good as it
should be, and even my English is inadequate at
times. . . .

CATHERINE: I think you just made Mary's point.

Eventually, Mary dropped off a little herself. It had been
such a long day already! At Amiens they were joined by an old
Frenchwoman with a soft halo of white hair under a black straw
bonnet, dressed in a widow's black crepe, who nodded at them
amiably and introduced herself as Madame Corbeau. Mary moved
to Diana's seat and told her to sit up properly, but Diana just put her
head on Mary's lap and continued sleeping. The old woman and
Mr. Justin Frank exchanged a few pleasantries in French. She lived
in Amiens and was going to Paris, where her daughter lived in the
dix-huitième arrondissement. Would they like to see a photograph of
her granddaughter? So pretty, and such a good girl. Ah, they came
from England, where it was always raining. Madame Corbeau
hoped they would enjoy France. Then she commenced to knit,
with a rapid clicking of needles. Halfway between Amiens and
Paris, she pulled a tin out of the basket that was her only luggage,
and out of that she pulled a package of waxed paper. *"Voudriez-vous?"*
she asked, holding it out to Mary. It contained rolled biscuits that
looked like little snails. Gratefully, Mary took one, then at the
woman's urging, another. They were filled with apricot jam, and
better than any English biscuits she had tasted. Justine took two
as well. Incredibly, despite the proximity of food, Diana did not
wake up.

DIANA: Hey, you never told me about the biscuits!
You should have woken me up.

CATHERINE: They couldn't have. It's one of the rules
of the Athena Club: Always let sleeping Dianas
lie.

DIANA: Where is that written? Seriously, show me.

Madame Corbeau ate a few biscuits herself, then recommenced her knitting, *click-click* to the sound of the train, *clack-clack* as the wheels went around. By the time they arrived in Paris, she had finished an entire sock.

Mary had been watching the city approach through the train window. First the fields and distant farmhouses had been replaced by detached villas sitting in their own gardens, filled with flowers and rows of vegetables. Then had come the first buildings of the famous capital.

Ah, Paris! It is the most beautiful city in the world. London is more grand, Vienna more intellectual, Budapest more charming. But Paris is certainly the most beautiful.

MARY: I prefer London, thank you.

BEATRICE: But you have not yet seen Florence! If
you had, you would acknowledge her as the most
beautiful of all cities. I still remember the sunset
turning her walls to gold. . . .

JUSTINE: Geneva is also very beautiful. I have only
vague memories, but I remember the blue sky
above, and the mountains in the distance.

DIANA: Mary's right, give me London any day. It may
smell of sewage, but it's our sewage.

CATHERINE: Well, I can't possibly think of a higher recommendation than that!

DIANA: That's sarcasm, right?

By the time they were approaching the Gare du Nord, Mary had sunk into the state of lethargy common after extended train travel. The movement of a train is quite different from that of a carriage, as our readers have no doubt noticed if they have experienced both. In a carriage, one is constantly jostled. The motion of the horses, combined with the condition of the roads, makes movement abrupt, unexpected—one never knows when a wheel will fall into a rut or hit a stone. But a train rides on its rails smoothly, evenly. One can even fall asleep to the *click-clack* of its wheels, as Diana was so effectively demonstrating.

It surprised Mary when Justine nudged her and said, "We're almost there."

She looked out the window. Now she could see the city itself, or at least its apartment buildings, with shops on the ground floors. It looked rather like London, only more French, although she could not specify in what its particular Frenchness lay. Mary shook Diana. "Sit up. We're almost there."

"Then tell me when we're there," said Diana without opening her eyes.

"No, sit up now. You've put my leg to sleep and it's going to be all pins and needles. Come on, sit or I'll stand up and dump you on the floor."

Diana sat up and rubbed her eyes, sleepily.

Slowly, feeling returned to Mary's leg. Why did something that caused no actual harm have to be so painful? It felt as though she were being pricked by very large pins and exceptionally sharp needles.

Madame Corbeau leaned over and tapped her on the knee. *"Il est beau, votre fils, madame. Regardez ses cheveux roux!"*

Mary smiled and nodded, although she had no idea what the old woman was saying. She had her waist bag, Justine had her carriage bag. They had Diana. Unfortunately!

Justine said something to Madame Corbeau that sounded polite, then made a small bow. As they followed her along the corridor and down to the platform, Diana said, "What did she say? She said something about me."

"She said you looked like a great deal of trouble, and she was right!" said Mary. "Come on. I have to figure out the ticket situation."

The Gare du Nord was considerably larger than the Gare Maritime. It seemed as though there were rail passengers everywhere, going in every which direction and speaking a babble of languages. And there were just as many pigeons as people. They strutted over the pavement, perched on lampposts, and flew up into the arch of the station as though it were the sky.

It took a while for Mr. Justin Frank to retrieve their trunk. When he had, he turned to Mary and said, "I think we had better hire a porter to bring it over to the Gare de l'Est. I could carry it easily, but it will be a long walk along the—it says on this map, Rue du Faubourg Saint-Denis. I do not want people to see me being so strong. This is not like Charing Cross, where I only had to take the trunk into the train station. I would be carrying it along a busy avenue in the middle of Paris. I believe it would be noticed. But I will need to pay the porter."

Mary nodded and gave him five francs—more than enough, but Mr. Justin Frank would need some money for miscellaneous expenses.

It was not really such a long walk—the two train stations were relatively close together. The Rue du Faubourg Saint-Denis reminded Mary of Baker Street, with its residences above shop windows, its carriages and costermongers, even an omnibus. Perhaps all cities were alike, really, at their heart? As they walked along the street, Mary next to Justine, and Diana scampering either ahead of or behind them as her fancy dictated, peering into shop windows, she asked, "What did that woman actually say to me on the train?"

"She said you have a handsome son, and mentioned Diana's red hair—her *cheveux roux.*" Justine responded absentmindedly, no doubt pondering the intellectual history of Paris, with its *philosophes* and *encyclopédistes.* Because that is exactly what Justine *would* be doing.

> JUSTINE: I was, actually. It is in Paris that the Enlightenment was born. I was thinking of men such as Rousseau, Diderot, Voltaire, and how they attempted to sweep away the darkness of superstition and ignorance that had clouded men's minds for centuries, like cobwebs.

> DIANA: I was thinking that I was hungry.

"Son!" said Mary, outraged. "How could she possibly think that Diana was my son! Do I look old enough to be the mother of a fourteen-year-old? Do I? Anyway, Diana and I look nothing alike."

"Well," said Justine, reasonable as always, "you look so composed and responsible, one might easily mistake your age. And Diana looks younger than her years. Perhaps you do not realize that you were stroking Diana's hair while she slept. So I can understand her mistaken assumption. . . ."

> MARY: I was doing no such thing. Maybe brushing it out of her eyes . . .

DIANA: Rationalize all you want, *ma soeur*. See, I
spoke French! Did everyone notice that I spoke
French?

"When are we going to eat?" asked Diana, who had been trail-
ing behind them. "I saw a bakery—at least, it looked like a bakery
although the sign above didn't look anything like *bakery* or even
bread. But it had loaves of bread in the window, and rolls shaped
like crescents. Can we go back and buy some? Seriously, I'm starving to death."

"After I figure out what to do about your ticket, and not a
moment before," said Mary, still feeling cross. "So you may as well
resign yourself to waiting. If you do die of starvation, it would be
most convenient for you to do so before I purchase a ticket, so we
don't waste any money."

"If I die, you'll have to carry my corpse!" said Diana. But she
did not fall behind again.

The Gare de l'Est was a smaller station than the Gare du
Nord, but just as crowded. It seemed to be filled with mountains
of trunks—clearly, these travelers were going on longer journeys,
and farther away. From here, trains departed for all points east:
cities such as Berlin, Warsaw, Munich, Vienna, and Budapest. The
Orient Express itself would go as far as Constantinople. Suddenly,
Mary felt elated—she was going to be on one of those trains! Well,
anxious and elated. Still, she felt like one of those lady travelers,
like the Mrs. Miles-Mowbrays of the world. At that moment, if
someone had suggested a camel-caravan, she would have mounted
her camel without hesitation.

She walked up to the ticket window after a mercifully short
wait in line. Two of the university students from the Dover-Calais
ferry had been ahead of her, but suddenly one made the familiar
gesture of searching for, and not being able to find, his wallet.

They both stepped to the side, and one of them waved her forward. She remembered that on the ferry, they had been discussing the latest biological discoveries with the absolute certainty that only medical students possess, and had gotten into some sort of argument over vivisection. They had been annoyingly loud.

"Mary Frank, picking up two tickets for the Orient Express to Vienna," she said.

"*Un moment,*" said the woman behind the grille. She was young and very pretty—*trés jolie,* Mary remembered from Mrs. Corbeau's description of her granddaughter —but wore an expression of disapproval that implied traveling anywhere was somehow fundamentally wrong, a symptom of our inconstant age, which must be always in motion, always going elsewhere. "*Non, mademoiselle,*" she said. "*J'ai trois billets pour vous. M. Justin Frank in one cabine, Mlle. Mary Frank et Mlle. Diana Frank in autre cabine, pour l'Express d'Orient, départ aujourd'hui. Et votre passeport, s'il vous plaît?* You must identify yourself for the tickets please."

Three tickets? This must be Mr. Holmes's doing. Mary felt some surprise, but more annoyance. She could have taken care of this problem herself. She was resourceful, wasn't she? He knew she was resourceful. Whenever they returned from this adventure, she would pay him back—somehow. She showed her passport, which had been tucked safely into her waist bag. The woman slid her tickets under the grille. Mr. Justin Frank, Miss Mary Frank, Miss Diana Frank, Paris to Vienna, departing 7:30 p.m.

"*Eh bien?*" Clearly the woman wanted her to move along, and indeed the line behind her had gotten longer.

"*Merci beaucoup, mademoiselle.*" Which was just about the extent of her French.

"*Pas mademoiselle—madame,*" said the woman behind the grille, giving her a withering look. Beatrice could not have been more poisonous.

"Look," Mary said to Justine, who was standing by the station wall with their trunk. The porter must have delivered it while she was waiting in line. "There was a ticket waiting for Diana as well." Wait, where had Diana gone? Ah yes, there she was, chasing a pigeon, which flapped away into the station, under the great arch. Like the Gare du Nord, this station was filled with pigeons, gray or brown or mottled. Train stations seemed to be their natural habitat.

"Mr. Holmes must have telegraphed for it," said Justine. "It's really most generous of him. I would like to take the trunk over to the Orient Express office. I can register it there, and they will load it onto the train when it arrives. Diana!"

At the sound of Justine's voice, Diana immediately turned and came over. Why couldn't she be that obedient when Mary called her, or Mrs. Poole?

"What? Are we going to eat yet?"

"Not quite yet. I need to deliver this trunk to the Orient Express baggage office. Can you hold that handle so it does not look like I am carrying it alone? It is not far."

"Sure, whatever. Just in case anyone forgets, I'm still hungry." Diana held the trunk by one handle while Justine lifted it by two others. Together they carried it across the concourse, to where a wooden sign on the wall said COMPAGNIE INTERNATIONALE DES WAGONS-LITS. Mary followed them. She should be grateful. She should be . . . but she was not. Her boots *click-clacked* precisely on the stone floor.

"Mary's mad about something," said Diana, after Justine had deposited the trunk with a uniformed porter and gotten a receipt for it. "I can always tell."

"Mary?" said Justine. "*Quel est le problème?* I mean, what is it?"

"Well, among other things . . ." Mary took a deep breath. He meant well. She knew he meant well. But perhaps sometimes, just sometimes, meaning well was not enough. "Among

other things, this ticket is for a Miss Diana Frank, and you"—
she turned to Diana—"look nothing like a Miss Frank." Not
in that getup. She looked, more than anything, like one of the
Baker Street boys. And sometimes kindness could be intrusive,
a burden. Sometimes it could turn into obligation. Did he not
realize that? No, of course not. She had meant to send him a telegram before they left Paris, but now . . . was it really necessary?
What could she tell him, other than that she was grateful? She
was tired of being grateful.

Anyway, there were more important things to do just now.
"Diana, we need to find you women's clothes."

"What? Why! I don't want to dress like a woman."

"Well, you have to, because your ticket says Miss Diana Frank,
and I don't think the conductor is going to believe that you're a
Miss anything dressed like that."

Diana snorted.

"You can make whatever unattractive sounds you please, but
we need to find you a dress."

Justine asked two porters without luck, but the woman who
sold cigarettes and bunches of violets in brown paper by the
entrance to the station told them they could find a shop selling
les vêtements pour femmes off the Rue d'Alsace. She had a face like a
dried apple and looked at them suspiciously, as though they were
planning to disguise themselves in order to rob the Banque de
France. But the shop was just where she had described. It was a
charity shop run by the Soeurs de Sainte-Catherine, although the
woman who ran it, pleasingly embonpoint and probably ten years
older than Mary, with eyes that seemed to be smiling even when
she was not, did not appear to be a nun. She was dressed rather
fashionably, *à la mode* as they say in France.

DIANA: I thought that meant with ice cream?

"You want a girl dress for the little boy?" she said, surprised.

"*Oui, madame,*" said Mary.

"*Mademoiselle.* But you may name me Nicollette!" Mademoiselle Nicolette insisted that she did not *parle très bien anglais*, but her English was certainly better than Mary's French! Really she ought to learn. If only she could have studied longer under Miss Murray. They had just started on French when Miss Murray left to teach at that private girl's school, and Mary had hired Nurse Adams to care for her mother, whose symptoms were getting steadily worse. Suddenly, although she was standing in a charity clothing shop in the middle of Paris, she saw again the dirt falling on her mother's coffin, the rain coming down and turning it to mud. Had it really only been three months?

"Yes, she is not really a little boy," said Justine, or rather Justin Frank. "You see, she is only dressed up for a jest—*un jeu*. But we have lost her proper clothing, so we must buy new ones. At least two dresses, I think, and the usual accoutrements. You know, what *les femmes* wear."

Goodness, couldn't Justine have made up something more convincing than that? But Mademoiselle Nicollette laughed and nodded. "*Vien, petite,*" she said to Diana, gesturing for her to come. They disappeared behind a curtained doorway that led, Mary presumed, to the back of the shop. She walked around, looking at the clothes, which were obviously second-hand, but of good quality. If they were not in such a hurry, she would have liked to look for herself. After all, there was a certain cachet to having clothes from Paris!

Ten minutes later, Mademoiselle Nicolette appeared again, smiling. "*Quelle jolie fille!*" she said. "I do not have believe it, when I see first."

"Well?" said Mary. Where was Diana?

"I hate it," came Diana's voice from behind the curtain. "And I hate you. And Mr. Great Detective can go to hell."

"For goodness' sake, just come out! We have a train to catch, remember? We have an hour and a half before it departs, so hurry up or none of us will get anything to eat beforehand."

Diana came out. She looked *jolie* indeed, dressed in more ruffles and frills than Mary had ever seen on her. She looked like a perfect French *demoiselle*. Her hair curled charmingly under a feathered hat perched at a fashionable angle.

"I'm probably going to kill you all in your sleep," she said.

"Lovely, please do. *Combien, mademoiselle?*"

"I have made up package, *une autre robe très jolie, une jupe, une chemise*, the stocking and others the gentleman must not hear, *n'est pas? Complète*. Only five francs, you see we are a *charité* and all the clothing it is donated."

Mary signed with relief. "I think you are the nicest person in France, Mademoiselle Nicolette."

"Oh, *seulement à Paris!*" said the woman, smiling. "*Bon voyage*, and the *Bon Dieu* go with you!"

Mary very much hoped He would.

On the way back to the Gare de l'Est, they passed a small restaurant called La Grenouille Enchantée, with a signboard on which sat a green frog, wearing a gold crown and licking its mouth with a long pink tongue.

"Seriously, I can't go any farther without something to eat," said Diana. "Especially if you want me to walk around in this getup. Why do women's clothes have to be so heavy?"

"All right," said Mary. "Let's eat here. But don't linger over your meal—we have a train to catch!" She had checked the prices posted in the window, and the place looked reasonable—at least by London standards.

"As though I ever do!" said Diana.

In they went. The waiter seated them at a small table close to the window and brought three hand-written menus.

"You shouldn't complain," said Mary. "Our brother Justin is the one carrying the bag with all your new clothes."

"Like he even notices. Escargot. What's that?" asked Diana.

"Those are snails, served with butter in their own shells," said Justine.

"I want some of those! Do they have frogs, too? Like that frog on the sign? I heard Frenchies eat frogs like they were chips. Snails and chips! Get it, like fish and chips? That would be a dish."

But the waiter informed them that frogs were out of season.

Mary ordered an omelet and a tomato salad, while Justine wanted a *soupe à l'oignon* and Diana insisted on her snails with, yes, *pommes frites*. She slurped the snails out of their shells and pronounced them very good. "What about dessert?" she asked, when all the shells were lying on her plate, like empty houses.

"Your stomach is a bottomless pit, you know that?" Mary wiped her mouth and put her napkin beside her plate. "Come on, the train is leaving in half an hour, and we want to be on it!"

When they reached the station, she had just enough time to exchange another pound for francs. On the train, all their meals would be included in the price of the ticket—they would have Mr. Holmes to thank for those meals, which Mary was not particularly happy about. But they would need money for tips and incidentals.

"Track Seven," said Justine. "There, you can see it from here. I have been told we can board at any time."

They made their way to Track Seven, and yes, there it was: the Orient Express, with COMPAGNIE INTERNATIONALE DES WAGONS-LITS written on each of the cars, and the gold crest of the company on the sides. They showed their tickets to the conductor before boarding. "Ah yes," he said. "*Les* Franks—an English *famille, n'est past?* First you will come to the cabin for the two *desmoiselles*, and directly after you will see the cabin for M.

Frank. It is shared with a university student, M. Waldman. Your trunk has already been delivered to your cabin, as you directed. If you would like to abstract what you will need for the voyage and have the trunk put with *les bagages*, you have only to tell your porter, Michel. *Et bon voyage, mademoiselles, monsieur!* We will be departing shortly for Vienna, Budapest, and Constantinople on the Orient Express!"

CHAPTER V

On the Orient Express

First they crowded into Mary's and Diana's cabin. It was arranged for daytime, with the seat facing forward, toward the engine. Justine dropped the bag with Diana's new clothes in it on the seat.

"Where are we supposed to sleep?" asked Diana.

"See that panel, up there?" said Mary. "This seat is one bunk, and it folds down to make another."

"Well then, I call the top bunk!" Diana sat on the seat and bounced up and down. "Not bad. And what's that little room?" She opened the door to the bathing facilities. "Hey, it's a WC! On a train! I wonder where the piss goes. . . ."

Suddenly, the whistle blew. Mary almost jumped, startled by the sound. Then there was a shuddering rumble, and the Orient Express pulled out of the Gare de l'Est. Their journey to Vienna had begun.

"Can I have the you-know-what?" said Mary to Justine.

"Have what?" asked Diana. "What are you talking about?"

Justine rummaged around in the carriage bag she had been wearing over her shoulder. She took out Mary's pistol.

"Hey!" said Diana. "Is that thing loaded?"

"Of course it's not loaded," said Mary. "I'm not an idiot. But it will be once we get to Vienna. I thought it best to be prepared for anything."

Justine handed the pistol to Mary. "Do you want the bullets now?"

"Yes, although I don't think we're in any danger on the Orient Express. After all, no one even knows we're going to Vienna, or why. It's not as though Dr. Seward is having us watched—more the other way around. He barely knows we exist, except as the man with one green and one blue eye who escaped from the Purfleet Asylum, and an obscure Miss Jenks. I wonder how Cat is doing, by the way? If she's found out anything else?"

"If she has, she will probably telegram to Vienna," said Justine.

> MARY: How in the world are our readers going to
> know who Miss Jenks is? She was only in the first
> book.

> CATHERINE: Then they should go back and read the
> first book. It's only two shillings, at bookshops
> and train stations. I would have mentioned that,
> but you told me to stop advertising!

"How come I don't get a pistol?" Diana flopped down on the seat again and crossed her arms, frowning.

"But I do not have a pistol either," said Justine. "You see, they are not always necessary."

"Yeah, but you can kill people with your bare hands," said Diana.

"What! I would never do such a thing." Justine looked shocked. Mary did not respond—it would have been neither polite nor kind to mention that Justine had, in fact, killed several people in just that way.

Mary opened the trunk and began taking out their nightclothes—her nightgown, then pajamas for Justin Frank, who would be sharing a cabin with another man, a stranger. She was worried about that—but of course he would not know Justin was a woman. Justine would be fine, wouldn't she? Anyway, she could defend herself. Diana, who had no nightgown, would have to sleep in her shift. Diana just stared at Justine, eyebrows raised.

"I mean, I would never kill intentionally. The man on the street in Cornwall, the Pig Man in Mary's house, those were accidents. I have never intended to kill anyone." Justine looked as though she were about to cry.

"Of course not," said Mary. "We know you would never do such a thing. Do you need anything else? I have pajamas and a robe for you here, but you had better choose a change of clothes for tomorrow. Also, where are your slippers? For goodness' sake, Diana, can't you make yourself useful? You're closer to the trunk than I am."

"No," came the response. "There's no room. You and Justine take up all of it."

Just then, they heard a knock on the door. Mary opened it. A man in the uniform of the Compagnie Internationale des Wagons-Lits said, "*Pardon, mademoiselle.* I am Michel, the porter for this car. We are serving coffee and a selection of desserts in the dining car. If you wish to attend, I will make up your beds in the meantime." He bowed and withdrew.

"Coffee?" said Diana. "Lovely coffee! Let's go."

"All right," said Mary. "I wonder if they have tea?" Perhaps she would have to get used to the continental practice of drinking coffee. It might be hard to find good English tea where she was going.

"Let me settle into my cabin, and I will join you," said Justine.

Mary nodded. This would be their home for two days. She looked around the cabin. It was small, but neat and elegant. Altogether, she approved of the Orient Express. Unfortunately, she would have to share it with Diana. . . .

DIANA: Better than sharing it with Catherine! She
    might have a nightmare and start prowling around
    the cabin in her sleep. She might even bite you
    without realizing it!

CATHERINE: Well, that's always a risk. I am a puma.

"Come on," Mary said. "You don't want to miss dessert, do you?"

"Hardly!" said Diana, jumping up. They left Justin in his
cabin, introducing himself to M. Waldman. Mary could hear the
murmur of their voices behind the closed door.

The dining room was as elegant as a hotel, with cloth on the
tables, proper silverware, porcelain cups for coffee, and . . . yes,
there was a teapot! Mary signed with relief. They found a table
under a window and ordered their drinks, then went to the dessert buffet. The dining car was full but not crowded—late August
was probably not the most popular season for traveling across the
continent. Most people had already taken their holidays and were
returning home, wherever that might be. Once she had chosen
a slice of raspberry torte and some almond biscuits—almost as
good as Madame Corbeau's apricot snails earlier that day—Mary
sat by the window and watched the suburbs of Paris rush by. Diana
rapidly devoured a slice of *gâteau au chocolat*, then went back for
seconds.

Mary let the warmth of the tea seep into her. It was a very
good oolong, and reminded her of tea in the parlor at 11 Park
Terrace. Really, she was exhausted. So much had happened
today. This morning she had been in London, and now here she
was, rushing through the French countryside toward Vienna and
then destinations unknown. Diana seemed perfectly fine, but
then she always did. Nothing seemed to tire her or affect her
ability to go from one thing to another without giving either

much thought. Sometimes Mary wished she could be so free of worries.

> DIANA: I do get tired. I get tired of you telling me
> what to do.

And Justine seemed at home here in France, in a way Mary could not be. In the restaurant earlier, she had ordered for all of them in French. Of course, she was the only one of them who spoke French fluently, and anyway she was Mr. Justin Frank. As the man of the family, he would be expected to make decisions for them all. He would be expected to handle financial transactions and take the lead except in those inconsequential instances where courtesy dictated that a woman should go first, such as through a doorway. Mary had to admit that Justine played a man to perfection, pulling out chairs for her and Diana, taking Justin's hat off at exactly the right times and in the right places. She wrapped her hands around her teacup and breathed in the rising aroma. Suddenly, she felt awkwardly English and self-conscious.

"I see you have found a seat. Mary, would you mind if Heinrich Waldman joins us? He is my cabinmate. Heinrich, my sisters Mary and Diana." Justin pulled out the chair next to Diana and sat, folding his long legs under the table. Her older brother Justin, she reminded herself, mentally reviewing the details of their story. She looked at up at M. Waldman and was surprised to discover that he was one of the university students from the ferry. He had been in front of her in the line at the ticket window, until he and his friend had drawn aside to discuss something or other.

"I do hope I'm not disturbing you," he said, in good but accented English. "If it is an inconvenience in any way, I would be pleased to sit elsewhere." He was tall and blond, with very blue eyes.

"Not at all. Please do sit. We've eaten already, you see, but I'm sure you're both hungry. There are plenty of refreshments left."

"I am most grateful to you, Miss Frank," he said, taking the chair next to hers. "I myself do not wish to eat anything, but I would welcome a cup of coffee."

"And for me as well," said Justin. "Heinrich tells me that he is Swiss, and returning from a vacation in England. I have told him that I studied for some time in his country, near Geneva. That is where I learned French, which so many Englishmen do not speak, although I'm afraid I never managed to learn more than a smattering of German. Of course Heinrich speaks both."

Ah, Justine had elaborated on their story! She had added the part about studying in Switzerland. Good for her. She would not have been able to disguise the excellence of her French from a Swiss national. Of course, she spoke English with a French accent, but it was slight—they had hoped foreigners would not notice. For a moment, Mary remembered the parlor at 11 Park Terrace, where they had sat with Catherine, deciding what they would say if anyone asked who they were and where they were going. *Make it as close to the truth as possible,* Catherine had said. *It's always easier to tell the truth than to lie, unless you're Diana of course.*

"Yes, my brother is studying to be a painter," said Mary. "I assure you it's not sisterly partiality when I tell you that he's supremely talented. We are going to Vienna so he can study at the art museum, the great big one."

"Ah, the Kunsthistorisches Museum," said Waldman.

"Gesundheit," said Diana. "I'm going to get more cake."

"You've had quite enough," said Mary, but before she could finish the sentence, Diana was already gone.

"And what is your field of study?" Mary asked, turning to Heinrich Waldman. Wasn't Heinrich a German name? She knew, because Justine had told her, that Switzerland was partly French and partly German. He looked German, or at least like the popular idea of a German. His eyes, she noticed, were very blue indeed.

"I am a student studying medicine at the University of Ingolstadt. I too will be going to Vienna, where I must visit the museum of *pathologische Anatomie*—ah, that is not a subject for the ladies!—before returning to university. Otherwise, I would disembark in München, since it is so much closer. I was traveling with a fellow student—I seem to remember that you were behind us in the ticket line, Miss Frank, when I so embarrassed myself by mislaying my purse! I was happy to find it again in another pocket. Unfortunately he was taken ill at the last moment and could not embark with me, so you see I am by myself. But I am very pleased to share a cabin with your brother."

"I'm very sorry to hear that," said Mary. "I mean, about your friend being taken ill."

"Ah, he will be better presently." Waldman smiled at her. "But you honor him with your sentiments, *Fräulein*."

"How is Switzerland now?" asked Justin. "I have not been there for many—that is, several years." While they had been talking, he had waved to the waiter and ordered coffee for both himself and Waldman.

"Well, you see," said Waldman, leaning back in his chair. What followed was a political and philosophical discussion that soon had Mary completely confused. How could the government of Switzerland be so complicated, with all those cantons and charters, or were they constitutions? Without realizing it, both Justin and Waldman soon switched to French, and then back to English, and then moved freely between the two as the subject seemed to warrant. She sat by the window as twilight fell and the gas lamps were lit in the dining car, drinking her tea, listening to their baffling conversation, and missing England very much.

When the porter came to tell them that their cabins were

ready for the night, Mary looked around for Diana. Where in the world had she gone? "Excuse me," she said, rising. "I must find our sister." The two men rose as well and bowed to her, then sat and resumed their conversation. Waldman took a cigarette out of a case in his breast pocket, no doubt for when the ladies had withdrawn and he could smoke. Diana was not in the buffet line. Mary scanned the dining car and saw her at the far end, sitting next to a woman in the most elaborate ensemble Mary had ever seen, in a shade of mauve that had surely never existed in nature, with a hat tilted at such a fashionable angle that it looked as though it were about to fall forward over her eyes

"Oh, hullo. I was wondering when you were going to notice I was gone," Diana said as Mary approached the table. "Duchess, this is my sister Mary. Mary, this is the Duchess. She has some sort of long name I can't pronounce."

"So pleased to meet you," said the Duchess in a high, cultivated voice —cultivated like those hothouse plants that can't survive outdoors and are wheeled out only on the most temperate days. She wore too much rouge. "You must call me Iphigénie. We are all *des amis*, are we not, on the Orient Express?"

"Yes, of course, ma'am," said Mary, somewhat befuddled. What did one call a duchess, other than Iphigénie? Surely it was something like "Your Grace." Continental duchesses were rather out of her experience. "I'm afraid it's time for my sister to go to bed."

"My sister is such a spoilsport," said Diana. But she stood up and said "Ta now," then followed Mary through the dining car. As she passed them, Mary noticed that Justin and M. Waldman were still in animated discussion, and the latter had lit his cigarette. Most of the other women had left already. Soon, the dining car would become an enclave of smoking men. Although she did not want to stay—by this point, all she wanted was a bed, or at least a bunk, to call her own—the thought annoyed her. Women were always withdrawing, it seemed.

BEATRICE: Exactly. That is why we must fight for liberty and equality.

CATHERINE: And divided skirts.

BEATRICE: Mock me all you wish, but the liberation of the female body is as important as the liberation of the female mind. With the vote and birth control—

CATHERINE: Beatrice! Do you want to get this book banned, particularly in America, where they're so prudish? There are some things you just can't say.

BEATRICE: But I should be able to! That is exactly my point.

Their cabin was made up for the night. Mary immediately changed into a nightgown. "Thank goodness I can get out of that outfit," said Diana. "Honestly, it makes me want to throw up."

"Not in here," said Mary. She found her *Baedeker's Austria* and lay in the bottom bunk, reading once again about Vienna, studying the fold-out map of the city. She found the Ringstrasse, the main thoroughfare of Vienna, which half-encircled the central city. Then she found Prinz-Eugen Strasse, the street on which Irene Norton lived. It was south of the Ring, and next to what looked like a long, rectangular park. Once they got to Vienna, they would find a cab to take them to her building. Cab fares were quite reasonable in Vienna, according to Baedeker.

Although she had responded to his telegram, Mrs. Norton would probably not receive Mr. Holmes's letter with a full explanation of the case until after they had already arrived. Mary hoped she would be able to help them. But there was no use lying awake and thinking about what they were going to do, or what might happen. She needed to go to sleep. Diana was already snoring in the upper bunk.

Mary rose, put her Baedeker away, then took her pistol and ammunition out of the waist bag where she had placed them earlier. She turned down the gas lamp, and tucked the pistol and small leather bag of bullets safely under her pillow before she lay down again. The pistol was not loaded—she knew better than to sleep with a loaded firearm under her head. In an emergency, it would not be particularly useful, except perhaps to bludgeon someone with. But its bulk under her pillow was reassuring.

She wondered if Justine was still in the dining car, talking to Heinrich Waldman. He was rather handsome, in a blue-eyed, blond, boyish sort of way. Quite the opposite of—well, it didn't matter whom.

> JUSTINE: We had returned to our cabin, but were still
> awake, conversing. Waldman was talking about
> the political and economic situation in Austria-
> Hungary, and I thought it would be best to learn
> as much as possible before we arrived. It was not
> particularly interesting—I find politics rather
> dispiriting, myself. But it was useful nevertheless.
> And then we got onto a discussion of Leibniz that
> kept us awake until the small hours. That was
> more interesting than politics, of course.
>
> CATHERINE: Oh, of course.

JUSTINE: Is that meant to be sarcastic?

CATHERINE: Of course not. Why would I *ever* be sarcastic about Leibniz?

JUSTINE: Ah, now I know you're being sarcastic!

DIANA: Who's Leibniz?

The next morning, they had breakfast in the dining car, again with M. Waldman. Mary expected that he and Justin would once again discuss politics, but this time it was to Mary he turned. Was she enjoying her travels? Did she find the continent very different from England? He himself had very much enjoyed his vacation in her country. He and his friend had gone on a walking tour of the Lake District. Was she familiar with Samuel Taylor Coleridge? Coleridge was his favorite poet. He much preferred Coleridge to Wordsworth. And her? Where did she come out on that great question?

Mary admitted that she liked Wordsworth very much, and had not read enough of Coleridge's poetry to judge, but both were said to be among the greatest English poets. While putting butter and jam on her roll—the breakfast on the train was what they called "continental"—she tried to remember what she had read by Coleridge. If only Miss Murray could have stayed longer, and she could have had a proper education!

She was rather flustered by his attention. For one thing, M. Waldman must be about her own age, or not much older. And he seemed even more handsome this morning. His hair was slightly rumpled, and he smiled more—particularly at her. He had a way of leaning slightly toward her as though they were sharing a secret. He seemed so direct, unlike some men she could name.

Now he was talking about his course of study. "I am most

interested in infectious diseases, Miss Frank," he said. "I wish to find out their causes, their methods of transmission. Great work has been accomplished in this area in the last decade—we have reduced outbreaks of cholera and typhoid, for instance. But so much remains to be done." His eyes were even more blue this morning, and very sincere. That was a noble ambition, was it not? To rid humanity of such scourges?

After breakfast, once their cabin had been made up for the day, he came and sat with her, chaperoned of course by Mr. Justin Frank. Now the two men discussed the scientific advancements of the day and their philosophical implications, but in a way that included Mary as well. Diana was bored to death, she informed them. "I'm going to get some air," she told Mary, and took off— who knows where! When Mary went to look for her before luncheon, she found Diana already in the dining car, sitting at a table with a Turkish rug merchant, a Viennese chocolctier, and her friend the Duchess. For several hours they had been playing some sort of card game. Apparently it involved gambling, for Diana had won ten francs.

"Where in the world did you get the money to gamble with?" Mary whispered to her fiercely as she dragged Diana back to their cabin.

"I stole it from you, of course," said Diana. "Ow! You're hurting my arm. You should be happy—I only stole five, and now we have ten!"

After lunch, Mary studied her German phrase book. *Danke schön. Wie viel kostet das? Wo ist das Museum der Kunst?* Justin lay in his cabin, taking an afternoon nap. He must have been up late talking to M. Waldman. She did not know where M. Waldman had gone. Probably for a smoke?

"He was flirting with you," said Diana. "I wonder why?"

"Because of course no one would flirt with me without an

ulterior motive," said Mary, exasperated. "I'm so composed and reasonable, and all that."

"Oh, come on! Don't tell me you bought into all that bosh about Coleridge and Wordsworth. What kind of man talks about poetry? Unless he's forced to under torture, or something."

"What do you mean, bosh? Why can't a man like poetry? Anyway, he's Swiss. Swiss young men are probably very different from English ones."

Just then, Mary heard a knock on the cabin door. Was it M. Waldman? But when Diana opened the door, it was the Duchess. *"Ah, ma chère Diane,"* she said. "Would you like to continue our *petit jeu*? The gentlemen say they are willing."

Diana looked back at Mary. "Well?"

"Oh, I don't care!" said Mary crossly. "Go do whatever you please." She immediately regretted it—after all, Diana still had ten francs to gamble with, and five of them were hers! But by the time she opened her mouth to protest, Diana had already slipped out the door.

> DIANA: What you really wanted to say was "Go to the Devil!" But proper Mary could not say that, could she?

> MARY: I seriously doubt the Devil would want you.

> MRS. POOLE: I do believe you would scare the Old Gentleman to death!

> DIANA: You bet I would.

At dinner they were joined by M. Waldman again. This time the conversation focused on the relative merits of the classical and romantic schools of art, as well as the innovations of the Impressionists. Justin admitted liking Monet, although yes, his technique could be sloppy. But his light! His choice of colors! He had experimented some with Impressionism himself. Waldman said that he preferred Courbet and Delacroix. Mary felt terribly ignorant. Why did Justine know so much more than she did? Of course, she had lived for almost a hundred years, and had spent much of that hundred years reading. Still, Mary resolved that, once this adventure was over and she was back in London, she would embark on a course of self-improving study. She would go to art galleries, listen to lectures on science and politics. She would read important books.

> CATHERINE: Most important books are not worth
> reading. Well, most books are not worth reading.

> BEATRICE: Surely you don't mean that, Catherine!

> CATHERINE: Oh, I don't mean mine. But realistically,
> only a small percentage of the books written
> are worth anything at all. Look at all the penny
> dreadfuls out there!

> ALICE: I rather like those. . . .

Halfway through dinner, Diana said, "May I be excused on account of boredom?"

Mary frowned and said "Go!" under her breath. Now M. Waldman was discussing innovations in music, which Justin admitted he knew very little about.

Diana smiled angelically, said "Thank you, dear sister," with as much sarcasm as possible, and went. By the time dinner ended,

Diana had not returned, so Mary looked for her—in the cabin, all up and down the corridor, in the dining car again. Finally Michel, the porter, told her that her sister had gone into the baggage car, presumably to retrieve a piece of luggage? Mary found her still there, arm-wrestling with the porter's assistant, a boy who looked about Diana's age and whose job was to bring out trunks when the passengers requested them.

She dragged Diana back down the corridor and told her to get ready for bed, or she would take away all the francs she had won. Anyway, she wanted the five Diana had stolen, and stealing was wrong, hadn't anyone taught her that? But as she was about to follow Diana into the cabin, she saw M. Waldman standing in the corridor by an open window, smoking a cigarette.

It might be bold of her, but . . . she walked up to him and said, "Thank you, monsieur, for such an interesting evening. I'm afraid I don't know as much as my brother about art, but I feel that I profited a great deal from your conversation."

He smiled down at her. He had a very attractive smile. "It was a pleasure to converse with such an intelligent and amiable woman, Miss Frank. And please, perhaps you will call me Heinrich? I hope you will let me continue the conversation when we are in Vienna. I would like to call upon you. And your brother, of course."

"Oh . . . certainly," she said. Call upon her! Intelligent and amiable! Mary felt both pleased and flustered. No man had ever wanted to call upon her before—only have her organize files and transcribe articles about the ears of murderers. But then she remembered that in Vienna, she would not be staying with friends and going to museums, as she had told M. Waldman . . . or Heinrich. She would be trying to rescue a woman who had probably been kidnapped.

"Perhaps if you could give me your address . . . ," he continued.

"We're not quite sure yet where we will be," she said. "You

see, although we are staying in Vienna, we may venture into the countryside as well, so our travel plans are not set. My brother has heard the Austrian villages are very picturesque." It was the best excuse she could think up at the moment. After all, she couldn't very well give him Mrs. Norton's address, could she? Who knew what they would be doing once they got there, or what sorts of dangers they would encounter?

"Of course," he said. "I will give your brother my address, and perhaps the both of you can call upon me, or send word? I will stay a week or two in Vienna before heading to Ingolstadt."

She nodded and held out her hand. "Good night, M. Waldman."

"Pleasant dreams, Miss Frank." She had intended to shake his hand, but instead he bowed and kissed hers, with continental courtesy.

She was glad of the darkness, because she was sure that her face was growing red. Mary Jekyll of 11 Park Terrace was not used to having her hand kissed. She turned and walked back to her cabin, not quite certain what had just happened.

Diana was already in bed, on the top bunk. "You know, you can be kind of an idiot sometimes," she said to Mary.

By the time Mary could ask her what in the world she meant and how she could talk to her sister like that, Diana was already snoring.

The next day proceeded much the same way, with Justin in intellectual conversation and Diana off somewhere or other, whether with porter's assistants or duchesses. By the afternoon, she boasted to Mary that she had accumulated thirty-two francs. That night, they would arrive in Vienna.

M. Waldman seemed slightly constrained. He smiled at her more rarely and hesitantly, directing his remarks to her less often. She worried that she had somehow offended him. Did he think that his interest, if that's what it was, might not be reciprocated?

Mary wanted very much to tell him where she would be, and how much she would like to see him again. When had a man of her own age been interested in her? When had she had the opportunity to meet such men at all? Never, that's when. She had always been the responsible one, the caretaker. And here was a man who seemed genuinely interested in her! Unlike some.

That night, they would be parting, forever as far as she knew. As soon as the Orient Express drew into the Vienna Westbahnhof, she, Justine, and Diana would need to hire a cab and take it to Mrs. Norton's apartment. It would be late, they would be tired, and she hoped there would be no problem finding the address. There would be no more time for the M. Waldmans of the world.

During dinner, he seemed unusually quiet. At one point he leaned toward her and said, "I will be sad at losing such a charming companion." She did not know how to respond.

What harm could it do, simply to let him know how to contact her? At least she could give him her address in London.

As they were once again packing their clothes and other necessities into the trunk, which had been brought up from the baggage car, she quickly jotted down her address at Park Terrace. She would find a way to give it to him before they separated.

Mary heard a knock on the door. Could that be—but no, it was the porter, coming to tell them that in a few minutes they would arrive in Vienna. He would take their trunk, which would be waiting for them on the platform. Mary nodded and gave him the customary *pourboire*. When he was gone, she checked to make sure she had her pistol and ammunition in her waist bag. Just in case.

"In Vienna, can I dress like a boy again?" asked Diana. She was kicking her heels against the bottom of the seat, impatient for their arrival.

"No," said Mary brusquely. "Come on, let's wait out in the corridor."

They both watched as the train drew into the Vienna Westbahnhof. It was past 11:00 p.m., but even at that hour, the station was lit by gas lamps. Through the train windows, Mary could see travelers waiting for trains next to piles of luggage. This was one of the great rail termini of Europe. The Westbahnhof never sleeps.

Just as the train stopped, Justine came striding down the corridor. "It's about time——," Mary began, but Justine grabbed her by the arm. It was such an unusual gesture for Justine that for a moment Mary stood staring at her, startled, not knowing what to do. "Come on!" said Justine, urgently. Usually she was so gentle, but now she gripped Mary's arm as though with steel pincers.

"All right, I'm coming!" said Mary. Justine was pulling her toward the train doors. "Be careful, you're hurting me."

She followed Justine down the steps, onto the platform. It was a confusion of travelers and their baggage. Where was Diana? Thank goodness, the girl was not dawdling for once. She was right behind Mary, although looking very put out.

"I'm sorry," said Justine. "But we need to find a cab, now! Where is the cab stand?"

"Herr Frank? You are Herr Frank?" Mary turned to see who had spoken. It was a young man dressed in the uniform of a footman, holding a sign that said "The Frank Family."

"Who wishes to know?" said Mr. Justin Frank, more suspiciously than Mary had ever heard him speaking.

"I am from the household of Frau Norton. She sent me to meet you at the train, and described you very exactly: *ein Herr*, very tall, and *zwei Frauen*. She said, tell to them that Meester Holmes sends his greetings. Her carriage is waiting for you before the station."

"Right," said Justine. "If you will help me to carry the trunk, we will follow."

Mary looked back at the train. There was M. Waldman, disembarking. He looked around the platform, as though confused or searching for someone. Was it her? She still had the piece of paper with her address on it. Was there time to run back, very quickly, and give it to him?

But the steel pincers closed on her arm again. "Come on," said Justine, and she had to follow.

The carriage, resembling a clarence but fancier, was waiting out front, its lanterns lit. The footman exchanged a quick greeting with the driver. The horses nickered and stamped their hooves. The footman helped Justine and Mary in—Diana refused his arm—then stowed the trunk and swung up on the footboard behind.

"Hü!" said the driver, and then the horses were clopping over the cobbled pavement. The carriage rumbled through the darkness of the Viennese night, down streets Mary could barely see, between buildings she could just discern in the darkness.

"What in the world was that about?" she asked. "My arm is going to be black and blue. I just wanted to . . ."

"I do apologize, Mary," said Justine. "But you see, I found something. I don't know why—I felt like a thief—but while Heinrich was out smoking, I searched through his bag. He was too perfect, you see. To friendly, too solicitous. He knew us only a little, yet spent all his time with us. And certain details, when he was talking about Switzerland—they were not quite right. It is a long time since I have seen my home country, but some things do not change in a hundred years. Even his accent, when speaking French . . . I wonder if he is truly Swiss?" She drew something out of her bag. Mary could barely see it in the dim light of the carriage lanterns, which anyway were not meant to illuminate the carriage, only to warn other drivers of its movements. She leaned close to the window and tried to examine it by the gas lamps on the city streets. She felt terribly jostled as the wheels bumped over cobblestones.

"What is it?" asked Diana, leaning over her.

"Stop that! You're poking me in the ribs with your elbow. You'll get your turn in the minute."

It was a piece of paper, an envelope. But it was empty, and she was about to ask Justine what in the world it signified when she saw that it had a seal: it seemed to be black, but would probably appear red in daylight. Looking at it closely, she could just make out the raised letters S.A.

> MARY: Did you have to go into such detail in this chapter? It makes me look like an idiot.

> DIANA: That's because you were.

> JUSTINE: You had no way of knowing that Heinrich Waldman was connected with the Société des Alchimistes.

> DIANA: No, but she was still an idiot. *Oh, Heinrich! What blue eyes you have!*

> MARY: It was definitely not one of my finest moments.

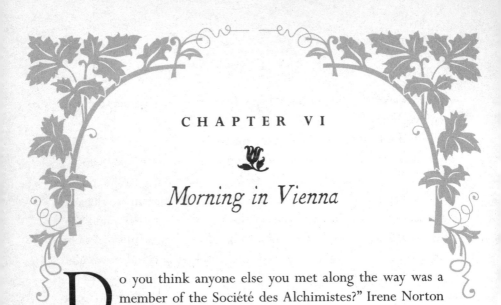

CHAPTER VI

Morning in Vienna

"Do you think anyone else you met along the way was a member of the Société des Alchimistes?" Irene Norton poured herself a cup of coffee.

They were sitting in a pleasant dining room, with morning light streaming through the windows.

"I can't think of anyone," said Mary. "That nice Madame Corbeau, who gave us biscuits? Mademoiselle Nicolette? I can't imagine either of them as members of the society. Maybe the Duchess, I don't know."

"She told me she was a spy for the Romanian government," said Diana. She took the pot and poured herself another cup of coffee, added five sugar cubes, and stirred vigorously.

"Then depend on it she wasn't," said Irene. "Spies don't go around telling people they're spies. More *crêpes*, anyone? Frau Schmidt made them especially for you."

Diana held out her plate, and to Mary's surprise so did Justine. "I ate these as a child," she said. "I don't know how I remember, but . . . yes, with a little sugar sprinkled on them. And then we would roll them up. I mean in my human childhood, in Geneva." She frowned as though trying to recall the occasion.

"Just a little more coffee for me," said Mary. She had already eaten four of the thin, flat pancakes herself. Weren't continental breakfasts supposed to be small?

"With jam or chocolate?" asked Irene. "Or both? I'm sure Diana wants both. You know, that name, Waldman, seems familiar for some reason. . . . But it wasn't among the names in Sherlock's letter." She has shown them the letter, five closely written pages describing them, their adventures solving the Whitechapel Murders, and the Société des Alchimistes. Mary had seen his signature on the final page: a scrawled *Yours as ever, Sherlock*. What did that mean? In what sense was he Irene Norton's, exactly?

Last night, when they had arrived and been shown up to Irene's parlor, she had risen from a chaise lounge and said, "Finally! I'm so glad you're here." Shaking their hands, she had added, "I hope we won't stand on ceremony. I want you to call me Irene. Sherlock's letter reached me yesterday. I want you to know that I've found out where Lucinda Van Helsing is being held. But there's nothing you can do for her tonight, and you must be exhausted. Do you want anything to eat? No? Then I suggest you all get some sleep, and we can talk in the morning."

Mary had been astonished. First, by the fact that Irene was obviously not an Englishwoman. She had a rich, deep voice with an undefinable accent. And second—"How in the world did Mr. Holmes's letter reach you before we arrived? I expected you to receive his telegram, but a letter couldn't have gotten here so quickly by post."

"Oh, Sherlock has his ways," she said, smiling. "Did you know his brother works for the British government? Queen and country and all that. Governments can send things more quickly than ordinary folks. But for goodness' sake, do take off your things! Hannah," she said to the parlormaid who had let them in, "can you see that Miss Jekyll, Miss Frankenstein, and Miss Hyde's luggage is unpacked?"

"Of course, *madame*," said the maid, with a curtsy. She gathered and carried off their hats and gloves.

"She speaks English!" said Mary after the maid had left.

"Yes, all my household staff speak English, German, and French," said Irene. "Except for the cook, Frau Schmidt, but she's excused on account of her pastries. Well, if you're not hungry, I'll have Hannah bring hot milk with honey to your rooms. That will put you to sleep, if sheer exhaustion won't."

"And Lucinda," said Justine. "You mentioned that you know where she is?"

"Yes, but I don't know how you're going to get her out, or even get in to speak with her. You see, she's in the Maria-Theresa Krankenhaus."

"Krankenhaus—that is a hospital," said Justine. "Is she ill?"

"It shouldn't be hard to get her out of a hospital," said Diana.

"Ah, but this isn't a regular hospital. It's an institute for the mad. And not just ordinary madmen, but those who are judged capable of harming others, or themselves. Convicted criminals are housed there, when they're not sent to the gallows. It's impregnable."

> DIANA: What do these alchemical chaps have about shutting people up in madhouses? They seem obsessed.

> MARY: We have often been told, by criminologists such as Lombroso, that genius and madness are closely related. Perhaps they see, in these madmen, a dark reflection of themselves. Remember Renfield.

> DIANA: I think they just like to lock people up, and madhouses are easier to get people into than gaol.

> CATHERINE: I thought you said Lombroso's theories were all wrong?

MARY: That's what Mr. Holmes says, and I agree with
   him.

DIANA: No surprise there.

That night, Mary had followed the maid down the hall to
a bedroom she would share with Diana. Their bed was already
turned down, their bedclothes laid out for the night. The trunk
was neatly unpacked. Justine had a sofa in the study to herself. It
was just long enough to fit all of her. Irene Norton's apartment
took up two floors in one wing of 18 Prinz-Eugen Strasse. So far,
they had only seen the second floor, up a flight of rather grand
stairs from the front entrance. But what they had seen was—well,
"elegant" was one word to describe it. "Sophisticated" might be
another. *Far more elegant than 11 Park Terrace,* thought Mary. But you
couldn't expect an English house to be as elegant as an apartment
in Vienna, could you? Particularly when that house was inhabited
by five young women, one of whom was Diana, who left a mess
wherever she went.

Mary changed into her nightgown, then went to find what
turned out to be a surprisingly modern bathroom, with heated
running water and a large porcelain tub on clawed feet. Gratefully,
she washed her face in the basin. She could feel all the grime of
travel washing away, then swirling down the drain. She dried her
face and hands on a luxurious towel, thicker than any English
towel she had used. The bathroom had an intricate pattern of tiles,
with designs of fish and other aquatic creatures, octopuses and
sea anemones, that she thought Beatrice would like. It seemed—
modern? Artistic.

On the way back to her room, she ran into Irene.

"I hope your bed is comfortable," said Irene. "I'm sorry I had to
put Justine in the study, but I only have one guest bedroom, and

the bed isn't long enough for her. These old European beds aren't exactly made for giantesses! If you need anything, just ring for Hannah. Sherlock speaks very highly of you, Mary. I'm looking forward to getting to know you better." She looked at Mary as though trying to decide what she thought of her.

"Thank you," said Mary, not quite sure what else to say. What in the world had Mr. Holmes written about her in that letter? Irene Norton, herself, was not quite what Mary had expected. She was beautiful, yes, and had not changed much from the woman in the photograph, although it must have been taken twenty years ago. But she could not imagine this woman as the mistress of a Bohemian king. She seemed—well, friendly, direct, and practical. Yes, there was something theatrical about her—her movements were graceful, and she gestured a great deal with her hands, more than an Englishwoman would have. She enunciated as well as an elocution teacher, and there was that accent, which Mary still could not place. But she seemed—effective, like someone you could rely on. Mary hoped she wasn't mistaken in that impression.

"Then we'll talk in the morning?" said Irene. She smiled, which made Mary feel as though she had somehow suddenly been approved of.

"Yes, of course," said Mary. "Well, good night, then."

"Sweet dreams," said Irene. "You know, I quite like your sister Diana. Although I have a feeling she's going to a handful. And I think Hannah brought up the milk. Just leave the glasses on the hall table when you're done."

Hannah had, but Diana had already drunk both glasses. Still, it did not take Mary long to fall asleep.

JUSTINE: I fell asleep almost immediately as well, although Irene had the most fascinating books! So many writers I had not read—she told me later that they were modern, writing in experimental styles. Sort of like you, Catherine.

CATHERINE: Well, not in the Astarte books. I don't know if this is going to sell as well as the Astarte books. I mean, people don't necessarily like to be experimented on. Not even by fiction.

In the morning light streaming through the dining room windows, clearer and stronger than the gray light of London, Irene Norton was not quite the woman of the photograph after all. Mary could see fine lines across her forehead and under her eyes. There were strands of silver in her hair, which had looked dark brown the night before but turned out to be a rich auburn. She was wearing a green dress with crimson embroidery on the collar and cuffs, sort of like a tea gown but probably one of those Reform dresses that Beatrice was always going on about. Mary had to admit that she preferred this Irene Norton. Her face had more character, as though she had lived a great deal in the intervening years. There was a sadness in her eyes that had not been there in the theatrical photograph. What would Mr. Holmes, who kept that photograph in his desk, think of her now? Watson had said she was the love of his life. Perhaps he would prefer this Irene Norton as well. Mary rather thought he might. *Yours as ever, Sherlock.* Irene called him Sherlock, when Mary had never called him anything but Mr. Holmes. But then, Irene called all of them by their first names.

"It's because I'm American," she had explained. "The accent? Oh, that comes from years of singing opera. I was quite a famous soprano in my day. Not as famous as Patti or the Swedish Nightingale. No, not like that. When you learn the Italian repertoire, and the German, and the French, you get a sort of mixed-up accent. You can't quite speak proper English—or American—any more. Hard to believe I was born in New Jersey, isn't it? But I fell in love and left the life of an opera singer. I wanted a woman's life—with children, you know. Well, I never got the children. Eventually the doctors told me I would probably never carry a child to term—that's what they call it, I think." She looked through the window as though remembering. Her eyes were bright with what Mary thought might be tears. "Then my husband died, and I could have gone back to the States. My father and brother are still there, and I think they expected me to come—if not to New Jersey, then maybe New York. But this has been my home for so long, and I've been happy here—very happy, once. My husband is buried here. It would be hard to leave."

"Is there any more?" asked Diana, shoving the very last bite of the very last *crêpe*, filled with jam and drizzled with chocolate, into her mouth.

"No, and Sherlock warned me about you," said Irene, smiling. When she smiled, Mary could see where those fine lines had come from. "Although I think you and I will get along very well. By the way, I sent him a telegram this morning, letting him know you had arrived. And I also sent one to your Mrs. Poole. I thought she would like to know that you're all here safely. I also thought she should be warned to watch out for the S.A. I've told her not to reply unless absolutely necessary."

"Thank you," said Mary. Well, that was one thing taken care of! She had been intending to send a telegram that day letting both Mr. Holmes and Mrs. Poole know they had arrived. After all, she had promised Mr. Holmes, and she knew Mrs. Poole would worry. But Irene was right—now they had discovered that the Alchemical Society was on their trail, they would have to be particularly careful.

"And what about Lucinda Van Helsing?" asked Justine. This morning, she was once again dressed in men's clothes, since those were all she had brought. Mary was also dressed, but Diana was still in her nightgown.

"Come into the parlor," said Irene. "It's almost nine o'clock, and I'm expecting a report."

A report? What kind of report? When Mary saw the parlor again by daylight, she wished she had a Kodak so she could take photographs for Beatrice. It was filled with exactly the sort of furniture Beatrice liked, made of various woods in interesting, unusual shapes. There were carpets in rich colors with stylized patterns, different from but somehow compatible with the upholstery on the sofa and armchairs. Paintings covered the walls. Mary suspected it was all very expensive, and in very good taste. Justine walked over to one of the paintings, hanging over the chaise lounge where Irene had been sitting the night before. What was Justine looking at so intently? Mary followed her and tried to make it out. The painting was of a woman in what looked like water, or maybe just wavy lines. She was swimming, or possibly drowning; it was difficult to tell. Her eyes were open, looking directly at the viewer, and her red hair floated around her, or were those more lines? The water part was green and blue, the woman was wearing a dark yellow and orange dress with strange patterns on it, and there was a great deal of gold leaf. On one corner was written *La Sirène*.

"This is magnificent," said Justine. "I've never seen anything like it. But I can't make out the artist's name?"

"It's by a friend of mine," said Irene. "His name is not known outside of Vienna, but it will be—I think someday soon, all of Europe will be talking about Gustav Klimt. I was the model for this one. I don't know if you can see the resemblance."

"No," said Diana. She was already sitting on the sofa with her feet tucked under her, just as she did at home. The sofa was upholstered in a green fabric with large red poppies on it that Beatrice would probably have fainted over.

BEATRICE: Not fainted. Women do not faint unless
they wear those abominable cages for confining
a woman's natural shape. Irene never wears such
a thing, and you can see how graceful she is, how
beautifully she moves.

MARY: Yes, thanks. We all love Irene, but do we need
to go on and on about her beauty?

BEATRICE: Of course her beauty is the least
interesting thing about her.

MARY: Yes, of course, I'm not disputing that—
but still. And why do you keep mentioning Mr.
Holmes, Catherine? This is supposed to be a story
about *us*.

Yes, Mary could see the resemblance between the painting
and Irene Norton, a little . . . although the watery woman was so
pale and angular. But then, she had never understood modern art.
Someday, she must get Justine to explain it to her.

"There's an intellectual and artistic ferment in Vienna, as
well as a political ferment. I think it will eventually transform
the arts, and perhaps our approach to life itself. But I'm worried
about the political part of it. It's like the ripples in a pot of water
before it starts to boil, made of up nationalism, sectarianism, anti-
Semitism. . . . I'm afraid of what will happen if Europe boils over.
But you're not here for a political discussion." Irene rang the bell,
and a minute later Hannah appeared. "Has Greta finished her
breakfast?"

"Yes, *madame*," said the maid. "I will send her in."

From a desk of very dark wood inlaid with what looked like

mother of pearl, Irene fetched a large scroll of paper, then unscrolled it on a low table in front of the sofa and put four objects on the four corners to keep it flat: a small bronze statue of a woman, probably a nymph judging by her state of undress; a green porcelain vase; a silver ashtray shaped like a leaf; and finally a book of poems with gilt poppies on the cover. She sat on the sofa next to Diana and said, "If you'll all come sit around the coffee table, I think we can have a—confabulation? A council of war? I just want to wait for—ah, here you are, Greta! *Guten Morgen,* my dear."

To Mary's confusion, Greta was a rather dirty boy, about Diana's age, perhaps fourteen or fifteen? She wondered if Greta could be a boy's name in German, or if she had simply heard it wrong.

"Have you had a good breakfast? I think we should speak English, for the sake of our guests. Come, sit down, all of you. These are the architectural plans for the Maria-Theresa Krankenhaus."

They gathered around, Mary and Justine sitting in two arm-chairs that matched the sofa, Diana cross-legged on the sofa next to Irene. The dirty boy walked up to the table and stood with his hands in his pockets, as though waiting for orders.

"These plans come from the architectural firm that designed the Krankenhaus, around the time the old state mental hospital, the Narrenturm, was closed down. It was replaced by a group of private asylums on the outskirts of Vienna: this was one of them. It was originally designed to hold criminals that the court had determined to be insane and a danger to the public, but came to house private patients as well. Most of those private patients are confined there by relatives because they are a danger to themselves or others. It has always been, essentially, a place of incarceration, offering little hope and less healing. I have a friend who is trying to change how the mentally ill are diagnosed and treated—he believes mental illness is not an inevitable hereditary tendency but a symptom of repressed thoughts and desires. If patients can somehow bring those thoughts and desires to consciousness, they can be healed—or so he says. He calls himself a psychoanalyst, because he analyses the psyche, the human mind—or soul, if we go back to the Greek. He interprets dreams, slips of the tongue—it's a controversial theory, and some of his colleagues think he's mad himself. But he helped me after my husband died, when I was so depressed that I could barely get out of bed. He was the one who confirmed for me that Lucinda Van Helsing was in the Krankenhaus, although he could not tell me where. But perhaps Greta can tell us more?"

"Yes, *madame*," said the boy. Like Hannah, he had a strong Austrian accent, and as soon as he started speaking, Mary realized that he was a she, although she made an even more convincing boy than Diana. Actually, she looked a lot like Charlie, and she had that same London swagger, although Mary supposed it was a Viennese swagger, here. Perhaps city urchins were much the same everywhere.

"She is here, on the third floor, but I do not know which room." Greta pointed to part of the scroll marked DRITTE-ETAGE. "My informant is one of the maids, a Swabian named Anika Krause who works in the kitchen and is responsible for taking food to patients on a cart. She remembers taking food to a young woman named Lucinda who sat on her bed, looking at the floor as it was brought in. There was an attendant—that is the right word?—*ein Aufseher* with her the entire time. When Anika came again to fetch the tray, none of the food was eaten. That was why she particularly remembers the woman—none of the food was ever eaten. And she wonders what such a young woman could have done to be confined on the third floor, which is for criminals."

"Ah, so that's why Sigmund couldn't find her," said Irene. "He told me he doesn't have access to the third-floor patients. What's the layout? He described the building to me in general terms, but I'm sure you'll have more detailed information. Like most visionaries, he's not particularly observant of the material world. I've seen him tip his hat to a hall stand."

"Yes, *madame*. The first floor is administrative. The second floor is for private patients, and the third floor is for criminals. The second and third floors have bars on the windows, and the rooms are locked only—I mean except—when the patients are allowed for exercise or recreation. On the second and third floors, the left wing is for women, the right for men. On the third floor, both wings also are kept locked. No one may go in or out except he has permission of the director. The private patients and criminals are not allowed to mingle—that is the right word, no? *Umgang pflegen*. There are guards at the front and back entrances of the Krankenhaus to make certain no one comes in. Deliveries come to the back door, where they are searched by the guards. I asked Anika if they could be bribed, but she says no, they are paid too well. Only those who work in the Krankenhaus —who have authorization—are allowed in or out. There are no visitors, not even family. Anika is searched every morning when she enters, as are all the attendants. I did not have to pay her for this information, *madame*. She is proud of working there, and boasted so much that I learned a great deal simply from listening to her. Indeed, I think paying her would have made her suspicious of me."

"And what about internal guards?" asked Irene. "Sigmund says there are no guards on the second floor. What about the third?"

"She did not tell me," said Greta. "And I did not wish to ask her more—I could see she was beginning to wonder why I was asking so many questions. I myself observed the hospital is surrounded by a high wall, nine feet I believe, topped with metal spikes. If you would like my honest opinion, *das, was ich glaube*—"

"Of course," said Irene.

"I do not think it possible. The Krankenhaus is not like any place we have previously . . ." She paused, looking suspiciously at them all, particularly Diana. "What I mean, it is not like breaking into a private house, or even the Hoffburg. It is more like breaking into a prison!"

"Thank you, Greta," said Irene. "As always, you've been most resourceful. Why don't you keep the funds we allocated for Miss Krause? And now you should probably get some sleep. I know you were out all night, on this as well as other business."

Greta nodded. "That other business . . ."

"Let's talk about that later, when we meet with the other girls."

Greta nodded again, then turned and strode out of the room, hands in her pockets.

"You see," said Irene, "I have my own Baker Street Irregulars, as it were, although I prefer to work with girls, often rescued from a life on the streets, like Greta. She's Hannah's younger sister. They were both in prison when I—well, rescued them, I suppose. Girls can go anywhere, do anything, indeed become anything. They're inconspicuous."

"See? That's what I'm always saying," said Diana. "But will Mary let me do anything? No."

"Well, any thoughts?" asked Irene. "I must admit that I'm stumped at the moment. How in the world are we going to get this girl out? Right now, we can't even get in to communicate with her. No visitors allowed, and no one goes in unless they're known to the guards at the front or back. There may also be additional guards on the third floor. Even if Greta's informant is wrong and the guards can be bribed—there are very few people who can't be bribed, if you find the right currency—it would take time, and Sherlock tells me you don't have time. What does that leave? Some sort of disguise? What sort of disguise will give us access to Lucinda? Or even to the Krankenhaus itself."

"What about the friend you mentioned?" asked Justine. "The one who is an interpreter of dreams."

"Unfortunately, I don't think he can do anything more for us," said Irene. "He has admitting privileges at the Krankenhaus, but that only gives him access to his own patients on the second floor. He's not allowed on the third floor, and might get in trouble if he were seen up there. When I got Sherlock's letter, I asked my girls to find out where the Van Helsings live in Vienna. About a year ago, Van Helsing rented a house close to the university, outside the Ringstrasse. His wife and daughter moved there, and he would come and go, as his research required. Several months ago, his wife was confined to a mental asylum—yes, the Maria-Theresa Krankenhaus. According to his housekeeper, Frau Müller, she died there a few days before her daughter disappeared. The police believe Lucinda was kidnapped by several men, probably to hold for ransom—their bootprints were found in the garden beds. But I figured if Van Helsing had sent his wife to a madhouse, he might have sent his daughter there as well, staging the kidnapping to deflect attention from his activities. So I asked my friend if he could look at the admissions book, and there was a Fräulein Van Helsing, as well the reason for her admission—neurasthenic, hysterical, suicidal. We're lucky that Van Helsing admitted her under her own name, or we wouldn't have found her—I suppose he felt that he could fool the police with a fake kidnapping, but the director of the Krankenhaus would know him and realize who Lucinda was. My friend looked around on the second floor and couldn't find her there. Even that was dangerous for him—aside from his controversial theories, he's Jewish, and it's becoming increasingly difficult to be a Jew in Vienna. If he's caught on the third floor, it will jeopardize his professional position. That's why I sent Greta to see if she could get more information. Greta is an expert at information, as you've seen. We need to find a way in so we can let Lucinda know we're trying to help her, and of course get her out. But how?"

They all sat silent for a moment.

"I have no ideas," said Justine, shaking her head. "I wish Catherine had come with us. She is so resourceful—surely she would have thought of something."

DIANA: Oh, you just had to put that in, didn't you?

JUSTINE: But I really did say it, at the time. At least,
I think I said it. Once it's written down, one
assumes the manuscript is accurate, rather than
one's memories.

"Well, we don't have Catherine," said Mary. She felt anxious and cross at the same time. She was supposed to be the resourceful one, wasn't she? At least, that had been her role in solving the Whitechapel Murders. But ever since coming abroad, she had felt discombobulated, as though she were still on that ferry, bobbing up and down on the ocean waves. Still, she should be able to come up with some sort of plan. She leaned forward and put her chin in her hands, looking more closely at the map. Even a place like the Krankenhaus must have its weaknesses. What were they?

"Oh, come on," said Diana. "It's obvious, isn't it? I mean, it's obvious to me."

"I think some sort of disguise might be our best option," said Mary. "You said Mrs. Van Helsing died there. Was there a priest for the funeral? Justine would make a good priest, I think. She might be able to get in that way, and then get up to the third floor. She's strong enough to break most locks. The guards might not suspect a priest. And as for getting Lucinda out, what about a coffin? You could conceal someone in a coffin. . . . A coffin wouldn't be searched, would it?"

"But we would have to wait for another a patient to die," said Justine. "That could take months. Or years! And how would I get up to the third floor dressed as a priest? I would be spotted immediately in such conspicuous garb. Even if I did manage it, how would I get Lucinda into a coffin, and what would I do with the corpse? There are many uncertainties in your plan, Mary."

DIANA: That was the stupidest plan *ever*.

MARY: It wasn't a plan. It wasn't supposed to be a
      plan. I was just proposing ideas.

DIANA: And ignoring mine, as usual.

"You're not listening to me!" said Diana, kicking the table.

"I doubt my friend Otto would appreciate your exuberance," said Irene. "He made that table especially for me. What is it, Diana?" She put a hand on Diana's shoulder, as though to both soothe and restrain her.

Now what did Diana want? Once again, Mary felt very sorry indeed that she had allowed her sister to accompany them. Maybe it would have been better if Diana had run off to Canada or Australia! At least Mary wouldn't have to deal with her tantrums.

"It's a prison, right? Or it might as well be. How did my dad get in and out of prison?"

Irene shook her head. "That's a part of your story Sherlock didn't tell me."

"He didn't get into prison," said Mary. For goodness' sake, what did this have to do with Lucinda Van Helsing? "He was arrested and sent to Newgate for the murder of Sir Danvers Carew."

"Yeah, but then he got out again! See"—Diana turned to Irene—"my dad, Mr. Hyde that is, was taken to Newgate Prison because he murdered someone, and who's to say that someone didn't deserve it? Being murdered, I mean. Anyway, he got out, easy peasy. Once he was in, he could see where the guards were, when they were coming or going. And he could pick the locks. At least, that's what I think happened—I don't know of course, because he left without saying goodbye. He's not the best dad, but he's the only one we've got, so shut up, Mary—I can see you're about to interrupt. Well, I can pick any lock that's ever been made."

"I wasn't about to interrupt," said Mary. "So what you're saying is, once you're in, you can get out—or at least up to the third floor to talk to Lucinda, assuming it's not guarded as well as locked, which we don't know. Well, how are you going to get into the Krankenhaus in the first place?"

"The same way Dad did."

"By murdering someone?" asked Justine, looking puzzled.

"I swear, none of you are thinking except me! You get into a prison by murdering someone, right? Well, you get into an asylum by going hysterical and neuras—whatever Irene said. Irene said her friend could admit patients, right? And once you're in, you can see where the guards are, how to get around them. They can't keep watch all the time—guards have to walk around, or go take a piss. Easy peasy."

"No!" said Mary. "Absolutely not. We are not going to send you into an institution for insane criminals. You're my sister, and I won't allow it. I don't care how great you think you are at picking locks. What if you can't get out again?"

"She could, if Sigmund admitted her," said Irene. "He would be the one deciding how long she stayed in the Krankenhaus. He could order her release, or transfer her someplace else. Unless she was caught, of course. Then I doubt he would be able to do anything to help you, Diana, and I hesitate to involve him any further. He's doing important work—I don't want to jeopardize his career. But . . . can you really pick any lock? Any lock at all?"

"Of course," said Diana scornfully.

"I want you to show me. Come on." Irene rose and motioned for Diana to follow her. What in the world was she doing? Was she going to make Diana demonstrate her lock-picking abilities? If so, how? Mary looked at Justine, who shrugged to indicate that she didn't know what was going on either.

Diana followed Irene, nose in the air like a duchess, still in her nightgown.

"Oh, for goodness' sake . . . ," said Mary, rising from the armchair. "Come on, Justine. I want to see what this is all about."

Irene led them down the hall toward the back of the apartment, then down a set of narrow stairs. This must be the first floor, where the servants lived? Yes, there was the door to the kitchen. Mary could see the large black range, a long central table at which Hannah and Greta were both sitting, and the usual accoutrements of a kitchen arranged around the walls. Strings of dried peppers and garlic hung from the ceiling. An older woman, presumably Frau Schmidt because she was wearing a cook's white cap and apron, was standing by the stove.

"Hannah, do you have a minute?" Irene called from the kitchen doorway.

"Of course, *madame*," said Hannah, coming to the door. "What do you require?"

"Not a maid, at the moment. I want to see who's a better lock-pick, you or Diana here."

Hannah looked at Diana appraisingly. "I am very fast," she said.

"Are you now," said Diana. "We'll see about that!"

"Then follow me," said Irene. "We're going to the office."

She led them to the end of the hall, which was . . . the end of the hall. It was a dead end, leading to nothing, paneled and with a painting hanging on it. The painting was of a blue jar filled with red poppies, which must be Irene's favorite flower.

Irene lifted the painting and turned a knob on the wall behind it. Mary was startled to see the wall swing inward. It was a door, after all.

"Just a moment," said Irene. "I need to turn on the light in here." Mary heard a click, and then the room was filled with light.

"It's . . . it's electrified!" said Justine.

"Yes, I had electricity installed in this room. For what we do here, we need light brighter than a gas lamp can provide. Come in, all of you." Irene held the door until they all followed her in, then shut the door behind them.

The room was about the size of Dr. Jekyll's study back at 11 Park Terrace, smaller than a parlor but larger than a morning room. There were no windows. Three walls were covered with shelves, which held books and file boxes. On the fourth wall hung a variety of weapons: swords, knives, pistols of various sorts, even a rifle. At the far end of the room was a large desk, which made it look like an office. But in the middle of the room was a table of dark wood surrounded by chairs that made it look more like a room for conferences, rather like the dining room at 11 Park Terrace where the Athena Club held its meetings—but with weapons.

"What is this room?" asked Mary, looking around with astonishment.

Irene did not answer. Instead, she lifted a box down from one of the shelves and put it on the table. She opened it and took out— what were they? Mary had to step closer to the table to see. They were metal . . . ah, locks. A variety of locks, both ancient and modern.

"Ten for Diana, ten for Hannah," said Irene, sorting the locks into two piles. She reached into the box again, rummaged around a bit, and took out a stopwatch, which she set on the table. Then she reached up and pulled two hairpins out of her hair, which was done up in style that managed to be simple and elaborate at the same time. How did Irene and Beatrice manage that sort of thing? Mary had no idea. "Here." Irene handed Hannah and Diana each a hairpin. "First to open all the locks wins. I'll time you. Ready?"

"Wins what?" asked Diana.

"My admiration and esteem. You should know that Hannah is very, very good. Probably better than you!"

"As if," said Diana, but she picked up the hairpin. Hannah gave her the sort of scornful look that is the particular property of a superior parlormaid.

Mary looked at the two girls, one still in her nightgown, the other in a prim black uniform with white cap and apron. Which of them would win? She pushed aside one of the chairs so she could stand closer to the table.

"Ready?" said Irene, picking up the stopwatch. "Go!"

It was rather beautiful to watch, like a ballet. First, both girls twisted the hairpins into their preferred shapes. Then with precise movements they picked up each of the locks in front of them, turning their hairpins in the keyhole, quickly and carefully. The lock would click, unusually loud in the quiet room, and then they would go on to the next one. Pick up, insert hairpin, turn, click. Pick up the next lock.

Who in the world was Irene Norton, that she had a parlormaid who could pick locks? Or a secret chamber in her house? Or a wall of weapons? Of course she was a friend of Mr. Holmes, but she was surely more than that! A thief, the leader of a gang of thieves, perhaps? Mary could not quite see Irene as a thief. Was she a detective, like Holmes?

There—while she had been distracted, Hannah had just put down her final lock. But Diana's locks were already on the table in front of her. Had she unlocked them all? Or were there still more to unlock? No, she was stretching and yawning with her mouth open as though she hadn't a care in the world.

"Hannah, six minutes, fifteen seconds. Diana, five minutes, forty-seven seconds. If you ever want to join our merry little band, you have a job waiting for you." Irene put the locks back in their box. "All right, I have one more thing I want to do here. Diana, why don't you get dressed? Hannah, thank you, you've beaten your own best time. Can we reconvene in the parlor in about fifteen minutes? Mary and Justine, if you'll stay for a moment, I'd like to have a word."

"You have beaten me square," said Hannah, holding out her right hand. "If you wish to, come to the kitchen later to see me and my sister. You will like her, I think. We will tell you some good stories, and Frau Schmidt always leaves a sweet in the cabinet for us, torte or strudel."

"Fair and square," said Diana, taking her hand and giving it a good, firm shake. "I'll come down when I get bored of this lot, which might be pretty soon. Also, can I borrow your sister's clothes so I don't have to go around looking so idiotic? Come on." As they left together, Mary heard Diana say, "You did good, you know. I've never met anyone nearly as quick as I am."

When Diana and Hannah had gone off, one to get dressed, the other presumably back to the kitchen, Irene turned to Mary. "I think Diana could do it. I think she could get through those locks. Ideally, she would establish contact with Lucinda Van Helsing. I don't want her to do more than that—just let Lucinda know we're coming for her. But even if she can't get to Lucinda, she could gather information on the asylum routine, most importantly whether there are guards on the third floor. If so, how many of them are there? Where are they stationed and when do they patrol? We'll need to know all that when we get in—however we get in! She's quick and clever—even quicker than Hannah, which I didn't think was possible. And she's the one who came up with this plan. The question is, are you willing to let her do it? I'm asking you in particular because you're her sister. I know the two of you don't always get along, but I also know you're protective of her, as you should be. This would put her in danger—there's no doubt about that. However, she's our best chance of establishing contact with Lucinda and getting the lay of the land, as it were. Once she reports back to us, we can figure out how to effect a rescue. What do you say?"

Justine responded before Mary could. "Irene, if you will forgive me—what is all this? The secret chamber, the weapons on the wall. I think we would like"—she caught Mary's eye—"yes, Mary and I would like some sort of explanation."

Irene laughed. "Am I a criminal mastermind? Or the leader of a radical political faction, perhaps an Anarchist? No, nothing so glamorous. When I was a young soprano traveling all over Europe, my country asked me to keep an eye on things. America is a young country, not yet a power in the world, but it wants to be. And it wants to know what's happening in Europe. It has a network of—well, observers. That's what I do—observe. Gather information. Whom are the generals supporting? Which financiers are having coffee together? Does the Emperor have indigestion? It's more important when an Emperor has indigestion than when ordinary people do—it can lead to all sorts of consequences. That sort of thing. Once, that work led me to a connection with the King of Bohemia, which is how I met Sherlock. I gave it up when I married, but after my husband died, I had no other work to do, no other reason to go on—it was too late to go back to singing. And so I took it up again."

"You're a spy!" said Justine.

Irene laughed again. She had a deep, rich, musical laugh. "A spy would never tell you she was a spy, my dear. Can we get back to the question of Diana? I'm going to contact my friend and ask him for help. I'm not sure I should, considering the danger to his professional standing if anyone finds out he was involved. However, I would rather explain the situation to him and allow him to make his own decision. Even if he's not willing to help, he can give us valuable advice. But first I need to know—will you allow her to do this?"

Mary realized they were both waiting for her to speak. "Diana's only fourteen," she said, stalling for time. "And Justine knows how difficult she can be. She rarely does what she's told."

"But remember how useful she was when you had to come into the warehouse to rescue me and Beatrice," said Justine. "I would not be here today if it weren't for her."

DIANA: Exactly, and don't you forget it!

"Yes, well, remember that afterward she helped Hyde escape!" said Mary. "She's only going to go in and make contact, right? And observe the guards? Nothing more? How long would she be in there?"

"I think we should give her three days," said Irene. "If she can't make contact in three days, we'll bring her out again and try something else."

Mary turned and stared very hard at the wall of weapons without seeing them. "All right," she said after a moment. "Talk to your friend, and let's see what he says. Anyway, maybe he'll say no."

Irene nodded. She walked over to the desk and sat down, then pulled an instrument that had been sitting on a corner of the desk toward her. Was it a microscope of some sort? It looked rather like a candlestick on a base. She picked up what looked like the candle snuffer—what in the world was she doing?

"You have a telephone!" said Justine.

"We are quite modern in Vienna," said Irene, smiling. "Can you give me some time alone? I think this conversation is going to take a while."

"Of course," said Mary. As she headed out of the room, she whispered to Justine, "So that's what a telephone looks like!"

"You've never seen a telephone before?" asked Justine.

"Only in advertisements. Not even Mr. Holmes has a telephone. Don't tell me you've seen one!"

"No, I have not seen one either. Not a real one."

They did not talk as they went back upstairs to the parlor, perhaps because there was too much to talk about. As they passed the door of the study where Justine had spent the night, she patted her waistcoat and said, "I think I've forgotten my pocket watch. I must have left it on the table by the sofa, or perhaps on the desk. Men's clothes require such constant thought! All the rules for when you must raise your hat . . ."

"I think women's clothes are equally difficult," said Mary. "It's just that we're used to them. Well, go find it, then. I'm sure we have a few minutes before Irene finishes her conversation on the telephone. So this friend of hers must have a telephone as well? I assume that's how it works, sort of like a telegraph but with speech."

She followed Justine into the study, which was darker than the rest of the second floor, with wooden shelves that reached to the ceiling and thick velvet curtains. The sofa Justine had been sleeping on was long and deep, perfect for curling up with a good book. Mary looked at the side table, but there was a book on it, rather than the pocket watch Justine was searching for. When she saw the title, she gasped.

"Oh. Oh no. I've been such an idiot!" Mary put her hands up to her face and covered her cheeks. If they weren't red with shame, they should be.

Justine held up the pocket watch. "There, you see, I left it on the desk where I would see it first thing, but forgot to put it into my watch pocket this morning. A man would not have forgotten. Mary, whatever is wrong?"

Mary could only point to the book, as though it explained everything. On its cover was written *Frankenstein: A Biography of the Modern Prometheus*. How had she ever considered herself sensible, responsible? How had she ever thought she could become a detective, like Mr. Holmes?

"Well, you see, the truth is that I've never read it," said Justine apologetically. "I thought it would be too painful to read about my father, and Adam, and my own supposed destruction. But it was sitting on the table, as though Irene had been consulting it, and I woke up early this morning, long before the breakfast hour. So I began to read. It was good, at first, to read about Switzerland and the Frankenstein family. But once I came to the description of Justine Moritz, I could not continue. . . ."

Mary sat down abruptly on the sofa. "You don't understand. *Waldman*. The name Waldman. I should have recognized it." She flipped hastily through the book. Justine might not have read it, but she certainly had, after they had solved the Whitechapel Murders and Adam had died in the warehouse fire. She had wanted to know as much about the Société des Alchimistes as possible. As Catherine had warned her, the book contained nothing—it had not mentioned the society at all. But she remembered a mention . . . yes, there.

"Waldman!" she said with a sort of triumphant anguish, then pointed to the page. "He was Victor Frankenstein's chemistry professor at the University of Ingolstadt. And that's where Heinrich Waldman was going to medical school. Oh, how could I have missed it?"

Justine sat down beside her on the sofa. "Truly? Where?"

She handed the book to Justine and pointed at the relevant paragraph. Then she put her head in her hands so they hid her face. "I don't know what's wrong with me," she said. It came out muffled, through her fingers. "Ever since we left England, I feel as though I haven't been myself. I forget things, I get confused. . . ." She had always known what to do, always been so sure of herself. She had been Miss Mary Jekyll of 11 Park Terrace. Who was she now, in this house that was not hers, in a foreign country? What was happening to her?

Justine put an arm around her. Mary was startled by the gesture. Justine so seldom touched anyone—she was always afraid that she might hurt them inadvertently. Now, her touch was deliberately gentle.

"You mustn't blame yourself. You see, the rest of us lost our homes long ago. Diana was taken to the Magdalen Society. Catherine was transported to Moreau's island, and Beatrice left her father's garden in Padua. I, of course, was taken from my native Switzerland when my father decided to reanimate me. But you have a home, one you have never left before. It's no wonder that you should feel out of sorts, as though you can't think clearly, away from it."

"Justine's right." Irene Norton was standing in the doorway. How long had she been there? "I felt the same way when I left New Jersey for the first time, to attend a conservatory in New York. I felt the same way again when I left the United States for Europe. I don't know you that well, Mary—not yet. But I think you're the sort of person who's used to being in control, and now you're not. Things are happening around you—things that are bigger than you suspected. That's why I asked if anyone else you met could be a spy for the Société des Alchimistes. Waldman—I knew I'd heard that name before, but I couldn't remember where. I assume he's a descendent of the Waldman who was

Frankenstein's professor. A great-grandson, maybe? What I can't figure out is, why he didn't give you a false name, which would have been easy enough. Maybe it was some sort of test, to find out how much you knew."

"Could it be a coincidence?" asked Justine, as though not quite believing in the possibility herself.

"There's no such thing as a coincidence when you're dealing with an organization like the Société des Alchimistes." Irene looked grim. It sounded as though she knew a good deal about such organizations herself. Anarchists? Socialists? Surely those were the sorts of groups Irene would know about. . . .

"I'm so sorry," said Mary. She felt thoroughly ashamed of herself. She was quite certain that Irene would not have made such a mistake. Would this get back to Mr. Holmes—to Sherlock? Justine's arm was a reassuring weight around her shoulders.

Irene looked surprised. "My dear, it's scarcely your fault. We all make stupid mistakes sometimes. I made one with Sherlock, initially. That's what human beings do. The only thing to do with a mistake is learn from it. Come on, I want to tell you the result of my conversation with Sigmund, but I want Diana there too, and Hannah and Greta to consult. So stop moping, Mary, and come into the parlor."

MRS. POOLE: Irene Norton is one of the most sensible women I've met. It's no use moaning over spilt milk. Best mop it up and move on, as my mother used to say.

DIANA: Unless the cat has lapped it up first.

MRS. POOLE: Those dratted cats! I don't know why I ever let you girls keep them.

When they were once again in the parlor, Irene rang the bell. A minute later, in trooped two impeccably outfitted maids in black dresses, with white caps and aprons. Dressed in their uniforms, Hannah and Greta looked surprisingly alike, although Greta was slightly shorter. Diana followed them in, looking considerably less impeccable. She seemed to have put on Greta's clothes from earlier.

"Here's the situation," said Irene, sitting on the sofa while they all stood around, waiting to hear what she would say. "My friend Sigmund has agreed to help, on one condition: he would like to meet Diana first, to assure himself that she will make a convincing mental patient. I told him that would be no problem—"

"Oy!" said Diana, angrily.

"But he would like to meet her himself. His reputation and admitting privileges are on the line. Nevertheless, he agreed it was important to help Lucinda, and evidently he has some sort of professional quarrel with Van Helsing, something about psycho-sexual development. . . . I stop listening when academics start mixing their Greek and Latin roots. That never leads anywhere productive."

Justine nodded, as though in agreement. Once again Mary wished she could have continued her studies under Miss Murray, so she would know what they were talking about.

"Mary, could you take Diana to his consulting rooms? I'm afraid you'll have to take a cab, since I need the carriage this morning. Also, he lives on the other side of the Ring, and I don't want you to be seen driving through the middle of Vienna in my equipage. As we've learned, the Société des Alchimistes is watching you, and I am watched as well, by parties that are as dangerous, if not more so. I'll send Hannah with you—she knows the address."

"All right," said Mary. "When do you want us to leave?"

"As soon as Diana changes back into women's clothes," said Irene.

"Why?" asked Diana, outraged. "I don't want to."

"Because you're supposed to be neurasthenic and hysterical. No one will question that diagnosis in a girl going through puberty."

"Puberty yourself!" said Diana, then whispered to Hannah, "That's a dirty word, isn't it? I'm pretty sure that's a dirty word."

"Justine and Greta, I need you to go to the Krankenhaus. Don't make contact with anyone or let yourselves be seen. Just get a sense for the neighborhood and find a place for us to keep watch while Diana is inside. Perhaps you can rent rooms in one of the nearby buildings? Make sure it has a good sightline. While Diana attempts to contact Lucinda, we will be watching from the outside in case she needs help. And we need to start thinking about possible scenarios for a rescue attempt. Everyone got it?"

Hannah and Greta said "Yes, *madame*," almost in unison. Justine nodded. Diana was still too angry at the prospect of wearing women's clothes to nod. She stood, arms crossed, with a frown on her face.

Mary put a hand on Diana's shoulder. "All right," she said. "Yes, if this is the plan, let's do it."

Fifteen minutes later, she, Diana, and Hannah were in a cab, rattling over the cobblestones of the Ringstrasse, the long, tree-lined boulevard that circles central Vienna. In her purse were enough krone for cab fare and whatever other expenses she might incur in Vienna, which Irene had given her just as they were leaving. It was far too much, she had told Irene—but then, she was not entirely sure of the exchange rate without consulting her Baedeker. Diana was staring out the window, complaining about something or other.

Mary was not paying attention to whatever Diana was saying. Waldman had been such a stupid mistake. She must be more vigilant, particularly now they knew someone from the

Société des Alchimistes was aware of them and their trip to Vienna. Someone was watching, perhaps having them followed. She looked down at the card Irene had given her, which she had shown to the driver:

Dr. Sigmund Freud
Berggasse 19, Alsergrund

She hoped Dr. Freud could help them.

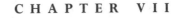

CHAPTER VII

The Address in Soho

"Drat those cats!" said Mrs. Poole.

"What have they done this time?" Catherine looked up from the dining room table, where she had been poring over a map of London.

"They chewed this telegram. I put it down for one minute so I could lock the door, and now look at it!" Mrs. Poole held up a piece of paper that did, indeed, look tattered and rather damp.

"Is it from Mary?" Catherine pushed aside the map. She had been trying to figure out the best way to get to Potter's Lane through the tangle of Soho.

"No, from that friend of Mr. Holmes, a Mrs. Norton. Here, take a look yourself."

Catherine took the telegram, put it on the table, and read the message on it.

> MARY JUSTINE DIANA ARRIVED SAFELY WILL
> TAKE CARE OF THEM AS THOUGH MY OWN
> DAUGHTERS DONT WORRY MRS POOLE BUT
> ADVISE CAUTION THEY ENCOUNTERED SA
> AGENT ON TRAIN DO NOT REPLY UNLESS
> ABSOLUTELY NECESSARY WITH BEST REGARDS
> IRENE NORTON

"What do you think that means, 'S.A. agent on train'?" Mrs. Poole sounded worried.

"It means that on the train, they met someone from the S.A., presumably," said Catherine. "Which means that the Société des Alchimistes has been watching us. Damn! We thought they didn't even know we existed. I think we're going to have to be a lot more cautious than we've been." She took the telegram from Mrs. Poole. "'S.A. agent on train.' Couldn't she have been more specific? Who brought this telegram?"

"A boy from the telegraph office," said Mrs. Poole. "He seemed like an ordinary telegraph boy, although he wasn't wearing his cap, and he had a strange accent. Not Irish. More like Australian, but not exactly. Why do you ask?"

"I don't know. I'm becoming suspicious of everyone, I suppose. Although I scarcely think a telegraph boy would be spying for the S.A., even if he were Australian!" Had she seen anyone around Park Terrace recently? She didn't remember anything suspicious. She would just have to be careful, particularly today, since she was going to find out what Seward and Prendick were up to. It would be better to wear masculine clothes for Soho. She had lost Reverend Josiah Crashaw's suit, but she still had the clothes she had stolen from the Flying Kaminski Brothers. They would have to do. She wondered what 7 Potter's Lane was, exactly. Probably a lodging house of some sort, or perhaps a pub? Why did Seward want to meet Prendick there, rather than in his office in Purfleet? She had no idea. Of course it would have been better if she could have gone there ahead of time, to scout out the territory. But there had been the rush of getting Mary and Justine ready to go, and then an article to finish for *The Woman's World* that would pay a very badly needed two pounds. She had told Mary to take as much money as she and Justine would need on their trip—and now they would have to pay for Diana as well, drat that girl! But it did leave the Park Terrace household in straitened circumstances.

Mrs. Poole frowned and put her hands on her hips. "I'm worried about Miss Mary and the rest of them, that's all. I wish they would write us a proper letter—telegrams are like those Egyptian hieroglyphs they have now at the British Museum. You never quite know what they mean. As for Alpha and Omega, and I don't know why you couldn't have called them sensible, decent cat names, like Tom and Puss—just keep them out of my kitchen. Two dead mice they left on the floor yesterday! I stepped on one of them this morning and had to clean the bottoms of my slippers with carbolic!"

"Well," said Catherine, reasonably, "I think that comes under the category of doing their jobs, don't you think? After all, you said they could stay as long as they caught mice. They must have overheard you. And two dead mice are better in the kitchen than two live ones, aren't they?"

"Hrumph!" said Mrs. Poole.

MRS. POOLE: I would never make such an undignified sound!

MARY: That's right, Mrs. Poole would never make a sound like that.

JUSTINE: Never an undignified hrumph. Not our Mrs. Poole.

BEATRICE: Indeed, Mrs. Poole would never make an undignified sound of any sort.

DIANA: You're all kidding, right? Why are you all laughing?

Just then, the front door bell rang.

> MRS. POOLE: It was actually half an hour later, but if
> you want to put lies into your book, don't let me
> stop you!

> CATHERINE: It's more suspenseful this way.

Mrs. Poole went to answer it, but Alice must have gotten there before her, because a moment later she walked into the dining room, followed by a giant of a man in a suit that did not quite fit over his bulging muscles. He looked like a sack of potatoes that had been stuffed into a sock.

> JUSTINE: That's not fair, Catherine! Atlas is the
> sweetest, gentlest man I know. He looks nothing
> like a sack of potatoes.

> CATHERINE: I thought you liked potatoes. Anyway,
> it's a good description, whether you appreciate it
> or not.

"This gentleman wishes to see you, miss," said Alice. "He says he knows you from the circus?"

"Atlas!" Catherine jumped up and almost ran around the table to give him a hug. How long had it been since she had seen him, and all her friends at the Circus of Marvels and Delights? Several months—she had not gone back since moving into 11 Park Terrace, although she had written to Lorenzo, letting him know what had happened to her and Justine. The circus Strongman hugged her back carefully.

"Hullo, Cat!" he said, with a wide grin on his face. It was a broad face, freckled, with blondish-brown hair spilling over the forehead in an unkempt fashion, which made him look rather like a lion. Its symmetry was marred by a nose that had once been broken and was now permanently crooked, but what might have been disfiguring on a different man was rather charming on his countenance.

CATHERINE: There, have I redeemed myself? Do you like that better?

JUSTINE: Yes. A lion is better than potatoes, and more accurate.

"For goodness' sake, sit down and tell me all about the circus," said Catherine. "I miss you all, you know!"

He sat in one of the dining room chairs, which creaked under his weight. "I came to give you the rest of the money from Lorenzo— he's very sorry he couldn't send it sooner! And to make sure you're all right, you and Justine. Is Justine here?" He looked around as though she might be hiding somewhere in the room, although it offered no places of concealment, particularly for a giantess.

"Well, now I know why you really came," said Catherine, sitting in the chair next to his. "No, she's away at the moment." No use telling him that Justine was in Vienna. He would only worry about her—he had worried about her enough when they were all in the circus together. On cold winter nights, he would come to their tent to make sure their stove was working, and he always inquired about her health, as though afraid she would catch a cold. "But I'll tell her you came by, Matthew." That was his real name, the one he had been baptized with: Matthew Taylor. When she had joined Lorenzo's Circus of Marvels and Delights, he had already been part of the sideshow, performing feats of strength and showing off his admirable, if somewhat overdeveloped, physique. He had originally come from Manchester, where his father and father's father had in fact been tailors until the factories had put them out of business. Catherine had seen him mend a handkerchief as neatly as a seamstress, although she had been amused by how small the needle looked, almost invisible in his large fingers. He had been a boxer until the broken nose and a concussion that had left him unconscious for several days. After that, he had decided on a less dangerous profession. Catherine knew for a fact that in his spare time, he wrote poetry, because he had written some for Justine.

> JUSTINE: It's rather good poetry. There's one that begins, "Where are you going, pale maid, so melancholy. . . ."

> BEATRICE: That's quite pretty, and describes you very well.

> DIANA: Poetry is such rot. Except Kipling. Kipling is prime, especially the one where they all die at the end.

> JUSTINE: You're thinking of Tennyson. "Into the valley of death rode the six hundred," is that not what you meant?

> DIANA: Yeah, that's the one! How did you know?

> JUSTINE: You left the book open on the floor in my studio. There is a streak of red paint down the center of the page.

> DIANA: Like blood!

"Well, here's your money," said Atlas, looking so disappointed that Catherine wished she could tell him something, anything—that Justine had spoken well of him, at least. But she hadn't mentioned him since they had left the circus. "Five pounds even, with his apologies for not sending the entire amount at once. The circus business ain't been too good lately. We ought to have been in Devonshire this month, but three towns said they wanted Bartoli's circus instead—it has an elephant. So here we are in London, staying at a boardinghouse in Clerkenwell. You should come by and visit—it's right on Clerkenwell Green, close to St. James's. Although we might not be there long—Lorenzo's got a new idea."

"Yes, what is it?" asked Catherine absentmindedly. The money would help, since their funds were so low at the moment. But she was already thinking ahead to the adventure of that afternoon. What would she find in Soho? Why was Seward meeting Prendick there? She would go to 7 Potter's Lane an hour before they were scheduled to arrive and see if she could conceal herself—perhaps there would be a closet, or a storage room of some sort? Somehow, she must find out what was going on.

"Some of us are going to Paris. We have a show there, for three nights. And then he's thinking farther—maybe Berlin! Imagine that. Me, Sasha, Clarence. The acrobats and contortionists. Madam Zora the snake charmer—she's new. Lorenzo says there's a fashion for such things now on the continent, anything unusual, macabre. I wish you were coming with us—we could use a Cat Woman or Giantess! By the way, Sasha says hello, and Clarence told me to give you a hug."

"I think you already did," said Catherine, smiling. "I wish I could, you know. I miss being part of the circus, and I've never been to Paris. But I have so much to take care of here."

"I can see that," said Atlas. "You look good, Cat. Like you've found a home. I'm happy for you—and Justine, of course."

Had she found a home? Catherine was still not sure. But she took his hands and squeezed them. "Matthew, the thing about Justine is—she's been through a lot. I'll let you know when she comes back, and then maybe you can visit. Bring flowers—you know she likes flowers. Don't give up. She had her heart broken a long time ago, and I don't know how long it's going to take to mend. But you can help. . . ." That wasn't quite right, it didn't describe what Justine had endured, but she wanted to put it in a way he would understand. Anyway, it was up to Justine to tell the whole story—how she had died and been resurrected—if she wanted to. And the story of Adam—well, that was certainly not Catherine's to tell.

"Bless you," said Atlas, squeezing her hands back a little too hard. He had such a nice smile, although at the moment it looked as uncertain as it was hopeful. Would Justine ever get over what had happened with Adam enough to trust another man? Catherine did not know.

"Well, when you see her, tell her I said hello, and that I look forward to seeing her again. Flowers, hunh? I'll remember that. I'm not good at those sorts of things, never have been." He rose.

"It just takes practice," said Catherine. She stood up on tiptoes to kiss him on the cheek—he had to lean down before she could.

And then, like a mouse, there was Alice in the doorway again. She appeared and disappeared so quietly! "Shall I let you out, sir?" She was holding a battered tweed cap.

"Thank you, missy," he said, nodding and taking the cap from her. "And do come visit us if you have time, Cat. It's Mrs. Protheroe's boardinghouse—I don't remember the address, but anyone in that area can direct you. We'll be there until the end of the week."

A minute later, Catherine heard the front door open and close. Ah, it had been good to see him! That had been a fine life, at the circus. Not easy, but interesting, and safe for a while. This new life—it was better in some ways, but less safe, she thought, for all that she was living in a posh house by Regent's Park. It had other kinds of danger, like the ones she would encounter in Soho.

"Miss?" It was Alice, at the door again.

"Yes, Alice? And for goodness' sake, could you just call me Catherine? Or Cat, if you prefer. Or Hey, you."

"Yes, miss. I was taking her luncheon to Miss Beatrice"— *Green sludge,* thought Catherine—"and she said she wasn't going with you this afternoon."

"No, it's too dangerous." Catherine drew the map to herself again. "I'll need to find a place to hide, probably someplace small. If Beatrice and I were hiding together, she might poison me. She wouldn't mean to, but she wouldn't be able to help it."

"Oh, I remember!" said Alice, with feeling. Of course, she had almost been poisoned by Beatrice in the warehouse by the docks, as described in *The Strange Case of the Alchemist's Daughter*, at all the finest booksellers, only two shillings.

MARY: Don't you think you've done that enough?

CATHERINE: When I've done it enough, I'll stop.

"I do wish the others were here," said Catherine. "Justine might be too tall, and Diana too wild, but Mary would come in handy, if only as a lookout."

MARY: Well, thank you for that, I'm sure! I'm much
more than a lookout.

Of course, she could have asked Charlie, but—this was about Prendick. Somehow, she did not want Holmes or his Baker Street

Irregulars involved. Whatever they knew, he would know, and this felt like her personal business. She would take care of it herself.

"What about me?" asked Alice. "I don't know that I'm *much* use, but I can look out as well as anyone one."

Catherine was astonished. "But Alice, you've told us over and over again that you just want to be a kitchen maid. No adventures for you, remember? You were most insistent."

Alice stared down at her feet and twisted her hands in her apron. "Yes, miss—Catherine. But it feels cowardly of me to let you go alone, when I could help. I feel that Miss Mary would expect it of me."

Catherine frowned. "Are you absolutely sure? We may be going back into danger, you know."

Alice looked up again and nodded. "Yes, Catherine. Absolutely."

Catherine waited a moment, and then another moment, in case Alice changed her mind. "All right, then. Come on over here. I want us both to memorize the streets in this section of Soho. And remember that it's going to look different once we're among the buildings."

> MARY: You know you didn't have to go. You didn't
>   have to prove anything—not to me, not to anyone.

> ALICE: I know, but I'm glad I did, despite everything
>   that happened after. We don't become who we are
>   without taking risks, do we?

> MARY: No, I suppose not. I just wish I could have
>   spared you a lot of pain.

> ALICE: If I had to do it over again, I would do the
>   same, you know.

BEATRICE: *Brava,* Alice. You are an example to us all.

It was around three in the afternoon when they left 11 Park Terrace. As they walked toward Marylebone Road, Catherine looked up and down the street—was anyone watching? A beggar, a cat's meat or rag-and-bone man, anyone who looked like an agent of the S.A.? But she saw no one except for Jimmy, one of the Baker Street boys, outfitted as a bootblack with a box and brushes. One or another of Holmes's Irregulars was always around, keeping a lookout. Otherwise, Park Terrace was entirely deserted. She gave Jimmy a small wave as she and Alice walked by, and he nodded an acknowledgment. On Marylebone Road, they caught an omnibus to Piccadilly Circus. Then they walked through a tangle of streets and lanes, going farther and farther into the labyrinth that is London.

Before they left, Mrs. Poole had told them both not to take any unnecessary risks.

"I agree," Beatrice had said, standing in the hallway as they were pulling on their gloves and donning the hats that would transform them into London clerks on their way home to lodgings. "How I wish I could come with you! Am I always to be left behind, more harmful than helpful to those I care about?"

"Well, as soon as I need anyone poisoned, I'll let you know," Catherine replied. Actually, it might be rather a good idea to poison Prendick. Surely he deserved it? She pushed the angry, resentful thought into a corner of her mind, where it could stay until she had time to examine it at leisure. Now was not the time for such thinking—now she needed to think clearly, logically. Ugh, she was starting to sound like Mary!

"I really don't know why Alice needs to go," Mrs. Poole said, looking worried. "I was hoping she could help me with the mending this afternoon. Is it really necessary to put her in danger as well?"

"Mrs. Poole, this is a little more important than mending!" said Catherine. "Anyway, at the moment she happens to be Alfred."

Alice was wearing a pair of Diana's trousers and a jacket that hung on her thin frame, although it was the smallest Catherine could find. Catherine was similarly outfitted in masculine clothes, although hers fit considerably better. "Come on, Alfred," said Charles, which was the name she had chosen for herself. She clapped her hand on Alice's shoulder in the most masculine way she knew how, and then before Mrs. Poole could raise any further objections, they were out the door and down Park Terrace, heading toward Marylebone Road.

The day was hot, the city close and airless, as though a glass dome had been placed over it. London smelled of sewage. There had been no room on top of the omnibus, and they had been forced to ride inside, on separate benches. At least they had more air, walking through the alleys and mews of Soho.

Following a map Catherine had drawn for herself, they came to Potter's Court, a semicircle of sad, drab houses around a thin sliver of park, like a half-moon. "But where in the world is Potter's Lane?" asked Catherine. Three lanes radiated from the court, but none of them were marked with signs. They walked down the first, then the second, then the third. The three lanes were indistinguishable, except that each was dingier and more depressing than the last.

"Excuse me, ma'am," said Alfred to a woman who was sitting on a stoop, smoking a particularly odiferous pipe. She looked a century old, but was probably much younger—there is nothing like poverty to wrinkle the brows and pucker the mouth, to bend the young, healthy body. "I'm looking for me brother, Joe we calls him although his name's Joseph, lives at Number 5 Potter's Lane. Bright red hair, you can't miss him. Can you tell me if this is the right street? Me mum's terrible worried about him."

Where had Alice learned to speak in the accent of the London streets? How shocked Mrs. Poole would be to hear her! Usually, Alice was most particular about how she spoke. Even when her vocabulary was not quite equal to it, she adopted the superior accent of a maid in a gentleman's household.

> ALICE: I'm a Londoner born and bred. I think people
> forget that, sometimes. When I first came to
> Mrs. Jekyll's residence, I used to imitate Enid so
> as not to sound low. I didn't want Mrs. Poole, or
> the other servants, to think I was nothing but a
> guttersnipe!

"Ah, you've come to the right place," said the woman. "Third house on the other side—you'll see the number right enough, although it ain't too clear from the road. What's your brother done that your mum's so worried about?"

"Taken to drink, more's the pity. And such a good boy once! But he fell in with a bad lot," said Alfred, shaking his head.

"Ain't that always the way," said the woman. "Well, I hope you find him, for your mum's sake!" She took another drag of her pipe, and Catherine noticed that her teeth were stained brown from the smoke.

"Thankee, ma'am," said Alfred. Catherine, or Charles, nodded and slipped her a penny, which promptly disappeared into a ragged pocket.

Sure enough, the third house down had a 5 painted on the door, although it was only half-visible because the paint on the door was peeling off in long strips. The next house had no marker at all, but logically, it must be Number 7. It was set a little back from the street, behind a small yard of dirt and dying grass. The front door was shadowed by the buildings around, the windows on the first floor boarded up. There was a second floor, with curtains over the windows, but no way to climb up to them.

"Can that woman see us?" asked Catherine.

"I don't think so," said Alice. "I can't see her around the corner of the building, so I don't think she can see me either. Why, what are you going to do?"

"You stand guard, although really there's not much you can do if anyone comes by. This will just take a minute." It took considerably longer than that, and at one point Catherine was worried that the hairpin she had stuck into the lock would break in half. But finally she heard a click. After all that effort, she certainly hoped they were at the right address and that the house numbers on Potter's Lane didn't skip around in some mysterious way, the way they sometimes did in London! Or maybe, just maybe, she had memorized the address wrong? Why in the world would Seward want to meet Prendick here?

As soon as she stepped through the doorway, she realized they were in the right place after all. She was so startled that she almost forgot to lock the door again behind her.

"Blimey!" said Alice. "I mean, goodness gracious. This is not at all what I expected!"

"Me neither," said Catherine.

Inside that dilapidated exterior, 7 Potter's Lane looked like one of the gentleman's clubs of Belgravia or Mayfair. Catherine was tempted to open the door again to see if they had suddenly been transported to another part of London. The walls were paneled in dark wood, and even in the dim light that came through the slats over the windows, she could see a mahogany hall table beneath a mirror with a gilt frame, beyond which stood an elaborate combination hat rack and umbrella stand. A wide staircase went up to the second floor. To their right was an archway into what looked like a particularly large club common room, with comfortable sofas and armchairs, a large fireplace suitable for sitting and reading by, and small tables arranged where ashtrays would be most welcome. There were paintings of distinguished-looking men on the walls, and heavy brocade curtains hung at the boarded-up windows.

"What is this place?" she whispered. It was so quiet that she felt it would be almost a sacrilege to speak aloud.

"Was," said Alice. "Don't you see, miss, there's dust everywhere. This place ain't . . . hasn't been dusted for ever so long. And look, cobwebs in the corners. If I left a place looking like this, Mrs. Poole would sack me for sure." Alice was right about the dust, although Catherine had not noticed until she had pointed it out. But then, it was Alice's job to notice such things. Even the mirror was covered with a layer of dust. Looking into it was like looking into a murky pool.

Catherine checked her pocket watch. "They're supposed to be here in an hour. We need to find a place to hide, but I want to reconnoiter a bit. I assumed 7 Potter's Lane would be a lodging house, or a neighborhood pub of some sort. I didn't think it would be—someplace like this. *What is it?* And why is it in the middle of Soho? I really wish I'd come earlier, to check it out."

"Don't blame yourself, miss," said Alice. "You've scarcely had time, with all the preparations for Miss Jekyll and Miss Frankenstein."

"And I had to write that wretched article—on hats! The things we do for money. Well, it's no use lamenting now. Let's see what we can discover in the next half hour."

The first order of business was to find a hiding place, so they could come back to it quickly. On the ground floor was the large common room they had noticed, as well as several smaller rooms for private meetings. One of them, right at the back of the house, was outfitted as an office, with a large desk and bookshelves.

"I bet they'll be meeting in here," said Catherine. "Seward is used to sitting behind a desk. He's used to being director, the one in charge. I bet this is the room he comes to automatically. But how can we be sure? And anyway, if he does come in here, where in the world can we hide?"

There were no hiding places. The room held the desk, a chair behind it, two chairs in front of it, and nothing else. The bookshelves were empty.

"They must have held books once," said Alice.

"And the desk drawers must have held papers, writing implements—but look, completely empty. You know, the other rooms were empty as well—no ashtrays on the tables. And yet look at this place!" The rugs were thick, the furniture upholstered in velvet, the picture frames of heavy gilded wood. "Come on, let's look upstairs."

But upstairs there were only bedrooms, and a bath with the water turned off. Here the wardrobes were empty, except for a few hangers. There was nothing in the bureau drawers. The beds had no bedclothes on them, only bare mattresses, some of which had obviously become the home of mice.

"What in the world was this place, when it *was* a place?" asked Catherine. Well, there was no time to speculate now. "We need to hide. Maybe in that hall closet downstairs?"

"I don't think we could hear much from there," said Alice. "There's something I noticed. If you don't mind following me, miss . . . Catherine."

Down the stairs they went again, Catherine wondering what Alice had in mind. But Alice had proven quite sensible so far, so she followed the kitchen maid back into the office. "There, you see," said Alice. "This room has a dumbwaiter. So does the large room up front. If you open it just a little, like this . . ." She lifted a small latch that Catherine had not even seen and opened what looked like a cabinet in the wall, halfway up, right next to the fireplace. Why hadn't Catherine noticed it? Perhaps because it was only a foot high, and its door was the same color as the paneling— indeed, made to look like a part of the paneling. It was certainly not large enough for either of them to hide in. Still, she should have been more observant! What was the point of being a puma if she didn't notice things?

"You see, if the door is open, anything said in this room will echo down the shaft of the dumbwaiter. Joseph, our footman that was, told me about a butler who blackmailed his master based on the things he'd heard through the dumbwaiter. Now we just need to see where it comes up from, which will be down below, I'm thinking."

Catherine stared at Alice's retreating back with respect. She had wondered if it would be a good idea to bring the kitchen maid with her. Well, here was her answer! She followed Alice, both amused and frustrated. Why, Alice was turning out to be as useful as Charlie!

On their way, Alice opened the dumbwaiter in the common room as well. Unless you were standing right next to it, you would never have noticed that it was open just a crack.

Then they descended into the basement, down the narrow set of back stairs so common in London houses. The first room they came to was a kitchen, with two windows at ground level, rounded like half-moons, that looked out into what an optimist might have called the garden. These were boarded up as well, but the boards had deteriorated enough that they could see each other, and the dusty stove, and the empty kitchen shelves, in the dim light. There, set into the dingy, soot-covered walls, they found the bottoms of the dumbwaiter shafts. "If we take out the frames, we'll be able to hear better," said Alice, beginning to take one out herself. Catherine helped her. At least she was still stronger than

Alice! Together, they lifted out the large wooden frames that normally ran up and down the shafts, delivering food and wine from the kitchen, and put them on the stone floor.

"And here's a pantry," said Catherine, opening the only other door in the kitchen. "If anyone comes down, we could hide in here. Let's put the frames in here so no one notices. Fifteen minutes until their meeting time!"

They stationed themselves by the dumbwaiters, which were on opposite ends of the kitchen, and waited for Seward and Prendick to arrive.

> MARY: I really think Alice should get a great deal of
> credit for thinking of the dumbwaiters!

> ALICE: I'm sure anyone would have noticed them,
> if they'd been looking. As soon as I walked
> into those rooms, I wondered how they would
> manage the food service, you see. So in a sense
> I was looking for dumbwaiters even before I saw
> them.

> MRS. POOLE: Don't be too modest, missy. You have
> a trained eye, and I know, as I was the one who
> trained it!

> ALICE: And an excellent training it was, too, Mrs.
> Poole.

They did not have to wait long. On her pocket watch, 5:00 p.m. passed, and Catherine wondered once again if she could have been mistaken—about the time, perhaps? Or the day? But no, at 5:15 p.m. she heard the unmistakable stomp of men's boots overhead. She looked over at Alice—but the kitchen maid was listening intently at her own dumbwaiter. There were voices above, but she could not hear what they were saying. What if she and Alice were wrong, and the two men went into another room altogether? All their preparations would be wasted. . . . But the voices were clearer now. They must be in the office, as she had predicted. She put her head inside the shaft to hear better. Yes, that was it! Their voices were echoing down. She waved frantically to Alice, motioning her to come over.

"What in the world possessed you to do such a thing?" That was Seward—at least, she thought she recognized his voice from the asylum. She had not heard him say much, but he had said it loudly enough at the time!

"Nothing. I mean, it was just an experiment," said another voice sullenly. Ah, that was Prendick. She would know his voice anywhere. She had heard it often enough on Moreau's island. If only she could forget it! But she knew that if they met a century from now, not having seen each other once in the interim, she would recognize it from a single syllable.

"And there was no one helping you, no one acting with you?" That was a third voice, one she did not recognize. How many of them were there? She had assumed it would be just Seward and Prendick.

"No, of course not," said Prendick. His voice was resentful, but she could detect an undertone of fear. Could Seward hear it as well? Perhaps, although her sensitive feline ears could detect what most humans could not. Remembering that, she moved a little, allowing Alice to lean in closer to the shaft. Alice would not be able to hear as clearly as she could.

DIANA: My ears can hear as well as yours. Well, almost.

CATHERINE: Who said you were human? Ow! Stop
         it. I meant that as a compliment, but I take it back.
         You are completely and entirely human. An animal
         would never be so annoying.

"So you just found the creature and—transformed it?" asked
the third voice.

Creature? What in the world were they talking about?

"I bought it off a sailor whose ship was departing on the next
tide, to Cape Breton or the Cape of Good Hope, something like
that. I don't remember exactly," said Prendick. "Why does it
matter? Anyway, who would help me? It's not as though any other
members of the society are left in London."

"It matters because I don't want Beast Men running around
London!" said Seward. "Luckily, this one happened to show up
at Lord Avebury's menagerie, and he assumed it was a rare spe
cies of ape. I happened to see an article he published about it
in the *Purfleet Gazette*, or I would have known nothing about it
myself. Quite proud of it he was. Well, he still has a photograph
to remember it by, but I removed the creature myself, in the dead
of night. And ruined a pair of trousers by doing so! Raymond, you
can see that I had nothing to do with this matter, can't you? It was
Prendick's doing entirely. I reported it to you as soon as I learned
of the matter myself."

"I believe you," said the third voice—that must be Raymond,
whoever he was. "But that does not explain why you summoned
me here, at this inconvenient hour."

Catherine could hear the steady thump of boots pacing above.
Back and forth they went. "This matter of there not being members of the society in London. Van Helsing and I want to change
that. He's going to Budapest for the annual conference. I'm going
with him, and Prendick, you're coming as well. Ostensibly, we'll

be presenting papers on a more effective means of transfusing the blood, but his real goal is to convince the Alchemical Society to reopen the English chapter so it can continue what Van Helsing and I have begun. After all, it's been fourteen years since our chapter was shut down so abruptly—and unjustly."

"What makes you think our esteemed Madam President will listen to you, or even Van Helsing?" Raymond's voice was dry, dismissive. "She was adamant, after Jekyll almost exposed the society to public scrutiny, that all experiments in transmutation should be done only with her personal approval. When she finds out that Van Helsing has been continuing those experiments behind her back, she is likely to be, shall we say, displeased."

"It's not up to her. He's going to ask for a vote of the general membership, which she can't override. Either the membership will be persuaded by our arguments and allow us to continue in this vein—excuse me, that was inadvertent. Or our resolution will be voted down and our experiments forbidden altogether. Van Helsing is prepared for that eventuality. Indeed, I think he would prefer it. He and Arminius Vámbéry, who is our primary contact in Budapest, have a faction of the society on their side, prepared to vote with us. Additionally, they've created—not an army precisely, but shall we say ground troops sufficient to make our argument by force, if it comes to that. Either a majority of the membership will side with Van Helsing, or there will be a bloodbath—and a change of regime. When he is president, we shall see some different policies in place, I assure you."

"Well," said Raymond. "I won't say I disagree with your assessment that a regime change would be helpful. *She* has held the office of president long enough. But I don't like it when things are done behind my back, Seward. I don't like it at all. What Hennessey described in his letter . . ."

"Hennessey was a coward," said Seward. His boots tapped out

a steady rhythm on the floor above, like a drum. "Van Helsing should have known better than to write to him about our plans. What did he do? Sent a letter to *her*. Well, I intercepted that right enough. We've had him watched since he retired from the asylum. I knew even then that he was close to a breakdown. He went through too much, five years ago at Carfax. It's left him—unreliable. But I didn't know he'd written to you as well, until you summoned me last Monday. Inconveniently, I might add. Not that I'm questioning your right to do so, both as asylum trustee and as the last chairman of the English chapter before the Hyde debacle."

"In his letter, Hennessy said your recent experiments shocked the conscience," said Raymond, accusingly.

"Well, did they shock yours? I think not, or you would not have come here today. And how are they any worse than yours, forty years ago, when you created Helen?"

"Well, we won't speak of that," said Raymond. "It's scarcely relevant to the current situation. What do you want now?"

"Your support," said Seward promptly. The drumbeats stopped. "Your word that you will not alert *her* to what we're doing. You're still our chairman, after all. We'd like you to take that position up again, once the English chapter is restored."

There was a long silence.

"And what's in it for me if I do?"

"Why, man!" said Seward. "Everything, that's all. What do you think a race of immortal men could do? Men who never die, never grow old, are never afflicted by infectious diseases. Men on whom wounds close, and who have the power of the alchemical sciences at their fingertips. They would be a race of Supermen! They would rule the world!"

"And if Lucinda dies, as Lucy did?" said Prendick quietly.

"What does that matter if the experiment succeeds?" Seward sounded angry—he was almost shouting. "The principle is what matters—the principle and the serum. She is merely the experimental subject. After September, what does it matter whether she lives or dies? Sometimes lives must be sacrificed for the greater good. Moreau knew that, even if you don't."

"Van Helsing would do that to his own daughter?" asked Prendick, but Catherine wondered if the two men above had even heard him. She had barely heard his words as they were whispered down the shaft.

"I've wired for two tickets to Vienna on the Orient Express. Prendick, you'll meet me at Charing Cross Station at quarter to nine on Thursday morning. We'll arrive in Vienna on Saturday night. Van Helsing will meet us at the station, and we'll check on our patient on Sunday. She should be fully transformed by then. He had to sequester her—evidently, there was some attempt at interference by Mrs. Harker, who was involved in the Carfax affair, but she's safe and . . . contained at the moment. We'll take her with us to Budapest—as proof of concept, shall we say? First, we'll meet with our supporters to show them what they can become if they stand with us. And then, we shall transform our moribund society! What will it feel like, gentlemen, to rule the world?"

Raymond chuckled. At least, Catherine supposed it was Raymond. However she felt about Prendick, she did not believe him heartless enough to be chuckling now.

"What about the poor creature I created?" Ah, that was Prendick right enough.

"It's in the coal cellar," said Seward, "And there it will stay to ensure your loyalty, or at least obedience, until this affair is brought to a conclusion. What do you think our Madam President would say if she knew you had created a Beast Man in the middle of London? And that it had been featured in a newspaper, even one as obscure as the *Purfleet Gazette*?"

"Well, I think that's settled, then," said Raymond. "I'll stand with you and accept reinstatement as chairman of the English chapter—only don't make me regret it! It's a risky enterprise, but worth the risk if it gets her blasted bootheel off our necks. Now, I don't know about you, Seward, but I would like my dinner. There's a place Jekyll and I used to go, near Tottenham Court Road, when the society was still meeting here. It used to serve an exceptional kidney pie, as well as a good old-fashioned porter. I wonder if it's still there?"

Catherine could hear laughter, although she did not know whose, and then boots on the floor again. And then a distant thud, as though the front door had been shut rather hard.

She and Alice both stayed perfectly still. Time passed: five minutes, ten. Finally, "I don't think they're coming back," she said.

Alice sighed, as though she had been holding her breath all this time.

"How much of that could you hear?" asked Catherine. Could a human have heard everything she had?

"Most of it," said Alice in a low voice, as though still afraid to speak much above a whisper. "But I didn't understand it at all. What was all that about, becoming immortal, invincible? It sounds ungodly, miss."

"I suppose you could call it that," said Catherine. "Although in a way it was Moreau's ambition too, really. He wanted to become a kind of god . . . well. This isn't the time to talk about theology. I didn't understand it all either, but there's one thing I'm sure of."

"What's that?"

"There's something—or someone—in the coal cellar." It was a Beast Man. That much was clear from the conversation she had overheard. But which one? Could it be a new one created by Prendick? Perhaps, but it was more likely to be one that had escaped the conflagration at the warehouse. She vaguely remembered a short, stooping figure dodging around Holmes, out the door and into the night.

"Alice, do you remember which of the Beast Men escaped, that night at the docks?"

Alice shook her head. "I was too sick from Miss Beatrice's poison to notice much."

"And I was too busy trying to save Justine from Adam's wrath. I know Holmes mentioned which one, but I've forgotten."

"Do you think that's what they were talking about?" Alice looked a little frightened. Of course, she'd been kidnapped by one of the Beast Men, acting under the direction of Hyde.

"It's all right. I don't think it's one of the large ones, the Bear or Boar Men. Here, hold my hand. I don't want to get separated." That was an excuse, of course. How likely were they to get separated in a straight hallway? But Alice seemed genuinely frightened. She clutched Catherine's hand as though grateful for the contact.

Together, they walked farther down the hall, where they had not yet ventured. Like the kitchen, it was lit by low half-moon windows that were boarded up, although some of the boards had long ago warped and fallen. It had several doors: the first led to what looked like the butler's chambers, the second to what had once been a pantry, with wine racks and cabinets for silverware, now empty, around the walls. The third was the right one. Catherine knew as soon as she opened the door because they were greeted by a pitiful screech.

There, lying on the floor, was the Orangutan Man. Yes, Catherine remembered now. He was the Beast Man who had disappeared down the back hallway, on the night of the fire.

The coal cellar had no windows; before they opened the door, it had been entirely dark. He stared at them, blinking his eyes in the light that came from the doorway. It was a dim light, but evidently more than he was accustomed to in his prison. And a prison it was. The Orangutan Man was naked, and there was an iron shackle around one of his ankles. A chain linked it to an iron ring in the wall from which a coal scuttle might once have hung.

"Those bastards," said Catherine. "Those bloody bastards."

The Orangutan Man put up one hand to protect his eyes. At the same time, he scurried backward, knocking over a tin pan that had probably once held water but was now dry. He was obviously terrified of them.

"We're going to get you out of here," said Catherine, dropping Alice's hand. She needed to get closer. "Do you understand me? I don't know how much human speech he understands," she said to Alice. "I'll have to pick the lock on that shackle. Wait here." But as soon as she started moving toward him, the Orangutan Man started screeching again. He bared his teeth and stood up to his full height, as though prepared to make a final stand.

"Catherine, I think it's too dangerous!" said Alice fearfully, still standing in the doorway.

"There are times when you can't think of the danger. But I don't know if I can get close enough to him. He smells puma, that's the problem. I can't get to that lock unless he lets me." His shrieks seemed to go straight through her sensitive cat ears, like sharp knives thrusting into her brain.

"What's that?" Suddenly, Alice darted forward and pulled Catherine back into the shadows in a corner of the room, where they would not be seen from the doorway. What in the world was Alice . . . but no, now Catherine could hear it as well, although the shrieks of the Orangutan Man were still ringing in her ears: footsteps coming down the stairs, and then down the hall. Suddenly, Edward Prendick was silhouetted in the doorway.

He was dressed in the same shabby suit she had seen him in last time, in the warehouse. The light in the doorway shone on his gray hair, creating a halo. Saint Edward! There was irony for you.

"You heard me coming, didn't you?" he said to the Orangutan Man. "Quiet, boy. Calm down, I'm not here to hurt you. I've brought you an apple, see?" He pulled an apple out of his jacket pocket and threw it toward the Orangutan Man, who plucked it out of the air and began tearing into it ravenously, core and all. From another pocket, an interior one, he pulled a flask and poured its contents into the Orangutan Man's dish. "There's water for you. Seward realized too late that he'd forgotten to bring any and let me come back. Lucky I had that apple, eh?"

The Orangutan Man drank the water up, then licked the tin plate with his thick tongue. It took only a moment, and when he had finished, he held out the ankle with the shackle on it. He looked at Prendick pleadingly. He still had half the apple in one hand.

"I can't," said Prendick. "I would if I could, but Seward would have my hide for sure. I'm in enough trouble already. I'm sorry. This is a rotten place for you, isn't it?" He looked around the coal cellar. *Now,* Catherine thought, *he will see us.* She glanced at Alice, who must be frightened, but the kitchen maid had her eyes closed, her hands clasped in front of her as though in prayer. Her mouth was moving—she seemed to be praying silently. Well, Alice could pray all she wanted, but Catherine was going to fight. She crouched down, preparing to spring at Prendick. If she killed him, well, he deserved it for all he had done—to her, to the other Beast Men. As soon as he noticed them, as soon as he noticed *her,* she would leap on him and tear his throat out. He would not have time to raise an alarm.

But his glance slid right over them.

"I'm sorry," he said again to the Orangutan Man. "I never meant for you to end up like this, old fellow. I never meant for any of this to happen. At least he left the door open for you—you've got some light. I'll leave it open as well, shall I? And I'll make sure he sends someone to take care of you while we're gone. Once we get back, he might let me take you away from here. You'd like that, wouldn't you?"

He tried to pat the Orangutan Man on the head, but the creature bared his teeth and growled.

"All right, then," said Prendick as though embarrassed. "I'm off."

He looked around the coal cellar again. Why didn't he see them? Catherine was baffled. Was he simply pretending not to see them? But no, he looked both so sincere and so completely broken that she might have felt sorry for him if he wasn't such a lying, manipulative coward.

MARY: You're being harsh, Cat.

CATHERINE: He deserved it. He left Archibald there, chained to the wall! I seriously doubt Seward would have remembered to send anyone. He could have died in that coal cellar.

ALICE: If you could have seen poor Archibald there, Mary . . . Truly, it was a pitiable sight.

Almost apologetically, Prendick turned. As he walked through the doorway, the Orangutan Man rose again and, with all his strength, threw the remaining half of the apple at Prendick's departing back. She could hear it hit with a dull thump. Catherine heard his footsteps hurrying down the hall and up the stairs—he was almost running. And then once again she heard the distant thud of the front door.

"You can open your eyes now," she said to Alice.

Alice opened her eyes and looked around. "He didn't see us. Thank goodness he didn't see us. I supposed he never thought to look in this dark corner."

"On the contrary. He looked right at us, twice. Just out of curiosity, what were you saying to yourself?"

"Well," said Alice, "at first I tried to recite the Lord's Prayer, but I couldn't remember anything past *hallowed be thy name*, so I just kept repeating *we're not here, we're not here, there's nothing here*. It was all I could think of. I'm so sorry, miss. I'm not brave, like you and the others. What is it, miss? You're looking at me so strangely."

We're not here, there's nothing here . . . Was it possible? But there was no time to explore that possibility now. "Come on, we need to get the Orangutan Man out of here before they decide to bring him an orange or something!" The mystery of Alice would have to wait until later.

She approached the Orangutan Man again, only to be met with the same screeching as before.

"Let me try," said Alice. "I'm a monkey, like him, or so Beatrice says—we're all monkeys, according to Mr. Darwin. Except you of course, but Mr. Darwin doesn't know about you, does he?"

Catherine nodded. She didn't know if it would work, but Alice might as well try.

Slowly, Alice approached the Orangutan Man. "Hush, hush," she said. "I won't hurt you." She held out her hand.

Suddenly, the Orangutan Man took it in his awkward digits. He held up his other hand. "Five man," he said, in a croaking voice that sounded as though he had not used it in days. "I am five man."

"Me too," said Alice, also holding up her other hand. "I am also a five man—or woman. Will you let my friend unlock that?" She pointed to his ankle. "I know she doesn't smell very good, but you can trust her."

"I am a five man," Catherine echoed, holding up her hands. How quickly it came back to her, the vernacular of the island! "Look, I was made." She pulled up one sleeve so he could see the scars—or she hoped he could, in the dim light. "I was made, like you. But now we are all men here, together. Men do not eat each other. You were taught this?"

"Yes, I was taught, by Master with the whip," said the Orangutan Man, nodding emphatically. He extended his ankle.

Did he mean Prendick? Catherine rather doubted it. The Master with the whip was more likely to have been Adam. Even on the island, Prendick had been a reluctant, ineffectual overlord.

It was the work of a moment to pick the large, clumsy lock. Once Catherine had removed the shackle, the Orangutan Man stood unsteadily, then fell —then stood again.

"Can you walk?" asked Catherine.

"Hold my hand," said Alice. "I'll help you." And that is how they walked out of the house on Potter's Lane, with the Orangutan Man holding Alice's hand and wearing the jacket she had taken off to cover his too-human nakedness.

Thank goodness it was starting to get dark! Hopefully it would make them less noticeable. They would have to walk all the way home. They could scarcely take a half-naked Beast Man on a London omnibus. As they made their way through the streets of Soho, Catherine wondered what in the world they were going to do with him.

CATHERINE: Honestly, I was afraid Mrs. Poole was going to have a fit when we brought him home!

MRS. POOLE: As though I ever have fits! And Archibald was such a good footman, even better than Joseph. Once, he climbed all the way up to the roof to replace the chimney pots. And he never once broke anything, which is more than I can say for Joseph, or even Enid! Who, by the way, are having their first child. If it's a girl, they're going to name her after me! Little Honoria. Isn't that nice, now? We'll have to go visit, Mary.

MARY: What do you think I should get them? A teething ring is traditional, I think.

MRS. POOLE: Ah, I still remember when you were teething. You never cried, not even then. The best baby, you were! At the time, I thought I'd just gotten lucky. Of course, now we know why. . . .

MARY: Cat, you're not going to include that in the book, are you? I mean, it's irrelevant what I was like as a baby. Also, embarrassing.

CATHERINE: We'll see.

CHAPTER VIII

Joining the Circus

T he first thing Mrs. Poole did with him, when they finally reached 11 Park Terrace, was put the Orangutan Man into a bath. "He smells something awful," she said. "And he needs to wear proper clothes. I think there's an old pair of Dr. Jekyll's pajamas around somewhere. They'll be far too big for him, but he can at least wear the shirt."

About an hour later, they were all seated together in the parlor: Catherine in her nightgown, cross-legged on the sofa; Mrs. Poole in one armchair and Beatrice in the other; Alice sitting on the floor, combing the Orangutan Man, who was properly attired in Dr. Jekyll's pajama top. Now that he had been bathed, he did not look much like a man—more like a boy with silky orange hair and large, soulful eyes. He reminded Catherine of Sasha, the Dog Boy. The two kittens, Alpha and Omega, were circling around as though trying to decide what to make of him.

"Mrs. Poole," said Catherine, "is there any more pig? I mean ham?" She looked at the remains of the supper Mrs. Poole had brought up—a platter of cold meats with pease pudding and a blancmange. Only Alice had eaten the pudding. Pumas, Catherine had reminded everyone, did not eat such things as peas, although she rather liked the blancmange, which was mostly milk. Beatrice was still sipping one of her usual concoctions. The Orangutan

Man had refused everything he had been offered, until Beatrice had looked orangutans up in the *Encyclopaedia Britannica* kept in Dr. Jekyll's study.

"Orangutans eat fruit," she had reported. "It says here that 'jackfruit or durian, the tough spiny hide of which is torn open with their strong fingers, forms the chief food of orangutans, which also consume the luscious mangustin and other fruits.'"

"What in heaven's name are durians or those other thing you said?" asked Mrs. Poole. "I don't know as I have fresh fruit—it's rough on the digestion, unless well cooked. But wait, I do have some pears I was going to make into a compote. I'll see if he likes those. Anyway, a compote is wasted on the likes of you! All I make, all day long, is meat or weeds. If I didn't have myself and Alice to cook for, I'd forget how to do it altogether!"

"It also says 'they construct platforms of boughs in the trees, which are sleeping places, and apparently occupied several nights in succession.' Did you know they come from Borneo and Sumatra? Orangutan means 'man of the woods.'"

"Well, I hope he'll do no such thing here, but sleep in a bed, like a decent Englishman," said Mrs. Poole.

The Orangutan Man liked the pears very much. He also liked Beatrice a little too much, saying "Pretty, pretty," as she walked by and reaching out to feel the hem of her gown. "You must not touch me," she said, kneeling down to where he was sitting on the carpet. "I am poisonous, do you understand?" Evidently, he did not, for he reached out again to touch her, with a look of wonder on his face.

"Great, even the monkey man is in love with you," said Catherine. "What now?"

"An orangutan is an ape, not a monkey," said Beatrice. Then she turned to the Orangutan Man and said, "Forgive me." She reached out to touch his hand and placed her palm on his—quickly, he drew his back and cradled it, as though he had been stung. "Do you understand now?" she said.

"Yes," said the Orangutan Man. "Yes, you are hurting me. Pretty hurting." He still looked at her with admiration, but did not attempt to touch her again.

"We need to give him a name," said Mrs. Poole. "We can't keep calling him the Orangutan Man. It's too long."

"What about Silky?" said Alice. "Because he has such silky hair."

"What about Lucky?" said Catherine. "Because he's lucky he survived the warehouse fire—I think he's the only one."

"Why don't you ask him?" said Beatrice. "I'm certain he can speak for himself." She turned to the Orangutan Man. "What is your name?"

He put his hand on his chest and said, "I am Archibald." Then he made a clumsy bow. Catherine had an impulse to laugh and ask if she could call him Archie, but he looked so dignified that she was sure he would be offended.

Solemnly, Beatrice curtsied back. "Archibald, I'm very pleased to meet you. Was that the name you were given when you were with Lord Avebury?"

Archibald nodded and looked happier than Catherine had ever seen him, although that was not saying much, considering the conditions she had found him in. They had probably not been much better at Lord Averbury's, where he would likely have been locked in a cage, but she was not surprised that he would have gone back there, or remembered his former self with longing. In her dreams, she too was sometimes still the puma she had once been.

DIANA: How many times are you going to mention that you were a puma?

CATHERINE: Why, does it bother you, monkey girl?

DIANA: You can't insult me by calling me a monkey.
Alice said she was a monkey girl too, and so is
Mary. Even Mrs. Poole is a monkey, according to
Mr. Darwin! Anyway, our readers are going to get
tired of you always talking about yourself.

MRS. POOLE: I am most certainly not a monkey!
What a wicked, heathenish idea.

CATHERINE: We are *not* getting into an argument
about evolutionary theory here, thank you very
much!

After Mrs. Poole brought up their supper, which they ate
informally in the parlor, Catherine explained the events of the day,
with interpolations from Alice and exclamations from Mrs. Poole.
Only Beatrice did not comment. Then they sat in companionable
silence, Catherine picking at a final slice of ham Mrs. Poole had
found for her. She slipped a bit of the ham to Omega, who was
scrawnier than his sister, and drank the tea Mrs. Poole had poured
out. There was nothing like a pot of tea, Mrs. Poole said, after a
long day of breaking into houses and spying on people.

"Catherine," said Beatrice. She was still nursing her own mug
of green goop. "I think you know what I'm going to say."

"I think I know what you're going to say too," said Catherine.
"I have a plan." Would it work? She was not sure.

Mrs. Poole stared at them both in turn. "What in the world
are you two on about?" She shook her head. "Here's what I don't
understand. First, who is this Raymond character, and why is he
important? And then—"

"Dr. Raymond used to be the chairman of the Alchemical
Society in England," said Catherine. "I suppose all the countries

have their own chapters? I don't know, of course—I'm just guessing from what Seward said. What I don't understand is, who's
Hennessey, and why was he writing to Raymond?"

"Don't you remember?" said Beatrice. "He was the assistant
director of the asylum, until he resigned. Mary told us that."

"How am I supposed to remember something Mary told us three
months ago?" It was exasperating. Catherine felt as though she had
been given the pieces of a puzzle and asked to put it together, but
some of the pieces were missing, some might belong to another
puzzle. . . . "So this Hennessey gets the wind up about something,
some experiments Seward and Van Helsing are conducting on Van
Helsing's daughter, meaning Lucinda. And he writes to Raymond,
who contacts Seward. I know, it's like one of those memory games,
where you have to recite it all back correctly at the end! The important thing is, whatever they're doing to Lucinda, they think it will
give them power—they'll be immortal, invincible."

"I've never heard such nonsense," said Mrs. Poole. She poured
herself another cup of tea.

"It's not nonsense," said Beatrice. "Look at me, Mrs. Poole.
Look at Catherine or Justine. If we are possible, I'm certain they
can create something that will give them the power they crave.
Catherine, you mentioned some sort of serum? Perhaps they have
discovered a substance that will prolong human life and enhance
the healing process. That has been a dream of the Société des
Alchimistes, or a certain faction of it, since Victor Frankenstein
introduced the idea of biological transmutation. And knowledge
is so easily perverted into a means of obtaining power. My father
was not a good man. His virtues were not positive ones, except
perhaps for his love of me, and you see how that has affected my
life—I am a monster, harming and killing those I love. But he
was not a bad one either. He did not crave power over others. He
believed that his research would eventually help humanity as a

whole evolve to a higher level. These men—they are a new generation. They wish to keep any scientific advancements they make to themselves. It is no wonder that the current president has forbidden their experiments."

"Do you know who the president is?" asked Catherine. "They kept saying *she* in the most peculiar way. Could the president be a woman?"

Beatrice shook her head. "That I do not know. My father did not discuss the politics of the Société in front of me, except when he was cursing its conservatism—and even then he said little about its inner workings. He told me I would know all when I became a member. The Société has had women members—in that way, it has been perhaps more progressive than other scientific societies. My father hoped I would be one of them. I suppose it could have a woman president—at least, theoretically."

"Well, it seems as though we don't know much!" said Mrs. Poole, sounding both worried and frustrated. "Except that Mary and the girls will be in more danger than we expected. They're supposed to be at that meeting in Budapest—I take it that's the meeting Miss Murray sent her telegram about. They're planning to take Lucinda Van Helsing there, and from what you tell me, there's going to be some sort of confrontation if Seward and the rest don't get their way."

"*Bloodbath,*" said Alice, helpfully. "That's the word he used."

"Thank you," said Catherine. "I was hoping to avoid mentioning that to Mrs. Poole, actually."

> MRS. POOLE: How you could keep that from me, I
> just don't know!

> CATHERINE: I would have told you, if Alice hadn't
> blurted it out—but without using that word. I was

trying to keep you from going into a panic about
Mary.

MRS. POOLE: I did not go into a panic!

ALICE: You kind of did, actually, Mrs. Poole.

"We have to telegraph at once!" said Mrs. Poole, rising from
the armchair and almost spilling tea down her apron. "Oh, my
dear Mary, what sort of danger have you gone into? These wicked,
wicked men! If your father were here I would give him such a
talking-to about his wretched society! There must be a telegraph
office open, even at this time of night. Mr. Holmes would know! I
must go talk to Mr. Holmes."

"Oh, for goodness' sake," said Catherine. "The bloodbath—I
mean, conference of the society—isn't scheduled until September
twentieth at the earliest. Do sit down, Mrs. Poole. Yes, of course
we have to do something, but we don't actually know where Mary
is, do we? We know she arrived in Vienna, but she may already
have left, if Lucinda Van Helsing is no longer there. Seward gave no
indication of where they're keeping her—just that she's transforming, whatever that means. And Mrs. Norton said not to reply to her
telegram unless absolutely necessary. I think Beatrice was about to
suggest what I was—Beatrice, what were you going to say?"

Beatrice took a final sip of her noxious decoction. "Mrs. Poole,
Catherine and I need to go to Budapest. Now that Catherine has
discovered Dr. Seward's plan, there's no longer any reason for her
to stay in London, and if Mary, Justine, and Diana are in danger, I
belong with them as well. There are drawbacks to both of our . . .
conditions, shall we say. But we are both powerful. We can both
fight. I think we showed in the warehouse that the five of us are
stronger together than apart."

"What about your plants?" asked Catherine.

"I suppose I'll have to cultivate new ones, assuming I return—as I intend to!" said Beatrice. "It will be sad to lose them, but this is more important."

"And what about me?" asked Alice. She looked half afraid of being asked to go, and half afraid of being left behind.

"Yes, what about you?" said Catherine. "You're not poisonous, and you don't have sharp teeth—also, I don't think Mrs. Poole would want you to go on such a dangerous adventure."

"Certainly not!" said Mrs. Poole. "You girls going is one thing—I worry about you, I worry terribly, but you've shown that you can take care of yourselves. Alice is only thirteen, and she doesn't have your, well, whatever you have. You know. As for sending a telegram—"

"Our monstrous qualities?" said Catherine. "No, don't protest—I know what you mean, Mrs. Poole. Although . . . something happened in the coal cellar. Alice, do what you were doing then, when Prendick didn't see us."

Alice looked puzzled. "You mean praying?"

"I mean closing your eyes and saying we weren't there. Do that again."

"Right now?" asked Alice.

"Yes. I want to see what happens."

Reluctantly, Alice closed her eyes. Catherine could see her lips moving.

"What in the world is supposed to happen?" asked Mrs. Poole.

"I'm not sure," said Catherine. "But in the coal cellar, it was as though we were invisible. Prendick looked right at us and didn't see us."

Alice opened her eyes. "And you think I had something to do with that? How could I have? I don't have any special powers, or anything. I'm just me."

"Never mind," said Catherine. "It was just an idea. Anyway, it was dark in that cellar, and maybe his eyesight isn't as good as it used to be. Who knows, it could have been affected by whatever happened to him after leaving the island." Did she believe that? Well, at the moment it was the only logical possibility.

"I understand that you need to go, and I certainly won't stop you," said Mrs. Poole. "But I think we should at least send a telegram to Miss Murray, warning her about Dr. Seward's plans. That's not a reply to Mrs. Norton, is it? By the time Mary and the others arrive, Miss Murray will be prepared. She was always a resourceful young woman when she was governess here. And there's another practical consideration. We have less than two pounds left in the bank. You'll have to borrow from Mr. Holmes, I'm afraid."

"Atlas gave me another five this morning," said Catherine. "But we need more than that if we're going to travel quickly. And I don't want to ask Holmes unless we absolutely have to. He has a way of interfering with one's plans. I have another idea. Beatrice, have you ever thought of joining the circus?"

Beatrice looked at her curiously. "No, not in particular. Why, Catherine? What do you have in mind?

BEATRICE: Now I understand why you and Justine felt so at home there. I've never felt such camaraderie anywhere, except here of course.

CATHERINE: Everyone in the circus is an outcast, an outsider. We're all running away from something. We're all, in one way or another, monsters.

MARY: I don't think that's the right way to talk about—

CATHERINE: I'm talking about the circus, Mary. You
can't correct me about the circus. I've been there.
I know.

The next morning, Catherine and Beatrice set out for
Clerkenwell. Once again, Catherine examined Park Terrace care-
fully as they left. She had talked to Charlie, asking him if any of the
Baker Street boys had seen anything suspicious in the area. "Not as
I know of," he had replied. "But I'll check with the other boys. One
or another of us is always around, on Mr. Holmes's orders."

In Clerkenwell, a woman selling newspapers and cheap paper-
backs from a stall was able to direct them to Mrs. Protheroe's
boardinghouse, near Clerkenwell Green as Atlas had described.
From the outside, it did not look prepossessing, but when did
circus folk lodge anywhere that did?

"Are you ready?" asked Catherine.

They were standing on the sidewalk across the street, which
was mostly empty, with only a few carts rumbling past and some
boys kicking a bottle as though it were a ball. This was not exactly
central London! Catherine could see the spire of St. James's
Clerkenwell over the roofs of the buildings, mostly small shops
with lodgings above them.

"Ready," said Beatrice. "Do I look like a circus performer?"

Catherine glanced at her. For the first time since escaping
from the house of Professor Petronius, she had left 11 Park Terrace
unveiled. They had not heard of or from him in three months—
what could be the harm? Or so Beatrice had said that morning.
Now she seemed to be enjoying the sunshine on her face, and even
the sooty London air. Well, good. No one should have to sequester
themselves all the time with a bunch of plants.

"You'll do," said Catherine, but her mind was on other things.
First, they had to get to Budapest, to help Mary and the others.

Second, or was this actually first, they had to get Lorenzo to let them join his touring troupe. And third . . .

That morning, Mrs. Poole had come up to her room. Catherine was still in bed, stretching under the covers. No use in leaving too early—circus folks weren't exactly early morning risers. "Well, you were right," she said. "I didn't believe you last night—I thought you must have been mistaken, or maybe Mr. Prendick was just near-sighted. But this morning I walked into Alice's room to bring her a fresh water jug, and she wasn't there! 'Alice, Alice where are you?' I called. And just like that, she appeared in front of my eyes. 'What in the world did you just do?' I asked her. 'Only what I did in the cellar,' she said. 'I repeated over and over that I wasn't here, and you didn't see me. Did you, Mrs. Poole?' 'Well, I never,' I said. 'Alice, you can make yourself invisible!' So you were right, miss, in what you said yesterday."

"It's not possible to make someone invisible," said Catherine. She pulled back the covers and sat up.

"Are you telling me to doubt the evidence of my own eyes? I saw her plain as day—or didn't. One minute she wasn't there, the next she was sitting on her bed as nice as you please."

"No, I'm not saying that, Mrs. Poole," said Catherine. "I'm just saying that when something is physically impossible, there must be another explanation."

"Hrumph. And are you going to tell Mr. Holmes about all this?"

"I will, I will, but can you give me until this afternoon? I'd like to get some things arranged without his interference—I mean help."

"Well, all right," said Mrs. Poole dubiously. "I suppose you know what you're doing, but I do wish Miss Mary were here. I found a blank telegraph form in the morning room desk, so I filled it out and gave it to Jimmy Bucket to deliver to the office in Camden Town, with the fee and a little for himself. I thought it would be less conspicuous than one of us taking it, just in case we are being watched. I told Miss Murray that you and Beatrice were coming to Budapest— C. M. and B. R. coming, I told her, like a code. And then I said something about beware danger from Dr. S. and Professor Van H. at the S.A. meeting. That should warn her, right enough."

"Yes, very subtle, thank you, Mrs. Poole," said Catherine, feeling annoyed. Surely the telegram was an unnecessary risk? She and Beatrice were going to Budapest, after all. They would certainly arrive in time. It would have been nice, she had to admit, to have Mary around. Mary was always so practical in her outlook. She was not as wise as Justine, or as knowledgeable as Beatrice, but she was the best planner. Catherine had the best instincts—of that she was convinced. But pumas were made for jumping and fighting, not planning. Ah well, she would simply have to take care of this situation as best she could—and she thought she knew how.

So she slid off the bed, which was rather high, stood on the bedroom carpet, which was soft under her bare feet, and said, "Mrs. Poole, are there any kippers for breakfast?" Once Mrs. Poole had departed to fry some for her, she went to Mary's room and looked into her closet. Today, she thought, she would need to wear feminine clothes. The blue dimity afternoon dress—yes, that was the stuff. It would look perfectly respectable. . . .

MARY: That's my favorite dress!

CATHERINE: Well, then I'm glad I chose so well.

Now she stared at the boardinghouse, with its shutters hanging awry. "Come on," she said to Beatrice. "It's the brick one across the street, next to the shoe and boot shop."

Beatrice nodded, and together they crossed over, between a

cart with furniture on it and one carrying sheep, which bleated continually in a way Catherine found particularly annoying. Silly creatures—a Sheep Woman created by Moreau had been her first kill on the island.

JUSTINE: How can you even mention such a thing?

CATHERINE: I'm a carnivore, remember? I can't eat weeds, the way the rest of you seem to.

They rang the bell and a woman in a patched apron let them in, presumably Mrs. Protheroe herself. She was rather like her boardinghouse—shabby and worn, but neat enough when you looked beneath the patina of time.

JUSTINE: Patina of time! I like that.

CATHERINE: Thank you. It's always nice when someone notices my finer touches.

Mrs. Protheroe smelled of lavender and mothballs. "The circus folks? I'll let them know you're here. They have use of the parlor for visitors. It's to the left down the hall."

As soon as Catherine walked into the parlor, a man who had been sitting on the sofa, reading the *London Times*, rose and nodded courteously. Then he looked at her more closely. "Catherine!" he said. "Is that you?"

"It's me, Clarence," she said, smiling.

In a moment he had wrapped her in a very thorough hug. Then he stepped back, still holding her by the arms. "How are you, Whiskers? Atlas told me you were doing well. But don't you look fancy! And who is your friend?"

Catherine looked back at Beatrice, who was standing behind her.

"This is Beatrice Rappaccini. Beatrice, my good friend Clarence Jefferson."

"Miss Rappaccini." Clarence bowed. He was a fine figure of a man, almost as tall as Justine, lean and broad-shouldered. His features proclaimed him a son of Africa, and indeed in Lorenzo's circus he was billed as the Zulu Prince, who performed his bloodthirsty native dances for anyone who bought a ticket to the sideshow.

"Mr. Jefferson." Beatrice nodded in response. Catherine could see that she was struck by his air of self-possession and the nobility of his mien.

DIANA: What the hell is a mien?

BEATRICE: I don't think Clarence would appreciate your romanticizing him, Catherine. And he is from Boston, not Africa, which anyway happens to be a continent that contains a multitude of peoples and countries. It is not simply one place.

CATHERINE: I know that perfectly well. I've known Clarence longer than you have. But he does actually look like that, including the noble mien. Which, for those who don't know how to use a dictionary, means his countenance, his demeanor—the way he looks. You could have looked up the word up yourself, Diana—you're not a complete ignoramus.

DIANA: Fine, I'll add that to my vocabulary list. Also *ignoramus*.

Clarence held out his hand toward Beatrice, as though to shake hers.

"Don't touch her!" said Catherine sharply. "She's poisonous. All right, as long as she has gloves on, but I still wouldn't get too close."

Clarence looked as though he were about to ask her what in the world she meant when in walked Lorenzo, with Atlas close behind him.

"Caterina!" He threw his arms wide, then put his hands on her shoulders and kissed her loudly on both cheeks. "*Mio bellissimo gattino!* It is so good to see you." He was a short, round man with the mobile face of a clown, which in fact he had once been. It could look sad or happy at a moment's notice, but now it looked particularly happy. "How have you been? You got the money I sent? I am so sorry—I could not send the entire sum earlier. It is the bills; they are terrible. Even here in this house, it is expensive to maintain so many. But we are a family, are we not, I tell my performers. We will not part until we have to. How are you? And how is *la bella* Justina? Sit, sit. Tell me all about yourself."

Catherine sat on the sofa where Clarence had been sitting and moved his newspaper to the side. "I will, happily. But Lorenzo, I have a proposition for you."

"A business proposition?" Suddenly, his expression was completely serious. "Tell me." He sat on the sofa beside her. Clarence motioned for Beatrice to take the only other comfortable chair, and he sat on a rickety wooden one that looked as though it might collapse under him. Atlas, who was always afraid that his weight would break whatever he sat on, leaned against the wall.

"This is my friend, Beatrice Rappaccini," said Catherine, gesturing toward Beatrice as though she were a shop girl displaying her wares.

"Ah yes, the beautiful lady," said Lorenzo. "I had indeed noticed her. How could I not have?" He turned toward Beatrice. "But Rappaccini . . . *sei italiana?*"

"*Sì, signore,*" she replied. "*Sono nata e cresciuta a Padova.*"

"*Ah, bella Padova! Spesso ho nostalgia del bel paese.* But forgive me, I am being rude. You can speak in English?"

"Imperfectly," said Beatrice, with her usual perfect command of the language. "I have learned much of the native tongue in this great city."

"We must talk more about Italy!" said Lorenzo. "I myself am a Florentine. Alas, it has been so long since I have seen my native land. . . . But Caterina, what is this business of which you spoke?"

Catherine leaned forward. Would he agree to what she wanted? She was about to find out. "Do you remember the Poisonous Girl, who was appearing at the Royal College of Surgeons several months ago? You said that you would give a great deal to have such an attraction in the sideshow."

"*Sì,*" said Lorenzo. Well, he was looking interested—puzzled and interested. That was something.

"Beatrice is the Poisonous Girl. I know you're taking the show to Paris. I want you to take us with you, to Paris and then if you're going farther—well, it depends on where you go. We need to get to Budapest, quite urgently, for reasons I would rather not discuss." She did not think he would ask. Circus folks did not ask personal questions. They all had things they would rather keep hidden.

Lorenzo looked at Beatrice with astonishment. "*È vero?* Is this true, that you are the Poisonous Girl?"

"Alas, it is," she replied. "I wish it were not so."

"Show me," said Lorenzo. "A kiss here." He tapped his cheek with one finger. "That used to be part of your show, did it not?"

Reluctantly, Beatrice rose and walked over to where he was

sitting. She leaned down and kissed him on the cheek he had indicated, next to his sideburn.

"Ah!" he said, darting back from her on the sofa. "That is—it sting like a wasp!" On his cheek was a fierce red mark, as though her lips had burned him.

"Alas that I do not have any ointment to soothe that burn!" she said. "You must put a cold cream on it, or it will blister."

"*Non importa!*" said Lorenzo, waving his hand. "You shall be our star! We will make much money. I will telegraph to Paris to add more shows. And then perhaps Frankfurt? Berlin and Prague have shown some interest, but I have not booked any other shows as yet. Now they will want us! Now they will give us the best and largest theaters! And of course Caterina will come along as our Cat Woman?"

"Yes, but we can't go to Berlin or Prague," said Catherine. "We could go to Vienna—that's on the way. If you book shows in Vienna and Budapest, we could go with you. But not as the Cat Woman and Poisonous Girl. You need to find new names for us." Would the Société des Alchimistes know them by their circus appellations? She had no idea, but she did not want to take that risk. If they could stop in Vienna, even briefly, so much the better—perhaps Mary and Justine might still be there, and if not, she could find out from Irene Norton where they had gone. "And we would like the same salaries Justine and I had, plus fifty percent of the profits from Beatrice's show."

"I can guarantee that it will be profitable, *signore*," said Beatrice. "The only proviso is that I will not kill a living thing. But I was the Poisonous Girl for many months. I know how to put on a show."

"I have no doubt, *signorina*," said Lorenzo. "Vienna may be a possibility. Let me see what I can do. And I will give you twenty percent. I will have to spend much on advertising, remember.

What would you like to be called? Of course for Paris, it will have to be in French."

Well! That was higher than Catherine had expected him to start with. "Forty percent. Imagine how a photograph of Beatrice will bring them in, especially the gentlemen!"

"I could be perhaps *La Femme Toxique*," said Beatrice.

"Ah, but photographs are expensive! Thirty percent. And *la bella Beatrice*"—he pronounced it "Beatriche"—"will be *La Belle Toxique*. As for you, Caterina—what name would you choose? It must still be one that will attract the audience, you know—we need to make money, after all."

"*La Femme Chatte?*" said Beatrice. "No, that is too much like the Cat Woman. What about *La Femme Panthère*? A puma is a type of panther, is it not?"

"Done!" said Catherine. "Puma, panther, whatever. I'll be the panther woman if you want me to." Thirty percent was more than she had hoped for. If Beatrice drew a large audience in Vienna, and there was no reason she should not, they would have plenty of money to make it to Budapest, whether or not Lorenzo could take them all the way. How much did the Société des Alchimistes know about them, anyway? She was not sure. But if they were traveling as circus performers, rather than as themselves, they would have a better chance of evading scrutiny. And what was more important, they would be among friends. Most importantly, they would not have to rely on Holmes.

> MARY: Why were you so determined not to take money from Mr. Holmes?

> CATHERINE: Because you did, and look what happened. You had everything planned out, and then you dropped it all in a minute because he

wanted you to, because he thought it would be
for the best. And you didn't even protest. You
may not mind being controlled in that way, but I
do. I had enough of that on Moreau's island.

MARY: You are such a puma sometimes!

CATHERINE: Thank you.

"We leave on Friday," said Lorenzo. "Early, mind! You must be at
Charing Cross Station at 8:30 a.m., no sleeping late! And if Signorina
Rappaccini could supply herself with some costumes appropriate
to her performance, I would be most appreciative. Or she could
borrow Madam Zora's, but I do not think they would quite fit!"

"We'll be there." That would give them two days to prepare and
pack. Well, if it had been enough for Mary, it would be enough for
them. "There's one thing more. Is Marvelous Martin still with you?"

"Of course," said Lorenzo. "He's up in his room, lying down.
You know he has his *emicrania*, his migraines."

"Yes, I know. Could I talk to him for a moment?"

"As long as our landlady does not object. She is depressingly
proper."

"I'll take you up," said Atlas.

Catherine smiled at him. "I could not have a better chaperone."
He blushed. It was amusing to make such a large man blush.

JUSTINE: Catherine, sometimes you are not very nice!

CATHERINE: When did I ever claim to be?

"All right, follow me," said Atlas. "He's on the second floor."
"Will you be all right here?" she asked Beatrice.

"Alas, it is I who am a danger to others, not the other way around," said Beatrice, drooping like a melancholy flower.

CATHERINE: And I do wish you wouldn't be so droopy about it. It's good to be dangerous.

BEATRICE: You're interrupting the story simply to tell me that?

CATHERINE: Yes, because you need to be reminded. Constantly.

Catherine followed the Strongman up the stairs to the second floor. She could smell a midday meal being cooked somewhere below. It consisted mostly of cabbages. Why were the English so enamored of cabbages? She was glad Mrs. Poole rarely cooked them. They were an affront to a respectable puma's nose.

"We're all worried about Martin," said Atlas. The stairs creaked under his weight, and the hallway was almost too narrow for him. "His headaches seem to be getting worse."

"I'm sorry to hear that," said Catherine. Really, whoever had chosen the wallpaper should be sent to prison for a good long time. It was criminally ugly, and the dingy light coming through a small, dirty window did not help. Poor Martin, stuck in a place like this. He had always been very sensitive to his environment—which was, he had told her, a common problem for members of his profession.

At the second door they came to, Atlas knocked softly. He opened the door just a crack. "Martin," he said. "There's someone here to see you."

"Come in," said the faint voice of the Marvelous Mesmerist.

CHAPTER IX

The Marvelous Mesmerist

tlas pushed open the door. The room was dark, with curtains pulled over the window. In the darkest corner, on a narrow bed, lay Marvelous Martin, the mesmerist of Lorenzo's Circus of Marvels and Delights. His eyes were closed, and his face was as pale as the bedsheet.

"Martin," said Catherine, going over to the bed. "Lorenzo says your headaches are getting worse. I'm so sorry."

He opened his eyes and gave her a wan smile. "Cat. How lovely to see you."

Martin looked exactly like a mesmerist should, with a gaunt, spiritual face, deep-set eyes, and long black hair that lay in disorder on the pillow. Up close, Catherine could see that the roots were coming in gray. So he dyed it? She had always wondered. Well, he was a showman after all—she had seen him powder his skin with chalk to make it whiter, more luminous under stage lights. But the pain in his face was entirely real.

"Martin, I've come with a question that you may not wish to answer."

He reached out one pale, thin hand, with the long fingers of a pianist. She took it and sat on the edge of the bed. "Anything for you, Cat Girl." He smiled, which made him look even more gaunt.

"Is mesmerism real? What you do—is it fake, like a stage magician? Or is there something to it?"

Martin closed his eyes again, and for a moment she was afraid she had offended him. But then he opened them and looked at her very directly, and with as much sincerity as a circus man, who is used to misdirecting the attention of an entire audience, is capable of. "Some of it is trickery, I'll admit. But the mesmerical waves? Those are real enough. Not everyone can sense or manipulate them—some who call themselves mesmerists are cheats and frauds. Even the great Dr. Mesmer may not have had significant mesmeric powers, although he convinced himself otherwise. But when I was a child, I could sense them all around me—like we were all living in the ocean, under water, but only I knew we were wet."

He shifted in the bed, as though uncomfortable, and Catherine said, "Here, let me." She adjusted the thin pillow, moving his head as little as possible, and smoothed out the blanket, which had been disarranged. Good Lord, she was turning into Mary! That was a fate worse than . . . well, if not death, then something else very distressing.

> MARY: There is nothing wrong with being me, thank you!
>
> DIANA: That's not what Dr. Freud said. And he's supposed to be the expert, ain't he?
>
> MARY: Isn't he.
>
> DIANA: Don't change the subject.

"I was only a poor boy," said Martin. "Destined for the fields or factory work. But I had the good fortune to attract the attention of a scientist, Dr. Henry Bell, who saw my potential. He came to our village to illustrate the power of mesmerism. I went with my mother, God rest her soul, to see his demonstration in the village pub, which had been turned into an impromptu lecture hall. There he was, standing at the front of the room in his high silk hat, and there I was in the back, a boy in ragged clothes with no shoes on his feet. But halfway through the show, he said, "For this next demonstration, I need an assistant. That boy, standing in the back. Yes, you, lad. Come on up." Later, he told me that even from across the room, he had seen the waves dancing over my head."

"What are the waves?" asked Catherine. "Also, would *eau de cologne* on your forehead help?"

"Perhaps," said Martin, looking doubtful.

"I have a handkerchief. Atlas, who would have *eau de cologne*, do you think?"

"Madam Zora might," he said doubtfully. "She's the type that likes to make herself fancy. I'll check, shall I?" He left on his errand, shutting the door behind himself a little too loudly. Martin moaned.

"We are not purely material beings," he continued. "Dr. Bell would say that we are not material beings at all, although I would not go that far. But we are surrounded by waves of energy. You've seen them in operation, even if you have not seen the waves themselves. If a husband and wife are happily married, their energy becomes entwined, so they think the same thoughts. A loving mother will know that her son has died or been injured, no matter the distance. Two sisters separated when young will be married on the same day, and not even realize it. It is the effect of mesmerical waves, traveling between people. They are often behind what we call the supernatural. A ghost is only the energy of a person that has died, not yet dissipated into the aether."

"Can the waves cause someone not to see me? As though I were not there, or invisible?"

"My dear," said Martin, "you've seen my act. I can convince people that I'm Queen Victoria, and they will bow down to me, calling me Your Majesty. I can make them believe they have turned into pigs, like Odysseus's men, and they will begin rooting about the stage." His deep voice echoed around the room majestically, as though he were standing on a stage at that moment. "Such a thing would be child's play, to one who could manipulate the waves. But"—and here his voice sank back to its usual timber—"why do you ask?"

"Here you go," said Atlas from the doorway. He must have realized that he had been too loud, because he came in as quietly as a mouse. He handed her an elaborate cut-glass bottle, rather large, with FLORIS written on the label. "Compliments of Madam Zora."

Catherine opened it—the scent of orange flowers was almost overpowering. She shook the scented water liberally onto her handkerchief, then laid it across Martin's forehead. He signed and closed his eyes again.

"Martin, if I brought someone over, a girl I know, could you tell me whether or not she has mesmeric powers?"

"Of course," he said. "And I presume she's demonstrated this ability—to make someone invisible?"

"I'm not sure. I just know there's something going on with her. But I'll bring her tomorrow—if you feel well enough."

He clutched her hand, but did not open his eyes again. "It should pass. It always passes, eventually. I find, as I get older, that I cannot control the waves as I once could—they are too strong for me. I'm afraid someday my physical frame will not be able to contain them."

"Well, not anytime soon, I hope," said Catherine. She squeezed his hand, then laid it on the blanket. "Until tomorrow, then."

He smiled, and it was not until she was downstairs that she realized she had left behind yet another of Mary's handkerchiefs.

MARY: How many have you lost at this point? Seriously.

CATHERINE: They're *handkerchiefs*. Little bits of fabric. Tiny little bits of fabric I could shred with my Cat Woman claws. . . .

MARY: They're a shilling a box, is what they are, and you owe me.

Downstairs, Beatrice was still talking to Clarence, but Lorenzo had been replaced by a woman that Catherine guessed must be Madam Zora, of the *eau de cologne*. She certainly looked foreign— her skin was as brown as Catherine's, and she had dark brown eyes outlined with a great deal of kohl. She was wearing some sort of multicolored robe, embroidered with gold thread, and her hair was entirely hidden by a turban of the same pattern. It was difficult to guess her age—perhaps a little older than Mary? She certainly looked the part of a snake charmer.

"How is he?" asked Clarence, who had moved to the sofa, next to Beatrice. For goodness' sake, hadn't he listened to Catherine at all? She had warned him that Beatrice was poisonous. This was the problem with Beatrice's beauty—it drew men in, and women too, no matter what you told them.

"Not well," she said. "Bea, do you have anything in that poisonous greenhouse of yours that can cure migraines?"

"Not cure them, no," said Beatrice. "But mitigate them, certainly. Migraines are caused by constriction of the blood vessels leading to the brain, or so my father believed. I can create a medicine from the common foxglove that will ease vasoconstriction, and at least decrease the symptoms—if taken in small doses. The medicine is always in the dose, as you know."

"I don't know, but whatever. I'll bring it to him tomorrow, with Alice."

"Alice?" said Beatrice, startled. "Why Alice?"

"I'll explain later. Madam Zora, I don't think we've been introduced."

"I'm failing in my social duties," said Clarence. "Madam Zora, this is Astarte, the Cat Woman of the Andes. Catherine, this is the great Madam Zora, who has traveled to England from the Mysterious East. There, she learned the art of charming serpents, so that, Medusa-like, she can walk across the stage carrying vipers wrapped about her arms and forehead. She can wear a python around her shoulders as though it were a coat. Cobras can bite her without causing the least inconvenience." He turned to Madam Zora. "Am I remembering it correctly?"

Madam Zora rose, put her hands together as though praying, and bowed. In a deep voice with an undefinable accent, she said, "I am pleased to meet you."

"Mysterious East, hunh?" said Catherine. "Whitechapel or Spitalfields?"

"Hackney, actually," said Madam Zora, grinning. Well, the accent wasn't undefinable anymore—this was the voice of London, inflected by the East End. "But my mother was born in India, right enough—Lahore, she told me, though I've never been there myself. My father was a soldier in the army—a sergeant, by the end. He married her even though he knew his family would disown him for marrying a native woman. They live in London now, running a hat shop on Shoreditch High Street."

"Did you learn how to charm snakes from her?"

"Not likely!" Madam Zora laughed. "She hates them, says they make the hair on her neck stand up. No, she doesn't approve of what I do, though my da's more understanding. I'm the rebellious one in the family, you might say. Ran away to the circus when I was sixteen, and learned my trade proper from Medusa herself. I mean Madame Medusa—that was her stage name at Baldessari's, which is what Bartoli's used to be called, before it changed management. She taught me the tricks of the trade. How did you know I wasn't"—here she affected the foreign accent again—"the mysterious Madam Zora?"

"No one in the circus is who they pretend to be," said Catherine. "Clarence isn't a Zulu Prince, and I'm certainly not the Cat Woman. I mean, I sort of am, but not the way I appear on stage."

"Is it true that poisonous snakes bite you, and you are not affected?" asked Beatrice.

"Sure, if I take their teeth out," said Madam Zora. "Most of them, I do it that way. Some I let keep their teeth if they're not too sharp, and I'm careful to get all the poison out before the show. That way the audience can see the teeth marks on my wrist— always impresses them."

"Ah, I see," said Beatrice, clearly disappointed. Catherine wondered why, then realized she was being stupid. Of course—it would have meant a great deal to Beatrice, finding someone who was not affected by poisons. She could have shaken hands with another human being without even the protection of gloves.

"I'm sorry," said Catherine. "I would love to chat longer, but Beatrice and I have a great deal to do before we leave."

"Yes, I heard you were coming with us to gay Paree," said Madam Zora. "We'll have plenty of time to chat, I'm sure!"

"It was a pleasure to meet you, Miss Rappaccini," said Clarence, rising and bowing.

"And you," said Beatrice, smiling and lowering her eyes in the way women do when they are about to become complete fools over a man.

BEATRICE: Catherine, that is absolutely not true!

DIANA: Oh, come on. Admit that you like Clarence.

BEATRICE: Clarence is simply a friend. A friend I do
not want to poison.

DIANA: Well, what if you weren't poisonous?

BEATRICE: But I am, and that is that. End of
discussion, as Mary always says.

MARY: Do I say that? Seriously, do I?

"Until tomorrow, then?" said Clarence, who knew perfectly
well what that reaction meant. Most men do, you know.

"No," said Catherine, "because I'm not bringing her tomorrow.
You've breathed in quite enough of her poison for one day. She'll
see you on Friday at Charing Cross. Come on, Bea!"

If Beatrice had not been poisonous, Catherine would have
dragged her out of that wretched boardinghouse. As though they
needed another problem, in the midst of so many. And men were
always, always a problem. Or a complication, anyway.

"Your friend Mr. Jefferson is a fascinating man," said Beatrice
as they walked toward St. Pancras, where they could catch an
omnibus. "He was telling me about Boston, his time at law school
there. Catherine, if he has a law degree, why is he in Lorenzo's
circus pretending to be a Zulu Prince? It does not make sense."

"First of all, if you expect things in this world to make sense,
you're going to be disappointed. Second, circus folks don't ask
one another questions. We all have things in our past, Bea, or we
wouldn't be there. He's never asked me why I'm the Cat Woman,
and I've never asked him why he's the Zulu Prince. And third,
Clarence happens to be my oldest friend at the circus. He's the

one who first helped me develop my act as Astarte. He's the only person I told about Moreau's island before I met Justine, and he's kept that secret like a true friend. I would really prefer for him not to be poisoned."

"Yes, of course," said Beatrice, sounding hurt. Was she thinking of her lover Giovanni, whom she had inadvertently poisoned, and who had died drinking what he believed to be the antidote? She must be. But all she said was, "The omnibus is coming. I didn't mean to make you angry, Catherine."

"You didn't. Really, you didn't." Inwardly, Catherine cursed— she had not meant to hurt Beatrice's feelings. There, you see? The situation was becoming complicated already. "I'm just worried— about everything. Mostly about Justine and Mary, and yes, even Diana. I want to be with them, in Budapest. Or wherever they are now. Let's just make sure we're there by the twentieth, all right? I don't want them walking into a trap, at least not without us. Mrs. Poole sent a telegram warning Miss Murray, but what is a governess going to do against Seward and Van Helsing—plus whatever forces they have at their command?"

"I know," said Beatrice. Quickly, with one gloved hand, she squeezed Catherine's arm—it was the most contact she would allow herself. "We'll get there in time to help them, I promise."

They mounted the steps of the omnibus and sat up top, where Beatrice always sat to avoid poisoning anyone.

"Well," said Catherine. "I suggest we stop at home to eat something, then go directly to 221B Baker Street. I promised Mrs. Poole I would tell Holmes what we were up to." Beatrice just nodded. She was probably still feeling hurt, but what could Catherine do? The truth was the truth, and sometimes it was unpleasant to hear. She didn't want Clarence to end up like Giovanni.

When they arrived at 11 Park Terrace, walking up from Marylebone Road, they found Watson waiting for them. As soon as they had let themselves in, Mrs. Poole appeared in the hall and said, "Dr. Watson, parlor. Needs to see you at once. Terrible worried, he is. I'll bring up tea."

Once they had removed their hats and Catherine had laid aside her gloves, they proceeded into the parlor. There was Watson, smoking his pipe and pacing up and down in front of the fireplace.

"Miss Moreau, Miss Rappaccini, have you seen or heard from Holmes?" He looked at them anxiously. "He hasn't been home since Thursday afternoon, when he said he had an appointment with his brother, Mycroft. It's not unusual for him to be gone for some time when he's on a case, but he gave no indication that he would not be coming home that evening—neither did he take anything with him. All his clothes, his toothbrush, his shaving kit, are still at 221B."

"That's strange," said Catherine, flopping down on the sofa. It occurred to her too late that it might look rude, but she was tired. "What was his business with his brother? Isn't Mycroft Holmes some sort of government official?"

"I have no idea why they were meeting," said Watson. "Holmes would not—or perhaps could not—tell me what it was about. And yes, Mycroft works in the government, although I do not know which branch. He has always been very discreet about what he does, and for whom. I got the impression that this was one of those hush-hush government affairs. Holmes seldom keeps anything from me, but Mycroft is involved at the highest level. I went to his club this morning and was told they had not seen him since last week. Unless of course the porters are lying, which is perfectly possible. It is the Diogenes Club, after all—the most secretive club in London. I thought Holmes should at least see Mrs. Norton's telegram, informing him that Miss Jekyll is safely in Vienna. I assume you received that news as well?"

"Yes, but she's in danger," said Catherine. "Not in Vienna,

but I found out that Seward and Van Helsing are planning to do more than present papers when the Alchemical Society meets in Budapest. They're planning to take power, by force if necessary. Do you know of anyone named Dr. Raymond? I remember that name from somewhere. . . ."

Beatrice sat down in one of the armchairs, elegant as usual. Catherine could tell that she was tired too, but did Beatrice show it? No, she did not.

> DIANA: How could you tell she was tired, if she didn't show it?

> CATHERINE: Well, I assumed she was, after all that walking.

> DIANA: That doesn't mean you could *tell*.

> CATHERINE: How about you go somewhere else and do something dangerous, like lighting yourself on fire? That should be fun.

> DIANA: Doesn't work, unless you have some sort of flammable liquid to douse yourself with.

> MARY: I'm not even going to ask how you know that.

"Dr. Raymond . . . ," said Watson, then pulled on his pipe. "No, I'm afraid not. Is he a member of the medical profession, or is his doctorate in something else?"

"You may be thinking of Mrs. Raymond," said Beatrice. "Remember, from the Society of St. Mary Magdalen, where Diana was being kept. Could she be involved with this somehow?"

"No, I remember now!" said Catherine. "Dr. Raymond is one of the trustees of the Purfleet Asylum. He's the one who summoned Seward, that day I went to the asylum and made a mess of things. Evidently, he was also the head of the English chapter of the Alchemical Society before it was disbanded—by decree of the president, whoever that might be. I assume he's a medical doctor, like Dr. Jekyll, but who knows. The important thing is that he's in league with Seward and Van Helsing—and Prendick. If he is a doctor—like you—could you find out anything about him?"

"I could look in the *Medical Directory* and ask around," said Watson. "But you mentioned Mr. Prendick. Did he then survive the fire in the warehouse? We suspected that he might have escaped out the back."

"However he did it, he's still alive—unfortunately." Catherine sighed and leaned back, letting her head rest against the upholstery. The thought of Prendick made her even more tired—she hated the idea of confronting him again, and yet, if she went to Budapest to help Mary and Justine, that was exactly what it would be—another confrontation.

"Can you tell me the source of this information?" asked Watson. "It sounds as though you have been investigating yourselves—commendable, although I hope you're not exposing yourselves to unnecessary danger."

"Not unnecessary, of course," said Beatrice, with a reassuring smile. He did not look particularly reassured.

"Tea, in the dining room," said Mrs. Poole, who had come in unnoticed. "It's long past time you ate, and Dr. Watson, I hope you will take some tea with us as well. It must be quite gloomy in 221B, with Mr. Holmes gone. It's a meat tea, you know—substantial enough for a busy gentleman such as yourself."

"It is rather gloomy with Holmes gone," said Watson. He

looked as though he had not given much thought to meals lately. "Thank you very much—I accept the invitation!"

Over tea, which was certainly more substantial than usual—evidently, Mrs. Poole thought gentlemen needed a good deal of food—Catherine explained the events of the last few days, with Alice, who had joined them, adding details. Watson was startled when Archibald brought in the sandwiches—excellent roast beef, the way only Mrs. Poole can make it—while Mrs. Poole carried in the large teapot on a tray. Catherine was amused by how suspiciously he regarded the Orangutan Man.

"Are you quite sure that creature is safe to keep here, with you?" he asked. "Remember that he used to work for your adversaries! He was there when Adam kidnapped Miss Frankenstein."

"We are all creatures here, Dr. Watson," said Beatrice. "God's creatures, I should hope. We can scarcely blame Archibald for having been turned into what he is."

"They had him chained up!" added Alice. "He's grateful to be here, really he is. And I'm teaching him to play checkers."

"Well, you know best," said Watson, shaking his head. "But I wish this journey you intend to make wasn't necessary, or that Holmes or I could go with you. I would offer to come myself, but I believe I had better wait here, in case Holmes needs me. He may be in danger."

"Anyway, I scarcely think you would fit into the circus, except as the Ordinary Gentleman," said Catherine. "Demonstrating the attributes of the perfectly normal, non-monstrous Englishman of the nineteenth century. Step right up, ladies and gentlemen, to see this paragon of normalcy!"

Alice could not help laughing, which was unfortunate because she was drinking tea at the time, and it came out as more of a sputter—with tea spilled on the table. "Oh, sorry, miss," she said, to no one in particular, and scurried out to fetch a damp cloth.

"Catherine, stop teasing and finish your tea," said Beatrice. "Dr. Watson, it's very kind of you to offer your protection, but I assure you that we can take care of ourselves."

"Of course, of course," he said, but not with conviction.

> MARY: Men never seem to believe that women can take care of themselves! And Dr. Watson is particularly annoying in that regard.

> BEATRICE: Mary, he was only trying to be chivalrous.

> MARY: I know. In a way, that makes it worse.

"And what about your plants, Miss Rappaccini?" he asked. Beatrice put down her delicious mug of pond scum.

> BEATRICE: How many different ways can you think of to mock my eating habits?

> CATHERINE: I don't know yet. I haven't finished writing the book.

"I'm afraid they will die in my absence," she said. "I am the only one who can take care of them in that toxic atmosphere— except Justine, who is immune to poisons. But of course she is in Vienna. Anyone who went into that room to water them would soon collapse from their fumes."

"Can you not create some sort of automatic watering system?" asked Watson. "I saw something of the sort when I served in Afghanistan, where there is little rainfall and all water must be preserved. It was an ingenious system of wooden pipes, but I believe the same effect could be achieved, at little expense, with rubber tubes. Once the system is in place, the water can be turned on from a central spigot, set very low so that the water flows to the plants drop by drop. They are never overwatered, nor do they dry out."

"I don't know," said Beatrice, doubtfully. "There is a spigot in the operating theater, but who could build such a system?"

"Why, I believe you and I could do it. I could install it wearing a patented Lung Protector Holmes purchased some time ago, for a case that required going down into a collapsed mine. It is a sort of mask that fits over the face and filters the air. It should protect me for the relatively short period of time it would take to set up the tubing."

Beatrice did not respond, but looked at him with concern. She seemed to have little faith that a Lung Protector, no matter how patented, could protect him from the poisonous effects of her medicinal garden.

> JUSTINE: But it worked, in the end. Did you know
> that the first such device was invented in Baghdad
> by three brothers? They describe it in *The Book of
> Ingenious Devices*, where they also propose a variety
> of automata . . .

> CATHERINE: Is this a novel or a scientific lecture?

The next two days were unusually busy ones. Alice accompanied Catherine to the boardinghouse in Clerkenwell with reluctance, and looked as though about to run away when Marvelous Martin sat up in bed and said, "Lord have mercy, I've never seen anything like it. It's like a hurricane, that's what it is. How can you stand it, girl, with all those waves crashing around you? I'll come twice a week and teach you how to control them."

He turned to Catherine. "Lorenzo doesn't need me on this continental jaunt of yours—he says I should stay here and wait until the circus returns to London. So I have some time to devote to little Alice, here. All I ask in payment is more of this—whatever this concoction calls itself." He held up the bottle of milky liquid that Beatrice had given Catherine for him. "I can't tell you how wonderful it is, to feel pain receding like the tide. Why, I might be wanting a bit of breakfast!"

"I don't think it calls itself anything," said Catherine. "But Beatrice said if it worked, she would make up more, to be dispensed in regular doses by Mrs. Poole. She says you must never exceed the dose, because what is medicine in small quantities is toxic in large ones. You understand, don't you?"

"Yes, yes," he said, although his attention seemed to have drifted away with the pain. "Now Alice, when you made yourself disappear, how did you do it? Can you show me?"

Catherine sighed. Sometimes she thought she was the only person in the world with an ounce of practicality.

> MARY: There are plenty of other people who are practical, you know!

> DIANA: And where do you get off calling yourself practical? You're a writer.

There was no time for passports, but then they would not be trying to pass themselves off as ordinary travelers. They would travel as *La Belle Toxique* and *La Femme Panthère*, circus performers. Mrs. Poole helped them with their theatrical costumes. Catherine's Cat Woman costume, which Clarence had kept for her, was in reasonably good shape, but she had some ideas about how to make it even more effective on stage.

CATHERINE: I gave him a good talking-to about the fact that Beatrice was *poisonous*, and he should leave her alone. He didn't seem very happy with me. But it was nice of him to have kept my costume.

JUSTINE: I'm afraid your warning did not have at all the intended effect.

CATHERINE: I should have known that telling Clarence to do anything would be completely useless. In fact, I think he took it as a sort of challenge!

Beatrice needed a costume appropriate for *La Belle Toxique*. A tea gown of Mrs. Jekyll's was remade in a more modern style. A more *artistic* style, Beatrice insisted.

"Although what is wrong with the fashions I grew up with, I don't know," said Mrs. Poole. "All this drapery—heathenish, I think it is. Give me a good stiff corset and petticoats starched so they stand up by themselves! That's what proper young ladies wore in my day."

"And you are more than welcome to them," said Beatrice.

Wearing his patented Lung Protector, Watson set up the system of rubber tubing that would water Beatrice's plants. It made him look rather like a frog, which sent both Catherine and Alice into fits of laughter, but scared Archibald so much that he would not come out from under his bed until Watson had gone.

On the night before their departure, Watson dined with them at 11 Park Terrace. "Have you heard anything more from Vienna?" he asked.

"Not yet," said Catherine. "I just wish I knew what was going on! And Holmes? No word from him?" She took more of the roast beef. Mrs. Poole made excellent roast beef, and it was even better the second or third day. Watson and Alice could eat the potatoes.

"None," said Watson, looking particularly dejected. "Miss Moreau, if you need any money . . ."

"We don't, actually. But thank you, Dr. Watson. You really have been kind and thoughtful these last few days. I'm not very good at thanking people, but I'm grateful for your help. More potatoes? And there's this green thing—haricots verts, Mrs. Poole called them, although I'm pretty sure that's not how it's pronounced in French."

"As am I, most grateful," said Beatrice, giving him one of her serious smiles. She seemed to be eating haricot verts soup. What in the world would she eat while traveling with the circus? Well, maybe they could pick her some weeds from the side of the road!

BEATRICE: You know I can go quite a long time with just sunlight.

CATHERINE: I know. That's so weird. You're just so weird sometimes.

BEATRICE: However you meant that, I will take it as a compliment.

"Well, it's only my duty of course," said Watson. Oh good, he was taking more of the pig food. It was difficult to tell by gaslight, but Catherine would have sworn he was blushing.

BEATRICE: Dr. Watson really is the staunchest, most loyal of friends.

JUSTINE: Just friends? You mean like Clarence?

BEATRICE: Well no, Clarence is a different kind of friend entirely.

MARY: Poor Dr. Watson. I really do feel sorry for him.

BEATRICE: You are all misunderstanding me.

CATHERINE: No, we're not.

Friday morning dawned bright and clear. By 8:30 a.m., Catherine and Beatrice were on the platform at Charing Cross Station, having said their goodbyes to Mrs. Poole and Alice, who had shown them how she could disappear at breakfast. "You see, Mr. Martin showed me how to do it! It's just a matter of controlling the waves. I don't actually disappear, of course, but you *think* I do. It's really quite scientific, once you understand that we are all surrounded by an energic field. . . ." It was probably a good thing they were leaving for the continent, thought Catherine. If Alice was going to go on and on about the principles of mesmerism, she would quickly become insufferable. The two pounds for Catherine's article had arrived just in time for her to make the cheque over to Mrs. Poole. She hoped that, together with whatever was still in the bank and the money Atlas had given her, would be enough to support the Park Terrace household until she and Beatrice returned—whenever that would be! Meanwhile, their travel expenses would be taken care of by the circus, and soon, she hoped, they would have plenty of money—she was sure the show would do well.

On the platform, next to a small mountain of bags and trunks, were Lorenzo, the Zulu Prince, Madam Zora, Atlas, Sasha the Dog Boy, the Twisting Jellicoe Twins, Colonel Sharp the Knife-Thrower, and various other acts that Lorenzo thought might be popular on the continent.

Catherine found a cabin for herself and Beatrice, pushed the top window all the way down, and forbade anyone else from entering. "Seriously, do you want to have fainted by the time we get to Dover?" she said to Clarence when he proposed joining them. "At least I'm used to Beatrice—if I need to, I can walk up and down the corridor. But you might not even notice what's happening before you lose consciousness!"

"You don't think I'm afraid of a little poison, do you?" asked Clarence, leaning up against the doorframe. He was smiling and had his arms crossed, which meant that whatever victory she won would be temporary.

"Well, at least let her get some rest!" said Catherine. "We've had to get ready for this trip in two days, and we were up past midnight finishing her costume. Even I helped sew, and I *never* sew. She's planning to sleep. Do you really want to watch her sleep?"

"All right," he said, still in good humor. "I'll check in with you at Dover. Don't you get poisoned either, Whiskers."

As Catherine watched the station platform slip by the train window, she wondered when she would see London again, and what in the world was happening to Mary and Justine. Had they found Lucinda Van Helsing yet? Why hadn't they sent another telegram? And was the Alchemical Society aware that she and Beatrice were leaving England? Were they being watched? She thought ahead with dread to the channel crossing. She really, really hated boats.

CHAPTER X

Consulting Dr. Freud

"How much longer do you think they'll be?" asked Mary. According to her watch, Diana had been in Dr. Freud's office for an hour. At one point she had heard shrieks of laughter—Diana's.

"I'm sorry there is nothing for you to read," said Hannah, looking up from the book of German poetry she had found on the bookshelves. The waiting room was comfortable enough, with its patterned wallpaper, its sofa upholstered in dark red chenille, its low table on which were arranged magazines—all in German. There was a large selection of books on the shelves in various languages: German, French, Spanish, Italian. But unfortunately the only ones in English were the collected works of Shakespeare and Sir Edward Tylor's *Anthropology: An Introduction to the Study of Man and Civilization.* Mary was not in the mood for either, so instead she had flipped through the magazines, looking at photographs of Austrian women in court dress, advertisements for soap and corsets and bottles of what she assumed were medicine. What in the world could the psychoanalyst and Diana be talking about for so long?

She walked to the window and looked out at the courtyard, which contained the stables. The window was open; she could smell the faint odor of horses and hay. It reminded her of London, but there was an undefinable quality to the sunlight, a particular brightness that indicated they were in a different climate altogether.

Suddenly, she heard the doorknob turn and the door of the office open.

"Ah, Fräulein Jekyll," said Freud. "My apologies for taking so long."

How was it that everyone on the continent could speak excellent English, while she could speak nothing else? It was embarrassing, that's what it was. She would have to ask Justine to help with her German pronunciation.

Sigmund Freud was an imposing man, with a thick head of brown hair and a beard that was just beginning to turn gray. He was smoking a cigar—Mr. Holmes would have been able to identify the type—and ash had fallen on the lapel of his wool suit.

"If you would please come in, I would like to speak with you for a moment."

"Of course," said Mary, confused. Why did he want to talk to her?

She followed him into his consulting room, then looked around, startled. It was much larger than she had anticipated. Here there were more bookshelves, filled with books and curios—pots, vases, figurines of various sorts, most of which looked ancient. On the tops of the selves perched classical busts. At the center of the room was a chaise lounge, and on it sat Diana, bouncing up and down so that the springs creaked.

"Stop that or you'll break Dr. Freud's furniture," said Mary.

"You can't give orders here. This is not your house," said Diana, although she did stop. "Well, are we done?"

"Yes, you and I are," said Freud. "But I would like to talk with your sister for a moment, privately. If I may?"

"All right," said Diana. "But you won't find anything interesting about her. She's not mad at all. She's as sane as sane can be." With her usual disdain for the proprieties, she marched out of the room. The psychoanalyst closed the door behind her.

"I disagree with your sister, *Fräulein*," he said, smiling. "I expect that I will find you as interesting as I find her, even if you are, as she insisted, *boringly* sane. I do not concern myself exclusively with madness, you know. My study is the human psyche, in all its forms and manifestations." His smile was a little frightening, through all that beard. Not because it was unkind, but because there was a particular intensity to his expression, as though he were looking deeply into your self, or perhaps soul. Mary found it disconcerting.

"I see," said Mary, although she did not. "And why do you wish to speak with me? Will you help us? Mrs. Norton indicated that you had agreed to help."

"First, please do sit. We will begin by discussing the practicalities. I see that you are a very practical young woman, an admirable quality. And then, if you do not object, I would like to ask you a few questions."

Mary sat on the chaise lounge since there was nowhere else, while Freud seated himself in a much less comfortable rolling chair.

"Your sister is certainly an interesting case," he began. He seemed to be frowning, and at first Mary wondered what in the world Diana had done wrong this time—had she made him angry? But no, she realized a moment later. He was merely puzzled, and it was the thick beard and eyebrows that made him look so formidable. Before he continued, he stubbed out his cigar in an ashtray.

"It will not be difficult to convince the asylum administration that she is mad. She is impulsive, irrational. Her language is most inappropriate. She showed me where she had previously cut herself. And yet, *Fräulein*, I do not believe that she is truly mad. She is not normal—certainly she is not normal. But she does not seem to suffer from her condition. Her nightmares give her no anxiety—indeed, she seems to enjoy them. She feels no guilt about expressing every thought and wish as it comes to her. She does not feel the need to conform to societal expectations, and her failure to do so does not worry her in the slightest. Indeed, if what she tells me is true, her mentality and behavior give her certain advantages. Of course she lied to me—it is part of her nature to lie. But I flatter myself that I can discriminate between the truth and a deliberate falsehood. While I spoke with Miss Hyde, it seemed to me that she was perfectly well-adjusted, that her actions made sense and would not be blamable, in a society different from ours. It seemed to me that it was our society which was at fault, rather than your sister."

"But this is the society we live in, not another," said Mary. "Its rules and conventions exist for a reason. They are the basis of civility, of concord. They allow us to live together as social beings. Diana, if you will forgive my saying so, Dr. Freud, is a pain in the arse."

DIANA: You said "arse"!

JUSTINE: Did you actually use the word "arse" in a conversation with Dr. Freud?

MARY: Well, I'm not proud of myself, but yes, I did.

DIANA: Mary said "arse"! Mary said "arse" to the great Dr. Freud!

MARY: And in retrospect, I think I was entirely justified.

"I'm quite certain she is," said Freud. "Yet I'm also certain that she's not hysterical, nervous, or neurasthenic. Narcissistic, yes. But without any actual sociopathology. She does, for example, love you, despite her protestations to the contrary. Yet you seem so opposite in temperament. And you do not share the same name. Do you have different fathers?"

"Different mothers, actually," said Mary. "But my father—you could say he took on a different identity when consorting with her mother. It was as though he became another person."

"I see," said Freud, leaning back in his chair. "I have heard of such cases—respectable gentlemen living two lives, even having entirely different residences and families. I am familiar with your father by reputation, *Fräulein*. He was said to be an excellent man in his field, if a bit unorthodox. But a professional reputation does not stop a man from being human—fallible, as we all are. Indeed, the higher a man holds his head in society, the lower he may descend in his secret life, as though the psyche is attempting to achieve a sort of balance, an equilibrium. I have long thought of the human mind as a battlefield, the site of a war between man's highest and lowest, most civilized and most primitive, impulses. Inside each of us is the primordial child, who wants only love, food, the fulfillment of its desires. It acts out of need, anger, the impulse of the moment."

"Well, that describes Diana precisely!" said Mary.

"And the adult, who knows not to give in to those impulses," said Freud. "You, for example, *Fräulein*, seem to me an admirable example of restraint, although your sister described it in slightly different terms."

DIANA: I said you had a stick up your arse!

MARY: You just wanted to say "arse" again, didn't you?

"Well," said Mary a little defensively, "I've had a great deal of responsibility since I was a child. After my mother went mad, I had a household to run—bills to pay, people who depended on me.

I couldn't go around doing or saying whatever I wanted, could I? There were obligations to fulfill, duties to discharge. . . ."

"Yes, your sister told me about your mother's illness, which interests me a great deal. And she—your sister, I mean. Is she also one of those duties?"

"Unfortunately!" Mary had not meant to sound quite so vehement, but it was true, wasn't it? "She really is the most . . ."

"Then why do you hesitate to send her into the Maria-Theresa Krankenhaus?" He leaned forward again, elbows on his knees, looking at her intently.

"Because she's my sister, and I'm supposed to take care of her." Obviously. Why was he asking her this? Surely how she felt about the issue was irrelevant. Diana was her responsibility, whether she liked it or not.

Freud smiled and leaned back in his chair. "Ah, *Fräulein*, you are wondering why I am interrogating you in such an annoying, impolite fashion, are you not? I have found that in the pursuit of psychological truth, one cannot remain polite. One is frequently annoying to one's patients."

But she wasn't his patient, was she? "Of course I would not have used those words if you had not inquired . . ." Mary began.

"No, of course not. You see, you lie differently from your sister. She will lie to get what she wants, without hesitation or remorse. You will lie to maintain the veneer of respectability and politeness, which is all that separates us from beasts. No, do not feel as though you need to respond—I will do as you wish and commit your sister to the madhouse. You understand that I am risking my career in doing so. I do this not for you, and not even for my friend Irene, but because I know a little of Abraham Van Helsing, and what I know, I do not like. He is a dangerous man—a man who pursues science for power rather than the dispassionate accumulation of knowledge. A man like that must be stopped. I do not wish to put your sister in danger, but it is clear to me that she will not feel the danger, as you and I might—to her, it will be yet another adventure. I will give her three days in the Krankenhaus. After that time, I will officially transfer her to another hospital—really, of course, into your keeping. I hope she succeeds in finding and establishing contact with this young woman, Fräulein Van Helsing."

Suddenly, he smiled. It was as though sunlight had unexpectedly broken through storm clouds. "And if you and your sister stay in Vienna for any length of time, I would like to see you again. It seems to me, *Fräulein*, that each of you has something the other lacks—as though your sister had received half the human psychic apparatus, and you the other. Is it true, as she tells me, that you never cry?"

"Not everyone goes around bawling at the slightest provocation," said Mary indignantly. How dare Diana have discussed her with this rude, provoking man?

"And you never thought of striking another person in anger? Or perhaps of kicking an inanimate object, such as a table when you have stubbed your toe upon it?"

"Why in the world would I do such a thing?" asked Mary. "It would do me no good, and would certainly not injure the table. Indeed, I am likely to hurt myself again, doing something so foolish. Although . . ."

"Yes?" said Freud.

"Well, I do think of slapping Diana! When she's being particularly impossible, you know." She hated to admit it, but it was true.

"Ah yes, Diana." The psychoanalyst seemed almost sympathetic. "Of course she would bring out your more primitive impulses. And you, I believe, restrain and guide her, despite her resistance."

DIANA: What utter bollocks.

"I certainly try," said Mary. "What exactly are you implying, Doctor? I feel as though there's some purpose behind this interrogation, but I cannot tell what it is."

"I wish it were so simple, *Fräulein*," he said. "No, this is merely an idea on my part—not even that, but the ghost of an idea that vanishes when I try to think of it directly. We speak about man—the *I*, the ego. And yet I believe that singular *I* is composed of disparate entities, at war with one another. As I mentioned, the human psyche is a battlefield. Those who are most wounded come to me, or end up in places like the Maria-Theresa Krankenhaus. It seems to me that you and your sister . . . No, I cannot come to conclusions on so little evidence. You will need to come back, and then perhaps we can speak again. But now you will be wanting your luncheon, and my wife is expecting me for mine. Tomorrow morning, I shall take your sister to the Krankenhaus—I will telephone Irene this afternoon to make plans. I hope that I shall see you again as well, Fräulein Jekyll, while you are in Vienna. And remember, when you have the time, I would consider it an honor if you would tell me the story of your childhood, of your dreams."

Mary rose. Of course she had no intention whatsoever of allowing herself to be psychoanalyzed! "Thank you, Dr. Freud," she said, politely but without enthusiasm. If this was psychoanalysis—poking your nose into the business of others—she wanted no part of it. Why in the world would someone as intelligent as Irene Norton find it either interesting or useful?

> MRS. POOLE: Quite right, miss. A man should know
>   the difference between right and wrong, and if
>   he doesn't, having some sort of complex—or
>   whatever word the psychological gentlemen use—
>   should not excuse him.

BEATRICE: But Dr. Freud has some remarkable
insights into human character. Have you read his
new book on the interpretation of dreams?

JUSTINE: No, do you have a copy?

BEATRICE: It's on my bedside table. You are welcome
to borrow it at any time. He argues that all of our
dreams are meaningful—that if we interpret them
correctly, we can understand what we truly hope
for and desire. For example, what did you dream
of last night?

JUSTINE: A lake, I believe. I could see myself
reflected in it, but then the clouds gathered over
me, and suddenly there was a great storm. It
started to rain, and I realized that I was cold, and
hungry, and lost. And the face in the water was
not my face anymore. . . .

BEATRICE: The lake is a symbol of the feminine.
Perhaps it represents your mother, and the rain
coming down represents the male principle that
disturbs the female? Rain is often a symbol of
the father, and the storm clouds are of course
associated with the father-god Zeus. So your
father, Frankenstein, who sought to be a god,
disturbed the feminine principle of creation,
and what emerged was you, as you are now—a
stranger to that other Justine.

CATHERINE: That's the stupidest thing I've ever heard.

Freud merely smiled. "Well, I think we are done then, *Fräulein*. Shall we rejoin your sister?"

Mary nodded and rose. Thank goodness that was over with! Of course, now the difficult part would begin.

Out in the waiting room, Diana was sitting crossed-legged on the sofa. "Oh, you're done, are you? Took you long enough."

"You were wrong, Fräulein Hyde," said Freud. He seemed to be glaring at her from under his eyebrows, but Mary could tell he was smiling. She rather liked him as a person, now that she knew him a little better. He resembled a tame bear that initially looked as though he might eat you up, but on closer acquaintance was considerably less intimidating. As for his theories—well, those were no concern of hers. She was interested in *facts*. Mr. Holmes believed in facts, not such vague hypotheses as to human nature. She wondered, indeed, what he would have thought of Dr. Freud's analysis of Diana—and of her.

"Oh? How am I wrong?" Diana stood up and crossed her arms, like a defiant child.

"I found your sister quite as interesting as yourself."

Diana shrugged as though she did not care, although Mary could tell she was offended. "Whatever. Can we go? I'm hungry."

"Yes, I believe this matter is settled," said Freud. "Hannah, can you tell your mistress that I will telephone her later today to discuss the details?"

"Of course, Herr Doktor." She put her book aside and drew on her gloves.

"Ah, Goethe," said Freud. "My favorite also."

"Is that how you pronounce it?" asked Diana. "Justine is always reading him. I thought it would sound more like 'goat,' with a 'th' at the end. That's how it's spelled, anyway."

"Thank you," said Mary to the psychoanalyst, ignoring Diana as much as possible. She was the one who was like a goat, always hungry, eating whatever she came across. Eating it or climbing on it! Mary held out her hand.

Rather than shaking it, Freud leaned down and kissed it. Well, she supposed that was how things were done on the continent! She would have preferred a firm English handshake.

"Until tomorrow," he said. "It has been a pleasure, *Fräulein*."

"Likewise, Doctor," she said, although she was not entirely sure it had. However much she might like him personally, she had no wish to be mentally dissected in that fashion.

> JUSTINE: Mary, would you ever go back to Vienna, to be psychoanalyzed by Dr. Freud? He might, perhaps, tell you some interesting things about yourself.

> MARY: He can't tell me anything I don't already know. That idea of his, about the different parts of the psyche, reminds me of what I was told in Styria by—

> CATHERINE: Oh no, you don't! We haven't gotten to that part of the narrative yet. I've told you over and over about the need to maintain suspense. You are the *worst* characters ever.

> MARY: We're not characters. We're people.

> JUSTINE: Although in a sense we are both, are we not? Since we have allowed Catherine to write about us in this way.

> CATHERINE: *Allowed?* If I remember correctly, I was

asked to write an account of our adventures. At a
meeting, with all members present.

"You see, it's impregnable," said Greta.

Justine looked up at the Maria-Theresa Krankenhaus.
Unfortunately, she had to agree with Greta. The mental hospital was
a rectangle of gray stone. It rose sheer for three stories—there was
no ornamentation, nothing one could climb, not even a drainpipe.
The windows were barred on the top two floors. No vegetation
grew over its forbidding facade, and even the grounds were absolutely bare, with no trees or shrubs to hide behind, only closely
clipped lawn. It was surrounded by a high stone wall, spiked at the
top. The building had two entrances, as Greta had described—
front and back, both guarded by armed men. There was only one
gate leading into the grounds, and that too was guarded.

"I could break into the Hoffburg and steal the Emperor's handkerchief from under his pillow more easily than I could get in
there," said Greta, shaking her head. She was once again dressed
in her shabby masculine attire, more appropriate than a maid's
costume for traveling around the city.

"Does he keep his handkerchief under his pillow?" asked
Justine, lowering the binoculars she had been using to survey the
hospital grounds.

"He does, actually," said Greta. Suddenly, she grinned, and
Justine could see the street urchin she had been behind the carefully trained maid. "Don't ask me how I know that."

Justine could not help smiling in response. "Very well, I shall
restrain my curiosity."

> DIANA: Wait a minute, you were telling Mary's story,
> in her voice and everything. And now you're
> telling Justine's.

CATHERINE: Well, Mary wasn't there, so I can't tell
this part from her perspective, can I?

DIANA: It just seems . . . weird.

CATHERINE: That's because you don't read modern
literature, just those penny dreadfuls and your
theater rags. Nowadays all the best writers
experiment with literary technique, like stream of
consciousness.

DIANA: Are you saying you're one of the best
writers? Because I don't think— oh, don't you
try to bite me! Your Astarte stories aren't exactly
Shakespeare, you know.

JUSTINE: Catherine, I seem to remember that Greta
and I were speaking in French.

CATHERINE: If you want this section to be in French,
you'll have to write it yourself.

"Perhaps I shall tell you another time how I learned where the
Emperor keeps his handkerchief!" said Greta, *in French*, for that
was the language she and Justine were speaking. "It is, at any rate,
an amusing anecdote. But now I think we had better return to
Madame Norton and let her know that we have found our observation post."

Despite its formidable appearance, the Maria-Teresa
Krankenhaus was located in an ordinary if somewhat disreputable
section of Vienna, outside of the Ringstrasse, to the north of the
Danube. Around its high stone walls were the usual buildings

and shops one finds in a city. Across the street from the hospital, Justine and Greta had found an inn that had a tavern on the first floor and rented rooms on the second and third. From a third-floor room that faced the front of the building, they could see quite clearly into the hospital grounds.

Greta had rented the third-floor room for four days, telling the proprietor that they might be going in and out frequently, as they were salesmen, in Vienna to sell their wares (which were, she hinted, a superior kind of hair oil). It was not a particularly attractive room—the paint on the walls was peeling, the mattress on the bed was stained, and the shaving stand had rusted. But it gave them the best possible view of the hospital. The proprietor looked at them from beneath bushy brows—the only hair that grew on his otherwise bald head. He had a long scar down one side of his face, and what seemed to be one glass eye because it was a different color than the other and sometimes moved independently. It was obvious, from the memorabilia behind the bar, that he was a veteran of one of that region's innumerable wars. What the hell did he care when they came in or out, he muttered through a particularly noxious cigarette clenched in a corner of his mouth, paying them little attention as he wiped down the bar. As long as they paid for their room and did not cause trouble, they could come and go whenever they pleased. From what Justine could tell, at least some of the rooms were occupied by women, and sometimes men, who brought in a series of guests they had evidently just met, for they were still exchanging names on the staircase. Did it bother her that this place was the resort of prostitutes? A little, but for the most part she felt sorry for these sons and daughters of sin. They could not help resorting to such low measures. If the world were only better arranged, if all men truly cared for their fellows as both the Bible and reason bade, such things would not exist. She blamed not the individual, but the system.

MARY: You really do sound like Justine! That's a little frightening, actually. It's as though you can get into each of our heads.

CATHERINE: I told you I'm a good writer. My Astarte stories aren't *meant* to be Shakespeare, thank you very much.

"All right," said Greta. "I think we've seen what we need to."

Justine nodded. She wanted, more than anything else, simply to go back to Mrs. Norton's apartment and lie down on the sofa in the study, perhaps with a damp cloth over her eyes. The last few days had been such a blur of activity—the train, and then the ferry, and the train again. And then sharing a cabin with Heinrich Waldman, keeping up the pretense of being Justin Frank. It had been exhausting, and since their arrival in Vienna, there had been no time to rest.

She was strong—physically, stronger than most men. Even Atlas was not as strong as she was. But there is another kind of strength, a sort of sheer endurance, and she had to admit that in that way, Mary was stronger. Mary could simply get up in the morning and go, whereas so much exhausted Justine—the sights and sounds of travel, conversations, the sheer presence of others. Even when she cared about them, as she did Mary and Diana, after spending several days in their company she would find herself developing a headache. In London, she had been able to climb up to her studio and paint. But here, there was nowhere she could escape, and no time in which to do it. They had to rescue Lucinda Van Helsing—all else was subordinate to that purpose. She knew that; nevertheless, she sighed and put her forehead on the windowpane, which felt solid and cool. Sometimes, she had to admit, she longed for the house in Cornwall, near the coast, where she had lived alone for almost a century.

MARY: Do you really long for that? For that kind of solitude?

JUSTINE: It does not mean I don't love you all. It's simply my nature. I hope you understand.

MARY: Of course we do. I mean, I'm not sure we really do, because we're not you. I can't imagine being alone for a hundred years. But it's all right.

DIANA: But you'd want *me* there, right, Justine? I wouldn't bother you.

MRS. POOLE: Your way of not bothering looks exactly like bothering, if you ask me.

DIANA: Which no one did!

"Justine, are you well?" Greta was looking at her with concern. "Yes . . . Yes, of course. We are done here, are we not?"

"Unless you've suddenly thought of a plan for rescuing Mademoiselle Van Helsing! No? Then I suggest we find our cab and return to Prinz-Eugen Strasse."

Justine nodded. It was good, at least, to be able to speak French. She had not realized how much she had missed her native language— the language in which her mother had spoken to her, and Madame Frankenstein had trained her, and Victor Frankenstein had taught her after reanimating the body of Justine Moritz. It came back to her so easily, like breathing. Speaking and thinking in it were so much easier, as though she were back in the mountains of Switzerland, drawing cool, clear air into her lungs, rather than the wet, heavy, sooty atmosphere of London.

She followed Greta down the stairs, stepping over a drunkard passed out on the second-floor landing. They found the cab where they had asked it to wait for them, in the mews several streets over. Soon, they were once again jostling over the cobbled streets of Vienna.

As they drove, Justine stared out the window of the cab at the apartment houses and factories in this section of the city. Then she turned back to Greta.

"How *did* you know where the Emperor keeps his handkerchief at night?"

Greta laughed. "That's the easiest time to steal it from him. As Madame Norton would tell you, the handkerchief of an Emperor, marked by his personal handkerchief maker, is useful in so many ways! It can, for example, convince someone that you are secretly his mistress, and therefore have his confidence. But I don't want you to think that I stole it from under his head! He was not in bed at the time. The advantage of being a maid is, if you're wearing the proper uniform, you can go anywhere, and no one will notice. But I don't think I should tell you any more, Justine, although I'm a good judge of character and you seem to be someone I could trust with the most secret information. I don't want to betray *madame*'s confidence, you understand. She . . . well, she saved our lives, my sister's and mine."

"Did she?" said Justine. She hesitated to ask how. She did not wish to intrude into Greta's personal life. . . . And that, right there, is the difference between Justine and the rest of us. We would not have felt such compunction.

MARY: I would certainly not have pried!

CATHERINE: But you would have *wanted* to. Your sense of propriety would have kept you from doing so.

BEATRICE: I confess, my curiosity would have prompted me to ask, even if politeness forbade it.

CATHERINE: Which is why Justine is far and away the best of us.

JUSTINE: Catherine, that's ridiculous. I have many flaws. I am sometimes more angry than you realize, and I do not forgive easily. When we were trapped in that castle in Styria, I could not find it in my heart to forgive—

CATHERINE: I said no spoiling the plot for our readers! Anyway, it's proof of your goodness that whenever you do anything less than charitable, you immediately feel guilty about it. Granted, I don't think it's very *sensible* of you—guilt never helped anyone change anything.

BEATRICE: Although guilt may result in ethical action later. One may, for example, determine never to harm another, after having once done grievous harm.

CATHERINE: Are you taking about your relationship with Clarence?

DIANA: I never feel guilty about anything.

MARY: We know!

Now it was Greta's turn to stare out the cab window, her face half-turned away from Justine. But the half Justine could see looked thoughtful. There was something soothing about the horse's hooves clopping on stone. At this point, they were traveling over the larger boulevards in the south of the city, with trees on both sides. Justine waited. Would Greta say anything? If not, Justine would certainly not ask again. When Greta turned back, Justine worried that she had caused the maid—or spy?—distress, perhaps even pain. Greta's eyes were filled with tears. She sniffed and wiped her nose with the back of one hand; then, as though remembering that she was Madame Norton's proper maid, she pulled out a rather dirty pocket handkerchief.

"Our mother died several days after I was born, of childbed fever. Our father cared for us, but he was a drunkard and a thief. It would have been better if he had been one or the other—as a thief he might have succeeded, for he was one of the best in Vienna, and as a drunkard he might have avoided thievery. But he stole while drunk and was captured. He died in prison, and we were sent to the Institute for Orphans and Foundlings, in the Margareten District. We had never been to school—Hannah knew how to read a little, but I did not know even that. The institute was—well, no better nor worse than many such, built for the warehousing of indigent children. They tried to starve us into submission, and if that failed, the switch would accomplish what hunger could not. Finally, we ran away. We did not know much, but our father had taught us one useful skill—how to steal. We lived on the streets for two years, surviving as pickpockets and thieves. One day, while Hannah was lifting a wallet out of the pocket of a particularly elegant gentleman, while I was distracting him by importuning him for money, we were caught. It seems the gentleman's manservant had been hurrying to catch up with him after settling a bill, and he had observed our trickery. Unfortunately for us, the gentleman was an official at court, who claimed that his wallet contained important state documents. He accused us of being spies, of conspiring

against the state. We were tried and condemned to hang for treason. Hannah was thirteen, I was only eleven years old at the time.
We thought we were going to die."

Greta turned and stared out the carriage window again. Now
they were driving by parks filled with tall trees, and buildings that
might have been universities or museums. How different from the
small, cramped streets they had come from!

"One day," she continued, still staring out the window, "as we
were languishing in our prison cell, having given up on the idea
of escape—don't think we had not tried!—a woman came to see
us. I still remember how she looked in the dim light from the
prison window—in a scarlet coat trimmed with fur, and wearing
a fur hat. I'd never seen anyone like her! I thought she might be
Empress Elizabeth herself. She was followed by one of the guards,
cringing and fawning. She ordered him to let us out of our cell,
and he complied, with a 'Yes, Your Highness.' We followed her
down those dark corridors, out of the prison and into the light of
day, which neither of us thought we would see again until the day
we were hanged in the prison yard.

"As soon as we stepped outside the prison, she grabbed our
wrists and said, 'Quick, into the carriage before they discover I'm
not any kind of Highness, and your release papers are forged!'

"We climbed as quickly as we could into the carriage, which
had a royal crest painted on it, and then we were rolling through
the streets of Vienna, just as we are now—free."

"And was that Irene Norton?" asked Justine.

"Of course," said Greta, smiling as though she were remembering
the episode. "Who else would have so much courage, to simply roll up
to the most impregnable prison in Vienna in a carriage painted with
the royal coat of arms, carrying false papers, and rescue two criminals
who had most definitely committed the crime of which they had been
accused? The crime of thievery, that is, not of treason."

"Why did she?" asked Justine. "It must have been a considerable risk."

"We are almost home," said Greta. "That is the wall of the Belvedere. In a moment, we will turn onto Prinz-Eugen Strasse. We asked her that as well. She said that if we were indeed spies, she wanted us to work for her, and if we were not, we could be useful to her as thieves. She arranged for us to learn various languages, how to fight with a knife and sword, how to shoot any firearm. She introduced us to the others. . . ."

"Then there are others like you, working for Mrs. Norton?" asked Justine. That was what Irene herself had implied earlier.

Greta laughed. "A whole—well, what is the word? Gaggle of us, I supposed. Only Hannah and I live with Madame Norton. For the others, there is a house, the location of which is so secret that I will not reveal it even to you! Although I like you, Justine, and if you ever take to spying—or thievery, either will do, I will certainly recommend you to *madame*!"

Justine was astonished. The Baker Street Irregulars seemed amateurish, compared with the operation Irene Norton was running.

"You see, now I've said too much," said Greta. "Anyway, we have arrived. This is 18 Prinz-Eugen Strasse."

Irene was not at home when they entered, and Mary, Diana, and Hannah had not yet returned from meeting with Freud. Greta headed down to the kitchen, saying something about seeing whether Frau Schmidt needed her help to prepare lunch.

What should she do? Justine knew, but did not particularly want to do it. Well, she would, whether she wanted to or not. If she had read Mrs. Shelley's book back in London, she might have recognized Heinrich Waldman's name. She had been putting it off long enough.

MRS. POOLE: To think he spent two nights in the

same cabin with you, knowing you were a woman!
No gentleman would do such a thing.

JUSTINE: I assure you, Mrs. Poole, he did nothing
improper. Although he did speak mockingly of
Leibniz's *Discourse on Metaphysics*, which I admit
shocked me a little.

When Mary returned from the psychoanalyst's office, she
walked back toward the bedroom she shared with Diana—who
had already disappeared down the stairs to the kitchen, saying
she would starve to death if she didn't get something to eat *tout
suite*. Well, at least Diana had picked up some French! All Mary
wanted, after meeting with Dr. Freud, was to wash her face and
put on something more comfortable than a walking suit. As she
passed the study, she heard something—what was it? A regular sound, low but steady. . . . Sobs, they were sobs, she could
hear them through the door. It was Justine! And she sounded as
though she were sobbing her heart out.

Sure enough, when Mary opened the door—it seemed
impolite, but helping her friend was more important than
politeness—she saw Justine sitting on the sofa, with her head
in her hands. Her shoulders were shaking, and she was crying
with a sort of abandon that was frightening in Justine, who was
always so gentle, so very calm. Mary walked over, quickly but
quietly so as not to startle her, and sat down on the sofa beside
her. She put a hand on Justine's arm.

Justine sat up and wiped her eyes with her fingers. Mary
handed her a handkerchief. That is one of the useful things about
Mary: She always seems to have handkerchiefs to hand out.

MARY: I won't if you keep losing them!

"I feel so foolish," said Justine. "But indeed, I could not help myself." Her normally pale face was red and splotchy.

"Is there anything I can do?" asked Mary. What in the world had set Justine sobbing in that way? Had someone been cruel to her? But who would be cruel to her here—not Greta, surely?

As though to answer her unspoken question, Justine handed Mary the book that had been lying open on the sofa, where she had put it. Was it some work of abstruse philosophy? Justine liked to read those, but Mary rather doubted they would make her cry.

"There," said Justine, pointing. "You see?"

Mary looked at the paragraph Justine was pointing to. Just beneath her long, slim painter's finger was written:

> The next morning, at daybreak, I summoned sufficient courage, and unlocked the door of my laboratory. The remains of the half-finished creature, whom I had destroyed, lay scattered on the floor, and I almost felt as if I had mangled the living flesh of a human being. I paused to recollect myself, and then entered the chamber. With trembling hands I conveyed the instruments out of the room; but I reflected that I ought not to leave the relics of my work to excite the horror and suspicion of the peasants; and I accordingly put them into a basket, with a great quantity of stones, and, laying them up, determined to throw them into the sea that very night. . . .

What in the world was this? Mary looked at the cover, on which was written, in gilding on crimson leather, *Frankenstein: A Biography of the Modern Prometheus*. Ah yes, Justine had said she was going to read Mrs. Shelley's book! Well, clearly that had been a bad idea.

"It's a lie," said Mary. "Just a lie, Justine. We know he didn't destroy you—or you wouldn't be sitting here right now, would you? We know Adam killed him on that island."

"Then why did she write it?" asked Justine. "The rest of the book, after that passage—it makes no sense. The monster Adam pursues my father to the Arctic—have you heard anything so improbable, so ridiculous? But reading that, about my own destruction . . . Oh!" And she burst into a fresh set of tears.

Mary put her arms around Justine. How could a woman who felt so frail—well, tall and frail, because Mary barely came up to her shoulder—be so strong? "It's all right, my dear," she said. "Cry all you want to. I'm not Catherine, but I'm here—whether you want to talk or not."

For several more minutes, Justine continued to sob. Then she sniffed and once again wiped away her tears, this time with Mary's handkerchief.

"I'm sorry, Mary," she said. "You would think that a hundred years might have healed those wounds. Sometimes I wish my father had indeed disassembled me and thrown my body parts into the sea, rather than reanimating me."

"You don't mean that," said Mary. "It's better to be alive—it's always better to be alive. Think of flowers, and your paintings, and think of us. What would we do without you? Catherine and Beatrice would miss you, and so would I. Besides, you're the only one who can do anything with Diana. If you had been destroyed, you would not have become my friend, and that would have made me so very sad."

"Ah, you would not have known anything about it!" said Justine, but now she was smiling through her tears.

"You know what I think we need?" said Mary. "We haven't had lunch yet, and it's almost two o'clock. Why don't you and I go down to ask if Frau Schmidt can make us a sandwich or something?"

"Now that is a very sensible suggestion, and one I was about to make myself!" It was Irene, standing in the doorway, dressed as a man in a brown wool suit and looking every inch the respectable

bank clerk or junior partner of an accounting firm. "Oh, honey!"
she said when she saw Justine's face. She walked over to the sofa—
she had a much brisker stride in trousers—and took Justine's face
in her hands. She looked at it searchingly—she did not have to
lean down far, since Justine was so tall, even sitting. Finally, she
said, "You know, Mary's right. What you need is something to eat,
and maybe even a little schnapps. And then some sleep. You're just
tired out, that's half the trouble. Come on, let's have a combination
Austrian lunch and English tea, with cakes and sandwiches—
although I'll stick to my coffee, thank you. I'll ask Frau Schmidt
what she's preparing for us—Greta said lunch would be served as
soon as we all arrived, and I think we're here now. Justine, why
don't you wash your face and meet us in the parlor? And seriously,
honey, it doesn't matter what Mrs. Shelley wrote a million years
ago. You're here. You're alive. That's the important thing."

"Not quite a million," said Justine, smiling. She sniffed—a
long, decided sniff. "Go, and I shall join you presently."

Mary followed Irene out into the hall. "Would you like me to
tell you about our meeting with Dr. Freud this morning?"

"Of course! But first, coffee, and I assure you that Frau Schmidt's
cakes are the best in Vienna. After this morning, I feel just like
Diana—as though my stomach were an endless, empty abyss! I
imagine she headed down to the kitchen as soon as you got back?
That was very smart of her, and probably what the two of you should
have done. So much of mental anguish is simply tiredness or hunger,
I always think, although I would not say that to Sigmund!"

> JUSTINE: Was it necessary to mention my splotchy
> face, Catherine?

> CATHERINE: That's how readers will know the story
> is true. You can't avoid having a splotchy face

when you cry. Unless you're Beatrice, but I'm
almost certain she doesn't cry real tears. It's
probably some kind of sap!

A few minutes later, they were sitting in the parlor again, just
as they had the day before, and much in the same places, as though
they had already become accustomed to these councils of war.
Irene, their general, sat in the middle of the sofa. Diana sat on
one side, with her legs crossed and her feet up on the cushions—
in boots! Mary felt like kicking her, but that would have meant
leaning across Irene and possibly kicking *her* instead. She rather
suspected that Irene would kick back. Why was it that Diana
always brought out her violent tendencies?

Justine and Hannah were sitting in the two armchairs, and
Greta was perched on what Irene had called a pouf, which seemed
a remarkably silly name for a piece of furniture, but then it was
a rather silly piece of furniture—a large, stiff cushion without a
back. How was one supposed to balance on it? But Greta seemed
to manage it perfectly well, leaning forward with her chin in her
hands.

On the low table between them was what might have been an
Austrian lunch, but it made for a very un-English tea. Irene was
finishing a cup of coffee. Justine and Diana had asked for coffee
as well, but Mary would stick to her tea, thank you very much!
She ate the last of a chocolate cake layered with apricot jam, with
a thick layer of chocolate icing on top, that she had to admit was
better than anything she could have had in England.

MRS. POOLE: Well, I never! As though anything on
the continent could be better than honest English
cooking. I'll take a treacle tart any day over some
foreign folderol.

MARY: No offense, Mrs. Poole, but I'll take the
folderol. It had chocolate and jam, you see.

"What I want Diana to do," said Irene, "is memorize the architectural map of the Maria-Teresa Krankenhaus. You'll have only
yourself to rely on in there, you know!" She frowned at Diana, as
though trying impress on her the seriousness of the situation.

"You think I don't know that?" said Diana, contemptuously.
She still had smears of chocolate on her chin.

"If you're caught, Sigmund may not be able to intervene," Irene
continued, as though Diana had not spoken. "So I want you to
take the utmost precaution. Figure out whether there are guards
on the third floor. If so, how many are there and what are their
routines? If you can, make contact with Lucinda, tell her we're
coming to rescue her, and wait for Sigmund to discharge you. But
if the third floor is heavily guarded, sit tight and don't do anything
foolish. Do you understand?"

Diana just crossed her arms and looked obstinate. That was a
danger sign––Mary knew it well. On the other hand, all signs from
Diana were danger signs, and what other options did they have?

"Meanwhile, Justine, Mary, and Greta will take turns watching from the room above the tavern. If something goes wrong,
give a signal of some sort—wave a handkerchief out the window,
for example. They will contact me, and I will contact Sigmund to
get you out. Hannah and I will work on a plan to rescue Lucinda.
Our best bet is probably blackmailing one of the guards. But that
sort of information takes time to gather. We need to know who
visits brothels, who is in debt for gambling on dog fights. Don't
worry," she said as they all sat around the table, worrying. "We'll
figure it out. We always do. Right, girls?" This was to Hannah
and Greta.

"We always have before," said Greta, dubiously. Hannah just

nodded. They did not seem particularly confident about this adventure.

"I've talked to Sigmund on the telephone. Tomorrow morning, I'll drive Diana to his office—so dress like a hysterical teenage girl," said Irene, looking pointedly at Diana.

"How is that any different from an ordinary teenage girl?" asked Diana. She took the last slice of cake without asking if anyone else might want it.

"It *is* an ordinary teenage girl." Irene put her coffee cup down on the table. "But for you, it will be like playing a part. Just pretend to be anxious and frightened. Cry a little, if you can. Don't go walking in there all cocky, or they'll know something is wrong."

"Oh, I'm an excellent actress," said Diana. "Mary won't let me act, but you'll see how convincing I can be!"

"All right," said Irene, giving her that doubtful look one always does give Diana. "Justine, I want you to get some sleep. I think you need it—the last few days have been an enormous strain on all of you, and I don't want you, in particular, overtaxing yourself."

Justine nodded reluctantly. But Mary knew that if she overtired herself, she might have one of those fainting fits that were Justine's single weakness—aside from her tender heart.

> JUSTINE: I don't think a tender heart is a weakness. Compassion makes us human.

> CATHERINE: It is if someone else has to go into your studio to clear out the spiderwebs because you refuse to sweep them away for fear of harming a spider!

> JUSTINE: Who are we to value the large over the small, the powerful over the weak? A spider has as much right to exist as I do.

MRS. POOLE: Not in this house, it doesn't!

"Mary, I want you to get some rest as well," Irene continued. "But first, could you come walk with me in the park? Since we've arrived, you and I have had almost no time to get acquainted."

"Of course," said Mary. Why her? Why her in particular, when Irene hadn't had time to get acquainted with Justine or Diana either? She felt a little—nervous? Apprehensive. What did Irene want to talk to her about?

After they had all risen and Hannah had taken away the remains of their un-tealike tea on a tray, she went back to the bedroom she shared with Diana to fetch her hat and gloves. Her afternoon dress would do, wouldn't it? For a walk in the park, anyway. It was a gray merino wool, and she would take a shawl. Of course it looked like nothing at all next to what Irene had changed into for the afternoon, some sort of burgundy silk embroidered at the neck and hem that must be one of those Aesthetic dresses Beatrice was always talking about. Irene didn't need a corset, with her figure. Really, she could have made an excellent advertisement for the benefits of Rational Dress.

Before leaving the bedroom, Mary glanced at herself in the mirror over the washstand. Plain, plain, plain . . . not unattractive, certainly, but nothing special either. Well, at least she looked respectable, which was what mattered, or so Mrs. Poole had always told her.

MRS. POOLE: Of course it is.

BEATRICE: But Mary, what's special about you is your expression. You're so—alert and intelligent, as though you were always observing the life around you, evaluating it, understanding it. When you look at yourself in the mirror, you have no expression on your face, except perhaps the common anxiety of women looking at themselves in mirrors—we all have that, I think. So you don't see what everyone else is seeing.

MARY: You're very kind, Bea, but I didn't ask to be complimented. I can't help that Catherine put those thoughts in my head. I'm not even sure I was thinking them at the time.

CATHERINE: But you do think them, don't you?

"Ready?" asked Irene, who was waiting in the front hall. She had put on a hat with black feathers that curved down over the brim and almost touched her cheek, very elegant and probably very expensive. "Come into the garden, Mary, for the black bat, night, has flown, or whatever it was Lord Tennyson said. Something something something and the musk of the rose is blown—I don't remember the rest. In my own way, I'm a good psychologist! I know that Justine needs sleep, and that you need to get out and walk around. Come to the park, and we'll talk."

They walked down the front stairs to the courtyard, then through the arched front entrance where carriages could drive in and out. Once they were on Prinz-Eugen Strasse, Mary expected them to turn left or right, but instead Irene led her across the street to the long stone wall. In the wall was a recessed door. Irene took a key out of her purse.

Where in the world were they going? When Irene saw Mary's expression, she laughed her deep, melodious opera singer's laugh. "Oh, my dear, you didn't think I was taking you to an ordinary park, did you? Welcome to the Belvedere!"

CHAPTER XI

A Conversation with Irene

To Mary's left was a long, rectangular garden—not like Regent's Park, with its perennial beds, but resembling a Turkish carpet, all flat swirls and curlicues of color made by bedded flowers carefully arranged around blue fountains. She thought it looked artificial, although the vista was magnificent. The garden sloped down, down, down to a stone building at its foot, over which she could see the city of Vienna with its rooftops rising up again, and behind them the green hills.

And to her right —well, there was another stone building. It was a palace, enormous and . . . palatial. That was really the only word she could think of. If someone had asked her to define the word palace, she could have pointed to that—classical in style and as elegant as a seashell, if a seashell had a hundred rooms, shining white in the afternoon light. Although it was getting on toward evening— orange and pink were just beginning to touch the sky.

"It's . . . ," she began.

"Much too big, and terribly out of date—who would want to live in such a mausoleum?" Irene looked up at it critically.

"Who does live in it?" asked Mary.

"A friend of mine—well, friend is an elastic term, when you're in my business. Let's just say that we find our acquaintance mutually satisfactory. When I told Franz that I like to walk here in the evenings, he gave me the key so I would stop picking the lock, which set a bad example, he claimed. I've told him that he should move someplace he actually enjoys living and turn this pile into an art museum, open it up to the people of Vienna. Can you imagine how much it would help the artists of this city if they could hang their artwork in a place like that? Gustav and Koloman and Max . . . Well, they shall have to make their revolution without state patronage. They will make it nevertheless, believe me. But I didn't bring you here to talk about art, Mary."

"What did you bring me here to talk about?" Was that too blunt? But then Irene was blunt—probably because she was American. One felt that bluntness would not be rude around her.

"Let's walk under the trees. I love seeing the sun set over Vienna, but the garden is nothing much to talk about. The Viennese, alas, have not taken to the English habit of informal plantings."

"I wondered about that. It seems so . . . flat. I was just thinking that it looks like a carpet."

"It's meant to be admired, not walked in. You can only see it properly from the second-floor windows, and from there it's quite impressive, although too precise for my taste. Come on, let's stroll down the avenue. 'Stroll' is the right word for a place like this." Irene took her arm. They walked in silence until they reached the shadow of the trees—chestnut trees, Mary thought, really rather elegant growing like this, in long rows. Then, Irene said, "How are you, Mary? That's what I wanted to ask. Since you've gotten here, Diana's been doing just fine—she's in her element, excited at going into a madhouse and proud as a peacock. I'm just worried she's going to try rescuing Lucinda Van Helsing by herself, for the glory of it. And Justine—she's been despondent, depressed, which makes perfect sense. This is the closest she's been to her home in a hundred years. She's speaking the language of her childhood, tasting food she last ate as Justine Moritz. Of course it would bring up emotions and recollections. And reading that book—the way she's responding is unfortunate, but perfectly natural. You, however . . ."

Irene paused for a moment, and they walked on in silence. Now they had come to a small stone house surrounded by shrubs and wildflowers—the first informal planting Mary had seen in this place. It made her feel a little more at home. Irene smiled. "This used to be a menagerie. There was a lion here, if you can believe it—Prince Eugen himself would look down from the second-floor windows to admire his menagerie, with the lion at its center. Poor lion . . . I'm sure it would rather have been roaming an African savanna than living in splendid captivity. By the way, I've seen no sign that you're still being followed by anyone from the Société des Alchimistes. Which tells us one of two things."

"What are those?" Mary was rather relieved that the conversation seemed to have moved away from her.

"Either they're not very good at this spying business, or so phenomenally good that I can't detect their emissaries. To be honest, I suspect the former."

"Why is that?" Mary asked.

"Because Waldman was clearly an amateur. He followed you on the ferry, then got on the same train from Calais, knowing you were unlikely to get out before Paris. It was, after all, the only stop where you could take a train farther east. Then he seized the chance of sharing a cabin with Justine. It was clearly a spur of the moment decision, and a bad one. Instead, he should have found a cabin farther down that train car and stayed in it with his friend, watching you from a distance rather than making contact. I've been wondering why he was stupid enough to use his own name, but at that point he could not have helped it—he had to use whatever was on his papers and luggage. I don't think he was supposed to make contact with you at all. Someone—whoever sent him in the first place—is going to be very angry. But you haven't answered my question. How are you, Mary?"

How was she? Mary did not know what to say. That was the problem in a nutshell—she did not know. She shook her head and opened her mouth, as though about to answer, but no words came out.

Irene waited. It occurred to Mary that if Irene Norton was really a spy, she was probably a very patient woman, like a spider in the middle of many webs. She was used to waiting.

"Dr. Freud said he would like to see me again," she said, finally.

"I just bet he would!" Irene laughed. "He collects beetles of all sorts, and you resemble a gray beetle that seems ordinary, but shine a light on it and it begins to shimmer like an opal—blue and green, all cool colors for you, I think. You know, when all of you had just arrived here, I admired your self-control. Here you were in a strange country, determined to rescue a woman you didn't know from a danger you didn't understand, all because a friend had asked you to. You were tired from a long journey, yet there you were, coolly making plans. Then later I realized it wasn't self-control at all— -it's simply the way you are, like Sherlock. He can't help it either. When there's a problem to be solved, he sits down and solves it: rationally, efficiently."

Mary opened her mouth to protest.

"I don't mean that you're emotionless, my dear. I just mean that your emotions are, themselves, efficient, rational. Please don't misunderstand me—I admire you very much and I would like to be your friend. But you remind me of Sherlock more than anyone I've ever met."

"I think that's a compliment?" said Mary. "I mean, I find him dreadfully aggravating, sometimes. . . ."

"Don't we all!" said Irene. "But . . . and this is what I was trying to say before. Despite that cool, calm exterior, you seem to be in distress. Am I right?"

"I think you're probably usually right," said Mary.

"Well, yes, of course," said Irene, with a smile that made it clear she was mocking herself rather than agreeing. "So what is it that's distressing you? Do you even know?"

And that was the whole problem—she didn't, not really. "I've never been so far from home before." But that wasn't it. "I suppose the thing is, I've gotten used to a sort of order in my life, a routine. Oh, living with Diana and all the others has interrupted it—the last three months have been nowhere near as quiet as it used to be! And I've been glad of that, really I have."

"But the others—Diana, Justine, and the rest—they've been living in *your* house, with you as their leader. Don't shake your head at me, Miss Jekyll! I know your club has no official leader, but you're the unofficial one nevertheless. And here all your routines are disrupted, all your plans subject to revision. No wonder you feel as though the ground is slipping out from under you."

Mary walked on for a while in silence. Then she said, "I thought I wanted adventure."

"You *do* want adventure," said Irene. "We none of us want to stagnate, to live behind closed curtains all our lives for fear the sun will fall on us too strongly—that was quite poetic of me, wasn't it? You're just not used to it, so you've gotten drunk on it, and now you have a hangover. That wasn't quite as poetic . . . ah well. And for all your strength, Mary, you have a weakness that Justine and I don't."

"What's that?" Mary felt half resentful and half curious. What was Irene going to say? And did she want to hear it?

"You can't punch a wall, or kick down a door, or burst into tears. For most of us, emotions are a safety valve—but not, I think, for you. I don't think you're capable of letting yourself go in that way, nor do I think it would bring you any satisfaction. Rather, it would be a further source of distress. What you need is a safety valve—something violent, but calm and rational. I know! Target practice!" Irene looked very pleased with herself. "You see, I can diagnose you as well as Sigmund, and I won't even charge you for my services."

Mary laughed. How long had it been since she had laughed? She could not remember. "That reminds me of a certain London gentleman of my acquaintance who is in the habit of shooting at his parlor wall!"

"I told you that you were like him!" said Irene. "Just for goodness' sake avoid some of his less healthful habits, and I don't mean destroying his wallpaper or playing the violin at all hours."

"What *do* you mean?" asked Mary.

"Oh, nothing. Ask John Watson sometime. Look, the sky is on fire!"

Indeed, the sky over Vienna was a blaze of oranges and pinks and yellows—all the colors of sunset.

"You know him so much better than I do," said Mary. "Do you think you might return to London someday? He would probably . . . I mean, Dr. Watson said you were the love of his life."

Irene looked at her in astonishment and then burst out laughing. "Oh, sweetheart! John is a wonderful man, a war hero—brave, loyal, kind. But there's so much he will never understand. Sherlock and I get along so well because we're complete opposites. In habits, temperament, the choices we make. Me and Sherlock—I don't think so. Honestly, I don't think any woman could be happy with a man like him, and I certainly never could be. I married Godfrey because I wanted what any woman wants—passion, devotion. I wanted to be loved like a woman, not a mystery to be solved. I would never be happy with Sherlock, and I seriously doubt that

he would be happy with me. Look, the first star!" She pointed up
at the sky, which was beginning to turn violet at the edges. Mary
followed her finger. Yes, there was the evening star, shining down
just as it did in London.

"Except maybe . . . I wonder if he would make you happy,
Mary?" Irene looked at her speculatively. "You're not quite like
any other woman, are you?"

"I would never presume—" Mary began, in confusion.

"Oh, honey," said Irene, taking her arm again. "Give me *some*
credit for knowing how a twenty-year-old *Fräulein* thinks. I was
there once too, you know. Come on, let's get back. If Diana
doesn't have dinner soon, she's going to destroy something, and I
have too many nice things to let that happen."

"Twenty-one," said Mary. "I'm twenty-one."

Irene laughed and pulled her along under the chestnut trees.
"Same difference."

> MARY: Why is this book so much more embarrassing
> than the last one?

> CATHERINE: Because you did more embarrassing
> things?

> MRS. POOLE: When she visited, Mrs. Norton said
> my treacle tart was the best she'd ever tasted, so
> how's *that* for your fancy European cakes?

> DIANA: Did you say treacle tart? I want a treacle tart.

By the time they got back to the apartment, Frau Schmidt had
already prepared a dinner of chicken in red sauce, with potatoes
and pickles.

MARY: It's called a *paprikas*. Pronounced *"ash."*

DIANA: And it is seriously the best food in the *entire* world.

The next morning, after Diana had kicked her awake, unintentionally for once (she must have been having a particularly active dream), Mary had a serious talk with the incorrigible Miss Hyde.

"Wake up," she said, shaking Diana by the shoulder. "I don't want you trying anything heroic, do you understand?"

"Go away," said Diana, without opening her eyes. "What are you doing here anyway? Go back to your own room." She pulled a pillow over her head.

"We're in Vienna. Don't you remember? To rescue Lucinda Van Helsing. Do *not* try to rescue her by yourself. Gather as much information as you can, let her know that we're working on a way to get her out, and then wait for Dr. Freud to come release you."

"Of course," said Diana from under the pillow. "That's the plan. Don't I always stick to the plan?"

"No," said Mary. "If you stuck to the plan, you wouldn't be in Vienna at all. But this is really, really important. If you try any heroics, you're going to get caught, and then we'll need to rescue the both of you—which will be inconvenient for us, and embarrassing for you. That is, if we can even pull it off. You might have to stay in the Maria-Theresa Krankenhaus forever! So don't try it."

"All right, whatever," said Diana, pushing the pillow off herself and onto the floor. "What's for breakfast?"

It did not much matter, because they had to eat so quickly. There were pastries and coffee in the dining room, but Irene told Diana to grab a couple of the pastries and drink her coffee as quickly as possible.

"Just drink it down, there's a good girl," she said, looking at her wristwatch. "It's almost cold anyway. We're supposed to meet Sigmund in an hour, and I don't know what traffic will be like on the Ringstrasse. Mary, you and Justine will go set up the observation post. At least one of you should be there at all times. Greta will help you, and you will always have either her or Hannah with you. Diana, remember, if you're in trouble, find a way to signal. A handkerchief out the window, a nightie, something that can be seen with binoculars. We'll send word to Sigmund, who'll come get you out. And if he can't—well, I don't know yet, but we'll do something. Come on . . . and that's not the right hat. You need something more frivolous if you're going to impersonate an average teenage girl. Try this one."

Diana, looking sufficiently frivolous in a confection of peach netting, followed Irene out the door, dodging a kiss from Mary along the way. "Remember!" Mary called after her. "No heroics!" Diana made what looked, to Mary, like a rude gesture, but as the door was already closing behind her, it was difficult to tell.

DIANA: It was a rude gesture.

MRS. POOLE: Knowing you, it would be.

Mary turned to Justine. "Ready?"

Justine just nodded. She was looking more composed this morning, after the emotional storms of the day before. "I'll be fine," she said. "Really, don't look at me so inquisitively. Irene was right: I needed some sleep and time to be alone. I'm better now, a little. Enough."

"All right," said Mary, doubtfully. She was still worried, but when Hannah came in to tell them that their cab was waiting below, they followed her down the stairs and into the courtyard.

At the inn, Greta was waiting for them in the third-floor

room. It was obvious that she had been sleeping on the narrow bed. The room had been made slightly less uncomfortable by the addition of thick pillows, a wool blanket, and a worn carpet for the floor. There were boxes of crackers and tins of soup stacked against one wall. On the rickety table was a spirit lamp over which food could be cooked, in a simple fashion. By the window was a set of binoculars and a retractable telescope.

"I'm glad you're here," said Greta when they arrived. "And not simply because of the pastries, although they are most appreciated!" Justine had brought several for her, wrapped in wax paper by Frau Schmidt. Greta took one, bit into it, and said through a mouthful of jam, "There is something worrying me."

"What is it?" asked Mary.

"Look down there," said Greta, pointing toward the street. "In the shadows by that building next to the wall of the Krankenhaus—it is a tobacconist's. And there, on the other corner, by that greengrocer's. You can see it better through the telescope."

Mary expanded the telescope and looked where Greta was pointing, but could not see anything strange or out of the ordinary. At the greengrocer's, a woman was putting potatoes into her string bag, and there was no one in front of the tobacconist's, although a moment later a man emerged puffing on a pipe. She wondered if Sherlock would have been able, at this distance, to deduce what tobacco he was smoking.

"I don't see anything in particular," she said. "Am I supposed to?"

"He may have moved," said Greta. "Sometimes they are there, sometimes not, and not always the same men—but always in the shadows. I think they are watching the Krankenhaus. That is only an intuition, you understand, but Madame Norton has taught me to trust my intuition. It will show you the truth when logic cannot, she always says."

Sherlock would certainly not agree with that! He had always

told Mary that intuition could lead you astray. Perhaps Irene was right, and the two of them would not have been compatible after all.

"What do these men do?" asked Justine.

"Nothing. That's what is so odd. They are not beggars or peddlers. They simply stand, sometimes looking down at the pavement, sometimes up at the walls of the Krankenhaus. Never many, two or three at a time. But there is something about them—they remind me of dogs that smell a rat in a drainpipe, and wait and wait for it to come out."

Mary frowned, worried. What Greta was describing reminded her of the last time they had been watched, by the Beast Men that Edward Prendick had created. But surely all the Beast Men had died in the fire? And Prendick himself was in London, not here in Vienna. Once again she wished that Catherine could have come with them. Perhaps Greta was imagining things? After all, she was Austrian, and Austrians were a romantic people.

> BEATRICE: Not any more so than the English! If you
> do not think the English are romantic, you have
> not read your national poets—Wordsworth,
> Coleridge, Scott . . .

> MRS. POOLE: I don't know what poetry's got to do
> with it. The English are a sensible people, always
> have been, always will be.

> BEATRICE: Except about the Queen and Empire!

> MARY: For goodness' sake, don't get into a political
> discussion with Mrs. Poole. Do you want our
> supper burnt? Not that it would matter to you, I
> suppose. How do you even burn weed soup?

Anyway, if there were strange men watching the Krankenhaus, there was nothing they could do about it now but observe, and wait.

"There they are," said Justine suddenly. Had she seen the men Greta was describing? No, there was Dr. Freud alighting from a cab just outside the gates of the Krankenhaus. He was greeted by one of the guards, and then he helped Diana out.

It was Diana, wasn't it? Even from this distance, Mary could tell that the girl following the doctor was slender, delicate, frightened. All her gestures seemed to proclaim her reluctance to enter those gates, and he was like a coaxing father, gently urging her forward.

Well! Diana was a good actress after all. Who would have thought she could play such a part?

DIANA: I *told* you!

Mary did not like seeing her go through those gates or disappear into the Krankenhaus itself, whose front doors seemed to swallow her up like a giant maw. Three days, she told herself. She would see her sister in three days.

"Well," she said, when she could no longer see either Diana or Freud, and the guard had returned to his post. "Now what?"

"Now," said Greta, "we wait."

They waited.

The hours passed slowly. One of them always kept watch. The other two read—Greta had provided them with a stack of books and magazines, although the magazines were in German and only one of the books was in English. Mary soon tired of *The Complete Poems of William Wordsworth*. Sometimes Justine sketched in a notebook she had brought with her. Sometimes, while Justine was watching, Greta taught Mary card games, at which she was better than she had expected. Sometimes one of them would go out to use the rather unsanitary restroom down the hall. Eventually, they had a sort of luncheon, and then a sort of supper, although the tinned food and crackers were not particularly appetizing.

When darkness fell, Mary, whose turn it was to watch, said to Greta, "I understand what you mean, now—about instinct. I don't know what it is, but I don't like them either, standing in the shadows like that. They even seem to avoid the street lamps. They're just watching, that's all. But watching what? Could they be guards for the Krankenhaus, disguised as ordinary men?"

"I do not know," said Greta, coming to the window. "They don't look like guards, though. The guards are mostly former soldiers. They have a way of holding their heads, as military men do. You can tell they have drilled and marched and obeyed orders. Those men in the shadows, not so."

"Then I don't know either," said Mary. She watched them because there was nothing else to watch with the binoculars, other than the ordinary routine of the Krankenhaus—guards changing, wagons filled with provisions going in and coming out empty, morning and evening. Might that eventually be their way in, and then out with Lucinda Van Helsing? Meanwhile, the men in the shadows did nothing.

Mary did nothing either, or nothing worth mentioning. She watched. She waited. Sometimes she slept. The three of them had arranged to sleep in turns, in the narrow bed—one at a time, so two of them would always be awake. And the hours kept passing.

Early next morning, Hannah arrived with a message from Irene—how were they, had anything happened, here was a salami, some poppy seed buns, and a jar of plum jam from Frau Schmidt. Gratefully, they ate slices of salami and buns smeared with jam. But they had nothing to report.

By that evening, Mary was heartily tired of staring at the

Krankenhaus. She had grown familiar with its bricks, blackened with soot. She had started ignoring the men who continued to lurk in the shadows, two or three at a time. After all, they did nothing but lurk—and sometimes smoke! That morning, they had been joined by a new man, who sat cross-legged by the walls of the Krankenhaus. But he seemed to be a beggar, a real one—he actually begged. Once, several of the guards walked by and told him to move on. He moved to the tobacco shop, and sat there with his hat in front of him. The other men stayed in the shadows, watching, smoking, eventually walking away only to be replaced by new ones. And that was all. Honestly, had she ever been so bored in her life? As she had throughout the day, she wondered what Diana was doing.

Meanwhile, Diana was mad. Of course, she was officially mad—she was, after all, an inmate in the Maria-Theresa Krankenhaus. But she was angry-mad, and at herself, which was a new and uncomfortable sensation.

She had been in the Krankenhaus for two whole days, and had not found Lucinda Van Helsing. Of course *she*, Diana, should have found Lucinda right away. Wasn't she the cleverest of them all?

That, at least, is what Diana believed.

> DIANA: If you're going to write from my point of view, then really write from my point of view. None of this "Diana believed" bullshit.

> MARY: Where, *where*, do you learn words like that?

> DIANA: What's wrong with words like that? It's all language, ain't it?

> MARY: Now you're just trying to provoke me.

The first night after Freud had committed her, she had picked the lock on her door and stolen out of her room. It had been easy peasy, just as she thought it would be. On slippered feet, for the inmates of the Krankenhaus were not allowed boots, she had explored the dark halls of the asylum. Although it was so well-guarded on the first floor, perhaps *because* it was so well guarded, there were no guards on the second floor—only a station where the female nurses sat, when they were not with patients. Presumably there was a similar arrangement in the men's wing. It had been long after midnight, when all the patients were presumably asleep. The night nurses sat in the nursing station in case of emergencies, knitting or gossiping among themselves. Walking around the second floor had been easy, and she had already taken the uniform of an asylum attendant, left just lying there for anyone to steal in a locked cupboard. Now it was hidden under her mattress. But of course, Lucinda was on the third floor, not the second . . . that was the whole problem.

Her first day, she had learned the routine of the Krankenhaus. Freud has signed her in, and she had met, briefly, with the director, a large man with red cheeks whose name sounded like coughing and who resembled a choleric pig, as though one of the Three Little Pigs from the fairy tale had grown up into a man. He had looked at her with a false smile filled with crooked teeth and said, "I am so sad, Miss Frank, to hear that you have become ill, but it is good that you have come to our beautiful city of Vienna to be treated by Dr. Freud. He is developing quite an international reputation, is he not?" The director nodded at Freud as though pleased, but Diana could tell he was not pleased at all. "So, you shall be staying with us for a little while, yes?"

"Just until her father returns from Berlin," said Freud. "I am very sorry, although not at all surprised, that she should have suffered this attack of nerves while he is away. We expect him back on Thursday, when I shall return, Miss Frank, to remand you to his custody. Meanwhile, we must make sure that you become strong and healthy again, must we not? And here in the Maria-Theresa Krankenhaus, you shall come to no harm, even from yourself."

"Yes, our patients are not allowed scissors or any other sharp implements," said the director. "Even needles are forbidden here, for the safety of our inmates—or rather, patients. If I may ask . . ."

"I stuck myself with a hatpin," said Diana in a shy, breathy voice that Mary would scarcely have recognized. She hid her face in her hands. "Over and over. I could not help myself."

"Very bad, very bad," said the director, in the same tone of voice he would have used to say *Very good, very good.* "We must make certain that the English miss does not do such a thing again. The second-floor matron will take your hat, with its offending pin—you will find that we do not need hats here!"

Sure enough, when Freud had taken her up to the second floor, a grim-looking woman in a gray uniform had taken her hat, her coat, her purse—anything other than the clothes she was wearing. Fortunately, as Freud had told her, second-floor patients, meaning the ones who paid, were permitted to keep their own clothes and allowed to bring comforts from home as long as they were of the most innocuous sort—pillows, books that were not French, photographs. The set of lock-picking implements that Irene had given her were well-hidden, sewn into the lining of her dress so cunningly that only a trained eye could have spotted them. She had watched Hannah sew them in herself. Sewing did, after all, have its uses! Perhaps someday she would learn to sew like that—after her experiences at the Magdalen Society, she had assumed that sewing was a boring waste of time. But if it helped you pick locks? If she could not make it as an actress, she might become a burglar, and such skills would come in handy.

The matron had spoken to Freud in rapid German, looking Diana up and down with disapproval—but she probably looked that way at everyone. Her frown was etched into her forehead.

"She says you will get everything back when you depart," said Freud. "You will be well here, yes? No more hysterical episodes, no more sticking the hatpin in the arm. You will rest and grow better, Miss Frank. I have asked for a very good room for you, with a view that you will like." Whether or not the matron could speak English, Freud was playing his part. That meant she would be in a room on the side of the Krankenhaus where Mary and Justine would be watching. They had not been absolutely sure whether he would be able to arrange for a room on that side—not that it mattered, since she wasn't planning on asking for help. When had she ever needed help before? "And you will have an attendant who speaks a little English—only a little, but it will be a comfort to you, to have someone who speaks your language. Now you must rest, Miss Frank. I will come for you at the appointed time. No unusual exertions between now and then, you understand?"

"Of course, Doctor," said Diana, with lowered eyes. Oh, Mrs. Poole would scarcely have recognized her!

Then he had taken her hand, pressing it with a final meaningful look—of course he could not say anything in front of the matron, but Diana could tell he was concerned. Well, he didn't need to be! She was Diana Hyde, and this was going to be easy peasy.

Then the matron had led her down a long hallway to her room, told her in German that she should rest—Diana could tell only because the dour woman pantomimed it at the same time, which almost made Diana laugh—and locked her in.

The room looked comfortable in a bland, impersonal way, like a mediocre hotel. Since she did not know what that night would bring, Diana lay down on the bed. She would close her eyes for a moment, just a moment, and make plans for the night. . . .

She was woken by the door opening, and remembered just in time where she was. "Hello, hello!" said the girl who had opened the door. She was not much older than Diana, dressed in the uniform of an attendant. She was pushing a cart with several trays of food on it. Well, well—it must be time for lunch.

"Klara," she said, pointing to herself. She was plump, and pretty despite her uniform—it was rather a feat, looking pretty with all one's hair pulled back into a white cap. She had a particularly wide, friendly smile—quite the opposite of the matron! She could not have been much older than Diana, but a large key-ring hung at her side, jangling with what looked like all the keys to the women's wing. It made her look very responsible.

"Dinner, yes? I speak leettle English," she said, taking a tray off the cart and putting it on a table in front of the window, which also looked as though it could be used for correspondence or whatever else tables were used for. It was the only one in the room.

"I don't speak German," said Diana, shaking her head and smiling back. This must be the attendant Freud had mentioned. "And that is lunch, not dinner."

"Lunch?" said Klara. "Lunch." She looked pleased with herself.

Diana sat down at the table. What in the world was that? On the plate was a waxy ball of cooked dough, the approximate size of a cricket ball, surrounded by some sort of watery stew.

"*Das ist ein Knödel,*" said Klara. "I come again, yes?" Then off she went, to deliver her other trays. *Knödel?* It tasted like Yorkshire pudding without any of the flavor. Diana missed Frau Schmidt's cooking! She ate half of it and tossed the other half out the window. The birds could have it. Yes, *Knödel* was definitely for the birds!

MRS. POOLE: Diana not finishing everything on her plate? I don't believe it.

DIANA: You've never tasted *Knödel*. It's like what they make walls out of.

Soon after she finished lunch, Klara returned for the tray. "Come," she said, pushing the cart in front of her. Diana followed her down the hall into a sort of common room, in which women were sitting in plush armchairs or on either side of a long central table. Some were talking to one another in low voices. Some were reading what looked like fashion magazines. One, sitting by the window, was singing softly to herself. The ones along the table were drawing with pastel crayons—there were no pencils, no paintbrushes. Were they considered too dangerous? There was a nurse sitting at the table as well, in the usual gray uniform and white cap. She smiled at Diana in the way nurses smile, as though you were a not particularly interesting insect they had just noticed, he kept under observation in case you were dangerous. Several other patients looked at her curiously, but did not greet her. d, yes?" said Klara, then waved goodbye and pushed her down the hall. So this was what madwomen did in the sat around and read fashion magazines, or drew silly d not seem so different from what most women did ry lives. Wealthy women, that is. Poor women had do than draw, or read magazines, or go mad!

think to get into conversations with several of them,
Krank might provide her with information on the
simply h none of them spoke English. Well, she would
By that she needed to know herself!

kicking son an hour, she was so bored that she felt like
herself by co ut of course that would not do. She amused
looking out the to be small and frail and nervous, sometimes
toward the inn w. Like the window of her room, it looked
ing, but they wou she knew Mary and Justine were watch-
tried to draw for a t be able to see her at that distance. She
she had imagined. H e, and discovered that it was harder than

did Justine manage to make all those

flowers look different from one another? Once, reminding herself to stay in character, she fidgeted and scratched at her arm.
The woman sitting next to her, who was drawing a tree that
actually looked like a tree, put a hand on Diana's, as though to
stop her. When she saw the scar on Diana's arm, from that day
she had cut herself in the Society of St. Mary Magdalen—had
it really only been three months ago?—she shook her head and
said, "*Non, ma chérie. Vous devez arrêter de faire cela. Vous êtes trop
jeune et jolie.*" Diana smiled, nodded, and continued drawing a
flower that looked like a bunch of noses stuck together.

After a period of time that seemed interminable but was
probably only a couple of hours, Klara came to take her back to
her room. "Sleep, yes? *Schlaf. Dormir.*" As the matron had that
morning, she mimed going to sleep, using her hands as pillow
Evidently, it was once again time to nap! This time Diana was n
tired at all—bored, yes, but not tired. However, she lay in
with her eyes closed, in case Klara or one of the nurses, or
the matron, chose to visit her. She visualized the archite
map Greta had shown her. The Krankenhaus was arranged
wings: men's and women's. They were connected by a cer
with a staircase, from the first floor to the third. From
ran two perpendicular corridors into the two wings,
building formed the shape of a cross. The patients'
arranged along those long, narrow hallways. All Di
was unlock her door, go down the corridor in the third
to the central hall, climb the stairs, and she woul one floor
floor. Lucinda's room would be along that same rded. How
up. Easy peasy, unless of course the third floor at all . . .
bored she was! She lay awake, not sleepy at all through a dark
Suddenly she was on the third floor, w be a forest on the
forest—it did not surprise her that there sh ked like a wolf. Any
third floor of the Krankenhaus. The guard

moment now he would find her and eat her up! But her red cloak would protect her, she was sure of that. After all, hadn't it been given to her by her mother? The wolf might howl, the wolf might bite, but Little Red Riding Hood was the most fearsome predator in this forest!

She was startled awake by a key turning in the lock. It was Klara, with what was evidently her dinner: boiled vegetables and more *Knödel*. She ate the vegetables and half the *Knödel*, because after all she needed to keep up her strength, then threw the rest of it out the window. As she did so, she saw that the sun was starting to set. Soon, her real day would begin.

> MARY: It's a good thing we didn't see you throwing the *Knödel* out the window. We might have thought it was a signal for help!

> DIANA: It would have been. A few more days of that diet, and I would have starved to death!

There were several things Diana established that first night. As long as she avoided the nurses, who mostly stayed in their station after midnight, she could roam about as she wished on the second floor, which housed the patients who had been admitted voluntarily or on their doctors' orders. On the first floor there were guards, but no patients—only administrative offices. These were useless to her anyway, so once she established that the first floor was securely guarded, she did not venture down again. The third floor was more complicated. At the top of the stairs, in the central hall between the men's and women's wings, sat a single guard. He sat there all night long, and as far as Diana could determine, he did not move except to, once every hour, get up, stretch, and walk up and down the length of the hall. He walked up the hall to the back window, then down the hall to the front window. Then back to his seat. That was it. As far as she could tell, he never left his post.

He had to leave sometime, if only to take a piss? But Diana watched for three hours from an alcove by the staircase that had probably, in the architect's mind, been intended for a statue of some sort. She stood as still as a statue, until the stairwell began to grow infinitesimally brighter from the approach of dawn. As long as she watched, he just sat on his hard wooden chair, smoking a pipe and reading from what looked like a prayer book— she could see his lips move. Every hour, he took his walk up and down, always within her sight. True, while walking up the hall he did have his back to her, but never for long enough that she could reach and pick the lock of the women's wing. She tried it once, and was almost seen. He never closed his eyes, and his routine never varied. It was very frustrating.

Finally, she had to go back to her room on the second floor, locking the door behind her, to begin a new day of flavorless gruel for breakfast, drawing in the common room with the other female patients, *Knödel* for lunch (this time with sausage), back to the common room to look through magazines or stare out the window, and *Knödel* for dinner (with a side order of despair or spinach, it didn't much matter which). At least she could work on Klara! When the attendant brought her breakfast, she said, "Klara, I think there is a friend of mine here—she is also sick, like me. Have you seen her? Perhaps I shall meet her today in the room where we all go to—" do nothing. But she did not finish her sentence.

Klara smiled and shook her head. "Slow please? I not so good English."

Diana signed. "Well, I not at all German, so you're ahead of me. My friend—Lucinda Van Helsing." She spoke slowly, the words distinct. "Girl—*Fräulein*—here." What did Lucinda look like? She didn't even know.

"Ah, Lucinda!" said Klara. "No, not here, three floor." She sat down beside Diana on the bed and took her hand. "No good," she said with an expression of sympathy. "How say—no so good, sick here." She pointed to her head. "Here." And she pointed to her stomach.

"She's sick? How sick?" asked Diana. But Klara merely shook her head. Perhaps she did not want to distress Lucinda's friend, perhaps she simply could not express what she meant in English. Whatever the reason, this was all Diana was likely to get out of her.

"Go now?" said Klara. "Make pretty *Blumen*." She mimed drawing.

"All right," said Diana. "I'll go draw some"—*bloody*, but she did not say that—"flowers."

As she sat at the table in the common room, drawing blue and green and purple flowers—the most unflowerlike colors she could find—she once again went over her mental map of the Krankenhaus. Last night, she had purloined an attendant's uniform from the closet next to the nursing station. That might come in handy, but it would not get her past the guard. What she needed was a distraction. But what?

The biggest problem with the Krankenhaus was the boredom. That in and of itself would have been enough to drive anyone mad. By afternoon, Diana was ready to tear someone's hair out—maybe even her own. But at last she had a plan. It had come to her at lunch, when she had heard Klara's keys clinking against one another. There was something pleasant and authoritative about the sound.

"*So schöne Blumen!*" said Klara, after putting her dinner tray on the table. She pointed to Diana's latest drawing, a mass of green squiggles. Seriously, she had given up on the flower business.

Knödel. Knödel Knödel Knödel. The only advantage of *Knödel* was that it could be eaten with a spoon, no fork or knife required. As

Diana reached for her napkin, to put it on her lap (wouldn't Mary be proud of her?), her elbow knocked against the tray. Bang! Metal clattered against the floor, porcelain smashed, and there was the *Knödel* in the middle of it all, miraculously undamaged. The broth that had accompanied it was everywhere, but mostly on Klara.

"Oh, I'm so sorry! So, so sorry," said Diana. "I am so terribly clumsy. How could I have done such a stupid, clumsy thing? I must stick something sharp into myself, to punish myself for such clumsiness and stupidity!"

"Nein, nein, es ist nichts," said Klara, putting a hand on Diana's arm, as though to stop her from doing anything to herself. Diana felt just a twinge of guilt—Klara seemed more concerned about her distress than about the fact that she had broth all down her uniform. But it had been necessary. "Is nothing, no," she continued. "I go more *Knödel*, for dinner, yes?"

"Sure," said Diana. "More *Knödel*, whatever." More food for the birds. She hoped the birds liked wallpaper paste. Hidden in her left hand were four keys from Klara's key ring.

At last, night came, her second night in the Krankenhaus. Beatrice might have thought of something poetic—at last you descend, oh night! Justine would probably have uttered some grand philosophical thought. But she was Diana, so all she thought was: *About bloody time.* If she did not establish contact with Lucinda Van Helsing tonight, she would only get one more chance. After midnight, after all the lights in the Krankenhaus had been extinguished, she put on the attendant's uniform, tucking her red curls under the white cap, which itched a little.

Pick the lock—easy peasy. Walk quietly down the hallway. In the nursing station, there was only one nurse, and she seemed to be knitting something or other. Once you realized that people were generally neither good nor evil, but simply oblivious, you could do pretty much as you pleased—or so Diana had found. Up the stairs, into the alcove. She could see the guard, sitting by the door to the women's wing. What was he doing? Lighting his pipe. He had just lifted the match to the bowl when *clink!* What was that? The noise came from the bottom of the stairs. Would he get up? No, after looking around startled, he had settled back down and was about to light his pipe again. *Clink clink!* Ah, now that must mean something. He stood up and set his prayer book down on the chair, with the box of matches on top. Since the noise had come from the bottom of the stairs, he should investigate. If someone had gotten in—how, he could not imagine, but somehow—and was moving around on the second floor, where the wealthy patients were housed, well, it would mean trouble for sure. Diana could see him thinking, hesitating, then starting down the stairs. Thank goodness, because there was only one key left to throw down the stairwell! She had been worried Klara would notice the missing keys, but she had waited until dinner on purpose. With soup on her uniform, Klara would not be able to finish the dinner service, and she would not need her keys again until the next morning.

Away from the door the guard headed, the probably ten stone of him lumbering down the stairs. He was conveniently loud!

Quick as a wink, she was at the door of the women's wing. It took less than a minute. By the time the guard returned, wondering who had dropped those keys on the second floor, assuming it could only be one of the night nurses, the door would be securely locked behind her.

And *click*, there it was, easy peasy. The hallway stretched before her, built according to the same plan as on the second floor, but oh how different! Here there was no wood paneling. The walls were bare, and probably white in daylight. Now only a little moonlight came through the window at the end of the hall. Unlike on the second floor, the gas lamps here were evidently turned off, and not just down, at night. The doors all had small windows through which patients could be observed, covered by metal grilles. Here, the Krankenhaus looked like what it was, at heart: a prison.

How was she going to find Lucinda Van Helsing? All she knew was that Lucinda was young—only a few years older than she was, according to Irene. It had not occurred to her that there would be no lights on this floor. She thought she would at least be able to see the inmates. Well, if she couldn't see them, then she must do this a more dangerous way. She would look into each room through the metal grille. And then, if necessary, she would ask if the occupant was Lucinda. The first room was easy—even in the darkness, she could see that the occupant had white hair. At the second grille she called "Lucinda," trying to sound both quiet and loud at once, but got no answer. However, from several doors down came a response—*"Ik ben hier."* Where had she heard it from? She walked over to the door from which she thought it had emanated and called through the grille, "I'm looking for Lucinda. Are you Lucinda Van Helsing?" An answer came from the next door over. "Yes, I am here." She looked through that grille. Moonlight came in through the barred window, but the room was still mostly dark. All Diana could see was a white figure sitting on the bed. It was the only piece of furniture in the room.

"I can smell you," came a whisper—from the figure? Yes, but in such a low, hollow voice that it almost seemed to come from the air itself. "Salt. You smell like the ocean. I saw the ocean once, at Bergen aan Zee. It was large, so large. I would like to drown in it."

Was this really Lucinda? Diana was looking for a prisoner—this was a madwoman. She spoke perfectly good English, with an accent of some sort. Wasn't Lucinda Danish, or Norwegian, or something? Maybe that's what she had been speaking, when she first answered.

"Seriously, are you Lucinda?" she whispered through the grille.

"No," said the figure. "I am her ghost, forced to wander the Earth. Or sit here, as the case may be."

Damn it all. Was this Lucinda, or should she keep looking?

"Did Wilhelmina Murray send you?" asked the women who might be Lucinda. "She said she would send you. . . ."

It was Lucinda all right. A prisoner *and* a madwoman! This was going to be even harder than Diana had thought.

Click! went the door when she turned the lockpick. But that was going to be the easy part of it. She shut the door behind her and said to the figure on the bed, who was definitely young, and probably blond, although it was hard to tell, "My name is Diana Hyde. I'm from the Athena Club. Miss Murray sent us your letter."

With two hands that shone white in the moonlight, the girl on the bed pushed back her hair, but all Diana could see were dark, shadowed eyes and sharp cheekbones.

"Too late, too late," she said in her sepulchral voice. "You should have come before I died and went to hell."

What was that supposed to mean? Whatever. It didn't matter, not now. Diana had a job to do, which did not depend on Lucinda Van Helsing's degree of sanity. "I'm supposed to tell you that we're going to rescue you. We just haven't figured out how yet." Despite Mary's warning, she'd been assuming that she would be able to rescue Lucinda by herself. But this basket case? She didn't think so.

Lucinda's hand shot out and clutched Diana's arm in a cold grip, stronger than she had expected. Ow, that hurt! "I will be gone. Even now I am going to that farther shore. I can see it, the black shore, the realm of oblivion."

"And that means what, exactly? Let go, you're hurting me."

Lucinda loosened her grip. "Death. I do not have much longer now."

She turned her face toward the moonlit window, and Diana could see it fully for the first time. She had seen faces like this before, in Whitechapel. Lucinda Van Helsing was starving. Yes, in a couple of days, maybe sooner, she would be dead.

So either Diana rescued her now, or they would lose her altogether. She sighed.

"Come on. I'll get you out somehow. We'll figure it out as we go along."

"Not without my mother," said Lucinda, in a low but perfectly ordinary voice. "She is across the hall, three doors down."

Her mother? But Irene had told them Mrs. Van Helsing was dead. Which meant either Irene had gotten bad information, or Lucinda was completely off her rocker.

Bloody hell. This situation was going from bad to worse.

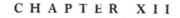

CHAPTER XII

Escape from the Asylum

M y mother needs blood," said Lucinda Van Helsing.
"And what might that mean, exactly?" Diana could
barely see the woman lying on the bed—she was a lump
of shadow under the thin coverlet provided to third-floor patients.
But what she saw—a skeletal arm stretched on the cover, a bony
wrist—did not give her much confidence. This woman was dying.
She could smell death in the room—it smelled like decaying lilies.

"She needs your blood, from your veins," said Lucinda, which
clarified exactly nothing. "To drink," she added. "It will bring
back her strength."

Seriously? "From my veins. You want me to cut open a vein, so
she can drink my blood?"

"Yes," said Lucinda.

Well, why not? She had done worse before. Diana drew the
small but very sharp knife out of her lockpick kit, cut into her forearm (the other one, not the one she had cut into at the Magdalen
Society—now she would have matching scars), and held it just
above Mrs. Van Helsing's mouth, or where she thought it was, by
feel. A dry, thin mouth that moved just a little at the touch of her
fingertips.

There—the cut was directly on it. And suddenly, she felt
something soft, wet—like a cat. Mrs. Van Helsing was licking
her forearm.

MARY: I can *not* believe you did that.

DIANA: What else was I supposed to do? What
would you have done under the circumstances?
Something sensible, no doubt. And Lucinda
Van Helsing would probably still be in the
Krankenhaus, or dead.

MARY: I would have thought of *something* other than
cutting myself so a woman I'd just met could
drink my blood!

DIANA: Technically, I hadn't even met her. I mean, we
hadn't been introduced or anything.

"That's enough!" cried Diana. Now, Mrs. Van Helsing was not
just licking, but sucking, gripping her arm with one strong, bony
hand. How could such a sick, frail creature be so strong?

"*Stop, Moeder!*" said Lucinda. She pulled her mother's hand off
Diana's arm, prying open the skeletal fingers. "Step back!" she
said to Diana. "She does not mean to harm you, but she cannot
help herself."

Diana stepped back. She felt dizzy. How much blood had she
lost?

Lucinda was speaking to her mother, rapidly, insistently, in a
language Diana did not understand. And then she was helping her
mother to sit up, to stand. When Mrs. Van Helsing stepped into
the moonlight, Diana gasped. She looked like someone already
dead, like the corpse of a woman, with dark, haunted eyes—wells
of darkness, she might have thought, if she was in the least poetic.
And so thin! As though she were in the last stages of consumption.
Like her daughter, she had long hair that hung down on either side

of her face, and she was dressed in a white nightgown. On the breast were a scattering of dark spots where Diana's blood had spattered.

Mrs. Van Helsing turned and threw her arms around her daughter with a cry that sounded almost inhuman. *"Mijn dochter, mijn liefste!"* she said. Lucinda had her arms around her mother as well, and she was sobbing—harsh, dry sobs.

For a moment, Diana put her hands over her eyes. She could not stand watching this reunion. It reminded her too much of the day they had taken her mother to St. Bartholomew's hospital, coughing blood into her handkerchief. And then the day Mrs. Barstowe had taken her to the graveyard by the hospital, where her mother had been lowered into a pauper's grave.

DIANA: Do you have to bring that up?

CATHERINE: You thought it, didn't you? That's what you told me. I could see that you were about to cry, even talking about it.

DIANA: Go to hell, you (the rest of this conversation has been omitted, as such language would be inappropriate for our younger readers, or indeed some of our older ones).

All the while, Lucinda was speaking to her mother, presumably explaining their predicament. Mrs. Van Helsing drew back from her daughter and pointed to the window. Then, she stepped to the iron bars and pulled the two central ones apart, bending them as though they were India rubber.

Diana stared, dumbfounded. Who, or what, was Mrs. Van Helsing? How was she still alive, when Irene Norton had told them she was dead? And how could she bend iron bars?

Lucinda turned and said, "My mother says we may escape through the window. We must climb down the wall, like the itsy-bitsy spider."

Trying to stay as far away from Mrs. Van Helsing as possible—the woman might still want her blood—Diana walked to the window and looked down.

"You have *got* to be joking," she said. It was sheer stone, with only the smallest cracks to hold on to, three stories down. And at the bottom? "Even if we make it down without falling, we'll be seen. Look, there are guards patrolling—there, and there." It was a clear, cloudless night. Her dull gray uniform might blend into the gray of the wall, but the moon, almost full, would shine on the white nightgowns. By the time they reached the bottom, guards would be waiting for them. "No, what we need"—it had worked once, it might work again—"is a distraction."

"Distraction—that is *afleiding*," said Mrs. Van Helsing. The woman knew English! Well, a little English, anyway. Her accent was even stronger than Lucinda's.

"Is there a closet on this floor?" asked Diana. "I have an idea—well, the start of one, anyway." Would it work? It would have to.

"I do not know," said Lucinda. "But there must be one, no? For supplies."

"Right," said Diana. "Can you help me look?"

Lucinda said something to her mother in rapid gibberish.

MARY: It was Dutch. The Van Helsings are from Amsterdam.

DIANA: Well, how was I supposed to know that?

MARY: Maybe because we mentioned it over and over again?

DIANA: You're assuming that I listen.

She turned to Diana. "It will be a door without one of the little windows."

"I *know* that!" Did Lucinda think she didn't know that? She wasn't stupid. "Come on." Diana stepped into the hallway, which was much darker than the room had been. If Lucinda thought she was going to be the one in charge . . . well, she just wasn't, that's all.

On the second floor, the closet had been located to the left of the entrance. Sure enough, there was one here too, right where Diana had expected it to be. She picked the lock and opened the door. In the closet, it was pitch black. Ah, she knew that box of matches would come in handy! Good thing she had pinched it off the prayer book, where the night guard had left it, before picking the lock to the women's wing.

> DIANA: Shouldn't you have said that back when I took it?

> CATHERINE: Our readers will naturally have assumed you took it. After all, it's *you*. If you saw a box of matches lying around, of course you would put it in your pocket.

> DIANA: I don't *always* steal.

> JUSTINE: Forgive me, Diana, but you do. I continually have to go into your room to retrieve my books.

> CATHERINE: And my clothes. Why are you always taking my clothes? Why don't you take Mary's?

MARY: And that brooch of my mother's that I said you
could not have.

DIANA: Whatever.

Diana took the box of matches out of her pocket and struck
one. The match flared and the interior of the closet was illumi-
nated by a flickering light. Shelves, filled mostly with what looked
like bedding and cleaning supplies. A mop in a bucket. But would
it contain . . . yes, there they were! Lamps. She had seen lamps in
the closet on the second floor, and had assumed there would be
some up here as well. And yes, there on a shelf were three lamps,
their reservoirs half-filled with kerosene. On the shelf below was
another gray uniform.

Diana lit one of the lamps. There, now she could see properly!
"Put this on," she said, taking down the uniform and handing it
to Lucinda. "I wish there were two, but this is the only one I can
find. I think everything else is sheets and pillowcases and bottles
of disinfectant."

Lucinda nodded. "You will turn around, yes?"

Diana stared at her incredulously. "We're in the middle of a
rescue operation, and you're worried about *modesty?*"

But she turned around, partly because she had been asked,
partly because she found the sight of Lucinda Van Helsing's face
disturbing. It was so very pale, the eyes so very sunken. Why was
she even bothering to rescue someone who was clearly in the last
stages of consumption? Once again she thought of her own mother,
coughing up blood. . . .

"I am ready," said Lucinda.

Well, at least she had been quick. Dressed in the gray hospital
uniform, with her hair up under a cap, she did not look quite so
conspicuous.

"Carry these lamps," said Diana, handing two of them to the newest member of the Krankenhaus staff. Lucinda nodded and took the lamps. She was obeying orders—good. She would need to, if Diana's plan was going to work.

Diana carried the lamp she had lit, and as many of the sheets as she could drape over the other arm. Once they were back in Mrs. Van Helsing's room, she tied the sheets to the bars on the window: some draped out of the window, down the stone walls of the building, some draped into the room. That would create the greatest spectacle.

"Open up the bowls on those two lamps—just lift the burners, like this—and sprinkle the kerosene on the sheets," she said. "We don't have enough to cover everything, but at least it will get the fire started. Now, I'm going to pick the locks on all the rooms. Here are the matches. Once I tell you to, set fire to the sheets. Do you understand? But not until the locks are picked, because we'll need to get everyone out as quickly as possible."

Lucinda nodded.

It took her only a few minutes to run up and down the hall, unlocking and opening the doors. All the patients were asleep but one, a woman who was pacing up and down, muttering to herself in the darkness. Finally, Diana unlocked the door to the central hall. She hoped the guard would not notice, but he was unlikely to check the door unless he heard something to alarm him. After all, he could scarcely expect anyone to break out from the inside! Only a few minutes now, and her plan would be set in motion.

There, that did it—everything was ready. She ran back to Mrs. Van Helsing's room. "You, get behind me," she said to Mrs. Van Helsing. The woman moved quickly—good. Diana just hoped she was strong enough to make a run for it. Would this work? It would have to, because if it failed—well, she did not think they would get another chance.

"Now!" she said. She saw the match flare in Lucinda's hand. It moved here and there like a firefly, setting fire to the sheets. "All right, come on! We need to get everyone off this floor. You stand by the entrance—make sure the guard understands there's a fire in here, and that everyone needs to get out. Hey, what's the German for fire?" Damn, she should have asked Lucinda earlier.

"Feuer!" said Lucinda as they both hurried out of the room, where smoke was already rising from the burning sheets.

"Right, thanks. I'll go that way, you go the other—make sure everyone gets out!"

Diana ran to the end of the hall, shouting *"Feuer! Feuer!"* Starting at the end, she made sure every patient was awake and out of her room. *"Feuer!"* she told them. "Run as fast as you can!" They probably did not understand her English, but they understood the word *"Feuer"* well enough, as well as her uniform and the pointing hand. She was one of the nurses, telling them there was a fire, telling them to get out. They ran down the hall, women of all ages in their nightgowns. She checked every room, making sure all of them were evacuating.

When she reached the entrance, there was Lucinda standing at the top of the stairs.

"Rufen Sie die Feuerwehr! Da ist es ein Feuer auf dieser Etage," she was saying to the guard, while herding patients down the stairs. He was looking confused, turning around and around as though looking for the fire—but then smoke started trickling out above Diana's head. Now she could smell it—thick, acrid. Where had Mrs. Van Helsing gone? Diana hoped she was already on the second floor.

"Ja, Schwester!" he said, nodding at Lucinda. Then he started shouting down the stairs. Diana watched him run to the men's wing and unlock the door. Good, he was going to get the patients in the other wing. That meant she wouldn't have to get them out herself.

She ran down the stairs, behind the stream of patients and Lucinda Van Helsing.

Patients in nightgowns, nurses rushing about—that was the scene on the second floor. Now she could smell the smoke down here as well. Her diversion was doing its work. Once she had gotten Lucinda and her mother safely out, Mary and the others would have to admit how very clever she had been.

> MARY: You put every single man and woman in that hospital in danger! You do realize that, don't you?

> DIANA: How? I set some sheets on fire. The hospital was built of stone. The fire would have burned itself out, eventually. It didn't even spread out of Mrs. Van Helsing's room. Anyway, no one got hurt.

> MARY: You didn't know that would be that case when you set the fire, did you? Someone could have been injured in the general confusion. And we only know that no one was hurt because Irene checked afterward. Why don't you ever stop to *think* before you do something rash and impulsive?

> DIANA: Because I *don't*. I swear, if you keep on at me about this, I'm going to start tearing my hair out. Or maybe yours!

> JUSTINE: Diana, why don't you come up to the studio with me? It's so peaceful there, and you can tell me about how you cleverly rescued Lucinda and her mother.

DIANA: No, I'm going out. At least Charlie and
the Baker Street gang aren't as insufferably self-
righteous as the lot of you!

For two days, Mary had been bored and worried. What was
Diana doing? Was she all right? She had watched and watched
from the window, sometimes through the binoculars, sometimes
through the telescope, but all she had seen were those men leaning
against the walls and the ordinary traffic of the street.

On the second night, she was sitting on the floor, playing
solitaire by the light of the single lamp they kept burning, when
Justine, who was keeping watch, said, "Diana was supposed to
signal if she needed help. Could that be it?"

Mary looked up from her game. "What is it? Is she waving a
handkerchief?"

"Not exactly."

Suddenly alert, Mary put the stack of cards to one side, went
to the window, and stood next to Justine.

The third floor of the Krankenhaus was on fire. Well, one
corner of the third floor, but the flames were reaching out of a
barred window and up into the night. *Oh Lord!* The building was
burning, and Diana was in there. . . .

"Greta!" she said. She leaned over and shook Greta by the
shoulder, sorry to wake her up—the girl had kept watch all day,
and deserved to sleep. But this was an emergency.

Greta opened her eyes and said, sleepily, *"Ist etwas geschehen?"*

Suddenly, an alarm rang out. Mary turned back to the
window. She could hear screams and shouts from the direction
of the Krankenhaus. The fire was climbing out, in defiance of the
bars. Now it had climbed to the roof! It danced there like yellow
hair blowing in the wind, spreading and spreading.

"Jesus, Mary, and the angels!" said Greta, who had come up

behind her. "They will have to evacuate the building."

"You don't think Diana . . . ," said Justine to Mary, with an appalled expression on her face.

Mary looked grim. "I would not put it past her."

> DIANA: You said to send a signal if I needed help.
> Well, I sent a signal. And created a diversion to get
> Lucinda out.

> MARY: I said to wave a handkerchief out the window!
> Or maybe your stockings!

> DIANA: What good would that have done? How
> were you even going to see a handkerchief in the
> darkness? Anyway, I didn't have a handkerchief—
> I'd left it in my room. And my stockings were on
> my legs, thank you very much.

> MARY: So you set the building on fire? And why are
> you dressed like that? You look like one of those
> newsboys who are always shouting about the latest
> crimes—or a chimney sweep!

> DIANA: I told you, I'm going out with Charlie. I don't
> wear your sort of la-di-dah clothes when I'm out
> with the gang. Ta, sister!

> MARY: I swear, some day I'm going to strangle her.

> JUSTINE: I do not think you are capable of that, Mary.

> MARY: Well, if not, it's a grave defect in my character.

"Come on," said Mary. "It looks like they're getting everyone out of the building. I don't know what's going on, but I think we should be down there."

Justine nodded. Greta grabbed her pistol from the side table, where she had put it before lying down, and lifted the lamp by its handle. Mary, the only one of them not dressed in masculine clothes, buckled on her waist bag and made sure her revolver was tucked inside. It was already loaded. Justine was not armed, but she did not need to be—her strength was as deadly as any firearm.

Quickly, and as quietly as they could on the creaking stairs, they descended the three flights, Mary and Justine following Greta's lamp. When they reached the entrance hall, Greta blew it out and put it on the hall table. She opened the front door of the inn, and they emerged into the street.

From here, they could see the long avenue in front of the Krankenhaus. It was rapidly filling with people, attracted by the alarm that kept ringing and ringing. Mary ran up the street and turned onto the avenue. She could hear Justine's and Greta's boots on the pavement—good, they were close behind.

To her right were the front gates of the Krankenhaus. There was already a crowd around them—people from the local shops and apartment buildings. She ran and stood at the edge of the crowd, trying to understand what was going on. She could see the proprietor of the inn where they had been staying, talking to a guard in rapid German.

"He says the fire brigade has been notified," said Greta, sounding out of breath behind her. "The others—they are wondering if the fire can spread, if they should get the women and children out of the nearby buildings. Is it possible that this is a coincidence, and has nothing to do with Diana at all?"

Was it possible? Perhaps Mary had simply jumped to conclusions. The fact that Diana routinely created chaos wherever she went did not mean she was responsible for this *particular* bit of chaos.

"Hey!" Something hit her on the arm.

She spun around. There stood Diana, dressed in a gray uniform, with a white cap covering her hair so not a single red curl showed. It was she who had hit Mary to get her attention.

"What the . . ." she said.

"Hell. The word you're looking for is hell. Come help me get Mrs. Van Helsing out. Actually, I think Justine would be more useful."

"Diana!" said Justine. "How is it you are out here?"

"Come *on*!" said Diana, pulling Justine by one wrist. Mary followed, checking to make sure Greta was behind her. When she looked back, Greta shrugged as though to say, *It's Diana. What did you expect?*

Diana was leading them to a corner of the gate, where it met the high stone wall around the Krankenhaus. Here, surprisingly, there was no crowd—all the local inhabitants were clustered at the other end of the gate, close to the guardhouse. Some were offering help, some warning the guards not to open the gates and let dangerous criminals loose in this part of the city.

When Mary looked at the gate where it met the wall, she gasped. Two of the bars had been pried apart, just wide enough for someone of Diana's size to slip through. Behind the gate were two women, one dressed in a gray uniform like Diana, the other in a white nightgown. That one was leaning on the one in uniform. Was the woman in the uniform a nurse?

"Mrs. Van Helsing is losing her strength," said Diana. "That's as far as she could bend the bars. I figured Justine could finish the job."

"Stand back," said Justine. She gripped the iron bars and pulled them farther apart, as easily as though she were parting a curtain.

"*Kommen Sie, Frau,*" said Justine, holding one hand through the bars she had just bent.

The woman in the nightgown took it. Staggering, she stepped forward and through the bars. *"Danke,"* she said to Justine in a faint voice. And then she sank to the ground, like a puppet whose strings have been cut by the puppeteer.

BEATRICE: That's a lovely image, Catherine.

CATHERINE: Thank you! I worked hard on it, you know. I'm not just a "mistress of the shilling shocker," as a reviewer recently called me. I can write as well as some of those literary johnnies. Anyway, the Astarte books sell for *two* shillings.

Justine lifted up the woman in the nightgown.

"He, was machen Sie da!" Who had shouted that? Inside the Krankenhaus grounds, one of the guards was running toward them. The fire was bright enough now that Mary could see him clearly. He had a thick mustache and the sort of expression guards tend to have when they realize you're trying to escape.

"Come on, hurry up," said Diana to the woman in the uniform, who lifted her skirt and stepped through the bars. "This is Lucinda Van Helsing. See, I got her out, all by myself."

At the sight of Lucinda escaping, the guard shouted something that Mary did not catch, but it was clearly intended to summon more of his kind. When he reached the bent bars, he stopped. He was far too large to fit through the gap, but he raised his rifle, aiming it right at them.

Mary pulled the revolver out of her waist bag and pointed it at the guard.

"Everybody, run!" she said. Oh, how she hated to do it, but she aimed at the guard's foot and shot—once, right into the toe of his boot.

The guard screamed, cursed, and doubled over. His rifle fell to the ground, but mercifully did not go off —instead, it just lay there while he grabbed his foot and made horrifying sounds.

Oh, this was dreadful! Mary had never imagined shooting someone would be so dreadful. The last time she had shot another living being, it had been a Beast Man, in self-defense. This was self-defense too, but somehow the fact that she had shot a human being, a fully human being created by God rather than vivisection, made it so much worse. However, it was a toe, not even the big toe—if he lost it, he could still live a normal life. And she had shot him in the precincts of a hospital. A hospital for the mad—nevertheless, it would have trained nurses and medical supplies.

She heard a clanging sound—yes, there was the fire truck, behind its team of horses. The gates of the Krankenhaus opened to let it through. Thank goodness—at least the building would not burn down.

Feeling guilty and ashamed about the guard she had shot, because she was Mary and she *would* feel that way even when she had simply done what was necessary, she turned and ran after Greta—the others had already disappeared into the darkness.

MARY: Later, I asked Irene to check on that guard. He retired and got a very good pension.

CATHERINE: Next, you're going to tell me that you knit him socks for Christmas!

MARY: Do you think he would appreciate that?

CATHERINE: No, I don't.

Greta turned left, into the street with the inn where they had been keeping watch. Ah, there were Diana and Lucinda Van

Helsing. Justine was still carrying the woman in her arms. Diana had called her Mrs. Van Helsing. But how was that possible? Irene had told them that Mrs. Van Helsing was dead, and Mary trusted Irene to know these things. Had Diana rescued the wrong woman?

"Should we go back up to the room?" she asked Greta. She had run so hard that she was almost out of breath. "We could probably hide out there for a while. Our supplies are still up there." Including, she realized, her pouch with the extra bullets. She had left it on the table after loading her revolver, placed neatly beside her sponge bag. How could she have been so stupid?

"I do not think so," said Greta. "They know there has been an escape, so once they put out the fire, they will begin searching all the neighboring buildings—probably with the help of the police. I think we must get as far away from here as possible. Behind the hospital there are stables—what you call the mews. Justine and I were there once before. It is so late, I do not know if we can hire a carriage, but we will have to try."

"Why don't you use mine?"

Mary turned. There stood the beggar who had been sitting on the pavement most of the day, but his voice—rich, operatic, feminine . . . "Irene!" she said.

"Come on," said the beggar, who was somehow also Irene Norton, although so cleverly made up that if Mary had not heard her speak, she would not have believed it possible. "My driver, Hermann, is waiting at the stables. It's only a few blocks from here."

Mary nodded. She did not want to admit how relieved she was to see Irene. Of course she would have led them all in Irene's absence, and made whatever decisions needed to be made. But sometimes it was a relief simply to follow, particularly someone as knowledgeable as Irene Norton, who would get them to safety.

Irene led the way into a dark alley behind the Krankenhaus. After her walked Justine, carrying the woman Diana had called

Mrs. Van Helsing. Then Lucinda and Diana—Lucinda, Mary noticed, was stumbling and holding her side, so she ran forward to offer the girl a hand, and a shoulder should she need it. But Lucinda shook her head and walked on resolutely alone, her arms wrapped around her torso, as though to protect herself from something. Behind them all came Greta, with her pistol drawn.

"Almost there!" Irene called back.

They were in a small square of some sort, with tenement houses on four sides, above shops that were closed for the night. In the middle of the square was a fountain, but no water ran from it. Although a pale moon still hung in the sky, Mary noticed that it was starting to lighten—dawn was coming. She was tired and shivering with cold, and she had shot someone. Why were adventures always so much less glamorous than they sounded? Lucinda Van Helsing had been rescued, yet all she felt was sick to her stomach.

Suddenly, she noticed that ahead of them, at the entrance to the alley they were heading toward, stood a man in a dark coat. Didn't she recognize him? Yes—that coat, that slouching attitude. He was one of the men who had lounged on the street near the Krankenhaus, keeping watch. But why was he here? Barring their way. . . .

"*Gehen Sie aus dem Weg!*" said Irene, waving her arm—clearly, telling him to stand aside.

The man just grinned. Mary could see now that he was tall, unshaven. A workingman of some sort, by his clothes and attitude. If she were Mr. Holmes, she would probably be able to tell what trade—

"*Ich habe gesagt, Sie sollen aus dem Weg gehen!*" said Irene. Out of the pocket of her ragged coat, she drew a pistol and pointed it at him.

"*Madame*, look behind us!" said Greta.

Mary turned to see what Greta was shouting about. There, behind them, was another of the loungers—and another to the side, standing by the fountain. Three men . . . no, there were more emerging from alleys, from doorways. How many? She counted seven altogether. There were no gas lamps in the square, but the sky was light enough now that she could see them clearly enough, although from this distance she could not make out their features. Seven of them—*And four of us,* she thought, at least if you did not count Justine, who was carrying the supposed Mrs. Van Helsing. She, Greta, and Irene were armed. Diana—well, Diana was resourceful and fearless. Could Lucinda Van Helsing fight? She had no idea.

A shot rang out. She turned back quickly, to see the man who had blocked their path crumple to the ground. Irene was standing like a woman who had just shot someone—which, of course, she had.

"Circle the wagons!" said Irene. "Lucinda and her mother in the middle."

Yes, all of them back to back—that made sense, although Mary wondered what wagons had to do with it. She glanced around quickly. Irene, Greta, and Diana were backing toward one another to form a circle, facing outward. Justine had just laid Mrs. Van Helsing on the ground in the middle. Lucinda was kneeling by her mother.

Mary stepped back as well. Five of them, like the points of a star—it was the best, most secure formation. They were close to the fountain. It would not protect them, of course. Still, if the men came from that direction, they would have to climb over or go around it, and that would delay them a minute or two. Sometimes, minutes counted. How many bullets did she have left? Five. She hoped it would be enough.

And then, the men were upon them.

There was one right in front of Mary—bearded, with a knit cap and a scowl on his face. This time she did not hesitate to shoot, in the shoulder so the shot would not kill. She wanted only to wound. At first she thought that she must have missed, because the shot seemed to have no effect. He swatted at where the bullet had hit him—yes, it had hit, she could see the blood on his pullover—as though swatting at an insect.

He kept coming toward her. She aimed, shot again—this time in the chest, aiming for his heart. She did not want to kill, but she had to stop him. She waited for him to stumble, fall—but he kept coming, although blood was soaking through the pullover, still from the shoulder, and now also from where his heart should be. In the early morning light, the bloodstains looked black on the dingy gray wool.

"You must shoot between the eyes!" cried Lucinda, behind her. "It will at least slow him down." Slow him down? It would blow his brains out the back of his head. But the man kept coming, so once again Mary took aim and fired, right at his forehead. He staggered back, dropped to his knees, and fell over onto the pavement. This time she felt, not guilt, but a flood of relief. What else had been happening while she was focused on this one assailant?

She glanced quickly around. Greta had shot one of the men, who was still crawling on the pavement toward her. Diana was fighting another—she had jumped on his back, holding a knife. It looked as though she was about to plunge it into the man's throat. Irene was facing two more. Justine stepped up behind one, placed her hands on either side of his head, and twisted—Mary could hear his neck snap. Another was menacing Lucinda, who was crouched over her mother, hissing at him like a kettle about to boil. Mary turned and pointed her revolver at him—two bullets left.

She heard a shot behind her, and then a string of curses. "What the hell is going on?" Irene shouted. "Why don't they die?" Two more shots rang out and echoed around the square.

Mary aimed, but the man was circling around Lucinda, like a wolf circling its prey. She could not shoot him without endangering Lucinda as well.

Suddenly, she heard someone yelling from above. It was a man in one of the tenements, who had opened a window and was now shouting at them, a long tirade in German. She understood only one word: *Polizei.*

Damn! They had to get out of there!

DIANA: Mary said "damn"!

MARY: I didn't say it. I thought it.

DIANA: How is that any different?

CATHERINE: Don't interrupt my fight scene.

In the seconds it had taken her to look up, the man by Lucinda had moved closer to her. He looked as though he were about to attack. Lucinda remained crouched over her mother, still hissing, fingers extended like claws.

"Get away from her!" Mary shouted. Would he see her revolver and move back?

The man turned toward her and snarled, like an animal. Inadvertently, she stepped back, startled by what she had seen: he had *fangs!*

Like a Beast Man. Could he possibly be one of Dr. Moreau's mad creations? No, that was impossible. All the Beast Men were dead; Catherine had told her that. But this was no time to think about what he might be. She had to kill him, that was all.

Lucinda leaped at him. And then they were a swirl of shabby coat and gray uniform. If only Mary could get in a shot! But she was as likely to hit Lucinda as her attacker.

Then Lucinda was on the ground—he had thrown her onto the pavement, not far from her mother. Mary could see a dark stain on her shoulder. The man crouched over her, fangs bared, mouth bloody. Had he *bitten* her?

He was still close to Lucinda, too close—she would have to be a very good shot indeed. *But I am a very good shot,* thought Mary. Two bullets. She would shoot once, then move in closer and shoot him between the eyes when Lucinda was out of the way.

Steady, aim . . .

The man was knocked back by a whirling mass of white. It was Mrs. Van Helsing, hissing and spitting like a cat. There was no way to shoot him now.

Mary ran to Lucinda. "Come on!" she said, and pulled Lucinda back toward the fountain. The man had his hands around Mrs. Van Helsing's throat, but she raked his face with her nails. He screamed, a high, thin shriek. Could Mary do anything? No, not while they were so close together. Well, at least she could get Lucinda to safety!

Once again, she heard cursing—the man in the window? Quickly, she looked up, but could not see him. She glanced around. Justine was fighting one of the men—Justine, fighting? When did Justine ever have to fight? With her strength, she could overpower any man in a minute. And there, by the fountain, was another of them—Greta was there as well, taking aim, but then Diana leaped on him with her knife. Stupid, foolhardy Diana! Why couldn't she let Greta handle it? He swatted Diana with the back of his hand as though she were a fly. She flew back onto the pavement, landing in a crumpled heap by the fountain. *Diana!* Was she all right?

"Mary, bandages!" shouted Irene. "Lucinda is down. Do you still have bullets? I'm out, and Justine needs help." Irene was running toward her. Behind her lay two of the men, dead. How many of them were still standing? Mary had no idea.

"Two bullets left," she said, holding out her revolver. *Bandages,* she thought. *Of course, for Lucinda.*

Irene grabbed the revolver and ran back to where Justine was still fighting—*still?* How strong were these mysterious assailants, who could match the Giantess in strength, who could take two bullets and keep coming?

But there was no time to think about that now. Mary tore strips from her petticoat—well, there went another petticoat!—and began to bandage Lucinda's shoulder. "Hold still!" she said. "You're badly injured—you need to hold still, or you'll lose too much blood. You don't want to die, do you?"

"Mijn moeder!" said Lucinda, holding out her hand. Mary looked up. Mrs. Van Helsing crouched over the man who had attacked her daughter. What was she doing? Mary could not see . . . There was a horrible tearing sound. Mrs. Van Helsing raised her head and— her mouth! It was covered with blood. Then she fell back onto the pavement, with her arms sprawled out.

"Moeder!" cried Lucinda. Without waiting for Mary to finish bandaging her shoulder, she leaped forward and knelt by her mother's side.

"Wait—" Mary followed her. Lucinda was holding her mother's hand. Mrs. Van Helsing's eyes were open, but it was obvious that she was fearfully wounded—her neck was a mess of blood.

"Ik hou van jou, mijn dochter, mijn liefste," she whispered to Lucinda. And then she closed her eyes.

"Nee! Moeder, nee!" Lucinda screamed and fell forward onto her mother's body. She was sobbing—heavy, wracking sobs. Mary lifted Mrs. Van Helsing's wrist—no, nothing. No pulse, no sign of life. What in the world could she do? She still needed to bandage Lucinda's shoulder, or the girl might die as well from loss of blood.

"We need to get out of here," said Irene, just behind her. "Is Mrs. Van Helsing—"

"Dead," said Mary. "I'm so sorry."

"Damn and double damn. I should have—I don't know what. But they were so strong! We've got them all—Greta shot the last one—but I think the police are coming." Irene put Mary's revolver in her pocket. "Can you take care of Lucinda? We need to get out of here."

"I'll carry Mrs. Van Helsing," said Justine. Mary turned—there were Justine, Greta, and Diana. Still standing, although Diana had a red welt on one side of her face.

"All right," she said. How in the world was she supposed to take care of this girl, doubled over and sobbing as though her heart were broken—as it probably was? She had a sudden and vivid recollection of the night she had sat silently, for hours, by her mother's dead body, with Mrs. Poole occasionally patting her hand. "Come on," she said to Lucinda, taking her by one arm. "Please, I need to finish bandaging your shoulder."

As gently as though she were lifting a flower, Justine picked up Mrs. Van Helsing.

Lucinda looked up. In the first light of dawn, her face was a horrifying sight—so pale, smeared with blood and tears. She held out one hand, as though reaching out to Mrs. Van Helsing, then dropped it back into her lap. In a voice filled with despair, she said, "My mother has died the true death."

"Come on," said Irene. "If the Viennese police find us here, we're all going to be arrested, and we don't have time to spend breaking out of prison. We need to get out of here *now*."

Mary held Lucinda's arm, half supporting her, half pulling her as they hurried across the square, with Irene leading them, Justine carrying Mrs. Van Helsing's body, and Greta in the rear, her pistol still drawn.

In the growing light, Mary could see the men more clearly as she walked past them, lying on the pavement. Rough men, large and strong, some with beards, some without, all in shabby clothes, like down-and-out laborers. Why had they attacked? Had they been sent by the Société des Alchimistes? Was this Heinrich Waldman's doing?

She hurried behind Justine, holding Lucinda's arm, out of the square and up the alley they had originally been heading toward.

Irene led them through what seemed like a maze of small, crooked streets, under balconies and lines hung with washing. They emerged at what Mary could immediately tell were the mews—a long line of stables and carriage houses. After the insanity of the previous night, there was something sane and reassuring about the smell of horses.

"Hermann!" Irene shouted. "Hermann! He may still be asleep," she added. "It's—what? Five o'clock?"

Mary glanced at her wristwatch—yes, almost five. She could just see the yellow edge of the sun rising over the buildings.

A man ran out from one of the stables. He was in shirtsleeves, with lather on his chin.

"Madame Norton!" he said. And then he said something in German, and Irene replied in German, and they disappeared into the stable together. Mary looked around for some place to sit. She felt light-headed, and judging from how much Lucinda was hanging on to her arm, the girl was about to collapse. How long had it been since any of them had eaten?

There was a bench in front of the stable, probably to assist with mounting the horses, or shoeing them, or something—she was not clear on the details of what one did with horses. In London, you called a cab and it came.

"Let's sit down," she said to Justine. "We all look as though we're about to fall over." Although actually Justine looked as though she could stand there all day, holding the dead woman in her arms, her face perfectly impassive—which meant that she, too, was feeling a sense of despair. Mary knew Justine well enough to judge her moods—stillness and silence were not good signs. Lucinda stood silent as well, looking down at the pavement. Greta had dark circles under her eyes. Only Diana looked perfectly fresh—as though she could do it all over again, if she had to, despite the welt on her cheek, which was rapidly turning glorious shades of blue and green.

"Go on, sit down," said Mary. "All of you, go sit!" They went—even Diana went quietly, for once. When they were all seated on the bench, there was no more room for Mary, so she leaned against a post with an iron ring in it. She looked at the faces in front of her, still not quite believing what they had just gone through. Justine cradled the body of Mrs. Van Helsing like a *pietà*—the Virgin Mary holding the dead Jesus in a church alcove.

Diana pulled the white cap off her head and combed her fingers through her red curls. "Well, that's over with," she said.

"I don't think it is quite over," said Greta. "There will be an investigation into the asylum fire. They will search for the missing patients—that is you, and Lucinda, and Mrs. Van Helsing—assuming you escaped while the asylum was being evacuated. Dr. Freud may even come under suspicion—we shall have to divert the investigators in some way. And remember, we have left seven dead bodies for the police to find."

"They are not dead," said Lucinda in a strange, singsong voice, as though she were intoning poetry. "They shall rise again, yea, even from their slumbers they shall rise."

"That's how she was talking when I found her," said Diana. "All crazy like that."

"Come on!" called Irene. She was standing by the large double doors of the stable. One of them had been open—now she opened the other. A minute later, out rolled her carriage, with Hermann, now properly coated and hatted, perched on the driver's seat.

"Get in," she said, opening one of the carriage doors. "Let's get out of this dismal place."

"Look!" said Diana. She was pointing back down the alleyway. There stood—no, it was impossible. Yet there he stood, the man Mary had shot between the eyes. Another man stepped out of the shadows and stood next to him, then another. Yes, they were, all three of them, men she and Irene and the others had fought—and killed.

"You have got to be kidding," said Irene. "Into the carriage, *now!*"

"Come on!" said Mary.

She made sure Lucinda climbed in first, then she climbed in herself. It was a tight fit for the six of them, plus the dead body of Mrs. Van Helsing. At least Justine had wrapped it up in her coat. With its eyes closed, it looked almost asleep—if one could ignore the terrible gash at its throat that no longer bled, but had left a stain on the coat collar. As soon as they were all in, with Diana half on Mary's lap, Irene shouted, "Hermann, *los jetzt!*"

"*Hü!*" shouted the driver. "*Hü, hü!*"

The horses started to trot forward—thank goodness, they would soon be out of there! But first they needed to pass the three men, who were blocking their path. As soon as the horses approached that blockade, they neighed and bucked—the carriage stopped, and for a moment it even rolled backward. Hermann shouted again, and Mary flinched when she heard the crack of his whip. Then she saw a dirty hand on the windowsill. One of the men was holding on to the carriage, about to—what? Try to stop it? Pull himself up? Irene drew Mary's revolver out of her pocket. She stood and moved to the window, as best she could in the lurching, crowded carriage—she was half leaning across Justine and the dead woman. Yes, the man was pulling himself up—now Mary could see his face, rough and dirty, deathly pale. It was the one she had shot, and there, on his forehead, was the hole where the bullet had gone in, crusted with dried blood.

Irene shot—right through one eye! With a scream, he fell back. Hermann cursed, and once again Mary heard the crack of the whip. Then they were moving again, at a stumbling walk and then faster, a trot that was taking them away from there, from that damn alley. Yes, she had said damn again, or rather thought it. This adventure was changing her, and she did not like it one bit.

"I've used all your bullets," said Irene, handing the revolver back to her.

"That's all right," said Mary. "There are more in the—well, the room at the inn. I guess we won't be going back there, will we? But it doesn't matter. We're alive. You kept us alive."

"I think we all contributed," said Irene. Mary had not seen her looking quite so grim before. "But those things—they're not men. No man looks at you with that empty stare, no man rises from a wound of that nature. *What are they?*"

"Lucinda knows," said Diana. "Don't you?" They all turned and looked at the pale girl who had squeezed herself into a corner of the carriage, as though trying to disappear.

"Lucinda?" said Irene. "If you know something that would help us . . ."

"They are demons of the pit," said Lucinda in that singsong voice. "Risen from the fires of hell to torment mankind. They have swum through rivers of blood. They wear the night as though it were an old coat, ragged, moth-eaten."

For a moment, they all just stared at her.

Then, "Grief has driven her mad," said Justine.

"Maybe." Irene looked at Lucinda skeptically. "Grief drives people mad less often than you would think, outside of novels. It may be hunger—the girl looks half-starved. We'll be home soon enough, and then we'll eat, rest—and hold our council of war."

War against what—or whom? Mary wondered. But she was so tired, and there was something curiously soothing about the motion of the carriage. She would close her eyes just for a moment. Just a moment, and then she would pay attention to whatever Irene and Greta were discussing. It was something about the men who had attacked them, and who they might be, and who might have sent them . . . then something about needing to get out of Vienna as soon as possible. Then somehow the carriage was flying, because the horses had wings, and when Mary looked down, she could see clouds below. . . . The moon had invited them all for tea, and the tea table was set with linen as white as snow, and she was having the most fascinating conversation with a white rabbit when Greta shook her awake and said, "Mary! Mary! We are here."

She rubbed her eyes and looked around. She was still sitting in the carriage, but except for Greta, it was empty. Where were they, and where had the others gone? Of course—as soon as she stepped out of the carriage, she could see that they were all back in the courtyard of 18 Prinz-Eugen Strasse. Justine and Diana were waiting at the door that led up to Irene's apartment, while Irene was ringing the bell. Mary breathed a sigh of relief. They had done it—they had rescued Lucinda Van Helsing! And they were all safe.

Then she saw that Justine was still holding Mrs. Van Helsing's dead body, and that Lucinda was standing away from the others, with her arms wrapped around herself. There was blood on her uniform—spots of it on her bodice and a long streak down her skirt. She was staring down at the pavement, paying no attention to the others.

Hannah opened the front door of the apartment. "What has happened to you?" she said. "You look like a collection of ghosts!"

Mary followed Greta to the front door, stumbling because she was so tired, while behind her the carriage circled around—she could hear wheels on the stones, and the clopping of hooves. She remembered the last thing she had heard before falling asleep in the carriage—something about getting her, and Justine, and Diana—with Lucinda, of course—out of Vienna as quickly as possible. Yes, they were back, but they were not safe at all.

CHAPTER XIII

Lucinda's Story

"Into the parlor, everyone," said Irene, when they had climbed up the stairs and were all standing in the front hall. "Justine, could you take the body—I mean, Mrs. Van Helsing—to the office? Please place her on the table. Greta, can you arrange her appropriately? You know—in a dignified manner. As you pass the kitchen, ask Frau Schmidt to bring up coffee and pastries. And bring some fresh bandages for Lucinda's wound—it should be looked at immediately. I've sent Hannah out to deal with the repercussions of this business. I know you're all tired as well as hungry, but I think we need to talk—now, rather than later."

How good it felt, to be entering Irene's parlor again! It seemed so—well, normal after the events of the past few days. Sunlight was streaming in through the windows, and someone had placed a bowl of tulips on a side table. They were the striped, frilled variety, like in a painting by Rembrandt. It all looked so civilized. As though the world of mental asylums, and fights in back alleys, and sudden death were a million miles away. How Mary wished they were!

"This isn't over, you know," said Irene. "As I told Greta, the four of you need to get out of Vienna as quickly as possible. Three patients are missing from the Krankenhaus—there's going to be an investigation. It will lead them to Sigmund, who will of course be shocked and distressed that his patient has disappeared. As soon as we've talked, I'll telephone him and tell him that we have Lucinda, and Diana's all right. He'll have to prepare a story for the asylum administration, and most likely the police as well. But there's another issue—the men who attacked us. Who are they? Who sent them? *And why didn't they die?*"

She turned to Lucinda, who was sitting on the sofa next to Mary. Diana had taken one of the armchairs.

"May I?" she asked, then pulled off the white cap Lucinda was wearing. Her long, flaxen curls, which had been hidden under it, fell down around her shoulders. Lucinda put her hands up to her hair, as though making sure it was still there, then pulled strands of it over her eyes.

"My dear," said Irene, brushing it back again, then sitting down next to Lucinda, on the other side from Mary, and taking her hand. "I know you've been through a terrible ordeal and suffered a great loss. I'm so very sorry. But you must tell us what happened to you and your mother—that is your mother, isn't it? Your housekeeper, Frau Müller, told me she had died, but perhaps that is what your father told her. Am I guessing right? I can't imagine what the both of you have endured. I hope you will tell us how the both of you came to be in the Krankenhaus—and, if you know, who those men are."

Lucinda clasped Irene's hand in both of hers. "Yes," she said. "I will tell you my story."

Mary wished she could say something to Lucinda—after all, she knew what it felt like, losing one's mother. But she could not think of anything in the least helpful. Irene was better at this than she was.

Just then, Justine and Greta returned. Behind them was Frau Schmidt, and—oh, heavenly! The smell of fresh pastries and coffee! For the first time, Mary understood the attraction of coffee. If you have been up all night, escaping from a burning mental asylum or fighting men who refuse to die when you shoot them in the forehead, or both, coffee is the perfect beverage.

MRS. POOLE: Give me good English tea, anytime.

BEATRICE: Technically, that is Indian or Chinese tea, Mrs. Poole. Tea does not grow in England. *Camellia sinensis* is a subtropical plant.

MRS. POOLE: Well, if tea isn't English, then I don't know what is!

Greta had a tin box in her hands. She went up to Lucinda and unwound the strips of torn petticoat that Mary had wrapped so hastily around her shoulder, then pulled back the collar of her Krankenhaus uniform.

"There is no dangerous wound here," she said. "It is merely a scratch. The blood must have come from her attacker. I will clean it with alcohol, but I do not think it needs a bandage."

Was that possible? Had Mary somehow been mistaken about the ferocity of his attack? She must have been, yet it had seemed at the time that Lucinda was grievously wounded.

"Well, that's a relief," said Irene. "I was worried about infection. Come, my dear. Have some coffee—it will make you feel a little better."

Irene poured out, and soon they were all sitting with coffee cups in their hands and pastries (one of each kind for Diana) on plates in front of them—except Lucinda, who had shaken her head to signal that she did not want anything. Irene said, "Are you sure? If you want a cup of coffee, just say so. And go on . . . You were going to tell us your story."

Lucinda looked down. The sunlight coming through the

windows turned her hair gold, and stray curls seemed to form a halo around her head. She looked like a young, pale, frightened Madonna.

"Rivers of blood," she said. "I swam in rivers of blood."

"Oh Lord," said Diana. "She's crazy. She's just crazy, that's all." Justine put a hand on Diana's arm as though to restrain her. Was Justine all right? She had, after all, been carrying a dead woman for the last couple of hours. She looked composed, drinking her coffee, a half-eaten pastry on her plate, but Mary could not help worrying. Well, at least she was getting some breakfast!

"Hush, Diana," said Irene. "Go on, my dear. Where were these rivers of blood?"

"In Amsterdam, and Paris, and Vienna," said Lucinda. She looked up. Her eyes were a pale green, like spring leaves. They seemed to be looking very far away. "I swam and was drowned, and I died three times. Three times they brought me back, as Christ rose after the third day. I was pierced, as he was on the cross."

"Pierced with what?" asked Irene.

Where in the world was this line of questioning going? Mary hated to agree with Diana, but the girl did seem—well, insane. Perhaps that was, after all, why Lucinda had been committed to the Maria-Theresa Krankenhaus. She took a bite of pastry and could not help her stomach growling directly after. How hungry she was! This one was filled with walnut paste.

"Needles," said Lucinda, matter-of-factly.

"Can you show me where?" asked Irene.

Lucinda rolled up one sleeve of her uniform. On her arm was a track of small dots, as though she had been marked with red ink.

Irene ran her fingers up and down Lucinda's arm. Then she rolled up the other sleeve. On Lucinda's other arm were identical red marks. "These rivers of blood—where did they come from?"

"They flowed from the garden of Gesthsemane," said Lucinda.

"And also my arms. They flowed and I drowned and died, but I was not buried. On the third day, I rose again as my father commanded."

"Your father," said Irene. "Do you know who your father is?"

"God in heaven," said Lucinda. "He is my only father. My earthly father has forsaken me."

Irene took a sip of coffee. "Ahhh!" she said, almost involuntarily. "I really, really needed that." She turned back to Lucinda. "All right, tell me about your father. Your earthly father."

"I have no father anymore," said Lucinda. "He has sinned, grievously he has sinned. He has consorted with demons, and surely the Lord will send him down to perdition."

"What the hell does that mean?" asked Diana.

"Hush," said Mary. "You haven't even finished what's on your plate. Are you Diana, or some sort of doppelgänger? Because the Diana I know doesn't leave food uneaten."

"Go to hell," said Diana, but she said it under her breath and stuffed her mouth with a poppy-seed roll.

"What sorts of demons?" asked Irene.

Lucinda was silent for a moment. Then, she said, "They drink the blood of the righteous, and they never die."

Irene took another sip of her coffee. "Did they drink your blood, Lucinda?"

"He washed me in the blood of their kind, and I rose baptized, as though I had been born anew. But I was lost, lost, to God and man alike. I am forever condemned, and I shall perish in hellfire."

Lucinda put her hands over her face and started to sob, as she had when her mother died—dry, wracking sobs that shook her body.

Irene put her arm around the girl's shoulders. "Oh, my dear. I know this has been so difficult for you. I'm sorry to make you talk about it again. Here, have a little coffee. Just a little. It will make you feel better, I promise." She held her own cup up to Lucinda's mouth.

"Well, if that's her story," said Diana, "I don't think much of it! I mean, she didn't actually tell us anything, did she?"

Lucinda put her shaking hands around the cup and took a cautious sip. Then, as though suddenly remembering what coffee was, she drank it down, almost gulping it in her eagerness. And just as suddenly, she was bent over, retching it all up again, onto the table and carpet. She shook and coughed and wept, while Irene held her, making what were probably supposed to be soothing sounds although Lucinda did not seem soothed.

Justine picked up the cup that Lucinda had dropped and put it back on the table. Mary wiped up as much of the coffee as she could with a napkin, trying not to think about where it had just come from—whether it was coffee or regurgitated coffee should make no difference, right?

"Disgusting," said Diana, which was about the least helpful comment she could have made.

"I will take care of it, Mary," said Greta. "I know where the cleaning supplies are, and you do not. So don't worry."

Reluctantly, Mary nodded. Greta was probably better at anything cleaning-related than she was. Still, she felt particularly useless.

"All right, I think you're going to bed," said Irene. "I shouldn't have kept you here, after all you've been through. Mary, can you help me get Lucinda to my bedroom? I think that's the best place to put her. Justine, Diana, once you've finished eating, I want you to get some sleep. And Greta, I'm sorry, I wish I could tell you to go to bed as well, but I think you'd better do what we discussed on the drive over—ask Hermann to go with you. Or better, take Georg. Hermann has enough to think about right now."

"Yes, *madame*," said Greta. "I'll find him right after I take care of that stain. If I didn't, Hannah would never let me hear the end of it!" Quickly, she drank the rest of her coffee, and then she left, pocketing the last walnut roll. Where was she going with Hermann—or Georg, whoever that was? Irene must be referring to the conversation Mary had slept through. In the carriage, Irene had told Greta to do something—Mary would have liked to know what, and whether it concerned her, Justine, and Diana.

But this was not the time to ask questions. She led Lucinda to the bathroom, so the girl could wash her face and brush her teeth. When Lucinda rolled up her sleeves to wash her face in the basin, Mary saw those red marks again, as though she had been bitten by two very persistent insects. She felt as though she should say something—but what did one say to someone who had just lost her mother?

> DIANA: "I'm very sorry for your loss." Even I know
> that!

> MARY: When I lost my mother, "I'm very sorry for
> your loss" did not help one bit.

Longing for a wash herself—she had not had a proper one for several days—she led Lucinda to Irene's bedroom.

Irene was there, rooting through the wardrobe. "I put a nightgown on the bed," she told them when they came in. "I'm just looking for some clothes for Lucinda. She'll need several dresses, and perhaps a suit for Budapest."

"Budapest?" said Lucinda, clearly startled. Hadn't Diana told her *anything*?

"We're going to take you to Budapest," said Mary. "Mina Murray is there. She asked us to bring you to her." This was probably not the best time to tell Lucinda that they needed her help convincing the Société des Alchimistes to stop its experiments in biological transmutation.

"Wilhelmina!" said Lucinda. "I would like to see Wilhelmina again. She was a friend to my mother. . . ." Once again, she put her face in her hands, and Mary heard a low sob.

"Come, my dear," said Irene. "Put this on, and tuck yourself into my bed—it's very comfortable, I assure you. I'll come back and check on you in a few minutes. All right?"

Lucinda took the nightgown that Irene was holding out and nodded.

Irene put her arm through Mary's, gave her a glance that Mary was pretty sure meant, *I want to talk but not here*, and led her out of the room. She closed the door behind her, then said, "Oh Mary, what a night! You always look so composed, as though you could manage anything, but you must be exhausted. I know I am."

"Thank you," said Mary, startled. She was glad to hear that she looked composed. She certainly did not feel it. "I am too. Exhausted, I mean. And not just physically. Somehow, the last few days . . ." Well, they had taken all her strength.

"I know," said Irene. "And I want you to get some sleep as well, but first there's something I need to show you. Come on."

Mary followed her down the hall. As she passed the bedroom she was sharing with Diana, she heard a loud noise, as though bees were buzzing around a hive. She looked in. Diana lay sprawled on the bed, still fully clothed. She was snoring.

Thank goodness she's safe, thought Mary. *Of all the stupid plans . . .* And yet it had worked. They had, indeed, rescued Lucinda Van Helsing. Unless Diana was right, and Lucinda was mad? In which case her mind might remain a prison from which she could never escape—like Renfield in the asylum at Purfleet, catching his flies, or Lady Hollingston, cheerfully discussing how she had murdered her husband.

As they passed the study, Justine sat up on the sofa. She was wearing the man's nightshirt and robe she had brought with her. "I have tried to sleep, but I simply cannot," she said. "After the events of last night . . . I have killed again, this time two men."

"I'm not at all sure you have," said Irene. "Come on. If you can't sleep, you may as well come with me and Mary. I'll show you too."

Justine stood and followed them on slippered feet. As Irene turned to climb down the stairs to the kitchen, Justine looked at Mary as though to ask, *What is this all about?* Mary shrugged and shook her head.

Were they going to the kitchen? No, of course not. Irene had told Greta to bring Mrs. Van Helsing's body to her office, so that was where they must be headed. Sure enough, Irene walked to the end of the hallway, lifted the painting of poppies, which looked unnaturally cheerful on this grim morning, and turned the knob hidden underneath. The wall opened inward, and once again they were in her secret office, with the weapons on the wall, the shelves of file boxes holding who-knows-what, and the desk with that modern mystery, a telephone.

The electric lights were on. The long table was covered with a white cloth that was probably a bed sheet, and on it, under another sheet, with only her head visible, lay Mrs. Van Helsing.

Irene walked to the end of the table and stood next to Mrs. Van Helsing's head. For a moment, she looked down sadly and stroked the dead woman's hair. Then, in a businesslike tone, she said, "You noticed the marks on Lucinda's arms, right?"

"As though she had been bitten by insects," said Mary.

"Not insects." Irene drew back one corner of the bed sheet. She lifted up Mrs. Van Helsing's arm and drew back the sleeve of her blood-stained nightgown. That arm was also marked with small red spots.

Justine stepped closer to examine them. "They follow the vein."

"You noticed that too?" said Irene. "Someone was drawing her blood, often enough to need multiple sites of insertion. There are marks on both arms."

"Then—they're the marks of a hypodermic?" asked Mary. "But why?"

"I don't know," said Irene. "But there's something else. I examined her while you were helping Lucinda. I did not have time to do it thoroughly, but I noticed this." She put one hand on the corner of Mrs. Van Helsing's mouth and, with her fingers, drew the lips apart.

Lucinda's mother had fangs.

"Like the man in the alley!" said Mary. "Well, that explains why she had blood on her mouth. She must have bitten him."

"Fangs?" said Irene. "The men had fangs?" She frowned, as though puzzled.

"Well, one of them did," said Mary. "I mean, I didn't see them all that clearly because it was in the middle of everything, but he was snarling at me, like a rabid dog. Or like a Beast Man. Do you think it's possible that these are Beast Men, like those made by Dr. Moreau?"

"No," said Irene. "I examined one of them before we left the scene—quickly, but I would have noticed if he was a vivisected animal. Sherlock described the Beast Men in his letter. No, he was entirely human—as is Mrs. Van Helsing."

"Could they be reanimated corpses?" asked Justine. "That would explain why they do not die."

"I don't know. But then why the fangs? You don't have fangs, my dear." Irene smiled at Justine. "I think we're looking at something new, something not described in Sherlock's letter. Those fangs are not the only strange thing about this body. When you were carrying her, I noticed there was less blood than there should have been—it coagulated quickly. And she's been dead for several hours, but rigor mortis has not set in."

"Is she not dead, then?" asked Mary. "Could she—rise again, like those men?"

"I don't think so," said Irene. "She has no pulse, no heartbeat—I think she is, as Lucinda herself told us, truly dead. But someone did something to her—changed her in some way. Look also at how thin she is. . . ." Irene drew the sheet back further. She was right—even covered by the nightgown, it was clear that Mrs. Van Helsing had been emaciated, almost skeletal. "How could she survive, starved in this way? And who would have starved her?"

"Professor Van Helsing?" said Justine. "We know he was conducting experiments. This has all the hallmarks of an experiment—unusual marks on the body, physiological and psychological changes. . . . Alas, I know all too well, having been an experiment myself."

"And who better to experiment on than his wife and daughter," said Mary, bitterly. "That's the pattern, isn't it? These scientists— no, I won't dignify them with that name. These alchemists believe that women, preferably young women, make the best experimental subjects."

"That," said Irene, in a cold, contemptuous voice, "is revolting."

"So what now?" asked Mary. "Do we—I don't know—fight Van Helsing somehow? He's not even in Vienna, is he?"

"He will be as soon as he finds out that his wife and daughter are missing from the Krankenhaus," said Irene. "Why did he have Lucinda and her mother confined? And why did he tell his servants that Mrs. Van Helsing was dead? Would he have announced Lucinda's death as well, eventually? Clearly he was trying to hide whatever he was doing to them—that's the only logical explanation. But what exactly was he doing? And what do those hypodermic marks mean? I wish Lucinda could give us some answers, but I think whatever her father did to her has affected her mind."

"Then you don't think she's just gone mad?" said Mary.

Irene shrugged. "Honestly, I don't know. All I know is that your friend Mina was acquainted with Mrs. Van Helsing, and knows when the Société des Alchimistes is meeting in Budapest. Clearly, she has more information about this business than we do. So no, you're not going to fight Van Helsing. What you're going to do is take Lucinda to Budapest, exactly as planned. You told me that you trust Mina. She has a plan, and you should follow it. Anyway, I want you out of the city when Van Helsing arrives. Let me deal with him—I can at least put his investigation on the wrong track. Hannah is already out trying to determine what the authorities know, whether they're trying to chase down the three escaped patients. . . ."

"Then—do we go by train again?" asked Mary. Did she have enough money to pay for tickets, for the four of them?

"No. I don't know who those men were, whether they were working for Van Helsing, or the Société des Alchimistes, or both. But the train is too obvious—if the society is still on your trail, the Staatsbahnhof, where the Orient Express departs Vienna, will be watched. I don't want you to run into Heinrich Waldman or, more likely, another of their henchmen. I sent Greta and Georg—that is my footman—to arrange for a private coach for the four of you. You'll leave before dawn, when there is the least amount of traffic on the roads. The coach will take you south of Vienna, then over the border to Hungary. It's slower, but less obvious, and you should still arrive in plenty of time. I'll pay for it, of course."

"You needn't—," said Mary, ashamed that she was accepting money yet again.

"But I want to," said Irene. "Those men attacked me too, remember? This is my fight now, as well as yours."

"You are too kind and generous," said Justine.

Irene smiled. "Or really, really mad at those bastards. When I shoot a man, I expect him to die! All right, now you're going to get some sleep, the both of you. You have a long, hard trip ahead of you—several days, even by the most direct route. *So go to bed.*" She pulled the sheet over Mrs. Van Helsing's face. As she did so, Mary saw Irene's lips move, as though in a silent prayer.

How could Mary sleep after all she had learned? There was so much to think about! But even as she followed Justine upstairs, Mary felt her eyes closing and struggled to keep them open. She would lie down next to Diana. . . .

Her dreams were filled with bees, and she wondered how they had flown all the way from England to Vienna.

When Greta shook her awake for the second time that day, the gas was lit. Mary sat up, confused about where she was. Why was it dark out the window, and why wasn't she in her own bedroom? Where was Mrs. Poole?

"I've drawn a bath and left out a change of clothes for you," said Greta. She was once again dressed as a respectable parlormaid. "Madame Norton says you should be prepared to leave within the hour."

"Leave? For where?" Mary rubbed her eyes. Hadn't Diana been sleeping next to her? Where had she gone?

"For Budapest," said Greta, and suddenly it all came flooding back—the events of the last few days, the plans for the next few. For a moment, Mary would have given anything to be back in England again, in her own parlor, with Mrs. Poole bringing in tea on a tray. "Madame Norton sent me to find a coach that would take you—for hire, as you say. With Georg's help, for he knows the stables hereabout—from gambling with the grooms, I'm afraid! It was not easy finding a coachman willing to take such a long trip. But a friend of Hermann's recommended a Hungarian who is familiar with the route, and the coach will be here soon."

"Right—Budapest!" said Mary. She was still so tired! How long had she slept? She looked at the clock on the mantel. The hands told her that it was 3:15—in the morning, presumably. Yes, of course in the morning, because it was still dark. She rubbed her eyes again. She had slept most of the day and half the night, but evidently it had not been enough. And she felt positively grimy. If only she could have changed into a nightgown! But no, she had simply lain down and fallen sleep in her clothes. Wait, hadn't Greta said something about a bath?

"There is food in the *salle à manger*," said Greta. "You should eat before you leave. Hermann says you will be traveling for three days, arriving on the third. Frau Schmidt has packed a hamper with sandwiches, but you will have to purchase your dinners at inns along the way, and I do not think you will get a good meal again before you reach Budapest."

"Three days!" said Mary. The train would have gotten them there so much faster. But then she remembered the men in the alley. . . . Did she want to meet them again in the corridor of the Orient Express? She shuddered.

When Greta had left, Mary bathed quickly—oh, how she wished she had time to soak in the luxurious bathtub! With the unerring instinct of a good maid, Greta had put out Mary's traveling suit. She dressed, folded the clothes she had slept in, and braided her hair, then pinned it up in a neat bun. She looked at herself in the mirror above the sink. Well, she still looked tired—but at least she was presentable.

When she entered the dining room, Diana and Justine were already there, finishing what looked like a substantial breakfast—potatoes, sausages, eggs, and a cucumber salad. Lucinda was sitting in front of an empty plate, eyes cast down. She was wearing one of Irene's dresses—Mary could tell it was Irene's from the richness of the fabric and the embroidery around the collar. Her hair had been pinned up, but strands still fell in ringlets around her face. She looked like the poor orphan in a novel by Mr. Dickens— pale and otherworldly.

When Mary saw the food set out in chafing dishes, she realized that she was ravenously hungry. She took a little of everything.

"I wish Beatrice were here to put something on that bruise," she said to Diana.

"What bruise?" asked Diana, shoving scrambled eggs into her mouth.

"You haven't washed your face, have you?" said Mary. "If you had, you might have noticed that half your face looks like Justine painted it."

"Actually, it looks more like the work of Monsieur Monet," said Justine, smiling. "He paints in those greens, blues, and purples, and there is something impressionistic about it. . . ."

Justine had made a joke! Had she ever made a joke before? Mary rather thought not.

> JUSTINE: I make jokes! I make jokes more often than you realize.

> DIANA: Yes, but you have to read all of Kant or Legel to understand them! That's why we never laugh. We don't even know you're joking. It's not a joke if no one gets it.

> JUSTINE: Do you mean Hegel? Friedrich Hegel?

> DIANA: Legel, Negel, Tegel. Who cares?

"I want to look at it!" said Diana. She sprang up and, because there was no mirror in the dining room, regarded herself in the silver lid of a chafing dish. "*Awesome!* It doesn't hurt at all. I guess one of those bastards landed a punch, damn him."

"I'll give you some cold cream to put on it," said Irene, entering the room. "Your luggage is packed and by the door. Hannah was able to retrieve the items you left at the inn near Krankenhaus. Those are packed as well. Mary, Greta brushed down the clothes you left in the bathroom and added them to your trunk."

"Thank you," said Mary. Greta seemed to think of everything.

"There's also a hamper of food, although it won't last you the entire trip. You'll be leaving in half an hour—I want you far away from Vienna by dawn. Tomorrow night, and the night after that, you will spend at inns along the way. Some time on the third day, if all goes well and the roads are as good as Herr Ferenc says they are"—she pronounced it Feretz—"you should arrive in Budapest. Miklós Ferenc is the coachman—Hermann doesn't know him personally, but a friend of his, who works in the stables at the Belvedere, recommended him, and Georg says he seems knowledgeable enough. He's a Hungarian, and knows all the roads, the places to stop and hire fresh horses. . . . While you were asleep, I telegraphed Miss Murray and told her when to expect you. I also telegraphed Mrs. Poole so she wouldn't worry."

"That's safe, right?" asked Mary. "They can't intercept a telegram, can they?"

"Anything can be intercepted," said Irene. "The telegraph, the mail . . . but I've taken every precaution. The first time I telegraphed Mrs. Poole, I sent it through the American Embassy—it was delivered by one of our attachés in London. I did the same thing again this time. That's the safest route, I think. By the way, I talked to Sigmund—he says to tell you Godspeed, and that he hopes to see you again someday. The both of you. He said you were interesting—the word he used was *unique*—from a psychological perspective."

"Is there time for seconds?" asked Diana. "I'm still hungry."

"If you eat quickly," said Irene. "Lucinda, are you sure you won't have anything?"

Lucinda looked up at her with haunted eyes and shook her head.

Irene went over to her and put one hand on Lucinda's shoulder. "I promise your mother will be buried in holy ground, with all the rites of her faith. Would you like to see her one more time, to say goodbye?"

Lucinda nodded.

"Come on, then. The coach will be here soon." Irene held out her hand. Lucinda took it and followed her docilely out of the room.

"Well, she's going to be a whole lot of fun on this trip," said Diana.

"Don't you have any compassion?" asked Mary. "She just lost her mother."

"You think I don't know that?" said Diana. "I lost my mum too, remember? So did you. So did Justine."

"That is all the more reason for us to show her sympathy and kindness," said Justine. She looked reproving—gentle, but reproving. Mary was not sure she had ever seen Justine look reproving before.

Diana glared at her, but did not respond. Instead, she shoved the rest of the potatoes she had taken into her mouth, then chewed with her mouth deliberately open, as though daring them to criticize her. Mary sighed. Three days in a coach traveling across the Austro-Hungarian countryside! It was going to be a long trip—and not just because of Lucinda Van Helsing.

In a few minutes, Greta appeared at the door. "The coach is here," she said.

"Thank you," said Mary. "And thank you for everything, Greta. I hope we'll see you again soon."

Greta grinned at them. "I hope so too. You would all make very good thieves and spies."

"I think that is the nicest compliment you could have paid us," said Justine, giving one of her rare smiles. "*Auf Wiedersehen*, Greta."

Their trunk was waiting for them at the bottom of the stairs. There was also a hamper, with blankets and pillows piled on it. Mary checked to make sure they had everything else: Justine's carriage bag, her waist bag. She patted it and felt the shape of her revolver. Who would have thought that Miss Mary Jekyll of 11 Park Terrace would find the feel of a revolver reassuring? And yet she did. She opened her waist bag and saw that her bullet pouch was back in it as well. It was once again full—the bullets she and Irene had fired in the alley, and then in the carriage, had been replaced. How very thoughtful of Hannah and Irene. Among their luggage was a leather traveling bag for Lucinda.

"Ready?" said Irene.

Mary nodded.

Irene opened the door. It was still dark, but the light of two street lamps shone into the courtyard. There, waiting for them, was a coach and pair of large, shaggy coach horses. Up on the box sat a coachman, holding the reins. Another man who was sitting beside him sprang down when they approached. He bowed and said "*Guten Abend, meine Damen,*" then lifted their trunk into the rear boot. The hamper and Lucinda's bag went into the coach, under the seats, and he piled the blankets and pillows on top. Irene spoke to him in German, handing over what seemed like a significant amount of money. He put it in a wallet, then opened the door of the coach and bowed again, saying, "*Bitte.*"

"Go on, get in," said Mary to the others.

"Me first!" said Diana. Of course, she always had to be first!

"Mary," said Irene, drawing her aside. "Try to see if you can get Lucinda to eat, or even drink something. I asked her why she wasn't eating earlier, and she said something about 'the bitter fruit of the forbidden tree'—I have no idea what she meant. But she needs to eat—they must have starved her in that place! There's something else worrying me. As I told you, the coachman is named Miklós Ferenc. The younger man is his son Dénes. He doesn't speak much German, and I suspect his father doesn't speak German at all. They speak only Hungarian—a completely impossible language! You'll have to do your best to communicate with them. I wish I could send you in my carriage, with Hermann driving you—but his wife is about to have their first child. I don't think she would appreciate my sending her husband off to Budapest just now. And Georg, while a perfectly adequate footman, is not trained to drive a coach, or even a barouche! You'd probably die in an accident if he were driving. Take care of yourself, Mary. And the others, of course. It's been a real pleasure getting to know you."

"You too," said Mary. Irene shook her hand—ah, there was that hearty English handshake! But then she put her hands on Mary's shoulders and kissed her on both cheeks. Well, Mary didn't mind. Irene was the most interesting woman she had ever met. They were not in competition, but if they had been, she would happily have lost to Irene Norton.

"Thank you—for everything," she said. Then Dénes Ferenc helped her up into the coach and closed the door behind her. The seats were cushioned and covered in some sort of dark velvet. Thank goodness—this was not going to be as excruciating as she had feared. At least they would not be bouncing around on wooden seats for two days. Diana was already curled up on the seat across from her, with her head on Justine's lap as though it were a pillow. Her eyes were closed. Justine just looked at Mary and shrugged. Ah well, if Justine didn't mind—at least Mary wouldn't have to do pillow duty! She covered Diana with a blanket and sat down next to Lucinda, who was looking out the other window, away from them. She wished there were something she could do—some way she could show Lucinda how very sorry she felt or offer consolation. Why was she so bad at these things?

Then she heard the sound of the whip, and the coach started moving. She looked out the window—there stood Irene and Greta, still visible in the light of the street lamps. She waved, and they waved back. Mary settled into her seat—not as comfortable as a train, but it would do—and drew a blanket over herself. She stared out the window at the streetlights of Vienna as the coach rumbled over the cobblestones. She was still so tired! She would close her eyes, just for a moment. . . .

When Mary opened her eyes, sunlight was streaming into the coach. Oh Lord, she had fallen asleep again, hadn't she? Across from her, Justine and Diana were both asleep—Justine leaning against the cushioned back of the seat, wrapped in a blanket, and Diana sprawled over the seat, with her head in Justine's lap, her mouth open. Good—after their adventures in Vienna, they all needed to rest.

But Lucinda was awake, sitting very straight and staring out the window on the other side.

"How are you feeling, Miss Van Helsing . . . Lucinda?" asked Mary. After all they had been through, surely they were on a first-name basis.

Lucinda turned around. She looked pale and hollow-eyed, but composed. "I am doing well, *danke*," she said. "We are heading into the jaws of doom, where the demons will drink our blood."

"Oh," said Mary. "Well, I'm very glad to hear that you're feeling better." The girl was mad, simply mad. What in the world were they going to do with her?

Lucinda just nodded, then turned back to the window. Mary looked out on her side. They were clopping at a brisk pace through very pretty countryside: The road wound through broad meadows alternating with fields of yellow flowers, obviously some sort of crop although she did not know what. Sometimes she could see farmhouses in the distance. The road was lined with tall trees. Poplars, at a guess? Poplars were tall and straight, right? The road was unpaved, but the coach seemed to be well-sprung, and she did not feel particularly jostled—or not any more than she would have been on the average London street. They must be quite far from Vienna by now. Judging from the position of the sun, it was late morning.

The motion of the coach was hypnotic. There was little else to do than stare out the window, unless she wanted to strike up a conversation with Lucinda. Once, indeed, she turned to the girl and said, "Are you quite comfortable? I could get out another blanket if you would like."

Lucinda replied, "I am covered in the blood of the lamb," as matter-of-factly as she might have said "No, thank you, I am warm enough." After that, Mary did not try again.

Around noon, Diana suddenly woke, sitting up and hitting Justine on the nose as she stretched. "I'm hungry," she said.

Justine opened her eyes and put her hands to her nose at the same time. "What . . . ," she mumbled, still half asleep.

"I'll see what's in the hamper," said Mary. There were sandwiches on buttered bread, some with cheese, some with ham, some with salami. There was a glass jar of cucumber salad, and another of what looked like pickled plums, beside a small basket that held hard-boiled eggs. In a brown paper wrapper, she found some of the rolls they had eaten yesterday, with either walnut or poppy-seed filling, as well as some jam tarts. She was particularly happy to find a vacuum flask of coffee. In one corner of the hamper, wrapped in a tablecloth, were four bottles of water, and beneath them she found four napkins. Thank goodness for Frau Schmidt. Without the Frau Schmidts and Mrs. Pooles, the world would probably stop spinning on its axis.

MRS. POOLE: And don't you forget it!

"Here," said Mary, giving one of the cheese sandwiches to Justine and one of the salami to Diana. She took a ham sandwich herself. "Which would you like?" she asked Lucinda, ready to reach once again into the hamper. Lucinda shook her head and shrank back into her corner of the coach. "All right, well, what about one of these jam things? They probably have some sort of German name. I think it's raspberry jam. Come on, I know you're hungry." Indeed, Lucinda was looking at the jam tart longingly. She reached out her hand, then snatched it back again.

"If she doesn't want it, I'll take it," said Diana.

"But she does want it," said Mary. "You do, don't you? Come on, I know you do."

So quickly that it startled her, Lucinda snatched the tart out of her hand and bit into it. She ate as though famished, in small, rapid bites, almost furtively, with her eyes closed. Once the entire tart had been eaten, she licked her fingers, then looked at Mary and said, in an almost normal voice, "Our cook in Amsterdam would make such *petites choses* for parties—when there were parties, before Papa became the Devil incarnate." Then she put her hands on her stomach, leaned over, and threw up on the floor of the coach, right next to Justine's feet.

For a moment, Mary just stared, not knowing what to do. Justine was quicker—before Mary could respond, she had moved next to Lucinda, squeezing in between her and the wall. She held the girl in her arms and offered her a handkerchief to wipe her mouth, then wiped it herself because Lucinda was so distraught that all she could do was sit, hunched over, with tears flowing down her face.

"All right," said Mary. "Clearly, that was a bad idea." With the tablecloth that had been in the hamper, she cleaned up the vomit, while Diana sat on the seat opposite with her feet on the cushion, offering helpful comments such as "That is so gross. Why did you tell her to eat? Don't you remember what happened with the coffee?"

"Of course I remember the coffee!" Mary snapped. The coach stank of vomit. She pulled down the window on her side as far as it would go, which was not far, then tossed out the tablecloth. It was not in her nature to litter, but they must get rid of the stench as much as possible, and anyway in a month the cloth would have disintegrated in the rain and mud. She used two of the napkins to wipe the floor, then tossed those out as well. For goodness' sake, why couldn't Diana help, for once? But no, she just sat there, complaining.

"All right, that's the best I can do," she said finally. Justine was still holding Lucinda, who was leaning against her, blond ringlets hanging over her tear-streaked face.

"What now?" she asked Justine. "She has to eat something, or she'll get sick. Maybe she already is sick, and that's why she's throwing everything up. Justine, does she have a temperature?"

Gently, Justine put her hand on Lucinda's forehead. "No, she's cold—cold and damp. I wish we had Beatrice here. She would know what to do."

> BEATRICE: Alas, even my medical knowledge would have been useless in such a circumstance. I have no cure for Lucinda's disease.

"Maybe she needs blood," said Diana.

"What?" said Mary, and "What do you mean?" said Justine, at the same time.

"When I was in the hospital, that Krankenplace, and we were trying to get her mother to come with us, she told me to give her blood, so I gave her some."

"Gave her some?" said Mary. "How?"

"Cut open my arm, of course. See?" Diana rolled up her sleeve. There, on her wrist, was a fresh scar, still red. "And then she drank it, right from my wrist."

"Oh, dear Lord," said Mary. "Why didn't you tell us this earlier? At Irene's, so it might have been useful to us, and we could have cleaned that cut properly?"

"I forgot," said Diana, shrugging.

"You *forgot*! How could you possibly forget letting someone drink your blood?"

"Well, there was a lot going on," said Diana defensively. "Also, you would have shouted at me, just like you're doing now."

"I'm not shouting!" said Mary.

Justine reached over and put a hand on her knee. "You are, though. Mary, I know you're upset, but quarreling won't help the situation. I'm worried about Lucinda."

And, indeed, Lucinda was leaning against Justine's shoulder with her eyes closed. She looked terribly pale.

Diana reached under her skirt and took out a small knife. "You'll see, she just needs some blood." She held the knife up to her wrist.

"Oh no, you don't," said Mary, grabbing her hand. "If you did that for Lucinda's mother, I don't want you doing it for Lucinda as well. I don't know how much blood you lost! I'll do it. And where in the world do you keep this knife?"

"In my garter, of course," said Diana. "It's useless otherwise, except to hold up my stocking."

Mary shook her head and took the knife, then placed it carefully on the seat beside her so the motion of the coach would not jog it onto the floor. She rolled back her sleeve above the elbow. She had never cut herself before. How much would it hurt? A little? A lot? Quite a lot, as it turned out. She watched the red flow of blood down her wrist—the left one, since she would need her right arm more.

"Hold her head, will you?" she said to Justine. Then she placed her wrist on Lucinda's mouth. This was mad—what in the world was she doing? On the other hand, it was no more mad than anything else that had happed in the last three days. Would Lucinda actually drink her blood?

At first, nothing happened. Lucinda leaned against Justine, eyes closed, as though asleep or in a faint. Then, Mary felt something on her wrist—it was a tongue. Lucinda was lapping at her blood, as though she were a cat lapping at a bowl of milk. All the blood that had flowed down Mary's wrist and arm, almost to the elbow, Lucinda carefully licked up. Then, still with her eyes closed, she put her mouth to the cut and began to suck.

It did not seem to hurt anymore, and Mary felt fine, just fine, although curiously light-headed. It felt as though the world were starting to swim around her, as though she were underwater, with the interior of the coach swaying like seaweed. Perhaps she had drowned, and this was the cabin of a wrecked ship. . . .

"That's enough!" said Justine. "Quite enough. Mary, are you all right?"

Justine's face swam into view. Was she all right? Probably. Maybe.

"You little bitch!" said Diana. "How could you do that to my sister?"

Mary giggled—she could not help it. Imagine Diana, of all people, coming to her defense!

"What?" said Diana. "Why are you laughing? Are you going into hysterics or something?"

"Give her coffee," said Justine. "I did not think Lucinda would drink so much, so quickly."

Mary felt the cold metal of the vacuum flask against her lips.

"Come on," said Diana. "Drink this, and I'm going to kill that little—"

Mary giggled again, almost getting coffee down the front of her dress.

"What?" said Diana. "Tell me why you're laughing!"

Mary drank from the vacuum flask—ah yes, why had she ever thought tea was superior to coffee? Coffee was the best thing in the world; coffee was life itself. . . . "Because you're littler than her," she said finally, after she had finished drinking. She handed the vacuum flask back to Diana.

"So?" said Diana. "I could take her with one hand tied behind my back!"

"I'm not so sure of that," said Justine.

Lucinda was sitting up now. For the first time, her cheeks were tinged with color. Her eyes were bright, less sunken and hollow than they had been. There was a spot of blood on her mouth, but as Mary watched, she licked her lips and then the spot was gone. In a stronger voice than she had spoken in before, she said, "I am damned, my soul is damned to eternal hellfire. I would prefer to die."

"Well, that's not going to happen," said Mary crossly. "Even if it takes all our blood to keep you alive!" She was starting to feel a little better, but she was still dizzy—the motion of the coach made her sick. "Diana, can you hand me a sandwich? Cheese, this time—and a hard-boiled egg. And some of those pickled whatever they are." She turned back to Lucinda. "We're going to get you to Mina in Budapest, understood? You're not allowed to die until we get there."

Lucinda stared down at her hands, which were lying in her lap. Justine stroked the girl's hair, as gently as a mother would have. Mary looked at Justine and held up her hands in the universal gesture of helplessness. Well, at least the wound on her wrist wasn't bleeding—all she could see was a red line where the cut had been. Justine shrugged, as though to say, *I don't know what to do either.*

Great, just what they needed. Here they were, rolling through the Austrian countryside, on the road for three days. It would be complicated enough taking care of all the usual things travelers faced on such journeys—making sure they had enough food as well as places to sleep, places to wash themselves. And now they had discovered that one of them needed blood to survive. Which wasn't exactly the sort of thing they could purchase at a local market, was it? How in the world were they going to make it to Budapest?

"Move over," Mary said to Diana, then switched to the other side of the coach. That would give Justine and Lucinda a little more room—and her too, although there was little enough in the confines of a coach, however luxurious it might be. She considered what had just happened. How often would Lucinda need blood? What sort of blood—would pig's blood do? She had no idea, and she did not think asking Lucinda would help, not unless she wanted to hear again about how Lucinda was damned and wanted to die. Her head ached.

Silently—thank goodness for small miracles—Diana handed her a sandwich, one of the hard boiled eggs, and the pickle jar, with a fork that had been lying at the bottom of the hamper, under the napkins. They were indeed pickled plums, and better than Mary had expected, both sweet and sour. She ate several, then wiped her mouth with one of the two remaining napkins. Diana also took an egg, cracked it against the windowsill, and started to peel the shell. When it was peeled, she bit into the egg and, with her mouth full, leaned over to Mary and said, in a not particularly quiet whisper, "Don't worry, if she attacks you or Justine, I'll kill her. I'll cut her throat with my little knife."

It was going to be very long three days.

DIANA: You never appreciate me, even when I'm being nice!

MARY: It was nice of you to defend me like that, Diana. I did appreciate it, you know. I do appreciate it, even now.

DIANA: Well, you're my sister. I mean, you're annoying, and you have a stick up your— Catherine doesn't want me to say that word anymore—but you're still my sister.

MRS. POOLE: That may be the most affectionate thing I've heard you say, Miss Scamp.

DIANA: Go back to your kitchen, you old (unprintable).

CHAPTER XIV

La Belle Toxique

B eatrice!"
Beatrice looked up guiltily. "I know, Cat. I'm sorry—
we were just coming to the end of a conversation. We've
only been talking about an hour, I promise. I watched the time,
truly I did."

"It's my fault, Whiskers," said Clarence. "I kept asking her
questions about Italy. I've never been. Imagine walking down the
streets of Rome, where men like Seneca and Marcus Aurelius
walked. . . . The only country in the world I want to see more
than Italy is Egypt. And I feel fine, really I do. I think I'm getting
used to it—sort of like getting used to the snow when I moved to
Boston, or getting used to rain in England. And look, we've got
the window open." He pointed to the train window, which was
pushed down as far as it would go. Outside, Catherine could see
the Austrian countryside flashing by. It looked . . . green.

"Beatrice's poison is not some sort of atmospheric condition,"
said Catherine. "You can't acclimate to it—not without becoming poisonous yourself. Is that what you want?" She glared at
him, frowning as disapprovingly as she knew how, then looked at
Beatrice. "But that's not what I want to talk to you about. I think
someone from the Alchemical Society is *here*—on this train."

"What do you mean?" asked Beatrice, startled. "Have you seen
someone who looks like a member of the Société?"

"No, of course not. What would a member of the Alchemical Society look like anyway, other than Dr. Seward? I mean, he looks perfectly ordinary. An alchemist in disguise could look like anyone. But I haven't seen anyone other than our own people. After breakfast I stayed in the dining car, talking to Colonel Sharp and Miss Petunia. Then I thought I would go back to my cabin— well, Zora's and my cabin, although it's mostly hers, considering how she leaves her stuff around. I'm surprised I haven't found one of her snakes in there yet! Anyway, I wanted to get my notebook, so I could write down my impressions of Paris. I thought maybe I could set one of the Astarte stories there—*Astarte at the Tour d'Eiffel*. Something like that. So I opened the trunk, and things were in the wrong place. Someone had obviously tried to put them back in the right place, but I'm a cat. I know when things are in the wrong place—I can just tell. So I went through all my clothes, our books and maps, even the toiletries you said couldn't fit in your suitcase. I took everything out, checked all the pockets. And then I realized—the telegram from Irene Norton was gone."

"Gone?" said Beatrice. "You told me you had put it someplace no one would ever find it."

"Yes, in your Bible, just inside the front cover. I didn't want to carry it around with me all the time—I figured it was safest if I hid it where no one would look. No one actually looks in a Bible, except Justine, and anyway I put it right down at the bottom, under all my clothes. Who would search down that far? But when I opened the Bible, the telegram wasn't there. And as I said, every-thing was disarranged—not so an ordinary person would notice, but I'm not an ordinary person. Now I wish we'd put my clothes in the suitcase and kept the trunk in your cabin. Although then all our maps would be infused with poisonous fumes. . . . Anyway, someone must have taken that telegram."

"Are you quite sure?" Beatrice still looked doubtful. "I know how cautious you are, Cat, but we've seen no sign that anyone is following us or even particularly interested in our movements. Yes, we were told that Mary and Justine encountered an agent of the Société des Alchimistes on their journey—although I wish Mrs. Norton had given us more information! But that does not mean the society knows where we are—or even who we are. And we have seen no one suspicious—this entire train car is filled with Lorenzo's performers. If a stranger were to board or enter from another car, he would surely be seen and remarked upon. Or do you suspect a fellow member of the circus? Surely not. I cannot imagine Sasha or the Jellicoes as agents of the Société des Alchimistes. Could you have put the telegram someplace else and then forgotten? Or perhaps it simply fell out of the Bible the last time you opened the trunk, and you did not notice."

Could that have happened? Catherine had certainly not put the telegram anywhere else, but could it have slipped out of the Bible at some point, perhaps while she was moving the trunk? No, since they had gotten on the train it had stayed securely under the seat, and she had simply slid it in and out, lifting the lid when she needed clothes. . . . Then what about while she had been searching through the trunk that morning, after she realized someone had tampered with it? Perhaps she should go back and look again. Beatrice might make herself silly over social causes, but she was fundamentally sensible and worth listening to. Catherine tried to think back . . . when had she last seen the telegram, anyway? Yes, it had been their first day on the train, when Beatrice had asked for a pot of rouge, no doubt to make her more attractive for Mr. I-don't-care-if-I'm-poisoned. She had checked to make sure nothing had broken or shifted while the porters were loading luggage onto the train, and there it had been, tucked securely in the front cover. There was no way it could simply have slipped out.

Today, Beatrice was wearing one of her Reform dresses—it

was green, and almost medieval in style. On their first day in Paris, before the evening performance, she had gone off by herself, telling Catherine only that she needed some air, and yes, she knew Paris perfectly well—she had been here before, for several months, meeting with learned men at the Sorbonne about her condition. Catherine had worried about her venturing out alone—what if she got lost, or poisoned someone? But several hours later she returned with a parcel wrapped in brown paper.

"Have you been shopping?" Catherine had asked. They didn't have much money, not having yet received any from Lorenzo, and Paris was expensive.

Beatrice had looked both pleased and a little ashamed of herself. "I should perhaps have gone to one of the museums or galleries—Paris is so rich in art and culture! But I found myself at the House of Worth, and one of his assistants was so kind as to show me the autumn collection, and then would you believe it, Mr. Worth himself came down from his office! He told me that I had an unusual look, and he would like to hire me as a model, so I had to explain who I was—*La Belle Toxique*, you know. Then he said that he would like me to wear one of his gowns, because it would be a good advertisement. There was one that had been made up for another customer, who had not wanted it after all, and he said with a few alterations it would look as though it had been made for me. So a seamstress fitted and altered it right there, and then his assistant took a photograph! And here, look! He said this model is called *la fée verte*."

She undid the parcel, and out spilled a gown of green silk that did, indeed, look as though it had been made for Beatrice. It was the perfect gown for a Poisonous Girl.

Of course, it made her look even more beautiful, which had not helped with the problem of Clarence! But Paris had been a triumph. Five shows—Friday evening, and matinee and evening shows on Saturday and Sunday, all filled to capacity with a crowd eager to see the Jellicoe Twins tie themselves into knots; Colonel Sharp throw his knives, assisted by the attractive, but distinctly bearded, Miss Petunia; and Atlas, the Strongest Man in the World, lift heavier and heavier objects. The Queen of Lilliput, the Smallest Woman in the World, recited poetry while standing on a table, the Dog Boy barked and howled, and the Panther Woman climbed a series of rope-and-plank contraptions to show her agility. The Kaminski Brothers demonstrated their acrobatic skills. The Zulu Prince performed his native dances with abandon. Madam Zora displayed her poisonous snakes. And then, the star attraction . . . *La Belle Toxique* came onto the stage. Beatrice had told Lorenzo that she would not kill anything living as part of her show. So instead, he called up audience members who had volunteered to let her breathe on them or shake them by the hand. They paid for the pleasure of reeling from her poisonous breath on their faces or feeling their fingers burn. The audience had laughed at those who came stumbling back down the stairs as though drunk, or cheered those who descended with blistered hands. Sometimes, she consented to kiss particular audience members on the cheek—an elderly politician, a beautiful young duchess, a poor sailor on leave. The Paris papers had labeled her *la vrai femme fatale*.

It was like being in the sideshow again, with a difference. On the ferry from Dover, Catherine had gone to Lorenzo and said, "Why don't you let each of us tell our stories? You know, how the Panther Woman of the Andes was born of a panther mother and human father, that sort of thing. These are French audiences, more sophisticated than your usual staid Englishmen. What do you think?"

Lorenzo looked at her skeptically. "Tell stories, eh? You think the audience will like to hear?"

"Of course. Everyone likes to hear stories. Look, I'll write them down and show them to you by the time we reach Paris. Then you can tell me what you think."

So she had spoken with Sasha, and Zora, and Clarence, and the rest of Lorenzo's performers, creating stories for each of them—a combination of their ideas and her storytelling abilities. In some cases, the story was an outright fabrication—(Clarence: "I was born the youngest son of Shaka Zulu himself. On the day of my birth, the priest of my tribe prophesied that when I was grown, I would travel across the great water to the land of a people as white as ghosts.")—in some, such as Beatrice's, nearly the truth. The show had been billed as *Une Rencontre Avec des Monstres*, and audiences had loved it. Lorenzo made so much money that he wired ahead to Vienna to book an extra show on Thursday evening. They had boarded the train again directly after their last Paris show. It was not an express, of course, but it would get them to Vienna in four days, just in time for their performance. And he told them that he already had an invitation from a theater in Budapest. Everything had been going so well . . . until about an hour ago, when Catherine realized that someone had been going through her trunk, and that the telegram from Irene Norton, with her address and a warning against the Alchemical Society, was gone.

"Cat, did you write her address down anywhere else?" asked Beatrice.

"No, it's not the sort of thing I wanted to write down, in case anyone found it. I have it memorized: 18 Prinz-Eugen Strasse. But that's not the issue. I've tried to think back, and there's no other way that telegram could be missing. Even if it fell out of the Bible, it would have been in the trunk somewhere. I really did look through everything, Bea. I took all my clothes out, went through the pockets. . . . The telegram wasn't there. And you know what? It must have disappeared between when I got dressed this morning and when I went back for my notebook, because if anything had been disturbed earlier, I would have noticed. I'm sure I would have. Someone here has been through my trunk and taken Mrs. Norton's telegram. I can't think of anyone who would want to do that except a member of the Alchemical Society. You're right, I don't think an outsider could have entered this car without being seen, in which case someone would have mentioned it—you know how circus folk gossip. And yes, Clarence and I know everyone here—have known them for years—*except Zora*. She's new. Do you remember how eager she was to share a cabin with me? She said she wanted to get to know me better. Why? I thought it was strange at the time, and now it seems . . . well, suspicious. If anyone in Lorenzo's circus is an agent of the Alchemical Society, it has to be her."

Clarence frowned. He could look quite formidable when he frowned. "Cat, it's not like you to accuse anyone without evidence. What exactly are you basing your suspicions on, other than the fact that Zora wanted to share a cabin with you?"

Catherine leaned forward. She felt like Sherlock Holmes discussing his conclusions. It all fit together so perfectly. "Look, Zora is the only person other than the porter with a key to our cabin. After all, it's her cabin as well. Anyone else would have been taking the risk that I was already inside, but that wouldn't have worried her—she could just have searched another time. And if she was seen entering, none of us would have thought anything of it—we would have assumed she was going to fetch something, or take a nap. Where was she after breakfast? She said she was going to feed the snakes, but where was she after that? She could have gone back and looked through the trunk then."

"You yourself have shown me how easy it is to open a locked door," said Beatrice thoughtfully. "You told me it took Diana only an hour to teach you how. And whoever looked through the trunk must have picked that lock—why not the door lock as well?

Certainly it would be a risk, but if someone could get in quickly, without being seen—"

"Yes, but that was *me*," said Catherine. "I can hear tumblers falling, remember? And it's harder to pick the lock on the cabin door—a trunk lock is child's play to anyone with a hairpin. Anyway, I didn't say I had any proof. Just a suspicion, that's all. Sherlock Holmes would follow up on a suspicion, wouldn't he? She's the most logical suspect."

Catherine remembered the evening they had boarded, standing on the platform in the Gare de l'Est while Lorenzo distributed their tickets. She was supposed to share with Miss Petunia—everyone had to share, except of course for Beatrice because of her poison. But Zora had grabbed her by the arm and said, "I'm sharing with Catherine! Come on, Cat Girl, it will be fun!" Miss Petunia had agreed to trade tickets and share with Mrs. Kaminski, who helped her sons set up and made sure the nets were securely tied. Even then, Catherine had wondered why Zora was so eager to share with her. It was not as though she and the snake charmer were friends.

"I think you should ask her," said Clarence. "Give her a chance to defend herself. It's only fair."

"You should have been a judge instead of a lawyer," said Catherine.

He laughed, but his laughter had an edge of bitterness. "They wouldn't let me be either in Massachusetts, Whiskers. Not after what I did."

"What did you do?" asked Beatrice. "You've never told me."

"Or me," said Catherine. She sat down next to Beatrice, the theft of the telegram forgotten for a moment. She and Clarence had been friends since she had joined the Circus of Marvels and Delights, but he had never told her why he was here, what had brought him to the sideshow. She had not asked—as she had told

Beatrice, one didn't ask questions in the circus. But now that Beatrice had brought it up, she was curious as well.

He sighed. "You really want to know?"

Beatrice nodded. Catherine simply waited. If he wanted to tell them, he would. Clarence was not the sort of man you could persuade or plead with.

"All right. It was the year I graduated from law school. Like the other black men in my class, I was inspired by Judge Ruffin, the first black man to graduate from Harvard Law and the first to become a judge in Massachusetts. I thought I was going to be just like him. Me, a poor boy raised by a widowed mother who used to clean other people's houses to pay the rent. Well, I went through Howard on scholarship, then Harvard on scholarship, and my first year out I worked for an organization offering legal aid to other poor folk—black, Irish, Italian, all sorts. I was sent to one of the counties in the western part of the state, to defend a black man accused of raping a white woman. That was the first time a judge called me 'boy.' I got my client off all right—the woman herself stood in the witness stand to say it wasn't rape. They wanted to get married. That was legal in Massachusetts, and she was of age, but her father didn't want her to marry a black man, so he told the sheriff that my client had raped her. She was visibly pregnant.

"My client walked out of that courthouse a free man, but there was a crowd waiting for him outside, and suddenly her brother stepped out of that crowd. He was the sheriff's deputy. He had a gun, and he said he was going to shoot that damn . . . his language isn't fit to repeat. He was determined to kill my client. Without thinking, I jumped on him and wrestled with him for the gun. It went off. . . . He bled to death in my arms. So I was tried for manslaughter in that courthouse, in front of that judge. Despite his jury instructions, I was acquitted—you could almost see him frothing at the mouth with fury and tearing his hair out, the day I walked out of that courtroom, a free man. Everyone in that crowd had seen it was an accident, but who was going to give me a job after that? It didn't matter that I was innocent. My face had been on the cover of the *Boston Globe* as the black man who'd killed a white policeman. My mother had died the year before of cancer, and my only other family was cousins down in Virginia. I had no money, so I got a job working the boiler on a steam ship bound for England. After we landed in London, I worked for a while down at the docks, in the East End. There, I met some men who were putting on a Zulu Extravaganza—not one of them was a Zulu, but they said that sort of thing paid well, and what did Londoners know about Zulus anyway? I was in that show for two years before it disbanded, but eventually one of the members left to get married, and another started a grocery business, so there weren't enough of us to go on. It was back to dockwork for me, until one day I saw an advertisement for Lorenzo's circus, and I asked him if he needed a professional Zulu. And I've been with the circus since."

They were all silent for a moment. Then Beatrice said, "Could you not use your law license in England?"

"I haven't bothered to find out," said Clarence. "I'm done with the law, and I hope it's done with me. Now, the lunch service is going to start soon. Cat, do you want to talk to Zora or not? If you're going to do it, you'd better do it soon. We'll be in Vienna in a couple of hours. I'd rather you had it out with her than go around spying and being suspicious. That's another kind of poison, especially for a show like ours."

"All right," said Catherine. "I suppose now is as good a time as any. And you need to get out of Beatrice's cabin. How long have you been in here, anyway? Beatrice said an hour, but I don't believe her. She doesn't even wear a watch."

"I came in after breakfast," said Clarence. "That was . . ." He took out his pocket watch. "Three hours ago?"

"Damn it, Clarence, you should know better! And you should have kicked him out, Bea. You know it's not good for him to stay in here so long, even with the window open. Do you want the same thing to happen again? You know—like with Giovanni?" She was so angry at them—at both of them. Why did people's emotions get in the way of rational thinking? Beatrice in particular should know better. The first man she had loved had become poisonous from spending too much time in her presence. Then, he had died. Why could she not think of the consequences?

"I am so sorry," said Beatrice. "I should have been more con-scious of the time. But it was so pleasant to talk. . . ." She looked conscience-stricken, and as though she were about to cry. Catherine was almost sorry for having spoken so harshly. After all, it must be difficult for Beatrice, not being able to socialize with the others. The circus—or in this case, the traveling sideshow—was a colle-gial group. Someone was always telling a story or demonstrating new tricks. There were card games and spontaneous sing-alongs that startled the staff of the dining car. Henrietta, the Queen of Lilliput, who was also Mrs. Colonel Sharp, had a particularly fine voice. Beatrice could not join in any of that. On the train, every cabin was an enclosed space in which her poison could accumulate. She had to spend most of her time alone. Catherine came to see her as often as possible, but even she could not spend all her time with Beatrice—she was not immune to Beatrice's poison either.

"Come on, Clarence," she said. "If I'm going to confront Zora, I want to do it now, and I want you to come with me, in case there's any trouble. Anyway, you need to get out of here. If I have to come to your funeral, it'll be your own damn fault."

"Cat, I'm *fine*," he said. "I can take care of myself, remember?" But when he stood up, he stumbled as his knees buckled under him, and he had to clutch at the luggage rack overhead.

Catherine just looked at him, too exasperated to say anything.

What was it with men, anyway? They always thought they were so strong, so rational—and really, they were just as emotional as women. Or more so! Here was Clarence, risking his health, even his life, for a conversation with the Poisonous Girl. . . . If he weren't her oldest friend, she would have remonstrated with him. Of course, if he weren't her oldest friend, she wouldn't have been so worried! And she cared about Beatrice, too. She wanted Beatrice to be happy —but not at the cost of Clarence's life.

"All right, Cat." He followed her into the corridor. "Whatever you were going to say, consider it said. I can see it all over your face—you look like a tabby turning its nose up at bad milk! I promise I'll be more careful. Now, where's Zora?"

Zora, it turned out, was sitting in the cabin she shared with Catherine. Next to her on the seat that was her bed at night, while Catherine took the bunk, were Sasha and an older woman Catherine did not recognize. She looked like someone's kindly grandmother, in a dress of black crepe with a lace fichu around her shoulders. She was wearing an old-fashioned black bonnet, and peered at Catherine through a pair of strong spectacles.

"Hello, Cat!" said Sasha in his strong Russian accent. That part of his story at least was true—he really had come from Russia, although from the slums of St. Petersburg rather than the steppes that stretch across that great empire. He looked nothing like a dog—today he was wearing an ordinary wool suit with a Norfolk jacket, and would have struck an onlooker as unusual only because of the copious amount of hair that grew over his face. "This is Frau Krähe. She is an old friend—she was a nurse at the orphanage in Moravia where I was sent as a boy. I was walking on the platform when we stopped in Wels, smoking a cigarette, when suddenly I thought, I know that woman purchasing a newspaper! And it was indeed she. Frau Krähe was just telling us that she got on in Munich, and is going to Vienna as well, to visit her granddaughter. She is several cars down. Is that not a strange coincidence?"

"I suppose so," said Catherine. "Pleased to meet you, I'm sure." She shook the small, crooked hand in knitted black gloves that Frau Krähe held out, not particularly pleased that Sasha was there, or his friend, although she looked like a nice old woman. She had hoped to find Zora alone so she could confront the snake charmer with her suspicions.

"I am always pleased to meet a friend of dear Sasha," said Frau Krähe, in a German accent that was even thicker than his Russian one, if that was possible. "How well I remember when he first came to us—a charming little boy, but very sick! We got him well again, on plenty of brown bread and clean mountain air. Now he smokes those vile cigarettes. Really, Sasha!" She shook her head at him, then turned back to peer at Catherine and Clarence through her spectacles. "And you are also with the circus?"

Then introductions were made all around, but Catherine wished both Sasha and his friend would leave so she could talk to Zora alone.

Instead, he finished telling the story of how he had been sent by himself, at such a young age, to the orphanage in Moravia. His father, who shared his hirsute condition, was also a sideshow performer, but had succumbed to the lure of alcohol and made barely enough to support his family. His brother and sisters had all been sent to orphanages as well—he had not seen them since they were children. Frau Krähe had helped him, more than he could describe. He owed her everything. . . .

"I want to talk to Zora for a minute," said Catherine, interrupting his story.

"Of course," said Sasha, standing up. "I shall save you all seats for the luncheon service, yes?"

"As for me, I have my luncheon in a basket that I purchased in

Wels," said Frau Krähe. "It is so easy, so convenient—these girls that come with baskets and sell them to the passengers for a few hellers. I have lovely goose pie, and a cheese, and grapes. But I hope to see you again, dear Sasha. I have so much to tell you still, and a little something to give you. When you are finished, perhaps you can come to my cabin and talk some more to me, *nein?*" She rose slowly, with a hand on her back—it was obvious that she suffered from rheumatism.

Sasha nodded, then followed her out of the cabin. When the Dog Boy and his friend were gone, Catherine turned to Zora.

"What?" said Zora defensively. "You've been looking at me strangely ever since you came in here. Out with it!"

Fine, if that was the way she wanted to do things! "Have you been going through my trunk?" asked Catherine. "There's something missing, and I think you took it."

"You think I went into your trunk and what—*stole* something of yours?" Zora was visibly angry. "And what is Clarence here for, to strong-arm me into admitting that I'm a thief?"

"Now, Zora," he said. "You know I would never do that." He looked distinctly uncomfortable. "I just wanted Cat to talk to you, so this could all be cleared up."

Zora stood up from the seat. Her fists were clenched at her sides. She looked as though she were about to hit someone. "I don't know what you would or wouldn't do, Clarence. You know, I've been called a thief before. Growing up in Hackney, going to the markets with my mother—the shopkeepers always kept an eye on us, in case we pilfered anything. Because we looked Indian, and you could never tell with those *wogs*, could you? The number of times I was told I wasn't welcome because I wasn't really English, even though I'd been born in London, same as them. I thought the circus was going to be different. I thought *you*"—she looked at Catherine accusingly—"were going to be different. But you know what? Why don't you just search my stuff. Go on. Whatever you're missing, jewelry or money—you just go ahead and look for it!" She bent down and drew her suitcase out from under the seat, threw it on top, and opened it violently, so that dresses and scarves spilled out. She shook the contents directly onto the seat cushions, then scattered them about. "Here you go, that's what you wanted, right? And if you find whatever you're looking for, you can go ahead and put me in gaol, or whatever they have for gaol here in Austria. I'm going to feed the snakes—they need their lunch too. They may be poisonous, but they've never made me feel like dirt. It takes a human being to do that."

She slammed the cabin door behind her, and Catherine could hear her boots stomping down the corridor.

"Whiskers," said Clarence, "you know I love you, but that was *not* your finest hour. You have no evidence that Zora did anything wrong. The least you could have done is asked her instead of accusing her. She's a member of this circus too, just like you are."

Catherine frowned. Whose side was he on, anyway? "Look," she said, impatiently. "She's the only one of us who's new, the only one who wasn't here when Justine and I were part of the circus, before we got tangled up with the Alchemical Society. Beatrice told you about the society—I don't think she should have, but she did. Do you think the sort of people who created me or Beatrice—or allowed those sorts of experiments—would have any moral compunctions whatsoever? If she's working for the society, then I'm not sorry I *offended* her."

Clarence regarded her from under lowered brows. She had never seen him look so judgmental. "They may have no moral compunctions, but you should."

Well, she was certainly not going to dignify that with an answer! Couldn't he see how important this was? Sometimes the end justified the means.

MARY: No, it doesn't. And you were insensitive, you
know. You can be, sometimes.

CATHERINE: Well, if I'd known then what I know
now, I would have acted differently. But I didn't,
did I? If we start criticizing ourselves for all the
decisions we've made, second-guessing ourselves,
we'll never actually get anything done. The past is
gone, and there's nothing you or I can do about it.
Do you regret that time you shot Holmes? I'm sure
you do, but what are you going to do about it now?
Nothing, that's what, because you can't. Except
wallow in your own guilt, which doesn't help
either him or you.

MARY: I still think you could have been nicer to Zora.
Or at least more polite.

CATHERINE: Well, excuse me! There were no
etiquette manuals on Moreau's island.

An hour later, Catherine had searched through Zora's suitcase, and then the entire cabin. She had even searched through the
trunk again, just in case she had somehow, improbable as it was,
overlooked something the first time. But she had found nothing.
There was no sign of the telegram, and no sign that Zora was
anything other than who she said she was—except perhaps that
she used a rather expensive brand of soap for a girl who had grown
up in the East End, which could simply be a matter of personal
taste. Catherine had tried to repack Zora's suitcase neatly—not
that Zora was a particularly neat packer!

"Now what?" asked Clarence, who had sat, arms crossed,

through the entire procedure. She could feel disapproval emanating from him in waves.

"I don't know," said Catherine. "I suppose she could be carrying it around on her?"

"Oh, you want to search *me* now?" Zora was standing in the doorway. "You just go right ahead. Come on, I'll strip to my skivvies for you."

"I really don't think that's necessary," said Clarence, frowning.

"All right," said Catherine. "Clarence, go away. I don't need you for this part."

Clarence looked incredulous. "You can't be serious."

"Go on," said Zora. "You're just as bad as her, Mr. Fake Zulu Prince, and I'm certainly not going to strip down in front of you. Get out, and shut the door behind you."

When Clarence had gone, with a final disapproving shake of his head, Zora untied the sash around her waist and unbuttoned her long robe, in a pink-and-orange paisley pattern that shimmered with gold thread, to reveal a perfectly ordinary shift and drawers. She was not wearing a corset—otherwise, she looked just like any other Englishwoman under her clothes. Finally, she unbuttoned and stepped out of her boots.

"I expected better of you," she said bitterly, standing in the middle of the cabin in her undergarments, on stockinged feet. "I wanted us to share a cabin because we were the brown girls in this troupe—I thought we could be friends. It was lonely being the new girl when everyone else had known each other for ages. But you're as bad as the Londoners who told me to go back to India, that my kind weren't wanted here. Are you satisfied now that I didn't take whatever you're missing?"

Catherine lifted the robe, shook it, looked—no pockets. Nothing in the boots. Well, if Zora had the telegram, it was certainly not on her person. "You could have had it on you before and hidden it somewhere while I was searching the suitcase," she said doubtfully. Could she have made a mistake? Perhaps Zora had wanted to share a cabin with her not because she was an agent of the Alchemical Society, but for companionship, as she claimed. It was sometimes difficult for Catherine to understand how these humans, born rather than made, liked to band together. No, *needed* to band together. Of course, she had friends as well—Justine was a friend, and so was Beatrice. But she was still essentially solitary. She probably always would be. Turning a puma into a woman did not take the puma out of her, not deep inside where it counted.

"I'm sorry," she said reluctantly, although she still felt that her suspicions had been reasonable. But she had not meant to hurt Zora, and she had learned that humans expect a show of regret and contrition when one is wrong.

"No, you're not," said Zora, buttoning her robe again and stepping into her boots. Then she banged out of the cabin with her boots still unbuttoned, muttering something about getting lunch before the service ended. When Catherine went into the dining room herself, after tidying the cabin, she saw Zora sitting with Sasha, Doris Jellicoe, and Colonel Sharp. The snake charmer glared at Catherine, then turned back to her companions, speaking to them in low, angry tones. She was telling them what had happened, wasn't she? Catherine wondered if they would be angry with her as well. She asked the steward for some mint tea, which was all Beatrice seemed to be ingesting on this journey. Well, at least it smelled better than her usual goop. Catherine herself was not hungry—that morning, she had been so tired of train food that instead of joining the others in the dining car, she had gone hunting. Luckily, the baggage car had been an excellent place to find big, juicy rats. They had been delicious, and she was still quite full.

DIANA: That's disgusting.

CATHERINE: And it's not disgusting when Alpha and
Omega leave decapitated mice on our beds?

DIANA: They're cats, not Cat Women. Anyway, you
said they think they're giving us gifts.

MRS. POOLE: Very kind of them, I'm sure. (Let
it be noted that Mrs. Poole's tone was entirely
sarcastic.)

When she entered Beatrice's cabin, holding the teacup carefully so as not to spill, the Poisonous Girl was sitting with her feet
up on the seat, staring out the window.

"Drink up," said Catherine. "We'll be in Vienna soon. Are you
all right? You look—pensive. Even more so than usual."

"I should not have kept Clarence so long," said Beatrice. "You
saw, when he left— my poison had begun to affect him. Catherine,
I do not want it to be the story of Giovanni again. I killed a man I
loved once—I do not want to repeat my sin, my crime."

Catherine sat down next to her. "Are you saying you love
Clarence?"

"What? No . . . I did not say that. How could I love him? I have
known him only a fortnight. I am referring to the general situation—
that once before, I killed a man."

"Well, first of all, you didn't," said Catherine. "What happened
to Giovanni was not your fault. Second, you were alone when that
happened, and now you're not. I'm here, and I won't let anything
happen—to either of you."

CATHERINE: Readers who are not familiar with the
tale of Beatrice and Giovanni can find it in the
first of these adventures of the Athena Club, in an

attractive green cloth binding that will appear to
advantage in a lady's or gentleman's library. Two
shillings, as I mentioned before.

BEATRICE: You would use the story of my grief to sell
copies of your book?

CATHERINE: *Our* book. I may be writing it, but you
are all as responsible for its contents as I am.
What is the point if we don't reach readers? And
honestly, Bea, you're not the only one whose
sorrows are being recorded here. I mean . . . Bea?

MARY: She's gone back to the conservatory. I think
you offended her—seriously offended her. The
way you offended Zora.

CATHERINE: Why do you humans have to be so
emotional?

"And what of Zora?" Beatrice asked. "Did you find the telegram among her effects?"
"I think only dead people have effects," said Catherine. "And
no, but I still think it's her. It has to be her, doesn't it? I mean,
who else could it be—Colonel and Mrs. Sharp? The Jellicoes?
I've known them for years." And yet, Zora had been so natural in
her denial, and in her anger at Catherine. She felt, not ashamed
exactly, but uncomfortable at having made the accusation, and
particularly of having searched Zora herself. Surely her actions
had been justified, considering the circumstances? She wished
she felt more confident about that. Human morality was complicated—it was so much easier being a puma! Suddenly, she stood

up again. "You know what? I'm going to find Clarence. I think he's mad at me."

"Surely not!" said Beatrice. "He's just a gentle soul."

"We are talking about the same Clarence, aren't we? He may be gentle with you, but I've seen him get angry before. You should have seen him when some drunk London clerks who had paid to see the sideshow started teasing Edith Jellicoe, making lewd suggestions. He kicked them out, and I'm not speaking metaphorically. When he's upset about something, he becomes a sort of righteous brick wall. And you don't want a righteous brick wall coming at you, or staring at your accusingly, which is what he's more likely to do. Drink up your tea, and then start packing. We'll be in Vienna soon."

Clarence was in the cabin he shared with Sasha, reading a book whose front cover was stamped *Essais de Michel de Montaigne*. Luckily, he was alone—Sasha must still be in the dining car.

"Hello," said Catherine, standing in the doorway. "I've come to apologize."

He looked up. "Because that's what we humans do, right?"

"You know me so well. Pumas don't apologize for anything— they just pounce. At least I didn't pounce on her, Clarence!"

"I'm not sure that would have been much worse." He shook his head. "You're kind of a mess, Whiskers. Not quite a cat, not quite a woman. You know, I'm not the one you should be apologizing to."

"What do you expect, considering my parentage and upbringing? Moreau's island wasn't a finishing school. If I find out it definitely wasn't her, I'll apologize very nicely, I promise—not that I think Zora will listen. We're slowing down, aren't we?"

Clarence looked out the window, and she followed his gaze. They were indeed slowing down. Now the train was running between shops and apartment houses. This was Vienna, and in a few minutes they would be pulling into the Westbahnhof. Tonight

would be their first show. Tomorrow, she and Beatrice would try
to find Irene Norton.

"Do you want me to help you with your luggage?" asked Clarence.

"Only if you're not still mad at me," said Catherine.

"Well, I am," he said. "Honestly, I think you should apologize to
Zora now, whether she listens to you or not—but that's between
you and her. Come on, let's go get your trunk. And then I'm going
to help Beatrice so she doesn't mess up that fancy dress she wants
to wear tonight. Though I don't see the point of a 'Parisian gown,'
as she calls it. She would look just as stunning in something that
cost a dollar in the Sears catalog!"

"But she would *feel* different on the inside," said Catherine.

Muttering that he would never understand women and clothes,
Clarence followed her down the corridor and into her cabin, to
fetch the trunk that had caused so much trouble that day.

> BEATRICE: That is very kind of him to say, but also a
> little patronizing, is it not?

> CATHERINE: Clarence is one of the good ones, but
> he's not a saint. Don't expect him to be. I once
> had to listen to him explain the Peloponnesian
> War while I was trying to mend my cat costume.
> That was before Justine came and started doing all
> the sewing. You *know* how I feel about sewing! Do
> you have any idea how boring the Peloponnesian
> War is?

> MRS. POOLE: That's men for you. I find the best
> course of action, when they start explaining, is to
> just nod your head, and maybe tilt it to the side
> a little. At the end you say, "My, how fascinating.

Whoever would have thought?" And then they're convinced you're a very clever woman.

BEATRICE: But surely it should not be like that! Surely one should be able to have a rational discussion with a member of the opposite sex without resorting to such subterfuges. Clarence and I have wonderful conversations, and when I disagree with him, he truly listens. Even Giovanni did not listen to me in that way.

CATHERINE: I told you, he's one of the good ones. Just don't let him get started on the Peloponnesian War!

CHAPTER XV

Evening in Vienna

From the Westbahnhof, the traveling troupe of the Circus of Marvels and Delights went directly to the theater. Lorenzo had arranged for their sets to be transported in a wagon, but the equipment had to be assembled and tested by the performers themselves. Atlas and Clarence did most of the heavy lifting. Catherine tested the ropes she would climb, the pieces of wood on which she would balance, catlike. Then she helped the Kaminski brothers, who were using some of the same apparatus. Beatrice was kept busy helping Zora with her snakes, who needed to be milked of their poison. It was so useful to have someone who was already poisonous! No snake bite could hurt Beatrice. When Catherine walked up to them and told them it was time for tea, Zora ignored her. Well, fine, if that was the way she wanted it! At least if Zora was an agent of the society, she was on notice that Catherine was not to be messed with.

Promptly at 5:00 p.m., Lorenzo stepped out in front of the curtain and said, "Ladies and gentlemen, *meine Damen und Herren*, welcome to an evening with monsters!" And the show began.

Catherine always had a great deal to do backstage—she was particularly good at putting up and taking down sets without making a sound. But finally, just before her own act, she found a few minutes to look out at the audience. The Queen of Lilliput was describing how she had come to England in a balloon drawn by a pair of tame albatrosses (always used for air travel in her kingdom). In a moment, she would begin to recite poetry by a famous Lilliputian poetess—Catherine had found it great fun to write Lilliputian poetry, although truth be told, she had stolen a number of stanzas from William Blake. This theater was smaller than the one in Paris, but it had electric lights! She thought they were a little too bright. However, the audience was large and appreciative, clapping loudly whenever Henrietta took an elegant, diminutive bow.

"Who is that woman in the front row?"

Catherine was startled to find Beatrice beside her, also looking out at the crowd.

"Which woman?"

"The one in the wine-colored evening gown with the garnet parure, who looks rather like a member of the royal family traveling incognito."

She examined the front row again. "Oh, that one. Why? Does she look suspicious in some way? Are you suggesting. . . ."

"Of course not! You have grown almost . . . what is the word? Paranoid, Catherine. You think everyone is a member of the Société des Alchimistes. No, I was simply admiring her, although now I think of it, she does seem familiar somehow. Perhaps she is a famous society figure, or an actress? The embroidery on her gown is magnificent."

Catherine stared at her. "You can see the details of her dress from here? Seriously? And what the hell is a parure?"

Beatrice drew back. "Yes, I can, and you should be able to as well—your eyes are sharper than mine. You simply do not notice such things because you do not think they are important. But the arts—even such minor arts as that of embroidery—contribute to the beauty and significance of life. If we did not have a sense of beauty, of taste and elegance and refinement, we would be little better than animals."

"Or plants!" said Catherine. "What have you got against animals—"

"Cat! You're up!" Atlas had tapped her on the shoulder. He was already in costume—a sort of Grecian tunic that left his arms and most of his legs bare, with leather sandals.

Catherine pulled her cat hood over her head, gathered up her tail, and bounded on stage.

> BEATRICE: I think we should thank Mrs. Poole for how very hard she worked on that costume. It really was spectacular—I could not tell where the real Catherine ended and *La Femme Panthère* began.

> CATHERINE: It was an amazing costume, Mrs. Poole. So much lighter and cooler than the one I used to wear in the sideshow. I couldn't have done all the stunts in the old one. You are a genius, you know!

> MRS. POOLE: Hrumph. Try to remember that when you girls have been on another of your escapades, and there are bloodstains on your shirtsleeves for me to get out! Or gunshot residue! Or when your trousers are torn from climbing all over the buildings of this city and need to be mended!

> BEATRICE: Mrs. Poole, you are always a genius, and we do not tell you enough. I would kiss you, but alas . . .

> MRS. POOLE: That's quite all right, miss.

By 7:00 p.m. it was over, and all Catherine wanted was her dinner. First they would need to transport their luggage, which had been stacked in the women's dressing room, to the boarding-house. Then they would finally get a meal. Performing always left her feeling both tired and hungry.

But when she opened the trunk to get her ordinary clothes so she could change out of her cat costume, she sprang back in surprise. "Bea!" she called. "Bea, come here!"

Beatrice was sitting before one of the mirrors, taking off her stage cosmetics with cold cream. She turned. "What is it, Cat?" She still had cream all over her face.

Catherine just waved her over. In front of the other mirror, Miss Petunia was adjusting her hat, and in one corner, Edith and Doris Jellicoe were trying to figure out the exchange rate from francs to krone. She did not want to say anything in front of them.

Beatrice, who had wiped the cream off her face and was now standing beside the trunk, asked, "Well, what is the matter?" Catherine lifted the lid and showed her what she had found on top of the clothes she had thrown in several hours before: the telegram from Irene Norton.

Beatrice stared at it doubtfully. "Is it possible that the telegram could have been here all along? That you simply missed it when you searched on the train?"

"*No*, it's not possible," said Catherine. She spoke as quietly as she could—the Jellicoes were on the other side of the room, but she did not want Miss Petunia to hear. "I changed just as the Kaminskis were setting up. That's when I put this dress in here, and the telegram's on top of it. Seriously, Bea! It's obvious someone took it, and now someone has put it back. Which means it's definitely one of the troupe—we're the only ones backstage. The question is, which one?"

"It must be a woman," said Beatrice. "A man would not come into this dressing room. Do you still suspect Zora?"

Catherine held the telegram up to her nose, then held it out to Beatrice. "Smell that."

Beatrice took it from her and sniffed it. "I do not smell anything. What am I supposed to smell?"

Catherine looked at her with a sort of pitying incredulity. "I don't know how all of you can go around with such a rotten sense of smell. It must be like being blind. What I *don't* smell is Zora's perfume. What I *do* smell is cigarettes. Whoever handled this had been smoking recently. And not just any kind of cigarettes—I'm starting to sound like Holmes, aren't I? These are strong ones, rolled by hand. Only one person in the troupe smokes these—he gets the tobacco by mail order from Russia."

"Sasha!" said Beatrice. "But how could he come in here without being noticed? And what could he possibly have to do with the Société des Alchimistes?"

"He could come in here when all of us were either performing or watching the show," said Catherine. "I'm sure there are times when the dressing room is empty. But if we confront him, it will be easy enough for him to deny he's involved—after all, he's already returned the telegram, and I'm probably the only one who can smell his cigarettes on it. Perhaps we should simply watch him, try to see if he makes contact with a member of the S.A. What about that woman in the front row, wearing the par—whatever you called it?"

"Excuse me. Are you Catherine?"

She turned around so suddenly that her shin hit a corner of the trunk. Oh, that was painful! She doubled over and held her shin in her hands—not a very dignified posture. Standing a few feet away from her was the woman in the wine-colored dress, now with a black wool cloak draped over one arm.

"And you must be Beatrice," she said, "I'm Irene Norton, and I need your help. Mary, Justine, and Diana have disappeared. They left Vienna a week ago, and nothing has been heard of them since. They seem to have vanished into thin air. I was hoping you could help me find them."

MRS. POOLE: How did Mrs. Norton know to find you at the theater?

CATHERINE: She didn't know—she guessed. She saw an advertisement for *La Belle Toxique* in her morning paper. Remember that Holmes had described us all in his letter. She figured a poisonous girl in the circus might be Beatrice, and when she saw there was a panther woman, she bought herself a ticket to our show. Good thing she did, too, or we would not have been on that train!

Catherine and Beatrice both stared at her. Beatrice was the first to recover from her surprise. "Yes, I am Beatrice Rappaccini. Mrs. Norton? We were going to find you tomorrow at your apartment. But . . . you say Mary and the others have disappeared? How . . . What is . . ."

"I'm sorry, I didn't mean to spring it on you like this." Irene looked at them with a rueful expression. "The problem is, we don't have much time. Van Helsing is leaving for Budapest tonight on the Orient Express. He's been here in Vienna, searching for his daughter. My associates and I have led him on a fine goose chase, I assure you! I thought we had him fooled, but now I suspect he may be the one who's fooled us. Did he order for Mary and the others to be kidnapped? Is he holding them somewhere—perhaps in Budapest? Someone needs to follow him. I'm hoping he can lead us to them."

Catherine frowned. "You think he realized they were trying to rescue Lucinda Van Helsing, and absconded with them in some way?"

"But they *did* rescue Lucinda!" said Irene. "Didn't you get my telegram? I sent it on Friday to Mrs. Poole—the same day I sent one to Mina Murray, telling her that Mary and the others were on their way to Budapest. They left that night, or rather early the next morning, by coach with Lucinda. I told Miss Murray to telegram when they arrived, but I haven't heard anything—in a week! They should have arrived days ago. I was so worried that I sent my footman, Georg, along that road on the fastest horse I could hire. About a day out from Vienna, their trail disappeared— somewhere after the city of Ödenburg, which the Hungarians call Sopron, the coach simply vanished. The innkeeper and his staff in Ödenburg could tell Georg nothing—one man and three women, with their coachman and footman, had stayed a night and left the next morning, that was all. That would have been Justine dressed in men's clothes, Mary, Diana, and Lucinda. One of the ostlers did say he thought the coach was heading, not toward Budapest, but in the opposite direction, toward Gratz. Georg searched along that road, but could find no evidence they had passed that way either. I'm worried sick. . . ."

"Excuse me," said Miss Petunia. "If you don't mind?" She pointed at the doorway.

"Of course," said Irene, and moved so Miss Petunia could pass by her.

The Jellicoes, Catherine noticed, were now packing up their costumes and cosmetics. "Friday was the day we left with the circus," she said to Irene. "We would have been gone by the time Mrs. Poole got the telegram. Have you heard back from her?"

"No, only from Watson. He's found your traitor—look." Irene

opened her purse, with was intricately beaded, with a silver clasp, then handed a neatly folded telegram to Catherine. On it was written,

REGRET TO INFORM YOU THERE IS A TRAITOR IN OUR MIDST. YOUNG JIMMY BUCKET CAUGHT PASSING INFORMATION TO A MYSTERIOUS LADY CROWE POSSIBLE MEMBER OF S.A. OR SO SAYS CHARLIE AND HE SHOULD KNOW. HAVE BEEN TOLD HE WILL BE COURT MARTIALED BY THE BAKER STREET BOYS. HE SEEMS TO HAVE BEEN THE LEAKY FAUCET BUT YOU SHOULD REMAIN ON GUARD. HOLMES STILL MISSING CAN YOUR LONDON CONTACTS HELP? TERRIBLY WORRIED. WATSON

"Poor Jimmy!" said Beatrice. "His sister is sick with tuberculosis, and his mother is a washerwoman—Mrs. Poole has employed her from time to time. She is a widow, and very poor."

Catherine took the telegram and read it again, frowning. "That doesn't excuse selling us out to the S.A., if that's what happened. And I don't feel one ounce of sympathy for Sasha, either. He's my second oldest friend here, after Clarence. At least, I thought he was my friend. I'd like to tear his throat out!"

"Sasha—is that the Dog Boy of the Russian Steppes?" asked Irene.

"Yes, Catherine suspects he may be an agent of the Société des Alchimistes. You see, she could not find the telegram you had sent—"

"Bea, I don't think we have time to explain everything," said Catherine. "Now that we know there's an agent of the S.A. in the circus, we can't stay here, and anyway, we need to find Mary and

Justine. And Diana, I suppose. But we have five more shows in Vienna! Friday evening, then Saturday and Sunday including the matinees. We can't just leave Lorenzo in the lurch."

"Is that Lorenzo the Magnificent, as it says on the poster?" asked Irene. Catherine nodded. "All right, tell me where to find him. I'll get this squared away. You just get ready to go. I'll be back in a few minutes."

"He has an office right next to the men's dressing room," said Catherine. "Around the corner and to the left."

"Right," said Irene, nodding. And then she was gone, although her perfume lingered on the air behind her. Catherine was not a fan of perfume generally, but Irene's was a deep musk that was somehow pleasant even to her nose.

She turned to Beatrice. "All right, let's get everything back in the trunk. I still can't believe that Sasha . . . I mean, he was my *friend*."

"You do not know his motive," said Beatrice. "Perhaps, like Jimmy, there is more to his story than you think."

"Whose motive?" Clarence was standing in the doorway. "I was wondering if you ladies would like to get some dinner."

"Oh, hello, Clarence," said Doris Jellicoe. "Excuse us, we want to get our dinners as well."

Catherine turned to see Edith Jellicoe nodding in agreement. "Yes, *excuse us*," said Edith, giving her a nasty look. What in the world was up with that? But before Catherine could ask, both of the Jellicoes slipped past her. She could hear their rubber-soled shoes squeaking down the hallway.

"It wasn't Zora, it was Sasha," said Catherine, turning back to Clarence. "Someone returned the telegram to my trunk—someone who smells like those vile cigarettes he insists on smoking."

"You're going to need more evidence than that," said Clarence. "You can't just keep going around accusing another one of us—the

Zora incident was a fiasco. She's told Lorenzo that she doesn't want
to work with you anymore, and I can't blame her. The Jellicoes are
mad at you, that's for sure!" He leaned forward and sniffed at the
telegram. "Anyway, I can't smell anything."

Well, maybe that's because you're not a puma, Catherine wanted
to tell him.

"You're American!" Irene was standing in the doorway. "Hello."
She must have come back from talking with Lorenzo. Well, that
was quick! Catherine wondered what they had discussed, exactly.
Irene held out her hand. "Irene Norton, née Adler, of New Jersey."

Clarence took her hand in both of his and shook it. "Clarence
Jefferson, originally from Virginia. I'd bow and kiss your hand,
Mrs. Norton, but I figure you might prefer an American greeting.
None of that aristocratic stuff!"

Irene laughed. "From a fellow countryman? Yes, please!" Then,
she turned to Catherine and Beatrice. "I've made it all right with
Lorenzo. You're going to leave the show tonight and rejoin it again
in Budapest. He'll tell everyone the Toxic Beauty and the Panther
Woman are sick. I've promised him another act to replace the
ones he's missing—Hannah and Greta, the famous sharpshooters!
Anyway, you seem to have caused a bit of a ruckus. I got the feeling
that he would be grateful for a break."

"And in the meantime, we shall try to find the others?" said
Beatrice. "We could travel the route they took."

"I think there's a quicker way," said Irene. "I take it that Mr.
Jefferson here is in the know?"

"Yes, you can say anything in front of him," said Catherine.

"All right, then. Van Helsing's been in Vienna for the past
five days. He arrived late Saturday night with two colleagues,
both English scientists—I assume they're also members of the
Société des Alchimistes. He may have found out that we rescued
Lucinda and then gone after Mary and the others, somehow. I

don't know how exactly. Alternatively, they could have been kid-napped by the Société des Alchimistes, in which case they're most likely in Budapest. Honestly, I assumed the S.A. was an amateur operation—until I read Watson's telegram. Getting one of the Baker Street boys to turn traitor isn't easy—they're very loyal to Sherlock. If Van Helsing turns out to be a dead end, go directly to Mina Murray—she should be able to give you more information on what the S.A. is doing. Instead of trying to follow the route Mary and the others took, which is what Georg tried to do, I suggest you follow Van Helsing. If he knows where Mary and the others are, he will lead you to them. And if not, you'll want to be in Budapest anyway. But he leaves on the Orient Express tonight. Can you be on that train?"

"You want us to spy on Van Helsing? Sure," said Catherine. "But I don't know how we're going to afford train fare. We don't have any money."

"I'll take care of that," said Irene. "The Orient Express leaves at midnight from the Staatsbahnhof. Why don't you come to my apartment? I'll give you dinner and tell you all about what's been happening here, since you don't know. And you can tell me about Sasha. I'll have Hannah and Greta keep an eye on him—they'll try to find out who his contacts are. He may be a member of the Société des Alchimistes himself, but it's more likely that he's working for them, like Jimmy Bucket. Mr. Jefferson, since Catherine and Beatrice seem to have taken you into their confi-dence, would you care to join us for dinner? I would be delighted to talk to another American. What do you think of McKinley? I'm a Republican, of course—my father was proud to fight for the Union. But I'm worried we're going to get ourselves into another war with Spain over Cuba."

And then Clarence said a great deal that Catherine did not understand about things like the Monroe Doctrine, and places like Guam and the Philippines, all while carrying her trunk through the back halls of the theater. She and Beatrice carried the rest of their luggage, while Irene argued. Catherine could not tell whether she was agreeing or disagreeing with Clarence, but they both seemed to dislike someone named William Randolph Hearst.

Along the way, Beatrice whispered to her, "Did you notice that Mrs. Norton's parure is missing?"

"I might have, if you would tell me what a parure is," said Catherine.

"That necklace she was wearing, and the matching earrings, and I think she also had a bracelet. She was wearing them when she came to the dressing room—they were very fine garnets, a dark red that matched her dress. She is no longer wearing any of them."

Catherine looked at her, puzzled. "Are you suggesting someone stole her jewelry?"

"No, I think that is how she paid Lorenzo to let us go for the rest of the Vienna engagement."

MARY: Which is yet another debt we owe to Irene.

Now they were in the lamplit street, and there was Irene's carriage waiting for them. Clarence handed them up and got in beside Irene, whom he seemed to treat with unusual gallantry. As they rattled away over the cobblestones toward 18 Prinz-Eugen Strasse, Catherine berated herself. She should have handled everything—yes, everything —better. The great solitary puma wasn't exactly doing so well. Thank goodness she had friends—Beatrice and Clarence, and now Irene Norton—to help her when she messed up. Maybe these humans were right to band together.

BEATRICE: When I first saw Irene's apartment, I thought I had—well, if it were not blasphemous, I would say that I thought I had gone to heaven. The furniture! The paintings! I could tell at once that she was a woman of taste and learning, a woman ahead of her time. Even the books. . . . Although some of them were very modern indeed! I admit the genius of Tolstoy and Ibsen. Nevertheless, I feel there are some values we do not need to overturn.

CATHERINE: The weapons! The telephone! Clearly, she was a lot more important than she was letting on. What sort of person sends their telegrams through the American Embassy?

MARY: Cat, should you be writing all this? I mean, Irene still lives in Vienna. Her secret room won't be a secret once this book is published.

CATHERINE: She said I could. Granted, she said no one would believe it anyway, the way no one believes Mrs. Shelly's biography of Victor Frankenstein. Everyone assumes it's fiction. She says people rarely believe in what they think to be improbable, although they often believe in the impossible. They find it easier to believe in spiritualism than in the platypus.

BEATRICE: So she thinks our readers might assume this is a work of fiction?

CATHERINE: Bea, you sound upset by that.

BEATRICE: And you are not? Do you not care whether readers understand that this is the truth of our lives?

CATHERINE: As long as they buy the book, no, not much. As long as they pay their two shillings a volume, and I receive royalties . . .

"It's almost nine o'clock, and you need to catch the train at midnight," said Irene, when they were all seated at her dining room table, with a very smart maid in uniform setting dinner in front of them. "By six a.m. you should be in Budapest. We know Van Helsing and his friends will be on that train—his housekeeper, who was loyal to Mrs. Van Helsing and has been keeping me apprised of his movements, saw the train tickets herself. I'm hoping he'll lead you to Mary and the others, or at least provide you with some sort of clue as to where they might be. My hypothesis is that the driver of the coach, a man named Miklós Ferenc, was in his pay—my coachman has since heard some things about Herr Ferenc that lead me to believe he was less trustworthy than we thought. Among other things, he left unpaid bills in Vienna. He may have taken them in a different direction, perhaps through Gratz to throw us off the trail? But Van Helsing will eventually want them in Budapest—at least, he will want his daughter there. Frau Müller overheard him talking about bringing Lucinda there, although he did not say for what purpose. What he intends to do with Mary, Justine, and Diana, I don't know. I'm desperately worried about them. But there's nothing you can do until you need to leave for the train station, so I suggest you finish your dinners, and then I have some things to show you that may help you in Budapest."

"And you will tell us how you rescued Lucinda?" asked Beatrice. "I'm so glad that she was all right."

"Well, sort of," said Irene. "See, it's like this . . ."

Over dinner, Irene told them about Dr. Freud, and the Krankenhaus, and Diana's daring if somewhat foolhardy escape. She told them about the altercation in the back streets with the men who would not die. Catherine listened intently enough, but part of her mind was elsewhere. Those two English scientists Irene had mentioned—they must be Seward and Prendick. If so, she would see Edward Prendick again. She both wanted and did not want to. She could not help thinking of the year they had spent together on Moreau's island, after Moreau and Montgomery had died. There had been bad days, when he had been morose and impossible to talk to. But there had been good days as well, when they had gone swimming together, or cooked fish over a fire, or hunted one of the Beast Men together. He had not enjoyed these hunts, but she had—she was still proud of the way she had dispatched the Hyena-Swine Man, with a single blow to the head and a bite through his throat. And then on rainy days they had sat in the cave they called their parlor, while he had told her stories about his childhood in Surrey, and being a student at Cambridge, and studying with the great T. H. Huxley himself at the Royal College of Science. He had a way of running his fingers through her hair. . . .

"Bea, I'm worried about the two of you going into such a dangerous situation," said Clarence. "Mrs. Norton, you've been describing all this very calmly, but a man who would conduct experiments on his own wife and daughter must be a man entirely without moral qualms. If Beatrice and Cat need my help . . ."

"That's very kind of you, Clarence," said Beatrice gently. "But you see, Catherine and I have natural defenses—I have my poison, and Catherine has her agility, her ability to see and smell beyond the human range, her fangs. You would not be protecting us—we would need to protect you."

"Got it," said Clarence. He looked a little nonplussed as he cut into his schnitzel.

"But it was chivalrous of you to offer," she added.

He gave her a swift glance, as though wondering if she were mocking him, but Beatrice simply smiled and continued with her dinner.

How nice it was to have a really thoughtful hostess! While Irene and Clarence dined on Wiener schnitzel and potatoes with little bits of green stuff on them (which Beatrice later informed Catherine was parsley—why would anyone put leaves in their meal?), Catherine had been provided with a thin, very rare steak, still bloody and absolutely delicious. She felt almost as though she had caught it herself. And Beatrice was enjoying a bowl of what looked like her usual green goop. Catherine imagined it probably tasted the same as always—Austrian goop was probably no different than English goop.

> BEATRICE: Actually, the vegetation of Austria is
> different from English vegetation, so Austrian
> goop has its own distinct flavor.

> CATHERINE: We really didn't need to know that.

> BEATRICE: You were the one who mentioned it!

They were served by the maid, whom Irene addressed as Hannah. Hadn't she said something about a sharpshooting act with a Hannah and Greta? But this Hannah did not look as though she could be a sharpshooter—like a perfect maid, she almost blended into the wallpaper.

After dinner, Irene said, "Catherine and Beatrice, I have some information to give you, and also some . . . well, equipment.

Clarence, would you prefer to go back to your lodgings, or stay here and wait until they're ready to go, then accompany them to the Staatsbahnhof? I can't go to the station myself—Van Helsing may recognize me, since I recently visited his house as Frau Müller's sister from Swabia! Who knows, he may be as good at seeing through disguises as Sherlock."

"He doesn't know me, but Seward and Prendick do," said Catherine. *Especially Prendick.* "Those are the two English scientists. They've never seen Beatrice, but they might recognize me."

"Then I think a disguise is in order," said Irene. "Let me think about what I might have. . . ."

"I'll wait," said Clarence. "The two of you will need some help with your luggage, and anyway, I'd like to see you safely on that train, even if you're not exactly going to be safe on the train itself!" He was talking to both of them, but looking at Beatrice as he said it.

Well, there it is: He's caught Beatricitis, thought Catherine. *I just hope he recovers—or learns to handle the symptoms!*

BEATRICE: I am *not* a disease!

"Then I have something for you, Mr. Jefferson," said Irene. From the sideboard, she handed Clarence a newspaper.

Clarence grinned. "The *New York Times*! I haven't seen one of these in years."

"There's a whole selection in the parlor, including the *Washington Post* and the *Boston Globe*. I like to know what's going on back home. And now, if you ladies will follow me downstairs?"

Catherine wondered why they were going downstairs, toward the kitchen and servants' quarters, but her admiration knew no bounds when Irene admitted them into her windowless sanctum and she understood, for the first time, that Irene Norton, née Adler, was not quite what she appeared.

"What *are* you?" she asked, standing in front of the wall of weapons.

"An opera singer," said Irene. "Alternatively, a collector of information."

"La Sirène!" said Beatrice. "I thought that I had seen you before. It was in an article about the great opera singers of the seventies and eighties. You were said to have been a wonderful Carmen, but the article asked what you were doing now. . . ."

Irene smiled. "That was in another lifetime."

"Does Mr. Holmes know about all this?" asked Catherine. She was looking appreciatively at a collection of knives, swords, and other edged weapons, including a machete.

"I'm glad you like my toys," said Irene. "Although Beatrice might prefer my medicine cabinet?" She walked to the desk at the opposite end of the room, then opened one of the cabinets behind it.

Beatrice, who had followed her, gasped. "But these are poisons! This is curare, from the root of the South American vine *Strychnos toxifera*. I have seen it growing in only one place— my father's garden. And this is digitalis, from the common foxglove, *Digitalis purpurea*. And aconitine, from *Aconitum napellus*, also called wolfsbane. Why do you have a cabinet of poisons?"

"Not because I poison people," said Irene. "Unless, of course, it's absolutely necessary." She was still smiling, so she must be joking—right? Catherine could not be sure. "Anyway, as you know, the poison is in the dose. Curare has been used to counter-act the effects of strychnine, for example. As for whether Sherlock knows, his brother Mycroft certainly does—we are counter-parts, of sorts—and I suspect Sherlock has deduced a great deal. He wouldn't expect me to be sitting idle here in Vienna. But I didn't bring you down here to show off my office. Choose what-ever weapons you think will be useful to you, and then come over here—I want to make sure you know where you're going."

Catherine gleefully chose a Webley revolver. If a Webley was good enough for Holmes, it was good enough for her! Although hers was smaller, a .32 that would fit comfortably in her hand or into a purse. Beatrice could not bring herself to touch the firearms. "I could not kill anything," she said. "Truly I couldn't." She was at last persuaded to take a stiletto in a leather sheath, purely for defensive purposes. Just then, Hannah entered with what looked like black fabric draped over one arm.

"I thought these might be best, *madama*," she said, holding up the fabric, which turned out to be two black dresses. Were they going to disguise themselves as widows? Or perhaps maids?

"Nuns!" said Beatrice. "You wish us to dress as nuns?"

"No one ever looks at a nun," said Irene. "Especially not men. It's a very useful disguise, almost like being invisible."

"Would it not be a sin——," said Beatrice.

"Not if you're saving your friends," said Hannah, speaking for the first time. Catherine was impressed by her English—she had assumed the maid would speak only German. "I assure you that God will understand, and if not, you can go to my confessor. He is used to absolving all sorts of sins!" She turned to Irene. "The tickets have arrived, *madame*. Greta had time to run down to the Staatsbahnhof. She's gone back to her post now, observing Professor Van Helsing's house."

"Thank you, Hannah. Catherine, I hope the two of you won't mind sharing a cabin for the night. I know of Beatrice's . . . effect on others, shall we say? But it would look suspicious to reserve individual cabins—nuns are not that wealthy. Will six hours in a train cabin be a problem for you? Forgive me, Beatrice, but I think it's best to be frank."

"I'll be fine," said Catherine. "We'll keep the window open, and I'll go walk in the corridor every hour or so. I just—does it have to be nuns? I'm not very fond of nuns, generally. Or priests either, for that matter. I got enough sermonizing for the rest of my life on Moreau's island."

"You don't actually have to take holy orders, and you'll find it a very useful outfit to hide a gun in," said Irene. "Among other things, it has pockets!" She took a document from her desk—no, it was a map—and unfolded it on the central table. "What I want you to do now is study this. Not all of it, of course—but if you're going to search for the others in Budapest, and possibly the surrounding countryside, you should get a good sense of the general layout. See, here is the Danube, which Hungarians call the Duna. On one side is Buda, on the other side is Pest. Here, in Pest, is the National Museum, and on this small street next to it is the address on Miss Murray's telegram. . . ."

An hour later, they were in a hired carriage traveling to the Staatsbahnhof—the three of them would not have fit in a cab. Clarence kept looking at Sisters Beatrice and Catherine, and then looking away. "Nuns," he said, for about the fifth time. "Did it have to be nuns?"

Sister Catherine, whose revolver was resting comfortably in the pocket of her habit, frowned at him, although she doubted he could see her expression in the darkness. "You know, I think Irene was right—this really is the best costume. It hides firearms and makes men uncomfortable. A perfect combination."

Beatrice, who was sitting on her other side, next to the window, said reproachfully, "Nuns are very holy women. It is an honor—and probably also a sin—to dress as one."

"Right," said Clarence. Then he whispered, so close to Catherine's ear that it tickled, "It's also really weird."

"You're going to have to get used to weird around us," she whispered back.

BEATRICE: I did go to confession afterward, and the

priest granted me absolution. But it is something I hope never to do again. We may solve mysteries, and carry weapons, and vanquish villains, but we need not do what is wrong in pursuit of what is right.

CATHERINE: Except sometimes.

By midnight, Clarence had helped carry their luggage to their cabin on the Orient Express, making sure the trunk was checked in with a porter and Beatrice's suitcase was stowed under the seat. This was so much more luxurious than the ordinary train from Paris to Vienna! Irene must have paid a great deal. Catherine felt a twinge of guilt. First her—what was it called again? Parure. And now this. Hopefully they would be able to pay her back someday.

MARY: I tried. She wouldn't let me.

"Bye, Whiskers," said Clarence, giving her a hug. "Take care of yourself."

"Clarence, could you do me a favor?" she asked, when he had stopped squeezing her. She had never gotten used to this human custom of wrapping oneself around another person as though one were a boa constrictor.

"Sure, what is it?" He looked at her apprehensively. What in the world did he think she was going to say?

"Tell Zora about me. I mean everything—Moreau's island and all. Tell her I'm a puma, or that I was a puma. I've lived with human beings for almost ten years now, but sometimes I still find your customs and society confusing. Maybe then she'll forgive me—or at least understand."

"Sure thing, Catherine." He smiled down at her. "I'll do my best."

She turned away for a moment to check that the window was

pushed down—standard procedure for riding in a train car with the Poisonous Girl—and when she turned back, she saw that he had his arms around Beatrice. Well, what of it? He was giving Beatrice a hug as well. But a moment later, as he said goodbye, she saw that blisters were beginning to form on his lips. Damn it, the man would never learn! Well, she hoped the kiss had been worth it. She looked at Beatrice and just shook her head. Beatrice winced and mouthed the word *Sorry.*

Once they were alone and the train was pulling away from the station, Catherine said, "Why don't you get some sleep? I told the porter not to bother making up the beds—we'll need to wake up in a few hours anyway—but he left us some blankets."

"I don't think I can," said Beatrice. "I'm so worried about Mary and the others. What do you think could have happened to them?"

Catherine shrugged to indicate that she had no idea. "I suppose Van Helsing must have found them somehow? Maybe he's keeping them somewhere, hidden until he can use Lucinda to convince his supporters to back him at the meeting of the society."

"But then why has he been in Vienna all this time?" Beatrice frowned. "I think the Société des Alchimistes found them and has taken them . . . well, I do not know where, or for what purpose."

"What would the society do with them?" asked Catherine, apprehensively.

"I have no idea," said Beatrice. "My father always spoke of it as a society of scientists dedicated to expanding the boundaries of knowledge. I would not have thought it was in the business of kidnapping people. But Lucinda, Justine, and Diana are all the results of experiments in biological transmutation. What will be the society's attitude toward them? I do not know."

"I still think it's Van Helsing," said Catherine. "But my powers of deduction haven't been particularly accurate lately! Well, there's one thing that gives me hope."

"What's that?" asked Beatrice, shaking out one of the blankets and wrapping it around herself.

Catherine smiled. It was a grim smile. "Diana's with them. There is no situation so well-planned that Diana can't introduce chaos into it. Whoever is holding them, wherever they're being held, is going to regret it."

Beatrice shook her head, but could not help laughing. Then they sat in silence, Beatrice curled in her blanket, thinking about a kiss—unexpected but not unwelcome—and Catherine checking her watch to make sure she did not spend too long in the cabin. There would be no sleep for her—every hour, she would walk out into the corridor to get away from Beatrice's poison for a while. The gas lamp flickered in the wind from the open window, throwing shadows around the cabin as the train sped through the night toward Budapest.

VOLUME II

From Vienna

to Budapest

CHAPTER XVI

The Blood Is the Life

Mary," said Justine, "I do not wish to alarm the others, but something is not right."

"What do you mean?" asked Mary. It was their fourth day of being on the road, or rather a series of roads, each of which seemed to have its particular textures, its differing amounts of rocks and ruts. She was so tired of being jostled all day, day after day, like a sack of potatoes. Her buttocks—yes, Mary, I'm going to use that indelicate word—was sore from sitting all day, even on the cushioned seat of the coach. All she wanted was to get to Budapest and find Mina, take a hot bath, and sleep in a proper bed.

Across from her, Diana had dozed off, and next to her Lucinda was also sleeping. She had been sleeping much better since they had figured out how to keep her fed.

"What I mean is—that farmhouse where we stopped to give the horses their oats? Dénes spoke to them in German." Justine looked at her meaningfully.

"Isn't that what people speak here?" asked Mary. "I mean, we're still in Austria-Hungary."

"Yes, but we should be in the Hungary part of it. The official language is German, but the common people speak Hungarian. Don't you remember our Baedeker?"

"Not as well as you do, evidently," said Mary. "Also, I don't think I could distinguish between German and Hungarian—what's the difference? And what are you implying—that we're traveling more slowly than we should be?"

"I don't know," said Justine, shaking her head. "But there is also a change in the countryside. Have you noticed—"

"Fewer farms, more forest? Yes, I've noticed." Mary frowned. She had not thought much about it—she had simply assumed that Hungary was not as civilized as Austria, sort of like Scotland in relation to England. "But what does that mean? If anything?"

"It's not just that," said Justine. "We've been traveling upward. Slowly, imperceptibly, but I have lived among mountains. The quality of the air is different here—we are higher up. I looked at all the maps carefully before we left England. There are no mountains between Vienna and Budapest."

"Then where do you think we are?" asked Mary. "I would check the Baedeker, but I think it's in the trunk. Maybe next time we stop, I can get Dénes to take it down, telling him I need a shawl or something?"

"I have no idea," said Justine. "We only studied the route we were planning to take. I do not think we are on that route anymore. Irene said it should take us three days to reach Budapest, depending on the condition of the roads. It is now the fourth day. I know this sort of travel is not as reliable as a train, and a private coach does not run to schedule, but . . . I am worried."

Damn. Damn and double damn. Could Justine be wrong? Mary looked out the window. It was starting to grow dark, and a fog was rising. The coach lanterns were already lit. The countryside around them was, not wooded exactly, but wilder and rockier than it had been around Vienna. The trees were different—she did not know how, except that they were taller and darker. She had seen all these things, but had not thought anything of them in particular. There had been other things to worry about—how to get Lucinda fed being the chief of them.

After the rather gruesome discovery that Lucinda would need blood for nourishment, the first day of their journey had been uneventful. They had stopped several times to rest the horses, once in a market town where Justine had bought peaches and cherries to supplement their food supply. As the sun was setting under orange and purple clouds, they had arrived at an inn. While Herr Ferenc and his son stabled the horses for the night and bargained for a fresh pair for the next day's journey, a stout, pleasant woman who seemed to be the innkeeper's wife welcomed them in German. Assured by Herr Justin Frank that they were all brothers and sisters so there was no impropriety involved, she led them to a room with two beds, a chest of drawers with a basin and pitcher, and a table with four chairs. Over the beds were two paintings of no particular artistic merit: one of the Empress Elizabeth, the other of the Virgin Mary. She told them that she would bring up dinner in half an hour, then left them to unpack their bags.

"I'm not sleeping with her," said Diana, pointing to Lucinda.

"You can sleep with me," said Mary. "Justine, would you mind—"

"Of course not," said Justine. "At least she does not snore!"

"No, she just drinks blood!" Diana retorted.

"Will she—I mean, is it like a meal for her?" asked Mary. "Will she need blood every time we eat? Because I don't think I can do that again today. I'm still not feeling entirely well."

"We could ask her," said Justine. She turned to Lucinda, who was sitting on the bed under the Virgin Mary. "Do you need to feed again? You know, on blood?"

Lucinda looked at her with haunted eyes. "When Jesus met with his disciples in Galilee, he offered them the blood of his veins and said, drink this in the remembrance of me."

"I don't think asking her is going to do any good," said Mary.

"Her color is better, and she seems stronger than before, but she's not sounding any more coherent. In fact, rather the opposite."

"Perhaps we should try to give her some, and see how she responds," said Justine. "I believe it's my turn. Diana, can you give me your knife?"

"I don't know what the two of you would do without me," said Diana. She reached under her skirt again and produced the knife, then put it into Justine's outstretched hand.

Just as Mary had, Justine cut her left wrist. But almost as soon as Lucinda put her mouth to the cut, she spit out the blood she had taken into her mouth so that it spattered in droplets onto the floor. She scooted away from Justine until she was huddled against the headboard, right under the Virgin. "You are dead," she said. "Dead and damned like me."

"Well! I guess your blood's not good enough for her," said Diana with a snort.

"Justine, I'm sure she didn't mean anything by it," said Mary.

"And yet she's right," said Justine, looking as sad as Mary had seen her since the day she had read Mrs. Shelley's book. "I have been dead a hundred years. My blood is tainted—it is the blood of a dead woman."

"Well, I guess it will have to be me again," said Diana, holding her hand out for the knife.

Mary looked at her incredulously. "After all the time you've spent complaining about Lucinda's need for blood, now you're volunteering?"

"I said it was disgusting," said Diana. "I didn't say I wouldn't do it. Hand me the knife already."

"Wait a minute," said Mary. "Does it have to be human blood? Lucinda, do you need the blood of a human being, or any blood?"

Lucinda just looked at Mary from her position under the Virgin. "Blood is life," she said. "Blood is a rose among the briars.

For a hundred years she slept, until the prince came to bite her awake."

"I don't think she's capable of giving you a coherent answer," said Justine.

"Then we'll just have to experiment," said Mary. "I saw a chicken coop near the stable. . . ."

Just then, the innkeeper's wife knocked on the door. *"Abendessen, meine Damen und mein Herr,"* she said. On a tray she had brought sausages, sauerkraut, and some sort of dumpling.

"Knödel!" Diana said in dismay. "You can torture me if you want to, but I'm not eating *Knödel*."

"Shut up!" said Mary under her breath, hitting Diana on the shoulder—only to have Diana turn around and hit her back. How could she have forgotten that Diana always hit back?

> MARY: I didn't forget. I just didn't want her to be rude in front of the proprietress.

> DIANA: You could put me in the deepest, darkest dungeon and torture me for a thousand years, and I still would not eat *Knödel*.

> MARY: You really are tiresome, you know that?

"Danke, gute Frau," said Justin Frank, tipping her. And then he said something that sounded like *"Hähnchen."* The innkeeper's wife responded in rapid German. "I'll be back in a minute," said Justin to the rest of them. He followed her out the door.

Ten minutes later, he was back with a large wooden bowl. Mary and Diana were already sitting at the table, eating their dinner—the *Knödel* was not as bad as Diana had described, and Mary wondered what all the fuss had been about. It was bland, but filling.

"What is that?" asked Mary.

"A hen," replied Justine. "I had to break its neck." She held the bowl so they could see it—or at least, a mass of feathers. It was obvious how much killing the hen had pained her. "I explained to the woman—Frau Lundhoff—that my sister had anemia, and she told me that an aunt of hers had suffered from the same malady. Here—" She held out the bowl to Lucinda. "Frau Lundhoff made a cut on the breast."

Lucinda took the bowl and stared down at the hen. Then, she turned away from them and lifted the bird—it was still beautifully feathered, and dangled from her hand. She lowered her head. A moment later, Mary could hear the most dreadful sound, a sort of sucking and slurping that turned her stomach. She regretted having eaten half a *Knödel*.

DIANA: See? I told you. Never eat the *Knödel*.

When Lucinda turned to them again, with the chicken back in its bowl, her face was smeared with blood. "Hell is empty, and all the devils are here," she said.

"What's that supposed to mean?" asked Diana.

"I believe it's Shakespeare," said Justine. "I shall help her wash."

"No, you eat," said Mary. "I'll wash Lucinda's face. And then we'd better get to bed. We need to start early tomorrow."

She washed the blood off Lucinda's face with water from the pitcher. It was no longer pale—now, Lucinda Van Helsing looked like a very pretty girl. You might have met her at a party in Amsterdam, dancing and talking about *beaux*. But as she looked up while Mary wiped her mouth and cheeks with a towel, Mary noticed that her eyes were unfocused, as though she were looking far away. And when Mary had helped her into her nightgown and tucked her into bed, while Justine brought the dishes back downstairs and Diana made her own ablutions, Lucinda said only, "I stood on the shore of the river, and the river took me. The river took us all. I pray that the good Lord will save us from drowning. Amen."

The next morning, Lucinda could no longer speak English. She looked better, brighter, happier—physically, she seemed to be in a better state. But her mind . . .

"I fear she is going mad," said Justine to Mary, after disposing of yet another dead, bloodless chicken. Mr. Justin Frank was once again dressed for traveling.

Mary was ready as well. She had cleaned Lucinda's face and made sure the girl looked decent, rather than a bloody mess. Diana was still pulling on her boots. "Hurry up!" said Mary. "Frau Lundhoff says the coach is waiting."

One more long day in the coach, getting out only when Herr Ferenc stopped to rest the horses and give them water. Then, they could get down, walk around, relieve themselves in the dignity of a nearby bush.

> MARY: Catherine! Is it necessary to include such a detail?

> CATHERINE: Do you expect our readers to believe that we had no bodily needs or functions for entire days at a time?

> MARY: No, but such things are simply—unstated. They go without saying.

> CATHERINE: It's very fashionable now to include realistic details, no matter how unpleasant or improper. Look at the French writers. Look at Émile Zola.

MARY: We are not French.

Mary was starting to feel like the servant girl in the fairy tale who is rolled down the hillside in a barrel, except in this case the barrel never stopped rolling. The steady but uneven motion of the coach put her into a sort of stupor. She mostly stared out at the countryside. Diana either slept or complained about the condition of the road, how hungry she was even though she ate more than Mary and Justine combined, how bored she was—so bored that she might throw herself out of the vehicle, just for something to do. Justine tried to read a book Irene Norton had lent her—the spine said *Also Sprach Zarathustra*—but finally she said, "I can't seem to concentrate at all, and I have to admit that modern philosophy sometimes seems to me a sort of poetic non-sense." After that, she played cards with Diana to keep her quiet. Lucinda, once again seated next to Mary, made the occasional comment in Dutch, or what Mary assumed was Dutch. She seemed entirely in a world of her own. Mary wondered if she even knew that she was in a coach traveling across the Austro-Hungarian countryside.

Had they been right to come and rescue her? To leave every-thing they knew behind when summoned by a telegram from the governess she had not seen in more than a decade and a letter from a girl she had never met, making a claim most people would have found unbelievable? Diana had fallen asleep again, thank goodness. Lucinda seemed to be asleep as well, slumped in the seat with a blanket wrapped around her. Justine was staring out the window, a German phrase book lying open on her lap. She had once again been complaining about the deficiencies of her German.

"We are doing the right thing, aren't we?" Mary asked.

Justine looked at her, startled. "Of course we are. Do you doubt it? One can usually tell the right thing to do, because it is difficult. And—look at her." She nodded toward Lucinda, curled into the corner, her face half-hidden by hair. She looked like a child taking its afternoon nap. "You would never have forgiven yourself if we had not responded to Miss Murray's telegram."

Mary smiled. One could always count on Justine to put things clearly. Lucinda had needed rescuing, so they had rescued her. This girl who drank blood was no different than Beatrice or Catherine, created by members of the Alchemical Society—and the men who had made her this way must be stopped. Despite the danger and discomfort . . . and Diana's snoring, which had just started up again. How did Diana manage to sound like a steam engine?

By the time they arrived at yet another inn, just as the sun was setting, Mary never wanted to ride in a coach again as long as she lived. Cabs and trains for her, thank you very much—or her trusty bicycle back in London!

This inn was markedly inferior to the one from the night before. Mary, Diana, and Lucinda shared one large bed, Mary between the two girls since Diana refused to sleep "next to that leech." Justine slept on the floor, wrapped in a blanket. Here there were no chickens, but Justine was able to purchase a piglet that squealed and wriggled in her arms. She asked them all to leave the room. Ten minutes later, when she told them to come back in, the piglet was dead and Justine was even paler than usual.

While Lucinda went off into a corner for her feast of blood— she did not like anyone to see her eating—Mary put one hand on Justine's arm. "I'm so sorry. You don't even eat meat."

"I would not willingly kill any creature," said Justine sadly. "But at least he felt no pain."

"Well, he was a pig," said Mary. "He would probably have ended up as sausages. I'm sorry." A tear trickled down Justine's cheek. "That sounds callous, but my point is that he would have come to the same end. And it is a question of Lucinda's life."

Justine just nodded.

The inn on the third night had been even more rural—a set of rooms over what was obviously the local tavern. That night, Lucinda feasted on the blood of another hen, and the rest of them shook their heads over a watery potato soup accompanied by slices of brown bread spread with lard. The supplies from Frau Schmidt's basket had run out. They paid for more bread and a large salami to take with them—overpaid, Mary thought. But what else were they going to do? They had to eat.

Now here they were, on the fourth day, and something was not right. They were driving into darkness and fog. The lanterns on either side of the coach seemed to illuminate very little. If Justine was right and they were not headed to Budapest—well then, where were they?

"We're going to stop somewhere for the night," Mary said to Justine. "Once we do, ask where we are—if we've no longer on course for some reason, we can find our own way to Budapest. We have money, we have a Baedeker. If necessary, we can commandeer the coach and horses. And if it comes to a fight, you're stronger than Herr Ferenc or Dénes, and I have my pistol. I don't suppose you know how to drive a coach? It's not the sort of thing Justine Moritz would have learned."

Justine shook her head. It was getting so dark that Mary could barely see. Thank goodness Diana and Lucinda were still asleep, although Diana was starting to turn her head and mutter in her dreams, which was a sign that she would be waking up soon.

"Well, I don't know either, but we'll figure out *something*. We always do." How Mary wished she had Irene Norton there to advise her! Irene would know how to proceed. But Irene was back in Vienna, with Greta and Hannah and a room full of weapons, all of which would have been useful right about now.

What would Irene do in this situation? Well, there was at least one thing Mary could do, before it got so dark that she could not see at all. In the last of the fading light, she took out her revolver and loaded all the chambers, then put it back into her waist bag. Logically, it weighed exactly the same as before, but now she found the weight of it reassuring.

"We are slowing down," said Justine. It was almost dark—the lanterns cast little light inside the coach, and Mary could barely see her. They had not been going very fast anyway, at a stolid walk—Mary had been thinking that the horses must be tired. But they were indeed slowing down. She could feel that they were climbing a slight incline—perhaps they would be there, wherever *there* was, soon?

"Are we there yet? I'm hungry." Diana was rubbing her eyes. Lucinda still seemed to be sleeping in her corner.

Abruptly, the coach came to a stop. Mary looked out the window, but it was dark and a fog had risen—in the dim light of the lanterns, it seemed to swirl around them.

"I guess so," said Mary. "I can see a light—it must be the inn-keeper coming to meet us. Come on. Wherever we are, I'm sure there's food inside. I just want to get out of this vehicle. I ache—well, everywhere at once!"

She opened the door and stepped down, then looked up, startled. This was not an inn—or if it was, it was not like any inn she had ever seen. Above her rose great stone walls, topped with battlements—she could see their teeth against the sky, which was turning from violet to indigo. There were small windows high up with peaked arches, and a round tower—this was a castle of some sort. It was half in ruins—another tower had partly tumbled down, and jutted into the sky like a broken bone. Where in the world were they? She looked around, startled and frightened. Dénes was climbing down from the driver's seat, although Herr Ferenc still held the reigns.

The innkeeper—or whoever held the light—was approaching. He held up his lantern. "Hello, Mary," he said, in a harsh, rasping voice.

By the light of the lantern, she could see his face—sharp, devious, never to be trusted, but also somehow attractive. This must be some trick of her tired mind. It could not possibly be . . .

"We've been expecting you all day," he said. "I'm—pleased to see you again, my dear."

For the first time in her life, Mary thought she might faint. How was this possible? How could he be here? She took a deep breath, reached into her waist bag, and took out her pistol, then pointed it straight at him.

"Hello, Father," she said. She had not meant to call him that—it had simply come out. "Mr. Hyde," she corrected herself. This was not her father, and never would be.

DIANA: But he is, you know.

MARY: Being a father is more than a matter of
  biological reproduction.

"Dad!" Diana had just stepped down from the coach. She still looked sleepy. "What the hell! Where are we, and what are you doing here? And why didn't you let me know where you were? You could have sent me a letter, a note, anything. But did you think of that? No, of course not. What kind of father are you, anyway? A damn lousy one, that's what."

"Shut up, Diana," said Mary. "This isn't the time." She turned back to Hyde, still covering him with her pistol. "Where are we? I'm guessing not in Budapest."

"No, and I think you'd better hand me that firearm, my dear," said Hyde. "It is mine, after all."

"There's no way I'm giving—"

"Mary, I think you had better. Look behind you." That was Justine's voice—she must have gotten down on the other side.

Mary turned—Herr Ferenc, still on the driver's seat, was pointing a rifle at her.

"Your friend is wise, *Fräulein*," he said in clear enough English, but with a foreign accent. Well, so much for speaking only Hungarian!

And there, just behind Justine, was Dénes—with another rifle. Damn! She saw it all at once: they had been deceived. Either Hermann's friend had deceived them, or Hermann himself. But how had Hyde known where they were? How had he arranged it? And where were they now?

> BEATRICE: It was certainly not Hermann. He is
> such a sweet man, and Frau Hermann is so kind.
> They have the nicest baby. . . . We met them last
> summer when we were in Vienna, visiting Irene.

> CATHERINE: I suspect all sorts of criminals have very
> nice babies too.

> BEATRICE: Cat, you're not seriously suggesting—

> CATHERINE: No, I don't actually think Hermann was
> the guilty party. I just don't think one's ability to
> reproduce says anything about one's moral character.

"Now give me the gun," said Hyde, holding out his hand and stepping closer to her. "Come on, Mary. I have no intention of harming you—or Diana either."

"You kidnapped us," said Mary accusingly. With reluctance,

she handed him the revolver, not bothering to turn the grip toward him so that he had to take it by the barrel.

"I prefer the word diverted," he said. "You may continue your trip once I have gotten what I need from you—well, one of you, that is. But first, I hope we can spend some time together. As a family, let us say."

"I'm not staying in this pile," said Diana. "No way, nohow."

Hyde smiled his crooked smile. "I'm afraid you have no choice, for the time being. It was not originally my intention to bring you here—but now that you are here, I am of course very pleased to see you, daughter. You are always welcome to stay with me as long as you wish."

Diana made a rude gesture.

"Ah, Miss Van Helsing!" he said. "Here at last is the guest we've been waiting for."

Lucinda stepped down from the coach, slowly, hesitantly.

Hyde put the revolver into his pocket and stepped forward, extending his hand. Mary stepped aside. What in the world was all this about? Lucinda, apparently—but why?

Lucinda came forward, stumbling a little. Clearly, she was still half asleep, or in some sort of trance. She took his hand, then looked over her shoulder at Mary and said, "We have arrived in hell."

"That's as may be," said Hyde. He seemed taken aback. "But you must be hungry, and we have dinner waiting for you—even for you, Miss Van Helsing. We have arranged for your particular pabulum, and I think you will find our preparations most satisfactory. I suggest that you all follow us inside. Although our primary aim in bringing you here was to secure Miss Van Helsing, I'm pleased to see all of you again, including you, Miss Frankenstein. If you will follow me, I shall tell you where you are, and how you came to be here—unless you prefer to stay out in the dark? It can be cold at night at this altitude. I recommend the comfort of our fire, and perhaps some brandy. The Hungarians make very fine brandy, much stronger than we have in England, and perfect for a night like this."

Diana followed, but Mary hung back for a moment—she was reluctant to follow Hyde anywhere, particularly into a ruined castle that looked as though it had come out of a romance by Mrs. Radcliffe or Sir Walter Scott, and anyway she wanted to wait for Justine.

"Where do you think we are?" she asked when Justine had drawn up beside her.

"I wish now that I had paid more attention," said Justine. "I have been trying to think of where on the map I saw mountains. I seem to remember that there were mountains to the south of Vienna—they reminded me of the Alps. If we have come south, then we are certainly off course."

"And we still have rifles pointed at us," said Mary, glancing back at Herr Ferenc and Dénes. "Come on, we may as well go in. We need food, we need rest, and we need to figure out where the—yes, where the hell we are. You know, I'm starting to sound like Diana."

DIANA: I know! It was great! I wish you would sound like me more often.

If only Catherine and Beatrice had been there! Then perhaps they could have fought Hyde and his henchmen. But there was just herself and Justine—she did not think she could count on Diana, who called Hyde "Dad" and berated him for—what? Not sending a postcard? As though that were somehow a worse crime than, you know, murder.

DIANA: I would have fought with you, if you'd wanted me to. He's my dad, but I know what a bastard he

is. And you're my sister. I'm not likely to forget
that, with you telling me what to do all the time!

BEATRICE: I wish we could have been with you as
well! But we were still on the train to Vienna and
did not yet know that you had disappeared under
mysterious circumstances.

Mary followed Hyde's lantern, walking under what looked
like a portcullis into—was it a courtyard? It must be, since she
was walking on gravel. The moon had risen, and it hung over them
like a shilling, or maybe here an Austrian krone, full and bright. It
was surrounded by clouds, and she could not see the stars. Here
too a mist swirled around them as they walked. And then there
was a large wooden door with iron fittings, which creaked when
Hyde pushed it open. She entered after Diana, then held the door
open for Justine. If only she had Catherine's eyes, and could see
in the dark!

MARY: I don't remember wishing I could see like you!

CATHERINE: Well, you should have. It would have
been so useful, don't you think? Honestly, I don't
know how you all do it, with your limited vision
and sense of smell. Although some days in London,
I wish I could have my nose removed! Ugh. . . .

They passed into darkness. Now they were truly inside, in
some sort of large space because Mary could hear boots echoing.
Hyde's lantern did little to dispel that darkness, which seemed
to gather around them like a great void. Then suddenly, light
blazed. Hyde was standing by the wall, holding a cord, and—was

it possible? The room was filled with light. Electric light, from naked bulbs around the room. They were placed, Mary noticed with surprise, in the iron sconces that had once held torches along the walls. She looked around—this must be the castle's great hall. It had stone walls rising to dark wooden beams, and a hearth large enough to roast a stag in. A long table ran down the middle of the hall, with benches on both sides. It was large, gloomy, and cold. Mary shivered. Sir Walter Scott might have been thrilled, but all she wanted to do was get out of this place as soon as possible.

At one end of the long table, she noticed, were set plates and bowls, napkins and cutlery.

"Come, Miss Van Helsing," said Hyde, leading Lucinda to a chair at the end of the table, the only chair in the room. "Sit and rest, for I'm sure you're tired after your long journey. And if you will all join her," he said to the rest of them, "I'll call for dinner to be served. It may take a little time to heat again—as I said, we thought you'd arrive earlier today. But now that you're finally here, we can show you that we're not entirely uncivilized, even in Styria."

Styria! That was to the south, wasn't it? Justine had been right. But what did Hyde mean by "we"? He was alone—could they attack him now? But what good would that do? He would surely call for Herr Ferenc, or Dénes, or both. And perhaps there were others around. . . . Mary did not like that "we." Diana was already seated on one of the benches, but like her, Justine had hung back.

"Act now or wait?" she whispered to Justine.

"It is better to wait," Justine whispered back. "We do not know what sort of situation we have fallen into. And surely we cannot escape tonight, in the fog and darkness. We must eat and rest, then plan."

"Well?" Hyde called. "Are you coming? I can promise you nourishing fare, although nothing as fancy as Viennese cuisine."

Mary could not think of anything else to do, not at the moment, so they might as well eat. Anyway, she had to figure out how Hyde had known they were in Vienna, why he had brought them here, why he was in Styria in the first place. The last time she had seen him, he had been headed for Newgate. What in the world was he doing in the Austro-Hungarian Empire?

Hyde rang a bell that was sitting on the table. Before it had stopped echoing around the room, a door opened in the far wall. In walked a girl, about Diana's age, wearing an embroidered cap and apron—probably a servant, but in a distinctively rural style, completely different from Hannah's smart sophistication. She was pretty, with brown hair in two long braids, and Mary thought that although she came to the table and stood by Lucinda's chair calmly enough, underneath she was frightened.

"Ágnes, I would like you to bring dinner as quickly as possible," said Hyde. "*Vacsorázni*, you understand? Our visitors are hungry."

"*Igen* . . . yes, Hyde úr," she replied with an awkward curtsey. "My brother, he already heating the *gulyásleves*." If she was a servant, she was not used to being one. Her English was heavily accented.

"Excellent," said Hyde, paying no attention to her nervousness. "Then you know already what you must do, don't you?"

"Yes," said Ágnes. She rolled up her left sleeve and closed her eyes.

What in the world was he going to do? Justine had already sat down on the bench next to Diana. Mary was still standing. She had the distinct feeling that something terrible was about to happen, and she could not do anything to stop it.

"There's nothing to be frightened of," said Hyde. And well he might—Ágnes was shaking like a leaf! All the blood seemed to have drained out of her face. From his coat pocket, he took a small leather case, then set it on the table and opened it. He lifted out something metallic—Mary could see it glinting in the light. A scalpel! The last time she had seen him with a scalpel in his hand, he had been in the warehouse by the Thames, preparing to remove Justine's brain.

"You will not harm that girl!" Justine had risen and was looking as angry as Mary had ever seen her, as angry as it was perhaps possible for Justine to be.

"I will do whatever I please, here in my own house," said Hyde. As he spoke, Mary heard a distinctive click and turned—there was Herr Ferenc standing by the door they had come through, with a rifle trained on Justine. "Ferenc úr there has a particular reason for being loyal to me, as has his daughter Ágnes." He looked at the girl. "You have agreed to this, have you not, of your own free will?"

Wordlessly, Ágnes nodded.

Agreed to what? But in a moment it was clear. The scalpel flashed, and then a line of red ran down Ágnes's arm. As quickly as a housecat springs on its prey, Lucinda turned, seized the girl's arm, and began sucking at the cut.

Ágnes gave a little scream, but stood still, seemingly resolute.

How had Hyde known that Lucinda needed blood and arranged for it beforehand? Who was Ágnes? He had called her Herr Ferenc's daughter, which also made her Dénes's sister. How had he persuaded her to become—well, Lucinda's dinner? Mary looked at Justine, who was still standing but sat back down after a moment. Justine looked at her and shrugged, as though she had no answers to give either. And Diana—well, Diana was looking on in fascination.

"That is *so gross*," she said after a moment.

"But necessary," said Hyde. "Although I think Miss Van Helsing has had enough for now. You don't want to drain your food supply, do you?" Gently, he withdrew Ágnes's arm.

Lucinda stared up at him, blinking. The blood smeared around her mouth looked particularly lurid under the electric lights. *"U bent zelf Lucifer,"* she said. Then, in a gesture that caused Mary to shudder, she licked the blood off her mouth, as a child might lick a smear of treacle.

"Lucifer, am I?" said Hyde, chuckling. Rapidly and expertly, he bandaged Ágnes's arm with gauze from the leather case. "While I cannot claim any facility in Dutch, your meaning is perfectly clear. However, there is one who has a much better claim to that name than I do! You shall meet him, by and by."

Whatever did he mean? Mary so was tired of mysteries and lies. "Tell us why we're here," she said. She was glad to hear that her voice sounded as contemptuous as possible. She had been worried it would come out weak or wavering. She was starting to feel a sort of despair she had not yet felt on their journey. No one knew where they were, not Irene, not Mina. It was just the four of them—well, three since Lucinda scarcely counted in her state—in a castle somewhere in Styria. They had no weapons, no means of transportation. What in the world were they going to do?

Just then, a young man slightly older than Ágnes came in, bearing a large tureen. It was obvious, from the resemblance, that he too was a member of the Ferenc family. A younger brother, perhaps? He was followed by Dénes, carrying a platter heaped with what looked like sausages—which is what they turned out to be, along with fried onions and mushrooms. It all smelled—well, heavenly. Despite the gravity of the situation, Mary heard her stomach growling.

"Excellent!" said Diana. She, at least, did not sound tired or dispirited. As soon as the platter was set down, she grabbed a sausage with her fingers and started chewing on it.

The young man served them a red soup filled with pieces of chicken and dumplings of some sort. Should she refuse Hyde's hospitality? But she was so very hungry! Mary tried a spoonful—it was excellent, although a little spicy for an English palate. She noticed that Diana was on her second sausage, but Justine was eating only the onions and mushrooms. Surely that wasn't enough, after the long day they'd had?

"You can have my soup," she whispered to Justine. "I'll eat all the chicken and then pass it to you. The dumplings are very good—nothing like *Knödel!*" Justine just shook her head.

"Miss Frankenstein, you're not eating," said Hyde. "Is the food not to your taste?"

He seemed genuinely concerned and solicitous. What a charlatan he was! If he had truly been concerned about Justine—or any of them—he would not have brought them here at all. To think that this man had once been her father! But no, better not to think about that. Mary put a sausage and some of the mushrooms on her plate. They were delicious.

"She doesn't eat meat," said Diana. "I thought you knew stuff like that, or are you not as smart as you pretend to be?"

"Ah, of course," said Hyde, ignoring the second half of her statement. "Miss Frankenstein is not the only one in this castle who subsists on a vegetable diet. Ágnes, can you fry up some eggs, and maybe some tomatoes? *Tojás és . . .* I don't remember the word for tomatoes. You know, red *gyümölcs.*" He cupped his hands, as though holding a ball.

"*Paradicsom,*" said Ágnes. Then she curtseyed again and left the room. Her brothers stayed, Dénes with his arms crossed, leaning back on his heels.

"Why have you brought us here?" asked Mary. If she wanted answers, she would have to talk to him, however much she would rather avoid it.

"Yeah," said Diana. "What's the deal, Dad? You could just have told us you wanted to see us."

"I don't think Mary would have come willingly," said Hyde. His smile was so much like Diana's! It was sickening.

DIANA: There's nothing wrong with my smile!

MARY: This isn't about you. It's about him. I'm not criticizing you.

DIANA: Well, you kind of are. If his smile is sickening, and it looks like mine—

MARY: I'm sorry, that's not the way I meant it.

DIANA: Did you just apologize? All right, who's kidnapped the real Mary. . . .

"And you see," Hyde continued, "I did not abduct *you*, much as your presence brings me pleasure—quite the family reunion, isn't it? My interest was in Miss Van Helsing. I was fortunate in that you extracted her from the Maria-Theresa Krankenhaus. And very clever of you that was, Diana. You get that from me, I think, although your mother was clever in her own way. Dénes would have had a much harder time doing so. After that, you simply came along with Miss Van Helsing—a bonus, as it were."

Diana clutched her knife. "My mother was—"

"What do you intend to do with Lucinda?" asked Justine, reaching over and putting a hand on Diana's arm. She sounded calm and collected- -thank goodness, because someone had to be. Diana put her knife down with a clatter and crossed her arms. Mary could tell that she was angry, just as she could tell that despite her air of control, Justine was tired and dispirited.

"Nothing worse than what her own father did to her," said Hyde.

From the case on the table, he extracted a hypodermic syringe. "If you would help me, János?" he said to the younger brother.

"You wouldn't darc!" said Mary. She rose, not knowing exactly how she was going to help Lucinda—but she would do something!

She heard a click behind her and turned. There stood Herr Ferenc, with the rifle pointed at her. Damn. So much for Hyde's statement that he had no intention of harming them! She did not doubt that he would allow Herr Ferenc to shoot them if necessary.

At the sight of the hypodermic, Lucinda snarled- -for a moment, Mary thought she was going to attack Hyde. But Dénes moved behind her and put his hands on her shoulders, restraining her in the chair. His brother rolled up Lucinda's right sleeve, then held her wrist while Hyde drew blood from the crook of her elbow. Lucinda did not struggle, but she hissed and glared at each of them in turn.

The younger brother drew back, frightened, even as he continued to hold her wrist, but Hyde seemed merely amused. "Thank you, Miss Van Helsing," he said, when the syringe was filled with blood. "This will be put to a good use, I assure you. My patient will be most grateful for your contribution to his recovery."

His patient? Whom could he mean? Mary looked at Justine. She shook her head and frowned, as though to signify that she had no idea either.

Just then, Ágnes returned with what looked like a plate of fried eggs and tomatoes, with a couple of savory biscuits. She put it in front of Justine. Diana immediately took one of the biscuits and bit into it.

"Well," said Hyde. "I have important business to conduct. Ágnes will show you to your rooms once you're finished eating. I suggest you do not try to escape. Ferenc úr and his sons will be on the watch. They are excellent hunters, used to both this castle and the surrounding woods. I would not want them to shoot you by accident. I am sure you are far too sensible to attempt such a thing, Mary, in this mountainous region, in a country you are not familiar with. I'm aware that I have not been a very good father to you, but I do not want either of my daughters shot."

Mary tried to think of a biting retort, but she was so tired! By the time he had left the room, she still had not thought of a suitable reply.

"He didn't even bring us here on purpose!" said Diana indignantly. "He just wanted her blood. Why does he want her blood?" She scrutinized Lucinda, as though trying to figure it out.

"Get your hands off Justine's supper!" said Mary. Diana had been about to take the other biscuit. "We all need to eat, so we're strong enough for . . . well, whatever comes next. And I suggest we continue this discussion in private. So finish whatever's on your plate, and then let's go up to our rooms, wherever they are." She looked at Ágnes doubtfully. Who was this girl, that simply let Hyde open up a vein to feed Lucinda?

Diana slurped up the rest of her soup directly from the bowl, then licked it clean with her tongue. "All right, I'm done."

"And I," said Justine. She had not eaten everything on her plate—there was a fried egg and some mushrooms left. But at least she had eaten; that was something. It would have to do.

Mary realized that she did feel better for the meal—but weary to the bone. What they needed, more than anything else, was sleep. She rose. "All right, let's go. Ágnes—" How much English did the girl understand? Mary had no idea. "Can you take us to wherever we're going to sleep tonight?"

Ágnes nodded, then gestured for them to follow her. Justine rose and went to Lucinda. As she approached, Dénes stepped back, but continued to watch her warily. "Are you all right?" asked Justine. "Did he hurt you?"

Lucinda stared back at her with unfocused eyes, as though she were not seeing Justine at all. Low, almost under her breath, she sang a song that sounded like the sort of thing a mother might sing to her child—some sort of nursery rhyme, perhaps. *"Slaap kindje slaap. Daar buiten loopt een schaap . . ."*

The song echoed around the room. Somehow, Mary found it stranger and more chilling than anything else that had happened that day. Lucinda's madness was getting worse, wasn't it? And no wonder, considering everything that had happened in the last few days. But what were they going to do? How were they going to get her out of here?

"Come on," said Justine, holding out her hand. Lucinda took it and rose from the chair, then followed Justine as a child might follow its mother, stumbling a little. Mary followed her and Diana came behind, last because she had quickly eaten Justine's egg and grabbed a final sausage.

"What! We have to keep our energy up, right?" she whispered when Mary gave her an exasperated look.

"Here way," said Ágnes, holding open the door for them. Then she led them along a narrow corridor. To Mary's surprise, it too had been electrified, with a few bare, dismal bulbs in the sconces along the stone walls. If this method of lighting was the future, as some claimed, Mary did not think much of it. Give her the warm glow of gas lamps! They followed Ágnes up a stone staircase to the second floor. Here there were no longer electric lamps, only the moonlight that came through small, arched windows. The room to which Ágnes led them seemed to have no modern innovations at all—it looked as ancient as the castle, with high ceilings that disappeared into the darkness. Although the moon was full and bright, Mary could not make out much in its light—just the general shapes of furniture. But as soon as they were all in the room, Ágnes struck a match and lit the candles in an iron candelabra standing to one side of the stone fireplace. It reminded Mary of the candelabras that stood by the altar in St. Marylebone Church. Then Ágnes lit its double on the other side of the fireplace. Finally, she lit the fire itself, which had already been laid.

"Ágnes, do you speak any German?" asked Justine. "*Sprechen Sie Deutsch?*"

"*Ein bisschen,*" said Ágnes. She sounded frightened, and very shy. Well might she be frightened, after that episode! Mary could not stop thinking about it. Her own father—well, not her father—cutting this girl's arm so Lucinda could feed! She glanced at Lucinda, who was simply standing there, staring blankly at nothing at all, still singing some sort of song under her breath. Diana, on the other hand . . .

"Look at this!" Diana was kneeling on a large four-poster bed with moth-eaten hangings that looked as though it had come straight out of the middle ages. She started bouncing up and down. "Best bed *ever!*"

Mary noticed with relief that their trunk and bags, even Frau Schmidt's hamper, were stacked against the wall. At least they would have their things again!

Aside from the bed, there was not much furniture in the room. A long, narrow table against one wall, on which were set a basin and mismatched pitcher. A chair that looked more like a throne, with an embroidered cushion on the seat, by the fireplace. Both were of dark wood and looked positively medieval, as though they had stood there since the castle had been built.

> MARY: Renaissance, not medieval. Most of the castle
> was built during the sixteenth century, although I
> believe its foundations date from the fourteenth.

> CATHERINE: And our readers will care why?

MARY: You may not care for accuracy, but I do—and
Carmilla will, when she reads this book.

CATHERINE: If I ever get the damn thing written,
with all these interruptions!

Over the fireplace hung the portrait of a woman, young and
rather attractive, with dark hair and eyes. She was dressed in a
medieval—or rather Renaissance—style, in a red velvet dress
with puffed sleeves and the sort of unattractive headdress women
wore in those times, elaborately embroidered in gold thread.
Around her neck was a gold cross set with rubies and pearls. The
painting itself was stiff and awkward, the perspective off, but her
face contained so much personality, was so vital, that it seemed as
though she were alive.

DIANA: Ha! I see what you did there.

Wait, was Justine speaking to her? Mary looked away from
the portrait, reluctantly because it had captured her interest. No,
Justine was conversing with Ágnes in German. Mary could tell
that Ágnes's German was not much better than Justine's. Both
of them spoke haltingly, Justine filling in with a few words in
English that Ágnes did not seem to understand any better than
her German.
"Why don't you lie down?" said Mary to Lucinda. "You must
be exhausted." Lucinda gave her a blank stare, but followed Mary
readily enough when she took hold of Lucinda's wrist and led her
to the bed. "For goodness' sake, stop bouncing!" she said to Diana.
"Can't you sit still for a moment?"
"I sat still all day in that bloody coach," said Diana. "Is there
anything left in the basket? I'm still hungry."

"You would be. Go look for yourself. I have other things to worry about than your appetite!"

When Lucinda was lying on the bed, staring up at the canopy, and Diana was searching through Frau Schmidt's hamper, Mary walked back to the fireplace, where Justine was still talking to the maid. As she approached, Justine turned to her.

"Ágnes says there is another room prepared for us as well," she said. "But I think we had better stay together. The three of you should fit in that bed, and I will put some blankets on the floor. Ágnes"—she turned to the maid—"can you bring us more blankets? *Teppiche*—I mean, *Decken*. *Und Kissen*—some pillows." Turning back to Mary, she said, "Ágnes tells me she was instructed to lock us in for the night. I would rather be locked in together than apart."

"I agree," said Mary. "Did you ask her where we are?"

"Styria, as we guessed, and a long way from Budapest." Well, as Justine has guessed! Mary could take no credit for guessing anything of the sort. "This is, or was, the castle of the Karnstein family. That"—Justine pointed at the portrait above the mantelpiece—"was the last of them, Countess Mircalla Karnstein. You can see her name engraved on the frame. Ágnes says she was a terrible woman —she used to bathe in the blood of virgins to preserve her beauty. If my German is correct, but I'm not certain it is, she says the Karnsteins were a family of vampires that preyed on the people of this country, long ago."

"Vampires!" said Diana. "Do you mean like *Varney the Vampire; or, The Feast of Blood*?" She had found something or other to eat—ah, some of the bread Mary had purchased that morning, at the inn where they had slept the night before. That seemed so long ago! There should still be part of a loaf—Mary had forgotten about it entirely. Diana took a bite of the piece she was holding in her hand, which she had evidently torn off, then walked over to them and stood looking at the portrait with considerable respect.

MARY: Honestly, Diana, you read the worst trash.

DIANA: It's no worse than Catherine's books. Ow, you bit me! That was completely unnecessary!

CATHERINE: Just like your remark was completely unnecessary, and also untrue. *Varney* is a melodramatic penny dreadful. What I write is experimental modern fiction.

DIANA: I bet you have rabies.

"There are no vampires such as those described in your serials, Diana," said Justine. "The term 'vampire' is merely a metaphor. Ágnes is describing a time when aristocrats lived on the labor of their serfs, as a vampire is said to live on blood. No doubt the Karnsteins were cruel masters, as was common under the feudal system. The superstition has likely persisted because of medical conditions such as Lucinda's, which I take to be an extreme form of anemia, created or perpetuated by Professor Van Helsing for some reason we do not yet understand. The important thing is that we are very far away from anywhere. The closest city is Gratz, but we have no way to get there and no one here will help us. The only servants in this castle are Herr Ferenc, his two sons Dénes and János, and Ágnes. I asked her why she allowed herself to be fed on in that way. Evidently, Mr. Hyde is seeking some sort of cure for a companion of his who also lives in this castle, but as a complete recluse. Ágnes has not seen him—only János is allowed in that room. Ágnes's mother is very ill. Hyde has promised that if he can cure his sick friend, he will cure her mother as well. He has told her that Lucinda's blood is powerful medicine. So you see, none of that family will help us."

"Well, I think we should continue this discussion at another time," said Mary. How much English did Ágnes understand? She did not know, but suspected that anything Ágnes overheard would be repeated to her father—or rather, Hyde. "Thank you, Ágnes," she said, turning to the maid. She took a gold krone out of her waist bag and handed it to her. Such gestures were never amiss when one was in a tight spot.

"*Köszönöm . . . danke,*" said Ágnes, curtseying. "I bring *Wasser und Seife.*"

When she had gone, Diana said, "Doesn't matter if she locks the door. I can unlock it, easy peasy."

"I think Hyde is well aware of that," Mary replied. "It's probably the first thing he would expect us to do. He didn't even take away your lockpick tools, did he?"

Diana shook her head and patted her pocket, where she had presumably put them. *She still has her knife, too,* Mary thought bitterly. *The only thing he's taken away is my pistol . . . .* His pistol, really, but after having abandoned her fourteen years ago, he scarcely had a right to reclaim it!

"Anyway, there's no point to us stumbling around the castle in the dark. Justine, can you get the Baedeker? We can at least find out more or less where we are on the map. And then I think we had better get some sleep. We'll be no good at all tomorrow if we're exhausted. We need to figure out what this is about, and more importantly, how we can get away from here!"

After Ágnes had brought up hot water for the pitcher and pointed out the chamber pot under the bed, they put on their nightclothes—Mary and Justine helping Lucinda, who seemed almost comatose. Mary tucked her and then Diana into the large bed—there would be plenty of room for her. "Scratch my back," said Diana—a thoroughly annoying request! But in a few minutes she was snoring, and Lucinda seemed to be asleep as well, so Mary could go back to the fireplace, where Justine was sitting on a pile of blankets and pillows spread out to form a sort of mattress. Mary sat down on one corner. It would not be a comfortable bed for Justine, but at least she would not be kicked by Diana in the middle of the night.

"I found Gratz," said Justine. She opened their small red Baedeker and unfolded the large map at the front of the book. "From what Ágnes told me, I believe we are somewhere here." She pointed to a place between the word Gratz and a red line that looked like the Hungarian border. It was nowhere close to Budapest. "We have come very far out of our way."

"Damn." Mary could not think of anything else to say. She stared into the dying fire, which sent shadows racing all over the stone walls and made the portrait of Mircalla Karnstein above them look sepulchral. Finally, she asked, "Do you think Lucinda's blood could have some sort of healing properties?"

Justine pulled one of the blankets around her shoulders. "That may be what Professor Van Helsing was trying to do with his experiments. We know blood is necessary to life. As long as we are alive it circulates throughout the body, as William Harvey showed. There is something in blood that heals—look how wounds close and skin repairs itself, so only a scar remains. Perhaps Van Helsing succeeded in making Lucinda's blood unusually powerful—we saw how those men watching the asylum healed from fatal wounds, and Irene believed they were his followers. I was surprised that your own wound healed so quickly, after Lucinda drank your blood. That could be the aim of his experiments—some sort of accelerated healing."

"There's more to it than that," said Mary. "Those men were also extraordinarily strong." She stared into the fire. How tired she was! Tomorrow . . . well, tomorrow she would have to confront her father. Hyde. She did not want to think about it.

"In the book Irene gave me, *Zarathustra* by the German philosopher Friedrich Nietzsche, there is a mention of an *Übermensch*, an over-man or higher man. Perhaps that is what Van Helsing is trying to create? It is, in a sense, what all these modern alchemists have been trying to create—Rappaccini, Moreau, even your father. Frankenstein simply wanted to conquer death. They seem to want more, to make man not only immortal, but godlike."

Mary looked at Justine. Her face was pale and calm in the firelight, but Mary could see the marks of strain, the lines of tiredness under her eyes.

"At this point, I wouldn't put anything past them," she said, wearily. "You know, I think this is the most trouble we've been in so far. I have no idea how we're going to get out of it."

Justine did not answer. Perhaps there was no answer—they would simply have to see what tomorrow brought.

Somewhere in the depths of the castle, she heard a cry, faint and far away. It sounded like some sort of animal. Perhaps a dog howling?

"I'm glad you're here," said Mary, putting her hand on Justine's arm. "I mean, I'm sorry we're stuck, especially in a place this dismal, and I feel a sense of responsibility because after all, Hyde is my father—sort of. But if we're going to be stuck, I'm glad you're stuck with me. If you know what I mean."

"I too am glad," said Justine. "You and the others—you have taught me the value of friendship, even—or especially—in difficult circumstances."

Would they get out of those circumstances? Mary stared into the fire, which was burning down to the embers. Tomorrow, they would have to find out.

CHAPTER XVII

A Castle in Styria

Mary woke with a start. She had been dreaming that she was back in the coach, driving over a particularly rocky road, shaken side to side.

"Wake up!" A freckled face hung over hers, like a pale moon with small brown spots. An obnoxious moon. Then Diana drew back and shook her again by the shoulders.

"What. Are. You. Doing." Mary shoved at her sister, ineffectually. "Get *off*. Are you actually *sitting* on me?"

"I had to wake you up!" said Diana. "Listen."

And there it was, the cry she had heard last night, but not as faint as it had been. This morning it was louder, and closer. It sounded like . . . she did not know what. An elephant being tortured? She had heard an elephant once, when she had gone to the zoo with her nursemaid—Mrs. Poole, when she was still just Honoria—as a child. Or maybe it sounded like a lion, but a lion with a toothache. There was a note of anguish in the cry.

Suddenly, the door of the room was flung open. It banged against the stone wall.

"I need more of Miss Van Helsing's blood." There was Hyde, standing in the doorway, wearing a white laboratory coat and holding the hypodermic in one hand.

"No!" said Justine. Mary rolled onto her elbow so she could see better, although it was difficult with Diana still sitting on top of her. What was going on? Justine had evidently just woken up as well, because she was still dressed in her nightshirt, sitting among the blankets on the floor. Now she stood up, although her feet were still tangled in the bedding.

"You will get nothing more, from Lucinda or any of us, until you explain why you brought us here." Justine sounded angry, defiant, and a little befuddled from sleep. "Why do you need Lucinda's blood? What are you hoping to accomplish?"

Where was Lucinda, anyway? "Seriously, get off," she hissed at Diana, and this time Diana moved, thank goodness. Mary turned back around—Lucinda was still sleeping next her. Sleeping deeply, it seemed—but her breathing was shallower and more labored than Mary would have liked.

"My dear Miss Frankenstein, I don't owe you or anyone else an explanation." Hyde pulled Mary's—his—pistol out of his pocket and pointed it at Justine. "János!"

Ágnes's youngest brother, who must have been waiting out in the hallway, came running into the room. *"Igen, Doktor?"* He was wearing a cotton smock. It reminded Mary of what Hyde had worn about the house, when he had pretended to be Jekyll's apprentice.

"I want you to draw Miss Van Helsing's blood, exactly the way I showed you." He handed the hypodermic to János. "Move away from the bed, please," he said to Mary and Diana.

"No!" said Diana. "If he comes near Lucinda"—she pointed at János, who was looking alarmed and confused—"I'll bite his ears off! And scratch his eyes out!"

Hyde did not respond. He merely pointed the pistol downward. A moment later, Justine jumped. A bullet had ricocheted off the floor, next to her bare feet.

"Oh, you just think you're the king of the castle, don't you?" said Diana. "You're nothing but a—"

"Shut up," said Mary. "He's perfectly capable of shooting

Justine. Come on." She pulled Diana off and away from the bed, toward Justine so the three of them stood together. Not the safest place in the room, but she wanted to present a united front.

Cringing and still looking at them suspiciously, János approached the bed. He pushed up one of Lucinda's sleeves, then extracted enough blood to fill the syringe again. How much blood could Lucinda lose? Surely not much more.

"You're going to kill her," said Mary. "Why? What is all this for?"

"I assure you, it's for a purpose of the greatest importance, far more important than any individual life," said Hyde. "If you would like to hear more, I'll explain it to you. I'll even show you . . . well, perhaps. But right now I have important work to do, and you probably want your breakfast. Come, János."

What sort of work? But Hyde and his assistant were already out the door, which shut with a bang behind them.

Justine rushed over to the bed. Mary could hear her speaking to Lucinda in English, then German, then French. Lucinda just lay there. Finally, Justine shook her by the shoulders.

"No response at all," she said. "What in the world are we to do?"

"She's not dead, is she?" asked Diana.

Justine put her hand against Lucinda's neck. "No. Her breathing is regular, and her pulse is steady, although slow." She raised one of Lucinda's eyelids, but again there was no response. "She is simply in a very deep sleep."

Mary signed. "As much as I hate to say it, I think we had better do as he —you know, Hyde—says and get dressed, then go down to breakfast. Of course he would offer us breakfast after almost shooting you! That's just like him. But we need to find out what's going on, and we won't find it up here, will we?"

No one had come to light the fire or refill the pitcher with hot water, so Mary and Justine washed their faces in the cold water left from last night—Diana refused to wash her face at all. And then they dressed themselves in the chilly room, turning their backs to give one another privacy. Diana grumbled again about having to wear girls' clothes, but Mary was so used to her complaints that she simply ignored them. Anyway, there were more important things to think about.

Mary would never have remembered the way—she stood for a moment in the hall, looking one way and then the other, trying to remember how they had come up—but Diana pushed past her and said, "Follow me. I know where to go. I always know where to go."

Luckily, Diana's sense of direction was almost as good as Catherine's.

DIANA: *Almost?* Are you serious? My sense of direction is as good as yours. Or better!

CATHERINE: There's no way your sense of direction is as good as mine.

DIANA: Oh yeah? Fine, we'll get Charlie to take us somewhere in the East End—Whitechapel, or Stepney, or the docks—we won't know where! We'll be blindfolded the whole way, and he'll drop us off in one of the alleys. At night! Whoever gets back to the Athena Club first wins.

CATHERINE: You're on. I'll pay for the cab.

MARY: Why are you fighting about this in the middle of a chapter?

Diana, whose sense of direction was *almost* as good as Catherine's, led them back to the stone staircase, and then down to the room where they had eaten last night. Mary worried about leaving Lucinda—would she be safe alone? But what else could they do? They had to eat, and then they had to figure out what was going on in this castle. Why had Hyde brought them there? What was his nefarious purpose? At least she assumed his purpose was nefarious. He was Hyde, after all, and that business with the hypodermic was certainly not what one might consider harmless. She could not blame herself for his crimes—she *would* not blame herself for them. But she was thoroughly ashamed that he was her father.

In daylight, the castle looked less imposing than it had the night before. At the end of the hallway on which their room was located, the wall was half tumbled down, with half a window frame set into it. Sunlight streamed in where stones had long ago fallen. They passed windows with broken glass, wooden doors that hung on rusted hinges. Some of them had burn marks. It was obvious that the castle had suffered a catastrophe of some sort, long ago. The stairs were worn by the tread of feet over centuries, but also chipped, so it was a wonder that none of them had tripped going up the night before. Everywhere there was dust and sunlight, and the sense of something that had been long abandoned.

In the great hall where they had dined the night before, many of the flagstones were broken or missing, and one corner of the ceiling was gone—through the hole, Mary could see the sky, which was very blue. The electric lights were turned off now, and the wires connecting them looked incongruous against the stone walls.

Breakfast had been left on the table—rolls, butter and jam, slices of ham under a mesh cover to keep out flies, and a bowl of pickles. Clearly some of the castle's inhabitants had already breakfasted, for there were plates with crumbs and smears of jam on them, as well as clean ones stacked by napkins and cutlery. There were mugs as well, but nothing to put in them.

"No coffee?" said Diana, frowning. "I want coffee!"

"I think we had better make some sort of plan for the day," said Justine, stacking the soiled plates to get them out of the way and taking a clean one for herself. She put a roll on her plate and sat down.

"My plan is to get coffee," said Diana. "There's got to be a kitchen around here somewhere. I bet I can smell my way to it!" She turned and headed back toward the door.

"Diana!" called Mary. "Don't go anywhere without us!" But Diana was already halfway across the room. And then, she was gone—off to find the kitchen, presumably.

"Damn. That. Girl." Mary sat down on the bench and put her head in her hands. "What in the world are we going to do?"

Justine reached over and put a hand on her back, then gave her what Justine probably thought was a reassuring pat. It did not feel particularly reassuring. "We'll think of something. I know this is a terrible position for us to be in, but I've been in worse. When I was on the island, and Adam had killed Victor Frankenstein, and I was forced to live with him as his wife. When I was alone for so long—a century, all by myself in that big house. Those were the saddest, most difficult times of my life, because I had no friends to talk to or share the difficulties with me. Certainly we are in the frying pan, as Diana might say, but we are together and we know there are friends elsewhere who are expecting us. Perhaps they are even now wondering where we are, and surely they will search for us if we do not appear when scheduled? Do not allow yourself to despair—Hyde may have his weapons and his henchmen, but we have one another."

Mary felt ashamed. Of course, Justine had been through much worse than this—forced to live with Frankenstein's monstrous creation on an island in the Orkneys, and then isolated for so long in a house on the coast of Cornwall. But she also felt heartened. They had faced adversity before and overcome it. Had they not killed Adam and solved the Whitechapel Murders? Of course, this was a different circumstance. They would not be taking a cab back home to Park Terrace from a castle in Styria! Would they prevail this time? Surely they owed it to themselves—and Lucinda, as well as the other members of the Athena Club, to try.

> CATHERINE: Reader, if you would like to hear more about these events, you have only to purchase the first of these adventures, *The Strange Case of the Alchemist's Daughter*, two shillings from reputable booksellers. Or you could read my latest story in *Blackwood's Magazine*, in the special Christmas issue.

> MARY: Justine and I were talking! Now you're interrupting in the middle of our conversation with an advertisement?

> CATHERINE: We need money. Unless you've decided that we don't need to pay the gas and water bills? Or discovered a stash of banknotes we didn't know about somewhere?

> MARY: No, you're right. We do need money. Especially since the diamonds Prince Rupert paid us with for saving his life turned out to be paste.

After breakfast—which was not as filling as Mary would have liked, but how filling could bread and jam be?—the first task of the day was to reconnoiter. Diana still had not returned.

"Well, she'll just have to find us," said Mary. "I can't worry about her right now. We need to get a sense of where we are—the lay of the land, as it were."

"Diana is quite good at taking care of herself," said Justine. "And somehow, I do not think Hyde would harm his own daughter."

"I would not put it past him," said Mary grimly.

DIANA: I wasn't with Dad. I found the kitchen, and Ágnes was in there making some sort of stew, so I stirred the pot while she made me coffee. Then János came in and we had an arm-wrestling contest. You know, he's a lot nicer when he's not scared witless by Dad. And then Ágnes wanted us to try the pastries she had made—they were a different kind, all in layers with bits of bacon inside, and you sort of peeled them off. She and János couldn't speak much English, of course, but you don't really need much English to say "Hey, try these pastries." I mean, the pastries say it for you.

MARY: We were imprisoned in a castle in Styria, trying to figure out how to escape, and you got into an arm-wrestling contest?

DIANA: And then I taught them how to play *vingt-et-un*, with me dealing. Don't look at me so disapprovingly! They didn't have any money, so we played for walnuts. Even when she'd lost all her walnuts, Ágnes wanted to keep playing. She'll be a gambling addict someday, you mark my words.

"But what about Lucinda?" Mary continued. "Diana may be able to take care of herself, but we can't just leave Lucinda up there alone, can we? Who knows what Hyde might do to her."

Justine sighed. "I don't think we have much choice. If we're going to rescue her, we must know where we are, what options we have. Even if Mr. Hyde were to come for more of her blood, we would not be able to prevent him, as we could not prevent him this morning. I think we shall have to leave her for now. What else can we do? There are only two of us."

"There would be three if Diana hadn't wandered off!" Mary wanted, more than anything else, to slap her sister.

> DIANA: See? I'm not the violent one. Or not the only
> violent one, anyway.

But that sort of thinking would not help; they had to deal with the situation as it was. "Come on," said Mary. "No one's threatening to shoot us at the moment, so I suggest we go outside and have a look around."

They made their way once again to the front door, then out into the courtyard. Or what had once been a courtyard. Most of the castle had long ago fallen to ruin. Mary could see low stone walls that had been rooms, now with grassy floors. The section containing the great hall still stood, as well as the arching front entrance where they had walked beneath a portcullis the night before. But everywhere there were signs of destruction and decay. Although the castle had once been covered with yellow stucco, most of it had chipped off or faded, leaving the underlying stone exposed. The other section still standing seemed to be a stable and carriage house, and in front of the stable door sat Dénes Ferenc, on a three-legged stool, cleaning some harness.

"Good morning," he called to them, cheerfully for a man who had pointed a rifle at them the night before. "If you are thinking to run away, the nearest village is in that direction." He pointed northward. Or at least Mary assumed it was northward, based on the position of the sun.

The castle was situated on a hill, from which they could see the surrounding countryside. Mary followed the general direction of his finger. There were forests, meadows, the light brown dirt of the road that wound here and there, sometimes appearing across a field, sometimes disappearing again into the trees. She could see nothing . . . no, there, in the distance, she could see a cluster of red roofs. But it was very far away, several miles downhill through difficult country. Toward her left rose a series of hills, culminating in the wooded slopes of high mountains.

> JUSTINE: They are not high! The high mountains of the Styrian Alps are farther east, and even then they are not like the Alps of Switzerland.

> MARY: Well, they seemed high to me! They were a lot higher than anything I'd seen before.

> JUSTINE: That's because you are English. England is an extraordinarily flat country.

> MRS. POOLE: As God made it. This sceptered isle, this seat of majesty, this other Eden just like paradise, this precious stone set in a silver sea, this England . . . something like that.

> BEATRICE: Why, Mrs. Poole! You are quite the poet.

> MRS. POOLE: Well, we did a fair bit of Shakespeare when I was in the Park Terrace Players. I was Viola once, and then Lady Macbeth.

JUSTINE: There is nothing in England I would call a
mountain.

MARY: I think you've made your point.

Justine tugged Mary by the sleeve and started walking toward
the stables. Mary followed, although she did not particularly
want to converse with Dénes—not after his deception! As they
approached, he smiled at them as though they were the greatest
of friends.

Justine could break your neck, thought Mary.

But they needed information, and who else was likely to supply
it? Of all the Ferenc family, he seemed to speak the most English.

"Where are we?" asked Justine. "Or are you not permitted to
tell us?"

His smiled turned into a sort of smirk. "What I am permitted to do is of no consequence. I am my own master, you see. I
help my father when he needs, but I am not like János, to jump
at every command." He swept his hand to indicate the castle,
both the standing and fallen parts of it. "This is the castle of
the Karnsteins since very long time. But the family it was very
wicked—Mircalla Karnstein, the last Countess, was terrible
woman. So the people, they burn the castle. Once, there was
village here, but no more. Everything was burned to get rid of
that wicked family."

"Your sister called her a vampire," said Mary.

He frowned. "Ágnes is a silly girl. We are not all silly peasants in Styria—we do not all have these superstitions. I myself am
studying to become an engineer at the university in Gratz."

"And Hyde," said Mary. "What does he want? Why did he hire
you and your father?"

"That I cannot tell you," said Dénes. "He hire my father, and

I help, but he does not tell us why, or what is so important about the girl, what he is doing with her blood. Only, he says it will help my mother—*édesanyám*."

"And those strange cries—," Mary continued.

"So now I ask—why do you dress like a man?" He looked up at Justine, shading his eyes with his hands. "You are not a man. You are too tall, yes, but you could be pretty girl. I myself would take you to dance in the village, even though the other men would look at me. But I do not mind! I like strong, brave women. I see you were very brave in Vienna."

"Um, thank you," said Justine, looking as uncomfortable as Mary had ever seen her.

"Yes, thank you indeed for that information," said Mary. "I think we will look around now a bit, if you don't mind."

"Suit yourself," he said. "That is the English phrase, is it not? Although a suit is also something you wear. It is a curious language, English. I am very good at it, I think."

"Yes, precisely, how very clever of you." Mary smiled her *you have overcharged me for the coal delivery* smile. It is a polite, frightening sort of smile: the artillery of the English lady. Next thing you know, she's going to hit you over the head with an umbrella.

MARY: I would never!

CATHERINE: No, you just shoot people.

"Come on, Justine. We have *things to do*." She drew Justine away by the arm.

Once they had rounded the corner of the carriage house and could no longer see him, she said, "The gall of the man! Take you to a village dance, indeed. . . ."

"I think he was trying to pay me a compliment," said Justine.

"Then he could have done it like a gentleman and not an idiot. Look, what is that?"

On this side of the castle were the ruins of what had once been a church or chapel—some of its walls were still standing, although its stone altar was bare to the sky, and grass had long ago grown over the floor. Around it they could see the remains of a churchyard—ancient gravestones here and there, mostly askew, and at its center a stone tomb, like a mausoleum but half buried in the earth. There was something written over the heavy wooden door—Mary could not quite see it. She walked closer, raising her skirt because the grass had grown tall here. Yes, now she could make out the letters, although they were partly covered with lichen:

MILLARCA KARNSTEIN
1680–1699

This must have been the wicked countess herself, although evidently the stonemason had misspelled her name. Well, now she was lying peacefully in her tomb. On this side of the castle, the landscape was wilder. The hill rose behind them, dark and wooded. There was no escape in this direction.

"Such destruction must have resulted from one of the peasant revolts so common in the seventeenth century," said Justine, looking around her at the remains of the church, and then back at the castle. From this side, it was even more clearly a ruin. "You can see there is damage from a fire within the house. It was not uncommon, in that era, for peasants to rise up against their masters, particularly in these old districts where the feudal system still lingered. They were seeking greater freedom for themselves, relief from the burden of taxation—"

"Right," said Mary. "Except now isn't the time for a lecture.

The question is, how are we going to get away from here? Not that I don't sympathize with the plight of seventeenth-century peasants, but seriously, we have to do something, and I simply don't know what."

Before Justine could reply, Mary heard it again—the cry she had heard earlier that morning. But now it sounded closer, as though it were coming through the stone walls of the castle.

"Mary!" That was Hyde's voice. She looked around her in all directions, but could not see anyone except Justine. "Up here!" She looked up, and there he was on the second floor— that must be the end of the hallway leading to their bedroom. She recognized the broken window frame. "I've been searching for you for the last twenty minutes. And where is Diana—isn't she with you?"

"No," said Mary. She wasn't about to tell him where Diana was—not that she knew herself!

"Oh," he said. "Well, I need you. And Miss Frankenstein, although he said not to bring her—but I think you had both better come. Just around the next corner, at the back, you'll find a small door. It should be unlocked. Go in and follow the hallway. Your first right will be my laboratory. I'll meet you down there. Can you do that?"

"If you tell us what this is all about," said Mary, frowning. He was not as domineering and dismissive as he had been that morning—no, he was almost asking her. Why? What had changed?

"I'll tell you, but just meet me!" His face disappeared from the broken window.

Mary looked at Justine and shook her head. She must have appeared particularly exasperated, because Justine said, "At least we'll find out what's going on."

Mary certainly hoped so.

Around the corner from the graveyard was what must have

once been a kitchen garden. There were still raised beds with paths between them, and here and there Mary could see sage or rosemary growing among the weeds.

>DIANA: You mean Justine could see them. Mary wouldn't know sage from . . . anything else green that grows in a garden.

>MARY: That's not necessarily true. I know it's—well, it has small leaves. And you use it to stuff the goose.

>CATHERINE: I was in Mary's point of view. I can't just change point of view whenever I want to. That's not how it's done.

>DIANA: Why does everything have to be from Mary's point of view? What makes her so special?

>CATHERINE: She's the easiest to write about. You're too chaotic, and I can't think like Justine—all that philosophy. Anyway, our readers would fall asleep if I wrote down all the things Justine thinks about—seventeenth-century peasants' revolts and the rights of man, and whatever Voltaire said. . . .

>JUSTINE: I do realize that, while I am interested in such things, our readers might find them tedious or tiresome.

>CATHERINE: I'm not criticizing, Justine. You know I'm glad you're the way you are, and I wouldn't wish you any different. But a narrative has to *move*.

DIANA: Yeah, but Mary wouldn't have recognized sage if it had bitten her.

MARY: Well, it doesn't bite. I do know that!

As she passed through the doorway, she felt once again the chill of the castle walls, the weight of the stone above and around her. The only light came from a small window at the end of the hall. She found a door on the right—there was another on the left a little farther down. But Hyde had said right, hadn't he? She pushed the door open. "Come on," she said to Justine, who was directly behind her, and then she entered.

If this was a laboratory, it was a poor excuse for one. There was nothing in the room but a long wooden table and a stool tucked under it. One end of the table had been burned long ago—here, too, that ancient fire had raged. On top of the table were instruments she immediately recognized: a microscope, a Bunsen burner, a scale with hanging balances. In the center of the table was an alembic, and ranged along one side were a row of glass bottles filled with different powders—his chemicals, she guessed. They were rather pretty, with their different colors. Next to them was a ceramic mortar and pestle. This was what the table in his laboratory had looked like, long ago, when her father had still been the respectable Dr. Jekyll. Except of course there had been shelves filled with scientific books—heavy tomes bound in leather with gilding on their spines—as well as stacks of official-looking journals. She remembered the table of elements hanging on the wall, and sunlight coming through the glass dome of the old operating theater he had used as his laboratory. Now all he had was this bare room, the most basic instruments of his trade, and a single book perched on one corner of the table. It was bound in leather and had a coat of arms stamped on it, with an awkward, medieval-looking dragon on a shield. Unless it was a dog with wings?

MARY: You'd better not let Carmilla read that!
Implying that her coat of arms looks like a winged dog. . . .

"He's still conducting experiments," said Justine.

Mary approached the table. "Of course he is. I don't think he ever stops. It's a sort of addiction with him." She was about to examine the book when Hyde pushed open the door, hard enough that it banged into the stone wall. His hair was disheveled as though he had been through a small tornado, or had been pushing his hands through it in exasperation.

"Mary," he said, "you've got to help me. Honestly, I'm at my wit's end. What's wrong with Lucinda's blood? You were in the coach with her for four days—you cared for her and kept her fed. Did you notice anything unusual? I mean, in the transformation process?"

Mary stared at him. The laboratory coat, pristine that morning, was now wrinkled. The pinched, crafty face looked tired. His brow was furrowed, and the charming, unreliable smile he habitually wore was absent. For a moment, she almost—*almost*—felt sorry for him.

"I have no idea what you mean," she said in the coldest, most contemptuous tone she could summon. "What transformation process? What did her father's experiment do to Lucinda?"

"My dear," he said, looking at her directly for perhaps the first time. Suddenly she realized that his eyes were exactly the color of her own—a shifting blue-gray. They were still her father's eyes, although his general appearance was so changed. He rubbed his hands together nervously, then began to pace back and forth. "Let's be honest with each other. You know as well as I do that Miss Van Helsing's blood has particular properties—or it should. I read Van Helsing's paper on the subject in the journal of the Alchemical Society. He explained the central principle quite clearly, although he did not provide the details of his procedure. By now, her blood should have the power to heal. If he knew I had his daughter—well, I met him once, a long time ago, when I was still a member of the society. He was known as an expert pugilist and a friend of Lord Queensbury. One would not want to get into a fight with such a man. But I would brave his anger to know why her blood does not work."

Ah, that was how his hair had gotten into such a mess! He was almost pulling at it in frustration.

Justine stepped forward. "I suspect we have considerably less knowledge of Lucinda's condition than you do. We have not read any papers. We know only that for some reason she must feed upon blood, and that she has slipped into a deep sleep—unless she has awakened since we left her?"

Hyde shook his head. "No, she's in a coma. I was hoping she herself could tell me more about her father's research—but it's no use. I can't wake her, no matter what I do."

"That's your own fault," said Mary sharply. "You shouldn't have drawn her blood this morning."

"Mary, you are too much my daughter to mistake correlation for causation. I drew her blood and she subsequently slipped into a coma, but those two events were not related. The amount of blood I drew from her was no more than a physician might take—it would not have had such a drastic result. Her decline is due to Van Helsing's experiment. But why? She should be stronger, heartier, more healthy rather than less. Her blood should have the power to heal all ills, to repair wounds, no matter how fatal."

"Like those men we fought in Vienna," said Justine.

"Exactly," said Hyde. "And let me commend you on a valiant battle—Dénes Ferenc saw it all and described it to me in the most vivid terms. I believe he was watching from a window in one of the nearby buildings."

"Perhaps that explains his statement to me earlier," said Justine.

"So you were spying on us!" said Mary. "For how long?" Ever since they had left England?

Hyde smiled—and there it was again, that wicked charm of his. Well, she would certainly not succumb to it. "Not you, my dear, although I am always delighted to know how you are doing. Dénes was watching the hospital, as well as the men watching the hospital—Van Helsing's henchmen, as you may have guessed. One day he saw a light flashing from a window of the inn where you were staying. He cleverly deduced a telescope and paid the innkeeper for information. Then he telegraphed me, and I telegraphed back. The nearest telegraph is in the village, but Ágnes does her marketing there, so it was not difficult for us to maintain contact. Mr. Ferenc really is a coachman, on the regular route between Vienna and Budapest. That made it easy to bring you all here. However, while I'm willing to satisfy your curiosity to the extent it is in my power, I really do have a pressing need for any information you might have on Miss Van Helsing—or rather, the quality of her blood."

"But we don't know anything," said Mary. "It's exactly as Justine told you. Lucinda needs to drink blood—she throws up if she eats any food, or even drinks anything other than water. She has puncture marks all up and down her arms. So did her mother, who died in that fight—maybe she wouldn't have died if Dénes had actually helped instead of spying on us! We know Professor Van Helsing was performing experiments on her and her mother, but we don't know what—or why he put both of them in a mental institution. Really, we have no idea."

Hyde ran his fingers through his hair again. He looked both dejected and frustrated at the same time.

"Why is it so important, anyway?" asked Mary. "What do you need her blood for? Why have you drawn it twice?"

He looked up at her, eyes wide, with a look of such sincerity that Mary was immediately suspicious. "Surely you must understand how beneficial this discovery would be to the human race. Imagine, Mary. We would be able to cure diseases with a blood transfusion! Anna Ferenc, for example: She's dying of cancer. Without a breakthrough like this, she will be dead within the year. Would you want to withhold such a cure from her? And imagine all the other lives that could be saved. . . ."

"And what's in it for you?" Mary did not trust him for a moment.

"Why, the advancement of knowledge, of course! Although one must live on something. I certainly would not refuse some sort of appropriate compensation, were it offered to me. My expenses, I regret, have been heavy of late—renting this castle, for instance. My personal fortune is almost gone."

"In other words," said Justine, "you would enrich yourself. The wealthy would purchase health and life, while the poor would continue to suffer. And how much life would they purchase? What exactly can this miraculous blood regenerate?"

"Ah, you have hit upon the very question I would most like to answer," said Hyde, gleefully. "The blood can heal—we know it can, for the men you shot rose again shortly after you had left them for dead. But can it prevent death itself? Can it conquer that grim destiny to which we must all come? If so—"

"You could create men who never die, and they would pay you handsomely, I'm sure," said Justine. "You are despicable, Mr. Hyde. You do not deserve our help, even if we were capable of giving it to you. Mary, I suggest we go up to Lucinda. We have left her long enough. We can at least make certain she is as comfortable as possible."

Mary looked at Justine with admiration. She was standing very tall, and seemed almost statuesque in her anger. She would have made a very good model for Nemesis, goddess of righteous vengeance.

JUSTINE: Goodness, Catherine. I would blush if I
were capable of it!

DIANA: Why can't you blush?

JUSTINE: I'm dead, remember? And alive, of course,
but—Lucinda rejected my blood because it is the
blood of a dead woman.

MARY: I'm sure she didn't mean that as an insult.

A cry of such anguish! And then the words "Edward! Damn
you, Edward!" They came from down the hall.

Surely Mary had heard that voice before? And the cry sounded
like those she had heard earlier—the tone was the same, but then
she had thought they were the cries of an animal. Now she knew
they were distinctly human.

She looked at Justine, then almost stepped back in surprise at
the look on Justine's face. It was terribly pale, and there was fear
in her eyes.

"That is not possible," said Justine.

"You know perfectly well it's possible," said Hyde. "You, better
than anyone, know how strong he is. If anyone could have survived that conflagration, it would be him."

Mary glanced from one of them to the other, confused.
"Who was that crying out? And what's impossible? Justine, what's
going on?"

Justine gripped her arm so tightly that Mary winced. For once,
Justine was not controlling her strength. Perhaps she was not even
aware of it. She stared at the stone wall as though she were seeing
something very far away.

With her other hand, Mary took hold of Justine's arm and

tugged at it. "You're hurting me. Let go—and tell me what's going on."

"He did not want you to see him," said Hyde. "Not as he is now—not until he had been healed by Miss Van Helsing's blood. But since you know—I think you had better come. He will not hurt you. He is no longer capable of hurting anyone."

Justine nodded, but Mary could see it was with reluctance. "I will see him. I think you have lied to us—the both of you have lied to us—long enough."

Mary wanted to ask them what in the world they were talking about. But Hyde was walking to the door, and Justine was following him, and all Mary could do was follow them both down the hallway and to the door she had seen earlier, on the left.

Hyde opened it. It swung inward with a loud creak.

Mary heard a cry—a terrible, desperate cry.

Justine was still standing outside the door, blocking her way, but Mary stepped around her. There, in a smaller room, as bare as a monk's cell, with only an iron bed in one corner, lay the unmistakable figure of Adam Frankenstein. A narrow, unglazed window let in sunlight, but his bed was in the darkest corner of the room. Although he was holding his hands to his face, she could see his coarse black hair, the pallor of his skin, the massive form under the thin blanket. It could be no one else. He was almost too large for the bed—his bulk filled all of it, and his knees were bent so he could fit between the head- and foot-boards. So he had survived the fire after all! And they had been so certain, so completely certain, that he was dead. She felt as stupefied as Justine.

"No!" he said. "Go away! I do not want you to see me like this!"

"Like what?" said Justine. Her voice was unnaturally calm, even for her. "What have the two of you been hiding from us?" She walked over to him and stood beside the bed.

"Justine, be careful! Remember the last time . . ." When Adam had tried to replace her brain with one that would be more obedient to his commands. Mary still remembered the battle in the warehouse, where Watson had been so dreadfully wounded.

Justine leaned down and pulled his hands away from his face. "He's not strong now. Are you, Adam?"

Before he turned his face away from them, toward the wall, Mary saw the dreadful ruin—all the left side burned, the left eye gone altogether. He pulled his hands away from Justine's, only to cough into them—harsh, hacking coughs that left blood on his fingers. The back of his left hand was burned as well.

"His lungs were damaged in the fire," said Hyde. "He's not supposed to talk. Most of his wounds are internal—they have weakened him considerably. I wasn't sure he would make it here alive, particularly since we had to cross the mountains. . . ."

"I'll talk when I damn well please!" said Adam. "What does it matter? I'm dying anyway. You haven't found anything in that book to cure me, and the blood has done nothing—nothing!"

"So this is why you kidnapped Lucinda—and us, incidentally," said Mary. "That whole rigmarole about helping humanity, and Mrs. Ferenc . . . You are such a liar!"

"I think we should try one more time," said Hyde. "Perhaps if I inject her blood closer to your heart—that might do the trick. If her blood doesn't work this time, I'll look in the book again. There has to be something in there. After all, the Countess is still alive, isn't she?"

"You are *not* taking any more of Lucinda's blood!" said Mary.

"Who's not going to take any more of Lucinda's blood? Hullo, Dad." It was Diana, standing in the doorway, with János behind her. "I heard a noise and figured I should investigate. Bloody hell, is that Adam Frankenstein?" She turned back to János. "No wonder you didn't want me to come down here!" She punched him on the arm—hard, by his expression and the fact that he clutched it immediately afterward. Then she turned back to Mary. "Do we have to fight him again, or what?"

"János!" said Hyde. "I want you to draw another vial of Miss Van Helsing's blood. My kit is in the laboratory."

Mary could see János darting in that direction. His boot heels echoed down the hall.

"No!" she said. "This has got to stop. First, because her blood isn't doing whatever you want it to, and second, because it's *wrong*."

János darted back past the doorway, in the opposite direction, with the hypodermic flashing in his hand.

"Diana—," she said.

"Don't worry," said Diana. "I'll make sure he doesn't get anywhere near Lucinda, even if I have to stick a knife into him!" She turned, and then Mary could hear her boots clattering down the hallway after János.

"She must not stop him," said Hyde. "I need to know why Van Helsing's experiment failed." He put one hand in his pocket. "Damn! That girl stole my pistol! How—"

Mary could not help smiling. Good for Diana! Annoying as she was, she always seemed to come through in a pinch. "She is your daughter, after all. What did you expect?"

"You don't understand," he said. He put his hands to his head, running his fingers through his hair again and then grabbing it as though about to tear it out. "The knowledge we could bring to the world! The insights we could gain into the mind of Nature herself! Why, it would be like Cortez, looking down at the Pacific—silent upon a peak in Darien. We would be the discoverers of a new continent of human knowledge!"

He stalked out of the room. With a glance back at Justine to make sure she would be all right—but Adam seemed harmless now, huddled under the blanket—she followed him back down the hall, into that sad simulacrum of a laboratory.

He went to the leather-bound book and opened it. "There must be something in here, some sort of explanation. In all of human history, only three people—two men and one woman—have discovered the secret of eternal health and life. Frankenstein was one of them, but his experiment was useless—who cares about resurrecting corpses? You've seen Adam—and Justine. Would you want to be like them, the walking dead? No, what we want, each of us whether or not we admit to it, is to live forever, young, unscarred by time or any weapon man can devise, vulnerable only to compete destruction . . . I thought, I was convinced, that Van Helsing was on the right track, that he had discovered the secret. Damn!" He hit the table with his fist, so that the jars and instruments on it jumped.

"This obsession with knowledge at the expense of human life, of ordinary human relations and pursuits, will destroy you," said Mary. She could feel anger building inside her. It was a novel sensation. "Look at what it has done already. Look at you! Alone here, with only Adam Frankenstein and your—yes, henchmen—for company. Was it worth giving up everything—our family, your reputation—for this?"

Hyde stared at her as though dumbfounded. "Mary, I never intended to hurt you or your mother. You must believe that. Ernestine—I went to see her, the first night we were in London. It had been so long. I wanted to see her face again, so I climbed up to the window and watched her for a while through the glass. . . . She was brushing her hair, and I remembered how I used to do that for her, when we were newly married, before so many things came between us. I thought once Adam's business was done, I could go back and tell her I had always loved her, ask her to forgive me. But a week later I learned that she was dead. I had left it too late."

"Because you killed her," said Mary accusingly.

"Killed? What do you mean? I never even entered the room,

although it would only have taken me a moment to unlatch the window from outside. All I did was look at her through the glass panes. She was sitting at her dressing table, with her back to me, and I could see the fall of her hair in the lamplight. She had the most beautiful hair, like a cascade of gold—the sort of hair goddesses have in Greek myths. I used to run my fingers through it. . . . She was looking into the mirror, but then she turned, and for a moment I could see her face—it was as delicate and pure as on the day I married her, although more lined with care and age. I thought for a moment she might see me—she seemed to be looking my way. But then she turned away again and blew out the lamp. The gas was turned low, and I could see no more."

"She saw you, all right," said Mary. She could barely look at him—her father, so different from the man he had been when she was a child. "What do you think make her so sick, so suddenly? She was raving about a face she had seen at the window. I never imagined she meant *yours*." She looked at him as coldly as she could, with contempt. This was the one thing she had wanted to tell him, the one thing she had wanted him to know ever since she realized what he had done.

He stared at her, bewildered. "Is that true?" Then he looked down and shook his head. "No, of course it's true. You would not lie—you are almost incapable of it. Your disposition would not allow such a thing. But I never meant to harm her. . . ."

"What do you mean, my disposition would not allow?" What had he meant by that? The phrasing struck her as peculiar.

Hyde put his hands in the pockets of his white coat and looked down at the floor. "I only mean that . . ." He was almost mumbling to himself.

"What?" said Mary. But did she want to know? She remembered what Dr. Freud had said about her—that she was as unusual, in her own way, as Diana.

Hyde looked at her with a troubled expression. "Ernestine wanted so much to have a child. When we married, we hoped—and several times she thought she might be pregnant, but it would turn out to be indigestion . . . or once, a bad tin of lobsters. And so we waited and waited. The lady's maid she had brought from Yorkshire, who married my butler Poole, had a baby—little Honoria that was—and Ernestine would take her for walks in the park or play dress-up and have tea parties as though the child were her own. Finally we consulted specialists, who told her that in all likelihood, she would never have a child. They advised her to take up charitable work! It broke my heart to see her longing for something she could not have. So I buried myself in science, and in the business of the Alchemical Society. Raymond, Lanyon, Hennessey, and I formed a sort of inner circle—and Carew as well, for we were friends in those days. How invigorated we felt! Darwin's theories seemed to open up new avenues of inquiry. We did not agree with him in all things, of course—we held with Lamarck, although the world might call us heretics. But we were happy to be so. We should return, we told ourselves, to the problem of biological transmutation. Raymond had been working on that problem, and had suffered setbacks. An experimental subject had proven—problematic, shall we say? Do not let that daunt you, we told him. Look at how the world treats all its visionaries! Inspired by the theories of Spencer and Galton—their errors as much as the areas in which they were correct—we redoubled our efforts."

"Carew! Wasn't that the man you killed?" asked Mary, astonished.

"What? Oh yes. We quarreled—he did not like the direction my efforts were taking. You see, at first I thought, why not attempt to raise humanity higher? Man could, and should, be made more rational than he was at present. Moreau had been working on the same problem—before he was hounded out of England by a bunch of sanctimonious antivivisectionists! His work focused on the biological, but I thought a chemical solution might be found to alter the balance of a man's personality, so that his angel was strengthened while his demon was lulled to sleep. But its effects would be psychological, not observable empirically. How could I know they had occurred? Clearly, I must ingest the chemical myself! I created a potion that would make me a better man, and so I was—for a time. I also wanted Ernestine to be happy, to have what she most wished for in the world. She was past the age when most women bear children, but with my growing knowledge of chemistry, I created a drug and secretly administered it to her—"

"You drugged my mother without her permission?" said Mary.

"For goodness' sake, I simply put it into her tea! I thought it would give her what she most wanted. And it did—you were born, Mary. You were her delight, what she most loved and cherished. She had given up on the possibility of having a child. To her, you were a miracle. I could not take that away from her by telling her you were the result of my science."

"And yet, you were trying to be moral—"

"Rational, Mary. Ethical. What I did was for the greater good. I made a decision that would be best for her, and for me. And I accepted the consequences of that decision."

"You 'accepted the consequences'? But . . . I was the consequence!"

"And a welcome one, I assure you! Your mother was happy, and you—well, you were the perfect child. You almost never cried. Once, I remember, you were walking in the park with Honoria, who had become your nursemaid, and you skinned your knee. She brought you home—she was sobbing, but you merely showed me the wound and said, 'Look, Papa, isn't that interesting? It's going to turn a pretty color.' You were the offspring of the man I was then. But I—well, I wanted to see what would happen if I went in the other direction. If I indulged my lower, baser instincts. It seemed to me there might be something worthwhile in the animal part of man after all, Moreau's theories notwithstanding. He thought humanity should be forced to evolve, to rise above our animal nature. I wanted to experience the animal. And so I began my slow descent into Hyde. Carew objected in stronger and stronger terms—finally, he proposed that I be expelled from the society. One night I met him in the street, coming home from— well, some sort of entertainment. There is no need for you to know what sort. He remonstrated with me one more time, calling me vile names, telling me in no uncertain terms how far I had fallen. I could not help it, Mary. It was as though I had been possessed by a great rage, a monstrous demonic rage that I could not control. Surely you cannot blame me for an action so automatic and instinctual?"

"Of course I can," said Mary. "You chose to become who you are. You chose to create—" She did not like that word. But what other word could she use? "You chose to create me. And what of Diana? And Diana's mother? She died in poverty because of you."

He seemed taken aback. "I really am very sorry about that. I cared for Colleen a great deal. But I could not stay. I was known for a murderer, hunted throughout England. What was I supposed to do, allow myself to be hanged?"

"Do you know what I think, Father?" Mary had not meant to call him that, but it was too late to take back the word now. "I think you are the most selfish man I have ever met. You stand here, justifying every single one of your actions, regardless of the consequences, regardless of the anguish you have caused others."

Bang! And then another *bang!* She recognized them instantly as pistol shots.

"Diana!" she said. "She has my pistol."

What had she been meaning to tell this man who was her father, and with whom she was so very angry, while he stood there looking chagrined, but not particularly ashamed or repentant? There was no time now. She turned and ran down the hallway. She paused for a moment at the door of Adam's room. Justine was still there, kneeling by the bed. Why was she kneeling? And why was she holding Adam's hands? She looked at Mary, startled and concerned. "What was that noise?"

"Shots," said Mary. "Either Diana's been shot, or she's shot someone, or both!"

Justine rose. "I'm coming. I'll be right behind you."

"Justine!" came the anguished cry from Adam. "Don't leave me! Don't leave me to die alone!"

Justine looked down at him for a moment. "God have mercy on your soul," she said. Then she ran after Mary, who could hear her boots clattering behind.

The hallway ran into another, perpendicular to it, like the top of a T.

"Right?" said Justine.

"Left, I think," said Mary. And yes, she had made the correct decision, because there were the stairs. They ran up, Justine taking the lead, two steps at a time. At the top of the stairs, Mary had to pause for a moment and put her hand to her side. She had a terrible cramp!

"Diana!" Justine was already at the door to their room. Mary ran to catch up and entered right on her heels.

They were greeted by a fearful sight. Diana was standing in front of the bed with Mary's pistol in her hand. Lucinda was still lying on the bed, as insensible as she had been that morning. János Ferenc was sitting on the floor, blood seeping through his trouser leg and spreading over the flagstones.

"It's not my fault!" said Diana. "I *told* him not to touch Lucinda. I even fired a warning shot. I *meant* to shoot him in the foot, but I'm not as good a shot as Mary."

DIANA: I did *not* say that.

"János! *Jézus Mária, mi történt?*" It was Ágnes at the door. Behind her was Hyde. She ran to her brother and knelt beside him, then took off her apron and tried to staunch the bleeding. The apron quickly became red. "You are a bad, bad girl!" she shouted at Diana. There were tears running down her face.

"My powders can stop the bleeding," said Hyde. "But we need to get him down to the laboratory. I can't carry him—someone will need to support him on the other side."

Justine moved forward, but Ágnes said, "No, not you! Not any of you! You will not touch him—I will do myself."

As Hyde and Ágnes lifted János, he gave a cry of pain, but he seemed able to walk well enough. Between the two of them, they supported him as he hobbled from the room, looking pale and frightened.

Mary held out her hand. "Give me the pistol."

"Fine!" Diana put it into her hand, none too gently. "You should be thanking me, you know. You wouldn't have your pistol back if it weren't for me, and I protected Lucinda. I think a *thank you* is in order."

"What's that?" Justine was looking about her, confused. Then Mary noticed it—a tapping sound, an insistent *tap tap tap*. Where was it coming from? The window!

There, at the window, was a face—the face of a woman. Her hand was raised, and she was tapping, *tap tap tap*. For a moment, Mary thought she must be hallucinating—not because there was a woman at the window, which could be explained logically in a number of ways, but because she was the exact replica of the woman in the portrait above the fireplace—of Mircalla Karnstein.

Tap tap tap. The woman made a motion—she was miming turning the latch.

Justine looked at Mary. "What should we do?"

"Oh, for goodness' sake!" said Diana. She walked over to the window, turned the latch, and opened one of the casements. "What do you want? We're a little busy at the moment."

"My name is Carmilla," said the woman. "I've come from Mina, in Budapest. I think it's time you were rescued from this place. Don't you think?"

CHAPTER XVIII

Escape from the Castle

Mary made the mistake of looking down while she was still considerably above the castle courtyard. The world swam around her: the dirt and gravel below, on which she might fall—Diana's face looking up expectantly—the rope by which she hung suspended against the wall—blue sky above. And there, in the window, Justine's face, looking anxious. Resolutely, she focused on the rope—*Just think of the rope!*—and started climbing down again, hand over hand, keeping the rope tightly between her boots, although her skirt and petticoat kept getting in the way.

When she reached the bottom, Diana said, "See? Easy peasy."

Mary looked up again. Now Justine was beginning her descent. Once Justine stood beside her, the woman who called herself Carmilla appeared at the window. First she pulled up the rope and disappeared inside. Then a large bundle appeared at the aperture. It looked like a week's worth of laundry tied up in a linen sheet, knotted at the top and tied to the rope. Except, incongruously, there was a foot sticking out, right at the top. . . . Slowly, she lowered the bundle. When it reached the ground and was sitting on the gravel, Diana made a cut on the top with her knife. She tore open the linen sheet. Inside was Lucinda, curled into a ball, still in her nightgown, still unconscious. Justine picked her up, cradling her as though she were a child, with Lucinda's head on her shoulder.

The rope fell to the ground. But how would the woman—Carmilla—climb down without it?

Mary was astonished to see her climb out the window, then crawl like a lizard, face-down, her fingers and toes finding purchase in the crevices between the stones. Now she understood why the woman had been barefoot when she had climbed into the room—she must have come up the same way! Mary also noticed her suit, which was unlike any she had seen before—resembling a man's suit, but tailored to a woman's body. It fit her like a glove. As she climbed down the wall, her long braid of dark hair swung down and preceded her. Halfway down, she stopped for a moment and looked at them, as though making sure they were still there and all together. How could she cling to the wall like that? Diana gave a low whistle of appreciation. "Blimey. Even I can't do that."

When Carmilla reached the bottom, she put her hands on the ground, then turned herself upright and brushed her hands against her trousers, leaving streaks of dust. "Could you hand me my boots? They're behind Diana. You are Diana, aren't you? Mina described you all quite clearly." Despite the seriousness of the situation, she sounded amused. Her voice was low and musical, with just the trace of an accent—Mary was not sure what sort, but then she was not very good at accents. Perhaps Justine would be able to identify it.

Wordlessly, Diana handed her a pair of tall riding boots that had been standing by the wall. Carmilla sat on the ground, pulled socks out of them, then pulled on the socks and boots.

"Who are you, and how do you know Mina?" asked Mary. Perhaps she should have asked that question upstairs, before this woman she did not know had climbed in through the window. But it seemed imperative to get Lucinda, and themselves, out of the castle as quickly as possible, before her father—Hyde, that is—returned. Even here, they remained in danger. One of the Ferencs, father or son, could spot—and then stop—them at any time. But what sort of woman crawled down a wall head-first?

"My carriage is down the road, around the bend where it can't be seen from the castle. I promise that I'll explain everything, but I suggest we depart before your father realizes we're gone. At the moment we outnumber him, but I always think it's better to avoid an unnecessary fuss. Here, I'll carry Lucinda."

Well, that would have to do as an explanation for now! Mary glanced at Justine, who handed Lucinda over, carefully—but Carmilla carried her just as easily as Justine had. She must be very strong? Lucinda was not large, but Mary could certainly not have carried her alone. She looked at Justine and raised her hands as though to say, *What do you think?* Justine shrugged and shook her head, as though to indicate that she didn't know what was going on either.

"Come, it's time we were gone." Carmilla turned and started crossing the courtyard, Lucinda in her arms.

"Lord!" said Diana. "She can climb like me—better than me, even. And she's as strong as Justine. Did you notice she looks just like—"

"Yes, I noticed," said Mary. She was worried, very worried. But the woman had said she came from Mina. . . . "Come on. I don't know if it's the right thing to do, maybe not, but it's certainly something. And we do need to get out of here."

As they neared the stables, Carmilla called out, "Laura, is everything all right?"

"Right as rain," came the response. The stable door was open, and inside Mary could see another woman, more properly attired in a walking suit, holding a rifle as though she was entirely familiar with its use. "They've been very good, haven't you, gentlemen?" She stepped aside, gracefully sweeping her skirt back with one hand while holding the rifle in the other. Behind her were Herr

Ferenc and Dénes, sitting on the ground with their wrists and ankles tied, their mouths covered with red kerchiefs—probably their own. Above them, one of the horses looked out of its stall as though wondering what all the excitement was about.

"Excellent," said Carmilla. "Then I suggest we go before Hyde realizes we're here. Miklós Ferenc will tell him soon enough who it was that took his prisoners, and then we'll have him following us, which will be a great bother, or refusing to pay his rent, which will be a great bore. Come on."

As they followed her out of the courtyard, Lucinda still in her arms, the woman she had called Laura joined them, walking beside Mary, who was in the rear of the procession. As they walked, she held out one hand, the one not holding the rifle. "You're Mary Jekyll, aren't you? I'm Laura Jennings."

Mary shook her hand, awkwardly because it was the left one, and also because she was trying to walk at the same time.

"It's so nice to meet a countrywoman of mine! You see, I'm English too, although I've never been to England. My father was an Englishman, but he spent his life in the diplomatic service, and my mother was Styrian. He and I always spoke English at home, and it's one of the great wishes of my life to see England for myself. London, the most important city in the world!—and the Lake District!—and the Cliffs of Dover!"

Mary looked at her curiously. She was older than her companion, and more conventionally dressed, although even as they made their way along the road winding down the hill, Mary noticed that her walking suit was exceptionally well tailored. It would have cost several guineas in London! She did indeed look thoroughly English, with the soft, rounded features and rosy complexion for which Englishwomen are famous, although her hair was braided in a crown around her head—not a particularly English hairstyle, and Mary would have liked to know how it was done. She looked practical and friendly, rather like a governess. Was she perhaps Carmilla's governess? But what sort of governess carried a rifle?

"Pleased to meet you," said Mary. "I don't suppose you could explain—"

"We will, I promise," said Laura, smiling. "I don't know how much Carmilla's told you already, although knowing her, I suspect the answer is nothing at all. That's one of the problems in dealing with these old aristocrats. They tell you to do things and expect you to do them without question. I assure you, the Count is worse. But here's the carriage."

And there it was—a particularly fine one, painted black with a crest on the door. Mary immediately recognized it: the dragon she had seen on the book!

The coachman—no, it was a woman, a very tall woman in a coachman's uniform—was standing by the horses.

"Magda!" said Carmilla. "*Mennünk kell*—as quickly as possible!"

Magda must be the coachman—or coachwoman, Mary thought, because she immediately nodded and opened the door. Carmilla climbed in and sat facing backward, with Lucinda draped across her lap. "Come on," she called out. "The sooner we leave, the better."

Justine climbed in after her, stooping so as not to hit her head, and Diana followed.

"Where are we going?" asked Mary. She frowned, worried. "Are we going to meet Mina?"

"First to our home," said Laura. She put one hand on Mary's arm. "I understand your concern, Miss Jekyll. I assure you, we're friends. Mina sent us to meet you, but when we discovered, at one of the inns along the way, that your coachman had talked about heading south—and when Carmilla realized he was Miklós Ferenc, for she knows him and his family—well, she knew where to look. I promise, we'll explain everything as soon as possible."

Mary nodded. It was reassuring, she had to admit, to speak

with someone so very *English*. It reminded her just a little of London, and Park Terrace, and Mrs. Poole. She wondered what Mrs. Poole was doing right at that moment.

> MRS. POOLE: Paying bills, like as not. We had little enough money after Catherine and Beatrice left! It was all I could do to keep Alice and Archibald fed—fruit isn't cheap, you know, even in August. Dr. Watson was a great help, insisting that if we were in genuine need, he would advance us whatever we required. Not that I would have liked to trouble him in that way, particularly since he had his own worries, poor man, with Mr. Holmes still missing. . . .

"Move over," said Mary. If it would have been at all ladylike, she would have shoved Diana with her hip. Carmilla's carriage was smaller than the coach. It had not been built for six passengers, one of whom was now sprawled across Laura's and Carmilla's lap.

Diana scooted an inch in the other direction. "There, that's all I can move, unless you want me sitting on Justine. Satisfied?"

Mary would have to be. Anyway, being squeezed between Diana and the side of the carriage, which luckily was padded with leather—really, it was the most luxurious vehicle she had ever been in—was a minor inconvenience beside the more serious one of having lost everything in their luggage—their clothes, their toiletries, even their Baedeker! All she'd been able to take had been her waist bag, which she had grabbed and buckled on before descending on the rope. It had her pistol in it, as well as her remaining pounds, francs, and krone. However, she should not complain. They were alive, out of Hyde's castle and headed . . . well, somewhere else.

"Where are we—oh!" Mary could not help exclaiming. What in the world was Carmilla doing?

Carmilla had pulled back the sleeve of her jacket and placed her wrist on Lucinda's mouth. Gently, she pried it open and pushed her wrist between Lucinda's teeth. "Come, little one," she said. "It's time to feed." Then she cupped Lucinda's jaw with her other hand so the girl's teeth clamped on her wrist. Mary could hear a distinct sucking sound, like an infant nursing. And yet Lucinda's eyes remained closed!

"What the hell?" said Diana. Mary would not have put it quite that way, but she shared the sentiment.

"She's dehydrated," said Carmilla, looking up at them. "You see how her eyes are sunken in their sockets. She must drink now, and after this at regular intervals. I should have Hyde publicly flogged for how he has treated her."

"Public floggings went out of fashion a long time ago, my dear," said Laura, sounding amused.

"Then privately flogged," said Carmilla. "I would have him thrown out, except that he's paid up until the end of the month."

"Paid up?" said Mary. "Whatever do you mean?"

"She means that Mr. Hyde is renting her ancestral home," said Laura. "The castle in which you were held captive has been in the Karnstein family since the fourteenth century. As soon as we learned that you were with the Ferencs, we suspected they were working for him. We came as quickly as we could, and just in time, I think. Miss Van Helsing really is in a terrible state."

Lucinda was still feeding. The sound made Mary's skin crawl—luckily, it was mostly drowned out by the rumble of the wheels, the clop of the horses.

"How is it she can feed like that?" asked Justine. "I did not see you cut your wrist. . . ."

Carmilla pulled back Lucinda's upper lip. Lucinda had fangs!

Just like her mother and those men in Vienna. The tips were sunk into Carmilla's wrist, and blood was seeping around them.

"But she did not have those before?" said Justine, astonished. "Surely we would have noticed them."

"Then they must have grown in recently," said Laura. "Normally, they would grow in shortly after she was infected, but we do not know how Professor Van Helsing's experiment will affect the course of the disease. It may not follow the usual timetable."

"What disease—what exactly was Van Helsing doing to her?" Mary asked. Lucinda seemed to be drinking a great deal! She must indeed have become dehydrated while they were held captive by Hyde. "If you want"—how she hated saying it—"I can contribute. Both Diana and I gave her our blood on the way to the castle, when we first discovered it was the only thing she could ingest."

"That was very generous of you," said Carmilla, smiling, although her raised brows looked a little ironic. She was much more attractive than the stiff portrait she resembled—her angular face, with its aquiline nose and high cheekbones, was mobile and expressive. She and Laura made an interesting contrast—one so English, the other so, well, Hungarian or Austrian, or whatever she was. "However, what Lucinda needs now is not your blood, but mine. I hope it will sustain her until we get to Budapest and we can consult on what is to be done. Her transformation is incomplete—that is the difficulty."

"Transformation into what?" asked Justine. "Mr. Hyde was trying to use her blood to heal—both Adam Frankenstein and Frau Ferenc, who is dying of a cancer."

"Anna Ferenc, who is far superior to her husband, both in intellect and morals, would choose death over the kind of healing Hyde offers her," said Carmilla. "She is a pious woman, and would dismiss his theories as blasphemy."

"And do you dismiss them in the same way?" asked Mary. She

still did not understand what was going on. What did Carmilla mean by a transformation, and how was Lucinda supposed to transform? Was this the transmutation Van Helsing had been trying to effect in his wife and daughter?

Carmilla smiled and shook her head. "My dear Miss Jekyll, or Mary if I may, this is the nineteenth century. Surely we are beyond such superstitions. My faith lies in science. Of course, the most advanced science may look like magic to a layman— nevertheless, I don't believe in anything that cannot be explained rationally." Without fuss, she removed her wrist from Lucinda's mouth. There, on the wrist, were two puncture wounds, with blood trickling down them. Before Mary's eyes, the wounds closed and the blood stopped trickling. It crusted on the skin, and Carmilla brushed it off in flakes. Then, she pulled her jacket sleeve down again.

"You're the woman in the portrait, aren't you?" said Diana. "The one over the fireplace." She sounded as though she were accusing Carmilla of a crime.

"That is not possible," said Justine. "The portrait was dated 1698. It was painted almost two hundred years ago. Perhaps she is a descendant—"

"You have a good eye, Diana." Laura smiled. "That *is* Carmilla, actually. Or was."

"I was a different person then," said Carmilla. "Physically, intellectually, morally. . . . Well, not entirely different—but I assure you, despite the resemblance, I am as unlike Mircalla Karnstein as Hyde is unlike Dr. Jekyll." She turned to Laura and took her hand, smiling back at her—a fond, affectionate smile. "You had something to do with that, *kedvesem*." Turning back to Justine, she added, "You are not the only one who has died and been reborn, you see. Although I claim seniority, since you were born only a hundred years ago—compared to me, you are an infant." Suddenly, she laughed. "Not that it's a competition, mind you! The Count is always telling me that I'm a child. . . ."

"Who is this Count?" asked Mary. "We are all—well, at least I'm very confused. How do you know Mina Murray? Who are you, the both of you?" She did not mean to sound rude, but they were in a carriage in the middle of Styria with two women they did not know, one of whom had just claimed to be two hundred years old, driving deeper and deeper into the forest. It was already afternoon—soon, it would be night. She did not even know where they were going. She put her hand on her waist bag, to feel the reassuring shape of her pistol. At least, if these women were not to be trusted, they could defend themselves.

"Yeah, and why does Lucinda suck blood?" asked Diana. "Is she a vampire, like Varney?"

"Miss Jekyll, you're right to be cautious," said Laura. "You do not know us, but I assure you that we mean you no harm—we are taking you to my home, where you will have food and a fire and a place to rest for the night. Tomorrow, we will take you to Mina in Budapest. We have known her for"—she turned to Carmilla—"is it five years now? When she first came to see the Count, after meeting him in England. Of course, she's had her own work to do, which takes her away from Budapest a great deal. Most recently, she was in Vienna. You see, she had been a friend of Frau Van Helsing's, and then served as Lucinda's paid companion—what you would call a chaperone—for several months after her mother was confined to a lunatic asylum. Somehow, Professor Van Helsing discovered that she was not there purely in a professional capacity—that she was allied with, shall we say, an opposing faction? So she was forced to flee Vienna, leaving Lucinda behind. When she heard that Frau Van Helsing had died and Lucinda had disappeared, I can't begin to tell you how frantic she was! She assumed Van Helsing had arranged for his daughter to be kidnapped, but had no idea where she might be, and she could not return to Vienna—Van Helsing's underlings knew her by sight. She hoped you would be able to help Lucinda in a way she could not." Laura paused for a moment, then added, "To be perfectly honest, Miss Jekyll, Carmilla and I did not think you would be able to find Lucinda—Van Helsing is a clever, unscrupulous man. But Mina said, 'I have confidence in Mary. If anyone can do this, she and the young women she has gathered around herself will be able to.' As soon as she received a telegram that you had rescued Lucinda and were headed to Budapest, she sent us to meet you on the road. When we realized that you had somehow gone astray, we wired her from Sopron, telling her that we would follow your trail. I imagine she is frantic with worry. She thinks very highly of you, and evidently her faith is justified."

If Mary were the sort of person who blushed, she would have blushed now. "Do please call me Mary," she said. "And you know, it was really our friend Irene Norton who discovered where Lucinda was being held, and Diana who rescued her. It wasn't my doing."

"Right. I was the one who recued her," said Diana. "I was the one who got her out of that Krankenwhatsit. All by myself."

"That must have been very clever of you," said Carmilla. She was doing that ironic thing with her eyebrows again. "You shall have to tell us all about it. However, we have arrived."

Mary looked out the window. They had been traveling through forest, but now the road wound through a meadow with scattered copses of birch and alder. She could see a stream, meandering between banks of flowering shrubs. There was a stone bridge across it. It was a picturesque wilderness, and reminded her more of England than any place she had seen so far in her travels. In a few minutes, they had drawn up to the front door of what looked like small castle, with several round towers topped by conical roofs resembling witches' hats. It was not as old or imposing as Hyde's castle—or rather, Castle Karnstein—but then it was not half tumbled down either. A fairytale princess could have lived there quite comfortably.

"I thought you said it was a house," said Diana.

"And so it is," said Laura, smiling. "A rather fancy house to be sure—but we are in the wilds of Styria, where such properties are cheaper, I assure you, than apartments in London! My father and I moved here after he left the diplomatic service. Alas, he died several years ago, and since I lost my mother when I was very young, I was left alone—except for Carmilla, of course. It's rather isolated, particularly in winter, but Carmilla and I like it here, don't we, darling?" She leaned over and kissed Carmilla, evidently meaning to kiss her cheek, but at the last moment Carmilla turned her head and they kissed each other on the lips. Laura laughed. It startled Mary— what was the relationship between these two women?

Just then, Magda opened the carriage door and Carmilla handed Lucinda to her, saying something in the incomprehensible language Mary was starting to recognize as Hungarian. Justine descended from the carriage after Carmilla, stumbling a little. Was Justine all right?

Diana shoved Mary with her shoulder and said, "Get out already!" Scowling, Mary turned to get out on the other side. She stepped down carefully—she was very tired, and the circular drive was covered with gravel. She did not want to turn her ankle on the stones.

"Not bad," said Diana. She had also descended from the carriage and was standing next to Mary, with her hands on her hips, looking up at the house—or castle.

MARY: It's called a *Schloss*. That's what small castles are called in Styria, Laura told me.

CATHERINE: Yes, but do you think our English readers are going to know that? Or our American

readers? I'm hoping for some American sales, if
the deal with Collier & Son comes through, and
there are no *Schlosses* in America—just teepees and
department stores.

BEATRICE: The slaughter of the native population is
a shameful stain on American history. Clarence
says—

CATHERINE: For goodness' sake, how are we going
to sell to readers in the United States if you go
on about the slaughter of the native Americans?
Who's going to want to read about that?

BEATRICE: Those who do not want to read about
it are exactly those who should be made aware,
Catherine. This may be a story of our adventures,
but we must not shy away from confronting the
difficult issues of the times. Literature exists to
educate as well as entertain, after all.

DIANA: You all went from *Schlosses* to teepees to a
political discussion, and you think *I* ramble?

The schloss was indeed *not bad*, in Diana's phrase. The afternoon light was shining on its windows and warming its stone walls,
which were partly covered in clematis and climbing roses. It was
surrounded by gardens in an informal English style, dominated
by one large oak tree of majestic proportions. Behind it grew the
dark pine woods so common in Styria, but they did not make the
schloss seem gloomy—rather, it resembled a jewel in a box lined
with green velvet.

The large, double front door was opened by what looked like a housekeeper in a proper black dress, with a proper white cap and apron—exactly what Mrs. Poole would have worn. As soon as it was open, two large white dogs bounded out into the courtyard and ran circles around Carmilla, barking excitedly. Mary hurriedly drew back behind Justine and Diana. She had no experience of dogs. They seemed to be leaping up and down, making the most terrifying noises, barks and howls! And there was Diana, right in their midst—as soon as she saw them, she had run up to them. Mary was worried—would they bite her?

But Diana was not the one she should have been worried about. As soon as Mary walked through the front door into the entrance hall—a pleasant hall, papered in a willow pattern, with furniture that glowed from frequent polishing—Justine sank to her knees, and then fell sideways onto the carpet.

Mary gasped and knelt beside Justine, forgetting all about the monstrous hounds. Once again, the Giantess had fainted.

"Is she all right?" asked Laura, kneeling down on the other side of Justine. "What a stupid question. Of course she's not all right, or she would not be lying on the floor. Does she perhaps have a wound she did not tell us about?"

"I don't think so," said Mary, loosening Justine's collar. "There's no sign of an injury on her, no blood anywhere." And surely Justine would have mentioned it if she had been injured? She was too sensible to keep that sort of thing to herself. "This happens to Justine periodically, after great emotional strain. Never during—always afterward. Can we perhaps get her to a sofa, someplace she can lie in comfort until she recovers?"

"I'll do that," said Carmilla, who had just walked in. She took off her jacket and handed it to the housekeeper, who was hovering over Laura, looking concerned.

The housekeeper said something to Carmilla that Mary did

not understand, and Carmilla responded—Mary recognized only the familiar words *sal volatile*. The housekeeper nodded and left on her errand.

Carmilla knelt by Justine and put one hand under her neck. Gently, she lifted Justine's shoulders, then slid her other arm under her knees. "Mrs. Madár will bring my medical kit. I've already told Magda to take Lucinda up to the green bedroom. If you will excuse me, Mary. . . ."

Mary stood and stepped back. As easily as she had lifted Lucinda, Carmilla lifted Justine—although her legs hung down in an awkward fashion so that she looked like a very large rag doll. Mary followed Carmilla across the hall and into the parlor—a charming parlor with beautiful old furniture, polished to perfection and just shabby enough to be pleasing. There were shelves filled with books, and a great deal of light from the windows, which were framed by curtains of Nottingham lace. Carmilla placed Justine on a large sofa upholstered in *Toile de Jouy*.

> BEATRICE: Would Mary have noticed all those details, if she was worried about Justine?

> CATHERINE: Those are from your notes, from when we stopped at the schloss last summer while we were trying to find Prince Rupert to get the money he owed us. I don't think Mary would have noticed those sorts of details even if she had not been worried. But I have to describe the room somehow, don't I? I can't have all of you moving around in indistinguishable spaces—the Train Station, the Castle Courtyard, the Parlor!

> MARY: What in the world is *Toile de Jouy*?

"Her pulse seems normal," said Carmilla. "And she's breathing normally. Mary, you've experienced this before. What do you recommend? Shall we attempt to revive her?"

Mary shook her head. "I've found the best course of action is simply to let her be for a while. She'll come to on her own. Meanwhile . . . Wait, where's Diana?"

"Playing with the denizens of the underworld," said Laura. She was standing by one of the windows. "Look."

Mary went to the window. There, still in the courtyard, were one red-headed girl and two large white dogs, running around and around, growling and barking. Diana was growling and barking the loudest.

"They won't hurt her, I assure you," said Laura. "For all their formidable appearance, Hades and Persephone are so gentle that I would trust them with an infant! Of course, they would not be gentle with anyone who attempted to harm this household. But they recognize Diana as a friend."

"I'm more worried about Diana hurting them!" said Mary, acerbically. They had important things to discuss—like what in the world was wrong with Lucinda—and Diana was playing with the dogs!

"My dear Mary," said Laura, putting a hand on her arm, "I haven't forgotten that we owe you an explanation. But you must be exhausted. It's too late in the day to leave now—nightfall would find us in the forest—so tonight you should rest and recuperate. We'll leave at dawn tomorrow. I'll ask Mrs. Madár to order some tea. Once we've eaten, Carmilla and I will tell you what we know, to prepare you for what you will find in Budapest. The situation waiting for us there won't be easy, I assure you. The Société des Alchimistes will not want to listen to us—and we shall have to make them. But it's no use worrying about that now. Tea should be ready in about half an hour. In the meantime, would you like to wash your hands and face?"

Mary would indeed! How long had it been since she'd had a proper wash? Or, indeed, a proper cup of tea? Both sounded heavenly.

> MRS. POOLE: It seems to me that traveling through Europe is positively uncivilized!

> MARY: Well, to be fair, we had been kidnapped. I don't think people are usually kidnapped in the course of their European travels. It's not the sort of thing you find mentioned in Baedeker.

Laura's bathroom was not as grand as Irene Norton's, but it had running water—quite cold, but Mary round it refreshing. She washed her face and hands with lavender-scented soap, then dried them with a soft, thick towel. She dampened the towel and brushed the dust off her dress as best she could. She must at least try to look respectable.

When she entered the parlor again, feeling a little more herself, Justine was sitting up on the sofa, her legs stretched along it under a plaid blanket. She was sipping from a porcelain cup with a floral pattern.

Laura was sitting in an armchair across from her, behind the tea tray, which was set on a low table. She was holding the teapot, as though she had just poured out.

"Do come in, Mary," she said. "Carmilla should be back in a moment. Diana was playing with the dogs too roughly, and I'm afraid there was an accident."

"Is she all right?" asked Mary. "What happened?"

"Oh, Diana's fine. But she bit Hades a little too hard on the ear. Carmilla went to bandage it up, and she insisted on going as well. Come sit and I'll pour you a cup. And there are sandwiches—ham or egg? I can't convince our cook to make them without paprika, so they're not quite what you would be used to in London. But think of them as a Styrian approximation."

Which might have been a good way to describe the parlor itself, now that Mary could observe it more closely. It looked so very English, as though someone had decided to stage a play and this particular scene was set in Typical English Parlor, Late Summer Afternoon. But the pillows were embroidered in darker, richer colors than they would have been in England, and the carpets were deeper, more luxurious. Despite its air of Englishness, the room was somehow undefinably foreign.

She sat down in the other armchair. "How are you?" she asked Justine, meaning not just *How are you right now*. Justine had been so quiet in the carriage. Of course, she was usually quiet—she was Justine, after all. But Mary still remembered her kneeling by Adam's bed, holding his hands. What had happened between them?

"I have recovered, thank you," said Justine. "Could I have another of those small cakes, Laura? They were very good—filled with apricot jam, I believe." Which meant that whatever it was, she did not want to talk about it at the moment. All right, Mary would wait until later.

The sandwiches, while delicious, did not taste English at all—but the tea, strong and hot, took Mary right back to the parlor at 11 Park Terrace. It was Mrs. Poole's favorite Yorkshire blend. She felt terribly homesick.

"You started without us!" Diana strode into the room, with Hades and Persephone on either side of her. Hades had a white gauze bandage on one ear, but did not seem otherwise the worse for having been attacked by a vicious wild animal.

DIANA: Hey!

Up close, the two dogs seemed even more formidable, and Mary could not help drawing back into her chair, although it was unlikely to protect her. They were almost pure white, except where they had gotten dirty playing outside, and so large that they came up to Diana's waist. She had one hand on each of their backs.

"Are those really dogs?" asked Mary. "They look . . ."

"Like wolves?" Carmilla strode into the room after them. One really did need trousers to stride. There was no striding in layers of petticoats. Just for once, Mary envied the striders. How freely they moved! Yet could anyone look more ladylike than Laura in her smart skirt and shirtwaist —she had taken off her jacket— sitting by the tea tray? Surely there was also value in looking, and behaving, like a lady.

MRS. POOLE: Of course there is!

"They are, partly." Carmilla sat down on the sofa by Justine's feet. "We call the breed *farkaskutya*—wolfdog. They have guarded the Karnsteins for generations. But Hades and Persephone are very sweet. My godfather gave them to me when they were just puppies." She ruffled Persephone's head affectionately, and the great white wolfdog put her head on Carmilla's lap.

"Is anyone going to give me something to eat? I'm starving." Diana sat cross-legged on the floor. To Mary's surprise, Hades lay down beside her. If Diana had bitten her ear, Mary would not have been nearly as friendly!

"Ham or egg?" asked Laura. "Never mind—I know you're going to ask for both. And cake, of course. I'll make you a plate. In the meantime, I think Carmilla had better tell you about the situation in Budapest. And about what is ailing Lucinda."

"Who will need to be fed again later tonight," said Carmilla. "She seems to be stable now, but she shows no signs of regaining consciousness. Either Magda or I will stay with her tonight, in shifts. We will make certain that she is well cared for, I promise. I hope that my blood will help her—at least until we can get her to the Count."

Mary put her cup and plate on a side table. "Why you? And why does she need to drink blood? What did Van Helsing to do her?"

Laura handed Diana a plate of cakes and sandwiches that could most accurately be described as "heaping." She looked at Carmilla and said, "I think you'd better tell them the whole story, starting from the beginning. *Your* beginning."

DIANA: You always do that so awkwardly. It wasn't
    as awkward in real life, you know. Laura just said
    "Go on, then. Tell them." And Carmilla did.

CATHERINE: If you think you can write this book
    better than I can, you're welcome to try!

Carmilla smiled, but Mary thought it was a sad, even bitter smile. As though sensing her mood, Persephone licked her mistress's hand and whined. Carmilla stroked her head.

"If you wish," she said, "I will tell you my story."

CHAPTER XIX

Carmilla's Story

I was born in the year 1680," Carmilla began, "the privileged daughter of a powerful family. Who in this region had not heard of the Karnsteins? My father, Count Karman Karnstein, was wealthy in land, if not in gold, a counselor to Archduke Leopold himself. It was a time of war—principally against the Turks, but also the French. And Catholics warred with Protestants, peasants with landowners. We did not see any of this, my sister Millarca and I. We were twins, born in the same hour, which was also the hour in which our mother died. She was a Hungarian lady, a Székely from Transylvania. Her last act was naming us: Millarca and Mircalla—Mila and Mira, as we were often called. It was the custom, in those days, to give twins names that were anagrams of each other, to confuse the Devil, who might otherwise steal one of them—such superstitions were widely believed. We were raised by a succession of nurses, and then governesses, largely unsupervised, for our father was often away at court in Gratz, or in battle against the Turks. We were said to be beautiful, and it was thought we would make promising marriages, perhaps to relatives of the Archduke himself. Mila was content with such a prospect—she was older than I by a quarter hour, and therefore the heir of Karnstein. She was also the more beautiful, more docile—the more reconciled to what was then considered a woman's life. She embroidered on silk, and sang like a nightingale, accompanying herself on the lute, and danced like a birch tree in the wind. And besides, she was good, much better than I was. It was she who took on the duties of lady of the castle, dispensing alms and medicines to the poor, who were numerous in those days. But I was the one who concocted the medicines. I had become fascinated, early, by the books in my father's library—he had copies of Dioscorides's *De Materia Medica*, Andreas Vesalius's *De Humani Corporis Fabrica*, even Harvey's *De Motu Cordis*, which described the circulation of the blood. While Mila studied music or sewed altarcloths, I rode my horse around the countryside, accompanied by a retinue—both safety and propriety decreed that a daughter of the Karnsteins could not ride alone. Portraits were painted of us, to show potential suitors—you have seen mine. I never cared for it, but Mila's hangs in my study, over my desk. It has been almost two hundred years, but I still miss her."

"Then that tomb in the churchyard—it was your sister's?" asked Mary. That would explain what she had assumed was a misspelling.

"Yes, alas," said Carmilla. "If we had not been so hurried today, I would have left her flowers." She looked down at her hands, then clasped them around her knees. She continued, but Mary could see that her eyes were shining with unshed tears. "One day, word came from my father that Mila was to be married—a very good marriage, to a nephew of the Archduke himself. His messenger brought a portrait of a handsome young aristocrat, Baron Stefan Alexander Matthias Vordenburg. Mila was pleased, if apprehensive. Soon, the aristocrat himself arrived. He was handsome in person as well, and he had very blue eyes. I thought they looked so sincere!"

> MARY: You can't trust men with very blue eyes. That
> should be included in manuals for gentlewomen,

right after the chapter on how to get in and out of carriages.

BEATRICE: What would you call Mr. Holmes's eyes?

MARY: Well, not very blue anyway! They sort of change depending on the weather.

"It was clear that my sister was in love with him," continued Carmilla. "But one evening, after we had been celebrating their engagement, he asked me to walk with him to the chapel. He said he wanted to talk to me. 'What about?' I asked him. We were walking through the graveyard. It held no terrors for me—was this not sacred ground? Were not all those who had been laid in those graves at rest, until the day they would rise to be with our Father in Heaven? Or so I had been taught.

"He did not answer, and I looked at him, wondering why he had brought me here—I was young, but not naive, and it occurred to me that engaged to one daughter of the house, he might be looking for another sort of favor from the other. Well, he would find no such favor from me.

"But what I saw on his face was not amorous desire—it was a snarl, like the snarl of a wolf! Before I could scream, he had caught me in his arms and bitten down on my shoulder. His teeth sank into my flesh, and he lapped up my blood, sucking, licking, while I cried out in fear and horror. I knew then what he was, for our superstitions speak of it—the *oupire*, or what you might call a vampire. Of course, I was being foolish—there is no such thing."

"No such thing as a vampire?" said Diana, who had been listening so breathlessly that she had left a slice of cake, uneaten, on her plate. Hades cautiously put out a long pink tongue, licked at it once, and then—just like that, it was gone. He licked the plate clean. Mary put one hand over her mouth to keep from laughing. Only the guardian of the dead could have taken a morsel of food away from Diana! She noticed that Laura was doing her best not to laugh as well.

"Of course not," said Carmilla. She stroked Persephone's ears. "Or not in the sense you mean, Diana. Spirits of the dead who rise from the grave to feast on blood? Who turn into bats and wolves, who fear crucifixes and cannot cross running water? Who can be defeated by garlic or sprays of wild rose? What nonsense. Of course, like much folklore and superstition, the legend of the vampire is based on a core of scientific fact. There is a blood-borne disease that gives its sufferers many of the attributes associated with vampires. Those who are infected become stronger, more agile. They develop keener senses. They can see in the dark, hear the beat of a bird's wing. Their canine teeth sharpen and elongate, as you have seen on Lucinda. My godfather believes that vampirism is atavistic—a revision to an earlier evolutionary state. And they can heal from wounds that would kill an ordinary man. Such is their immunity to disease and the ravages of time that they can live for centuries without aging. But they pay a heavy price for such abilities—they must live on blood, and there is a mental deterioration—they begin to go mad.

"This disease, the Baron's retinue had brought from Gratz. Sometimes the *oupire*'s desire is only to feed. Sometimes, particularly in the first stages of madness, it wishes to reproduce others of its kind. That is what he wished. I was terrified, and fought him with all my might. I snatched the knife in his belt—in those days, a man of his class would never have been without a weapon. I stabbed him in the chest, but he laughed exultantly and held my face to the wound, so that my mouth was filled with his blood. I must have ingested some—enough.

DIANA: That is *so gross*.

BEATRICE: I do not think it is polite to criticize
another way of eating, no matter how unusual.
Many of us have our own . . . dietary restrictions.
I, for, example, am limited to vegetable matter,
which is easiest for me to ingest in liquefied form.

DIANA: That is also *so gross*.

"The next thing I remember is waking up in a small room, in
the highest tower of the castle. It was evening—the room was
in shadow. I hurt—my whole body hurt, as though I had been
dropped from a height and all of my limbs had been broken,
although I could feel they were not, that I was still whole. As I
looked about me, terrified, a darker shadow detached itself from
the wall and moved toward me. I screamed and crouched on the
floor, looking about for any avenue of escape. If need be, I would
jump out the window and end my own life, rather than endure any
further indignities.

"'Mira!' said the shadow. 'My dear Mira, do not be afraid.' He,
for it was clearly a he, spoke in Hungarian, the language of my
mother, which I had learned from my nurses. When he stepped
into the light, I could see that it was not Baron Vordenburg, but
my godfather, the Count, who had an estate in the Carpathian
Mountains. I had met him several times—he was the head of my
mother's family, a wealthy and respected man although there
were some who called him a heretic for his views, which were
unorthodox. 'My dear, I have come for you,' he continued. I said
nothing—I could not speak. 'Come, we must leave this place, and
quickly. The peasants have heard that it has become the haunt of
vampires, and they are coming to burn it down.'

"'Mila!' I cried. 'Where is Mila?' He must rescue her too—after all, he was godfather to us both. I could not leave without her.

"'Mila is dead,' he said gently. 'Truly dead, and better so. She will not become one of those who rise again once the vampire blood is in their veins. I have left her body in the wine cellar and locked the door so the peasants will not find it. I promise that after they have done their worst, I shall come back and make certain she is buried in holy ground.'

"'But, *keresztapa*,' I cried—that is godfather in Hungarian—'What shall we do? We cannot simply desert everyone in the household!'

"'Mira,' he said to me, 'There is no one left alive. I do not know how long even you . . .'

"Just then we heard a sound—chanting, from far off as yet. He looked out the narrow window. 'I can see them coming,' he said. I crawled to the window—I had scarcely enough strength to stand. In the distance I could see, winding up the hill, torches—a procession of torches.

"'We must go,' he said. 'Mira, can you climb upon my back and hold on very tightly?'

"I told him that I could. I clung to his back as he climbed down the stone wall of the tower, my limbs trembling, terrified every moment that I would fall—or that he would, but he seemed as secure on the wall as a spider.

"'My carriage is waiting in the woods,' he said.

"As soon as we had gotten into his carriage and were driving away as fast as the condition of the road and the darkness allowed, I begged him to explain what had happened in the castle, and how he had come to be there.

"It had been no coincidence, he told me. He too had been in Gratz, conducting some research in the scientific archives of the university. There had been an outbreak of vampirism in the city, and he had heard such things of the Baron as had made him suspicious. So he had followed as soon as his research would allow, but arrived too late. Then he explained to me the dreadful disease of vampirism, which I had contracted. And which, he now confessed to me, he too had contracted long ago. He, too, was an *oupire*. Before I go on, would anyone like more tea? It gets cold here in the evenings. Laura, should we light the fire?"

Mary was startled. She had been so absorbed by Carmilla's story that she had forgotten where she was. Indeed, it was getting dark in the parlor. While Carmilla waited, Laura called for some lamps and lit the fire that was already laid in the fireplace. The housekeeper arrived with two lamps, which she placed where they would shed the most light. A parlormaid followed her with another tray of cakes and a fresh pot of tea. Diana promptly took two of the small cakes, and Mary prevailed on Justine to take one, as well as a glass of sherry that Laura poured out of a cut-glass decanter. She herself accepted another cup of tea, grateful for its warmth and strength.

"Then what?" asked Diana, her mouth full of cake. "Get on with it already."

Mary would have reproved her, but she also wanted Carmilla to get on with it.

Carmilla ruffled the hair on Persephone's neck and scratched behind her ears. The wolfdog stretched her neck on Carmilla's lap and barked just once, as though to indicate that the stroking should continue. "In order for you to understand the rest of my story, and also what has happened to Lucinda, I must tell you a little about the disease of vampirism, which is as terrible in its own way as syphilis or tuberculosis. You see, vampirism makes its sufferers stronger physically, but it destroys the mind. In weeks, perhaps months, the vampire goes mad. It becomes little more than an animal. Although vampires can live for centuries, they seldom survive so long. In their madness, they harm themselves or attack others, often members of their own family or village—then, they are hunted and killed according to ancient custom. My godfather thought I too would go mad—but I did not. There are only a few of us who have contracted the disease and retained our sanity intact. We do not know why. My godfather told me that one other member of the Société des Alchimistes was able to make the transition —an Englishman: John Ruthven, Lord Glenarvon. Ruthven believed it had something to do with the moon. He was convinced that he needed to lie in moonlight on a regular basis."

"And was that the reason?" asked Justine. "Did it have something to do with moonlight?"

"No, nothing whatsoever." Carmilla sounded disgusted. "The result was not reproducible—we lost several peasants that way. Either Ruthven was a credulous romantic, or he was deliberately misleading us. My godfather thinks the latter, but Ruthven died fighting for Greek independence, so I incline to the former theory!"

"Wait, do you mean your godfather is a member of the Société des Alchimistes?" asked Mary, astonished.

"Was at one time," replied Carmilla. "He was expelled when the current president came into power. She did not approve of his methods, and she was probably right. Even I was appalled by some of his experiments, and my conscience is not stainless—I too pursued some of those avenues of inquiry, before I met Laura. She has made me . . . more compassionate."

Diana looked at Carmilla with distrust. "Ágnes said you bathed in the blood of virgins to stay young. Is that true? Also, what's a metaphor? Justine said a vampire was a metaphor. . . . Is that some kind of monster?"

Carmilla laughed out loud. "The respectable Mrs. Madár would be quite irate if I filled our bathtub with blood, I assure you! No, that's another of the ridiculous superstitions concerning the *oupire*. I bathe in water brought up by Júlia, the chambermaid, with ordinary soap. When I want to be particularly luxurious, I scent my bath with Hungary water. That is all. I do not age because of the disease, and I drink the blood of animals—at least, I do now. As I said, Laura has been a good influence on me."

"The president of the Alchemical Society is a woman?" Mary put down her teacup and leaned forward. Perhaps she had heard wrong.

"Does that surprise you?" asked Carmilla. "Many prominent members of the society have been women, particularly in the last century or so. It is rumored that the first female member of the society was Hypatia of Alexandria, but the records of the society do not go back that far. Of course there were fewer female members when I first contracted the disease of vampirism. At one time, my godfather wanted me to join the society myself, but it seemed to be made up of tiresome old men, seeking wealth and immortality. I might have joined in the early part of the century, when Lord Byron and his circle were livening things up—that is the English phrase, is it not?"

Laura nodded and smiled, as though amused. "Yes, very English indeed."

"Wait, I'm lost," said Diana, frowning. "You were in the carriage with your godfather, the Count. What did you do then? No one wants to hear about the history of the Alchemical Society."

"Actually, I would like to," said Mary. She would like to very much indeed. If they were going up against the society, they would need to know as much about it as possible.

But Carmilla was already continuing her story. "Well then, we were in the carriage. My godfather was certain I would go mad. But he fed me with his own blood, as I have fed Lucinda. A week later, we reached his castle in Transylvania. There, I stayed with him for many years. I had nowhere else to go; my home and fortune were gone. My godfather helped me adjust to the disease. Vampirism is not easy for its sufferers. At first, I was always starved for blood, like an anemic. But his tenants knew, when they slaughtered an animal for their own food, that they should collect the blood and bring it to the *boyar*—for that is what they call the nobility in that region. They knew what he was, but they were proud to serve under such a man. Their parents, and their parents' parents, could remember the *boyar* in the castle. He had already lived for centuries. In his human lifetime, he had been one of those who had beaten back the Turks and defended the border for Christendom. They thought of him as a war hero.

"We waited for the symptoms of madness, but they did not come. How was it that I had survived the onset of the disease with my sanity intact? My godfather had been infected with vampirism in the dungeons of the Turks—it had been a common form of torture in those days, both among the Turks and the defenders of the Holy Roman Empire. A soldier would be infected, then released to find his way back to his own men and spread the infection. In the early days of his condition, he had attempted to infect his soldiers, to make them stronger, harder to kill. But almost immediately, their minds would begin to deteriorate. In a few weeks, they would be no better than animals. He found that he could prolong their period of usefulness through mesmerism, but a mesmerized soldier obeys orders, nothing more. He cannot think for himself.

"I was interested in this phenomenon, as I had been interested in medicines and diseases before my transformation. Together, we began a period of experimentation, using subjects who were on the verge of death. The plagues that swept through the countryside those years provided us with many such subjects. And we experimented directly upon the blood. Was there some factor we did not yet know about that would ensure success in one case but not another, as in a blood transfusion, which in more cases than not kills the recipient, but sometimes saves a life? He wanted to understand the blood itself. During periods of relative peace with the Turks, he communicated with their scientists, who were so far ahead of Europeans in their understanding of human physiology. He still remembered his encounters with Turkish physicians while he was a prisoner of the Sultan. The Turks were our enemies, but one of them, a physician named Mustafa Ahmet bin Abdullah, had become a particular friend, and had nursed him tenderly through the onset of his illness. He had originally wondered if he had survived with his mind intact because of their greater knowledge of the disease, but when he saw that I was spared at well, he realized there must be some other cause. He wrote to the physician of the Grand Vizier in Constantinople, hoping for but not expecting a reply, because war had broken out once again. But he did get a reply—the Turks had also attempted to create invincible warriors, with no greater success. The Grand Vizier's physician did not know why the two of us had been spared madness."

"How did these soldiers, and the peasants dying from plague, feel about being infected with the disease?" asked Justine. Her mouth was set in a thin, disapproving line.

"That is exactly the question I asked her," said Laura. She nodded at Justine, as though to signal her agreement and sympathy.

"Yes, Laura has explained to me *at length* why what we did was improper and immoral, and why you must always ask permission of your experimental subjects," said Carmilla. She did not appear particularly contrite. "But this was the eighteenth century, a time of almost continual warfare, when diseases ran rampant over the countryside. You inhabitants of the modern age cannot imagine what it was like. Even Justine is a child of the Enlightenment. Do not judge me by the standards of a different era. I did what I thought was most appropriate under the circumstances. Can you say that you would have done any differently?"

Justine continued to look disapproving, but did not reply.

"And did any of these experiments work?" asked Mary. Of course Justine was right—what Carmilla and her godfather had done was unconscionable. Nevertheless, if it had yielded any information that would help Lucinda, they should know.

"No, not one." Carmilla frowned as though dissatisfied. It was evidently the scientific failure that vexed her, not the moral problem of having experimented on unsuspecting subjects. Mary did not quite know what to think. Carmilla was helping them, and yet—was she any better than Rappaccini or Moreau? "We did have some partial success," she continued. "Magda is one of them—she was one of the Count's soldiers, mortally wounded in battle. To save her life, he gave her his own blood. To look at her, you would think she was an ordinary woman in her middle years. And yet, she was born more than a century ago. At first, we thought she might escape the madness of vampirism entirely. Alas, it was not to be. Sometimes, she will wake screaming or believe she is still at war, and must be restrained. Well—all that is in the past. When the region became more stable and the Turks retreated, I returned to my castle. I did not live there often—it held too many memories for me. For the most part, I stayed with my godfather in Budapest. But one summer I came down once again, craving my native countryside—and that is when I met Laura."

She smiled at Laura, who could not help smiling back. Mary wondered once again what there was between these women. They seemed more than merely companions.

"She accepted me for what I was. She did not see me as either a monster or the Countess Karnstein, but simply as Carmilla, which was the name I had adopted—a new name for a new woman. I did not know, at the time, that my godfather had once again taken up experimenting with the transmission of vampirism. He thought the emerging science of blood transfusion would allow him to purify the blood, and therefore control what was being transmitted. You've seen one of his failures—the madman Renfield."

"Renfield!" said Mary. She remembered that sly, strange little man, sitting in his room at the Purfleet Asylum, ingesting flies in the belief that they would give him eternal life.

"Yes, Renfield was a fellow member of the Société des Alchimistes. He volunteered for my godfather's first experiments in transfusing infected blood. You have seen the results—madness, with none of the benefits of the disease. No heightening of the senses, no exceptional strength, no eternal life—only a degeneration of the mind that led to his confinement in a mental asylum. That is why Dr. Seward and Professor Van Helsing contacted the Count. When Seward became the director of the asylum, he read through Renfield's files. He and Van Helsing were also seeking a means of extending life, and they believed my godfather's experiments would give them a way forward. At that point, he had already been expelled from the society, but was continuing his research independently at his castle in Transylvania. They asked him to come to England. He helped them—at first. But there was an accident, a terrible accident. A young woman died. He decided that he could no longer support either their methods or their aims, so he refused to work with them any longer. Now, his goal is to undermine them, to have their experiments banned by the society and the both of them expelled."

"Is that why he and Mina are working together?" asked Mary. Some things were starting to fit into place.

"Well, that's one reason," said Laura. She seemed amused—Mary was not sure why. "But Mina can tell you all about that herself, tomorrow. I know this isn't a fashionable hour to go to bed, but we've finished the tea and cakes, so I suggest we do exactly that. Carmilla promised to tell you her story, and she has. We need to leave at dawn if we're going to make it to Budapest by nightfall."

"Nightfall!" said Justine. "How is that possible? We are still several days away from Budapest, are we not? By carriage, I mean."

"Ah, but you haven't seen my horses!" said Carmilla. She laughed, as though at an amusing, but evidently private, joke.

"Just tell them!" said Laura, gathering the teacups and putting them on the tray.

"Why spoil the surprise?" asked Carmilla. "They will see for themselves tomorrow. I'm going to feed Lucinda. Magda has been sitting with her, but I would like to check on her condition myself. And, of course, she needs blood."

"I want to make sure she's all right too," said Mary.

"And I," said Justine.

"I'll meet you up there and show you to your rooms," said Laura. "Although Diana might prefer the kennel!"

Mary looked down. There, on the carpet, was Diana, fast asleep with her head on Hades's flank. The white wolfdog looked up, as though to say, *What? Nothing to see here.* No wonder Diana had been so quiet for the last few minutes.

> DIANA: I wish we had dogs like that. Cats are boring. All they do is sleep and catch mice.

> CATHERINE: *Excuse me?* Dogs are well and good in their place, but cats are nature's perfect predators. A cat has all the weapons it needs at the end of its paws and in its mouth. It takes orders from no man. It is a natural assassin. Cats are not boring.

> DIANA: Except when they go on and on and on about how wonderful they are!

Lucinda's condition had not changed: she was still unconscious, although she drank Carmilla's blood eagerly.

"Well, she's not dying," said Laura, checking her pulse. "That's a good sign, at least. If we can keep her in this stable state until she has reached the Count, we may be able to save her."

Lucinda looked so thin and pale under the covers. Someone, probably Magda, had changed her into a fresh nightgown and brushed her hair, then braided it so it would not tangle.

"Thank you for taking care of her," said Mary. If only they had not trusted Miklós Ferenc! Yet how could they have known? And it was Hyde's fault after all! If only Hyde had not arranged for Miklós Ferenc to kidnap them in the first place. . . . But for that, he would have to be a better man, a better father. If only, if only— you could fill a bucket with "if onlys," and it would get you nowhere at all. They were like air. If Hyde were a better father, the father she and especially Diana needed, he would be a different man, more like the father she had known as a child. Yet even then, she had barely known him. Whatever he was now had always been there in him, as a potential. The thought made her feel sick and ashamed.

"Come on," said Laura, putting a hand on her arm. "Carmilla will stay with her for a while. I'll show you to your rooms. You really do need to get some sleep."

She showed Justine to a somber room paneled in dark wood, with a canopied bed at one end. "This used to be my father's room," she said. "Some of his nightclothes might fit you. Look in that chest of drawers. He died several years ago, but I could not bear to throw anything of his away."

The room to which she led Mary was considerably more cheerful, papered in a pattern of birds perched among flowering branches. It contained painted furniture and two narrow beds— Diana was already curled up on one of them, sleeping. She was still in her clothes.

"I asked Mrs. Madár to have her carried up," said Laura. "There's a nightgown laid out for you on the pillow—we're about the same size, I think. I'm sure you're very tired, but—Mary, would you like a bath? I told Júlia to bring up some hot water. I thought you might like to wash off the dust of the journey. I asked Justine earlier if she would like one, but she said she just wanted to sleep."

A bath! More than anything else in the world, Mary suddenly realized, she wanted a bath. To wash all the events of the last few days off her . . . to feel fresh and clean for the first time in a week!

"Oh, yes please!" she said, more fervently than she had intended.

Suddenly, without warning, Laura gave her a quick, tight hug. "You're going to be all right, my dear," she said. "You'll see, you're with us now. We'll get you to Budapest, and the Count will help us—if anyone can save Lucinda, he can. He's a bit . . . formidable, but you'll get used to him. He's rather like a friendly lion—he keeps his claws sheathed around friends. And Mina will be there. I don't know anyone in the world as reassuring as Mina."

Mary wanted to cry, and almost thought she might. It was the nicest thing anyone had said to her in days. She was so tired! Tired of traveling, of trying to take care of them all. It was lovely to be among friends.

"Thank you," she said, and would have said more, but Laura was pulling her down the hall toward a bathroom in which the ceramic stove had already been lit. The old-fashioned enameled tub was filled with steaming water, and a scent hung in the air, like a bouquet of herbs and flowers. She could smell lavender, mint, lemon . . .

"Go on," said Laura. "There's a robe on the hook, a tooth-brush and tooth powder in the cabinet, cold cream in the drawer. Use whatever you want. If you leave your clothes outside the door, Júlia will take care of them. And there's more water in the bucket, which you can heat on the stove. We don't have such luxuries as hot running water here in rural Styria, but we do well enough, as you see! I'll wake you tomorrow morning, bright and early." When she had closed the door with a final "Get plenty of sleep!" Mary silently blessed her. Thank goodness there were people in the world who cheered and helped, like Laura Jennings! She would try to be one of them—the women who made others feel comfortable and at home.

> BEATRICE: You are one of those women, Mary. Look at how you've made a home for us here.

> DIANA: You don't make *me* feel comfortable. Mina let me wear whatever I wanted, and she didn't criticize me all the time.

> BEATRICE: Diana, aren't you even a little grateful to your sister for providing a home for you—for all of us?

> DIANA: Only on alternate Tuesdays.

It was almost an hour later that Mary left the bathroom, damp and scented and so sleepy that she had been worried she was going to fall asleep in the water. It would have been a sadly anticlimactic end to her adventures if she drowned in a bathtub! As she made her way back down the dark hall, she saw a light under the door of Justine's bedroom. Could Justine have left the lamp burning? She should check and make sure that Justine had not fallen sleep.

She knocked quietly on the door and heard a *"Kommen Sie herein!"*

She opened the door and looked in. Justine was sitting up in bed with a book in her hand.

"I thought you'd gone to sleep," said Mary. "I was afraid you'd left the lamp burning, and I thought I'd better check."

"I assumed you were the maid," said Justine. "Alas, I have tried, but I have not been able to sleep. I was just reading."

Mary wrapped the robe more tightly around herself. The floor was cold under her bare feet. She walked over to the bed and looked at the book in Justine's hands. It was a large book, bound in leather, and on its cover was written *The Holy Bible*. "Do you want to talk about it?" she asked.

Justine put the Bible down on the coverlet beside her. "You mean . . ."

"Whatever happened with Adam. Whatever the two of you were talking about, while I was trying to deal with my father. I mean Hyde. Before we heard the shots."

Justine looked down at her hands. For a long moment, she was silent, and Mary wondered whether she would say anything at all. Then suddenly, she put her hands over her face and began to sob—violent, choking sobs that shook her body. Mary was so startled that she did not know what to do. She was not good at this sort of thing—all the others knew that. They came to her for logical reasoning, not emotional reassurance. What in the world should she do—or say? Then she thought, *What would Laura do in this circumstance?* Of course . . . She sat on the side of the bed beside Justine, scooted over so she was right up next to her, and put her arms around the sobbing Giantess.

Justine looked up at her, startled, as though wondering what in the world Mary, of all people, was doing there. But then she returned to crying—more quietly now, more calmly. In a few minutes, she sniffed and wiped her eyes, then her nose. "I'm sorry. I did not mean to do that."

"Justine, what happened? I mean, you don't have to talk about it if you don't want to. But sometimes it's better just to tell

someone. Sometimes . . ." Oh, for goodness' sake, how did one
do this? There ought to be a rule book. Why was ordinary human
sympathy so difficult?

Justine sniffed loudly and wiped her face with her hands. It
was red and splotchy. One never looks attractive after a hard cry.

DIANA: I bet Beatrice does.

CATHERINE: That's because she's like a plant. They
don't look much the worse after a storm. They just
bend back up again.

BEATRICE: Catherine, that makes absolutely no sense.
A storm can destroy vegetation. It can break
branches, flatten reeds. . . .

CATHERINE: I was being poetic.

"It is difficult to talk about," said Justine. For a long moment,
she did not say anything, and Mary thought that might be the end
of it. She wondered if she should bid Justine good night and go to
bed. It was late, after all.

But then Justine said, "He asked me to forgive him. He wanted
me to pray with him and asked for my forgiveness."

"That . . . doesn't sound like Adam," said Mary, doubtfully.

"Oh, he railed against me for not loving him. Railed—that is
right, is it not? He could not understand why I did not see myself
as his chosen spouse. Made as we are, he said, who else would ever
want us?"

"Yes, that's more like him! What a—" Mary tried to think
of the right word. Fiend? Monster? How could one describe the
despicable cruelty of someone like Adam?

"But he also asked me to forgive him. He still hoped his condition could be cured—he thought Lucinda's blood, if he could get enough of it, might cure him. He did not understand why it had not done so already. But if he died, he wanted to die with my forgiveness."

"And?" There were streaks on Justin's face where tears had run down to her chin. Mary wished she had a handkerchief. Instead, she wiped Justine's cheeks with the sleeve of her nightgown. "Did you forgive him?"

Justine looked at her with red, puffed eyes. "How could I? After all he had done . . . And I could not lie to him, Mary. There was no forgiveness in my heart, so there could be none on my lips. I told him so. I told him that he should ask forgiveness of God, whose compassion was infinite. He would forgive Adam—I, in my human frailty, could not. I told him that I would pray with him, and so we prayed together. I had never known him to be religious before."

"So that's what I saw when I came to get you. I wondered . . ."

"Yes, although I think perhaps he just wanted to hold my hands. Mary, was I wrong not to forgive him? I've been reading the Holy Book, and everywhere it tells me that we should forgive those who have sinned against us. Have I become a sinner myself, in not forgiving his sins?"

"Hell no!" Oh goodness, Mary had not meant it to come out like that. "No, of course not," she added more gently. "Anyway, if God can forgive him for murdering seven women—or more, we do not know the full extent of his crimes—then I strongly suspect He can forgive you for not being more charitable. Adam does not deserve either your forgiveness or your compassion."

Justine smiled wanly. "You sound like an avenging angel."

Mary had to smile at that image of herself. "On your behalf, I'll be happy to hold the flaming sword of . . . I don't remember. Whoever guarded the gates of Eden or something like that.

Anyway, what matters is, you need to forgive *yourself*, and also go to sleep. Laura said we would need to leave for Budapest at dawn. We should both get some rest."

"All right." Justine leaned back against the pillows. She certainly did not look happy, but she seemed more at peace. "Thank you, Mary. I feel as though, on this journey, we have gotten to know each other so much better."

They certainly had! There was nothing quite like being kidnapped and escaping together to increase one's understanding of another person. Mary was silent for a moment. Then, she said, "Justine, I don't know if I should ask this, but . . . Laura and Carmilla. Are they—"

"Together?" said Justine. "Yes, they are a couple. Have you not read Sappho?"

"That's Greek, right? I never learned Greek. She was a poetess, I do know that." Absentmindedly, Mary smoothed the cover, then realized it was her mother's gesture. That was just how her mother had tucked Mary in at night when she was still a child. She felt a sudden impulse to tuck Justine in, and wondered if Justine would be offended. "I'm glad they have each other. Just as I'm glad we all have one another—even Diana!" She squeezed Justine's hand and said, "Good night. May I take the lamp? The hall is quite dark." Justine nodded, then pulled up the coverlet and closed her eyes. Mary gave the coverlet a final pat before making her way down the hall to her own bedroom.

When she finally climbed into her bed, Diana was snoring— ordinarily, it would have annoyed her, but tonight she was reassured by the sound. All three of them were free, and together, and safe—at least for one night. Tomorrow would bring more dangers and obstacles, but . . . the rest of the thought slid away into dreams.

She woke to Laura shaking her. "Time to get up, I'm afraid.

We'll leave as soon as it's light enough to see the road. Júlia has put out fresh clothes for all of you, and there are pastries and chocolate waiting for us downstairs. Diana is already having breakfast."

She would be! Mary rose groggily and murmured a vague good morning. After Laura had left the room, she washed her face in the basin, which had obviously already been used once—by Diana, she supposed, because there was water splashed everywhere, and the towel was crumpled. Then she put on the walking suit that had been left out for her. It was the most fashionable outfit she had ever worn—without decoration of any sort, but cut with great precision, in a dark blue cashmere that felt almost like silk. It must be Laura's? And there were fresh underclothes as well, which felt positively luxurious. By the time she descended to the first floor—a maid she had not seen the night before directed her to the morning room—Justine and Diana were both sitting at a table, having their breakfast. She was not particularly pleased to see that Diana was once again in masculine attire. Probably one of Carmilla's outfits, for the trousers were rolled up at the cuffs but otherwise fit well.

Of course, Justine was also dressed as a man. "Good morning," she said to Mary gently. She looked better and stronger than she had the night before. "Laura gave me one of her father's suits." The trousers were a too short and the jacket hung on her slender frame, but they fit well enough. Once again all three of them looked clean and respectable—although dreadfully tired. Even Diana, usually so energetic, stifled a yawn. One of the dogs, Mary was not sure which, was sitting under the table, looking up at Diana and whining, as though for its own breakfast.

Mary had just enough time to eat half a pastry filled with some sort of sweet cheese and drink half a cup of thick, dark chocolate before Laura came into the room and announced, "All right, we're ready. Carmilla is waiting for us out front."

"But I haven't finished," said Diana, her mouth filled with what she had just chewed, and hanging open in dismay.

"Bring whatever you want with you," said Laura. "But come on—the motor is running."

The what? But as they stepped outside the schloss, onto the circular drive, Mary realized what Laura had meant and why they would be in Budapest that evening. Carmilla was standing in front of a motorcar! And there was the other dog beside her. When it saw Diana, it barked once.

Not that Mary had ever seen a motorcar, but what else could it be? It looked a little like a clarence, with an open seat up front for the driver and an enclosed carriage behind for passengers, but there were no traces at all. Instead, sticking up from the floor in front of the driver's seat were a wheel, presumably to steer, and several levers that probably made it go. It was black, and shone as though brand new. Mary could scarcely believe her eyes. A motorcar? In the wilds of Styria?

"Bloody brilliant!" Diana strode past her, hands in pockets, and walked around the motorcar, admiring it from all angles. One of the wolfdogs loped beside her—the one from the breakfast room? Yes, it must have followed her out, because there they both were, the two white wolfdogs, circling and sniffing, the way dogs do.

"Just what Carmilla needs!" said Laura in a tone that meant the opposite. "Someone to admire her prized possession. Do you have any idea how much that contraption cost? It was why she agreed to rent Castle Karnstein to Hyde in the first place!"

"Are you complaining about this beauty again?" said Carmilla, smiling. "You won't be complaining when we arrive in Budapest by nightfall! It can go three times as fast as a horse, and it never tires. We would have driven it to the castle yesterday, but Laura said it would be too noisy for a rescue operation."

"You could have bought a dozen horses and a landau fit for

Queen Victoria at that price!" said Laura. "It's broken down once already, remember?"

"Someday, no one will use horses anymore. Everyone will travel by motorcar," said Carmilla. "Come look at her, Mary, Justine. Isn't she beautiful? She is a Benz phaeton, designed for me by Bertha Benz herself. No one else has a motorcar like this—not yet! Karl Benz may have patented her design, but Bertha is the brains behind the Benz company, as you say in English. Magda is bringing Lucinda down. There is room for three of you inside, but one of you will need to sit up front with us."

"I call the front!" said Diana, raising her hand as though she had the answer to a question in school. Mary could not imagine why anyone would want to sit in that front seat, which looked so precarious behind a complete absence of horses. She shuddered just a little at the thought that they were going to be driving in that *machine* all the way to Budapest.

"Look, I'll show you where the petrol goes," said Carmilla.

Just then, one of the dogs started growling and running back and forth. It was a little larger than the other, so it must be Hades. Persephone stood still, but her ears were pricked up. She was turned away from them, looking toward the road that led to the schloss. Hades turned back to Carmilla and barked a warning.

"What is it?" asked Justine. "What do they sense?"

Carmilla stood still as well, as though listening. Then she said, "A carriage, coming this way. Laura, tell Magda to bring Lucinda down *now*. We need to leave as soon as possible. It will be here in a few minutes."

"*Itt vagyok, grófnő,*" said Magda. Mary turned at the sound of her voice. She was standing right behind them with Lucinda in her arms.

"Get in, everyone!" said Laura. "Hades and Persephone never

give warning without good reason. I suspect . . ." But she did not say what she suspected. Instead, she said something to Magda in Hungarian. A moment later, Lucinda was stowed in the back of the phaeton.

"I think we'd better sit on either side of her," said Mary to Justine. "Perhaps we can squeeze Diana in as well. . . ."

"No way!" said Diana. "I'm not sitting in that stuffy carriage with you and creepy Lucinda. I'm sitting up front, where all the excitement is." Mary did not like the idea, but this was no time to argue. Carmilla was already doing something with one of the levers. Suddenly, Mary heard a roar, as though a lion had jumped out of the forest and was about to attack them. She had been about to climb into the motorcar, but she was so startled that she almost fell back. She looked wildly around for the source of the noise, then realized it was the motorcar itself. It was shuddering under her hand, as though she were in the middle of an earthquake.

"It's all right, Mary," said Justine, who was already sitting inside. She had to speak loudly to make herself heard. "It's just noise, that's all. You'll see, it's quite comfortable in here!"

"But now you see what I don't like about it!" said Laura. "The noise, and then the petrol has a stench . . . Well, I suppose we mustn't stand in the way of progress!" She seated herself in the front, next to Diana. Hopefully she would keep Diana from doing anything stupid while the motorcar was moving!

Mary climbed into the back of the motorcar reluctantly. Was it really going to shake and shudder like that all the way to Budapest?

Laura turned and said, through the window that allowed passengers in the back to converse with the driver. "Are you both comfortable? Is Lucinda quite all right?"

Well, no, not exactly—she was still unconscious, lying on Justine's shoulder with her eyes closed. On her lips was a fresh spot of blood—she must have fed already that morning. But she seemed as well as could be expected under the circumstances. She was in some sort of loose dressing-gown, and Magda had wrapped her up well in a plaid blanket, probably the same one that had been on the parlor sofa last night.

Then Mary heard it, even over the noise of the motor car—carriage wheels, and the whinny of horses! Coming up the road was a vehicle she immediately recognized, with Miklós Ferenc on the box. It was the coach in which they had been kidnapped! When the coach turned into the circular drive, she could see Dénes Ferenc on the seat above the boot, holding a rifle. And there, with his face at the open window, was Hyde.

"I was wondering how soon he would show up," said Laura. "Carmilla! We need to go!"

"Then you were expecting him?" said Mary.

"Of course! Although I didn't know how soon we would have to confront him again. The Ferencs would have told him that we had rescued you—I knew he would follow as soon as he could. We were safe at night—the roads around here are too treacherous to travel in the dark. You could end up at the bottom of a ravine, or driving into a tree. But it looks as though he must have left before dawn. Carmilla, aren't we leaving?"

"Not yet," said Carmilla. "Not . . . quite . . . yet. Is our Home Guard in place?"

What in the world could she mean? Mary looked back toward the schloss. There, emerging from the front door, were Mrs. Madár, and the maid that had given her directions the night before, who was probably Júlia, and another maid, and another, and what looked like the cook. All of them were carrying weapons of some sort, either pistols or rifles or what appeared to be pikes, and they formed a line behind Magda, who stood with her arms crossed, with Hades and Persephone on either side of her. Everything about her seemed to proclaim, *You shall not pass.* Somehow, the two dogs looked larger and fiercer than Mary remembered—now it was clear that they were partly wolves. They were both growling in the direction of Hyde's coach. If she had seen them like this last night, she would not have dared touch them, and would have tried to keep Diana away for fear they might attack.

The coach stopped. Dénes Ferenc jumped down from his seat and walked to the door where she had seen Hyde's face a moment ago. Was Hyde about to descend? Was Carmilla planning to confront him? Mary had no idea what was going to happen.

"Now!" said Carmilla. She shifted one of the levers, and suddenly the motorcar leaped ahead. She was driving it straight toward the horses! Terrified of this roaring machine, they reared up, one trying to turn away from the noise, the other backing into the traces. The coach lurched back and then from side to side. Dénes Ferenc ran to get out of the way. Were they going to hit the horses? No, at the last moment Carmilla swerved to the right and drove around the coach. As they passed, Mary could see Hyde's face at the window. He seemed to be shouting something, but she could not hear what it was. Then they were roaring down the drive and onto the road, between banks of wildflowers.

When they were completely out of sight of the schloss, Carmilla slowed down just a little. Mary was grateful. She felt sick from the motion and noise. She looked over at Justine, who seemed pale but resolute.

"Are you all right?" she asked.

"If in the future everyone travels in motorcars," said Justine, "I would prefer not to live that long."

MARY: But you probably will, you know. Among all

of us, you're actually the most likely to live that long.

JUSTINE: I would rather not think about that.

Since most of my readers have never ridden in a motorcar, or perhaps even seen one, I should describe how it felt to Mary and Justine to ride in one through the Styrian countryside.

DIANA: Hey, what about me?

CATHERINE: I imagine to you, it was just one glorious rush. You like that sort of thing! If anyone ever builds a genuine flying machine, you'll be the first to go up.

DIANA: Damn right, I would! Wouldn't it be glorious to fly through the air like a bird?

JUSTINE: Or Icarus.

Riding in a motorcar is nothing at all like riding in a carriage, or even a charabanc. Instead of the *clop-clop* of horses' hooves, there is the steady roar of the motor. You are moving so fast that you cannot examine the countryside at your leisure: forests, fields, lakes all flash by you, as they do when you're in a train. But in a train, you can stand up and walk along the corridor, have a conversation with your companions. None of that is possible in a motorcar. And the motion is more like a carriage than a train. By the end of several hours, Mary felt so tumbled about that she did not know if she would be able to walk when the vehicle stopped. Her buttocks were aching.

MARY: Could you please keep my anatomy out of your
book? I don't know why you insist on referring to
the baser aspects of life.

CATHERINE: Because it's funny? Particularly when
it's you. . . . Oh, all right, I'll take it out before
publication, I promise. You will stride through the
book buttockless, like one of the angels.

DIANA: If angels don't have buttocks, what do they
sit on?

CATHERINE: Their faith in God?

MARY: That doesn't even begin to make sense. Plus,
I'm pretty sure it's blasphemous.

They stopped around noon in a meadow and had lunch out
of a basket under the watchful eyes of several cows. Carmilla fed
Lucinda again with her own blood. Mary looked away—although
she had fed Lucinda herself, she found the sight disturbing, particularly since it produced no change in Lucinda's condition. She
remained comatose, and slumped against Mary when she got back
into the motorcar.

They were out of the forest now, motoring through farmland
and sometimes even villages, where their passage would be met
with cries and consternation, mothers snatching their children out
of the way and startled chickens fluttering to the side of the road.
Once, Mary caught a glimpse of an old woman in a kerchief crossing herself. She sympathized with the impulse. No matter how
much Carmilla slowed down as they neared a village, the passage
of a motorcar must have looked, to these farmers and their wives,

like the advent of some mythological beast—a squat black dragon, a metallic ogre.

They broke down once, and Carmilla spent an hour repairing something underneath. Diana handed her various tools, while the rest of them sat by the side of the road eating whatever was left in the basket and swatting away midges. Mary saved some rolls and the end of a salami for Diana, knowing there would be complaints otherwise. It was mid-afternoon, and hot. She worried about Lucinda, who was still lying in the motorcar, wrapped in a blanket, but when she went to check Lucinda's temperature, her skin was as cool as though she'd been sitting in an icebox. Laura and Justine were talking Austro-Hungarian politics, which was as boring, she thought, as British politics. But she was glad to hear Justine talking—she had been so quiet during the drive, and Mary worried that their conversation last night had made her uncomfortable or perhaps even angry, although when did Justine ever get angry? But she and Laura seemed to be having a very pleasant discussion about something or other that had happened in the last century, probably a war of some sort. Mary was tired and numb from riding in the motorcar for hours at a time, so she just stared at the fields around them and the distant mountains. Finally Carmilla emerged from beneath the motorcar, covered with dust. There was a streak of black oil across her left cheek, but the engine was running again.

Even with the delay, by nightfall they were in the suburbs of a large city. Cottages surrounded by small gardens turned into apartment houses with shops on the street level. They did not look like the gray buildings of London, or even the brighter ones of Vienna, but were painted in various colors—pale yellow, sage green, a sort of burnt sienna, sky blue.

"How beautiful!" said Justine. They had slowed down enough so she could peer out the window and examine the buildings closely—indeed, they were at that moment stopped behind a cart. How strange it was to be in city traffic again! Noisy, odiferous— yet Mary realized that she had missed it. She was a city girl, after all. As they drove along a broad avenue, the street lamps were being lit, pedestrians were bustling along--men from offices or factories, no doubt, and women from working in shops or private houses, going home to prepare dinner, too sophisticated to take much notice of a motorcar, although they got some curious looks. Home! She missed London and 11 Park Terrace. What were Catherine, Beatrice, Alice, and Mrs. Poole doing now? Probably sitting down to their dinners. She glanced at her wristwatch and mentally subtracted an hour for Greenwich time. Yes, safe at home, eating their dinners in the dining room— or drinking weed tea, in Beatrice's case. Thank goodness they were all together and safe, not here in a foreign country where she could not even read the street signs, with Lucinda Van Helsing sleeping on her shoulder! She was about to say so to Justine, but the Giantess had also dozed off. Ah well.

> CATHERINE: Of course, we were on the train traveling to Vienna, so our situation wasn't so different from yours!

> BEATRICE: Except that we had not been kidnapped.

> CATHERINE: Well, yes. It is always better not to be kidnapped. So advantage to us, I guess.

Just as Mary looked back out the window, the motorcar turned into a narrow street between a leafy park and a row of ornate buildings. At one of them, Carmilla stopped and sat idling. Mary had grown so used to the motion of the motorcar that the cessation of motion startled her. Laura climbed down and rang a bell beside the large carriage door, then climbed back in. A few minutes later, the door swung open. Carmilla turned into the arched entrance and drove through the passageway into an inner courtyard at the center of the building. There, she parked the motorcar to one side.

"We're here," she said. "Come on, let's go find Mina."

But when Mary got out of the motorcar, on legs that felt like rubber so that she thought she might fall at any moment, Mina was there. Mina, looking just as she had seven years ago when Mary had last seen her, except perhaps a little more tired. Looking just as kind and sensible, holding her arms out and giving Mary a hug as well as much-needed support when she felt as though her legs might buckle, saying, "Oh, my dear, I'm so glad you're here safe and sound! And my, how you've grown!"

CHAPTER XX

Morning in Budapest

The Orient Express traveled through the night toward Budapest.

Catherine looked at her watch. They would be there in a couple of hours. She had to admit that she was tired—she had not allowed herself to shut her eyes at all, and although she was naturally nocturnal, the lack of sleep was starting to affect even her. Every hour, like clockwork, she had gotten up to walk along the train corridor. Once, she had nodded to the conductor as he passed, and he had said something in French that sounded very respectful. She had reminded herself that he was saying it not to the Puma Woman, but to Sister Catherine, distinguished by her nun's habit and the rosary in her left pocket. In her right pocket was the pistol Irene had given her. Its weight was reassuring, although really she could defend herself perfectly well, thank you. She was a puma, after all. But now it was time to walk along the corridor again, to make sure she would not be affected by Beatrice's poison. She wasn't going to make the same mistake as Clarence!

Beatrice was sleeping in the corner by the window, wrapped in a blanket. Well, let her sleep. In a couple of hours they would be in Budapest, and they would have to figure out how to get to the address Mina Murray had sent them. Catherine assumed there would be cabs in Budapest, just as there were in London and Paris and Vienna. It was a civilized city, wasn't it? They should be able to show the address to the cabbie, who would take them to the right place. Even if he didn't understand English, he would understand that.

But as she stood up and stretched, Beatrice turned her head and opened her eyes. She mumbled, as though still half asleep, which she probably was, "Mmmm, everything all right?"

"Yes, everything's fine. I'm just going to walk around for a little while. Although . . ." There was one thing that had been bothering her. "I'm a little worried that we didn't see Seward or Prendick on the platform. I hope Van Helsing's housekeeper was right about the tickets? They could have gotten on before or after we arrived, and anyway the platform was so busy that even if we got on at the same time, we could have missed them."

"We'll probably see them on the platform in Budapest," said Beatrice, but her eyes were already closing again. She shifted her shoulders, as though trying to get more comfortable on the stiff seat. "We'll make certain to watch for them. And make certain they do not see us. . . ."

All right, time to walk in the fresh air of the corridor. Catherine wished that, as she could not get any sleep, she could at least have a cup of coffee, but the dining car would not be open until after they had disembarked. As the next best thing, she stepped into the small lavatory and splashed cold water on her face. She was startled by her reflection in the lavatory mirror. With her hair pulled back and her face surrounded by a white coif under the black veil, she did not look like herself at all. Well, that was a good thing, under the circumstances.

She made her way along the corridor toward the dining car. The train was dark—the moon had already set, and there were no lights under the cabin doors. Everyone seemed to be sleeping. No, that was not quite correct—from the door of one cabin, right at the end of the car, a sliver of light shone into the corridor. She strolled that way, slowly because when she reached the end of the car, she would simply have to turn around and walk back again. Someone was certainly awake—she could smell the sweet, heavy odor of a pipe.

As she approached the sliver of light, she heard a voice. At least someone else on that train other than herself was awake. Or several someones, because she heard another voice reply. Suddenly, she was completely alert, as she would have been if, in the middle of the night in the Andes, one of the mountain deer had wandered by her den. Yes, Van Helsing's housekeeper had been right—he was on this train, in the cabin with the light under the door. At least, that was Seward's voice, and he was saying something. She tried to make it out, but it was difficult to hear over the noise of the train—just then, the whistle drowned it out entirely. When that horrible screeching had stopped—she rubbed her sensitive puma ears through the rough cloth of her veil—she pulled back the coif wrapped around her head to expose one ear, then put it right next to the door. Now she could hear more clearly.

"I think we should go directly to Professor Vámbéry's apartment," said Seward. "We can drop off our luggage, have breakfast, and then proceed to this abbey he described. In his letter, he told you that he'd assembled a small army. Well, I for one would like to inspect our troops. It's not that I distrust Vámbéry—I'm not saying that, exactly. But I like to see things for myself, as you know, Van Helsing. And then, we can arrange to meet with those members he identified as most likely to join us. Tomorrow will be soon enough for that."

"But should we not look for Lucinda?" asked Prendick. "You said whoever took her from the asylum might have transported her to Budapest. What if her symptoms have gotten worse? You told us yourself that you confined her so she could have constant care.

You have not seen her for several weeks. Should we not at least attempt to determine where she is? And how will you convince your—well, your faction—without her?"

They don't have Lucinda! Catherine pressed her ear against the door, straining to hear. If they didn't have Lucinda, they might not have Mary, Justine, and Diana either. But then where could Mary and the others possible be?

"I know where she is," said Van Helsing. "Or where she must be. The men I had watching her could give me little information on who had abducted her—most of them have sunk irretrievably into madness. Only one remains capable of speech. When I asked who had attacked him, he repeated a single phrase—'*Frau mit einer Pistole.*' A woman with a pistol."

"Mrs. Harker, no doubt," said Seward. "That damned interfering—"

"Exactly," said Van Helsing. "If she has taken my daughter to Budapest, as I believe, she will no doubt have sought the protection of the Count. In his home base, he is too powerful for us to challenge, at least until we have the might of the society at our backs. Then, we will drive him out of Budapest. Let him return to his ancestral castle in the Carpathians. He can do us no harm there."

"Although I grant you that it will be more difficult without Miss Van Helsing," said Seward. "She would have served as a visible demonstration that the experiment is, if not a complete success, at least worth pursuing. If she is with the Count, as you believe, could Vámbéry not negotiate—"

"I do not think so," said Van Helsing. "He knows that Vámbéry is working with us, and he will do nothing to aid us in our endeavors. No, we cannot expect help in that quarter. Light a match, will you, Seward? My pipe, it has gone out."

So Van Helsing did not have Lucinda, *and* he did not know

that Mary, Justine, and Diana had been involved in rescuing her. *Who in the world is Mrs. Harker?* Catherine wondered. *Another member of the Alchemical Society?* That was the logical explanation. If Mary and the others had disappeared on the way to Budapest and Van Helsing knew nothing about it, the Alchemical Society must be responsible.

"Well then, we shall simply have to convince them, as we convinced Raymond in London." That was Seward again. She was beginning to hate his voice. It was so self-assured, so smug, as though Dr. John Seward never questioned his own judgment. "The society must allow us a free hand in our experiments—no more stifling research at the whim of our esteemed Madam President. The important thing is to bring the motion to a vote as quickly as possible at the general meeting. And if we are voted down, that's when we bring in reinforcements."

"I would rather accomplish our goals peacefully if possible," said Van Helsing. "Of course if it is not possible—"

"But the important thing is to accomplish them," said Seward. "It's the result, not the method, that counts."

"Even if the method results in death and destruction?" Ah, that was Prendick's voice. She had in the past accused him of cowardice, but she had to acknowledge that there was some value in being an essentially peaceful man. At least he was not planning a bloodbath! And he cared what became of Lucinda.

"If the vote goes against us, we can't answer for the consequences," said Seward, in his smug, self-satisfied way. She would have liked to scratch his eyes out.

"Mr. Prendick, surely you're not losing your resolve?" asked Van Helsing. "Our research will bring incalculable benefits to mankind. That is worth any price, to an objective mind. You should have learned that from Moreau. When he and I were young men— ah, that was a time! Before the Antivivisection League sapped the life out of science in England. He had the right attitude—increase of knowledge is worth any price. What is an individual life beside the vast sum of knowledge? Think of how much was lost when the forces of barbarism ransacked Rome. Consider, friend Edward, how slowly we have rediscovered what we lost, as though building the library of Alexandria again, brick by brick. And how much, in this century and the one to come, we may add to it! Biological transmutation opens up vast realms of possibility. We may learn more than we ever dreamed of the plasticity of life! And what stands in our way? One woman who says 'No.' And who is she, gentlemen, to say to us, 'You shall not'? She may once have been Queen of Kôr, but here she is only one among the members of the Société des Alchimistes. Yes, she is our president, but I do not think she will be for long. I believe the members of the Société are ready to be convinced."

"I certainly hope you're right," said Seward. "But if not, I want us to be ready. Buck up, Prendick. You didn't used to be so squeamish. What happened to the Edward Prendick who worked with Moreau?"

"You're confusing me with Montgomery," said Prendick. "Saying that I worked with Moreau mischaracterizes—well, there's no point in arguing. The both of you have your idols, to which you bow down. The pursuit of knowledge for Van Helsing, and for you, Seward, the quest for power. I was not born a humble man, but circumstances have humbled me—I have no idols anymore. If you will excuse me, gentlemen, I would like to get some air."

But that meant . . .

Catherine had time only to move halfway down the corridor and adjust her coif and veil to provide as much coverage as possible before Prendick came out of the cabin and shut the door behind him. She pulled the rosary out of her pocket, stood very still, and pretended to pray. How did one pray, anyway? One put one's hands together and recited . . . something. She tried to remember the Lord's Prayer as she had heard it when she used to attend church with Sir Geoffrey and Lady Tibbett, but the only thing that would come to her was the insane litany she had learned on Moreau's island: *His* is the hand that makes, *his* is the hand that wounds, *his* is the hand that heals. Moreau's had been the hand that had unmade her, and then made her again in another image. *His* is the lightning-flash, *his* is the deep salt sea. Damn Moreau to hell, forever and ever, amen.

"Good morning, Sister." Prendick was standing beside her. "You're up early." He sounded very tired, even more tired than he had sounded in the former headquarters of the Alchemical Society in Soho. There was a sort of desperate resignation in his voice. Could she pretend that she didn't speak English? But it was the only language she *could* speak.

"Good morning, my son," she replied. That was the sort of thing nuns said, right?

Almost immediately, she could sense that something had changed. He had not moved—rather, he was standing unnaturally still. It was like the moment when a deer smells the puma that has been stalking it. You can tell it is aware because there is a tension in its stillness. For a few minutes, he did not speak. Then he said, "Do you think there is forgiveness for sin, Sister?"

What in the world could she say? "God forgives all those who have a contrite heart." Surely she had heard Justine say something like that before.

"But if our sin is so bad that it blackens our soul forever . . . Well. I have found, Sister, that hell is inside the human heart. Even if God forgave me, even if she whom I wronged forgave me, I could not forgive myself."

She had no idea how to respond. He knew, didn't he? He knew who she was. Would he go back to Seward and Van Helsing, and tell them? She put her right hand on the pistol in her pocket. She could shoot him. . . . Although she did not like the idea of shooting Edward Prendick. He had left her to die on Moreau's island, and yet, somehow, she did not know if she could point the pistol at him and pull the trigger. Not point blank.

"No," he continued. "All I can do now is atone. Forgive me for talking to you like this, Sister—a strange man whom you've never met. It is the darkness that has given me courage. Bless you—may God, if He exists, bless you and keep you safe from harm." The sentence ended in what sounded like a choked sob. He turned and walked down the corridor, back toward the dining car.

Catherine looked at his retreating back. Had he not recognized her after all? No, she was certain he had. But he was—atoning, whatever that meant. At the moment it seemed to mean that he would not raise any sort of alarm.

She walked quickly back to her own cabin. Beatrice was still asleep, wrapped in the blanket so that only part of her face was showing, like a half-moon. Catherine wanted to wake her, simply to have someone to talk to, but no—let the Poisonous Girl sleep. Her hands were shaking, and her head hurt. She put her head in her hands, as though that might help somehow. What time was it? Almost 4:00 a.m. She would close her eyes, just for a few minutes. . . .

When she woke, the sun was shining through the window. Beatrice was shaking her.

"Wake up, Cat," she said. "The conductor says we will be in Budapest in fifteen minutes. We need to figure out what we're going to do there. How are we going to find Van Helsing? We don't even know if he's on the train. And how long have you been asleep? Are you all right? If you had woken me, I would have stood in the corridor for a while, so you could rest."

"He is on this train," said Catherine, sitting up. She was

feeling light-headed. That was the effect of Beatrice's poison, even though the window had been open all night. How long had she been asleep in it? Certainly longer than she had intended! *I'm just as bad as Clarence, damn it,* she thought. *And with less of an excuse.* She should have known better. "And I know where he's going. He's staying with Professor Arminius Vámbéry. You remember—Van Helsing mentioned him in that letter Diana stole, when we were solving the Whitechapel Murders. He's another member of the society."

"Then how do we find Professor Vámbéry?" asked Beatrice. "We have no idea where he lives."

"Follow Van Helsing, I guess," said Catherine. "The way we would follow anyone in London. But he doesn't have Lucinda or any of the others. He doesn't even know they were the ones who rescued her. I heard him and Seward talking about it last night."

"Last night?" said Beatrice.

By the time they had drawn into the Nyugati railway station, Catherine had told Beatrice all about the night before. Beatrice looked at her apprehensively. "Do you think Prendick will tell them?" she asked.

"I have no idea," said Catherine. "That's just a risk we'll have to take. I wonder if there's someplace we could store our luggage for a while. Somewhere at the train station, so we can come back for it later. If we're going to be following Van Helsing *et al.,* I don't want to be lugging a trunk around."

"I shall speak to the conductor," said Beatrice. "He knows a little English, but he is more comfortable in French. Look, we are drawing into the station now."

"Why didn't I think of that? You're much more awake than I am." Catherine drew the wallet that contained their money out Beatrice's suitcase. "Here's a krone for the tip. Or is that too much? Irene gave me some hellers—I think the little ones are called hellers. Never mind, just give him the krone. If Mary were here, she'd know the exchange rate!"

The conductor assured them that he would take care of their luggage, which would be left in the storage area allocated for passengers on the Orient Express—or so Beatrice translated. But when she offered a tip, he shook his head and said something in French. She made the sign of a cross and then intoned in Latin—at least it sounded like Latin. He thanked her—well, he looked as though he was thanking her, and he called her *ma Soeur*, which even Catherine knew was "sister" in French.

"What in the world was that about?" asked Catherine as they climbed down the steps onto the platform.

"He asked me to bless him," said Beatrice. "I am not entirely certain that my Latin was correct—my knowledge of the language is scientific, not conversational. But a blessing is never out of place, I think. Do you see Van Helsing or the others? I do not know what they look like."

Of course, Catherine did not know what Van Helsing looked like either, but yes—there was Seward, ahead of them in the crowd leaving the train station. Next to him was a heavyset man with white hair and an equally white beard, wearing a frock coat and top hat. That must be Van Helsing. She could not see Prendick. Ah, there he was—strolling up to Seward and gesturing toward the street. Perhaps he had found a cab. They must find one as well.

"Come on!" she said to Beatrice, pulling her by the sleeve. "There they are—and I don't want them to get away." When they emerged from the arching front door of the station, she saw Seward and Van Helsing standing on the street corner, talking to each other, while Prendick supervised a porter who was loading their bags into a hackney carriage, like the famous London growlers. There was a cab stand—the cabs looked mostly like hansoms, although there were a few traps among them. Catherine walked up to the first one. The cabbie bowed when he saw her and said something incomprehensible in Hungarian.

"I don't suppose you speak English?" she asked. He just shook his head.

"*Lei parla italiano?*" asked Beatrice. "*Parlez-vous Français? Sprechen Sie Deutsch?*"

"*Ja, ein bisschen,*" he said. He looked at them curiously—these two obviously foreign nuns.

"*Gut. Dieser Wagen* . . . I don't know. Oh goodness, how do you say 'follow'? *Folgen.* I think my Latin is better than my German, and that is poor enough."

But the cabbie seemed to understand, or perhaps he understood Catherine's frantic pointing and the krone she showed him. A minute later, they were pulling into traffic, the horse clopping on the cobbled streets just as horses did in London. Ahead of them was the carriage Prendick had hired.

They drove down a broad avenue between grand apartment buildings. There were carriages and carts on the road, but not many—it looked like a quiet summer morning. Budapest reminded Catherine of Paris, except that the buildings were more colorful, and somehow the sunlight was brighter. She felt stifled under the black cloth of her habit.

Ahead of them, she could see a bridge—they were approaching the river. She remembered the map Irene Norton had shown them, with the Danube bisecting the city. Were they going over that bridge? No, Van Helsing's carriage turned left, down a road that ran alongside the river.

"Where do you think we're going?" asked Beatrice.

"Well, we're still in Pest, not crossing over to Buda," said Catherine. "Sorry, that's not very helpful, is it?"

"Actually, it is," said Beatrice. "Miss Murray's address is in Pest—5 Múzeum utca, by the National Museum. I took the precaution of memorizing it, in case we were separated. I think we are slowing down?"

Yes, because the carriage ahead of them was slowing down as well. It drew up to the curb in front of an apartment building that faced the river. Beatrice rapped on the back glass. "*Anhalten hier, bitte!*"

The cab drew up to the curb. They were still far enough behind the carriage that Catherine hoped they would not be noticed.

By the time they got out and Beatrice had paid the driver, Van Helsing and Seward had crossed the street and disappeared into the front door of the building. Prendick, who was following at a slower pace, carrying both his valise and someone else's, crossed just in front of their cab as it drove on down the street. Then, he disappeared into the dark doorway.

Catherine and Beatrice stood by the side of the road. Behind them, steps led down to the Danube. A little farther along, boats and barges were tied to the river wall. Upriver, she could see construction—were they building another bridge? There seemed to be enough bridges already. It looked as though they had just begun. Across the river in Buda rose a forested hill, topped by a palace complex. It looked quite grand. This side of the river was not as grand—wagons rolled down the street, workmen called to one another on the barges, and down the street from them, across from the apartment building, a beggar woman was sitting on the curb, with a hat on the ground in front of her. The sun shone down on them all. It was hot, bright, and dusty.

"What now?" asked Catherine. She had not planned any further than this. Mary was the one who made elaborate plans. Pumas were not planners—she had a tendency to act on impulse. Her impulse to follow Seward and Van Helsing had brought them here, and now she was not quite certain what to do.

"We could go directly to Miss Murray's address," said Beatrice. "I believe if we walk down to the next bridge and take a left, we will get to the museum. It is a long walk, but would likely be easier than finding another cab. There do not seem to be any cab stands in this part of the city. However, did you not say that Seward wanted to—how did you put it—inspect his troops? They were keeping men somewhere, men trained and willing to fight for them. Should we wait until they come out again and follow? It would be useful, I think, to determine where they are keeping their army, as it were. But we might have to wait for some time, if they breakfast first. What do you say, Catherine? Shall we go directly to Miss Murray, or wait and see if we can gather any more information?"

"You sound just like Mary," said Catherine. "She lays it out like that: on the one hand, on the other, *etcetera*. I'd rather wait and see if they come out again, but we can't just stand around in the street wearing these!" She held out the cloth of her nun's habit, which she was beginning to heartily dislike. It was hot and itchy. "Also, I wouldn't mind some breakfast either."

"I think that if we take off the coifs—here, I will show you." Beatrice unpinned her black veil from the coif, then took off her coif and bandeau. She stuffed them into her pockets and tied the veil around her head as though it were a kerchief. Her hands were still gloved, but her fingers were as nimble as though they were bare. "You see?" she said. "Now I look like a poor widow from the country."

Catherine immediately did the same thing, although less nimbly. That was the one drawback to having been a puma—her former paws were not as flexible as human hands. Oh, that felt so much better! She rolled up the sleeves of her habit. Yes, this was more like it—at least she could get some air on her neck and arms! "So we just stand here, looking like poor widows? I suppose we could beg, although there is a previous claimant to that position"—she pointed toward the beggar woman, who was still sitting, looking down at her hat—"if we had something to beg with! Even a bucket would do."

"As we were driving past that bridge they are constructing, I believe I saw—wait, I shall be back in a moment." Before Catherine could protest, Beatrice was hurrying up the street, toward the construction site. Catherine herself had not looked at it closely—it had been on Beatrice's side of the cab, and all she could see now was a structure of wooden slats where stones were being raised. There were workmen walking around the site, calling to one another. What had Beatrice seen there? She felt like calling, "Don't poison anyone!" But of course Beatrice would be careful.

What now? She would simply have to wait and watch the building in case Van Helsing or Seward came out. While Beatrice was gone, could she perhaps find out more? If she could get into the building and find Arminius Vámbéry's apartment, perhaps she could put her ear to the door and overheard what they were planning, just as she had done on the train. Of course Beatrice would think it was too dangerous, but then Beatrice wasn't here, was she?

Catherine lifted her habit and sprinted across the street— men's trousers would have been so much more practical! In the shadow of the apartment buildings on the other side, out of sight of the windows above, she walked down to the building Seward and Van Helsing had entered. She put her hand on the front door handle, turned it downward, and—it opened! Well, that was easy. She let herself into a small lobby with stairs leading up to a second door. There was a row of mailboxes on the wall, with Vámbéry's surname on one of them. Good so far! Now, the second door.

But the second door was locked. Did she have anything . . . No hairpins this time, since her hair had been held back by the coif and bandeau, but she did have the two pins that had held her veil in place. Quickly, she bent one into an *S* shape—it was not really long enough, but she did her best. And then she inserted it into the lock. As soon as she tried to turn it, the half she had inserted broke off, and there she stood, holding a stub of metal. *Damn and double damn!* She tried the second pin. It broke off, just like the first. Fuming at herself, she walked out into the sunshine again.

DIANA: Didn't you wish I was there!

CATHERINE: I don't think you would have done any better than I did, with what I had.

DIANA: Oh please. I would have gotten into that building so quick. . . .

Beatrice was waiting for her where they had been standing before, holding a large wicker basket. "I bought this from two women—I think a mother and daughter? They were selling gingerbread to the construction workers. They were happy to sell me the entire basket at once! We can stand here selling the pieces that are left—then we will not look so conspicuous. And look," She drew out a white piece of cloth and handed it to Catherine. "Tie it around your waist. I do not think they understood my German, but sometimes krone are as effective as words!"

It was an apron. As Catherine tied the apron strings behind her, which made it a little easier to move in the voluminous habit, she said, "I was just going to see if I could pick the lock of the building. You know, so I could find Vámbéry's apartment."

"I know exactly what you were going to do," said Beatrice, disapprovingly. "And I would have told you not to. How would it help us, or Mary and the others, if Seward or Van Helsing found out that we were following them? We would put ourselves needlessly in danger. Worse, we would no longer be able to gather information to help Miss Murray. Really, Catherine, I'm surprised at you! Here, hold the basket."

Catherine stood silent, feeling thoroughly chagrined, while Beatrice took another apron out of the basket and tied it around her waist. She pulled off her gloves and stuffed them into one pocket. Peasant women did not wear gloves like fine ladies! Then she said, "Look, I purchased a sausage from a man who had brought it for his lunch. You mentioned that you were hungry?" Which made Catherine feel worse, but it was a very good sausage, spiced with paprika, and once she had torn it apart with her teeth, puma-fashion, she felt a little better.

The only thing they were missing was water, but there was none of that around, except in the broad green river behind them. Beatrice did not seem to need anything—for several hours, she stood in the sun, looking as fresh as a poisonous daisy, selling pieces of gingerbread to passers-by in either German or pantomime. She never seemed to wilt. Catherine, increasingly thirsty, finally risked a few handfuls of water from the Danube. Well, at least it looked cleaner than the Thames! But she was a puma, used to drinking from muddy pools and malarial streams—she hoped it would not do her too much harm.

Just when she thought they would have to abandon their post and go find Miss Murray—perhaps Seward had decided not to inspect those troops today after all—Beatrice said, "I see one of the men from the carriage. Is that Seward or Prendick?"

It was Seward. With him was a man Catherine did not recognize, with a dark beard and mustache, in a light summer suit—he must be Arminius Vámbéry. The two men emerged from the doorway of the building, then turned downriver.

"Come on," she said to Beatrice, tugging at her apron. "Let's see how far we can follow them without being seen." As they passed the beggar woman, Beatrice put the basket down beside her, leaving the remaining gingerbread. She just grunted—Catherine supposed it was a sort of thanks.

They hurried after the two men, trying to stay far enough behind that they would not be spotted. But Seward and Vámbéry were deep in conversation and never looked back. They turned off the road that ran along the Danube and walked quickly through a labyrinth of narrow, twisting streets, where buildings blocked out the sun and laundry hung from balconies. Even with her excellent sense of direction, Catherine worried that she was starting to get lost. But no—she could still smell the river. As long as she could smell the river, they would be fine.

Suddenly, Beatrice pulled her back by her sleeve into a doorway. "What is it?" she whispered. "Ow!" Beatrice had accidentally touched her arm. It stung.

"You said they were going to an abbey," said Beatrice, just as quietly as she had. "Look!"

At the end of the street, Catherine could see a high wall covered with yellow stucco. Over it rose a red-tiled roof and a bell tower with an ornate copper turret.

"How do you know that's an abbey?" She licked her wrist where Beatrice's touch had burned it.

"Did I—oh, I am so sorry!" said Beatrice, looking dismayed.

"I'm fine—I mean, ow, but it's not important at the moment. How is that an abbey? It's just a wall." Her experience with abbeys was—well, nonexistent. Monks and nuns lived in them, right? Like in the romances of Mrs. Radcliffe.

"There are many such abbeys in Italy. You see the tower of the church directly above? And look, Dr. Seward and his friend are stopping at the gate." As she spoke, she took her gloves from her pocket and pulled them back on again.

Catherine stepped out a little from the doorway. Yes, there was the front gate. Just then, she heard a deep *clang*—Vámbéry had rung a bell, and it echoed down the street. In a few minutes, a man in a brown robe, one of the monks she supposed, came to the gate. Vámbéry said something in Hungarian, and the gate was opened for him. He and Seward passed through. The gate closed shut behind them with another *clang*.

Then there was silence. The narrow street was empty, except for dust and sunlight. *It must be around noon,* thought Catherine.

"Now what?" she asked. "Should we try to get closer, to get a sense for what this place is?"

"If it is like the monasteries in Italy," said Beatrice, "it will be completely surrounded by that wall—the front gate, and possibly a small gate in the back, will be the only means of ingress and egress. I have an idea. It is not a very sensible idea. Perhaps as we are traveling together, I am becoming a little like you, Catherine."

Catherine grimaced. "You say that like it's a bad thing. All right, what's this idea of yours?"

"First, we must return to being holy sisters again."

Ugh, that was the last thing Catherine wanted. But she was intrigued—Beatrice so seldom led. She was always the one who held back, who gave good counsel. Where would she lead now? So Catherine once again put on the coif, turning around so Beatrice could tie it up the back, then tying Beatrice's. Then the bandeau, and finally the veil. How was she going to pin it on again with two broken pins? But the blunt ends, which she had kept in her pocket, went through the rough cloth and held it well enough.

"What about our aprons?" she asked.

"If we leave them in the street, it will look as though they fell from a balcony where they were drying," said Beatrice. "Follow me, and do not speak—hold your rosary and pretend you have taken a vow of silence. I cannot get us inside—only men are permitted to enter such a community. But I can at least ask for information. *Veni, panthera.*"

Why exactly was Beatrice speaking Latin? But Catherine followed her to the end of the street, which opened into a small square. Along one side was the yellow wall with the gate in it. Through the gate, Catherine could see a church, the same color as the wall, with the red-tiled roof and bell tower she had noticed earlier. Next to it was a large rectangular building that looked like a dormitory.

Beatrice pulled the rope that rang the bell they had heard earlier, just as Seward had done. In a few minutes, the same monk in brown came forward—or at least, a similar monk in brown. How could one tell them apart?

"*In nomine Dei, salvete, Frater,*" said Beatrice. And then she continued to speak in Latin. Catherine's Latin had only ever been rudimentary. Prendick had taught her some on the island, but it had mostly consisted of his own schoolboy declamations. Of what Beatrice was saying, Catherine could only understand one word: *aqua*.

The monk replied, then nodded and walked back toward the dormitory. He disappeared through a doorway.

"Look, there!" said Catherine, just loud enough so Sister Beatrice would hear. In front of the church stood Seward and Vámbéry. Another monk in a brown robe emerged from the church, and then there was a conversation of some sort—the monk was gesticulating a great deal. He motioned for them to follow him, and they all entered through the large church door.

Just then, the monk Beatrice had spoken to returned with a two tin cups of—ah, heaven! Cold, clear water. Even if they got no information out of this encounter, the water itself would be worth it.

Beatrice exchanged a few more words with the monk, then returned the empty cups and expressed what Catherine assumed was their gratitude. She followed Beatrice along the wall and then into another narrow street, where they were out of earshot of the abbey.

"It is called the Abbey of St. Ignatius," said Beatrice. "He says there are about forty monks, and they live in complete seclusion from the world. His abbot is a very holy man. How holy, I wonder, if he has to do with the likes of Seward and Van Helsing?"

"And what are these forces Seward was talking about?" asked Catherine. "I didn't see an army. The place looked as peaceful as—well, a church."

"Could he have meant the monks?" Beatrice looked puzzled. "But why would a group of monks fight for Van Helsing? I don't understand—"

"I could try to get in and look around," said Catherine. "There may be a place along this wall where I can climb up. . . ."

"No," said Beatrice. "Cat, I know you like to go off on your own and investigate. You are like Mr. Kipling's Rikki-Tikki-Tavi—your motto is 'Run and find out.' But now is the time to find Miss Murray. She may be able to tell us how these things connect, and the most important thing of all."

"What's the most important thing?" asked Catherine. She sniffed the air. The river was to their right, and not as far away as she had initially assumed.

"Who is Mrs. Harker? If this Mrs. Harker has Mary and the others, our first duty is to find her and make certain they are safe. If I had known this detour would take so long, I would have urged you to contact Miss Murray first and then investigate Seward and Van Helsing. I see now that your instinct is to stalk—it explains a great deal."

"You should be grateful," said Catherine. Of course she had an instinct to stalk—she was a puma. What right did the Poisonous Girl have to criticize? "If it weren't for me, you wouldn't even know about Mrs. Harker, whoever she is. If we take the next right and walk a few blocks, we should get back to the river. Once we're there, we can find the Franz Joseph Bridge. The road that crosses that bridge leads to the National Museum."

Granted, they hadn't found out as much as Catherine would have liked, but they had found out something. Now to join Miss Murray and combine whatever information they had so they could rescue Mary, Justine, and Diana—and of course Lucinda as well—from this Mrs. Harker and the Alchemical Society.

CHAPTER XXI

The Purfleet Vampire

Mary walked down the grand staircase, feeling a little overwhelmed and intimidated. She had been so tired the night before that after Mina had welcomed them and given them a light supper, she had gone directly to bed. There had been so much more to discuss, but Mina had said, "There will be time enough tomorrow. And the Count will be back—he's expected late tonight, far too late for you to wait up. It will be better to discuss everything when we're all together."

Now, this morning, she felt mostly human again—and hungry! Last night, she had not paid much attention to her surroundings. She had gone to bed in a large bedroom, grateful to, for the first time in their travels, have a bedroom entirely to herself. No Diana to snore her awake! This morning, she had looked around that bedroom with astonishment. It was very large indeed, with a high, painted ceiling on which Greek gods and assorted nymphs seemed to be disporting themselves with pagan abandon. It was difficult to tell because the paint was so faded, the plaster intermittently cracked. The bed was magnificent, although the hangings were faded as well, the once-crimson brocade now pink, with frayed edges and threadbare patches where sunlight came through. But the linen was old and fine, smelling of lavender. The basin in front of the windows was hand-painted with roses. Out of those windows she could see the linden trees in the park around the National

Museum, a white neoclassical building just visible through their leafy branches. She could hear a cacophony of birdsong.

She had washed her face and dressed quickly, and then found the staircase again. It was carved of gray marble, with fancy balusters. On the walls, as she descended, were paintings so large that Mary wondered how they had been hung up. There were military scenes that featured men stabbing each other with swords or spears while horses screamed and rolled their eyes, and forested landscape with tiny huntsmen in the foreground, walking along with rifles over their shoulders, dogs running at their heels, tongues lolling. Evidently, their hunts had been successful, because they carried the carcasses of ducks or deer. Here and there, grim men or women in ruffled collars stared down at her. She felt that they would have disapproved of her intensely.

Of all the houses she had stayed in on her travels, this was certainly the most magnificent. Irene's apartment had been modern and artistic. Carmilla's castle—well, that had been a medieval ruin. Did it even count as a house? Laura's schloss had been comfortable—like an English country house transported to the Styrian countryside. But this was truly a palace. A sort of town palace, which made sense if they were staying with a count. This must be how counts decorated, with suits of armor scattered here and there instead of potted plants. Still, it seemed rather bare, and as she walked along the corridor on the second floor, hoping she would run across the others, or breakfast, or both, she noticed that everything was very old. The demi-lune tables against the walls were in the style of a previous century, the mirrors above them tarnished. She spotted an open door—even the doors were twice as tall as she was! And there were Mina, Justine, and Diana having breakfast.

"Good morning!" said Mina. "I hope you slept well. You're on the park side, and I always find the birds wake me up at dawn. I like rising early myself, but I hope they didn't disturb you." She

was looking very much as Mary remembered her—in a respectable gray dress with white collar and cuffs, her dark brown hair
pulled back into a simple chignon. She did not look much older—
some lines under her eyes and an even more composed manner,
that was all. There was something thoroughly reassuring about
seeing her here, presiding over a large, rectangular table of dark
wood with baroque ornamentation as she had presided over the
table in the dining room of 11 Park Terrace.

"I did, thank you. But I would probably have slept through
a battle—with cannons!" Mary yawned and hastily covered her
mouth with her hand. However much sleep she had gotten, it had
evidently not been enough. "May I join you? I see some chafing
dishes." They were arranged along a sideboard as baroque as the
table. In this room as well, there was an air of faded grandeur.

"There's everything," said Diana with her mouth full. "Eggs
and sausages and pancakes, very thin ones that look like *crêpes* but
Mina says they're called *palacsinta*, and there's jam to put in them
and sugar to sprinkle over them, and coffee and chocolate and tea,
and some fried fish that are very good, and some vegetables but I
didn't try those."

"The Count does not eat—which may be why he always pro-
vides so much food!" said Mina. "Come sit. Can I pour you some
coffee? Or would you prefer tea? And then I want you to tell me
all about your trip. Justine says you encountered . . . your father.
That must have been so difficult for you."

Mary just nodded. She did not want to talk about Hyde right
now. How frustrated he must have been to watch them drive off!
No, she would not think about it this morning. It was a beautiful
day, she was with friends, and there was food in chafing dishes on
a long sideboard. She took a delicate porcelain plate and loaded it
with eggs, toast, and grilled tomatoes. The cutlery was of heavy
silver, beautifully polished.

She sat down next to Justine. Diana was regaling Mina with details of their life in London, including the antics of Alpha and Omega. By the look of her plate, she had already eaten a substantial breakfast.

"How are you doing?" Mary asked Justine in a low voice.

Justine gave her a tentative smile. "Better, I think? Sleep knits up the raveled sleeve of care . . ."

That was Shakespeare, right? Mary *thought* it meant Justine had slept well.

"And you?" asked Justine.

"I'm still pretty raveled," she said. "Maybe breakfast will knit me up again." She spread butter on her toast.

"Mary," said Mina, "when the two of you are finished, I would like to speak with you, if I may."

"And me!" said Diana.

"Certainly," said Mina in her pleasant, reasonable voice. "Unless you would rather go down to the stables. One of the Count's wolfdogs recently gave birth, and there are five puppies in a basket filled with straw. Of course, if you would rather not play with them, I completely understand—puppies are such a bother. And our conversation will be very interesting—all about making plans and allocating responsibilities."

Mary smiled. Yes, that was the Miss Murray she remembered. She had been a very good teacher, a superior governess. Had she handled Mary in the same clever way?

"Oh, well, I think you all can take care of that," said Diana. "I want to see the puppies. Are they like Hades and Persephone?"

"Yes, but smaller and fluffier," said Mina. "I'll ask Attila to take you down." She rang a silver bell on the table and a footman appeared through a door in the wall that did not look like a door at all—it was disguised as part of the wall itself. He must have been waiting in an adjacent room in case he was needed? He seemed quite young, just a little older than Diana, dressed in the most ridiculous getup—knee breeches? In this day and age? Mary felt like laughing, but he looked so dignified that she hastily put a hand over her mouth.

Mina spoke to him in what seemed, to Mary, a fluent stream of Hungarian. He bowed to Diana and said, *"Hier entlang, Fräulein."* Diana smirked, shoved a last forkful of *palacsinta* into her mouth, and followed him out of the room. *She's going to be insufferable, isn't she?* thought Mary. The last thing Diana needed was a footman treating her as though she were an aristocrat!

"You speak Hungarian," she said. "When did you learn?"

Mina laughed ruefully. "Only a little, and not very well. I just told him to take young lady to stable to visit tiny dogs, more or less. I'm not even sure I put it in the imperative. Attila is a good boy, a sort of footman in training—his father is the Count's majordomo, what we would call a butler. He's around Diana's age, and she can amuse herself trying to make him understand English. I assume she'll get him into trouble of some sort, but at least we'll have time to talk. We have a great deal to discuss. Don't worry, Mary, there's no rush—you don't need to gulp your coffee. Whenever you've finished, we'll go to my study. The Alchemical Society meets in three days, and we need to figure out what we're going to do."

"Good morning! Mina, I see you are making plans with our guests."

Mary looked up, startled. There, in the doorway, stood a man dressed all in black. He appeared to be foreign, but of course that made sense because this was a foreign country. He had prominent features —dark eyes, high cheekbones, and an aquiline nose. Black hair waved back from his face and down to his shoulders. She would not have called him handsome, but he was certainly striking—the sort of person who captured your attention when he entered the room. His accent reminded her of Carmilla's, but it was heavier, more noticeable in his deep voice. He was not particularly tall, but stood very straight, like a military man.

"Vlad," said Mina, turning toward him and holding out her hand. "We were just about to go to my study, to talk and plan. Do you have time to join us?"

He walked to Mina's chair and took her hand. "Of course, *kedvesem*. And anyway I would like to meet Miss Jekyll, whom I have heard so much about—all good, I assure you." He bowed to Mary. "Also it is a great honor to meet Miss Frankenstein. I did not know Victor well when he was a member of the Société des Alchimistes, but I met him once at a conference in Geneva."

"You met my father?" said Justine. She sounded —startled, nonplussed. Her fork clattered against the side of her plate.

"He was a brilliant student," said the man in black who must be the Count, because he looked exactly as one would expect a count to look, if he had lived for hundreds of years and was a vampire. Or had been infected with vampirism, as Carmilla preferred to put it. Mary had no idea what to think. Why was he holding Mina's hand? And what did *kedvesem* mean? Carmilla had used that word for Laura, back at the schloss. What there something between the Count and Miss Murray?

He bowed to Justine as well. "There are those who believe that his experiments were foolish, that he should never have meddled with the material of life itself. But that was a different time—we felt that we were bringing light to a world still tainted by the darkness of medievalism. Mina would argue that we were wrong, but how can one judge the past by the standards of the present day? Victor was a brilliant young man, and I was sorry to hear of his death. He would have been proud of such a charming, intelligent daughter."

"Thank you," said Justine, looking both pleased and embarrassed.

"I'm so sorry," said Mina. "I haven't properly introduced you. Mary, Justine, this is my friend Vladimír Árpád István, Count Dracula. If everyone is finished, perhaps we can move this discussion to my study? It will take some time, and I think we will be more comfortable there."

"Excellent," said the Count. "Then I shall order—what are you drinking? Coffee, Miss Frankenstein? And for you, Miss Jekyll? Well, more coffee, then, to be brought into your drawing room."

"It really is a study, *not* a drawing room," Mina said after he had gone, presumably to order more coffee for them. "The Count is old-fashioned in some ways. Sometimes I have to keep him from treating me like an aristocratic lady, circa 1600! Seriously, he's going to turn me into a socialist. Come on, it's on the other side of the courtyard."

Mary followed her out of the dining room and into the hallway. On one side, it had windows that looked down into the courtyard where Carmilla had parked her motorcar the night before. On the other side were doors that presumably opened into rooms like the one they had just come out of. The house seemed to be arranged around that courtyard. She walked down the hall, not quite knowing what to think. Mina looked just like the Miss Murray she had known in London, who had taught her the multiplication tables and the major capitals of Europe. Yet here she was in Budapest, in an old, run-down palace, with this aristocratic man who clearly had some sort of understanding with her. Mary felt a sudden longing for England and Mrs. Poole.

Sunlight streamed in through the tall windows. She walked with Mina while Justine hung back a bit, looking at the paintings.

"Most houses in Budapest are built like this," Mina continued. "There's usually a courtyard in the center where the carriages turn around, with the carriage house and stables in back. This hallway goes all the way around on the inside, so if you get lost, just follow the hall—eventually it will get you wherever you want to go. Of course, there's almost always a servant to direct you. Honestly, I can't get used to having so many. Three footmen, plus one in training! I asked Vlad why he has so many footmen, and he said they were needed to stand decoratively behind the chairs at dinner, and also to get drunk on his wine! I *think* he was teasing, but he always says everything with such a straight face that I can't be sure."

"It's quite a change from the days when we would sit in the parlor and mend stockings together!" said Mary. She smiled, in part because she was afraid what she had said would sound judgmental. It was no business of hers who Mina chose to associate with. And if she was a little discomfited, well, she must try not to show it.

"Oh goodness, you don't think I've given up mending stockings, do you?" Mina looked shocked. "This is all well and good"—she gestured around, as though indicating the palace as a whole, with its marble staircase, its paintings of sour-faced ancestors, its footmen—"but I'm almost broke. Van Helsing never paid me for chaperoning Lucinda, and I spent my last krone getting out of Vienna as quickly as possible once he discovered who I was really working for. I have a small income from that particular employer—but it's scarcely enough to keep me in stockings and *papier poudré*. I'm fortunate the Count is letting me stay here, but none of this is mine. Look." She stopped, bent down, and lifted the hem of her dress so Mary could see the underside. It was obvious that the dress had been turned—taken apart and then reconstructed, with the former outside now on the inside. That side was considerably more faded than the side now showing. No wonder the dress looked so smart and respectable!

"But I thought you and the Count . . ." Mary did not quite know how to say it. Had she somehow misinterpreted their easy familiarity? Perhaps such things had a different meaning in Europe.

"Oh, that, yes." Mina smiled, as though amused that Mary was being so reticent. "It is what you think—there is an understanding between us. Which is why I won't take any money from him. It's, shall we say, a matter of honor."

Ah, there was the old Miss Murray after all! That, at least, was reassuring.

"Justine?" Mina called back. "How are you finding the pictures?"

"Very interesting, thank you," said Justine.

Mina laughed. "My dear, I'm sure you have many skills, but lying isn't one of them. They are dreadful, aren't they? A regular procession of Draculas, who were unpleasant people, for the most part. Well, most aristocrats were unpleasant back then—killing each other, raiding each other's territories, marrying off their daughters for land or gold."

"I do like the landscapes," said Justine defensively, joining them once again. "Some of them remind me of Switzerland. Although of course I would prefer them without the hunting scenes. I do not understand the slaughter of animals for sport."

"You really are the best of us," said Mary in a low voice, giving Justine's hand a quick squeeze. Amid so much that was strange, she was glad of a familiar face, a familiar system of values. Justine could always be relied upon.

"Ah, here we are," said Mina. "My study." The Count was leaning on the wall next to the door, reading a letter. Standing beside him was a maid in a uniform with a stiff white cap, holding a tray with a coffeepot and cups. "You could have gone in without me," said Mina, opening the door.

"I told you this was your room, beloved—I would not enter it without your permission," he replied, a little stiffly Mary thought.

Mina took the tray from the maid, said "Köszönöm, Kati," and went in. The Count stood by the door and waited until they had all filed in, then entered and closed the door behind him.

Mina's study was not large, but there was room in it for a desk covered with neat stacks of paper and two armchairs in front of the fireplace. There were bookshelves along every wall, filled with books of every description—some of them serious scientific tomes, some travel guides, some novels—as well as stacks of journals and magazines. Sunlight came through one large window, brighter than English sunlight but less harsh than the sunlight of Vienna.

CATHERINE: Of all the rooms we saw in our travels, the only one I envied was Mina's study.

"Please sit down, all of you." Mina put the coffee tray on a low table between the armchairs.

Mary sat in one of the armchairs and poured herself another cup of coffee. Usually she would not have two, but this morning, she needed it. Justine stood hesitating, but Mina pulled out the desk chair and sat on that, so she sat in the other armchair and looked around her, at the book titles. The Count remained standing and leaned back against the desk.

"What about Carmilla and Laura?" asked Mary. "Should they not be here as well?"

"They are testing a hypothesis of mine," said the Count. "I will explain later. First, I think we need to hear from Mina. *Kedvesem*, will you begin? Unless you wish me to. . . ."

"No, I'd better start," said Mina. Suddenly, she looked very serious. "I'm going to tell you a story, and I'm afraid you're not going to like it, either of you."

What in the world could she mean? Mary looked at Justine, in the other armchair. She had her hands clasped on her lap and was listening intently. Well, Mary would follow her example. She leaned back against the cushion, took another sip of coffee—really, coffee seemed the appropriate beverage for continental adventures, tea was simply not strong enough—and prepared to listen.

"You must understand, first, that my father was a university professor," said Mina. "He was an early supporter of Darwin's theory of evolution and natural selection, although he held, with Wallace, that consciousness in man was given by God—natural selection alone, he maintained, could not have created such a complex phenomenon. He was also a believer in spiritualism, which sometimes put him in conflict with his scientific colleagues. My mother died when I was young, bearing her second child, who did not survive. I think he believed in the spirit world from the hope that he could someday contact her, that her consciousness, at least, had survived in some form. After her death, he left the University of London, where he had been teaching, and moved to one of the new women's colleges springing up in the countryside—Blackwood Women's College, it was called, after Eugenia Blackwood, a wool-merchant's widow and ardent suffragist who had founded it in the 1870s. My mother had been a firm proponent of education for women, a New Woman before her time, and he wanted to honor her memory. I grew up in the heady excitement of women allowed to experience higher education. He would hire students to be my nurses and tutors, and himself undertook to teach me the natural sciences. When the time came, I matriculated—my time at Blackwood was, I can say without hesitation, the happiest of my life. Living and learning with other women in those old brick buildings, strolling across the lawn discussing literature, philosophy, art. . . . We were young, and so very hopeful that a new era was coming for our sisters, whether they were fine ladies doing the London season or factory girls in Manchester. Time has proven us partly right."

For a moment, Mina was silent. She had a smile on her lips and a look in her eyes, as though she were very far away, on the green lawns of her college once more. Mary could not help envying her. No one had ever considered educating her in that way.

"During my final year at college," Mina continued, "my father became ill with a lung complaint. I told him I could leave school for a year to nurse him, but he would not allow it—he told me that I must never take my opportunities for granted or stop working toward my goals. Not long before graduation, he died. He was never able to see my diploma." Quickly, almost surreptitiously, Mina wiped her eyes. The Count put one hand on her shoulder, as though to comfort her.

"So I left Blackwood Women's College, alone in the world and unsure what to do with myself. Our only source of income was my father's salary, and our meager savings had been spent on his medical bills. I would need to work, which for a woman of my class and educational status meant either governessing or teaching in a school for girls. Where would I go? I applied at an employment agency and, while waiting to hear back, cleaned out the house I had shared with my father for so many years, cataloging our possessions for sale. If I sold most of our things, it would give me a sum I could put in the bank for emergencies. Our lease was up at the end of the month. Mentally, I prepared to move on with my life.

"One day, I heard the front door bell. Minutes later, the daily woman, a Mrs. Higgins, came up to the attic, where I was going through old trunks, and said, 'Miss Murray, there's a gentleman here to see you. Says he knew your father in London.'

"I went down to the parlor. There, standing next to the fireplace, was an older man with white whiskers, in an old-fashioned frock coat.

"'Miss Murray,' he said. 'Please accept my condolences. I was deeply grieved to hear of Professor Murray's passing.'

"'Did you know my father?' I asked. 'Mr. . . .'

"'Dr. Faraday. Simeon Faraday, at your service. Yes, we were both members of the Royal Society. At one time, he was very active on a subcommittee I chair—the Subcommittee on Bibliographic Citation Format. I don't suppose he's ever mentioned it to you?'

"I had known, of course, that my father was a member of the Royal Society, although he had not attended a meeting or been active for many years. And a Subcommittee on Bibliographic Citation Format sounded exactly like the sort of body he would join—he was always a stickler for correct, exacting scholarship.

"I asked Dr. Faraday to please sit down, and told Mrs. Higgins to bring us tea. After some pleasantries and reminiscences of my father, he leaned forward, put his elbows on his knees, and said, 'Miss Murray, I did not come here solely to express my condolences. I also came to offer you an employment opportunity. Forgive me for interrupting your time of grief with business, but would you be willing to hear what I have to offer?'

"'Dr. Faraday,' I said. 'I am a woman alone in the world, eager to prove myself useful and make an independent living. If you know of a place for someone with my qualifications, I would be grateful for any information, and perhaps a recommendation.'

"'It is, indeed, because of your qualifications that I am here,' he said. 'When my fellow members of the Subcommittee on Bibliographic Citation Format were searching for a suitable candidate for the position we have in mind, I immediately said, what about Murray's daughter? The subcommittee voted unanimously that we should put our proposition before you.'

"Mrs. Higgins had brought in tea, and I poured out, wondering what sort of employment opportunity a subcommittee of the Royal Society could possibly have for me.

"For a moment, he looked at me seriously, from under a particularly bushy set of white eyebrows. Then he said, 'Miss Murray, have you ever heard of the Société des Alchimistes?'"

Mary leaned forward. *What* had Mina just said? Had she heard it correctly?

"Then you knew of the Alchemical Society before you became Mary's governess," said Justine.

"Yes," said Mina simply. "I knew."

"I don't understand," said Mary. "Do you mean that you knew about the Alchemical Society all along? All the time you were my governess? And did you know that my father . . ."

"Yes," said Mina again. "I knew. In order to explain, I need to tell you what Professor Faraday told me that spring morning, and what I learned later in my work with the subcommittee. You see, almost from the founding of the Royal Society in the seventeenth century, a group of the fellows felt the need to combat and contest what they felt to be false or unethical science—to expose fraud, to investigate and stop abuse. Only in this way could the legitimacy of genuine, beneficial science be maintained. The fellows knew that such unorthodox activities brought science into disrepute. So a committee was formed for such purposes—to debunk taxidermed monstrosities and ineffective nostrums. However, debunking fakes was not the most important task of the committee—more important was combating the use of science for nefarious ends. In this, the committee's most constant adversary was the Société des Alchimistes."

"And this committee—," said Justine.

"Was initially named the Committee on Scientific Fraud and Abuse. But in the early nineteenth century, after the Frankenstein scandal—for the Société des Alchimistes could not hush up entirely the rumor that one of its members had created a monster—it was thought best to keep the work of the committee secret. Science was growing more respectable, but also more powerful, and the Royal Society did not want it known that such atrocities could be committed in the name of discovery and knowledge. Better to deal with them quietly, to keep the public unaware. So it was renamed the Subcommittee on Bibliographic Citation Format, although its mission remained the same."

"Why in the world—," said Mary.

"Was it named that? Because if you heard there was a meeting of the Subcommittee on Bibliographic Citation Format, would you ask to attend? Well, you might, Mary, with your precise mind! But I assure you that most people would not. That day, Professor Faraday told me the subcommittee needed a young woman, an educated young woman, to perform a particular task. He explained it to me, and asked if I would be willing."

"What was that task?" asked Justine. Mary glanced at her, startled. Had she ever heard that tone in Justine's voice? She sounded . . . angry. Could Justine be angry?

"You must understand," said Mina, "that the subcommittee's purpose is to safeguard the reputation of genuine scientific effort. It does not often interfere. What it does is observe and, if necessary, rectify the situation as unobtrusively as possible. When it heard a rumor about a giantess roaming the coast of Cornwall, it sent one of its agents to investigate. William Pengelly found this giantess living peacefully in an abandoned manor house, subsisting on fruits and vegetables."

"My friend Guillaume!" said Justine. "Are you saying that he was—"

"Yes," said Mina. "He was working for the subcommittee. I have seen his report—it's twenty typed pages, with a final recommendation."

"What did he recommend?" asked Mary. This conversation was sending shivers up her back—she felt prickles along her arms. *Someone walking over your grave,* is what Cook would have said, remembering old Yorkshire superstitions.

"Pengelly recommended that Justine be left alone, and that

the subcommittee protect her in any way it could. Which it did."
Mina turned to Justine. "Why do you think no one disturbed you
in all that time? You were protected in ways you did not know.
From curious poachers, from heirs who wanted to break the entail
on the property . . ."

Justine shook her head. "I do not know what to say. All that
time . . . and Guillaume, whom I thought was my friend."

"He was," said Mina. "It was because of his report that you
remained undisturbed for almost a century."

"And what would the subcommittee have done if Mr. Pengelly
had made a different recommendation?" asked Mary.

"It would have rectified the situation," said Mina, mildly.
"Mary, I can see that you're about to protest. I assure you that the
subcommittee only acts when it absolutely must. It did nothing to
harm Justine."

"But it could have?" said Mary.

Mina looked at her steadily, seriously. "Yes."

"And what about this task you mentioned?" asked Justine. "Was
it—"

"What Dr. Faraday asked me to do," Mina continued, "was
apply for a post as governess in the house of the late Dr. Henry
Jekyll. I was to watch and see if the notorious Mr. Hyde returned.
I was told of Jekyll's experiments, of how the respectable chemist
was also Hyde. If I saw even a shadow of him, I was to inform the
subcommittee at once."

"You spied on me!" said Mary. She stared at Mina incredulously.

"Yes, I did," replied Mina. "And I can't apologize to you, as my
apology would not be sincere. I was fulfilling my responsibilities
to the subcommittee, and carrying out the task for which I was
hired—work that my father would have approved. I'm sorry, Mary,
for shocking you with this revelation. I know it's difficult for you to
learn that I deceived you, but unfortunately that is the case."

"Then, all that time . . . ," said Mary, not quite knowing what to believe, what was true or not anymore.

"I can tell you that everything I taught you—history, geography, literature—all that was real. My affection for you was real. But on Thursdays, which were my half-days off, I would go down to Burlington House in Piccadilly, where the Royal Society has its offices, and report to Dr. Faraday. There was never much to report. You were a delightful, intelligent child. Perhaps overly conscientious—too calm, controlled, and reasonable for your age. But like Justine, you posed no danger, and Hyde never attempted to contact you. We did not know, then, about Diana, or we would have had an agent inside the Society of St. Mary Magdalen as well. When you had to let me go so you could afford a permanent nurse for your mother, it was with real sorrow that I left. Teaching you was one of the great privileges of my life."

"Oh," said Mary. She had no idea what to say, or even think. More than anything, she felt a profound sense of disappointment, and also of displacement. Was any facet of her life not affected by her father's experiments? Perhaps she would discover that Mrs. Poole was an agent of the Alchemical Society, or that Alice had been created through scientific experimentation! Was nothing in this world stable and ordinary?

> MRS. POOLE: I understand your reaction, miss. You
> must have been in a state of shock. But to think of
> *me* as an agent of those evil men! For evil is what I
> call them, despite their fancy titles—doctors and
> professors! Evil is as evil does, I say. I'm glad you
> girls are—well, that you *are*, however you came
> to be. But I would not give any of those alchemical
> johnnies the time of day.

ALICE: The thought of me being created by
alchemists! I'm an ordinary girl, like any other.

MARY: Not quite ordinary. An ordinary girl can't
disappear, among other things.

ALICE: But mesmerical powers are entirely natural.
Martin has them, and he's not a monster—just a
man who's different from others. Like Atlas being
tall and strong, or the Jellicoe twins being able to
tie themselves in knots.

MARY: If you say so, Alice.

"And do you still work for this organization?" asked Justine.

Mina drank the rest of her coffee, then put the cup down on
the desk. *She's stalling,* thought Mary. *What doesn't she want to say?*
With obvious reluctance, Mina said, "I am currently employed by
the Subcommittee on Bibliographic Citation Format. The position
allows me to draw a small salary, and it is of course why I am here
in Budapest, with Vlad. After I left Mary's employ, the subcommittee asked me to teach at Whitby Ladies' Academy on the Yorkshire
coast, so I could keep an eye on a student named Lucy Westenra.
Her father, Lord Westenra, had been one of the financial backers
of the English chapter of the Alchemical Society. He had recently
died, but his wife, Lady Westenra, was continuing his contributions. Haunted by her husband's death, she was interested in ways
of prolonging life. It was she who urged the Purfleet Asylum to
hire Seward, so he could learn more about poor Renfield and his
experiments with spiders and flies. Dr. Hennessey, the assistant
director, who was also a member, had told her about his peculiar-
ities. And it was she who introduced Seward to Van Helsing. You

see, the English chapter had been disbanded after the murder of
Sir Danvers Carew threatened to expose the Alchemical Society
and its activities to the public. But there was a group of younger
members who refused to give up: Seward and Arthur Holmwood
were its leaders. Holmwood was a young aristocrat with plenty of
money—he is now Lord Godalming, and remains involved with
the society only indirectly, as one of the trustees of the Purfleet
Asylum. Seward and Holmwood were joined by Jonathan Harker,
a young solicitor whose firm represented the Holmwoods, and
an American named Quincy Morris, an adventurer who was not
particularly interested in science. He had hunted grizzly bears and
bison in the American west, traveled up to the icy lands of the
Arctic, and trekked through South American jungles, so why not
search for the secret of eternal life? It was yet another adventure.

"I befriended Lucy. That too was a true friendship, Mary,
although you may well doubt my sincerity, after all I have told you.

"Lucy was not like you. She did not particularly care for study.
She was interested in dresses and parties and flirting with eligible
bachelors. And why should she not be? She was young, beautiful,
and wealthy, destined to become a society lady, perhaps even a
political wife. She was not at all intellectual—she preferred magazines and French novels to history or philosophy. At the same
time, she was romantic, idealistic, and generous to a fault—
deeply stirred by the suffering of others. I once saw her give her
gloves to a girl on the street who was selling roasted chestnuts and
burning her fingertips. The travails of a cart-horse could bring her
to tears, and cabbies dared not use their whips around her, for fear
of a lecture. She had a great deal to learn about the world, but her
instincts were sound. In the sphere of life into which she had been
born, she could have made a real difference.

"We became friends, and when she left Whitby Academy, she
asked me to come with her as a paid companion. So I entered the

social world of the Westenras, in their house on Curzon Street. And that was where I met Seward, Holmwood, Morris, and Jonathan Harker, who would become my husband."

"Your husband!" said Mary.

"Yes. I am married." Mina looked down at the coffee cup in her hands. Mary noticed that she wore no rings at all. "I am, technically, Mrs. Jonathan Harker. I have asked him for a divorce, but he has refused to grant me one, despite the considerable evidence of my desertion and . . . disloyalty. He believes that someday I will get over this madness, as he calls it, and return to him. Return to being a solicitor's wife in Exeter. After what I saw—after what they did, those men who wanted to live forever, and who were willing to sacrifice anything, or anyone, to prove their theories."

The study was so quiet. Sunlight streamed through the windows, shining on motes of dust. Somehow, in that stillness, it felt as though Mary's ideas about the world, and Mina specifically, were tilting and whirling, like a ride at the country fair.

DIANA: Mary's never been to a country fair.

CATHERINE: Yes, well, I have. There were often fairs around the circus as we traveled throughout England.

DIANA: I'm just saying, you're supposed to be in her point of view here.

CATHERINE: Oh, so suddenly you're a writer!

DIANA: You're the one who told us about point of view. Why even have writing rules if you're going to break them all the time?

"But why did you marry Mr. Harker if you knew of his involvement with the Société des Alchimistes?" asked Justine.

"I did not realize at the time how involved he was," said Mina. "I knew that Lady Westenra had invited Professor Van Helsing to come to England from his native Amsterdam. He stayed at the house on Curzon Street for several days, then joined Dr. Seward in Purfleet. And I knew the men were up to *something* at the asylum. Mr. Holmwood kept going out there, as did Quincy Morris. I thought Jonathan was just Holmwood's solicitor. He was so earnest, so determined to do well in his career! When Lucy walked with Arthur Holmwood in Hyde Park, I would walk with Jonathan, ostensibly chaperoning her. He was interested in the political and technological developments of the day. And he too had lost his parents—we had that in common. Slowly, I fell in love with him, and he with me. There was an innocence about him, a loneliness, a need . . . He needed me, I thought, and I needed him as well. I had never been in love before. It was a delightful new sensation—to be loved and to love in return, to believe that I would spend my life with someone. After we were married, I decided, I would no longer work for the Subcommittee on Bibliographic Citation Format. I would concentrate on being a good wife, a helpful partner for a rising young solicitor. I was—younger than I am now, and perhaps naive. I missed the signs that there was something going on."

"What sort of thing?" asked Justine.

Mina looked up at the Count. "He'll have to tell you—at least part of it, since I didn't know at the time. But Seward had found out about Vlad's experiments with blood transfusion—from Renfield, you know. He had pieced together the madman's ravings, and Van Helsing had asked around, discreetly, among the membership. Some of the older members of the Société des Alchimistes still remembered a paper Vlad had given forty years before on the possibility of transfusing vampiric blood. He found the paper in the archives of the society, and then . . . he contacted Vlad." She reached one hand out to the Count, who took it. "You'll have to tell this part, my dear. You know it better than I do."

He smiled, but it was a bitter smile. "I do not appear to advantage in it, do I, beloved? Well, we shall not worry about my vanity. Van Helsing contacted me through a mutual acquaintance, the linguist and ethnologist Arminius—or Ármin, in Hungarian—Vámbéry. He asked me to come to England. He thought that with his methods—for he had been researching the transfusion of blood for many years, and was considered an expert on the subject—we could transfer the positive aspects of vampirism without the madness that is its almost inevitable result. I arranged for the purchase of an old manor house behind the Purfleet Asylum—Carfax, it was called. Mr. Harker came out to my castle in Transylvania, to bring me the deed and help me transport some delicate apparatus as well as a number of notebooks."

"I should have seen it then," said Mina. "I was so stupid! Everything seemed normal. Lucy was preparing for her wedding day, as I was preparing for mine while Jonathan was away. Hers would be a grand affair—half the fashionable people in London were invited, it seemed. I still remember her dress of Carrickmacross lace over white silk—the Westenras traced their ancestry to that area of Ireland. It was dreadfully impractical—when could she wear it again? But all the society girls were marrying in white, as the Queen had done. My much more modest brown silk would serve me well on the honeymoon we were planning to take in Cornwall. There was a great deal for me to do in anticipation of Lucy's wedding—I was needed to address invitations, help her select the flowers and music, pacify six bridesmaids, each of whom wanted to dress in a style that was flattering to her individually. And then of course there was her mother—Lady Westenra was an impulsive, impractical woman who loved her daughter, but was completely under the influence of Van Helsing. Her husband had believed in him, so she did as well—unfortunately. Dr. Faraday had warned me about Van Helsing, but at that time we knew very little about his activities, apart from the papers he had published—as far as we knew, they were relatively orthodox, dealing with the uncertainty of blood transfusion in medical situations. Why did it sometimes work and sometimes not? Van Helsing thought there might be factors in the blood that had not yet been discovered. . . . If only I had known his real interest! I might have averted the eventual disaster.

"When Jonathan returned, we were married in a quiet ceremony, with Lucy as my sole bridesmaid. I handed in my final report to Dr. Faraday, who urged me to continue monitoring the situation. But no, I told him. I wanted to be a wife, and someday a mother. He would have to find someone else to spy for him. That night, Lady Westenra held a small party for us—just Holmwood, Seward, Morris, Van Helsing, and a friend of his who had recently moved to England—a Count Dracula."

"That was the first time I saw you," said the Count.

"You frowned at me the entire evening," said Mina. "I remember looking up several times—I was seated next to Mr. Morris, who kept going on and on about a hunting trip to the Brazilian Republic. I was bored by his exploits, which consisted of shooting a great many things along the banks of the Amazon—monkeys and pumas and snakes. Each time I looked up, you were staring at me from under those dark eyebrows, as disapprovingly as possible!"

"But I *was* disapproving!" said the Count. "Here was a beautiful, intelligent woman, who had just that day married Harker, a man I had already classified as a harmless idiot! Oh, he was a gentleman—he could talk well enough about points of law or what he had read in *Punch*. He had been informative about British politics and customs on our trip from Transylvania to London. But within a year or two, he would begin to bore you. You would see his intellectual narrowness, his provincialism. Additionally, I had already decided that you and I were destined for each other. Your marriage to him was an unfortunate, but hopefully temporary, obstacle."

"Destined!" said Mina. She laughed, as though despite herself. "There speaks the romantic Hungarian! And also the arrogant Count, who thinks he can simply take whatever he pleases. Did you think I would have no say in the matter?"

He answered mildly, "I recognized that if we were indeed destined, you must accept that for yourself. You would come to me in your own time, and not before. I had only to wait. And in any event, I had other worries to consider. Van Helsing had been conducting tests on my blood. Soon, he would begin transfusing it into Lucy. She said she was willing—but she was so young, and it was obvious to me that she was influenced in her decision by her fiancé. Her mother, who might have counseled her otherwise, was unaware of what we were doing. Lady Westenra did not understand the details of Van Helsing's research—she merely wanted to continue what her husband had started, and indeed Van Helsing himself concealed information from her. She had a heart condition—he said our methods might shock her, even if she agreed with our aims."

"And what were those methods?" asked Justine. There it was again, the anger in her voice, and beneath it, a deep disgust. It startled Mary out of her own sense of loss, her sense that somehow she had lived her entire childhood without understanding anything. First she had heard her father's confession, and now Mina's. Had nothing been the way she thought it was? She felt curiously numb, as one does when a wound has gone so deep that one does not feel it, our nerves being on the surface. A surface wound will hurt us more than a deeper blow.

The Count responded to Justine as a surgeon might, when you ask how he performs his surgery—in calm, clinical tones. "He would withdraw my blood, then filter it—he thought the madness of vampirism was caused by certain impurities he had identified. Then, when he was certain the blood was pure, he would inject it into Miss Westenra. Already at that time she was beginning to change—"

"I remember her at that party," said Mina, once again wrapping both hands around the coffee cup as though they were cold. "She looked almost feverish. I ascribed it to the excitement of the upcoming wedding. I should have known—I should have stayed! I will always blame myself for missing the signs, for not suspecting she might be the subject of some experiment. After all, Dr. Faraday had warned me about Van Helsing. But I did not think Lady Westenra would do anything to hurt Lucy, and at the time, I had never heard of vampirism. The next morning, Jonathan and I left on our honeymoon. A week later, we returned to Exeter, to a new semidetached house Jonathan had rented, for we could not yet afford to purchase. I was ready to furnish and decorate it, to make it a home for us. . . ." She sat silent for a moment, looking down at her coffee cup. "But there were letters waiting for me. Three from Lucy—the first ordinary, if a bit distracted, but what girl would not be distracted before her wedding? The second rambling—she mentioned nightmares in which she swam through rivers of blood. The third—she spoke of being in hell, of burning in hellfire. She said that she was surrounded by demons who wanted to drink her blood and eat her soul. I showed them to Jonathan. He said there was nothing to worry about, since Van Helsing was there—if Lucy was ill, he would surely be treating her. It was not what he said, but the way he said it—I remember we were standing in the kitchen, for I had not yet hired a maid-of-all-work, and he looked away from me, out the window into the back alley. That was when

I began to suspect that he knew . . . and had not told me what Van Helsing and Seward were attempting. I sent a telegram to Dr. Faraday and bought a ticket on the next train to London.

"When I arrived at the house on Curzon Street, it was already too late." She looked up at the Count. "I think you should describe this part. You were there—I came later, too late to save dear Lucy."

"Alas, I was there, but still I could not save her," he said ruefully. "I told them they were going too far, too fast. It was obvious to me that Miss Westenra was slipping into madness. Hennessy, who was assisting, also remonstrated—he was beginning to question their methods and aims. But Seward and Van Helsing refused to halt their experiments, and Holmwood, who believed in Van Helsing, was all for pressing forward. Morris did not care either way so long as it was an adventure. Since they would not listen to me, I told Lady Westenra. Both she and Lucy had come to stay at Carfax, in order to facilitate Van Helsing's experiments. If she could understand the seriousness of the situation, perhaps she could persuade him to stop. She had, at least, the power to cut his funding. I still remember the day I brought her into the room where they were injecting Lucy with more of my filtered blood. She looked at the chair into which her daughter was strapped— for Lucy became delirious during the transfusions, and she was gaining in strength. Van Helsing was afraid that while in that state, she might try to attack us. Lady Westenra saw the men around her daughter—respectable, scientific men. She saw her daughter open her eyes, look at Van Helsing, and scream. I have mentioned that Lady Westenra had a weak heart. At that moment, she clutched at her chest and collapsed onto the stone floor. She struggled to speak, but could get out nothing. Her hands waved ineffectually in the air. Seward rushed to her, but there was nothing he could do—in a few moments, she was dead. Van Helsing was angry, hysterical. He accused me of interfering with his experiment. Morris

pulled the large kukri knife that he always wore out of its leather
scabbard and stabbed me in the chest. Such a wound could not
kill me, but it could weaken me. They dragged me down to the
cellar and locked me there, in what had once been a storage room,
without aid or nourishment. Then I believe they returned to the
laboratory upstairs. . . . I do not know, but that is what I conjecture. And they found Lucy gone. She had burst her restraints,
drained the blood of her dead mother, and departed.

"I was in that cellar room for three days. By the end, I was delirious with hunger and loss of blood. If Mina had not shown up . . ."

"You would not have seen your four hundred and sixty-third
birthday," said Mina grimly.

"She gave me her own blood," said the Count. "Without her,
I would not be alive." He reached out his hand, as though to take
hers again. "You see, I knew from the moment I saw you that we
were destined for each other."

"I won't allow you to tell this as a love story," said Mina. She
did not take his hand in response. "It's a tragedy. What they did—
what you all did—was indefensible. And yes, I know you tried to
stop them, but I lost a friend and pupil. My poor, dear Lucy . . ."

"What happened to Lucy? I mean, after she escaped," said
Mary. But she almost did not want to know. Whatever had happened to Lucy was also happening to Lucinda. Would events
repeat themselves?

Mina put her coffee cup on the table. Mary could see that
the coffee was still only half drunk—and probably cold. "They
chopped her head off. I'm sorry, I don't know how to say that any
more gently. Somehow, she had made her way to Hampstead. I
suppose some sort of instinct drew her back to London. . . . The
police began finding children on the heath with puncture marks
on their throats. They talked about the beautiful lady in white
who would ask them to come for a walk. One little girl said she

was so pretty, she must be a princess from a fairy tale. I know because it was reported in the *Westminster Gazette*, but I did not see that article until later—all I knew was that Lucy had escaped, and they had gone after her. I told Vlad to leave England as quickly as possible—before Van Helsing and the others returned. I was sure they would return—after all, they would need his blood for their infernal experiments. Then, I went to the asylum and asked when Seward was expected back. Tomorrow, Dr. Hennessey told me, so I took a room in the Royal Hotel for the night. The next morning, I returned to the asylum and waited. Lunch came and went—the attendants gave me soup and bread, which I ate with some of the patients—a Lady Hollingston who had murdered her husband, and several other examples of *femina deliquente*. It was early afternoon before Seward returned with Holmwood, Morris, and Van Helsing. I remember sitting in his office at the asylum while he asked me, suspiciously, where I had been, what I had seen. I told him I had been so worried by Lucy's letters that I had come up by the first train, and not finding them at the asylum, had gone to Carfax. There, I had seen the laboratory they had set up. I had found the Count, but he had attacked me—I could show the mark on my wrist where I had given him my blood as evidence of an attack. And then, he had escaped. Where was Lucy, I asked Seward. Why had her letters been so strange, so disjointed? I looked around at those men, standing there so sure of themselves—Holmwood staring out the window, Morris leaning against a filing cabinet—with concern and dismay. I did not want to betray that I knew what they were, what sorts of experiments they were engaged in.

"Seward seemed relieved that I did not know more, and explained it all to me in the most reasonable terms. They had been conducting an important experiment in blood transfusion, attempting to cure the Count of a dread disease—the blood disease of vampirism, which turned its victims mad. Lucy and Lady

Westenra had been most interested, and had come to see their procedures. But the Count, whose disease had progressed more than they anticipated, had attacked and infected Lucy—her mother had died of the shock. Now Lucy was out there somewhere, with vampiric blood in her veins. They must stop her before she too became that dreaded thing—a vampire!

"I pretended to accept their story. But inside, I was seething with anger. If I could have summoned lightning to strike them down at that moment, I would have. It would have given me pleasure to see their smoldering ashes. Instead, I told them I would go to London and wait at the house on Curzon Street, in case Lucy should return there. Seward seemed relieved. If I had only known that they were planning on hunting her that night! I took the train to London—it was late afternoon by the time I arrived at Fenchurch Street Station, but I went directly to Dr. Faraday's house in Bloomsbury. It was he who showed me the article in the *Westminster Gazette*. After I had tendered my resignation from the Subcommittee on Bibliographic Citation Format, there had been no one to keep an eye on Lucy directly, but a member of the subcommittee who lived near Hampstead Heath had brought the article to his attention. He had already summoned the members, who were meeting the next day. I told him I would come to Burlington House at the appointed time, and took a cab to Curzon Street. There was still a chance that Lucy might decide to come back home, and I did not know what else to do—wandering around Hampstead Heath by myself at night was unlikely to be useful! But that was the night they killed her."

"Chopped her head off!" said Diana. She was standing at the door, with her hand on the collar of a beautiful white dog, one of the Count's wolfdogs no doubt. "What did they chop it off with, and did it roll on the ground afterward?"

"How long have you been standing there?" asked Mary.

"You didn't even notice me!" said Diana, scornfully. "None of you, except the Count—he's known the whole time. That's why you winked at me, didn't you?" She walked into the room and stood in front of Count Dracula. "You knew as soon as I opened the door. And I thought I was so quiet!"

The Count smiled. "You smell of wolfdog and breakfast, mixed. It is a good smell, but a distinctive one. I think Hóvirág here likes you. That is a kind of flower, the *hóvirág*. It is as white as snow."

"Well, as long as I smell *distinctive*. Now, why did they chop off her head? I want to hear this part." She sat down on the carpet in front of the fireplace. Hóvirág lay down beside her and put her head in Diana's lap. She seemed to have accepted Diana as her mistress.

"How much have you heard, Diana?" asked Mina. "I don't want to repeat myself."

"From the chopping her head off part. So she was a vampire, was she?"

"It is more accurate to say that she had contracted the disease of vampirism," said Mina.

"You are splitting threads, *kedvesem*," said the Count. "Whether or not you call us vampires makes little difference."

"Splitting hairs," said Mina. "It's hairs. I'm not going to argue with you about semantics, not now." She sounded impatient and a little angry. "The point is . . ."

"Why did they chop her head off?" asked Diana again. She was seated right by Mary's feet. Should Mary kick her? The thought was tempting.

> DIANA: I wish you'd tried it! Hoho would have bitten your foot off.

"They chopped her head off because vampires are difficult to kill," said the Count. "Vampirism destroys the mind, but it makes the body stronger. It is able to heal from wounds that would kill a man. If you wish to kill a vampire, you cannot simply stab him through the heart, or shoot him in the head, or even break his neck by hanging. You must wound him in a way that makes it impossible for healing to occur. Decapitation is one such way. Or the vampire can be burned. In my native Transylvania, burning was one of the traditional ways to kill both vampires and witches."

"There are witches?" said Diana.

"No, of course not," said Mina. "Only poor old women accused of making a pact with the devil because the other villagers fear or dislike them. Diana, I appreciate your curiosity, but if you want to find out what happened to Lucy—"

"All right, I'll be quiet," said Diana, frowning. Then, she added with more interest, "Did they burn her up too?"

"She lies in the Westenra vault," said Mina. "Van Helsing himself signed her death certificate, as well as her mother's. I stayed in London for the funeral, then went back to Exeter, back to Jonathan. Dr. Faraday had told me to look through his papers, even though I assured him that Jonathan knew nothing, that he had no knowledge of the experiments. I was wrong— Holmwood had described what they intended to do in the letters instructing Jonathan to go to Transylvania and assist Count Dracula with the purchase of Carfax. Jonathan had not known everything, but he had known enough. I did not confront him with the letters—that would have alerted him to my involvement with the subcommittee. I merely told him that our marriage was a mistake and that I was leaving him. And then . . . well, I left. I returned to London, to Dr. Faraday and the Subcommittee on Bibliographic Citation Format, determined to stop Van Helsing. I swore that I would watch and wait, and that someday, somehow, I would avenge Lucy's death."

"But Mrs. Van Helsing wasn't decapitated, or any of those

other things," said Mary. "She was bitten through the throat, and then she died. If she was a vampire—"

"Creating a vampire through blood transfusion introduces additional uncertainties," said the Count. "Renfield went mad without becoming a vampire. Lucy transformed, but the procedure accelerated the effects of vampiric madness. We do not know exactly what Van Helsing did to his wife and daughter, or how it affected the transformation process. Whose blood was he using? And how did he process it before transfusion? Theoretically, all blood infected with vampirism should work in the same way. However, it seems clear that Mrs. Van Helsing's transformation was incomplete. In the last few days, Lucinda has drunk my blood as well as Carmilla's. We can only pray—those of us who pray— that when she wakes, she will have both the strength of vampirism and her sanity intact."

"I would knock, but the door's open. Judging from that last sentence, I seem to have come at exactly the right time."

Who had said that? Mary turned her head, trying to find the source of the statement. It was Laura, standing at the door.

She stepped into the room, looked around at all of them, and said, "Lucinda's awake."

CHAPTER XXII

The Egyptian Queen

L ucinda was sitting up in bed, leaning on Carmilla. The
Countess had one arm around the girl, who was indeed
awake. Her hair tumbled down her shoulders, and she
looked at them with frightened eyes.

The bedroom resembled the one Mary had slept in—an
ancient four-poster bed with faded hangings, frescoes that must
have been painted in the last century, a chair drawn up by the bed
that could accommodate a crinoline, or even panniers. On one
wall hung a tapestry with frayed edges. Woven men in feathered
hats hunted a unicorn—they had speared its withers, and blood
flowed from the white hide. Their dogs bayed at its heels. Mary
guessed all of the Count's rooms were similarly decorated, except
of course the servants' quarters. This was probably how counts
decorated in general, at least Hungarian ones! In that enormous
bed, Lucinda looked small and fragile.

The Count walked to the side of the bed, lifted Lucinda's hand
from the counterpane, then bowed and kissed it. And that was
probably how counts greeted young ladies, at least in Hungary!

"You are very welcome to my home, Miss Van Helsing," said
the Count. "If I can do anything to make you more comfortable,
please inform me."

Lucinda looked up at him. Her eyes were large in her thin face,
and there were shadows under them. "Hail, Prince of Darkness,"

she said. "Have you come to save me from hell? I have been among devils, and you are the chief of devils, but an angel also. I think you are the angel Gabriel, who told our Lady that she was with child. You are the messenger of God, but what message do you have for me? My mother is dead, and she will not rise again, no, never." She said it in the same calm tone in which she might have said, "Good morning. What's for breakfast?"

"I told you she was awake," said Laura. "Not lucid."

"She's been speaking like this since she woke up," said Carmilla. "But at least she is conscious. She hasn't fed yet. I offered, but she refused."

"You will not refuse me, child, will you?" asked the Count. He sat on the side of the bed, then put a hand on Lucinda's cheek and stroked it, tenderly. "You must feed. You will not get better without feeding."

"Will I be damned to eternal hellfire?" asked Lucinda, as though inquiring about a thoroughly practical matter—the grocery bill, for instance.

"No, child. The god you believe in forgives all, and redeems all. You know this because you learned it at your mother's knee, did you not? Others may be punished, but you are innocent. I promise you—that is my message to you, from God if you will. Now come, drink." He put his hand behind her head and pulled her closer to him. She leaned forward, placed her mouth on his neck, and then . . .

Ugh, not this again! The terrible sound of Lucinda sucking and lapping blood. Mary put her hand over her mouth.

"That is *so gross*," said Diana, who had her hand on the collar of the white wolfdog. She pulled at the wolfdog's ears. Hóvirág did not seem to mind.

"You get used to it after a while," said Mina, matter-of-factly. Mary did not think she would ever get used to it! How in the world did Mina . . . Well, that was yet another issue, wasn't it? Mina and the Count. But Mina was married to another man, who was back in England. She could not quite wrap her head around it.

"Mary, you'll be all right here, won't you?" asked Mina. "I need to send two telegrams—one to Irene Norton and one to Mrs. Poole, letting them know you've arrived safely. The telegraph office was already closed by the time you arrived, or I would have sent them yesterday. It should be open by now. Mrs. Poole would never forgive me if I kept her in suspense, and I'm sure Mrs. Norton is starting to worry —it's been a week since you left Vienna. When I come back, we'll do some shopping. We may have a lot to think about, but all of you need new clothes, so I think a trip to Váci utca is in order."

"Would you ask Mrs. Poole to let Mr. Holmes know we've arrived? I was supposed to send him regular updates, but Irene warned us not to telegraph from Vienna once we realized that we'd been followed by the Alchemical Society, and there was no way to contact him after we'd been kidnapped." Should Mary send him a telegram herself? No, there was too much to tell him. Later that day, she would sit down and write him a long letter. Mrs. Poole would let him know they had arrived in Budapest, and then she could fill in all the details. She felt a little guilty that she had not written to him yet—but there had been so much else to consider, and so little time!

When Mina had left, with a wave to the Count, who was still, ugh, functioning as Lucinda's breakfast, Mary looked at Justine. How had she taken the revelations of that morning? After all, she had been—well, under observation as well by the Royal Society. She herself was not sure what to think. This Mina was not quite her Miss Murray anymore. Had that Miss Murray even existed?

"I feel the same way," said Justine, shaking her head. "As though it is all too much."

"How did you know what I was feeling?" asked Mary.

"Because you have not said anything for some time. You said almost nothing while Mina was speaking."

"Neither did you."

"What is there to say? On this journey, which of our assumptions have turned out to be correct? I thought Adam was dead, and he is not dead. You thought Mina was simply your teacher, and she is more than your teacher. I do not know what to think of this subcommittee—what has it done to combat the activities of the Société des Alchimistes? In the case Miss Murray described, it seems to have been singularly ineffective. It could not save Miss Westenra or even stop Professor Van Helsing." Justine shook her head. "I simply do not know. . . ."

Yes, that was exactly the way Mary felt! She simply did not know . . . about so many things. Her father, for instance. How had his experiments affected her? Had they made her what she was? Had they given her the temperament that even Mrs. Poole had noticed when Mary was a child?"

MRS. POOLE: You were a perfect child, my dear.

MARY: That's the whole problem, isn't it? Children aren't supposed to be perfect.

"There, that is better, is it not?" asked the Count. Gently, he laid Lucinda's head back on her pillows. She still had blood on her mouth.

Carmilla wiped it off with a handkerchief. "She looks better, at any rate. Thank you, *keresztapa*. Now we shall see if your theory works. . . ."

There was so much for Mary to think about, but this was not the time. Although it never seemed to be the time. They were always rushing from one thing to another, frying pans to fires to more frying pans! Once again, she longed for her quiet room in the house at 11 Park Terrace, and Mrs. Poole talking about bills. Adventures were all very well, but after a while one began to long for regular meals, for time to read a good book or take a walk in the park.

Laura sat down at the foot of the bed. "Vlad, will you stay with Lucinda, or shall I? Carmilla's been with her all night and needs a break. And there's no need for Mary, Justine, and Diana to be here. Mina is planning on taking them shopping as soon as she gets back. In the meantime—"

"If you could stay with her while I arrange my affairs for the day, I shall return and spend the afternoon here," said the Count, rising again.

"Right. I'll take over, then." Laura walked to the other side of the bed. When Carmilla stood up, she kissed her on the lips, the affectionate but perfunctory kiss of a couple that has been together for a long time, and said, "Get some sleep, sweetheart! I'm serious—I know you're incredibly powerful and all that, but even you're not invulnerable. Besides, when you don't get enough sleep, you're also irritable and grumpy." Then, she took her place by Lucinda's side.

"Yes, *ma gouvernante*," said Carmilla, with a mocking smile. She did not look particularly grumpy, but she did stifle a yawn.

"Don't even start," said Laura, shaking her head. "Go sleep!" She put her arms around Lucinda, so that Lucinda's head lay on her shoulder, and stroked Lucinda's tangled curls. "Shall I tell you a story? Or sing to you? Tell me what you would like."

If Lucinda responded, it was so low that Mary could not hear.

When they had followed the Count and Carmilla into the hallway, Carmilla turned to them and said, "I'm under orders. I shall see you all in about seven hours, yes?"

"Go," said the Count. "You have certainly done your duty. Now you must allow us to do ours. Miss Jekyll and Miss Frankenstein, perhaps you would like to sit in the music room until Mina returns? Yes, you too, Miss Hyde. And yes, you may bring Hóvirág. *Farkhaskutyák* are not normally affectionate toward strangers, but she seems to have taken to you."

Mary just nodded. At the moment, she did not much care where she went. She just wanted to sit and think about all that had happened that morning.

The music room was also on the second floor, just past the room in which they had eaten breakfast. It contained what Mary recognized as a harpsichord—did anyone play harpsichords in this day and age? By the fireplace was a stiff, ornate sofa and several armchairs.

"Earlier, you mentioned a theory," said Justine to the Count, when they were all seated. "What is this theory of yours?"

A theory? Mary did not remember him mentioning—oh yes, he had. Some sort of theory about vampires.

The Count smiled at Justine. It was a charming smile. Mary had to remind herself that he was more than four hundred years old, because he looked—well, about Mina's age. He was handsome in a way that seemed completely European, or at least not at all English, with those high cheekbones and dark hair that fell to his shoulders, dark eyes that seemed so much deeper than—well, than lighter eyes would have. Blue-gray eyes, for example, which were so inscrutable. You could never tell what Mr. Holmes was thinking. But the Count—Mary could see why Mina would be attracted to him. There was of course his courtesy, which seemed to belong to another era. And yet, he was a military commander who had defended the borders of Christendom. There was, in him, a sense of hidden power. Mary imagined he could be quite dangerous, if he chose.

JUSTINE: Catherine, you're turning the Count into a romantic hero.

CATHERINE: I'm not turning anything. He is a romantic hero. Think about how useful that is, for a novelist! Clarence is far too sensible, Holmes is completely undemonstrative, and you keep insisting that Atlas is just a friend. Every novel needs a romantic hero of some sort, and the Count is absolutely perfect for the position. He actually goes around being passionate! I mean, he probably sneezes passionately. And he has great hair.

JUSTINE: But he has killed people, and not only in war. He has infected men and women, we do not know how many, with vampirism. Are any of them still out there, feeding off and infecting others? He himself does not know. And it is partly his fault that Lucy died.

CATHERINE: That makes him an even better romantic hero. They're supposed to be dangerous. You're supposed to believe they've killed people and might again. Think about Manfred or Montoni. And he regrets it, or says he does, which is also a plus. Trust me, the Astarte books would not sell nearly as well if Rick Chambers weren't so conflicted all the time. Romantic heroes need to be passionate and conflicted and *brooding*.

BEATRICE: Clarence can be quite passionate, you know.

"Yes, my theory," said the Count. "I know only three cases of vampirism in which the victim was not driven mad. Myself, an English nobleman named Ruthven, and my goddaughter Carmilla. I am a materialist. For a long time, I believed it must be some substance in the blood that caused us to retain our sanity, when so many had not. So I experimented—on the blood itself, and on men—even occasionally on women. Carmilla told me that you have met Magda. She was one of my warriors—it was as unusual for a woman to be a warrior in that place and time as it is now, but she was stronger than most men. She is my greatest success—yet even in her, there is mental instability. That was the most I was able to achieve, on a purely material basis. Lucy was my greatest failure. In her, the madness developed even faster than it does in ordinary cases of vampirism. After that debacle, when I returned to my castle in Transylvania, injured and demoralized, alive only because of Mina's heroism—truly I have never known a woman with her courage—I once again read everything I could upon the subject. The literature is filled with conjecture and superstition. When I could take no more, I turned to the most recent scientific journals, and there I found what I thought might be a new avenue of inquiry. It is only recently that the mind has been studied in a scientific way, and in this discipline the English and Germans have been preeminent. I read Maudsley, Myers, Krafft-Ebing, Freud— whom I understand you met in Vienna. I would like to meet him myself, someday. I find his theories provocative, although not entirely convincing. What they showed me is that the mind affects the body much more than we previously thought. Trauma can alter and condition physical reactions. If trauma, why not the opposite? I did not have a word for what I meant, so I called it 'eutrauma'— the good wound. Love is a eutraumatic experience.

"I thought once again of my own transformation, of Ruthven's, of my goddaughter's. And I realized there was a commonality.

Each of us had been cared for, in a continual, consistent way, by another. In my case, there was my friend Ahmet, a young physician in the Ottoman court who sat with me day and night during my transformation. We were enemies, or so we had been taught by the rulers to whom we owed allegiance, but he cared for me as though he were my brother. He spoke to me, read me poetry, held my hand. In Ruthven's case, it was a Greek maiden named Ianthe, who stayed with him and fed him with her own blood. It was to avenge her death that he died fighting for Greek independence. And in Carmilla's case, I was so afraid she would die alone, or the madness would come upon her while I was away, that I never left her side, even when I myself was about to drop from hunger and exhaustion. Those who are infected with vampirism are seldom cared for—their own families abandon them, frightened for their own lives and sanity, frightened of the superstitions that surround vampires. In Magda's case, she was left alone for long periods of time by her companions. I told them to take care of her, but we were in the midst of a siege, and I could not care for her myself. They were frightened of her strength, and of her ferocity when she hungered. When I thought of these incidents, it occurred to me that the missing ingredient might be psychological—the consciousness of being cared for, of being loved. Therefore, one of us will sit with Lucinda at all times. We will hold her hand, speak to her, sing if necessary. I hope—I have lived too long to believe in a just or merciful God, but if one does exist—I hope to God that I am right."

"It is, at least, a plausible theory," said Mina. Mary looked up. She was standing by the doorway with her hat and gloves on. "Horvath úr had telegraph forms, so I've entrusted my telegrams to Attila, who will take them to the office on Kerepesi út—which means more time for shopping. We'll save Lucinda, somehow. At any rate, no matter what happens, we'll take care of her—we won't let her suffer the same fate as Lucy." Her face looked grim. "But I also want to make sure we stop Van Helsing from continuing these experiments. Who knows what other victims he might find, what other young women he might convince to undergo these transfusions until he either succeeds or stops trying? Although I don't think he'll stop trying. Immortality is a powerful incentive."

"But . . . how are you planning on stopping him?" asked Mary. "You said there was a meeting of the society, and something about Lucinda—"

"We are not powerful enough to stop him directly," said the Count. "He must be stopped by the society itself, and for all practical purposes, that means Ayesha." He pronounced it Aye-shah.

"And who is this Ayesha?" asked Justine.

"She is the president of the society," said the Count.

"She's a lot more than that!" Mina took off her hat and put it on the harpsichord, then pulled off her gloves. "Ayesha is—well, she showed up about . . ." She turned to the Count. "How long ago was it?"

"About fifteen years ago, I believe?" he said. "Forgive me, I am not always exact as to dates and times—at my age, they do not mean the same to me as they once did. However, it was a year before the Carew murder—Miss Jekyll, I do not mean to give you pain by reminding you of the past. But she became president of the society shortly after what we called the English scandal broke out. She disbanded the English branch of the society and forbade experiments in biological transmutation without her express permission. The headquarters of the society were moved from Vienna to Budapest, in a further effort to insulate it from scandal. As for Ayesha herself . . . how can one describe her?"

"She's a woman," said Mary. "That surprises me. While this is the nineties, I would not have expected men like Professor Van Helsing and Dr. Seward to accept a female president. They seem . . . well, I would not ask them for contributions to the National Society for Women's Suffrage!"

"Ayesha is . . . formidable," said the Count. "She is a woman of great beauty and power. And she is the greatest alchemist that has ever joined the society. There have been only three members of the society who have learned how to transcend death. The most recent was Victor Frankenstein, who created you." He bowed to Justine. "As we know, he was killed by the monster Adam. Before him, a medieval alchemist named Sebastian Melmoth learned how to prolong his own life. He lived for centuries, but became so tired of witnessing human suffering that eventually he committed suicide."

"And Ayesha?" asked Mary. "What about her?"

"I've never met her," said Mina, "so I don't know how formidable—or beautiful—she might be. But she claims to have been a priestess of Isis in ancient Egypt. I don't know how familiar you are with the history and religion of that region? It's not the sort of thing I would have taught you, Mary—and anyway, a great deal more has been learned in the last few years from the latest archeological data. Isis was one of the great goddesses of Egypt, worshipped at temples throughout the land, most famously at Philae, in Nubia. She was supposed to have resurrected her husband, Osiris, from the dead—it was rumored that the priestesses of Isis had also learned the secrets of life and death, and could defeat death itself. One finds references to such powers in Strabo and Ptolomy. Well, Ayesha showed up fifteen years ago with two Englishmen—a Mr. Leo Vincey and his friend and former guardian Professor Horace Holly, who had been a member of the society since his university days. They had been captured while on an expedition in British East Africa and she had saved them, somehow or other. I don't know why she decided to accompany them back to Europe, but once here, she joined the society. After the English scandal broke out and the president resigned—he was widely blamed for not monitoring the English situation closely enough—she decided to run for president herself. So far she's been reelected to three consecutive terms."

"Ancient Egypt!" said Diana. "You mean like mummies? I read a book once about a mummy. Its tomb was cursed, and everyone who went inside it died. That was an excellent book—lots of blood and bugs!"

"Surely that's impossible," said Mary. "If she was a priestess of Isis in ancient Egypt, she would be thousands of years old." Although how impossible was it? She was, at that moment, conversing with a woman who was a hundred years old and a man who was even older, who had lived for centuries. But thousands of years? Surely no human being could live that long.

"Dr. Faraday believes her story, and he's not a credulous man," said Mina. The Subcommittee on Bibliographic Citation Format takes her very seriously indeed. Evidently, she has knowledge of scientific techniques that had been lost for centuries. But as I said, I've never met her myself."

"If you saw her, you would not doubt it," said the Count. "When she speaks of the places she has been, you feel as though you were there with her—in Egypt when the Sphinx was young, in Imperial Rome, walking among the Caesars. And her Greek is exceptionally pure, or so Arminius says. I am not a linguist."

"Yes, well," said Mina skeptically. "Men can be extraordinarily credulous around a beautiful woman."

"But these experiments in biological transmutation—they have been performed since she became president of the society," said Justine. "Moreau created Catherine only ten years ago. The society must have given permission for his experiments. Why would she forbid Van Helsing?"

"Creating Beast Men on an island in the South Seas did not threaten the society," said Mina. "But infecting men and women with vampirism in the middle of London or Vienna? That's a different thing altogether. We know Van Helsing applied for permission before experimenting on Lucy, and was denied. He proceeded anyway. As far as we know, he never asked for permission to experiment on Lucinda. He's breaking the rules of the society. That's what we need to show Ayesha. But to do that, we need to show her Lucinda. We need her to *see* what Van Helsing's been doing."

"Then why don't we do that?" asked Mary. "If we could meet with her before the conference . . ."

"Ah, that is the difficulty!" said the Count. "You see, when she ran for president, she did not run unopposed. She promised to control and monitor such experiments, but I—at the time, I believed they should be allowed. I ran against her, with the support of Arminius and a significant faction of the society. There were heated words, tactics used . . . I did not always act as honorably as I should have. After she won the presidency—it was close, it came down in the end to seven votes between us—I was expelled. When Van Helsing contacted me, I was in disgrace. I helped him as much to take my revenge on her, and on the Société des Alchimistes, as out of scientific interest. After Lucy's transformation and death, I came to see how foolishly I had acted, how culpable I was. But I remain in disgrace, an outcast from the society. I am no better in her eyes than your father, Miss Jekyll."

"Oy! He's my father too," said Diana. She scratched Hóvirág behind the ears, and the wolfdog put her head on Diana's knee.

"So . . . what are we going to do?" asked Mary. She was confused—all this history, all these people. The most important thing was stopping Van Helsing, and then getting the society to stop these experiments altogether. If the only one who could stop them was this Ayesha, then they would have to talk to her, convince her. "How do we find Ayesha, if she won't talk to the Count?"

"That's why the meeting of the society is so important," said Mina. "This annual conference—it's where the members present their papers, speak on panels, hold plenary sessions, that sort of thing. It's not so different from what the Royal Academy does, when it meets. On the first day, there's always a general meeting of the membership. Everyone attends—there will be hundreds of members from all over Europe, some from even farther away since the society is becoming increasingly international. We think there's an excellent chance of getting in among the crowd, then presenting the entire membership with our evidence. Ayesha can't refuse to hear us in that forum."

"And that's on Monday," said Mary. "In other words, we have two days to prepare."

"Two days, and we have a great deal to do," said Mina. "But in the meantime, you all need clothes. And you haven't seen Budapest yet. Let's go shopping!"

> CATHERINE: That was the day we arrived in Budapest. If you had reached Budapest earlier and Mina had been able to send a telegram the day before, we wouldn't have been so worried about you, and we might have been able to find out more about Van Helsing's plans.

> MARY: If Carmilla had driven any faster, I don't think we would have survived the journey!

Half an hour later, they were walking along a broad avenue, between shops and apartment houses. It was both like and unlike walking through Vienna. The buildings were shorter and more colorful, more individual—each one seemed to have been designed by a different architect, who had his own ideas about how buildings should be decorated. Each was painted in the colors Mary remembered from the previous day: yellow, green, blue, pink, a kind of ocher. Some had classical motifs, some swirling example of *l'art nouveau*. Nymphs and gargoyles peeked out from corners or under balconies. Everywhere, at the level of the street, there was bustle—carts transporting and selling wares, horses snorting and stamping, the clang of an omnibus. Old women held out bunches of lavender that you could buy for a heller, although here in Hungary it was called a *fillér*, Mina told them. The sidewalks were filled with pedestrians. They were dressed more brightly than in London—the summer dresses of the women were particularly attractive, in floral prints or light cotton embroidered with patterns of vines and flowers. But they did not look much like the national costumes Mary had seen when researching Austria-Hungary. In cut and color, they were closer to ordinary English clothes.

> BEATRICE: People do not wear such costumes except
> on feast days, usually in the countryside. City
> dwellers dress much the same anywhere you go—
> whether London, Paris, Vienna, or Budapest.

Pigeons strutted in the streets or circled overhead. And on everything fell the sunlight, so much brighter than in London, warmer than in Vienna. Despite the events of the last few days, despite the events that were to come, it was nice to be walking down an ordinary street, among ordinary people, doing something as normal as shopping.

"That's the Great Market Hall," said Mina. "To your left. We need to turn right onto Váci utca, but first—do you want to see the Danube?"

There was general agreement that yes, they wanted to see the

Danube, although Diana really, really wanted to feed the pigeons. Mina said the pigeons got enough to eat without people feeding them on the streets, thank you very much. It felt as though they were tourists, seeing the sites in this foreign city. Mary wished they had not left their Baedeker behind in Castle Karnstein.

"Straight ahead, then," said Mina. Straight ahead was an ornate iron bridge over the river. "That's the Franz Joseph Bridge—Ferenc József híd, they call it here. It was finished just last year—thank goodness, because the construction in this area made traffic unbearable. Come on, from the bridge we can see the central city." They walked to the iron railing of the bridge and looked upriver. The Danube was narrower than the Thames, but twice as busy, with ships and barges going up and down between ports in Vienna, Bratislava, Budapest, and Belgrade. Whereas the Thames was dark and choppy, the Danube was a calm, light green. It looked like a jade serpent winding its way through the city.

"This side of the city is called Pest," said Mina. "Pest is where the business is conducted, where the government meets, where the university is located. And that side is Buda. There you can find the villas and gardens of the nobility. Look, there is Castle Hill, with the palace of the Hungarian kings." She pointed upriver. Mary could see it, in the distance—a high green hill with a castle complex on top.

"I wonder what would happen if I jumped?" asked Diana.

"You would learn a great deal about gravity," said Mina in the same calm tone Mary remembered from her childhood. "Most of it unpleasant, I imagine. We're not in a very fashionable area here," she continued. "But Vlad prefers it. He says Buda may as well be asleep, and the fashionable area of Pest, near the Oktagon, is too public for him. He would have to socialize with his peers, engage in political discourse—he hates that sort of thing. Here he can be in the city and yet retain a measure of privacy. Come on, we can

walk back along the river, but right now we have an appointment
with Carmilla's seamstress. I sent Kati ahead to let her know we
were coming this afternoon."

Váci utca was a narrow, busy street with shops, restaurants,
and a church every few blocks. There were a lot of churches in
Budapest, Mary thought—certainly more than in London. It
reminded her that they had not gone to church in a while—not
since they had left for the continent. How long had it been?

"When did we leave London?" she asked Justine, who was
walking beside her. Diana was ahead with Mina, who was holding her hand to keep her from wandering off and looking into
every shop window. At least she had stopped complaining about
not being able to bring Hóvirág!

"Two weeks ago," said Justine. "Exactly two weeks ago today."

Only two weeks! How could so much have happened in such a
short time? It felt as though they had been gone two years.

"How are you, by the way?" she asked Justine. Amid so much
turmoil, it was easy to focus simply on the problems of the moment,
or one's personal concerns. But the last few days had been as difficult for Justine as they had been for her—perhaps more so. Hyde
was bad enough, but Adam . . .

Justine smiled wanly. "I'm all right, I suppose. I feel rather
the way I imagine you do. I had just gotten used to the Société des
Alchimistes, and now there is the Royal Society and its subcommittee with the ridiculous name. But how do you feel, Mary? Miss
Murray lived with you for many years. And all that time . . ."

"I've been trying not to think about it," said Mary. She waved
away a girl trying to sell her ribbons from a basket. "We'd better
hurry—they're getting too far ahead of us. I don't want to get lost
in Budapest. Maybe if I don't think about it, it won't matter very
much?"

"I doubt that is the case," said Justine. "Human hearts and

minds don't work in that way, although perhaps it would be better if they did. You cannot stop either thinking or feeling. When I am troubled, I find the consolations of religion and philosophy—"

"Come *on*," said Mary, grabbing her by the arm. "Now I can't see them at all. Could they have gone into a shop?" The consolations of religion and philosophy weren't going to matter very much if they got lost in a strange city where they could not speak the language.

Mina was waiting for them at a shop entrance. Presumably, Diana had already gone in? Above the door was written ILONA COUTURE. "This way," said Mina. "I want to introduce you to Madame Ilona herself. She'll know exactly how to outfit all of you."

Madame Ilona turned out to be an older Hungarian woman, tiny and rather like a bird, dressed in a plain but very well-tailored black dress with a white collar and cuffs. She greeted Mina with a kiss on both cheeks. "You wish three *costumes*, yes? One for *la femme*, one for the gentleman, and one for the little boy?" Justine and Diana were still dressed in masculine clothing—she must have assumed they were male.

"Three *femmes*, *madame*. And three outfits each, with all the necessary undergarments. Two feminine, and one masculine, I think." Mina turned to Mary and Justine. "That should do, don't you think? Three outfits for each of you—a dress, a walking suit, and men's clothes."

"Is it necessary for us to have men's clothes?" asked Mary. "I don't really think—"

"My dear, there are certain things you'll need to do in the next few days that may require men's clothes. You will need to be versatile."

"Well, I don't want any girls' clothes!" said Diana. "Why do I have to wear skirts? They always tangle in my legs."

"Because if you're going to be a spy, or even a thief, you need to be able to fool people," said Mina. "That sometimes means appearing as a boy, sometimes as a girl. You wouldn't have been able to rescue Lucinda all by yourself if you weren't dressed as a girl, would you?"

It had scarcely been all by herself! *We were right there,* thought Mary. *We helped too. Diana would never have gotten away from the Krankenhaus without the rest of us.*

But Diana said "Oh, right," and did not quarrel with Mina's clothing selection again. Which just went to show that Mina was good at this sort of thing—at dealing with girls, including difficult ones. Mary felt a bit as though she were looking behind the curtain of a magic show. Had Mina been as persuasive—she might as well use the word *manipulative*—at 11 Park Terrace? *But perhaps all it means is that she's a good governess,* thought Mary. She *had* been a good governess—at least, Mina had taught Mary more than anyone else, certainly more than her own mother or father. She should be grateful for that.

Madame Ilona was discussing fabrics with Mina, and a woman in an identical black dress, who seemed to be a shop clerk, was measuring Justine. Then it was Mary's turn to be measured: around the neck, across the shoulders, down the arm, around the bust and waist, down the back, down from the waist to her ankles. She had never been measured so thoroughly before.

"I have ready an attractive *costume* for *mademoiselle*—it will take only a little change," said Madame Ilona.

"*Madame* sells ready-made clothing that can be altered to suit the wearer," said Mina, "as well as making clothing to order. Her husband does all the men's tailoring. I've ordered one dress that can go from day to evening, one walking suit with a shirtwaist, and a man's suit for each of you. And of course an assortment of unmentionables. Once we're done here, we need to get you new boots, then hats, gloves, and purses. That should do it, I think."

"This is going to be very expensive!" said Mary. "I don't think we have enough money—"

"Neither do I!" said Mina. "But the Count is paying for anything we purchase today. He insisted. Think of it as supplies for the coming . . . whatever it's going to be. Supplies for the battle, shall we say?"

"But you don't accept money from him," said Mary. "You made that very clear."

"My dear, that is an entirely different situation. I am . . . well, I am not his mistress. I am an employee of the Subcommittee for Bibliographic Citation Format, and I pay for myself, out of my own salary. The three of you are in a different position. You are friends of his goddaughter who lost your possessions through misadventure. It is the duty of a good host to supply you with necessities."

"That sounds like a lot of rigmarole," said Diana. "Do you like that word? Catherine taught it to me. *Rigmarole*."

> MRS. POOLE: It's nothing of the sort. Miss Murray was exactly right, and I'm glad you had someone there to think about the proprieties. While you could accept such assistance from the Count, she certainly could not—not if she wished to be thought of as a lady!

> CATHERINE: The rules about what a lady can and can't do are bloody complicated.

> MRS. POOLE: And that is exactly the sort of phrase a lady should never use.

> CATHERINE: Bloody hell. I don't know how proper ladies manage to do anything in this world.

MRS. POOLE: Miss Murray manages quite well,
 without cursing or complaining. You could do
 worse than take her as an example, my girl!

The final step was meeting Madame Ilona's husband—
Mihaly úr, Mina called him—so he could discuss the cut of
their masculine jackets and trousers. Then, after saying fare-
well to Madame Ilona, her husband, and the shop girl, whose
name Mary never managed to catch —she could not quite tell
which were words and which were names, in Hungarian—they
headed up Váci utca, first to a boot shop, then to a milliner's and
haberdasher's. By this time it was the middle of the afternoon,
and they were exhausted. Even Diana walked without speaking,
hanging onto Mina's arm.

"One more stop," she said, "but I think you're going to like
this one. In London, we'd be having tea right now. You're not
going to find an English teashop in Budapest, so I'm taking you to
Gerbeaud."

"What's Jerbo?" asked Diana, which was the way Mina had
pronounced it.

"That," said Mina, pointing across the square at a large white
building, four stories above the shops at street level, with an ornate
classical design. On it was written, in prominent letters just under
the top story, GERBEAUD. "Come on, I'm hungry."

"It's a *pâtisserie!*" said Justine, when they had entered through
the front door. The room in which they were standing had red
velvet curtains at the windows, and small marble-topped tables
were scattered throughout. Ladies and gentlemen sat at the tables,
drinking coffee or chocolate, eating pastries and cakes on delicate
porcelain plates or ice cream from crystal dishes. Across the room
was a long counter, also topped with marble, where clerks stood
to receive orders. At one end of the counter was a glass case, in

which were arranged slices of cake and pastries of various sorts that customers could purchase. There was a great deal of gilding and dark wood.

"Let's find somewhere to sit," said Mina. "I'm dying for some coffee."

They found a table, and then Mina directed them through the menu—them being Mary and Justine, because of course Diana had immediately gone to the glass case, where she was examining the contents as carefully as a judge might examine the evidence in a murder trial.

"If you haven't tasted Hungarian pastries before—and no, they're not the same as Viennese pastries, not at all—I suggest we order several slices so you can share and taste everything. For one thing, Hungarian pastries aren't as sweet, and for another, some of the flavors are . . . unusual, for an English palate."

"You must choose for us," said Justine. "Indeed, I do not recognize anything on the menu, except perhaps the Kugler. That's German, isn't it?"

"All right," said Mina. "One slice of Dobos torte, one slice of Eszterházy cake, a Gerbeaud slice—you must have one of those—a Rigó Jancsi, which is the most romantic cake, I think, named after a gypsy violinist who invented it for the princess he loved—and what else?"

"Goodness," said Mary. "I think that's quite enough for the four of us."

"I want one of the cakes with all the layers," said Diana. She sat down and put her elbows on the marble tabletop." Mary swatted at her arms, as she might have swatted at a fly. "What? Oh, right. I'm supposed to be *ladylike*." Diana put her hands in her lap and sat up straight, with mock correctness.

"That's the Dobos torte," said Mina. "I'll order two slices of that, and coffee all around. Oh, and a *krémes*—like a Napoléon.

That will introduce you to the Hungarian *gateaux*, at least." When the waiter approached, she ordered in what sounded like fluent Hungarian—but she assured them it wasn't at all. And then there was a great deal of chocolate filling and apricot jam and ground walnuts and caramel on top, and sweet, strong coffee that made Mary feel as though she could probably conquer the Société des Alchimistes single-handed, if she were to attempt it in the next half hour.

By the time they were finished—plates scattered with crumbs, coffee cups empty—Mary was completely full and a great deal happier than she had been for a long time. Was it all the chocolate, or sitting here, in a café in Budapest, with Justine and Diana—and with Mina, because this was the Mina she remembered, telling them about the history of the city, from when it was the Roman town of Aquincum to the coronation of the Empress Elizabeth. She had always been able to make history sound interesting—the account of real people living their real lives, and not just a series of dates.

As they left Gerbeaud, Diana lagging noticeably behind—she had eaten the most, and looked the most tired—Mina said, "Before we head back, I want to show you one more thing. It's not far." Only a few blocks away, the narrow streets gave way to a park with tall trees. To their left, Mary could see another bridge over the Danube, and the Castle Hill rising above it. How far they must have walked! "There," said Mina, pointing across the park. "That's the Hungarian Academy of Sciences. It's also the current head-quarters of the Société des Alchimistes, where they'll be holding their conference, starting on Monday. Before that, we'll have to do some scouting—make sure we know where the entrances are, how to get in and out without being seen."

"And on Monday—what exactly?" asked Justine.

"That will depend on Lucinda," said Mina. "What state will she be in by then? I hope tomorrow she'll be able to get up and walk around a little. We need her strong enough for. . . whatever happens." Her brow was furrowed with worry. "Come on, we've been gone several hours. Let's get back, check on her, and start making plans."

As Mina had promised, they walked back along the Danube. Most of the way, stone steps led down to the water. Diana ran up and down them, then lagged behind complaining that she was tired and her boots hurt.

At one point, Mina stopped. "Do you see that building?" she said. "The white one with the geraniums in the window boxes. That's where Arminius Vámbéry lives, in an apartment—I think it's on the second floor."

"That is Van Helsing's friend, is it not?" asked Justine.

"At the moment. Vámbéry's great passion is knowledge—of languages, cultures, all the things that make us human. He is one of the few Europeans to have traveled extensively in Turkey and Persia, as far as Khiva, Bokhara, and Samarkand, disguised as an adherent of Islam. He convinced the Hungarian Academy of Sciences to allow the Société des Alchimistes to hold its meetings and conferences in its headquarters, after it was determined the society should leave Vienna. He will ally himself with anyone who promises him more information, greater understanding. He was Vlad's friend at one time . . . and may be again in the future. But at the moment, he is Van Helsing's ally."

Across from the apartment building, an old woman was sitting at the top of the steps that led down to the river, smoking a noxious pipe, with a dirty cap in front of her and a basket at her side that seemed to hold all her possessions. Her clothes were ragged, and she had the stench of someone who had not bathed in a long time, evident even under the stench of the smoke. As they passed, Mina said, "*Jó napot, Mária Petrescu. Hogy van ma?*"

"*Jó, jó,*" said the woman, nodding and blowing smoke out of her mouth. Her face was brown and wrinkled, like a piece of paper that had been crumpled and smoothed out. Her eyes, small and dark like apple seeds, watched them intently.

Mina leaned down and said something to the old woman, too low for Mary to hear. The woman responded, and Mina dropped a krone into her hat.

"Come on," she said. "We need to get out of here. Van Helsing and Seward arrived this morning, and they are staying with Vámbéry. I thought they would stay in the society's guest house on Castle Hill, but evidently not. I don't want to run into them here—they would recognize me at once."

As they hurried back along the street, Mary said, "That woman—you seemed to know her. Is she a spy of some sort? Does she work for the Count?"

"That is Mária Petrescu, and she works for me," said Mina. "She is what they call here a *cigány*, one of the Romani people. There is a great deal of prejudice against them—it is difficult for the Romani to find work, so many of them are reduced to begging, but I pay Mária to be my eyes and ears. She's been watching Vámbéry's apartment. He's planning something, but so far I haven't been able to figure out what. I don't have the resources here that I had in Vienna. I just know that he's going out more often than usual—and not to the university. Also, he's very careful not to be followed. But where is he going? That, I don't know. I need Sherlock Holmes's Baker Street boys, don't I, Mary?" She smiled, and Mary smiled back before she remembered that she was angry and disappointed with Miss Murray. By that point, Mina was already walking in front, leading them back to Múzeum utca.

Across the street, under the linden trees that overhung the tall metal railings around the park, a peasant girl in an embroidered apron was selling bunches of lavender. Mary wished she could buy one, but she did not want to waste their hellers.

As they entered, the maid she remembered from earlier in the day—Kati was her name, wasn't it?—said something to Mina in Hungarian.

Mina looked confused. "I don't understand. What does '*apáca*' mean? *Mit jelent az 'apáca,' Kati?*"

Just then, on the stairs above them, appeared the last thing Mary expected to see, although perhaps it was not so surprising in a Catholic country: two nuns in black habits, walking down from the second floor. Were they coming to ask for some sort of charitable donation?

"Catherine!" said Justine. "How is this possible? And Beatrice!"

What in the world? Mary looked more closely at the nuns and almost tripped over Diana, who was of course in the way. "Cat! Bea! What are you doing here? How did you get to Budapest?"

"I could ask the same of you," said Catherine. "We were told, on the unimpeachable authority of Irene Norton, that you had disappeared. We came to find you, and to warn Miss Murray that Professor Van Helsing is amassing an army of sorts, to attack the Alchemical Society if he doesn't get his way. Dr. Seward says it's going to be a bloodbath."

CHAPTER XXIII

At the Café New York

"We have to warn them," said Mary.

"I do not see how," said the Count. "Ayesha will not admit me to her presence, and neither will any member of the society who is loyal to her. Indeed, we do not know who is loyal to her and who is not. Who, then, are we to warn?" He stared out the window, brow furrowed.

They were once again sitting in the dining room, having breakfast. The night before, they had sat up late, telling each other their adventures since they had parted in London. So much had happened in that time! Mary did not feel like the Miss Jekyll who had left the security of 11 Park Terrace anymore. But then, who was she now? She had no idea.

"And you never got the telegram from Mrs. Poole?" Catherine had asked. "She wired to tell you that we were coming, and hinted somewhat cryptically about Seward and Van Helsing's plans. Although we're still not entirely sure what they intend to do at that meeting, are we?"

"I certainly never received that telegram," Mina had responded, shaking her head. "Could she have mistaken the address? Although I never knew Mrs. Poole to be careless about anything—she was a most conscientious housekeeper. Or perhaps it simply went astray. The telegraph office here in Budapest is generally reliable, but such things do happen."

"Catherine, did she not give that telegram to Jimmy Bucket, to bring to the telegraph office?" Beatrice had taken off her veil and coif. With an audible sigh of relief, Catherine had followed her example. "You remember Dr. Watson identified him as a traitor among the Baker Street boys, although I do not like to use that word for a boy such as Jimmy. We do not know what motivated him, or what excuse he might have for his actions."

The night before, Catherine had pulled Mary aside as they walked up the stairs to the second floor. "I have to tell you— Holmes seems to be missing. Shortly after you and Justine left, he went off to investigate something or other. Very hush-hush government stuff, I think. He didn't tell Watson what it was, or where he was going. Of course, he may even be back by now—I don't want to worry you. But I thought you should know."

Mary had been dismayed to learn of Jimmy's defection and Holmes's disappearance. Where could he have gone? Surely he would be all right—he was the great detective, after all. She had been intending to sit down and write him a long letter—but it was pointless if he was not even at 221B Baker Street. It had been difficult for her to fall asleep, wondering and worrying about what was happening back home.

Now she picked at her breakfast, trying to interest herself in the eggs and mushrooms, which really were excellent. But she seemed to have no appetite this morning. If Jimmy had taken that telegram, what had he done with it? And more importantly— *where was Mr. Holmes?*

She needed to stop thinking about it and focus on the problem at hand. Here they all were again this morning—Catherine and Beatrice in their own clothes, for their trunk had been fetched the night before from the train station, and Justine in a brand-new dress delivered this morning from Ilona Couture. Mary looked down at her own dress from the seamstress, in a soft blue cotton voile, beautifully sewn, and could not help feeling a little lighter in heart, despite their troubles and the mysterious disappearance of Mr. Holmes. Such is the power of a new gown. Diana, looking like a boy, for she had refused to wear the new dress Madam Ilona had sewn for her, was slipping pieces of sausage to Hóvirág.

"But we must try to warn them," said Justine. "Surely it is our moral obligation to try and prevent bloodshed."

"And maybe if the president of the society—if Ayesha can see that we're on her side and trying to help her, she'll stop these experiments once and for all," said Mary. "If we can tell her what Van Helsing is planning ahead of time—but what is he planning, anyway? We don't actually know."

"He mentioned *supporters* and *troops*." Beatrice sipped her decoction, whatever it was. In a house where some of the inhabitants drank blood, hers was no longer the most unusual dietary requirement. "I assume his supporters are members of the Société who have pledge to vote as he directs. As for his troops—what Dr. Seward called an army. Could they be like the men you fought in Vienna? Is it possible that he has more of those men here, in Budapest?"

"Men infected with vampirism under Van Helsing's control," said the Count. "If so, he is using an old tactic—one that I described to him myself. Even a few such men would wreak havoc among the members of the Société des Alchimistes. It is a society of scientists, not warriors. They come to this meeting to give papers, discuss their research. If Van Helsing were to unleash maddened vampires at such a meeting, it would be a massacre."

"Which means we have to warn them," said Mary. "If Ayesha won't see you, could you send her a message somehow?"

"What about through Mr. Vincey?" asked Mina. "If you told him she was in danger . . ."

The Count shook his head. "Beloved, Leo despises me more, if that is possible, than Ayesha herself. He despises me on her behalf, which is an even stronger motivation."

"Well, we have to do something!" said Mary. "Can't we at least try to contact this Vincey person, whoever he is? And if it doesn't work, we'll try something else. We only have two days. I don't think we can afford to neglect any possibility of averting what you yourself called a massacre."

"If Van Helsing wins, everything goes back to the way it was, right?" said Catherine. "Whoever wanted to could conduct experiments in biological transmutation with no oversight whatsoever—bringing corpses back to life, or making girls poisonous, or turning pumas into women. Well, we're not going to let him win. We're just not." She bit down on a piece of spicy red chicken with grim determination.

"That would not be the worst, if he succeeds in his aims," said Mina. "Eventually, we could be faced with the prospect of powerful men living forever, controlling our world in ways we cannot yet imagine. Vlad, I agree with Mary. I think we have to try—if not Leo Vincey, then Professor Holly."

"Holly is even less likely to listen to me than Leo," said the Count. "He and I disagree on certain points of science—which, as you know, are the most important disagreements of all, to men of intellect. Very well, I will send a message to Leo Vincey, and we shall see whether he replies. Ladies, if you will excuse me. . . ." He bowed to them all, then Mary could hear his boot heels clicking across the parquet.

Catherine leaned over and whispered, "*Where* did Miss Murray meet someone like that? He looks like a young Sir Henry Irving in something suitably dramatic—*The Bride of the Isles* or *Macbeth*!"

Oh, for goodness' sake! This was no time to be mooning over vampiric counts. "He drinks blood," Mary whispered back. "Probably *human* blood. Although of course it could just be chickens."

Catherine shrugged. "So? I eat meat. That's no different. Do you think his hair just flops like that naturally?"

"Well, he's at least four hundred years older than you are!" Mary had forgotten how annoying it could be, having all of them together—as though they were back home at 11 Park Terrace! Nevertheless, she was glad to have Catherine and Beatrice here in Budapest. They were all stronger together. Less amicable, but stronger.

Mina put her napkin on the table and stood up. "All right, I think we should check on Lucinda. Laura and Carmilla have been with her since Vlad and I went to bed, late last night. They must be exhausted. And then, we need to decide how to spend the rest of today. There's a great deal for us to do before the meeting of the Alchemical Society."

Mary rose as well. Yesterday had felt like an interregnum of sorts. Today, events seemed to be moving much more quickly— she did not quite know what was going on or where it would all lead. At home in London, things had been so much more orderly,

MRS. POOLE: I should think so!

ALICE: Well, on an ordinary day. But we don't have
many ordinary days anymore, do we, Mrs. Poole?

MRS. POOLE: We do our best. You can't say we don't
do our best to run a proper household.

When they entered Lucinda's room, she was sitting up, leaning back against her pillows. Carmilla was sitting on the bed beside her. Laura was seated in an armchair by the bed, looking so tired that Mary immediately said, "Do you want one of us to take over?"

"Oh, would you?" said Laura, gratefully. "Vlad and Mina

were here until midnight, and then Carmilla and I took our turn. Honestly, I feel as though I'm going to fall over and go to sleep right on the floor!"

"And how is she doing this morning?" asked Mina. Lucinda certainly seemed better—she had lost those dreadful hollows under her cheeks. She was playing with a pack of cards that had different figures on them: a woman with a star over her head, a man hanging upside down, Death riding a white horse.

"You can ask her yourself," said Laura. "Although she's still not making much sense, I'm afraid."

"Tell them how you're doing, my dear," said Carmilla, putting her hand on Lucinda's arm. "A little better, yes? You recognize Mina and Mary and Justine—and of course Diana, whom you met under such difficult circumstances. But I see that we have some guests?"

"I'm so sorry," said Mary. "Mrs. Poole would be appalled at my manners. These are Catherine Moreau and Beatrice Rappaccini. Cat, Bea, this is Countess Karnstein and her friend, Miss Laura Jennings. And of course Lucinda Van Helsing."

Lucinda looked up. There were red spots on her cheeks, as though she were still feverish. "I am doing very well, thank you. Truly, it is as though I have come into the realm of the angels. Strange, is it not, that Lucifer should reign over heaven? And yet he, too, was once an angel. Perhaps someday even he shall regain his wings. . . ."

"She's as loony as she ever was," said Diana, shaking her head. "Come on, Hoho. Up on the bed."

"That dog does *not* belong on the bed," said Mary, trying to catch the wolfdog loping past her, but there was nothing to take hold of unless she wanted to grab the thick white hair on Hoho's neck. By the time she reached for the wolfdog, Hóvirág had already jumped up on the bed and put her head on Lucinda's feet. Well, at least Lucinda did not seem to mind! She kept staring down at her mysterious cards. Diana scrambled up after the wolfdog and began looking through the pack as well.

"Any news from the world outside of this room?" asked Laura. "What is your plan, Mina? What do you need us to do?"

"Today, all I need is for you, in particular, to get some sleep," said Mina. "Tomorrow, when the Academy of Sciences building is closed, for all official buildings close on a Sunday, we'll need to do some scouting. How do we get in, and hopefully out? Where are the various doors? What sorts of locks do they have on them? How easy are they to pick? That sort of thing. Vlad has been inside the building, but he retains only the vaguest notion of where things are. Imagine walking down hallways and not remembering the general layout! I supposed that's what happens when your head is filled with schemes for making men immortal."

"Surely we should do more than that," said Mary. "We need to investigate this Abbey of St. Ignatius. What were Seward and Professor Vámbéry doing there? If Van Helsing is keeping what he calls his troops there, or in that neighborhood, we need to find out more. How many of them are there? And are they in fact men infected with vampirism, as we suspect?"

"Men infected with vampirism!" said Carmilla. "I see that Laura and I have missed an important discussion. If there are such men in Budapest, I would like to know where they are, and how many. If you need someone to investigate this abbey, I volunteer."

"You will need a way either to climb the wall or get through an iron gate," said Beatrice. "The wall is plaster over stone—there are no foot or hand holds. Mary described your abilities to us last night, Countess, but I do not think even you could climb that wall."

"I can pick the lock, easy peasy!" said Diana, looking up from the cards.

"There's no way I'm letting you go any place where there are more mad vampires," said Mary. "Don't you remember the last time? We could have been killed in that alley in Vienna. We only got out because there were so many of us, and Irene was there with her coach."

"Who made you queen?" said Diana, with a disgusted look on her face.

"If the bars are iron, I may be able to bend them," said Justine with characteristic modesty. Bending iron bars had been part of her show in the circus—it was child's play to the Giantess. "And I do not think these vampiric men could hurt me. I am, as you know, already dead. . . ."

"Then you and I shall go together," said Carmilla. "No, Laura, I do not need to rest! I'll be perfectly fine. And please, Justine, Beatrice—call me Carmilla."

"It sounds as though you're making plans," said the Count. Mary had not heard him come in, but he was standing right behind them. "Leo Vincey replied by return of messenger—why so quickly, I wonder? He has agreed to meet with us at the Café New York. Miss Jekyll, would you be willing to come with me? I do not think Leo will listen to me alone, but if you tell him what you know, what you've discovered about the activities of the society in England . . . And perhaps Miss Morcau could come as well, to tell him about the conversation she overheard."

"Of course," said Mary. "But what about Lucinda?"

"I can stay with her," said Beatrice. "That is, if my nature will not endanger her. As you know, I am . . . toxic to most animal life."

"Miss Rappaccini, give me your hand," said the Count. "Your bare hand, if you would not mind removing your glove?"

"No, I cannot—" Beatrice drew back from him.

"I promise you, it will be all right." He held out his hand. She drew off one glove and put hers into it, gingerly, cautiously, as though afraid of what might happen. He leaned down and kissed the back of her hand, long enough that she grew alarmed and drew it away.

The Count straightened and smiled, then showed her the palm of his hand. It was a little red, but as she watched, the redness disappeared. In a moment, neither his lips nor his hand were marked in any way.

"Your poison, although efficacious, works slowly," he said. "My body has time to repair itself before it can do any real damage. Carmilla is constituted the same way, and Lucinda will be soon—she is almost fully transformed. Even now, you cannot truly harm her. You can touch us, you can be in our company, without alarm."

Beatrice looked bewildered, but relieved. This was a new sensation for her, no doubt—simply not hurting another by her touch. The only previous companion safe from her poison had been Justine. "Thank you," she said to the Count. "Thank you for what you have shown me. I shall stay here gladly. And perhaps Diana can stay as well, if I keep the window open? The room is large and well-ventilated. I see she is teaching Lucinda some sort of card game."

"Because no one wants me to go with them!" Diana grumbled.

Mary ignored her. Diana might be unhappy, but she would be safe, at least for today.

"And I shall write a long letter to Dr. Faraday, bringing him up to date on the situation. Well, then," said Mina, "I think it's going to be quite a day, for all of us. Except Laura—you, my dear, spend far too much time taking care of everyone else. Go to sleep—governess's orders!"

> DIANA: It was *so boring*. Except for the part where I invented a completely new card game. Lucinda's almost as good at it as I am. Beatrice kept reading these stories. . . .

BEATRICE: Laura told me it might help if I read aloud. Mina had given us a book of fairy tales. *Blue Fairy Tales? Blue Book of Fairy Tales?* I do not remember the exact title. I was never given fairy tales to read as a child, only scientific treatises. How I would have enjoyed them! Although I do not understand how a shoe could fit only one woman in an entire kingdom.

DIANA: It was a magical shoe.

BEATRICE: Still, that is not logical. I can accept pumpkins turning into coaches, and lizards into footmen, but a shoe will fit many women of the same size. How could the prince know he was choosing the right one?

Fifteen minutes later, Mary and Catherine were waiting downstairs at the carriage entrance, properly hatted and gloved for an excursion.

"I think the brougham will be quicker and less conspicuous than the landau," said the Count. "Unless you prefer the landau? With the three of us, the brougham will be a little tight."

"No, the brougham would be perfectly fine, thank you," said Mary. She glanced at Catherine. Catherine rolled her eyes. Nervously, Mary looked at the Count to see if he had noticed, but he had already turned away from them. He was walking toward what looked like a groom, holding a bay mare by its bridle. She poked Catherine in the ribs with an elbow.

"What!" whispered Catherine. "Why did you hit me?"

"I didn't hit you. That wasn't a hit. And behave yourself! You don't roll your eyes at a *count*, for goodness' sake. Or even behind his back. Anyway, he's our host, and Miss Murray's . . . well, friend."

"Oh, Miss Jekyll, would you prefer the brougham or the landau?" Catherine spoke in a high, mincing voice, imitating someone— probably Lady Tibbett, who had reluctantly taken her in when she first arrived in London, and thrown her out after Catherine had bitten her Pomeranian.

"I thought you liked the Count—he has that floppy hair, like Sir Henry Irving! Why are you making fun of him?"

"I'm not making fun of him specifically—I'm making fun of people who have both broughams and landaus. What even is a landau? We poor circus folk don't travel in those sorts of high-society circles, you know."

"It's an open carriage for riding in the park, and if you continue like this, I won't tell you what happened in Castle Karnstein or about the conversation I had with Hyde—the things I didn't want to mention in front of Mina and the Count. Seriously, behave yourself—this isn't a game, Catherine. You should have seen those men of Van Helsing's. We could have gotten ourselves killed in Vienna."

"Yes, ma'am!" said Catherine. "You know, I'd forgotten how annoying you can be."

"You too, but I'm glad to see you and Beatrice all the same. Honestly, I feel much better about all of this now that we're together again. As Beatrice once said back in London, we're stronger together than apart. As long as we don't kill each other, that is."

"Agreed. And we really were afraid the three of you had simply vanished into thin air. Disappearing without a trace like that! What were you thinking?"

"Well, it wasn't *our* fault," said Mary. "Kidnapped, remember? Kidnapped means we didn't have a say in where we were going."

"Miss Jekyll, Miss Moreau, if you are ready?" The Count was waiting to hand them in to the brougham.

"After you, Miss Moreau," said Mary, trying to sound as much like Lady Tibbett as she could. Catherine rolled her eyes again.

Yesterday, she had walked through the back streets of Budapest. Today, she was driving along grand boulevards, with ornate buildings on both sides. The areas Mary had seen so far had been smaller, more modest, but this part of Budapest was as spectacular as Vienna.

"What in the world are those?" asked Catherine.

Mary, who was sitting in the middle, leaned forward and looked where Catherine was pointing. What *were* those indeed? They looked like individual train cars moving along a set of tracks down the middle of the avenue. It was—it must be— "A tram system," said Mary. "But there are no horses moving the trams. How do they run?"

"On electricity," said the Count. "There is a cable under the street that delivers electricity to the cars, so they appear to run as though by magic! Although of course it is science."

"We don't have such a system in London," said Mary.

The Count smiled. "When I was in England, I noticed that Englishmen generally assume the east is uncivilized, incapable of technological innovation. But you see it is not so. We have innovations here in Hungary that you do not have in your country. When Jonathan Harker came to Transylvania, he noticed the peasants in colorful garments. He did not notice our up-to-date farming equipment or advanced irrigation techniques."

Mary stared at the trams. How strange that they should share the street with carriages and carts! But no stranger, perhaps, than Carmilla's motorcar driving through villages that had never seen such a contraption before.

"I've noticed that about England," said Catherine. "When I wrote my first story—'Astarte and the Spider God' that was, which I'm now turning into a novel although I'll probably have to call it something different—I created an Englishman, Rick Chambers, who thinks everything English is the best. Until he falls in love with Astarte, of course!"

"Ah, Miss Moreau, I found your story delightful. Mina pointed it out to me in *Lippincott's Magazine*. I particularly liked the portion where Rick Chambers tries to rescue Astarte from the spider-god, and she must rescue him!"

"You read my story?" said Catherine. Her voice sounded curiously toneless.

"Yes, and enjoyed it very much! I believe Mina saved that issue. Perhaps tonight you can autograph it for me?"

Mary watched Catherine's face slowly flush. Goodness, who knew the Cat Woman could turn so red? She mumbled something that sounded like "sure" and then stared resolutely out the window. Authors were certainly strange beasts! Shouldn't she have been pleased by the compliment?

But Catherine said nothing more until they arrived at the Café New York, alighted from the brougham, and walked through the front entrance. Then she said, "Oh. My. Word. What is this, some sort of temple to coffee?"

Marble columns rose to high ceilings painted with classical scenes—there were a lot of cherubs. From the central hall, she could see two floors filled with small tables. At those tables sat men in suits, or sometimes military uniforms, and women in afternoon dresses, wearing hats with sweeping feathers, carrying beaded reticules. Chatter, cigarette smoke, waiters bustling to and fro—and gilding everywhere, casting a sort of golden haze around the customers so they looked as though they were sitting in an enchanted place, a Mount Olympus of coffee. The smells of coffee, cigarettes, perfume. Suddenly, Mary wondered what it smelled like to Catherine, with her cat's nose.

CATHERINE: Absolutely foul. How people can stand
to stink up their environment in that way, I don't
know.

It's . . . a little overwhelming," said Mary doubtfully.

"Can I just curl up in a dark corner?" asked Catherine. "I don't know how anyone can hear anything in this din."

"The Café New York opened several years ago," said the Count—said or shouted, it was difficult to say which. "It is the most fashionable coffeehouse in Budapest, a place to see and be seen, as the English say. I do not come to such places myself, but this is where Leo asked to meet us." He said something in rapid Hungarian to a passing waiter, who pointed him toward the back. "Come," he said, gesturing for them to follow him. They made their way through that noise and spectacle. Mary was grateful that when they reached the back of the coffeehouse, it was a little quieter.

"There," said the Count, pointing. "But he is not alone."

At the table where he was pointing sat two men. One, the younger, must have been in his late thirties or early forties. He was exceptionally handsome in a way that would have made any woman turn to look at him on the street—as though the Apollo Belvedere had stepped off its pedestal and put on a modern suit. But there were the beginnings of lines over his forehead and under his eyes, and his hair, golden and curling, was peppered with gray. The other was perhaps twenty years older, and his opposite in every way— short, broad-chested, pugnacious-looking, with a heavy beard and a nose that had at one time been broken and healed badly. Whereas his companion was more attractive than most men, he could with justice have been called ugly—although in an arresting way that drew your eye. He was smoking a rather large pipe.

"Hello, Dracula," said the man with the golden hair. "You seem to have brought companions. Ladies?" He rose and bowed. At the same time, his companion rose just enough for politeness and nodded. He did, however, place his pipe in an ashtray.

"Miss Jekyll, Miss Moreau," said the Count, gesturing toward the Apollo, "this is Leo Vincey. And his companion, whom I did not expect to see here, is Professor Horace Holly of Cambridge University."

"Jekyll! Moreau!" exclaimed Professor Holly. "Then you're the result of those damned experiments."

"Holly!" said Leo Vincey. "Where are your manners?"

"Forgive me, ladies," said the professor, although he did not sound particularly penitent. "I am, as Leo can tell you, deficient in the social graces. I must admit that as a scientific man, I am fascinated to meet you—particularly Miss Moreau. I have always felt that I myself am half ape—a throwback, an atavism, in some sense. It is delightful, therefore, to meet a young lady who is half cat. If it were not infernally rude, I would ask to study your physiognomy. . . ."

"But it is, in fact, infernally rude," said Vincey. "Dracula, fascinating as your companions may be, what I'm interested in is your message—what is this danger to Ayesha from Professor Van Helsing? And I may as well tell you that Van Helsing has pre-empted you—I received a message from him yesterday morning. He seems to think you've kidnapped his daughter from a mental institution. He says she has a persecution complex—believes her own father is turning her into a vampire. Evidently, she has inherited her mother's mental instability. Is this true—have you indeed kidnapped Miss Van Helsing?"

"It is most certainly not true!" said Mary. "He really was turning her into a vampire—or trying to, anyway! He and Dr. Seward have been conducting experiments in biological trans-mutation. Their goal is to revive the English branch of the Société des Alchimistes. Tell them, Catherine."

"If the society doesn't vote to allow research into biological transmutation again, he intends to take over the society," said Catherine.

"Take over? How? He doesn't have the votes." Vincey looked skeptical.

"With an army of vampires that he controls through some sort of mesmerism," said Mary. "At least, that's what we think he's doing. Arminius Vámbéry is helping him."

Vincey looked at her for a moment, then burst out laughing. "My dear Miss Jekyll, that sounds like the plot of a penny dreadful. I don't trust Van Helsing any farther than I can throw him, but he is a gentleman and a man of science. If you'll forgive my asking, why should I trust *him*"—he pointed at the Count—"who has betrayed us in the past, and the two of you? Dracula may be manipulating you, or you may be manipulating him for all I know. I have no reason to trust the daughter of Dr. Jekyll—who, may I remind you, also betrayed the society, and whose whereabouts remain unknown—and the creature who killed Dr. Moreau. Have either of you actually seen this supposed army of vampires?"

"No, but—," said Mary.

"And did you kidnap Lucinda Van Helsing from a mental institution where she was receiving treatment?"

"Yes, but—"

"And is she indeed mad?"

"Well yes. But—"

"Then give me one reason why I should trust you or your preposterous story."

"Because we're trying to help you!" Mary clenched her fists. She would have liked to punch Leo Vincey in that beautifully classical nose.

"You should listen to them," said Dracula. "You do not know what has been going on. Ayesha does not know—"

"She knows a hell of a lot more than you do," said Vincey. He stood up. "Holly, I think we've heard enough. As for you, Dracula, I suggest you restore Miss Van Helsing to her father, or place her in some institution where she can be cared for as she ought to be. Do not contact me or attempt to contact Ayesha again. Good day, ladies."

"Will you at least tell her?" asked Mary. "Tell the president . . . tell Ayesha what Van Helsing intends to do."

"I shall do nothing of the sort. She has a conference to run and a speech to write—she does not need to be bothered with nonsense." Vincey pushed in his chair, said "Come, Holly," and walked away from them toward the front of the café, weaving between the small tables. Professor Holly gave them one glance before following him.

"Well, that went splendidly," said Catherine.

"We tried," said the Count, shaking his head. "If they will not listen to us, what more can we do?"

They did not say anything more until they were halfway home, when Catherine burst out, "Moreau deserved it, you know. What I did to him, he fully deserved."

Mary put her hand on Catherine's and squeezed it once, in a way she hoped was reassuring, then continued to hold her hand as the brougham made its way back to Múzeum utca. What now? Perhaps when they got back to Dracula's house, Justine and Carmilla would have returned with some news about this army of vampires.

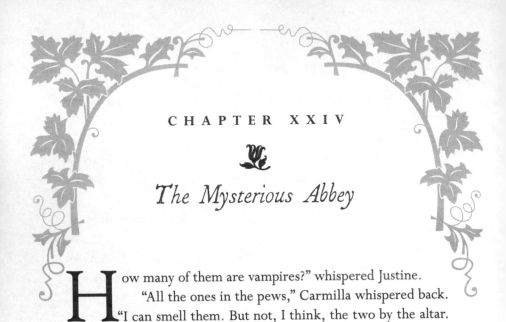

CHAPTER XXIV

The Mysterious Abbey

How many of them are vampires?" whispered Justine.
"All the ones in the pews," Carmilla whispered back.
"I can smell them. But not, I think, the two by the altar.
They are not yet infected."

Silently, Justine counted the men kneeling in the pews below.
Twenty-four. All vampires, if Carmilla was right, and Justine suspected she was.

This morning, Mr. Justin Frank and the dashing young Count
Karnstein had left 5 Múzeum utca and made their way to the Abbey
of Saint Ignatius—Szent Ignác in Hungarian, Carmilla had told
her. As soon as they had left the house and were walking down the
avenue toward the Danube, Carmilla said, "Would you prefer to
speak in French? I know it is your native language. It was the language of the nobility, when I was a child." Justine had nodded, and
so their conversations had proceeded in that language. Despite the
danger and difficulty of their errand, it made Justine happy to be
conducting it in her mother tongue. She had so few opportunities
to speak French in London!

They had decided on male attire because if they were caught
breaking into the abbey, they might be able to pass it off as a prank
of some sort—young men did that sort of thing, did they not?
Young women trying to get into an abbey filled with monks would
arouse more suspicion.

It had been easy getting into the abbey itself. They had found the small back gate and Justine had bent open the bars, then bent them closed again after they had passed through.

"We need a vantage point from which we can get a general sense of what is going on," Carmilla had said. Luckily, the stucco on the back of the bell tower was broken away in places. Using those as handholds, she could climb up to the belfry and let down the rope conveniently concealed around her waist, under Count Karnstein's jacket. It was just after noon—no one seemed to be around. Perhaps the monks were eating their midday meal? Justine had climbed up the rope. In the belfry, beneath the great brass bell, they had waited. There were windows on each side. From there, they would be able to see anyone coming and going.

They did not have long to wait. Sooner than Justine had expected, a line of monks filed out of the dormitory and made its way to the church below. Why now? As far as she knew, it was not one of the liturgical times for prayer. She crouched down so that only her head was above the windowsill—she did not want the monks to see her.

"There are two men with them," said Carmilla, who was crouched beside her. "I mean, men who are not monks."

Justine had not seen those, but then her eyesight was not as good as Carmilla's. Now all the monks had filed into the church. In one corner of the belfry, there was a narrow stone staircase spiraling downward. Carmilla went to the staircase, disappeared down it for a moment, then reappeared and motioned for Justine to come as well. One spiral down, there was an aperture that allowed them to see what was happening below. They could see the monks, all but two of them, sitting in the pews. But those men in brown cassocks did not look particularly violent or vampiric, and she wondered whether Carmilla could be right—could her superior sense of smell really identify vampires at that distance?

The other two were standing on either side of the altar as though waiting. For what?

A side door opened, and in came a man who was obviously not a monk, because he was wearing an ordinary frock coat and trousers, although he had put some sort of chasuble over his garments. She recognized him at once from Catherine's description the night before: "He looks like Father Christmas in modern dress." So that was Professor Van Helsing! He had a white beard and a halo of white hair. From above, she could see the bald spot on the top of his head.

After him walked another man—younger, trimmer. Was that Dr. Seward? He was clean-shaven, and Catherine had described Professor Vámbéry as having both a beard and mustache. Justine would have recognized Prendick from the last time she had seen him—administering ether to her on the terrible night when Adam had tried to replace her brain with that of another woman who would love him in a way Justine never could. She shook her head as though to drive the thought away—there was no time for that now. She must concentrate on what was happening below. The other man was most likely Seward. He was carrying the sort of ornate chalice used for communion.

Now Van Helsing was standing at the altar. Seward, if it was he, placed the chalice in front of him, then stepped back toward the apse, leaned against one of the stone columns, and crossed his arms. For a moment, Van Helsing looked down at the chalice. Then, he raised his hands and started speaking—in German, so Justine could not understand all of it, particularly as it did not seem to make much sense. *Rivers of blood—the day of atonement—feasting upon the heretics and blasphemers.* His voice, which had the resonance of a frequent lecturer, echoed throughout the stone chancel. She looked at Carmilla, wondering if the Countess would have any clearer idea of what was going on than she did—after all, she spoke German. But Carmilla shrugged as though to say, *I don't know either.*

Van Helsing raised the chalice. He intoned something—wait, that was in Latin. *The blood of our Lord—granted eternal life—take, drink.* Those weren't the words of the communion prayer! Or they were, but in the wrong order, saying the wrong things: no humility, no call to participate in the community of the church. They were all about eternal life, purchased through blood, granting glory forever and ever. Justine shivered—she had never had such a presentiment of evil. Not even Adam, who had murdered so many, had caused her to feel such a sense of dread. That any man should desecrate what was holy for his own purposes . . .

Van Helsing's oration ended. Now one by one, each of the monks in the pews rose, came up to the altar rail, and knelt on the cushion. Van Helsing went to each and held the chalice to his lips. As each drank, he looked that man deeply in the eyes and said something, too low for Justine to make out.

"It's not wine," whispered Carmilla. "It's blood. I can smell it even from here."

But somehow, Justine could have guessed that. It was all of a piece with this hideous mockery of the communion rite. Catherine had described to her how Moreau had perverted religion on his island. Here was Van Helsing doing it in the middle of a European capital.

"Can you hear what he's saying to them?" she whispered, but Carmilla shook her head.

Twenty-two—twenty-three—twenty-four. Each of the monks drank, each returned to his place in the pews. Finally, Van Helsing spoke again in German. "In the name of the Father, the Son, and the Holy Spirit, which is in you, now and forever. Amen."

Seward was still leaning against the column, watching casually, as though this were a theatrical performance and he were merely a spectator.

Then, one by one, the monks in the pews filed out of the church, leaving only the two who had been standing on either side of the altar. They still stood there, hands tucked into their cassocks.

Van Helsing turned to one of them. "Will you tell the abbot that I am most grateful for his assistance, and that I will be making a large donation shortly? It seems as though everything is going according to plan." Or at least that was the best translation Justine could make of it. *Spende*—donation or payment. *Vorhaben*— project or plan. She thought that was right.

The monk bowed and mumbled something too low to hear— whereas the professor's voice was calibrated to a lecture hall, he probably spent his days in quiet contemplation.

"Are we quite done here?" asked Seward in English— presumably he did not speak German.

"You are impatient, friend John," said Van Helsing. "But it is important to thoroughly inculcate into our troops the proper ideas, so that when the time comes, they will act as we desire. Remember, in two days we will ask them to fight, and possibly die, for us."

"Yes, yes," said Seward. "I must say, though—as a man of science, I find this mumbo jumbo distasteful. Why can't you just hire mercenaries? Why do you have to go to such lengths?"

"Any men we hire could be hired by another party to betray us. You do not know Ayesha as I do. She is ever vigilant, and unites the cunning of a woman with the objective, rational mind of the highest type of man. It is a fearsome combination. If men are to obey you without question, they must believe in the cause for which they are fighting. Our supporters in the Société des Alchimistes believe in the promise of science—that it can deliver heretofore unimaginable power and benefits to mankind. And so we have convinced them in that way. These creatures you find so distasteful believe in God and the eternal life He delivers. Even though their minds have been corrupted by disease, they continue to believe. That is what they will fight for, and they will not betray us. But come, let us not quarrel. We still have preparations to make before the start of the conference. Whatever happens at the general meeting, the rest of the conference will go on, and you are scheduled to deliver your paper. I shall look at it once more and let you know if I think any further revisions are necessary." Van Helsing put his hand on Seward's arm, and then the two of them walked along the nave to the back of the church. They went out through the large double doors.

Justine watched as the two monks spoke with each other in low tones. Then one took the chalice and left through a door that probably led to the vestry. The other folded the altar cloth, then followed him.

When they were gone, Carmilla said, "And he looks like such a nice man! A grandfather who would buy you the toy train or stuffed bear your parents cannot afford for your name day." She shook her head. "I think we had better report back at once. Mina will want to hear what we are up against. But how to fight them—that is the difficulty. You are strong, as am I, as is my godfather. But we are only three. The others have their guns and knives—but what will those do against vampires? And the way Van Helsing controls them—that is the way my godfather used to control his vampiric soldiers, by implanting certain ideas in their heads. On the battlefield, they will do whatever he commands."

They climbed down from the bell tower the same way they had come up: Justine on the rope, which Carmilla released after she had reached the ground, and Carmilla crawling on the tower itself, head-first. But as they approached the gate, Justine heard a shout.

One of the monks was rapidly approaching across the grass. He must have been working in the garden, because he was carrying a trowel. Justine had no idea what he was saying—it was a stream of Hungarian.

"*Hallo! Hallo! Ist das der Biergarten?*" said Carmilla. Her voice was thick, her words slurred. She grabbed Justine by the arm and leaned on her. "*Wir suchen den Biergarten.*"

The monk looked at her, startled. "*Nein Biergarten. Nein Biergarten hier. Wie kommst du hier?*" Evidently, his German was rudimentary. How was Justine going to answer his question? She could not explain that they had gotten in by bending iron bars. . . .

Propping up the evidently drunk Count Karnstein, Mr. Justin Frank said, "*Das Tor ist kaputt. Sehen Sie?*" To show that the gate really was broken, Justine pushed it hard with the palm of her hand. She hoped he would not hear the metal latch snap in two under the pressure.

"*Geh! Geh!*" he said, waving his hands at them as though shooing chickens. "*Das ist nein Biergarten! Du bist hier nicht!*"

Mr. Justin Frank and Count Karnstein left hastily through the broken gate, but not before the Count had made the angry monk a drunken bow.

> JUSTINE: Carmilla also made what I think was a rude gesture, but I do not know enough about such gestures to understand what it meant.
>
> DIANA: I can teach you, if you want. I know lots of them!
>
> MARY: Yes, you're fluent, as we know.
>
> DIANA: Look, here's one! And here's another one.

JUSTINE: Diana, do you really think it is necessary to
express yourself in such a crude, unsophisticated
way? Underneath that rough manner, you are a
clever, affectionate girl.

DIANA: What's your point?

By the time Justine and Carmilla reached the house on
Múzeum utca, Mary and Catherine had returned from the Café
New York and were sitting in the music room, both looking glum.

"Your plan did not work, I take it?" said Justine. She had already
given her hat and gloves to a footman at the door.

"They wouldn't even listen to us," said Catherine. She was
curled up on the sofa, with her feet on the cushions, while Mary
sat more properly in one of the armchairs. "Leo Vincey—what an
arrogant, idiotic—and he had stupid hair. All those little curls, as
though he were trying to imitate some sort of Renaissance Cupid!"

"I think if Mr. Vincey hadn't been there, Professor Holly might
have listened to us," said Mary. "He was insulting—but I got the
sense that he is insulting to everyone. Meanwhile, Beatrice has
spent the last couple of hours with Mina—they're working on
some sort of top secret project they won't tell us about. And
Diana's off somewhere with that apprentice footman, who must
be named after Attila the Hun. Which I suppose makes sense,
this being Hungary! Lucinda is asleep—Laura and the Count are
staying with her. I think Laura has been doing double duty—she
seems to be staying with Lucinda twice as much as anyone else.
And we're—well, we don't quite know what to do with ourselves.
How can you plan when you don't know what you're planning for?
But the two of you must have found out something. Justine—does
this vampire army exist?"

"I am sorry to say it does." Justine remembered those monks, drinking blood as though it were communion wine. "There are twenty-four men Carmilla identified as vampires. We observed them engaging in—well, it was the most ridiculous, and yet the most disquieting, ceremony. Carmilla believes Van Helsing is controlling them through the power of suggestion—a sort of mesmerism."

"Yes, Laura is like that," said Carmilla, shaking her head. "She nurses the servants when they are sick, and every wounded animal that comes near the schloss. I make the medicines, but she cares for them. I shall remind her not to overtax herself. There are many here who can share that duty with her."

"Twenty-four doesn't sound like much of an army," said Catherine.

"And yet twenty-four vampires will destroy a company of ordinary soldiers, and throw a battalion into disarray," said Carmilla, bringing her attention back to the present discussion. She sat down in the other armchair, while Justine perched on the harpsichord bench. "I saw it myself in the border wars, when the Count was still creating vampiric soldiers. He, too, would mesmerize them—to fight until they were incapable of continuing. Arminius Vámbéry would be familiar with the technique from his historical research."

"It is a terrible practice," said Mina. She was standing in the doorway. "I'm very glad to see you all safely home. So we were right, Van Helsing has vampire troops at his command. Well, that's bad. On the other hand, I estimate he only has thirty to forty supporters in the Société des Alchimistes, which is fewer than I feared."

"How do you know the number of his supporters?" asked Mary.

"This morning, as Mária Petrescu watched from across the street, a steady stream of men and women went into Arminius Vámbéry's apartment building at approximately the same time. She counted them—there were thirty-six. Some may have been tenants, but most were clearly visiting Vámbéry, and by implication Van Helsing. Even from where she was sitting, she could see activity in Vámbéry's apartment, and Van Helsing himself walked some of the guests to their carriages afterward. When those guests had departed, Van Helsing and Seward went out."

"That must have been when they went to the abbey," said Justine.

"Of course, those may not be all his supporters," said Mina. "He may see more tonight, or perhaps tomorrow although it is the Sabbath. Nevertheless, I do not think he has a majority, which is why he's counting on force to carry the day. Vlad tells me these annual conferences are attended by members from all over the world. He estimates there will be a hundred to a hundred and fifty members in attendance. Van Helsing's faction will be no more than a third of that. However, I'm not sure it matters in terms of our plans. If Van Helsing wins, we will have to act. If he loses, we will still have to act. And to that end—there's something Beatrice and I would like to show you. If you'll come into the dining room, I think it's time for a council of war."

A council of war! Justine did not like the sound of those words. When had war ever led to benefits for mankind? Indeed, it sometimes seemed to her that history itself was simply a long account of bloodshed, to little purpose and for little gain. And yet, men such as Van Helsing had to be stopped—she knew that as certainly as she knew there was good in the universe, and it must combat evil. If it chose to do so through her, she would not refuse the battle.

MARY: Isn't that a bit melodramatic? I mean, I know you're describing Justine's thoughts, but still . . .

CATHERINE: Justine and I were in the circus together for years. That is exactly how she thinks. Imagine if Joan of Arc had read a lot of obscure German philosophy and were over six feet tall. That's Justine all over.

JUSTINE: Catherine, you give me too much credit. I am neither as good, nor as eloquent, as you make me out to be.

CATHERINE: See? What did I tell you?

In the dining room, Beatrice was standing by the table, on which were arranged an assortment of weapons—pistols and knives, as well as what looked like lengths of cable. Behind them was a collection of glass bottles, some of which were filled with a bright red liquid. Were those weapons of some sort as well? Mary could not imagine how.

"I'm very glad to see you back!" said Beatrice to Justine and Carmilla. "And I hope your errand was more successful than Mary's and Catherine's. They have been complaining that their journey was useless."

Justine approached the table and looked down at that strange assortment. "I believe so. We discovered that Van Helsing has twenty-four vampire followers—although they more closely resemble acolytes. Unless they were not all present at his unholy mass . . ."

"He would have wanted them all there, to reinforce his power over them," said Carmilla. "He has placed them in some sort of religious trance, induced by mesmerism."

"That sounds like something out of Catherine's stories," said Mary. "How in the world are we going to fight a bunch of mesmerized vampires?" How would they fight a bunch of vampires, whether mesmerized or not? She had no idea.

"Even I would not have come up with that," said Catherine.

"Spider gods, yes. Mummy curses, certainly. Mesmerized vampires? I doubt it."

"What about crosses? Or garlic?" Diana was standing in the doorway, with Hóvirág by her side. What in the world had happened to the wolfdog? It was almost completely black with soot. Diana was mostly clean, although she had a long black streak down one of her cheeks and the side of her neck. "Attila is locked in the coal room. You might want to get him out. He's been pounding on the door for a while."

"And why would Attila be locked in the coal room, exactly?" asked Mina, who was still standing by the door.

"He said no girl was more clever than a boy. She could be *as* clever, but she could not be *more* clever. So I told him we should each allow ourselves to be locked in the coal room, and whoever got out fastest would be the most clever. I went first and got out, easy peasy. He's probably been in there long enough. I thought if I let him out too soon, he might want to say that boys are more clever again. And then I would have to do something else to convince him."

"And I take it that is coal dust all over Hóvirág?" said Mina.

"What? Oh, yes. What's the Hungarian word for coal-flower? I think we should call her that now. She *loved* rolling around in it."

Hóvirág let out a plaintive bark.

"Come on, you," said Mina to the wolfdog. "Let's get you bathed before you roll on one of the carpets, although I doubt it would hurt any of them much. Diana, you have managed to be a bad influence even on one of the Count's *farkaskutyák*. I'll be back as soon as I get Attila out. Beatrice, could you continue without me?"

"Of course," said Beatrice. As Mina led the sooty wolfdog out of the room by her collar, Beatrice explained, in a voice we have since come to identify as Beatrice Lecture Voice, "The difficulty in fighting those who have been infected with vampirism is that they are extraordinarily strong and can heal from almost any injury. Knife and bullets wounds can slow them down, but will not kill them. The only ways to truly stop them are decapitation, dismemberment, and burning."

"What about crosses—," said Diana again.

"These particular vampires love crosses," said Carmilla. "And while I personally do not like garlic—I can always taste it in the blood of a regular garlic-eater—it will not harm a vampire."

"Diana's suggestion is not as silly as it sounds," said Beatrice. "As you said, you can taste garlic even in the blood. While I was sitting with Lucinda, I noticed that she had particular sensitivities—to light, and sound, and odors. All these senses are heightened in vampires, and can make them more vulnerable. They are stronger and can heal more quickly, but they are also easier to wound in the places they are most sensitive."

"See, I was right," said Diana. "Beatrice says I was right."

"For example," continued Beatrice, "Mary, will you help me demonstrate?"

Mary stepped over to where Beatrice was standing. What in the world was she helping to demonstrate? She had no idea. Beatrice picked something up off the table—a metal cylinder that had been hidden behind one of the pistols. She held it to her lips and blew into it. Suddenly, Mary could hear howls from the courtyard. Were those the Count's wolfdogs?

"What in the world?" she said. What were the wolfdogs responding to?

"That. Was. Awful." Catherine was holding her hands over her ears.

Justine looked at her as though wondering what had just happened, and Diana said, "What was that all about?" But Carmilla was doubled over, with her hands on her ears as well.

"Forgive me!" said Beatrice with contrition. "I had no idea it would produce such a powerful effect. Carmilla, are you all right—"

"It's brilliant," said Carmilla, standing up once more. She took her hands away from her ears. There was blood on her fingers. "Painful, terribly painful—but also brilliant."

"But what is it?" asked Mary. What were Catherine and Carmilla talking about?

"It is a common dog whistle," said Beatrice. "I borrowed it from the Count's groom, who uses it to signal the wolfdogs. They were first invented by Sir Francis Galton to determine the range of hearing in human beings and animals. Human ears cannot hear it—as the rest of you saw, Mary was not affected at all. But those of a dog can—or a cat, or a vampire. A cat can hear sounds higher than a dog, and a vampire, I conjecture, can hear even higher. We can use it to distract and disable Van Helsing's troops. But those of you with particularly acute hearing will have to carry India-rubber earplugs to protect yourself from its sound."

"And what are those glass bottles?" asked Justine. "Are they, too, weapons of some sort?"

Beatrice held up one of the bottles, which had an atomizer attached. "These are filled with paprika, the spice commonly used in Hungarian cooking, distilled in alcohol. If you spray it into their eyes, it will burn—and they will be blinded, at least temporarily. When I told Mina what I intended to make, she found these bottles in a perfume store. They will dispense the paprika spray evenly and effectively."

Carmilla looked at her with respect and a little trepidation. "That is fiendishly clever!"

"And the bottles that do not spray?" said Justine. "They seem to be filled with a clear liquid."

"That is chloroform," said Beatrice. "It will also burn on

contact, but its primary use is as an inhalant. If you place a hand-kerchief soaked in it over the nose and mouth, it will render the victim unconscious. The Count allowed me to test a little on him to make certain it would work. As I suspected, vampires are sus-ceptible to its effects, just as they can be shot or stabbed. However, they recover more quickly—you must secure them before they are able to revive."

"How in the world were you able to make that?" asked Mary. Beatrice had indeed been busy while they were away.

"Mina bought one of the ingredients at a pharmacy. The other is a simple cleaning agent—the butler was able to supply a large bottle. But you must be careful with both of these things—they will harm ordinary human beings as well as those infected with vampirism."

"I can carry a pistol, right?" said Diana.

"You've never even shot one," said Mary. "Once you've learned how to use a pistol safely, then you can carry it into a fight." The last thing any fight needed was Diana with a firearm! She was as likely to shoot one of them as one of their enemies.

> DIANA: You wouldn't even teach me. I had to get
> Holmes to do it.

> MARY: Yes, and I still think that was a misjudgment
> on his part. You're enough of a danger without a
> pistol.

> DIANA: Is that a compliment? Because I think that's
> actually a compliment.

"In this case, a pistol will be the least effective weapon," said Mina, who had evidently just come through the door—without the wolfdog, this time. "Even a knife can do more damage. And remember that the conference will be filled with members of the Société des Alchimistes. We will be in crowded rooms, where shooting off a pistol can be particularly unwise. We want to prevent a bloodbath, not create one. Your goal is not to kill—which would be difficult anyway. Beatrice, can you demonstrate the restraints?"

Beatrice nodded. She lifted one of the cables off the table. It had some sort of locking mechanism attached. "These were provided by the Count. Apparently, they can restrain vampires."

"Or at least that's the theory," said Mina. "They're made of the same material as the cables for the funicular up Castle Hill. Vlad himself will carry them in a rucksack. Restraining the vampires will be his responsibility. We can talk later about which weapons each of you prefers to use. Does anyone have questions?"

"Where's Hoho?" asked Diana.

"Being bathed by Attila, who will hopefully get a little cleaner as well. Now, unless you want to dine on chloroform and paprika spray, I suggest we move all these items to the sideboard. I've ordered an early dinner—you've all been running around today, and I suspect you're hungry. There's nothing more we can do until tomorrow, when the Academy of Sciences will be completely empty and we can 'case the joint,' as they say in America. In the meantime, I suggest we talk about something else. We need to take our minds off this, at least for a little while, or we'll all go mad, like Lucinda!"

Mary was relieved to talk of other things for a while. Over dinner, which was excellent, as were all the meals in Count Dracula's house—ironically, since the host himself did not eat—Catherine described the various circus performers and their acts, including Madam Zora, the Zulu Prince, and Sasha the Dog Boy. They speculated about why Sasha might have taken Irene

Norton's telegram. Had the Société des Alchimistes bribed him to steal it, or was he perhaps being blackmailed, and if so, with what? Catherine pointed out that the circus must be performing in Vienna right now—it would be close to the end of the Saturday evening show. Justine said she sometimes missed being the Giantess, and Beatrice admitted she had enjoyed her time as a circus performer. Catherine started teasing Beatrice about Clarence, but Mary stopped her—the Poisonous Girl was looking distinctly uncomfortable. Beatrice changed the subject to Irene Norton's apartment, which was the most elegant she had ever seen, and how she proposed to redecorate the parlor when they got home to Park Terrace. Justine mentioned that she would like to paint the Styrian countryside, if they could see it again when they were not fleeing Mr. Hyde. Carmilla invited her to visit the schloss at any time and described various Hungarian superstitions about vampires that still survived in rural districts. Catherine asked if she knew anything more about mesmerism—how was it that Alice could make herself disappear, or seem to? Diana was fascinated by Beatrice's description of Archibald. "I bet he's more fun than the lot of you," she said.

When dinner was brought in—a sort of fried noodle that Mina called *krumplis nudli*, with bean soup and cucumber salad, ham hocks for Catherine and a linden flower tisane for Beatrice—Mina asked the footman to turn up the gas, as it was beginning to get dark. After eating more than her share of *nudli*, Diana stood up, told them she was bored to death, and left to go see whether Hoho had recovered from her bath. Mary stopped her from taking one of the pistols on the sideboard on her way out. The girl was an incorrigible thief!

Only Mina was quiet. Mary looked at her inquisitively, but Mina just smiled and offered her a second helping of soup. Mary herself would have enjoyed dinner more if she were not so worried about Mr. Holmes. Where had he gone, and was he back with Dr. Watson yet? She kept telling herself there was nothing she could do about the situation, so there was no use worrying. Instead, she tried to focus on the conversation—so comfortable, so ordinary, as though they were back in the Athena Club! But she could not keep from wondering what was happening at 221B Baker Street.

Just as they were finishing their dinners, Kati poked her head in the doorway and said something to Mina that included the words "Katrin Moreau."

Mina looked puzzled. "Catherine, Kati says there's someone here to see you. He won't come in—he's waiting for you outside. He says it will only take a moment, and that you know him from the island?"

Catherine dropped her fork. It clattered loudly on the plate.

"What is it?" asked Mina sharply.

"Edward Prendick," said Beatrice. "Cat, are you all right?"

Catherine stared at her plate for a moment. Then she pushed her chair back and rose. "All right," she said. "I'll go talk to him."

MARY: Yes, you do have to write about this! You
    wrote about all the difficult, embarrassing things
    that happened to the rest of us. You wrote about
    my conversation with Hyde. You wrote about
    Justine and Adam. You wrote about Beatrice and
    Clarence. And Diana—well, Diana doesn't get
    embarrassed about anything, so that doesn't count.
    It's not fair if you don't write about yourself in the
    same way.

CATHERINE: I wrote about what an idiot I was,
    thinking Zora had stolen the telegram. Wasn't that
    embarrassing enough for you?

JUSTINE: But your conversation with Prendick was important—not only because of the information he provided, but also because of how it affected you. Catherine, this is not simply a story of our adventures. It's a story about us—our emotions and relationships. Without that, it would indeed be like one of your Astarte books.

CATHERINE: There's nothing wrong with my Astarte books!

DIANA: Except that Rick Chambers is kind of stupid.

Prendick was waiting for her in the carriage entrance. In the light of the gas lamp by the front door, he looked just as he had on the train—like himself, but more tired, perhaps older. It was not only his hair that had turned gray. He himself had turned gray, as though he were slowly turning into a ghost.

"Catherine," he said. "As soon as Van Helsing mentioned Count Dracula, I knew where I could find you. They don't know I'm here. I know you don't want to see me. I know you probably never want to talk to me again, but I had to warn you. Please, please stay away from this fight. You don't know what forces you're up against."

Catherine raised her hand, as though to stop him, but he took it and held it to his chest, just over his heart. "I know you hate me, I know you will always hate me for abandoning you on the island. But please listen."

"I don't hate you," she said. That was not entirely true, but she did not want to admit how she felt. It allowed him too much power over her. She had loved him once, and that had allowed him too much power over her as well. She had learned her lesson. "I despise you as a coward," she said. That was not entirely true either.

"Despise me all you want," he said, with a sort of quiet desperation. "It can't be more than I despise myself. I will tell you one thing, however. I never meant to leave you and survive—when I stepped onto the raft I had built, I believed I was going to my death. I was saved only by chance. When I saw you again in London—"

"Where you were creating Beast Men, like Moreau!"

"Catherine, believe me, I never would have done so if they had not forced me."

She stared at his thin, drawn face. She would not pity him— no, she would not. "You made a choice. You chose to become one of the Masters with the whips. You chose to leave Archibald—the Orangutan Man—chained up in a cellar."

He looked startled. "How did you know—"

"What do you want, Edward? Why have you come here?"

"To dissuade you from entering this fight." He held her hand, which was still on his chest, with both of his. "My love . . ."

She pulled it away. "Nothing you say will either persuade or dissuade me—not in this or any other matter."

"Then, I wanted to give you this." Out of his breast pocket, he pulled a piece of paper. "I wrote it all down in case you would not see me. Please, Catherine. Be careful."

Reluctantly, she took the piece of paper he was holding out. Without a word, with only a final look at her, like a man seeing land for the last time, he turned and disappeared into the dark street.

Catherine stared into the darkness after him. Then, she unfolded the piece of paper and read what was written on it in his spiky handwriting, which she recognized from long ago on the island, when he had taught her to write. It was a detailed description of Van Helsing's plans.

CHAPTER XXV

A Meeting of the Society

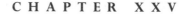

T he next morning, at breakfast, Mary was startled to see Laura come into the dining room with Lucinda on her arm. Lucinda was dressed! And out of bed! Well, that was a positive development.

"How is our patient this morning?" asked the Count, rising and bowing. He was as courteous as ever, but Mary could tell that he was surprised and concerned.

Mina rose and went to her. "Are you all right, my dear? I'm very pleased to see you up this morning. That is, if you're not tiring yourself out."

"She's been doing much better," said Laura. "This morning she heard the church bells and said that she wanted to go to church. At least, I think that's what she meant."

"I wish to sing in the heavenly choir," said Lucinda, looking at them all with great sincerity. "I wish to join my voice with the angels and archangels."

"There's a Catholic church on Kecskeméti utca, only a few blocks from here," said Mina. "I'm afraid this is a household of nonbelievers—neither Vlad nor Carmilla attend mass. I don't suppose some of you—"

"I shall take her," said Justine. "It has been several weeks since I have attended mass—not since we left London. I would like to go."

"As would I," said Beatrice. "Justine and I can take her. That is, if she's strong enough?"

"If she begins to feel unwell, I can always carry her back," said Justine.

"I don't suppose there's a Church of England in Budapest," said Mary, smiling. "I would like to go to church as well, but I don't think the Archbishop of Canterbury holds sway here."

"What about a Calvinist service, if you don't mind that it's non-conformist?" asked Mina. "There's a church in Kálvin tér where Laura goes sometimes. We could take you and Diana to a service there. Of course, it will be in Hungarian. . . ."

Mary did not mind. Diana did, but then she would have disliked being dragged to any blasted church service, as she told Mary. Still, Mary insisted that it was for her own good. With Mina there, Diana actually behaved herself instead of making faces or kicking the pew in front of her. Laura translated the Hungarian sermon as best she could—she said her Hungarian was not particularly fluent, since she had grown up in the Austrian part of the Austro-Hungarian Empire. "My French and German are all right," she said, "but for Hungarian you really need Carmilla!"

When they returned, Mary was startled to hear music floating down the stairs. Was that the harpsichord in the music room?

Suddenly, Mina gripped her by the arm. "Oh, thank goodness. That's a good sign. Come on, I want to see—"

See what? What was a good sign? Mina was almost running up the stairs. Mary looked at Laura, who seemed just as surprised as she was. "I've never heard anyone play that instrument," said Laura. "I didn't even know it was in tune."

It wasn't, completely—but the music that floated down from the second floor was melodious, despite a few sour notes.

Mary entered the music room just behind Mina. There was Lucinda, sitting on the harpsichord bench, playing as though her life depended on it, with her fingers dancing across the keys, her hair in wild curls around her head. Beatrice and Justine were standing by the harpsichord, listening to her performance.

"She asked to come up here as soon as we returned," said Beatrice. "Apparently, she had seen the instrument earlier, when passing this room."

"Lucinda," said Mina, kneeling by the bench, "my dear, are you all right?"

Lucinda's fingers crashed on the keyboard. She turned on the bench, and Mary could see that there were tears streaming down her face.

"*Mijn moeder!*" she said. "*Mijn moeder is dood.*" Mina sat on the bench and put her arms around Lucinda. The girl sobbed on her shoulder as though her heart were broken, which it probably was. But why now? Lucinda had not cried about her mother's death since that day in Irene's apartment. She had been so far gone in her madness. . . .

Slowly, her sobbing grew quieter. She looked up from Mina's shoulder. "Where am I, Wilhelmina?" she said. "What is this place? I remember a castle in the forest, where I was pierced by thorns. But no, that is a fairy tale. Am I still in Vienna?"

"You're in Budapest, with me," said Mina, stroking her hair. "How much do you remember of what happened?"

Lucinda shook her head. "Dreams. Nightmares. The shadows came for me. They brought me to the dungeon where the king had imprisoned my mother. No—that is a fairy tale again. My mother—" Tears still ran down her face. "But I remember—her. She gave me blood." She pointed at Mary. "And her." Now she was pointing at the door, and there stood Diana, lagging behind at usual. "She burned the castle to the ground and set me free."

"Something like that," said Diana. "Is she—is she sane again?"

"Hush!" said Mary, scowling at her.

"How did this happen?" Mina asked, looking at Beatrice and then Justine. "How did Lucinda regain—well, her composure, let us say."

"The organ started playing," said Justine. "And the choir sang—young boys with voices like angels. Then suddenly, I felt her gripping my hand. She looked at me, and for the first time I could tell that she truly saw me. I would say it was a miracle, but I believe it was the music."

"Lucinda has always been a gifted musician," said Mina. "She studied with a famous composer in Amsterdam, and her mother thought that someday she might be a pianist. Perhaps the music reminded her of who she was and brought her out of her dreams." She turned to Lucinda again. "My dear, forgive me for asking you this, but do you remember anything about your father? About his experiments?"

Lucinda put her hands over her eyes, and for a moment Mary thought she was not going to answer. Then, she said, "He took my blood. And he—with the needles, I do not know the word in English. He put blood into me, blood that he said would change me, make me stronger. Make me live forever. But I could feel the shadows gathering around me, in my mind. I was lost in the dark forest. . . ."

Mina put her hand on Lucinda's arm. "Do you think you could describe this—to other people? Quite a lot of other people? At a very large meeting."

Lucinda looked at her with wide, frightened eyes.

"Surely we can't subject her to such an ordeal," said Mary. Lucinda looked so young, so vulnerable. "She has just regained her—well, composure was the word you used. Would bringing her to the meeting of the Alchemical Society endanger it again? Could she sink back into—you know."

"Looniness," said Diana.

"Mary's right," said Laura. "You can't possibly expect her to appear in front of all those people, not in this state. Can't we do it some other way?"

"No, we can't." Mina's voice was unexpectedly sharp. "This is why you brought her here. Presenting her to the general meeting was the whole point. When Van Helsing killed Lucy, he destroyed the evidence of his crimes. He will never be brought to account for her death. But Lucinda is the evidence—the marks of transfusions on her arms, her vampiric madness. We need the members—and Ayesha—not only to hear, but also to see what Van Helsing has been doing. Now that she is once again—well, not entirely herself, but more so, Lucinda can tell her own story. That will be even more powerful than if I were telling it. Mr. Prendick has informed us what he is planning. If she could speak as soon as Van Helsing makes his motion, I think it would have the greatest effect. Lucinda, can you do that? You will help save other girls who might suffer the same fate and stop your father from committing atrocities."

This was a Mina that Mary had never seen, the Mina employed by the Royal Society as a spy, for purposes she still did not entirely understand. The Mina whose primary concern was stopping Van Helsing, no matter the cost. Would she ever be able to think of her as Miss Murray again? She felt sick at heart.

She was still feeling dispirited later that afternoon, when they broke in to the Hungarian Academy of Sciences.

> DIANA: I was the one who broke in. I picked the lock, just like I rescued Lucinda. At least she gave me credit!

> CATHERINE: You got us in, then Mary made a map while you wandered around aimlessly, looking at the paintings, making fun of the men in wigs. Beatrice formed plans for the contingent up in the

balcony, while Justine and I planned for those of
us on the floor of the meeting room. So I think
the credit goes to all of us.

The Academy was as impressive on the inside as it was outside. There was the great hall where the meeting itself would
take place, the grand staircase leading up to the second floor, the
balcony where observers could watch what was happening below.
Tomorrow, the hallways would be filled with members of the
Alchemical Society, the conference rooms with scientists giving
papers. How many of their projects, Mary wondered, would
involve some form of biological transmutation? And . . . had her
father ever given a paper on her or Diana? Somewhere, there must
be copies of papers by Rappaccini, Moreau . . . even Frankenstein.
She wondered what they would say.

When they returned to the house on Múzeum utca, Mina said,
"This evening, I want all of you to get some rest. Do something to
take your mind off the Société des Alchimistes. You'll be sharper
and more ready tomorrow for having rested."

MARY: As though we could have! I think I paced
nervously most of that evening. I may have worn
a hole in my bedroom carpet. And of course I
worried about Mr. Holmes.

JUSTINE: Beatrice and I read in Mina's library. You
should have joined us. When I am nervous, I find
Kant's *Observations on the Feeling of the Beautiful and
Sublime* always calms me.

BEATRICE: I'm afraid that I read a copy of *La Nouvelle
Mode*. I could not concentrate on anything more

serious than a fashion magazine. But where was
Catherine?

CATHERINE: Rooftop. I had a lot to think about, and I
always feel better on mountains.

Just before Mary was about to go to bed, there was a knock on
the door. "Come in!" she called.

It was Mina. "Mary," she said, walking over to the bed and sitting at the edge of the mattress, "there's something I want to talk to
you about."

"Yes?" said Mary. Would Mina say anything more about all
those years she had lived in the Jekyll household, spying for the
Subcommittee on Bibliographic Citation Format? And did Mary
want to hear it?

"Tomorrow, I'd like you to be the one who makes our case in
front of the society. You're Mary Jekyll, your father's daughter.
You have a credibility I don't. Could you do that?"

"I guess so," said Mary. "But what do I say—"

"Just let Lucinda talk, and then make your case to Ayesha. No
more experiments. No more monsters."

Mary winced at that word. Did Mina have to use it? *Is that what
Mina thinks I am?* she wondered.

"All right," she said. She would do it—not because Mina asked,
but to stop men like Van Helsing. So there would be no more
Lucindas . . .

Mina smiled. "My dear, you were always my favorite student.
Good night, sleep well."

And you were my favorite teacher, thought Mary. *Truly, my only
teacher.* After Mina left her room, she tossed and turned half the
night before falling into a deep, dreamless sleep.

She woke the next morning dreading what the day would bring.

There was breakfast, as usual, but only Diana seemed to have any
appetite. Even Catherine chewed on some bacon desultorily.

Mary looked around the table. All of them but Diana seemed
tired and anxious. Even the Count looked worried, and he knew
better than any of them what they were up against.

Lucinda was the only one other than Beatrice wearing a
dress—a white muslin that made her look like the heroine of a
melodrama. Had Mina chosen it for effect? Of course she had!
Mary stole a glance at Mina, who looked weary but resolute. For
a moment, Mary longed for the days when Miss Murray had been
her friend and companion, the woman she had most looked up
to in the world. This Mina was so different! Like Mary, she was
wearing a walking suit that would not restrict her movements.
The rest of them were in masculine attire and had done their best
to look like respectable members of the Société des Alchimistes.

"Here are the things I want you to keep in mind," said Mina.
"First, there will be guards, but they are the usual Academy of
Sciences guards. As far as we know, the Société des Alchimistes
has not hired any additional guards of its own. The guards won't
be able to tell us from the members by sight. What they will be
checking are these." She opened a small bag and scattered some
metal objects on the table. "When I was still Lucinda's chaperone,
I took a wax imprint of Van Helsing's seal. These are for those of
us who will need to get through the front door."

Mary reached for one and recognized it immediately. She had
first seen it on the body of a murdered woman in Whitechapel—
poor Molly Keane, her very first case with Sherlock Holmes! It
was a metal seal, suitable for hanging on a watch chain or wearing
as a pendant. Engraved on it were the letters S.A.

"Diana, Vlad, Laura, and Beatrice, you will be breaking in
through the back door, the way we entered on Saturday, so you
won't need to identify yourselves at the entrance. I want you to go

directly to the balcony—no getting distracted, Diana!"

"As if!" said Diana under her breath, so only Mary could hear.

"Find and take care of the vampires Van Helsing has positioned there before he can give his signal. You may find other observers as well—Vlad says provisional members, who have no voting rights, sometimes sit in the balcony. Try not to chloroform any of them by accident. Diana is there to break in, Beatrice and Laura to do the chloroforming, Vlad to restrain them. Remember these men are phenomenally strong. Also, they bite.

"Mary and I will go in through the front lobby with Lucinda. We'll find a place to sit by the meeting room door, and won't identify ourselves until Van Helsing calls for a vote. First, Ayesha will give the president's welcome to the members, then the membership will discuss old and new business—that's when Van Helsing will raise the issue of biological transmutation. And that's when we're planning to speak up. Catherine, Justine, and Carmilla will also go in through the front and position themselves about the meeting room. Catherine and Carmilla will be able to detect the vampires by scent. Justine, follow their lead. If they attack—and we don't know how this meeting will go, any number of things may happen—you must deal with them and do your best to protect the members around you. Disable the vampires as fast as you can—Vlad will join you as soon as he's done in the balcony to restrain them with the cables. Any questions?"

Mary looked around the table. Catherine was shaking her head, and no one else seemed to have questions either. Suddenly, Diana asked, "Can we bring Hóvirág? I bet she would be useful to bite vampires!"

"No," said Mina. "Any other questions?"

There were none.

"All right," she said. "It's seven o'clock. First group goes by the Danube, second group by Váci utca, third group by Kecskeméti

utca. You should be in positions by a quarter to eight. The meeting starts at eight sharp. Group one leaves first, wait five minutes,
then group two, *etcetera*. Ready?"

No, not ready, thought Mary. But she was beginning to learn
that one never was truly ready for the difficult things in life. They
happened, and one either rose to the occasion or failed to do so.
The trick was simply to rise to each occasion as it came.

She was in the third group. Fifteen minutes later, she, Mina,
and Lucinda were walking down Múzeum utca. Birds were calling
to one another in the linden trees that hung over the park fence.
The lavender seller was standing in her usual place. *"Levendula!
Levendula egy fillér!"* she called. Perhaps after this was over, Mary
would buy herself a bunch? Surely she would deserve it.

They crossed the square—Kálvin tér, Mina had called it yesterday, when they had gone to the Calvinist church, then made
their way down Kecskeméti utca, a narrow street that led between
shops, apartment buildings, and more churches—just how many
churches were there in Budapest? The air was clean and fresh, and
the streets seemed quiet for a Monday morning. Their boot heels
clicked against the cobblestones. She had asked Mina if they ought
to disguise themselves in some way, but Mina had said no. They
were going to speak in front of the society. They needed to do so
as themselves, to earn the trust of the members—and perhaps
Ayesha herself. The three of them would not carry weapons, and
their only disguise would be a small hat with a veil for Lucinda.
It was the sort of thing any fashionable woman would wear in
summer, to protect her face from the sun—but it would keep Van
Helsing from recognizing his daughter in the crowd.

The narrow streets opened up to a square, and once again she
could see Gerbeaud, the coffeehouse where Mina had taken them
on that first day. Mary wished—how she wished!—this were an
ordinary morning, when all they needed to do was see the sights

of Budapest, and perhaps stop for some ice cream. But they passed the coffeehouse and proceeded down a street with grand hotels on either side until they came to the park.

Across it, Mary could see the Academy of Sciences, looking exactly the way it had looked on Sunday: official and imposing, like a more ornate version of the College of Surgeons in London.

Mina turned to Lucinda. "Are you all right, my dear?"

Lucinda nodded, but Mary could tell she was nervous. She reached out and took Lucinda's hand. "All you have to do is tell your story," she said.

"I think I can do that," said Lucinda. Her small, cold hand clutched Mary's tightly.

"And what about you, Mary? Are you ready?" asked Mina.

"As ready as I'll ever be," said Mary. She missed the reassuring weight of her pistol.

Mina looked at her watch, a pocket watch with the seal of the Alchemical Society on its chain. "Quarter to eight. Five more minutes, and then we'll go in. Just enough time to walk through the park."

What Mary had really been worried about was getting into the building, but it turned out to be surprisingly easy. There were two turbaned men in front of them who looked Indian, speaking a language Mary did not understand. They showed their seals and proceeded into the marble lobby. Then Mina and Mary stepped up to the front desk. Mary pulled Lucinda with her—she was lagging a little behind. The guard at the desk simply looked at their seals and nodded. And then they were inside. Up the steps, to the right—that was what she remembered.

The hallway outside the meeting room was filled with members of the Société des Alchimistes, drinking coffee, greeting one another, making introductions. For the first time, Mary caught a glimpse of this organization her father had belonged to, an organization that had meant so much to him—until his expulsion.

They spoke in a babble of languages—she could make out German, French, and surely that was Italian? And that—no, she had no idea. Perhaps one of the Central European languages? And the members! Men and women, although not as many women, she thought. In the sorts of frock coats one might see in London, but also long jackets ornamented with embroidery, or tunics and loose pants of colorful silk, or in the case of several women, what looked like Indian saris. Several men were wearing fur hats. There was clothing she thought might be Turkish or Greek, and a party of members who appeared to be from the Orient—perhaps Japan? But did she really know the difference between those eastern countries? There was Burma, and China, and Indochina . . . It had been a long time since she had studied geography with Miss Murray. Suddenly, she felt dreadfully ignorant about the world.

Mina led them through the crowd to the meeting hall, which looked just as it had on Saturday, large and paneled in dark wood, except that now it was filled with people. Some of them were already seated, although many were still circulating. Mina found three chairs next to the door. Mary sat down gratefully, feeling less conspicuous that way. She looked around her. At the front of the room was a dais with a podium set on it, and two tables on either sides. She could see Leo Vincey seated at one of them— his golden hair shone in the sunlight coming through the large windows. Professor Holly was standing next to him. She did not recognize anyone else up there, but they all looked very important. No doubt they were various officers of the Alchemical Society and its national branches. The room itself was filled with chairs—at least a hundred, probably more. So this was what a meeting of the Alchemical Society looked like!

Bang. Bang. Bang. Exactly at eight o'clock, a gavel rapped loudly at the front of the room. Mary looked at the podium. There stood a woman—was this Ayesha? She did not look much like a priestess of Isis. Indeed, she reminded Mary a little of Nurse Adams—she had the same air of grim determination, although Nurse Adams had been more plump, and this woman had gray hair. She felt a hand in hers—Lucinda had once again taken her hand. She gave Lucinda's hand what she hoped was a reassuring squeeze.

"*Mesdames et messieurs, Damen und Herren,* ladies and gentlemen. Welcome to the annual conference of the Société des Alchimistes. If you would, please take your seats. . . ." She had a heavy German accent—well, that was certainly different from Nurse Adams, who had been proud of being a Londoner born and bred!

There was a general bustle as the remaining members filed into the room and found their seats. The room grew quiet.

"I would like to remind you that there will be coffee in the hallway for the duration of the conference, and we once again thank the Café Gerbeaud for catering this annual event. Please remember to pick up your conference badges and schedules on the second floor. We will begin with a welcome by the president, then any business of the society. The first paper sessions begin at 10:30 a.m. sharp. Moderators, please make certain that presenters stay within the time allotted to allow discussion afterward. Lunch will be served in the dining room, after which we will have the afternoon paper sessions, and then panels. Tonight's reception will begin at 5:30 p.m. in the hall outside the dining room with a selection of Hungarian wines and cheeses. Please remember that translation services should have been arranged in advance. All papers must be given in English, French, or German unless an alternate language has been approved beforehand. If you need assistance accessing any conference events, and I speak as one who has suffered from rheumatism myself"—there was scattered laughter—"please speak with either myself or Lady Crowe. And now, without further ado—Madam President."

She stepped back from the podium. Ayesha took her place.

Mary knew at once that *this* was Ayesha. She looked exactly the way one would expect a priestess of Isis to look. She was tall— almost as tall as Justine. She had the brown skin of a Nubian, the high cheekbones and large, dark eyes familiar to us from paintings on Egyptian tombs. Her hair fell around her in a hundred long black braids, down past her waist. She was dressed in a cloth-of-gold gown that looked as though it had survived from the time of the Pharaohs.

> BEATRICE: Actually, it was a *robe à l'Egyptienne*
> from the House of Worth. Mr. Worth told me
> the recent archeological discoveries of Professor
> Flinders Petrie would make all things Egyptian
> fashionable, whether in clothing, furniture, or
> architecture—as indeed they have!

Ayesha moved to the podium gracefully and with an air of absolute command—the way a cobra moves before it's about to strike.

> MARY: Don't you think that's a little judgmental?

> CATHERINE: She does in fact move that way, and
> cobras are beautiful animals. They're also very
> useful—they keep down the rodent population,
> like cats.

> MARY: You are the only person who would think
> being compared to a snake is a compliment.

> CATHERINE: Also, she's as dangerous as a cobra. You
> can't deny that.

"Welcome," said Ayesha. "*Willkommen. Bienvenue.* And for our most recent members, *konnichiwa.*" Her pronunciation, in whatever language, seemed flawless, although there was a musical quality to her voice that made her English, at least, sound foreign. It was a deep voice, and it resonated around the room. "You are not here to listen to me, but to one another, so I will keep my remarks brief. This is the fifteenth year that I have had the honor to be your president. In that time, we have made great progress in expanding our membership, both in Europe and in countries that have not previously had a branch of the Société des Alchimistes. I am pleased and proud to announce new branches in Rhodesia and the Empire of Japan, which has a long and honorable tradition of alchemical accomplishments, older even than those of the European nations. Will the Japanese and Rhodesian delegations please stand up?"

Two groups on different sides of the room stood and bowed. There was a great deal of applause. Mary would have applauded automatically, as one does when others are applauding, but she was still holding Lucinda's hand.

"Thank you. I am also proud to report that we have increased the participation of women in the membership and our research." Here again there was applause, and a few calls of "Hear hear!" from feminine voices. "We are creating a society poised for the twentieth century. During my tenure as your president, we have made discoveries that will lead to incalculable benefits for mankind, while also maintaining important guidelines on alchemical research. That research must continue—we cannot stop the process of human discovery—but it must be done in a way that preserves the reputation of the society. I am proud of what our society has accomplished in its long history, and what it continues to accomplish. A new century is almost upon us. As we meet this week, I urge you to listen to one another, learn from one another, and think about how you and your colleagues can expand the bounds of human knowledge. Once again, I would like to thank the Hungarian Academy of Sciences for allowing us to share its headquarters, particularly for this annual conference. Professor Vámbéry, will you convey my thanks to the academy?" She looked at one of the men sitting at the table to her right—that must be him, thought Mary, with the pointed beard and mustache. He nodded and smiled.

"Now, is there any old business?"

A man stood up—not just any man—it was Dr. Seward.

"I would like to propose reinstituting the English branch of the society."

The man sitting next to Seward stood up as well. He was an older man, white-haired and genial—Van Helsing. "Madam President. I second Dr. Seward's motion, and I also propose that we abolish the approval process for experiments in biological transmutation." Mary recognized his accent as Dutch because it sounded so much like Lucinda's. "These two matters are inextricably linked. The restrictions on such experiments were put in place at the same time as the English branch was, how you say, disbanded, and for a similar reason—the actions of Dr. Henry Jekyll. I submit that we have not had a problem since, and there is no reason members of this society should be forced to go through such a process simply because of the actions of one man. I myself have had proposals rejected several times—"

"Indeed, Professor Van Helsing?" said Ayesha. "It seems to me that both of these items should more properly have been introduced as new business, since they are not currently under discussion in any of our committees, nor under consideration by the administrative body of this society."

"However, Madam President, we have discussed these matters before, many times—" Van Helsing sounded frustrated.

"Nevertheless, as you have tabled these motions, the membership can certainly discuss them now. First, is there a second for your proposal?"

"Second," said Arminius Vámbéry.

"Well then," said Ayesha. "Both motions are before the membership. Can you tell me, Professor Van Helsing, why such experiments should proceed without the prior approval of the society? Is the approval process so very onerous?"

There was something in her voice—a sharpness of tone. Suddenly, Mary thought, *Ayesha is playing with him, the way a cat does with a mouse.*

Van Helsing replied, looking around as though speaking to the room, making his case to the other members, "This procedure is cumbersome and unnecessary. We have not had a problem with biological transmutation since Dr. Jekyll's unfortunate experience. Members of this society have carried out such experiments successfully and with great effectiveness. I myself have petitioned to conduct such experiments, and the paperwork involved——"

"Do you call Dr. Moreau's research safe and effective, Professor? I authorized his experiments because they were limited in geographical scope, had clear experimental goals and methodologies. . . . And look what happened."

"Moreau was scarcely responsible for a wild animal breaking out of its shackles and attacking him!" said Seward. "Madam President, the pursuit of science almost always involves unforeseen consequences. Should we pursue knowledge less zealously simply because it sometimes leads us into dangerous territory? You yourself have said——"

"Any statements I have made in the past, I am well aware of," said Ayesha sharply. "Does anyone else in this room have a response to this particular proposal?"

This was the moment. Mary stood up. "I do, Madam President!"

She had thought half the night about how to do this. Be rational. Be persuasive. Speak calmly, and in a clear voice. Do not let them see how nervous you are.

"And who might you be?" said Ayesha. "I do not recognize you as a member of this body."

"I am not a member," said Mary "But my father was. I have evidence that pertains to the question before you."

There were murmurs among the membership. No doubt people were wondering who she was, why she was speaking.

"What evidence is that?" asked Ayesha.

"The evidence of Professor Van Helsing's daughter, Lucinda!"

"Stand up," Mary whispered to Lucinda, tugging at her wrist. "Stand up and pull back your veil!" Lucinda stood, reluctant, unsteady, reaching up with one hand to pull the veil away from her face. For a moment, Mary thought she might fall down, or even faint. Was she just frightened, or was she unwell? If she should fail in this . . .

"Indeed? Miss Van Helsing, could you please approach? If you have something to say, I would like to hear it."

Lucinda was shaking like a leaf in a high wind, and she had knocked her hat askew so it was now at a perilous, if admittedly rakish, angle. She would never be able to walk up to that dais alone.

"Come on!" said Mary. She pulled Lucinda along with her down the row, with audience members looking at them curiously and moving their feet out of the way, and then up the central aisle.

It was strange and fascinating, walking past all those—well, those alchemists, like her father, regarding her with curiosity, incredulity, astonishment, except some who did not seem to speak English and were asking companions to translate for them and explain what was going on.

She continued to pull Lucinda until they stood before the dais, in front of the podium. Ayesha looked down at them, expressionless. She would have been imposing even without the height of the dais. Mary quailed just a little.

>DIANA: She did not! She didn't look like she was quailing at all.

>MARY: Well, I was, and more than a little. Also, Lucinda was hurting my hand.

"And who might you be?" said Ayesha, looking at Mary.

"I am Mary Jekyll, the daughter of Dr. Jekyll." She heard gasps from the audience. "Lucinda, tell them," she whispered.

"I object," said Van Helsing. "My daughter is mad, quite mad, diagnosed by an eminent specialist in Vienna. A week ago, she was kidnapped from the mental asylum where she was being treated. Now she has been brought here, displayed before you in this fashion. This is highly injurious to her mental health, to her progress—"

"Thank you, Professor Van Helsing," said Ayesha. "Your objection is duly noted. Miss Van Helsing, what do you have to say for yourself?"

Mary squeezed Lucinda's hand in what she hoped was an encouraging way.

Lucinda looked up at Ayesha. She opened her mouth . . . but nothing came out. She looked at Mary with terrified eyes. Lucinda wouldn't be able to speak, would she? The girl was simply too frightened. Would they be dismissed? Disbelieved? And there was Van Helsing, looking so respectable, so very righteous! What in the world was Mary going to do?

She looked up at the president of the Alchemical Society and said, "Professor Van Helsing has been giving his daughter transfusions of vampiric blood in an effort to make her immortal and invulnerable. He also conducted similar experiments on her mother. When Mrs. Van Helsing began displaying symptoms of the madness that typically accompanies vampirism, he had her confined in the Maria-Theresa Krankenhaus in Vienna. Later, he confined Lucinda there as well. Her mother is now dead as a result of his experiments in biological transmutation. Lucinda almost died too. She would have, if we had not rescued her from the asylum."

"And have you any proof of this accusation?" asked Ayesha.

Had she? Had they? It was Lucinda's word against Van Helsing's.

Lucinda looked at her and smiled—the first genuine smile Mary had seen on that pale face. It was a gentle, innocent smile. Then she crouched down and leaped—up to the dais, up on the table. Before Mary could react, she had lunged toward Arminius Vámbéry and bitten him on the neck! He shrieked—a surprisingly high shriek for such a large man. Lucinda raised her head and turned back to the audience. Her hat was completely to one side, and there was a long streak of blood down the front of her white dress. She looked at Ayesha, her mouth red with fresh blood, and snarled.

The room erupted into gasps and screams. Members looked at the dais and one another, trying to understand what was going on.

"This is nonsense!" shouted Van Helsing. "You have no proof it was I who did this to her! Those who have kidnapped her are in league with Count Dracula. It must be he who transformed her in this way!"

"Professor Van Helsing, you are in contempt of this body," said Ayesha. "A procedure for your expulsion will immediately commence—"

Van Helsing stood on a chair. "I call for a vote of no confidence in the president!" he shouted. "Who is with me?"

There were hands raised—perhaps a third of the membership.

Arminius Vámbéry's was not among them, but he was using his hands to try to stop the bleeding from his neck. Professor Holly was pressing something, probably a handkerchief, to the wound. It was rapidly turning red. Most of the members seemed too astonished to respond.

"The society has become moribund!" shouted Van Helsing. "Why do we concern ourselves with trivialities when we could discover the secrets of life and death? Why do we undertake inconsequential research when we could advance human evolution through artificial selection, make humanity swifter, stronger, more intelligent? Why do we lurk in the shadows when we could become the new governors, the true legislators, of a better world, a world ruled by science and scientists? Man has ceased to evolve—the wisest and most honest of us admit it. If we, who understand the processes of nature better than other men, including the benighted fools who call themselves respectable scientists, will not save humanity from itself, if we will not extend our benevolent power over mankind and its institutions, men will surely degenerate and perish. Come, my brothers and sisters, who is with me?"

Among the audience, Mary could hear some calls of "That's right! Listen to Van Helsing! It's time for a new president!"

"You're mad, Van Helsing," shouted Leo Vincey, pounding on the table. "You're not seeking some sort of benevolent rule, but personal power."

"That's right!" Mary heard from at least one corner. There were obviously arguments going on among the membership. Some were with Van Helsing, some with Ayesha—a great many seemed to simply not know what was going on.

"Professor Van Helsing had asked for a vote," said Ayesha calmly. "By our rules and regulations, any member may make a motion of no confidence at any time. I assume that if I am voted out of power, Van Helsing will be nominated for the presidency by

Dr. Seward. If he is elected, his proposals will prevail—a return to experiments in biological transmutation without oversight and restoration of the English branch, with Dr. Seward as its *de facto* if not titular head. Let us take a vote: right here, right now. Members of the society, if you would like Van Helsing to replace me as president, raise your hands."

There were hands raised, but fewer than last time. Van Helsing's words had had an effect, but not the one he intended.

"And who would prefer me to remain as your president?"

Those who had voted *nay* were overwhelmed by those who voted *yea*—Ayesha had well over a majority.

"Come on," said Mina, gripping Mary's arm. "We need to get Lucinda out of here. This is when all hell breaks loose." How had she gotten to the front of the room? But Mary had not been paying attention to anything but the drama between Ayesha and Van Helsing.

"Aanvallen!" shouted Van Helsing.

That was the code for the attack. In the audience, men rose— how many? Mary could not count them all. They hissed and snarled, then began attacking the members seated around them. One of them bit down on a man's throat—suddenly, there was blood and screaming. Some members at the front of the room craned their necks to get a better look. Some began moving toward the doors, first out of caution and then in a panic, not yet certain of what was going on, but sensing that something was. Mary noticed a few sneaking out along the side aisles—had they been informed beforehand of what would happen? Van Helsing had probably warned his supporters.

A vampire jumped up on the dais and shrieked, head thrown back, fangs bared. And then, as though a pot had suddenly boiled, the entire room erupted into chaos. Most of the members were rising, shouting to one another, running toward the doors . . .

She had expected a dramatic battle, like their showdown in the warehouse with Adam Frankenstein. But this was less a battle than a melee. This was screams and shouts, and not knowing what was going on, being unable to see over the heads and shoulders of the crowd. She wondered how Beatrice and Laura were doing up in balcony. And somewhere in this crowd were Carmilla, Catherine, and Justine. She hoped they were all right. But she could not help them now—she and Mina had to get Lucinda out of this mess.

In the balcony, Beatrice had stood in the back, behind the seats, until Van Helsing had begun speaking. Then, as quietly as she could, she had positioned herself behind one of the men Count Dracula had pointed out as vampires. There were six of them, sitting among perfectly ordinary audience members whom she must protect from harm. When Mary had begun to speak, she had clamped a piece of cloth soaked with chloroform over his mouth. Almost immediately, he had slumped over, unconscious. Well, that wasn't so bad, was it? But when she looked around, she realized that she had been lucky. The man Laura was attempting to chloroform had torn the cloth out of her hands and turned around to attack. Laura was backing away from him, toward the balcony door. The other spectators in the balcony had realized something was wrong. Some of them were heading toward the door, but a few were trapped in a corner. The Count seemed to be occupied fighting two of the vampires at once, and she could not see Diana at all. In her pocket, she had the paprika spray. She pulled it out, ran to the vampire attacking Laura, and sprayed it into his eyes. He clawed at his face, backed away, and kept backing until he was against the edge of the balcony. For a moment, he swayed, hands over his eyes as though playing a grotesque game of hide and seek—and then, suddenly, he fell backward over the baluster. Laura was doing better now, spraying another of the vampires—two down, and Dracula was still fighting one. The other had sprung up onto the baluster and crouched there like a monkey. Diana streaked past her—she had a knife in one hand. Before Beatrice could say "Diana, don't!" Diana's weight had carried both her and the man she had just stabbed over the edge, down to the crowd below. Beatrice looked around. Laura's vampire was now sitting on the floor, hands bound with the cables—there were another two beside him. Dracula must have been busy. That left one still to capture.

Where was Diana? Beatrice looked frantically over the baluster, but could not see her. Why did Diana always have to do the opposite of what she was told? Beatrice hoped she was safe, somewhere down below. Then, she heard her name called. She turned to see a short, squat, powerfully built man with a thick beard. He said, "Miss Rappaccini? I'm Horace Holly. We'll take it from here, thank you. Ayesha requests your presence and that of your friends, including Count Dracula"—he uttered the name as contemptuously as possible—"in the library. If you will restrain that creature in the corner—I assume he too is one of Van Helsing's minions—we will take it from here. Would you follow me, please?"

On the floor below, Justine looked up just in time to see Diana and the man she was clinging to fall over the edge of the balcony and land on a knot of people trying to flee through the back door of the meeting hall.

> CATHERINE: Diana, when I call you Monkey Girl, you
> should take it as a compliment. I don't know why
> men like Moreau and Van Helsing think evolution
> is so great. Human beings have lost a lot in their
> evolutionary trajectory. You have no idea how much
> better off you would be with tails!

DIANA: I wouldn't mind a tail! Do you think you
could sew one on me? One that works, I mean. I
bet Dr. Moreau could have!

MARY: Oh Lord, that's the *last* thing you need.

That moment of distraction had cost Justine. The very large
vampire she had just hit over the head with a chair rose again and
drove the splintered leg of the chair halfway into her side. She
lurched back from the impact, then reached down and drew the
chair leg out. She examined her side where it had entered, under
the rib, dispassionately. She could feel the pain, but intellectually she knew that such a wound could not harm her, so she must
ignore it for now. Where was that vampire?

Catherine had jumped on his back and bitten his shoulder. He
roared and tried to grab her, turning this way and that, like a dog
chasing its own tail.

Justine raised the chair leg and looked for a place to stab him
without also stabbing Catherine. Perhaps in the chest? If only he
would stop turning around and around!

"I'm all right!" shouted Catherine. "Take care of Carmilla!
Behind you—"

Justine turned. There was Carmilla, surrounded by three of
them, trying to protect a woman who had been part of the Japanese
delegation and seemed to be putting up a good fight herself, duck-
ing and weaving out of the way of a surly-looking fellow who had
his fangs bared, ready to bite. The Japanese woman kicked him in
the stomach as he lunged at her.

Mina had been right—pistols would have been worse than
useless in this crowd, although it was thinner now. So many of the
members had gotten out, or were trying to get out, through the
two sets of doors. There were shouts, cries, the sound of chairs

banging against one another, and among it all, noises as of wild animals. In that echoing chamber, she could barely hear herself think. How many of the vampires were left? One of those who had attacked the Japanese woman was within her reach. Justine stabbed him with the chair leg, but it scarcely seemed to affect him—he kept coming despite the piece of wood sticking out of his stomach. She grabbed him around the throat. If she could hold on long enough, squeeze hard enough, she could cut off his air so he would pass out. That might stop him for a while. She saw his face go purple. Slowly but surely, he slumped in her hands.

Just then, Carmilla cried out—she had been stabbed in the chest! Justine could see a red streak running down the front of her shirt. The vampire who had stabbed Carmilla was holding a large, wicked-looking knife with what was now a bright red handle. Justine stepped in front of her.

"Now you will have to deal with both of us," she told him.

She was fairly sure he could not understand her—his eyes had that film of delirium and incomprehension she remembered from the fight in Vienna, and anyway he probably didn't speak English—but he grinned and raised his knife, as though looking forward to using it again. She pulled the bottle of paprika spray out of her pocket and sprayed it in his eyes. Ah, that had done the trick! He was writhing on the floor. How many of them could she spray? How many were in her vicinity? One more coming at her, but another three behind him. She pulled out the strongest weapon in her arsenal—the small metal cylinder that made such a piercing noise, for those who could hear it. When she had told Beatrice that she would not carry a weapon, neither pistol nor knife, Beatrice had said, "Then you should be the one to carry this." But first, she must warn Catherine and Carmilla so they could protect themselves from the sound.

"Carmilla!" she shouted. "I'm going to use the whistle!" But where was Catherine? A moment ago, she had been battling one of the vampires. . . .

But Catherine was no longer there. The fight had carried her to the other side of the room, close to the dais. The vampire she had bitten was down, but there was another lunging for her. She bared her fangs and growled. She would rip the meat off his bones! And then she would drag his body up a tree, and feast on it for days.

"Get away from her!"

Who had yelled that? She turned, snarling. There was Edward Prendick, standing by the dais, shouting at the vampire she had bitten. Damn, she thought that vampire was down, but no— although his arm was limp and bloody, he was crouched, ready to spring at her. Well, let him come. She would tear him limb from limb. She grinned, and motioned to him—*come on, I dare you.*

The vampire sprang, and she braced herself for the impact, but at the last moment Prendick stepped between them. What was he doing?

He took the full impact of the spring, falling back onto the floor. The vampire crouched over him, slavering. Then, it bared its fangs and bit down.

What was that high, shrill noise? It must be the whistle! She put her hands over her ears and fell to her knees, then crawled over to Prendick as best she could. The vampire who had attacked him was even more affected than she. He had curled into a ball like an animal protecting itself, with his hands wrapped around his head. Beside him was Prendick, lying on the ground. Was he—yes, he was still alive. Ignoring the whistle as best she could, she knelt beside him, examining the bloody face, the disaster that was his neck. How bad were his injuries? She would have to wipe the blood away before she could tell. He looked up at her and smiled, the way he had on the island when he had first told her that he loved her. "Catherine," he said, reaching for her face. For a moment, he touched her cheek. She let him, although it distracted her from what was more important, assessing how badly he was hurt. Then his hand dropped, and he was still. He looked up at the ceiling with eyes that would never look at her, or anything else, again.

"Catherine, are you all right?" It was Justine, staring down at her, the whistle in her hand.

Catherine looked up. She could feel tears on her face. Damn Moreau and his island! Pumas didn't cry. "He's dead," she said. "He tried to protect me. The idiot! Such a damn idiot! Such a god-damn . . . Didn't he know I'm so much stronger than he is? Why didn't he just let me fight?" She looked down again and stroked his hair, getting blood on her fingers. Then, she closed his staring eyes. "Moreau made me, but Edward taught me to be human." She was surrounded by chaos—she could still hear the battle around her, although it seemed to be happening someplace else, a place as distant as Moreau's island. She picked up the body of Edward Prendick and cradled it as though it were a child.

Beside her, the vampire that had curled into a ball, the one who had killed Prendick, uncurled himself. He stood and seemed to look around for the source of the terrible noise that had incapacitated him. Seeing nothing, he grinned and crouched, as though prepared once again to attack.

Catherine looked up at Justine and said, "This one is mine."

Suddenly, with a look of anguished astonishment, he crumpled to the ground. Behind him stood Ayesha. Her hand was raised, but there was no weapon in it. What had she done? She looked down at Catherine as though assessing the situation, then turned and moved back toward the center of the room. There was still one vampire menacing the Japanese woman. Was that it? Surely there had been more! Justine and Carmilla could not have dealt with all those vampires so quickly! Carmilla was close to the Japanese woman, but could not help her—she too had been affected by the whistle and was sitting on one of the chairs with her head in her hands. Ayesha walked over to the vampire, raised her arm, and held her hand a few inches from his head. Nothing happened. Then, the vampire raised his hands to his head, screamed in pain, and crumped to the ground. He did not get up again. Ayesha bowed to the Japanese woman, hands together palm to palm, and led her toward the door.

Catherine stared up at Justine in astonishment. "What the hell was that?"

Justine knelt by the body of the vampire who had killed Edward Prendick. "There is no wound on him. But look, there are two red marks on either side of his temples. It is as though a current has passed through him, as though he has been burned by electricity."

"Catherine!" It was Carmilla, standing just behind Justine, hands still at her temples and blood down her shirtfront, soaking into her jacket and waistcoat. "Is that Prendick? Is there anything we can do?

"He is beyond help, Countess."

Catherine turned to see the gray-haired woman who had spoken before Ayesha, standing in front of the dais. "I am Frau Gottlieb. Ayesha would like to speak with you." She looked down at Edward Prendick. "I'm very sorry for your loss. I assure you that we shall treat Mr. Prendick's remains with the utmost respect. Now, if you would all follow me to the library? Madam President would like to meet you."

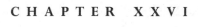

CHAPTER XXVI

Madam President

T he library was on the second floor. It was a large room
with shelves on every wall, filled with what looked like
scientific books and journals, all the way up to the ceiling.
The topmost ones could only be reached by a rolling ladder.

Justine was startled to see that Mary and the others were
already there. Mary was standing in front of an enormous oak
table. Beatrice and Laura were sitting at the table with Lucinda,
who was quietly sobbing into her hands. Laura had her arm around
Lucinda. Mina and Dracula were talking quietly in one corner,
near the ladder.

"Oh, thank goodness," said Mary. "We were so worried about
you!"

"What happened?" asked Justine. Carmilla went over to Laura
and murmured something—probably asking if she was all right.
Catherine sat down on one of the chairs and stared at her hands,
which were still spattered with blood. Beatrice leaned over and
handed her a handkerchief.

"I don't quite know," said Mary. "All hell broke loose, and
then a woman—older, with white hair and spectacles—told us
to follow her and led us here. Mina, Lucinda, and I have been
waiting here since. And then Count Dracula, Beatrice, and Laura
came with Professor Holly, who went off again without giving any
explanations. What's going on out there—*and where is Diana?*"

"Have you perhaps misplaced one of these?"

It was Ayesha. She must have entered right behind them. She was holding Diana by the collar. Diana was twisting and turning, evidently trying to kick the president of the Alchemical Society in the shins.

"Diana! Stop that at once!" said Mary.

Diana scowled, but when Ayesha released her collar, she ran to join the rest of them by the table. She plopped herself down on a chair and started kicking its legs.

Ayesha examined them as though they were particularly interesting insects, of a species she had never seen before.

A woman entered behind her. She was older, white-haired, wearing a pair of strong spectacles. She smiled at them like a kindly grandmother, as though she were about to hand out biscuits and good advice. Then she turned to Ayesha and said, in a well-bred English voice, "Madam President, the situation has been contained. We have seventeen wounded and three dead, including Mr. Prendick. Professor Van Helsing is locked in one of the basement storage rooms, but Dr. Seward managed to escape. Professor Vámbéry disavows any knowledge of today's events—he assisted Mr. Vincey in the capture of Van Helsing, and is currently being treated for a nasty bite."

"How very like Arminius. Van Helsing was a fool to depend on his loyalty." Ayesha turned back to them. "How is your wound, Countess?"

Carmilla unbuttoned her shirt collar and looked at her chest. "Already healing, Madam President."

"Good." Ayesha looked at each of them, comprehensively and dispassionately. "I have no time to spare for you today. I have wounded members to care for, and order to restore to this conference. The first paper sessions begin in half an hour. Miss Murray—" She turned to Mina. "It is a great pleasure to meet an agent of the Subcommittee for Bibliographic Citation Format. I am also pleased to meet such an interesting group of young women. Miss Jekyll, Miss Moreau, Miss Rappaccini, Miss Frankenstein, and, of course, Miss Hyde, if you will await me tomorrow at 3:00 p.m. in Count Dracula's house, I will speak with you further. You will not mind, I am sure, Vlad, if I avail myself of your hospitality. Lady Crowe will show all of you out."

She turned, and as gracefully as a cobra or a cat, she walked out of the room.

"What in the world—," said Mina. Which was, more or less, what they were all thinking. They stared at each other in astonishment.

"If you will follow me," said Lady Crowe. "And may I say that it's lovely to see you again, Mary, Justine, and Catherine? And of course little Diana?"

They all stared at her, startled. Then, "Madame Corbeau!" said Mary at the same time as Catherine exclaimed, "Frau Krähe!" Mary recognized her as the kindly grandmother from the train to Paris, Catherine as Sasha's childhood nurse from the train to Vienna. She was both and neither.

"Bien sûr," said Lady Crowe, smiling her grandmotherly smile. *"Natürlich.* However, much as I would love to chat with you again, we are busy today. As Madam President said, she will meet with you tomorrow. In the meantime, I have ordered for a basket to be packed, containing sandwiches from our luncheon and some excellent wine. You must be tired and hungry. The park is a popular place for a picnic, or you could go up to the castle district this afternoon. I think you've earned yourselves a rest, and perhaps some sightseeing."

They all stared at her. They had just fought vampires and incurred wounds, both internal and external. And she expected them to go on a picnic?

"Come on," said Mina, looking at Lady Crowe as though she had no idea what else to say. "Let's get out of this place."

They followed her out of the library, down the steps, and into the bright light of a Budapest morning, tired and uncertain about what they had accomplished. But the sun shone down on the Danube, and in the park, the birds were singing.

> JUSTINE: Is it not strange how such things can happen—momentous things, things that seem to change the world itself, and yet they do not. The river flows, the sun shines, the birds sing. Nature is indifferent to man, which is perhaps why we can find in it a source of healing. We may be wounded, but it is not—despite our weariness, it renews itself continually. I find that thought comforting.

> DIANA: I probably would too, if I knew what the hell you were going on about!

> JUSTINE: Come to the library. I shall read you some Wordsworth, who can explain it so much better than I can.

As they were finishing breakfast the next morning, Mina leaned over to Mary and said, "Would you like to go for a walk in the park before our meeting with Ayesha?"

"Yes, I'd like that," said Mary. She looked around to see if any of the others might want to join them, but Mina said, "I meant just you. We haven't really had a chance to talk since you got here, and I think it's time."

Anyway, all the others seemed occupied. Laura had asked Lucinda if she would like to go back to Styria and live at the schloss for a while, so she could learn how to be a proper vampire. Carmilla and Magda could teach her how to get the blood she needed, control her powers, and not accidentally kill people. Count Dracula was off doing whatever counts did on a Tuesday morning, which evidently included things like managing their estates and responding to complaints from tenant farmers. Catherine and Beatrice were talking about their circus act. A telegram had come that morning from Lorenzo:

CIRCUS ARRIVING WEDNESDAY CAN YOU PREPARE
FOR THURSDAY EVENING SHOW THEY WANT
THE POISONOUS GIRL

Catherine had thought of some ingenious new ways Beatrice could demonstrate her poisonousness. Justine was trying to persuade Diana that she should take the two puppies she had sneaked up in her pockets back to their mother in the stable. Later, Mary would have to once again patiently explain to her that no, they could not take any wolfdogs back with them to England. Hóvirág looked on inconsolably, having lost her very own human to these new distractions.

"All right," she said. They hadn't talked, not really, since Mina had told her about the Subcommittee for Bibliographic Citation Format, and so much had happened since then! She thought back to the events of the day before. It was all confused in her mind—standing with Lucinda at the front of the room, looking up at the dais where Ayesha stood listening to them, trying to get Lucinda out when the fighting began, being taken to the library by the woman who had called herself Madame Corbeau . . . She was still trying to understand exactly what had happened. It would be good to get out and walk around!

As they crossed Múseum utca and then walked to the entrance

of the park that surrounded the museum, Mary was reminded of the walk she had taken, not long ago, with Irene Norton. But this was certainly not like the Belvedere! The museum was a large neo-classical building set within a small park of gravel paths between tall trees. Along the paths, there were patches of grass, scraggly bushes, and statues of what Mary assumed were famous people. It was a beautiful morning, cool and sunny. Mothers were out walking with their children, who were either in perambulators or running around, shouting just as children shouted in London, but in Hungarian of course. Young men who looked like bank clerks or university students sat on the park benches, next to shop girls and nursemaids.

"We should to go the museum sometime," said Mina. "It houses artifacts from Hungary's history, going back to the reign of King István, perhaps even farther—I haven't been for a while. The funny thing about living in a place is, you never do the things you would if you visited! Mary, I'm sorry that your visit has been all intrigue and fighting and vampires."

Mary looked at her—she was wearing a respectable but not particularly fashionable straw hat—and laughed. "You sound just like Miss Murray, my old governess. You must meet her sometime! I'm sure the two of you would get along. Mina, do you remember when we used to go to the British Museum?"

"Of course I remember. Come on, let's walk around back. It's a fairly short circuit." Mina led the way, her boots crunching on the gravel. "You liked the Elgin marbles best, if I remember correctly. And all the red pottery, although some of the images were quite inappropriate for a young English miss. Once, you asked me whether there were any pots left in Greece, since the British had taken so many. I was sorry to leave, especially when you were still so young—far too young to take over the management of a household. And I was sorry to interrupt the education of such a bright mind. That's so often what happens to girls—they are educated up to a point, and then they are called upon to take up household duties, to care for other children or aging parents. It's a shame, really."

"Well, hopefully I turned out all right," said Mary, smiling although she was a little apprehensive about what Mina would say.

"My dear, you turned out splendidly, and very much as I thought you would." Mina walked for a moment as though lost in thought.

A small boy in a brown suit almost crashed into them. *"Gyere ide, Gyuri!"* his mother shouted. At least Mary assumed she was his mother. Birds were calling overhead. Mary had no idea what sorts of birds they might be. Justine would probably know. She tended to know these things.

Then Mina said, "Mary, can you forgive me for the deception I practiced? I was younger then, and it did not strike me as wrong to deceive a child of seven, particularly when I had an important reason for doing so. After all, you would never know of it. Well, I've learned my lesson—learned many lessons over the years. The benefit of growing older is that you make different mistakes. If you can't bring yourself to, I will understand, you know."

They turned onto the path at the back of the museum and walked under the shade of tall linden trees. Mary thought for a moment about how to respond. "I was angry with you. I suppose I still am, and I'm not sure what to do with that anger. I'm not very good at anger, as you know. Right now, after everything that happened yesterday, I'm just grateful that we're all alive! And I'm grateful for what you did, trying to help Lucinda—and all of us. Is Ayesha really going to call on us at Count Dracula's house? Somehow, it's hard to imagine. . . ."

"Her in Vlad's reception room? It's quite a grand reception room, far too grand for daily use, but you're right, it's difficult to imagine her in an ordinary setting. She belongs in an Egyptian temple, or perhaps a sublime landscape of some sort. How about the Alps? Where Lord Byron could write a poem about her . . ."

"Perfect!" Mary laughed, then grew serious. "What do you think she'll do to Professor Van Helsing? And do you think she'll agree to stop these experiments once and for all?"

"I don't know. Yesterday, did it seem to you . . ." Mina paused for a moment—they had walked all the way around the museum and were now on the other side. Then she said, as though startled, "The girl who sells lavender isn't at her usual post. She's been there every day for the past week."

"Oh," said Mary. "I didn't notice. Perhaps she's sold all her stock. But what were you going to say? About yesterday . . ."

Mina frowned and looked down at the ground. She kicked at the gravel with one foot. "Just that it seemed too easy. I know, three people died, including Edward Prendick, and more than a dozen were injured. But it could have been much worse. It could have been a real bloodbath. Instead, as soon as Beatrice and Laura subdued all of Van Helsing's henchmen in the balcony, Professor Holly appeared to clean up. When Catherine, Justine, and Carmilla were in trouble below, Ayesha herself came to blast the vampires with her power—and wouldn't I like to know how that works! I mean, does she need to touch them? I don't think so. Does she need to be close to them? And what does she do, exactly? I suspect it's like electricity, a sort of invisible lightning. At any rate, after Lucinda attacked Arminius and Leo Vincey pulled her off him, Lady Crowe came and led us to the library. It all seems rather—convenient. Almost rehearsed."

Mary was not entirely sure what to say, except perhaps—"It worked. I mean, we're here, and Van Helsing's been captured, although Seward got away. And Lucinda's herself again."

"That's the most important thing, of course," said Mina. She was silent for a moment. Then, she said, "Mary, there's a specific reason I asked you to come out today." She reached into her purse and took out an envelope. "This came in the mail for you."

A letter for Mary? "Is it from Mrs. Poole?" she asked, eagerly. It must be—who else would write to her at Mina's address? Perhaps it would tell her that Mr. Holmes had returned—the mystery solved, the criminal apprehended and handed over to Lestrade.

But as soon as Mina handed her the envelope, Mary could see that it was not from Mrs. Poole. She recognized that spiky, almost indecipherable handwriting. The envelope was addressed to Miss Mary Jekyll c/o The Countess Karnstein. Reluctantly, she opened the envelope and read the single sheet it contained.

> My dear Mary,
>
> I was disappointed to hear, from Ferenc *père et fils*, of your abrupt departure. I would have liked to spend more time with my family—you and Diana. I see myself in the both of you—different facets of myself, of course. Perhaps someday soon we can spend more time together. Despite our differences of opinion and temperament, and some unfortunate misunderstandings—there was no need for Diana to shoot János, who is a good boy if an inadequate assistant—I am proud of my daughters, one so fiery, the other so sensible.
>
> It is because you are so sensible and will know what to say that I write this to you: please tell Miss Frankenstein that Adam died the night after you left. He did not go peacefully, but raged against his creator and the woman who had rejected him. The last word on his lips was "Justine."
>
> I hope you are well, and please give my love to Diana. Tell her that I will try to send her some postcards from Switzerland. After we returned from England, in the expectation that he would not survive

his injuries, Adam made me the executor of his estate, part of which comes to me. If you ever wish to visit me, I shall have a somewhat gloomy castle with inadequate plumbing for you to stay in. But the view is magnificent. How shall I sign this letter? Perhaps with the name by which you knew me once, and may perhaps know me again.

Your loving father,
Henry Jekyll

Mary stared at the letter, and then up at Mina.

"What is it, my dear? You look as though you've seen a ghost."

Mary just held out the letter—how in the world was she going to explain it? How did one explain a man like Hyde? She watched as Mina read it—what would Miss Murray say? She was startled when Mina burst into laughter.

"I'm so sorry, my dear," said Mina, handing the letter back to her. "I know this is a serious matter—but he's just incorrigible, isn't he? Don't you dare feel guilty for escaping from his clutches, and don't let Justine feel guilty for Adam's death. She has an overdeveloped sense of responsibility—as you do, sometimes. So now Mr. Hyde will move into some castle in Switzerland, to do what—try to become Dr. Jekyll again? Oh—" She wiped tears of laughter from her eyes. "I'm so sorry. Some parents are impossible, aren't they?"

Mary put the letter into her purse. She must have looked thoroughly defeated, because Miss Murray smiled and said, "I know what you need. Do you remember what we used to do after our trips to the British Museum?"

"Tea and scones," said Mary. The memory was a happy one—how she had loved those outings! Then, she looked puzzled. "Are we going to get scones? Here, in Budapest?"

"Well, it's not quite teatime," said Mina. "And what would Mrs. Poole think of me if I spoiled your appetite for lunch? But there is a place around the corner that sells ice cream, and I don't believe there's any particular time of day when ice cream is appropriate—or not! They have the most wonderful flavors—coffee, sour cherry, hazelnut . . ."

> DIANA: Why didn't you take me? Why didn't I get any ice cream?

> MARY: You got plenty of ice cream while we were in Budapest! And strudel, and those biscuits you pull apart in layers, and those fried dough things . . . If you didn't have a stomach made of iron, you would have been sick the whole time.

> DIANA: But I didn't get any ice cream *that day*.

At three o'clock, they were all seated in a room they had never yet entered: Count Dracula's reception room. It looked exactly how Mary would have expected, based on the Count's style of decorating: all dark wood, velvet chairs, and gloomy paintings.

"Do you ever spend any time in here?" Mary asked. Then she realized the question might be rude. Goodness, was she getting as bad as Diana?

> DIANA: As if!

> MRS. POOLE: Miss Mary could never be that rude.

> DIANA: She doesn't have the imagination.

"Of course not," said Carmilla. "Isn't it a dreadful room? It's only ever used to receive ambassadors and other dignitaries. I have no idea why Vlad doesn't redecorate. Honestly, this entire house needs some cheering up." She turned to the Count. "You should let Mina do something with it—anything, really!"

Mary, Beatrice, Catherine, and Justine were in their best dresses—even Diana had been persuaded to wear her new dress from Ilona Couture, although she was now seated on the floor with her arms around Hóvirág, probably getting it covered with dog hair and slobber. Lucinda was looking ethereal in the white dress she had worn the day before, which had been cleaned. Mina and Laura were both in respectable gray and looked as though they could have been sisters. Carmilla was in her trouser suit, and Count Dracula was wearing a military outfit of some sort with a great many medals. They looked as though they were ready for some sort of audience—as, in a sense, they were.

At three o'clock exactly, Horvath úr, the Count's majordomo, entered and announced Ayesha—at least Mary assumed that was what he had done, since the president of the Alchemical Society followed him a moment later, but it was in Hungarian, so he could have said anything, really. Goodness, she was being both rude and flippant today—what was wrong with her? Well, other than what had happened the day before.

Ayesha was not alone. She was accompanied by two other women: the gray-haired one who had spoken before her at the podium, and a younger one who was carrying her purse and parasol.

Dracula rose and bowed. "Welcome to my house, Princess of Meroë, Priestess of Isis, Queen of Kôr."

Ayesha looked him up and down. Today, she was dressed in an afternoon ensemble of dark blue silk with silver stars woven into the fabric. Over it, she wore a blue-and-silver shawl that made her look just a little like a moonlit night, which was probably the

intended effect. Mary had been right—she looked just as imposing when she wasn't standing on a dais.

"My dear Vlad, you know perfectly well that flattery will get
you nowhere," she said. She took off her shawl and handed it to the
young woman behind her, who draped it over her arm. "I have no
intention of reinstating you in the Société des Alchimistes. Van
Helsing has confessed—not only to the experiments on his wife
and daughter, but also to the murder of Lucy Westenra. And may
I say"—she turned to Mina—"how very sorry I am for the death
of your friend. Anyway, my kingdom is long gone, overrun by
the British in their thirst for African gold and diamonds. I am no
longer any of the things you called me. You may call me Madam
President. Or Ayesha, if you wish." She smiled, in a way that did
not reach her eyes.

"What will you do with my father?" asked Lucinda. "Will you
punish—"

"He will not be physically harmed, but he will be punished, in
the worst way a scientist can be punished. His research will be
discredited. He will be forced to retire from his university appointments, and he will never again be allowed to publish a paper in a
respectable journal. I think he would prefer death! We will, of
course, continue to monitor his activities, to make certain he does
not return to performing experiments in biological transmutation.
Those are forbidden to him now, under any circumstances. I have
personally dispatched the creatures he mesmerized into following
his commands."

"You mean you killed them!" said Justine. "Surely that was not
necessary? They were not responsible for their actions. Perhaps
they could have been released in some remote area—"

Ayesha looked at her with raised eyebrows. "So they could
menace rural villages? These were not wolves, Miss Frankenstein,
but human beings who would inevitably be drawn back toward

human habitation, where they would feed and attempt to create others of their kind. I assure you, the death I gave them was less painful than what they would have suffered from superstitious villagers! As for Dr. Seward and Arminius Vámbéry, they too will be dealt with appropriately in time. Arminius, at least, remains useful to me, although I will put an end to his operations at the Abbey of St. Ignatius, which Van Helsing described after some . . . persuasion, let us say. I'm sure the Archbishop of Esztergom will want to know what the abbot has been up to! I doubt making vampires is his idea of the proper role for a monastic community. Although the Royal Society may not give us credit for doing so, we do take responsibility for our own."

Mina rose. "Madam President, how did you know—"

"About you? About the Subcommittee on Bibliographic Citation Format? My dear Miss Murray, I learned a long time ago that the most precious thing in this world is information. Is that not right, Frau Gottleib?"

"Just so, madam," said the gray-haired woman standing next to her. Yesterday, she had spoken with a German accent. But today . . .

At the sound of her voice, Mary started, then stood up. "But that's impossible," she said, leaning forward and peering at the woman. The room was so dark and gloomy . . . if only she could let in more light! She wished she could pull back those heavy velvet curtains.

"Good afternoon, miss," said Nurse Adams, in the accent of a respectable hospital nurse who had never left London in her life. Her voice, her expression—everything was different than it had been the day before! She was still thinner than Nurse Adams had been, with gray hair rather than brown, and yet in every other way . . .

"This is Eva Gottleib, currently the secretary of the Société des Alchimistes," said Ayesha. "Eva had an English mother and received her training in London, although her nationality is

German. Many years ago, when I needed an agent in your household, and you, Miss Jekyll, needed a trained hospital nurse to care for your mother, she applied for the position. She spent seven years in your employ, until you could no longer afford her services. You see, like the Royal Society, we too like to keep an eye on situations of interest!"

Mary sat down in the velvet chair with a thump. Nurse Adams was Eva Gottleib? This was getting ridiculous! Next, she was going to discover that Mrs. Poole—

> MRS. POOLE: Not me, miss. Whatever anyone else
> may be, I'm Honoria Emmaline Poole, thank the
> good Lord. To think that Nurse Adams, who was
> so proper, and so particular about her tea, should
> be a German! It just goes to show that you never
> know about people.

"Heinrich Waldman was one of your spies as well, was he not?" asked Justine.

"Oh, Heinrich!" Ayesha sighed. "What a stupid young man. He was returning from England, and Lady Crowe thought he could keep an eye on you on the train from Paris to Vienna, since she had other business to attend to. He was never supposed to make contact. Then he lost you in Vienna, and we could not find you again until you had come to Budapest, to stay with Vlad. You see, despite all I am telling you, we are an organization not of spies, but of scientists. This is not what we ordinarily do. We were keeping watch here, of course—we knew about Miss Murray, and anticipated that this would be your eventual destination."

"The lavender seller!" said Mary.

The rest of them stared at her, and Laura raised her eyebrows, as though to say *What you are you talking about?*

"That's her! The lavender seller." Mary pointed at the young woman holding Ayesha's shawl. "You're the one who's been selling lavender across the street, aren't you? I recognize you now . . ."

The young woman held out one hand as though offering a bunch of flowers, and said, "*Levendula, csak egy fillér!* Yes, I am your lavender seller, Miss Jekyll."

Mary looked over at Mina, who had noticed the absence of the lavender seller that morning. Mina nodded and gave her a small smile. *I bet she realized that girl was the lavender seller as soon as they came in,* thought Mary. *Well, at least I noticed it eventually.*

"Very good, Miss Jekyll," said Ayesha. "This is my assistant, Ibolya Kovács, who will begin medical school in Zurich next month, since the medical school here in Budapest is too prejudiced to admit women. She has indeed been monitoring your movements since you arrived. You seem to be learning from your friend Mr. Holmes."

Mary was not at all sure of that. There was so much she had missed, so much she had not seen. Where were her powers of observation, of deduction? When she saw Mr. Holmes again, he would no doubt lecture her about all the things she should have noticed. The thought made her feel particularly gloomy.

"And I really ought to return something that belongs to you." Ayesha reached into the purse that Ibolya was holding and took out a piece of paper. She handed it to Mary.

It was a telegram. Incredulously, Mary read it aloud. "'To Miss Mina Murray. C.M. and B.R. coming to Budapest. Beware danger from Dr. S. and Professor Van H. at S.A. meeting. Bloodbath! From Mrs. H. Poole.' How in the world?"

"Please tell Mrs. Poole that I appreciate the advance warning. Leo and Holly have confessed to me that you and Miss Moreau tried to warn us as well. It was very stupid of Leo not to listen to you. He can be impulsive and judgmental, allowing his emotions to determine his actions—I have no doubt that his old rivalry with Vlad disinclined him from taking your message seriously. And Holly is too influenced by him. I assure you that they are thoroughly ashamed of themselves."

"But if you knew," said Mary, staring down once again at the telegram as though she could not imagine how it had gotten there, and then looking up at Ayesha, "why didn't you do something? You could have warned the members of the Alchemical Society beforehand, or hired guards to keep Van Helsing out, or . . . well, any number of things. And if you knew we were coming, why didn't you keep us out? I don't understand. . . ."

"You are describing practical considerations, Miss Jekyll. My primary considerations were political. I wished to remain the president of the society. I wished to retain the confidence of the membership, so I could implement the changes I believe will be necessary to take it into the new century. The best way to do that was to let Van Helsing attempt a coup, and fail. I thought I could count on you to make certain he did fail, without my appearing openly in the matter. He failed quite spectacularly, did he not?"

"But people *died*," said Mary. "Three of your own members died. How can you justify—"

"Child, I did not come here to discuss ethics," said Ayesha. Her cool, appraising glance made Mary feel like an insect indeed. "You came to the annual meeting of the Société des Alchimistes all the way from England, by way of Vienna, bringing Miss Van Helsing with you, because you wanted something from me, something you thought I could provide. What is it?"

"We want you to stop these experiments," said Catherine. "You yourself said they were failures—even Rappaccini's and Moreau's. Look at me, look at Beatrice, look at Justine. No one should be allowed to do what our fathers—our creators—did."

"Is that what all of you want?" asked Ayesha. "Is that what you came to ask of me? Miss Jekyll? Miss Rappaccini? Miss Frankenstein? Miss Hyde?"

"Well, I don't know," said Diana "I mean, that's not what I wanted, particularly. Ow! Why did you kick me, Mary? I hope Hoho bites you!"

"Yes," said Mary. "Yes, it is what we all want. Look at the harm that's been caused, the people who have died, because of these experiments. Look at us. . . ."

"I am looking at you," said Ayesha. "I am looking at all of you, and what I see are intelligent, capable, independent young women. Why should I stop experiments that have produced your like?"

"Because we are monsters," said Beatrice. Her voice was soft and low, but it resounded around the room like a note played on a musical instrument.

"Indeed?" said Ayesha. "Then I am a monster as well—indeed, the chief of monsters! Do you know how long I have lived?"

"About two thousand years?" said Mary. Approximately, if you considered when the temple of Isis must have existed at Philae . . .

Ayesha nodded. "Compared to me, Miss Frankenstein is as the infant of an hour, Countess Karnstein as a day-old child, Count Dracula as a toddler barely learning to walk. As a priestess of Isis, I learned that death is not the inevitable end of human life, but only another state of matter, which is also energy. The priestesses of Isis were the alchemists, the great scientists, of the ancient world. They are gone now, and only I remain. . . ." For a moment, she was silent, as though mentally back in the past. Mary had never seen anyone look so sad, and so very alone.

"But . . . you *chose* to be who you are," said Justine. "We did not choose. We were created without our knowledge or consent."

"Nevertheless, you should consider yourselves fortunate," said Ayesha. She looked at Justine with respect, but no sympathy. "You have one another, I can see that . . . I, Ayesha, envy you. I cannot give you what you want. I will not forbid experiments in biological transmutation—we cannot stop scientific progress, and the next century will see advances in the biological sciences that as yet we can barely conceive. But I will give you two things you have not asked for. First, membership in the Société des Alchimistes. If you wish, you may join our organization. Second, I will allow you to examine the archives of the society so you can see the theories that went into your own creation. You can read your fathers' papers, the records of their experiments. Perhaps those will convince you how very special, how singular and extraordinary, you are."

She turned to Catherine and addressed her specifically. "Miss Moreau, you have suffered a grievous loss. A funeral will be held this Wednesday for Edward Prendick. He will be buried as a member in good standing of the society. I hope you will attend. Now, I have a plenary session to chair. Frau Gottleib will arrange for your access to the archives. It has been a pleasure meeting such a group of extraordinary young women. We shall meet again, I am sure of it."

And then she was gone, before they had finished rising and bowing to her.

"Well, that was . . . ," said Mary. She stood there, mouth still open. She was not certain how to finish the sentence, and no one else finished it for her.

JUSTINE: She *chose*. We did not choose. We did not get the opportunity to choose what we are.

MARY: I know, and you can keep telling us that as often as you like. But it's not going to convince Ayesha, is it?

CHAPTER XXVII

Evening in Budapest

That night, the Athena Club held an emergency meeting in Mina's office. Present were Mary Jekyll, Diana Hyde, Catherine Moreau, Beatrice Rappaccini, and Justine Frankenstein, together again as we had been in London. We were sitting in armchairs or on the floor, with no sense of ceremony or decorum, exactly the way we would have sat at 11 Park Terrace. Mary had not bothered to turn up the gas, but there was a fire in the fireplace, which gave enough light for us to see each other.

What were the members of the club thinking that night, after all that had happened—the travels, the adventures, the adversities we had endured? Mary was thinking of the letter she had received that morning. There had been no time earlier in the day, but tonight, after this meeting, she would have to tell Justine about Adam's death. Catherine was trying not to think about Edward Prendick. She did not know how to feel about what he had done, sacrificing his life for her. Did it wipe out all the cowardice he had shown before? She could not help feeling a great sadness that he was gone. He was the only person in the world who had known her as a puma. With his death, she had lost a part of herself. And yet, she could not entirely let go of her anger toward him. It was a complicated feeling, and she did not like complicated feelings. Beatrice was thinking about Clarence, who was going to be in Budapest in a couple of days. She needed to make a decision about him, and she did not know how. Once before, she had been selfish—she had loved Giovanni and wanted to be with him. She had not thought of the consequences, and he had died. Did she want to risk that happening again? Diana was thinking through various schemes to bring Hóvirág back to England. And Justine was longing for the estate in Cornwall where she had lived alone for a hundred years. She did not often long to be alone again—she valued the friend-ships she had gained, although sometimes she found the other members of the Athena Club a little overwhelming. But tonight she felt sick in her soul, and would not have minded being there again, on the cliffs by that restless, eternal sea.

"First order of business," said Mary. "Does anyone want to talk about what happened yesterday?"

"I was *awesome!*" said Diana. "You should have seen the way I jumped down from that balcony. I landed on someone—I don't know who, but anyway I saw that vampire trying to escape out the door and stuck my knife into him, and he turned around and was about to bite me but Ayesha got him from behind. How does she do that, anyway? It was like she just reached out and he fell over. He had these red marks on his face, as though she had burned him with her fingers. I want to be able to do that."

"Anyone *else* want to talk about these events?" asked Mary. But everyone else was silent. Finally, Justine said, "Fighting is so romantic in poetry, but in real life it is always ugly and com-plicated. I'm simply glad that Lucinda is safe and Professor Van Helsing has been captured."

"Right," said Mary. "We stopped Van Helsing, and he won't be able to kill any more girls, or their mothers, to advance the progress of mankind." Her tone was as sarcastic as we had ever heard from Mary. "Seward is still out there—I doubt we've heard the last of him, but there's nothing we can do about that right now. Second order of business: Ayesha refuses to stop the experiments.

What can we do about that? Anything? Also, she offered us membership in the Alchemical Society. Anyone want to take her up on that offer?" Ah, now *that* was the most sarcastic. We had not previously noticed Mary's talent for sarcasm, but we were certainly noticing it tonight. At least, Catherine certainly was. "Anyone want to join the Alchemical Society? Let's see a show of hands."

Clearly, Mary was expecting none, and was surprised to see one hand raised: Beatrice's.

"Are you serious?" she said. "No, let me rephrase that, borrowing one of Diana's favorite words: Are you bloody serious?"

Beatrice, who was sitting on the floor, put her arms around her knees and said, in her usual gentle tone, "We cannot force Ayesha to do as we wish—she is clearly more powerful than any of us. But we have not yet started trying to convince her. Our meeting with her this afternoon need not be our final meeting with her, and her refusal need not be the final word on the matter. I have been thinking—like a scientist, as my father trained me, and I have an idea. It is not fully developed yet, and I do not wish to present it before I have considered all its consequences. Furthermore, it may come to nothing. Mary, I understand why you and the others may not wish to join. The Société has caused considerable harm. But consider—the Athena Club would have a voice in the Société des Alchimistes."

"Considerable harm!" Mary looked flabbergasted, which is not an expression we are accustomed to seeing on her face. "All these scientists, these alchemists—including your father and mine—were conducting their experiments as members of the Alchemical Society. They presented their ideas at its conferences, published in its journal—even when their research wasn't authorized, like Van Helsing's, their ideas originated in the society. You know what they're responsible for? Turning you poisonous, among other things. Even after seeing Lucinda and hearing her story, Ayesha refuses to stop. Do you really think you would have any influence as a member?"

"If you think I'm joining the society that allowed Moreau to create Beast Men . . . ," said Catherine. "Ayesha authorized those experiments. *Personally.*"

Justine shook her head. "Forgive me, Beatrice—I understand your logic. But I could not bring myself to join."

"No," said Mary. "Just no. I could not bring myself to do it either. The society has been spying on me for years—do you think it will stop spying on on us now? Diana, what do you say?"

"Not bloody likely!" came the response. "Anyway, who wants to go to their stupid meetings, to be bored to death by scientific papers or bitten by vampires?"

"I see," said Beatrice. "Then I too will refuse her offer. I am, first and foremost, a member of the Athena Club, and I will abide by what the majority wishes."

"Actually, I think you should join," said Catherine. "The fact that we don't want to doesn't mean you shouldn't. As far as I'm concerned, they're a lot of bloody murderers. However, if we want a voice in the Alchemical Society, you could be that voice. I don't believe you would change anything, any more than Mary does—why should Ayesha listen to you? But at least you could tell us if there were any more experiments going on. If they're going to spy on us, we should spy on them—and a spy on the inside is the best kind."

Beatrice looked around at their faces in the firelight. "What do you all think of Catherine's position? Do you agree that I should join the society? Of course I would do it on behalf of the Athena Club."

Mary looked undecided, but said, "Catherine does make a good point. It's really your decision, Bea. I mean, we don't have any rules about that sort of thing. We don't have any rules, actually, except the one about never waking up Diana."

DIANA: Is that actually a rule? Seriously, is it?

Beatrice nodded. "Let me think about it tonight, and I shall decide tomorrow. What about Ayesha's offer concerning the archives?"

"I think we should send a message to Nurse Adams—I mean Frau Gottleib—tomorrow morning," said Mary. She still could not believe that Nurse Adams had lived with her for seven years as a spy for the society. Betrayal and deception, that's what the Société des Alchimistes was all about. "I would certainly like to see what's in the archives. Anyone else?"

Justine and Beatrice said "Yes" and "I would" simultaneously. Catherine shook her head. "I couldn't care less what Moreau wrote about me." Diana just said "Boooring!"

"Third order of business," said Mary. "I think we should offer Lucinda membership in the Athena Club. We've never decided on a criteria for membership—we've never had to. But I think she meets it. I mean, she's like us—"

"A monster," said Catherine.

"—a young woman affected by experiments of various sorts," said Mary pointedly. "Those experiments have altered her physically and psychologically. She will never entirely recover from them."

"So?" said Diana. "We barely even know her. What's the point of letting Loony Lucinda into the club?"

"The point is, we can help her," said Mary. "Isn't that what the club is for, so we can all help each other? Consider: she has lost her parents and her home. We do not know if she has any source of income. She needs a place to live, and friends to care for her so she can recover as fully as possible from what her father did to her. We can be those friends."

"I second the motion," said Justine. "This is, as Mary says, why we founded the Athena Club—to help one another. Why else did we come all this way to rescue Lucinda?"

"Third," said Beatrice. "She's a trained pianist. Perhaps she can give lessons, once she is more recovered from her ordeal. That could be her contribution to our common fund. It would not be expensive to purchase a piano that had been used by a church or music hall."

"Fourth," said Catherine. "I can set up the typewriter in my room so she can have the old governess's room. Or I could use the study downstairs? It's not as though I absolutely need a writing room. I mean, Justine needs the studio for her painting, but I can write anywhere, as long as I can shut the door so Diana doesn't bother me."

"Good," said Mary. "If there are no objections—"

"I object!" said Diana. "She drinks blood. Are *you* going to find blood for her in London? Because I don't think Mrs. Poole is going to do it!"

> MRS. POOLE: You girls have asked me to find you a lot of strange things since you moved in together and began these adventures of yours, but blood! Going down to the slaughterhouses like an anemic with a bottle to fill . . .

> BEATRICE: And yet you did just that, Mrs. Poole, when Lucinda came to visit us. Really, I think you're a treasure. What would we do without you?

> MRS. POOLE: Well, someone's got to take care of things, with all the gallivanting you do!

"Diana," said Mary, "are you seriously going to object to letting Lucinda join, after all we've been through together? We've never voted on membership before, but I think adding a new member should require unanimous approval. So you can stop the Athena Club from offering her membership—do you want to?"

Diana frowned and put her chin in her hands, looking as recalcitrant as possible. Would she really object to Lucinda joining? Then she said, "Oh, all right! No, I guess not. But if she bites me, I'm biting back!"

"Fourth order of business," said Catherine. "I think Mary should become the president of the Athena Club. If we're going to deal with an organization like the Alchemical Society, we need an official spokeswoman. Mary's been doing that anyway—I think we should let her continue."

"Second," said Beatrice and Justine simultaneously.

"You have *got* to be kidding," said Diana. "That's just going to make her even more annoying."

"But I don't want to be president," said Mary. She looked at all of them, startled by Catherine's proposal. Where in the world had it come from? She had never expressed a desire to lead the club in any official capacity. "I thought we agreed that we would not have a president. I appreciate your confidence in me, Catherine, but that's a lot of responsibility. I don't feel as though—"

"Oh, she doesn't want to do it," said Diana. "Third! Mary for president."

"Sorry, Mary," said Catherine. "I think the motion has carried by majority vote."

DIANA: I told you it would make her more annoying.

JUSTINE: But it is also a great deal of work for Mary, arranging everything, being responsible for the running of the club. I'm sure she's very tired of being president sometimes.

DIANA: That's what makes it worth the annoyingness!

It was a busy week for the Athena Club. The next day, Mary, Beatrice, and Justine went to the Academy of Sciences, by arrangement with Frau Gottleib. At the last moment, Lucinda asked if she could go with them.

Mary looked at her, startled. "Why, Lucinda? We're just going to work in the archives, although Beatrice has a scheme of some sort that she won't explain to us. . . ."

"I wish to speak with my father," said Lucinda. She looked pale and tired, but composed. She had not said anything yet that day that sounded mad or even unusual—until this request.

"Surely that is unwise," said Justine, looking concerned. "You are still not very strong. Such a confrontation . . ."

"I wish to speak with my father," she repeated again. She sounded determined.

Mary looked at Justine and Beatrice with an expression that clearly said, *What should I do?*

"This may be necessary for her," said Beatrice. "It was necessary for me to confront my father after Giovanni's death. Sometimes we cannot heal until we have confronted those who have harmed us."

Mary was still not sure it was a good idea—but Lucinda had the right to make her own decisions. Would she decide to join the Athena Club? When Mary had asked her that morning, she had looked a little frightened, as she often did, and said that she did not know. Well, that too was hers to decide, and Mary would not press her on it.

At the Academy of Sciences, they were met at the front desk by Lady Crowe, who took them up to Ayesha's office on the third floor. As they crossed the lobby and went up the stairs, they passed men and women arguing, or perhaps just conversing vehemently, about scientific ideas in a variety of languages. Apparently, the

chaos of the general meeting had not affected the annual conference of the Alchemical Society.

On the way up, Lady Crowe said to Beatrice, in her aristocratic English accent, "My dear Miss Rappaccini, Sasha tells me
his theft of the telegram has been detected—apparently, a Zulu
Prince and a Madam Zora are very angry with him. I think if you
knew the circumstances, you would forgive him, as would they.
You see, as a child, Sasha was sent to me in London. His father
was a drunkard and his mother could not support the family. The
other children did not share Sasha's and his father's hirsutism—
they were taken by orphanages or, if old enough, trained for
service. But no one wanted Sasha. He was living on the streets of
St. Petersburg, eating whatever scraps he could beg or scavenge.
A fellow member of the Alchemical Society noticed him and
immediately thought of me—he knew that I was interested in
congenital abnormalities. He paid for Sasha's passage to England.
I took Sasha in—he lived with me until he was old enough to
join the circus. Unfortunately, I was not able to cure his condition, which remains beyond the reach of the alchemical sciences.
But he has always been loyal to me. When Ayesha learned that
you and Miss Moreau were traveling with the Circus of Marvels
and Delights, I remembered that Sasha had mentioned working
for Lorenzo, and asked him to investigate. It seemed a fortunate
coincidence. I hope you will forgive him and speak for him to the
other members of the circus. It sounds as though Madam Zora
may feed him to her snakes!"

"And Jimmy Bucket?" asked Beatrice. "What of him? You know
the Baker Street boys have found him out." She looked at Lady
Crowe accusingly.

"Ah yes," she said, with no sign of guilt or shame. "That was
a simple matter of bribery. Young Jimmy has been keeping the
Jekyll *ménage* under observation since shortly after Nurse Adams,

that is Frau Gottleib, left. His family is very poor, and his sister's treatments are expensive."

"And is anyone else spying on us for the Alchemical Society?" asked Mary. Unlike Beatrice, she did not feel particularly inclined to forgive Jimmy Bucket. Were there other Jimmy Buckets keeping watch over them? The thought made her angry.

Lady Crowe smiled at her. It was a sweet, grandmotherly smile. "Here we are, Miss Jekyll. Ayesha is expecting you. And if you have time later, do stop by and have tea with me. I'm coordinating events in the general assembly room. We still have a conference to run, you know! But I am always interested in anomalies, abnormalities—monsters of nature, if you will. I would love to chat further with such interesting young women."

Mary stared at her back as she walked down the stairs. She had not necessarily expected Lady Crowe to answer her question, but to ignore it in such an obvious way? And then ask her to tea, smiling just like the kindly Madame Corbeau? *Well,* she thought. *Appearances certainly are deceiving!*

JUSTINE: Perhaps she simply forgot to answer your question?

MARY: Do you seriously believe that?

Just then the office door opened. Standing in the doorway was Leo Vincey. "Please come in," he said, in a not very pleased tone.

Ayesha's office was more functional than Mary had expected, with a large writing desk, glass-fronted bookshelves, a typewriter on a typing stand, presumably for a secretary—the usual accoutrements of a business office. Somehow, she had imagined the president of the Alchemical Society in a grander space. However, a large window provided a magnificent view of the Danube and the hills of Buda beyond. Ayesha was seated at a round conference table. Today she was wearing a dress the color of marigolds, with black embroidery on the collar and cuffs. Professor Holly, who was seated to one side of her, rose as they entered. "Ladies," he said, rather as one might say "wild animals." "Leo and I would like to beg your pardon for disbelieving you. We were mistaken, and I have been informed that I was rude. I find that I often am without realizing it—the peril of being an old bachelor."

"Although I think the mistake was understandable, under the circumstances," said Leo, with a smile that he probably thought was charming. Oh, Mary did not like him! He might be handsome, but he was too arrogant by half, as Mrs. Poole might say.

"Thank you, Professor Holly," she said in her most dignified tone. "Your apology is accepted. Madam President?" As the president of the Athena Club, she would act as spokeswoman—one president to another.

Ayesha regarded them for a moment, then said, "I'm glad to see you today, Miss Jekyll, Miss Rappaccini, Miss Frankenstein— and surprised to see you here, Miss Van Helsing. Tell me what has brought you."

Lucinda stepped forward. "I wish to see my father."

Ayesha looked surprised and concerned. "Is that wise? He is still here, being held in a storage room until the end of the conference, when I will have time to deal with him. But are you prepared for such a confrontation?"

Lucinda did not answer. She looked steadily and defiantly at the president of the Alchemical Society.

"Very well," said Ayesha. "Leo, could you take her down? Frau Gottleib is on guard at present."

"I'll go with her," said Justine. "Come, Lucinda. I shall be with you the whole time."

When Justine and Lucinda had left, followed by Leo Vincey,

Mary said, "We have considered your invitation to join the society and view the archives. We accept the second of those offers. As for the first—Beatrice?" She was not entirely sure what Beatrice was going to say. The Poisonous Girl had some sort of plan. She had not wanted to discuss it beforehand, and Mary had not pressed her. As president, she trusted the judgment of the other members.

"Madam President," said Beatrice, stepping forward. "My fellow members of the Athena Club do not wish to join the Société des Alchimistes. However, I will do so—on one condition."

"Indeed? And what condition is that?" asked Ayesha. For the first time, Mary saw her genuinely smile with amusement. Evidently, people did not often give Ayesha conditions.

"Instead of deciding whether to allow experiments in biological transmutation yourself, on an *ad hoc* basis, you will form a committee to create a set of research protocols and review individual proposals. The committee would approve or disapprove proposals based not on the best interests of the Société des Alchimistes, but on ethical and moral grounds. I would be one member—you would choose the other two."

"And why should I do such a thing, Miss Rappaccini?" Ayesha was smiling broadly now. Mary hoped it was an *appreciating Beatrice's audacity* smile rather than a *considering how to destroy us* smile.

"I listened to your speech at the meeting, and what you said to us yesterday in Count Dracula's parlor," said Beatrice. "You are trying to prepare the Société for the coming era. You are making it more modern, more international. But, if you will forgive my saying so, your perspective on these issues is antiquated. You are not Pharaoh, to decide the life or death of others. It is not modern to rule by fiat. If you wish to create a society for the twentieth century, you must consider the welfare of the experimental subject and, if possible, obtain that subject's consent. That is the way in which the scientific community is tending—why should alchemists be left behind?"

Ayesha threw back her head so that her long black braids almost touched the floor and laughed until it echoed around the room. Professor Holly looked at her in astonishment.

Mary quailed a little and glanced at Beatrice. She seemed undaunted, despite just having insulted a woman who could zap people to death in a way Mary did not understand. Were they about to be zapped, like those vampires?

"So you think I'm antiquated," Ayesha said finally, through intermittent laugher. "Perhaps. And perhaps, after millennia of being Princess and Priestess and Queen, I have gotten used to ruling and being obeyed. This position of Madam President—it is a new experience for me. Do you know why I joined the Alchemical Society, Miss Rappaccini? After all I had seen—after the destruction of the temple of Isis at Philae by the troops of Augustus, after the burning of the library of Alexandria—I grew tired of humanity. I traveled south, and in the mountains above the Zambesi I found a kingdom whose subjects were long dead, its monuments fallen into ruin. I claimed its throne—there was none to dispute my claim, and so for centuries I ruled as Queen of Kôr. There, based on the teachings of the temple and my alchemical research, I discovered how to prolong my life indefinitely. I thought I would live in those underground caverns until, from boredom or despair, I ended my own existence. Then the British started encroaching on my kingdom to create their protectorate. I am not an admirer of your British Empire, Miss Jekyll. It shares the rapacity of the Romans. Your colonial administrators cleared the forests for coffee plantations, blasted the mountains in search of metals and gems, poisoned the river with their manufacturing. They brought disease and privation to the tribes surrounding my kingdom. Could I fight the British Empire alone? I might have tried, but by a strange chance Leo and

Holly found my hiding place and asked me to return with them. . . . Well, here I am. So you see, you are right, Miss Rappaccini. I am, in a sense, a survival from another world. Is there any place for me in this one? I thought there might be, in this society that continues, in its haphazard way, the research of the priestesses of Philae. Miss Jekyll, you have a question for me—I can see it in your expression. Ask, and I shall answer."

"How do you zap people?" asked Mary. "I mean electrocute, if that's what you do. What sort of power allowed you to kill those vampires without touching them?"

Ayesha smiled. "In the temple of Isis, I was taught to sense and manipulate the energic powers of the Earth. That is how the priestesses were able to heal both themselves and others—and also to kill, although the High Priestess forbade us to use our powers for such a purpose. That is why my sisters in Isis fell to the spears of the Romans. Only I was able to escape alive. As you can see, I no longer have such moral qualms."

"What are these energic powers?" asked Beatrice. "Do they have anything to do with mesmerism?" She thought of Alice, back home in London, learning how to control what Martin had called mesmeric waves. Was that at all related to Ayesha's story?

"Mesmerism! Sheer quackery," said Holly. "Don't let anyone fool you into thinking mesermism is a science, Miss Rappaccini. Except perhaps the science of separating money from the credulous!"

"Do not dismiss what you do not understand," said Ayesha. "The theory behind mesmerism is valid, despite the fraud perpetrated by its practitioners. To you, Miss Rappaccini, Miss Jekyll, this table, these shelves filled with books, the floor upon which we stand, all seem real and solid. But I assure you they are not. They are formed of energic waves, as are even you, Holly-the-skeptic. Mesmerism is the lowest level of the discipline I learned at Philae. Even an eight-year-old novice at the temple of Isis could create illusions—a priestess would have scorned to do so, concerning herself solely with the manipulation of the real. All matter is energy. This is an understanding man has lost, but may someday regain. Well, let us look forward to that future. In the meantime, Miss Rappaccini—Beatrice, if I may—I shall form this committee. The other members will be Holly, because every committee needs a skeptic, and—"

Just then, the door opened and Frau Gottleib entered. "Ayesha? Leo says Mary and the others are here to look in the archives. Oh, forgive me! I did not know you were in the middle of a meeting."

"—yes, let us make it yourself, Holly, and Eva Gottleib, who shall be the chairwoman. We shall try your system for one year, and see whether it is indeed better than mine. Are you satisfied, Beatrice?"

"Yes, Madam President," said Beatrice. "That is exactly what I was hoping."

MARY: Was it really?

BEATRICE: Well, I would have liked to be
    chairwoman myself, but that would perhaps have
    been too much to ask for.

MARY: You should have asked. What could she have
    said, no? Or, you know, she could have reached
    out her hand and electrocuted us with her energic
    waves. Never mind, I'm glad you didn't ask.

As Mary and Beatrice were entering Ayesha's office, Justine and Lucinda were following Leo Vincey down into the basement of the Academy of Sciences. When they reached the basement storage room where Professor Van Helsing was being held, they found Frau Gottlieb sitting outside, with a pistol in her hand.

"What are you doing here, *Liebling*?" she said to Lucinda. "You do not need to see this man."

"He is my father," said Lucinda. "I wish to speak with him."

Frau Gottlieb shook her head, but she took a set of keys out of her pocket, unlocked the door, and let them in. The room was obviously used to store files—there were shelves filled with file boxes on three of the walls. Light came in through one small window on the far wall. Under that window was a fold-out cot with a pillow and blanket. Professor Van Helsing was seated on it, hands on his knees, looking perfectly composed. His white hair, high forehead, and clear, calm eyes made him look like a benevolent deity.

Justine did not know what to expect—how would Lucinda respond to seeing her father again under these circumstances? When he saw her, Van Helsing rose and said, *"Hallo, dochter."*

"Je hebt mijn moeder vermoord!" said Lucinda. Suddenly, without warning, she crouched and sprang toward her father. With the instinct of an athlete, Leo caught the fabric of her skirt, which started to rip in his hand. Lucinda turned, snarled at him, and raked his face with her fingernails. For a moment, Justine was too startled to respond, but had the presence of mind to catch Lucinda around the waist and hold her fast.

Van Helsing said something in his deep, soothing voice. Lucinda answered back, loudly, rapidly, but as it was all in Dutch, Justine had no idea what they were saying. When we asked Lucinda about it later, as she was preparing to depart for Styria, she said, "He told me that I should be proud of having contributed to science. He told me that we all make sacrifices for the benefit of mankind, for human progress—that he had made sacrifices as well. If Justine had not held me back, I would have ripped out his throat."

Somehow, with Leo's help, Justine managed to drag Lucinda out of that room and into the hallway. She would have been strong enough to do it alone, but Lucinda kept flailing—there were arms and legs everywhere. She felt as though she had somehow caught the legendary Kraken.

"What happened to your face?" said Frau Gottleib, staring at Leo. Justine turned to look—he had four red claw marks across that handsome cheek. "I shall get the carbolic, *nein?*"

Leo collapsed into the chair she had been sitting on. "Just get that hellcat out of here. Lock the door and give me the pistol. I'll stand guard. Find a cab so Miss Frankenstein can take her home, then bring me some bandages."

It was with relief that Justine put Lucinda into a cab and took her back to Count Dracula's house. As they drove through the streets of Budapest, she could not help thinking about what Mary had told her the previous evening: that Adam was dead. She had tried not to feel anything about it, because when she allowed herself to, she felt not grief or loss, but only an overwhelming sense of relief. Adam would never trouble her again. Perhaps it was, after all, for the best—he had gone to meet his original Maker, and might now, at last, find the peace and forgiveness he had craved. Surely she was justified in feeling relief and even joy on his behalf? For the first time since she had learned that Adam was still alive, the world seemed brighter and clearer, the future filled with possibilities. Surely there was no shame in feeling that!

When the cab reached Múzeum utca, Lucinda turned to her and said, "If I join your club, will I need to come live in London immediately? I think that first I should learn to manage my condition. In that room, I almost killed my father. If you had not held me back, I would have. . . . Laura has invited me to go with her and Carmilla to Styria. I think perhaps that would be the best place for me, for a while."

DIANA: Bloody right! Get it? *Bloody?*

MARY: Lucinda was a lovely guest, the last time she
and Laura visited. I'm just sorry Carmilla was
too busy helping Mina with secret subcommittee
business to join them. I think you're jealous
because when Lucinda's here, she gets more
attention than you.

DIANA: Jealous of a vampire? Not *bloody* likely!

While Frau Gottleib was leading Mary and Beatrice down
to the basement of the Hungarian Academy of Sciences, where
the files of the Alchemical Society were located, Catherine was
staring down at Edward Prendick's gravestone. It said Edward
Prendick, S.A., with the dates of his birth and death underneath,
then *Requiescat in Pacem*. She did not believe in a life ever after, but
she hoped he was resting in peace.

Laura took her hand. Thank goodness Laura had offered
to come with her! At least there had been two mourners at
Prendick's graveside. It was a beautiful resting place—high
on a hill outside the city, with tall trees shadowing the gravestones and wildflowers growing between them. "When I'm in
Budapest," said Laura, "I'll come here and put flowers on his
grave for you."

"Thank you," said Catherine. She walked off a little way and
looked toward the city, spread out in the distance. At her feet,
poppies waved in the wind like small red flags. "You know, I still
don't know whether I loved him or hated him. Loved him, certainly, at first. And then hated him. And now? I don't know. . . .
It's complicated."

"Relationships are always complicated," said Laura. "Look at

Mina and Vlad. They are very different sorts of people. Will their relationship last? I hope so, but one can never be sure."

Catherine picked a blade of grass and started chewing on it. "You and Carmilla seem like a perfect couple. You're different, but you complement each other."

"We do," said Laura. "And yet, we met under the most inauspicious circumstances! Carmilla had fallen in love with an Austrian woman—young, beautiful, elegant. She wanted to remain so forever, and asked Carmilla to turn her into a vampire. Carmilla warned her of the consequences, but she insisted. Carmilla gave in—and her beloved went mad. What is worse, she went on a rampage, killing a series of prostitutes in Vienna. When we met, the woman's guardians were hunting Carmilla. They knew what she was, and almost killed her—the true death. I gave her shelter and time to heal from her injuries. The physical injuries healed. The emotional ones? I'm not sure they ever will. It took a long time for her to trust me."

"But she did come to trust you, finally," said Catherine. Was she like Carmilla? She certainly had her scars, both internal and external. It was difficult for her to trust anyone.

Laura smiled. "She did. And I have no desire for eternal life. The present is enough for me, thank you very much. Come on, let's get back to the city. We've focused on death enough for one day. There's a life waiting for us. Also, lunch."

"When we get back," said Catherine, after climbing into the Count's carriage, which had been waiting for them below the graveyard, "I'm going to climb up to the roof, to sit by myself for a while. I need some puma time."

But when she reached the house on Múzeum utca, there was a surprise waiting for her.

"I'm going to check on Lucinda," said Laura, as she stood in the front hall, taking off her hat and gloves. "If you ask the Count, he'll tell you how to get up to the roof—I mean, other than by climbing! He should be in his study—it's two doors away from Mina's."

As Catherine reached the second floor, wondering if Count Dracula's study was two doors before or two doors after Mina's, Justine met her in the hallway and said, "Kati just told us you had arrived—at least, she said something about Katerina and Laura, so I assumed you were back from the funeral. Look who's arrived in Budapest!" Out of the music room behind her stepped Clarence and Madam Zora. Behind them came Sasha, stepping out tentatively as though unsure if he would be welcome.

"Hello, Whiskers!" said the Zulu Prince.

"Clarence!" said Catherine, giving him a puma-strength hug. Then she turned to the snake charmer. "Zora, I'm sorry for everything. You don't have to forgive me. I just want you to know that I'm perfectly aware of what an idiot I've been."

"Are you really a puma?" asked Zora, with her hands on her hips, looking at Catherine skeptically.

Catherine pulled back her top lip to show her fangs, then unbuttoned the top buttons of her shirt. She held the collar open to reveal the scars from her transformation.

"Well, you're certainly something," said Zora, looking at the pale lines that shone against Catherine's darker skin. "I'm not saying I forgive you, but—" She held out her hand. "I'm Surita. That's my real name, when I'm not in the circus."

"Thank you," said Catherine, and shook her hand. In the circus, any revelation, any sharing of a confidence, was a gift.

"Well, Cat Girl," said Sasha in his heavy accent, hanging back. He still smelled like that damn cigarette smoke.

Catherine walked over to him and punched him hard on the arm. "*What* were you thinking? What kind of friend sells me out like that?" She punched him again to make her point.

Sasha retreated into the music room, rubbing his arm. "Let me explain. . . ."

Clarence, still standing in the hallway, told Justine, "We arrived just this morning. You know, Lorenzo could use a Giantess, if you want your old job back. And Atlas would be thrilled to see you, but he's so shy that he wouldn't come with us this morning, in case he might not be welcome."

"How silly of him," said Justine. "I would be happy to see him, Clarence. Truly I would."

By the time Mary and Beatrice returned from the Academy of Sciences, the circus performers were all laughing and talking between mouthfuls of the apple strudel and a horn-shaped pastry called *kifli*, filled with poppy seeds and raisins, that Kati had brought in with coffee. Clarence and Catherine were telling stories about the early days of Lorenzo's Circus of Marvels and Delights, Justine was listening thoughtfully as usual, and Zora was asking questions about what it had been like when the circus was at its height and toured all over the countryside. Diana, who had appeared seemingly out of nowhere shortly after the food, was sitting on the floor, asking Sasha what it was like to be half dog. Sasha was patiently explaining to her that he was, in fact, fully human—just a little hairier than most.

When Beatrice entered, Clarence rose and moved toward her. Gracefully, she reached out her gloved hand. Looking disappointed, he shook it, letting it go reluctantly. Catherine introduced Mary, who had never met the performers of Lorenzo's circus.

"Very pleased to meet you all," she said, sinking into an armchair. Coffee, that was what she wanted. It had been a long day.

"Beatrice, can I talk to you?" asked Clarence in a low voice.

"Of course," said Beatrice, with what she hoped was a friendly smile. "I am always happy to talk."

He frowned. "I mean alone."

She looked at him a moment, then said, "In the hallway?"

"All right." He followed her into the hall, with its battered suits of armor and grim portraits. Beatrice stood by one of the windows, where sunlight filtered through threadbare brocade curtains. She felt uneasy and unhappy. She had spent most of that afternoon with Mary in the basement of the Academy of Sciences, trying to determine which files would be necessary for their research. In an old issue of the *Journal de Société des Alchimistes*, published in English, French, and German, she had found an article by a Dr. Giacomo Rappaccini in which he had described how to make a laboratory rat immune to poisons through repeated exposure to certain vegetable alkaloids. At the time of publication, he had been only twenty-four years old.

"Bea, I'm just going to say what I need to say." Clarence looked down at her, affectionately but also apprehensively. "I care about you very much—more than that. I'm falling in love with you. You're a beautiful, intelligent, compassionate—"

"Poisonous."

"—woman. Well, yes, that too."

"And that is everything. There is no way that I know of to make myself less toxic. I have been to doctors all over Europe. None of them have found a cure for me. This morning I read a paper by my father—in it he detailed the procedure he would later use to make me poisonous to others. The poison is so inextricably part of me that eliminating it would require my death." Beatrice looked out the window at the courtyard—it was just beginning to rain. Then she said, as directly as she could, because it was necessary, "You will never be able to kiss me or hold me for more than a few seconds. There will never be any intimacy between us. It does not matter how we feel. There can never be anything more between us than friendship."

"How *we* feel," he said, pointedly. "So you feel it too."

She would not lie to him. "Yes, and that is what makes this more painful than I can say. Please do not make it any more painful for me, Clarence."

"Honey, if you love me, that means anything's possible. Didn't Giovanni get used to your poison after a while? Maybe I can slowly acclimate myself to it—you know, over time."

She stared up at him in astonishment. "But you would become poisonous, as I am! You would no longer be able to touch other human beings, to spend time with them as you do now."

He reached out and stroked her hair, but only briefly—it too carried her toxicity. "If we can be together, I'm willing to pay that price."

She looked at him with an expression of horror. Here was the story of Giovanni, playing itself out over again. "That is not your choice to make, or not your choice alone. If you were ever to regret it, if a day came when you no longer loved me and wished you could rejoin humanity—do not shake your head, you do not know what the future holds—you would blame me. And then we would become each other's torment. I will not allow you to make that choice, nor will I allow you to impose it on me. I offer you my friendship. I cannot offer you more."

He looked down at her as though trying to evaluate how serious she was. Evidently, she looked serious enough, because he said, "All right. I accept your friendship, of course. We'll always have *that*, no matter what happens. But I'm not giving up—there's got to be some sort of solution. If Edison can invent the electric light bulb, we can find some way to be together."

She shook her head, but she had to smile at his willingness to hope. Americans were so optimistic! Alas, after all the doctors she had consulted, the medicines she had tried, she knew better than to think there might be a cure for her condition. Clarence would be convinced of that in time.

MARY: America does not have a monopoly on
optimism.

CATHERINE: You certainly can't call the English
optimistic. You're such a gloomy lot.

BEATRICE: It is the rain. The constant rain, drenching
the flowers in the park.

JUSTINE: Also, the lack of mountains. If England had
a proper mountain, like Mont-Blanc near Lake
Geneva . . .

MARY: You are all being ridiculous.

"Beatrice!" It was Mina, standing by the door of the dining
room. "Can you tell everyone that dinner is ready?"

"Of course," said Beatrice, with relief. She was glad to have
an excuse to end this conversation with Clarence. However much
she cared for him, she would not allow her affections to cloud her
judgment. Not this time.

When she entered the music room, she found Mary talking
about their meeting with Ayesha. "I don't know whether to believe
her about these energic waves," Mary was saying. "But their effect
is real enough. I mean, she really did electrocute those vampires."

"Alice really can make herself disappear," said Catherine. "At
least, she can make other people believe she disappeared, which is
more or less the same thing."

"It sounds like we need her in Lorenzo's," said Zora. "The
Vanishing Girl! Is she there? Is she not there? You decide! She
would be a sensation."

How lovely it was to have them all together—the Athena

Club and the circus performers! Cut off from others as she was, Beatrice felt the pleasures of company and camaraderie even more keenly than the others would have. "Come into the dining room," she said, "Mina says dinner is ready."

Talking and laughing, they all followed her down the hall to find a feast prepared for them. Tureens and platters filled with chicken *paprikas*, one soup that seemed to be fish, another that was probably cauliflower, small dumplings that looked nothing like *Knödel*, cucumber salad, potatoes with parsley, stuffed eggs . . .

"Mrs. Horvath has outdone herself," said Mina. "I told her not to bother with courses. Our tastes are not so refined that we need service *à la Russe*, I think. Come, sit. There's room for everyone."

The table was already raucous by the time Carmilla came in, with Laura and Lucinda following arm-in-arm, although of the three of them, only Laura ate. Carmilla and Lucinda were served, discreetly, glasses of something red that was not wine. Finally, in the middle of dinner, they were joined by the Count himself, who took the empty seat at the head of the table.

Mary looked around at them all. The circus performers were describing their acts to Laura, who paid rapt attention. Carmilla, Lucinda, and Justine were discussing travel plans. Diana was whispering to Attila, who was serving as footman—no doubt about some new mischief. The Count was holding Mina's hand.

The Athena Club had not achieved everything it had set out to on this journey, but it had achieved a great deal—Lucinda was safe, Professor Van Helsing was in the custody of the Alchemical Society, and Beatrice might eventually persuade Ayesha to stop these experiments altogether. That afternoon, she and Beatrice had spent considerable time in the archives, identifying the files they wanted to examine with more care. She was looking forward to a quiet week in the basement of the Academy of Sciences, where the files were kept.

Mina rose. "My dear friends, both old and new—I am very happy to see you all here. First, I have something for the members of the Athena Club. When I had the seals of the Alchemical Society replicated, I also ordered these." Out of a bag beside her dinner plate, she took several small objects that clinked against one another. What were they? Mary could not tell. Mina handed them to the diners sitting next to her. "Could you please pass these down to Mary, Diana, Catherine, Beatrice, and Justine? I hear Lucinda will also be joining the Athena Club, so I shall order one for her as well."

When one of the small objects made its way to Mary, she realized that it was a silver watch fob, slightly smaller than the fob she had found in the hand of Molly Keane so long ago, which had turned out to be the seal of the Alchemical Society. It was decidedly more elegant than the seal of the S.A., in the style Beatrice called *l'art nouveau*, with a ring where it could be hung from a watch chain, or any sort of chain the wearer preferred. It too was a seal—it was set with a carnelian, on which was carved the image of a wide-eyed owl, with an olive branch on one side and the letters AΘE on the other.

"It is the owl of Athena," said Justine. "This symbol was stamped on the currency of Athens for a thousand years. Mina, how did you decide—"

"I thought you might like a seal of your own," said Mina, smiling. "Now you can send your own secret letters. That is, if this gift is acceptable to the Athena Club? Madam President, I do not wish to impose." She turned to Mary and bowed.

Mary looked down at the seal, then around the table. They were all staring at her as though expecting something. Well, of course they were—she was the president of the Athena Club. When Catherine, Beatrice, Justine, and Diana had elected her, she had been filled with trepidation. It was gratifying, in a way, that they had chosen her as their leader—but trying to lead the Athena

Club was going to be like trying to herd a flock of London sparrows! However, now that it was done and decided, she would have to rise to her role and the occasion.

So she rose. "Mina—Miss Murray, on behalf of the Athena Club, I would like to thank you for this very generous gift. Henceforward, we shall adopt the owl of Athena as our symbol—I didn't know she had an owl, but this really is splendid, and he looks very wise, doesn't he? I would also like to thank Miss Jennings, Countess Karnstein, and Count Dracula for their hospitality. Without your help, we could never have accomplished as much as we have these last few weeks. The Athena Club thanks you, and hopes that you will all"—she looked around the table—"come visit us in London."

She sat back down, feeling a little flushed. There—she had done the best she could. She hoped that she had represented the club adequately.

First Catherine clapped, and then the entire table burst into applause, with several cries of "Brava, Mary!" and "Hear, hear!" If Mary was the sort of person who blushed, she would have blushed now. Instead, she looked around at all the diners gathered around that table, smiling or grinning, filled with a delicious feast—the Cat Woman, the Zulu Prince, the Dog Boy, the Giantess, the Poisonous Girl, several vampires . . . She felt gratified to be part of such a strange, wonderful gathering.

CATHERINE: Of monsters.

MARY: Well, metaphorically, perhaps.

CATHERINE: If you insist.

CHAPTER XXVIII

The Mesmerizing Girl

W orking in the archives of the Alchemical Society was considerably more tedious than Mary had imagined, although Beatrice seemed to find it interesting, and Justine perused dusty old documents with quiet persistence. Dr. Jekyll had written a *lot* of papers. They were in a theoretical, scientific language that Mary had difficulty understanding—all about good and evil, and Swedenborg, and a man named Louis Vivet. At one point, going to use an upstairs lavatory, she ran into Heinrich Waldman on his way down.

"Hello, Miss Frank!" he said. "Miss Jekyll, of course I mean . . ." He grinned and bowed, a bit clumsily because he was standing on two different steps. "I am here presenting a paper on the nervous system, particularly the nervous diseases of women. Perhaps afterward, I can take you to lunch? There is a very good café nearby, on Arany János utca."

"I don't think so," said Mary. "My nervous system is in very good order, thank you." Why had she ever thought he was handsome? He had a weak chin. And his blue eyes were watery.

DIANA: I'm glad you finally got over creepy Heinrich.

MARY: I was never not over him. I mean, I was never as enamored of him as your statement seems to imply.

JUSTINE: Forgive me, Mary, but you were, in fact, both flattered and gratified by his attention. If he had not turned out to be a spy for the Alchemical Society—

MARY: None of you ever tease me in this way about Mr. Holmes!

JUSTINE: We like and respect Mr. Holmes. He is far superior to M. Waldman.

DIANA: Also, yes we do.

By the end of the week, Mary was thoroughly sick of sitting in the basement of the Academy of Sciences, sorting through old journals and file boxes. Justine and Beatrice had spent every day in the archives with her. Catherine had spent all her time with the circus, preparing for their first show. That evening, she and Beatrice would be performing as *La Femme Panthère* and *La Belle Toxique*. The rest of them were invited to sit in the front row. Diana had been busy alternately pestering Attila to take her down to the dogs, or Mina to take her out for ice cream (or cake, or *pogácsa*, or *lángos*, or any of the other treats that Budapest has to offer).

The day before, Laura and Carmilla had left for Styria in the motorcar, taking Lucinda with them. Carmilla had promised they would all visit at some point, when Lucinda was stronger— Laura was particularly excited at the prospect of seeing England at last. Count Dracula's house seemed quieter without them— until Diana had decided to bring all the puppies upstairs, and their mother had very properly objected to such an unorthodox procedure! It is not, in general, a good idea to separate one of the great white wolfdogs of Count Dracula from her progeny.

That afternoon, Mary was sorting through the Frankenstein documents. She, Justine, and Beatrice were trying to establish exactly when Victor Frankenstein had been recruited as a member of the Société des Alchimistes. They were going, systematically, through any material relating to their parentage—after the Frankenstein material, they would start on Moreau. The basement room where they worked was lit by two small windows that gave adequate, but not excessive, light. In the middle of the room was a large table, almost exactly like the one in the library two floors above. Scattered across it were file boxes they had already looked through, ready to be returned to their places on the shelves, as well as notebooks in which they were taking notes, pencils, and India-rubber erasers—for Frau Gottleib would not allow them to use pens around those old documents. Mary could not help being startled every time the former Nurse Adams spoke in a German accent.

"Ach, you are going to break my back, you girls!" said Frau Gottleib. She put her hands on her back and leaned one way and then another, trying to stretch, then picked up one of the boxes to be replaced. Mary thought she might need to stretch as well, or perhaps walk around for a while—she had been sitting at that table for hours! The room was so quiet, with just the sound of rustling papers, the occasional comment from Beatrice or Justine when they found something worth noting. Afternoon sunlight fell on dust motes floating in the air. She was just about to stand up when Catherine burst in. At least, it felt like bursting—suddenly, the quiet basement room was all Catherine and noise.

"Telegram!" she gasped. Evidently, she had been running very hard. She put her hand to her side.

"What in the world?" said Mary. "Slow down—you're going to give yourself a cramp."

"Telegram from Mrs. Poole! I got back from the circus and this was waiting—" Catherine looked down at the telegram in her hand. Between gasps for air, she read, "'Alice kidnapped Archibald inconsolable Holmes still missing now Watson too send help.'"

Mary heard a loud *bang*.

She looked around, startled. Frau Gottleib was staring at her with an expression of horror. The box she had been carrying lay at her feet, its files half spilled out. "Alice kidnapped!" she said. "You must return to London at once!"

"Well, of course we'll go back," said Mary. "Who in the world would kidnap Alice? It must be some sort of mistake. But why are *you* so concerned, Frau Gottleib? I mean, when you were Nurse Adams, you barely knew Alice except as the scullery maid."

Frau Gottleib sat down on one of the uncomfortable wooden chairs that surrounded the table. "Her name is not Alice. Yes, that is the name she was given at the orphanage, the name she believed to be hers. But when I arranged for her to come to your household, I knew who she truly was—Lydia Raymond, the daughter of Helen Raymond, who was brought into being by a Dr. Raymond in one of the most dangerous experiments ever conducted by a member of the Société des Alchimistes. It harnessed the energic powers of the Earth itself—ah, Ayesha could tell you the details better than I can. But those powers flowed with unprecedented force through one person: Helen Raymond, who left a trail of death and destruction in her wake. It was not only because of Jekyll's experiments and Carew's death that Ayesha ordered the English branch disbanded—she did not want Dr. Raymond to find the child or resume his experiments."

"Wait, what? What do you mean, you arranged for Alice to come to my household?" said Mary. "It was Mrs. Poole who hired her."

"Dr. Raymond!" said Catherine. "He was the chairman of the English branch until it was disbanded. He was going to be chairman again if Seward and Van Helsing had taken over the Alchemical Society."

"The director of the Society of St. Mary Magdalen was a Mrs. Raymond," said Justine. "It was she who arranged for those poor girls to be murdered by Adam and Mr. Hyde. Is that merely a coincidence?"

"I do not believe in coincidence," said Frau Gottleib grimly. "It was I who suggested to Mrs. Poole that she hire a scullery maid, I who arranged for the orphanage to send Lydia—called Alice—to your household. There, at least, I could keep an eye on her. If she has inherited her mother's ability to manipulate the energic powers of the Earth, she is a very dangerous girl."

"Alice? Dangerous? How could Alice possible be dangerous?" asked Mary, incredulously.

"Well, with her mesmeric powers—," said Catherine.

"Have those begun to manifest themselves?" asked Frau Gottleib. She did not seem surprised. "Then she is both a danger to others and in danger herself, for others may try to use her to their own ends."

Oh, for goodness' sake. Wasn't this how their whole adventure had started in the first place? With a kidnapping and a telegram? Well, at least this time Mary knew what to do.

"All right, Justine and I can start back on the Orient Express tomorrow. Catherine and Beatrice, can you follow us as soon as your shows are done? We'll need to borrow money from Count Dracula, because I don't think we can afford train fare. And Diana—well, she can come with us, or go with you, but I'm pretty sure she won't want to be left out. Come on, let's go. I'm sorry, Nurse—I mean Frau Gottleib, sorry, I keep forgetting. Would you mind putting the boxes back on the shelves? We'll have to come back to Budapest—there's so much more we need to look at. We were only just getting started. But right now I think we'd better get back to Múzeum utca and tell Mina that we need to leave at once."

Justine and Beatrice were already replacing documents in

their file folders. Catherine was waiting impatiently, the telegram in her hand. "Come *on*," she said.

As they walked quickly back through the streets of Budapest while the sun shone on the Danube, talking about what to pack, Mary wondered what could possibly have happened to Alice. Was she truly Lydia Raymond, the result of yet another cruel experiment? Was Lydia the daughter of Mrs. Raymond, who had eluded justice in connection with the Whitechapel Murders? Mary remembered the grim, unsmiling director of the Magdalen Society, who had seemed so proper, but had sold the young women in her care to Mr. Hyde so Adam could harvest their body parts to create another Justine. And Dr. Raymond—was he yet another of these mad alchemists who acknowledged no boundaries in their quest for knowledge and power? She was more worried than she wanted to admit about Mr. Holmes—and now Dr. Watson was missing as well! In her head, she was already running over the schedule of the Orient Express and calculating expenses. How soon could they be back in London?

CATHERINE: All these questions, and more, will be answered in the third volume of these adventures of the Athena Club, assuming this volume sells sufficiently well—two shillings in bookstores, train stations, and directly from the publisher. And should anyone wish to bring out an American edition—

MARY: You really have to stop it with the advertisements!

CATHERINE: If our readers want to find out what happens to Alice, they will need to buy the first

two books! Of course, if they want me to leave
Alice in peril . . .

Alice sat in a forest glade. All around her grew ferns, their
fronds swaying gently, the shoots curling like fiddleheads. She
was sitting on a mossy stone, in the dim, dappled light that fell
through oak and birch leaves high above. The air was cool, fresh.
It smelled of last year's leaf mold. She could hear birdsong—
somewhere close, a chickadee was singing its two notes.
Everywhere around her, the forest was rustling—ferns swaying
in the breeze, branches rattling against one another, a stream
burbling along out of her sight but close enough that she could
hear it. Suddenly, she could hear birds everywhere, a cacophony
of song. A shy rabbit hopped past. Then, a few minutes later, a
doe and her fawn ambled through the undergrowth. The fawn
looked at her with large, dark, sympathetic eyes. She would have
liked to talk to it, but she knew it would not say anything to
her that she could not have said to herself. She would have liked
to stand up, walk around under the trees, among the ferns—
perhaps drink from the stream. But there was a bright green
snake wrapped around her left ankle. While it was there, she
would not be able to stand up.

"Lydia." The voice was harsh, imperious. "Lydia, stop this at
once." The forest around her wavered, then started to break apart
as though it had been made of smoke. Wisps of it swirled around
a woman in a gray dress with iron-gray hair. Next to her stood a
tall man with an aquiline nose, a high forehead, and a receding
hairline.

"I told you I would be able to find her for you," he said. "Now
that she's here, we have everything we need to implement our
plan. In two weeks, a month at most, you will be sitting on the
throne of England."

"If she cooperates," said the woman in gray.

"I'm sure she will. Won't you, my dear?" he said to Alice. "I don't believe I've introduced myself properly. I'm Professor Moriarty, and this is Mrs. Raymond—your mother."

"Hello, Lydia," said the woman he had called Mrs. Raymond. "If I had recognized you at the Society of St. Mary Magdalen, I would have treated you very differently. You could have joined me in our enterprise. I'm glad you escaped from Hyde and his henchmen." She paused for a moment. Alice did not respond. "I'm pleased to see you again, daughter," she added. But she did not look pleased, or if she did, then her pleased face had a grim, distinctly *displeased* expression on it.

The last wisps of illusion dissipated as the mesmeric waves broke and scattered. Alice looked around the damp stone cell, with its single dim lantern and bucket latrine. A chain hung heavy from her left ankle.

"You will be a good girl and do what Professor Moriarty wants, won't you, Lydia?" said Mrs. Raymond.

Alice closed her eyes and told herself that she was not there—no, not there at all. *I'm not here, I'm not here, I'm not here,* she thought, as intently as she knew how. But she knew it would not work. Not this time.

TELL THE WORLD THIS BOOK WAS

| GOOD | BAD | SO-SO |

ACKNOWLEDGMENTS

I may have written the words, but this novel would not exist without the help of a great many people. I could not have written it without visiting the magnificent cities of London, Vienna, and Budapest, to walk the streets and imagine what Mary, Diana, Beatrice, Catherine, and Justine experienced. Farah Mendlesohn and Edward James invited me to stay at their beautiful house in London and guided my research into the late Victorian era. Katherine Pendill and Seger Bonebakker hosted me in their equally beautiful apartment in Vienna and helped me visualize the era of the Secession movement. Csilla Kleinheincz taught me so much about Budapest that I did not know, and corrected the Hungarian phrases in this book. I would like to thank all of them for their help and hospitality. My characters speak Italian, German, and Dutch, but I do not, and my French is not as good as Justine's. I am grateful to Lesley Yoder, Ilaria Patania, Sasha Vivelo, Bernhard Stäber, Horus Odenthal, and Simone Heller, who helped me with those languages. Any mistakes are the result of my not following their excellent advice.

A heartfelt thanks goes to my agent, Barry Goldblatt, who believed in these characters before I wrote about them, and who kept me sane during the process of writing this book. Another goes out to my wonderful editor, Navah Wolfe, who sometimes understood this book better than I did and could tell me exactly how to make it better, as well as the whole team at Saga Press, particularly

Bridget Madsen, Tatyana Rosalia, KeriLee Horan, and the designer, Krista Vossen. She and the cover artist, Kate Forrester, made this book more beautiful than I could have imagined. Elena Stokes, Brianna Robinson, and Taylan Salvati at Wunderkind PR were tireless at organizing publicity for the first book in this series, bringing it to the attention of readers who will hopefully also like this second adventure of the Athena Club. I am most grateful for all of their work and support.

Finally, I would like to thank my daughter, Ophelia, descended from a respectable line of mad scientists, who inspires me every day. The first time she laughed at one of Diana's antics made all my efforts worthwhile.